THE HEART OF THE CONTINENT

NANCY CATO

THE HEART OF THE CONTINENT

St. Martin's Press
New York

Library of Congress Cataloging-in-Publication Data

Cato, Nancy.
    The heart of the continent / Nancy Cato.
        p.   cm.
    ISBN 0-312-02927-6
    I. Title.
PR9619.3.C394H43   1989
823–dc19
                                    89-30124
                                        CIP

First Edition
10 9 8 7 6 5 4 3 2 1

For Bev and Bronnie, without whose help
this book would never have been finished.

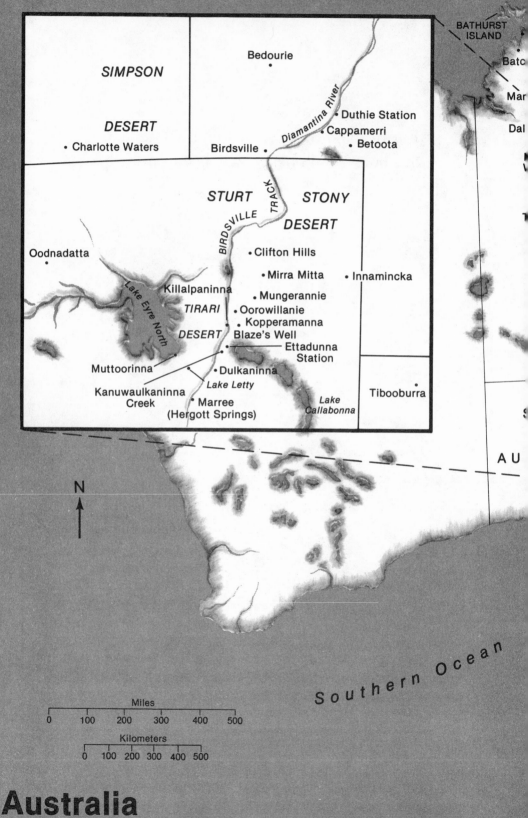

Australia

Arafura Sea

Milingimbi
Mission
ELCHO ISLAND

Gulf of

laningrida

mundie

GROOTE
EYLANDT

erine

Coral Sea

ataranka

Carpentaria

Birdum

Nutwood
Downs

Borroloola

Cooktown •

MORNINGTON
ISLAND

Downs

• Anthony's
Lagoon

Normanton

Cairns •

Brunette
Downs

Burketown •

Doomadgee
Mission

Croydon

ek •

Forsayth

HERN

• Camooweal

Townsville •

• Barrow Creek

Cloncurry

Julia Creek

ITORY

Mt. Isa

McKinlay

lice Springs

Tobermorey

Kynuna

• Winton

urg

Boulia •

SIMPSON

Bedourie

• Longreach

Rockhampton •

ck

DESERT

Birdsville

QUEENSLAND

• Charlotte
Waters

Betoota •

• Windorah

STURT STONY

LIA

DESERT

• Charleville

Tibooburra

Brisbane •

Marree •

Lake Torrens

Lake Frome

FLINDERS
RANGE

Broken Hill

Coffs Harbour •

Port Augusta

Quorn

NEW SOUTH WALES

Clare

Spencer Gulf

Sydney •

Cootamundra •

Adelaide

Canberra •

VICTORIA

• Melbourne

South Pacific Ocean

Tasman Sea

TASMANIA

The very heart of the continent and most of the great space we temporarily inhabit is threatened with destruction . . . Sand blows across bare tracts where a failure to exercise intelligent restraint has wasted the land with greedy, reckless overstocking . . . We have placed too much of it in the hands of men who cannot be trusted to use it well.

Ray Ericksen, *West of Centre*

BOOK ONE

CHAPTER ONE

"Wait for me! Wa-ai-t!" Laughing, gasping for breath, Alix MacFarlane ran after her friend, tripping on her long skirt. The grass of the parklands was as dry and slippery as straw.

"Come on! We'll be late, and old Blue Nose will have us up before Matron. Can't you *hurry?*"

"I am hurrying. But I've got a stitch in my side."

They were walking home through the park to the North Adelaide Hospital, to save the penny tramfare. Their total wages amounted to five shillings a week, and every penny counted. As probationers they had received nothing in their first year, only their keep and the privilege of working a twelve-hour day and learning the occupation of nursing. Now, in their third year, 1911, they still worked just as long hours, as well as attending lectures.

"Come on, MacFarlane. It's that Berlin bun you had for tea. You know you shouldn't have—"

"I know. I couldn't afford it, either. But oh! It was yummy." Alix licked her lips reminiscently, tasting again the golden, doughy fried dumpling with its coating of sugar and the slit in the side (saved till last) filled with cream and raspberry jam.

It was nearing the end of a long hot day in late summer; already the cooling, blustery "gully wind" was beginning to sweep across the city as the colder air on the top of the eastward hills began to slide down the steep gullies to the plains below. The hills, catching the last of the light, were rounded, smooth, and golden-grassed against the sky, shadowed with viridian and cobalt. As the girls crossed the parklands, where smaller trees had been eaten off to the same level above the ground by grazing cows, the sparse gum-trees began to lash and bend in the strengthening wind, shedding curved shells of bark and a few twigs of narrow leaves.

"Mab Kingston! Stop a minute!"

Alix (who had been christened Alexandra) leaned against a smooth bole, panting, and dragged off her hat. The soft, pale-brown curls, pulled into a bun at the back of her head, were starting to come down. Her hair was so fine and silky that she always had trouble anchoring her stiff, starched, cone-shaped uniform cap on top of it, however many pins she used. "Old Blue Nose will have to wait. I can't hurry any more."

The Sister they called Old Blue Nose was not old, probably no more than thirty, but to the girls she seemed ancient. She had an unfortunate tendency to indigestion, which made her bad-tempered, and in the cold Adelaide winters her usually red nose turned purplish. The young nurses likened her silent cruising round the ward, looking for faults, to the cruising of a blue-nosed shark.

Mab came back a few steps and leaned on the other side of the tree, where small black ants crawled up and down like traffic on a city thoroughfare.

"We should've spent the penny on the tramfare," she said. "If we get docked our free time for being late we'll be even worse off."

"I'm sorry, Kingsy. But I had to have a breather."

"All right, little 'un." She squinted down at her fob watch. "We've got five minutes yet; that includes getting into uniform."

They were nearly there; the hospital grounds adjoined the terrace that bounded the parklands on this side. Alix smiled at her friend. They were "Kingston" and "MacFarlane" to each other most of the time, no soft feminine first names; but though Alix was taller, she was so thin, with a tiny waist, that patients referred to her as "the little nurse"; and the wiry Mab, ever protective towards her, often called her "little 'un." Alix's face was too thin and pointed for beauty, but her soft hair, naturally red lips, and cornflower-blue eyes caused the unthinking to refer to her as "a pretty little thing," a phrase she hated.

Mab Kingston had straight, sandy, wiry hair, a rosy complexion, and a wide, straight mouth that looked uncompromising when closed, but could relax into a cheerful grin in which there seemed to be more than the normal number of teeth. Patients were scared of her until they saw her smile.

They raced into the entrance of the nurses' quarters and into the room they shared, where they flung their outdoor clothes on the floor and were into their uniforms and running down the tiled corridor fixing their caps by one minute to six.

"Made it!" muttered Mab out of the corner of her mouth as they glided decorously into the ward. The evening meal was over and they had only to do the rounds with supper and medications, hustle the last visitors out of the ward, take out the flowers, and settle the patients ready for the night nurse to take over.

They had already worked a nine-hour day, but the regulations said that they must not work more than three hours without a break. After an early morning cup of tea they came on duty from six to nine, then had half an hour for breakfast. Three hours later, at half past twelve, they stopped for lunch, worked for three hours, and then had two hours off.

At six they were back on duty again till nine, when they usually snatched a cup of tea and a piece of bread and butter in the ward kitchen before falling, exhausted, into bed. At five-thirty in the morning they had to be up again, and ready to go on duty at six.

It was not so bad in summer, when the mornings were often the best time of the day, before the blazing sun rose high above the eastward hills and beat on the shimmering plain. Even so North Adelaide, being a little higher than the rest of the city, would catch whatever breeze there might be.

The hospital's wide verandas, which acted as overflows for the wards, were provided with canvas blinds that had to be dropped in the afternoons and rolled up again in the evenings—a process as complicated as hoisting a sail. The heavy wooden weight, big as a mast, was pulled up by a series of ropes and pulleys, with the canvas rolled around it. Alix hated coping with the blinds. She was deft with bandages but no use with anything that required physical strength and mechanical knowledge. Mab, the practical one, was her opposite in all things. When Mab attacked the blinds they seemed to roll themselves into neat sausages, while for Alix they hung crookedly, half-furled, and drunken-looking.

Twice a week the nursing students had time off for lectures, where they made notes in exercise books in hurried, cramped writing. Physiology, anatomy, biology, invalid cookery, dressings, bacteriology, trolley-setting, bandages. . . . The practical lessons were the best, when they had to turn out coddled or lightly scrambled eggs, milk jellies and egg custards, or practise elaborate bandages and splints on the bodies of volunteer patients.

The worst thing, Alix found, was being treated like a half-witted child and not being allowed to answer back. By the end of the day her stiff, starched collar was beginning to chafe her neck. When spoken to by Sister, etiquette demanded that she stand with her starch-cuffed hands behind her back, heels together and shoulders straight. Sometimes she longed to do something outrageous, swear or poke out her tongue; but she stood there answering meekly, "Yes, Sister. No, Sister."

She remembered how a finicky senior nurse had made her life as a probationer a misery. While Alix was preparing bread and butter for the patients' supper, the senior would come in, watch critically, and say, "Don't hold the knife so, Nurse, but so. And when you cut off the crust begin with the left side first, then turn the bread so, and so, and so. And don't place your first finger so far down the knife, Nurse."

Shut up, get lost, Alix muttered under her breath, but aloud she said "Yes, Nurse. Thank you, Nurse." When the senior had gone, she threw the knife across the pantry, and bolted a piece of bread and butter to force down the anger in her throat.

At night in their narrow cell with its tall window, two iron bedsteads, tiled wash-stand and single wardrobe, and a "duchess chest" with swinging mirror which they had to share, the girls talked about their future, when

11

they should have completed their third year of training and become certificated sisters.

"D'you want to work in a hospital?" asked Mab.

"No! Heaven forbid! Think of the night duty!"

"Think of the Dragon [their name for the Matron] and the Blue-Nosed Shark. There'd be someone like them in every big hospital, I bet."

"Perhaps a country hospital?" said Alix. "I'd like to see other parts of Australia. Queensland, the Northern Territory—"

"Too hot."

"Well, Western Australia then."

"Too far."

"Mother will want me to come home to live, and make eyes at a beau, and put myself on the marriage market," Alix predicted. "I'll have to get right away from Adelaide."

"At least my old man doesn't care what I do, as long as I'm self-supporting and don't ask him for help," said Mab. Her mother had died two years before, having been nursed by Mab in her last illness.

"Well, we've got plenty of time to think about it. I'm going to sleep."

And she promptly did so, without a single toss or turn, her healthy, tired young body shutting off consciousness like a velvet blind until the alarm clock shrilled at five-thirty next morning.

CHAPTER TWO

Alix's determination to take up nursing had horrified her mother.

"I don't know how you could even *contemplate* such a thing!

"Your father would never hear of it.

"I certainly don't approve! A nurse is only a glorified servant girl. . . . And such an indelicate occupation. You would be required to wash men patients *all over*. Of course, as a young girl you don't realise quite what this means, but I assure you the experience could be quite a shock. . . . How can I face my friends and say my daughter has gone to train as a *nurse?*"

So, with many verbal underlinings, Mrs. MacFarlane had received the news of Alexandra's ambition.

What made Frances MacFarlane so bitterly opposed was her own uncertain position in the tight little circle of Adelaide "Society"; her father was the brewer of Carter's Lager. When she changed her name from Carter by marrying Major Robert MacFarlane, retired British Army officer, she felt her position improved. Her ambition now was for an official invitation to a Lord Mayor's Ball or a garden party at Government House.

She was a little round woman with curly dark hair and sharp blue eyes. The tall and solid Major MacFarlane had found her irresistible, with her tiny pearly teeth between which she would catch her rosy bottom lip, as was her habit. He had no family in Australia to disapprove of her connection with "trade"—not that it mattered in a young community where the upper crust consisted simply of those who had money, or property, as against those who had neither. He owned property in the city besides having an interest in a couple of flour mills in the country.

There had been many battles before Alix finally got her way, for her mother was as obstinate as she was herself. In vain she claimed that she had a vocation, a call towards nursing, "almost like the vocation of a nun," as she had told her father.

"Good heavens! I hope you haven't got any ideas about entering a convent!" he said, blowing out his fine, silky moustache with a great breath.

"No, no, Father; I just want to be a nurse."

"Well, your mother won't hear of it, I'm afraid, and that's that."

13

Alix sulked for a week, but she knew her father would not take her side against her mother.

A combination of outside events helped her to get her way in the end. A disastrous fire destroyed her grandfather's brewery, and the bank from which old Will Carter had borrowed for rebuilding threatened to foreclose. His daughter Frances could not bear the disgrace if her father should be declared a bankrupt, so she appealed to her husband to sell his assets in the city and bail out Carter's Brewery.

Major MacFarlane agreed unwillingly. It was a bad time to be selling property. Then, when he had realized his assets, little remained after paying his father-in-law's debts.

"I really don't know," he said gloomily to his wife, "how I'm to keep my head above water. There's only the income from the two flour mills left, and with the price of flour dropping every day—"

"This Depression can't last."

"And the upkeep of this big house, and having to pay a manager for each of the mills. . . . Now if I'd had sons who could take over the management for me—"

"Robert! It's not fair to throw that in my face now." Frances bit her bottom lip and dabbed at her eyes with a lace handkerchief. It was an old sorrow; their only son had not lived above a day, and after that a series of miscarriages had left Frances unable to bear any more children. Alexandra was their only child. And what sort of a child have I produced! Frances said to herself in despair. Not interested in young men, no sign of getting married, and now this mad idea of becoming a nurse. . . .

As though he had heard her thoughts, her husband brushed back his long moustache with a determined hand.

"And in fact, if Alix is not goin' to get married and take herself off our hands, she'd better take up this nursing idea. It will give her her keep and a bit of pocket-money, which I won't be able to afford."

"Robert! You wouldn't give your permission? I should die of shame— a daughter of mine, washing dirty bedpans!"

"Well, the gel seems set on it as a career. And after all I saved you from dying of shame, as you said, when I rescued your father from bankruptcy. Now you'll just have to put up with it."

So Alix, just turned eighteen, enrolled at the North Adelaide Private Hospital, which her mother thought a little more genteel than the Public Hospital.

The work was far harder than Alix had expected, but she never seriously regretted her choice.

"Oh, Nurse!"

An elderly patient called to Alix in a quavering voice. He had just come back from surgery, and had not yet learned that young Nurse

14

MacFarlane, with her soft blue eyes and pretty hair, concealed beneath her delicate features a will of iron.

The ward was Men's Surgical; the old man had had twenty-seven stitches in a badly gashed leg, opened down to the bone by the iron-bound wheel of a runaway cart.

"Nurse, can I 'ave a 'ot-water bottle? I got the ducks an' drakes somethin' cruel," he said, shivering exaggeratedly.

"Now, Mr. Barrett, you know we aren't allowed to give hot-water bottles to patients just back from the theatre. Didn't you ask Sister Bryant before she went off duty?"

"Yairs; but I thort—"

"It's a safety precaution in case you're still sleepy from the anaesthetic. If you're unconscious a hot-water bottle could burn you badly without your being aware of it."

"Yair, but I ain't unconscious, am I?"

"I'm sorry. I'll get you another blanket instead."

"Cripes, you nurses is 'ard-'earted," he complained.

"Is your leg keeping you awake? Sister left you a sedative if you need it."

"Na, don't like takin' them sleeping pills. I'll be right."

Alix went to the window and looked down at the deserted grounds of the North Adelaide Hospital. It was early in the morning and she was on night duty, gliding about with a small lamp, administering a cool compress here, a glass of water there.

One of the men, a solid, muscular bushman with a nose that looked as if it had been broken, had been admitted with liver damage from a prolonged drinking bout. He suddenly went into delirium tremens, shouting that there were snakes in his bed.

"Mr. Wilkins! Calm down now, you are disturbing the other patients."

He glared at her with no comprehension in his wild glance, and threw back the sheet.

"Mr. Wilkins! You are not to get out of bed."

He thrust her slight frame aside and ran towards the windows, two floors above the ground. "'Ave ter get out of 'ere!" he yelled. "They're after me—snakes—devils—!"

Alix ran and got between him and the windows. "Mr. Wilkins—listen to me! The snakes are gone now. Look!"

He paused and a light of dawning intelligence showed in his bloodshot eyes. "Gone? They'll be back, don't you worry."

"What colour were they?"

"Eh? Red—and purple, and yeller, with big fangs."

"Well, they're gone now. Come and I'll make you a cup of tea in the pantry."

She did not dare take her eyes off him.

15

"Nurse!" came a whisper from Mr. Barrett. "D'you want me to tackle 'im?"

"No, no, you know you're not allowed to walk yet."

"Well, you yell if you need help."

She tried to calm the patient with a cup of weak tea, but as he reached for the cup his eyes began to roll wildly. He started back, and struck the cup from her hand.

"It's no good! They're gunna get me!" he yelled. He grabbed a sharp knife from the sink and with his other hand ripped open his pyjama jacket. "I might as well end it now," he muttered, gesturing towards his bare chest.

With desperate strength Alix grasped his wrist, "Give me that knife!"

But he shook her off and backed away from her. With a trembling hand she mixed a Seidlitz powder into some milk.

"Here, Mr. Wilkins. Drink this. It's guaranteed to drive away demons."

"Yair, but what about snakes?"

"Snakes, too. Drink up."

This time he took the cup and drained it, though he kept the knife pointed menacingly towards her. She looked quickly at the fob watch pinned to the front of her uniform. Three A.M.—it would be three hours before she could expect any help.

Alix went to a cupboard where games, jigsaws and packs of cards were kept for the patients. She took out a pack of cards.

"Mr. Wilkins! D'you remember you told me you were good at cards? What about a game of euchre?"

"Eh?" Once again the dazed look of half-comprehending came back to his ruined face.

She sat down at the night sister's table and cleared it of papers. Then she shuffled the cards and started to deal two hands. The man came unwillingly to watch. He sat down in the chair opposite and picked up his hand, but kept the knife close beside him on the table.

"Ha! A right bower," he gloated, then shot her a look of suspicion. "I shouldn't 'a told you that, should I?"

She ignored him and began to play, first taking the notepad and pencil that dangled from her waist and putting them ready for scoring. She prayed he would have good cards.

After half an hour he had become absorbed in the game—she let him win most of the time. He seemed to have given up all ideas of self-destruction, when he began to get restless again. He picked up the knife.

"Get away! GET AWAY!" he yelled suddenly, kicking at something on the floor.

"What is it, Mr. Wilkins?"

"Ruddy great centipede, that's what!"

16

Alix had a horror of centipedes. She looked under the desk with a shudder. There was nothing there.

"No, no . . . that's not a centipede. . . . You didn't know I had the joker, did you?"

"Eh?" The vague, puzzled look came back into his eyes. She judged it was safe to risk moving away.

"Let's have another cup of tea, and then you'd better get back to bed."

"No! It's full o' snakes."

"I'll make sure the snakes are all gone."

Reassured by the quiet murmur of their voices over the cards, most of the patients had gone back to sleep, except the one who had offered assistance.

Now he asked in a stage whisper, "You want help in getting 'im back to bed, Nurse?"

"I'll be all right, Mr. Barrett. He's much calmer now."

"Well, you're game as Ned Kelly!"

For a moment she saw herself as if looking at a scene from outside, and she was amazed. Here she was in the middle of the night, playing euchre with a crazed patient by the dim light of the one lamp, with a ward full of incapacitated men and no help within call. She ought to be terrified, but her main fear was that the patient might do himself an injury.

"Eh, what about giving 'im my sleeping medicine?" Mr. Barrett whispered.

"Good idea."

She mixed the powder into a cup of tea, and at last got the patient back to bed.

The next day Mr. Barrett tried to tell Matron, on her morning rounds, of the bravery of the "little nurse."

"She should be given a medal, that's what."

"I'm sure Nurse MacFarlane was only doing her duty, Mr. Barrett."

"Yes, but she kept her head and calmed 'im down, big hulking brute. Hours she played cards with him, till she got 'im back to bed."

He glared across at the shape of Wilkins, now thoroughly sedated and snoring heavily. Alix had gone off duty. It was not until the next week that she learned Mr. Barrett had whipped round the ward for a suitable present for her, and had put in the biggest contribution himself.

She was back on duty a week later, and re-bandaging Mr. Barrett's leg, when he handed her a little packet. "Got my brother to get it engraved for you," he said. "Just a little reward for bravery, like."

"But Mr. Barrett . . ." She unwrapped the tissue paper and found a piece of notepaper wrapped round a small silvered medal with her name and "Oct. 19" on one side, and "For bravery" on the other. The paper was inscribed in Mr. Barrett's best copperplate: "To Nurse MacFarlane, with the best wishes of Ward 7, in recognition of her brave action when alone in the Ward and faced with a patient suffering from the D.T.s."

She was embarrassed, but she thanked him and slipped the medal into her pocket.

Later that morning she had to accompany Matron on her morning rounds of the ward, as it was Sister Bryant's morning off. The surgeon, that godlike man, would be doing the rounds with Matron, and Alix felt her palms grow damp, her mouth go dry with fear and excitement. Just to see Dr. Hamilton in the distance made her heart turn over. He was not young, for the fair hair had receded from his high, broad forehead, but he was an imposing figure, tall and broad-shouldered, in his white coat, and he carried himself with the conscious dignity of one whose word was law, before whom medical students quailed and ward sisters became obsequious.

"Are you ready for rounds, Nurse?" came Matron's crisp tones. Her bosom jutted out to an extraordinary distance under the starched white uniform, giving Matron's figure the appearance of a schooner in full sail before a following wind. (The young nurses had a theory, quite unjustified by science, that this mammary overdevelopment had been caused by "thrills"—unspecified, but to do with adventures with men in her youth.)

Dr. Hamilton accompanied Matron, and they proceeded round the ward with Alexandra a few deferential steps behind.

"Well, Jack, how's the leg?" asked Dr. Hamilton, when they stopped at Mr. Barrett's bed.

"Orright. I'll be out of 'ere in no time."

"Well, we'll see about that."

His long, sensitive fingers were deftly unwinding the bandage, which went the length of the man's lower leg.

"That's an excellent reverse spiral," he said approvingly as he unlapped the rounds of bandage, each with a sharp turn or fold at the front of the shin, and each exactly above the next fold. "Who was responsible?"

Alix gulped, but no sound came from her throat.

"Nurse?" said Matron sharply.

"I—I was, Dr. Hamilton."

"Good work, Nurse."

"Thank you, sir." Alix's cheeks were pink, her soft blue eyes luminous with adoration, but the doctor did not look at her. He was examining the suture with a pleased expression. "I did a very neat job here, though I say it myself. It was a nasty gash."

"Yes, Doctor," murmured Matron.

Alix went about her work for the rest of the day singing inside, though she didn't dare sing aloud. The great Dr. Hamilton had noticed her! (Well, he'd noticed her bandage.)

18

That night she burned the light late and kept Mab awake while she read her "bible," as Mab called it—the well-thumbed 1900 edition of *Modern Methods in Nursing*.

Under "Bathing—the Bed-Bath" she read, "The chest and abdomen dried and covered, the genitals are carefully washed under cover. In many cases patients are able to do this for themselves with some little assistance from the nurse. With helpless or unconscious patients it must not be neglected from a false notion of delicacy, the skin in these parts becoming easily inflamed and sore from the natural secretions, unless kept scrupulously clean."

Her mother would have a fit! Mrs. MacFarlane was full of false notions of delicacy, so much so that she had left Alexandra to discover the facts of menstruation for herself, so that she spent two days of panic before a school-friend enlightened her.

"'Care of the Back—Prevention and Treatment of Bedsores,'" she read.

"For Pete's sake, MacFarlane! Do you have to read out loud?"

"Oh! Sorry."

Alix read on silently, but forming the words with her lips so as to memorize them.

"After the daily bath, the back, hips, and other points of pressure should be rubbed with alcohol and dusted with powder. Besides pressure from the weight of the body, the common causes of bedsores are moisture, wrinkles in the bedclothes, crumbs in the bed, want of cleanliness, and bruising from the careless placing of a bedpan. . . ."

"Crumbs!" murmured Alix.

"What?"

"Crumbs in the bed! A cause of bedsores. Can you imagine Sister if she found crumbs in a patient's bed?"

"Hardly! She would faint with shock and horror."

"Listen: 'From earliest days pupils should be taught quiet and dignified behaviour while at their work. . . . No conversation on personal topics should be allowed in the wards, and no raised voices or noisy movements.'"

"And no reading aloud in bed after work! Put the lamp out and go to sleep."

Alix did so, and placed the heavy book under the bed. But she did not go straight to sleep. She lay awake pursuing one of her fantasies about Dr. Hamilton. In one she rescued him from in front of a bolting horse, bravely leaping up and catching the maddened animal by its bridle. He then thanked her tenderly, bowing his big fair head to kiss her hand. . . .

In another scenario, desperate with unrequited love she flung herself before a horse-tram and was brought, dying, to the hospital for him to operate on. She let him know that it was for his sake she had suffered this fate, because she could not bear his indifference. Then, stricken with remorse, he made a superhuman effort and saved her with a successful operation. And then, and then . . . but at this stage she dropped off to sleep.

CHAPTER THREE

In June 1911 Alix and Mab graduated together as fully trained nurses. They each received a purple-enamelled Maltese Cross along with their certificates. They were photographed in the group of their year, in their pale blue uniforms buttoned down the front, without their white pinafores, and wearing the tall blue velvet caps and blue velvet capes that made up their dress uniform.

Alix was glad the long grind of probation and study were over; but she realized with a sinking feeling that she would probably never see Dr. Hamilton again, unless she could be admitted for urgent surgery, and become his patient. But she felt extremely healthy.

She would never love anyone else, she felt sure, and she meant to dedicate herself to relieving mankind's suffering and tending the sick. She didn't want to specialize in midwifery or child nursing, though Mab had decided to enrol at the Queen Victoria maternity hospital for six months. Alix, after working part-time at a private hospital, was impatient to nurse under the most difficult conditions and in the most distant places.

When she met Mab on the Beehive Corner for an ice-cream soda, she was full of suppressed excitement. She had read the report of a lecture by John Flynn, the Presbyterian minister who had been on a travelling mission in the outback with camels. He spoke of his plans to establish something he called the Australian Inland Mission, to open the first of a chain of hostels through the loneliest parts of Australia, staffed by trained nurses. Alix decided to apply. Mab had finished her midwifery and was "specialling" an elderly patient; they could both get away.

"How's your patient?" Alix asked when they were seated in front of their drinks.

"Crotchety as ever. I don't think I can stand it much longer. He's impossible."

"Good!" said Alix.

"MacFarlane, you're up to something, I can tell. When your eyes have that blue innocent look, I beware."

"Well, you see . . . Listen, Kingsy, there's a most marvellous opportunity for two trained nurses to run a hostel in the far north of South Australia. Remember I told you about the A.I.M. . . .?"

And she launched into an enthusiastic description of the isolated outpost where they would be entirely alone, without a doctor nearer than three hundred miles away.

"I've written to arrange an interview. But you have to come too. Their letter says, 'In such an isolated place, it is most important that the two appointees are compatible.' It's at Hergott Springs, that used to be the terminus of the northern railway before it was extended to Oodnadatta. It sounds just perfect for us."

Mab said teasingly, "What, you're asking me to leave the flesh-pots of the city, for heat and dust-storms and Aboriginal kids with runny noses and ringworm? You must be mad."

Nevertheless, before they parted Alix had Mab's promise to think about it. A week later she wrote, "Free at last! I've told the old curmudgeon I'm leaving. He immediately had a turn for the worse, on purpose I believe. But I can get away in a month."

Alix enrolled at a dental clinic and learned something about extractions. The more qualifications they had the better their chance of acceptance.

In three weeks they had their interview, conducted by a dour Presbyterian minister who painted a daunting picture of the hardships that awaited them.

"There's one hotel at Hergott Springs, and a store, and that's about it. Apart from the springs themselves, which are mineral water, and of course the railway station. The town's a railhead for cattle which are droved down the notorious Birdsville Track, ye'll have heard of that, a real perisher—"

Seeing Alix's face alight with interest, he gave her a sharp glance from under his sandy brows. "And I hope ye're no' looking on this as just a wee adventure," he said severely. "It will mean work, hard and lonely work in deeficult conditions—"

"Don't worry, it's the nursing which interests us."

"Aye. That's settled, then. We'll send your train-tickets next month— second class, I fear. The appointment is for two years, when you will be relieved. . . . Weel, that seems to be all."

He rose and shook their hands. For the first time a smile warmed his frosty face.

"Ye're a pair o' brave lassies, and I wish ye the best for the future as A.I.M. Sisters. It's grand work ye'll be doing."

Outside Alix danced along the pavement. They had the job! They would be travelling north in the fabled "'Ghan," the little steam train named after the Afghan camel drivers, along the line pioneered by the teams who helped build the Overland Telegraph Line all the way north to Darwin. They in turn had followed in the steps of the explorers, lured northwards by the shimmer of vast blue lakes which turned out to be dry clay-pans filled with salt.

She went home to break the news to her mother.

"Going to the far north! Out in the *bush!*" Frances cried when Alix informed her of the appointment. "A young girl, alone and unchaperoned—"

"Not alone, Mother. My friend Mab Kingston is coming too."

"Well, two young girls, then. I've never *heard* of such a thing—"

"Mother, I am twenty-two years old and a trained nurse. I'm not a child any more."

"No, and you should be thinking about getting married," said Mrs. MacFarlane, changing her tack. "You'll soon be an old maid at this rate. Your father and I were looking forward to our grandchildren, and now—"

"I certainly don't intend to get married until I've seen a bit of Australia and used my nursing skills where they'll be most useful. It would be wicked just to get married and waste three years of training and all that I've learned."

"I can't see that at all."

"No; well, we don't see eye to eye on most things, do we?"

"Oh! You're impossible, Alexandra." And her mother swept away with an indignant rustle of her taffeta skirts.

Now, in her bedroom at home, in the eastern suburbs just below the curve of the Adelaide Hills—what was known as the foothills, though it was in fact a sloping plain little higher than the rest of the city—Alix took her "bravery" medal out of her drawer and looked at it. She didn't have a silver chain suitable for hanging it round her neck, and anyway it would have embarrassed her. What to do with it? She felt she couldn't just throw it away.

She looked out the window at the round hills, still green with last winter's rains, grazed by sheep into a series of tiny terraces as they moved around the face of the hill. She put away the "citation" from Mr. Barrett carefully, wrapped the medal in a piece of tissue paper, and put it in the pocket of her skirt.

"I'm just going for a walk, Mother," she called.

"Where? If you're going down to the corner shops, you can get me—"

"No, I'm just going for a walk. It's such a lovely sunny afternoon."

At the top of their street houses gave way to empty paddocks, not yet subdivided. Then she was on the lower flanks of the hills, striding vigorously, leaning forward against the slope. Small sticks and prickles did not cling to the firm weave of her long gabardine skirt, which she now kilted up above her ankles.

She would not look round, though she was aware through the corner of her eye of the suburbs, the flat plains, dropping away below her. She wanted to get to the very top before she looked.

A strong wind buffeted her suddenly, and the green turf flattened out before her feet. She had climbed one of the lower slopes of Mount Osmond, and now at about eight hundred feet found herself at its summit.

23

A few lichened rocks protruded in grey slabs from the grass, and hard dry sheep-dung rolled under her feet. She turned, the wind in her hair, and gasped with delight.

The Adelaide Plains stretched out before her, close and yet far below, to the pale blue line of the Gulf to the west, the smoky chimneys of Port Adelaide. House-roofs looked near enough for her to bounce a pebble off them, yet she knew the nearest must be a mile away. Some grey clouds bunched about the westering sun, but a single ray shone through and lit the grass to brilliant emerald.

She looked at that effulgent ray with a feeling of superstitious awe. She had come here to dedicate herself to God and suffering humanity. She began circling, picking up grey stones with some clay attached to them, breaking off weathered pieces of quartzite from the outcrops, and piling them together. She took the medal from her pocket, made a little cache for it in the ground, and built her cairn on top.

Then she knelt on the short turf, raised her arms to that dramatic sky, and dedicated herself to her career.

"O God," she prayed, "make me unselfish and single-minded, and give me the gift of healing. I promise to go wherever I shall be called. . . . Amen."

She half-expected an answer from Heaven, a wisp of flame on her cairn, a thunderclap from a clear sky, something. But the gold ray faded, the clouds moved away and left a sky like a clear blue lake, and in the pauses of the wind she heard the melancholy "baa-aa" of the grazing sheep moving below the hill-top.

Feeling a little deflated, she began a swift, stiff-legged, jolting run down the slope. She spread her arms as though flying, and then, overcome by high spirits and the wide sunny prospect below, she lay down and rolled. She ended up, breathless, against a small tree, with a piece of rock sticking into her back. She had torn one of her black cotton stockings on a thistle —oh well, it wouldn't show, it was well above the hem of her skirt.

She arrived home ravenous, with glowing cheeks, feeling she had passed an important milestone in her life. Frances MacFarlane looked at her daughter sourly.

"What on *earth* have you been doing, Alexandra? There are bits of dried thistle in your hair!" She added grimly, "Your father wants to see you in his study." This was her term for the small room which was really an office; the Major studied little there but accounts and share prices and the price of flour.

"Now, my gel," he said as Alexandra appeared, demurely dressed in a blue poplin skirt and white shirtwaist with a high collar. "Harumph!" He coughed unnecessarily to give himself time to think. "Er—your mother thinks, she tells me, you have some idea of going off into the wilds on this nursing caper—"

"Father, I—"

"Hear me out, if you please. Business is looking up, and I'm now in a position to launch you in society, with a dance to open the season or whatever she considers necessary."

"And what about what I consider necessary? I'm grown up, I can decide what I want for myself. Look, Father, I've been out in the real world, dealing with life and death, with people, not 'social acquaintances.' I don't want—"

"Your mother has set her heart on this, Alexandra. I'm afraid if you cross her it may affect her health."

"Don't worry about Mother. She's tough. She's wiry like me. You can bend and twist us as much as you like, but we won't break." She knew he didn't care twopence for the dance, he just wanted to make his wife happy.

"You see, Father, 'this nursing caper,' as you call it, is my whole life, and I intend to carry on with it."

"Not in some far northern town, I hope. We'll miss our girl, you know."

He looked so despondent that she jumped up and gave him a kiss. "Cheer up. It's not for a while yet, and I'll still be in South Australia."

Yes, but out there in the back of beyond, she thought, the red centre, the Never Never, that was where they would be going; beyond that mysterious blue plain to the northward whence came in summer the scorching breath, the red dust haze of the vast inland. She could not wait to see it.

CHAPTER FOUR

The little train was travelling due north over a barren plain. Dried grasses grew along the edge of the line where a rare thunderstorm had caused water to collect below the edge of the permanent way. Among them were some clumps of white everlasting daisies.

The third occupant of the compartment climbed down from her bunk, rubbing her eyes, glanced out the window, and her tousled orange hair seemed to stand on end.

"Gawd! Look at it! Will you just look at it?" She appealed to the others.

"Yes. It's immense, isn't it?" said Alix.

"Just miles and miles of bloody desert! I hope it ain't like this where we're going."

"I'm afraid so, only more so. What did they tell you at the employment agency in Adelaide?"

"Just—just that I was needed to be a plain cook, nothing fancy, at a hotel somewhere up north. Hergott Springs. I thought it sounded nice, sort of. I mean, springs—it must be fairly green, with plenty of water. Though they told me it was a hot place."

Alix and Mab exchanged a glance. "Did they tell you the *springs* were hot?" asked Mab.

"Eh?"

"Artesian water. It's hot where it bubbles out of the ground. And you can't drink it!"

"And all around the town is gibber plain and sandy desert. I hope there'll be some trees, but somehow I doubt it. Maybe date palms, like an oasis, you know."

"Gawd! What have I let meself in for?"

It was late morning when they pulled into the station at Hergott Springs after two days of travel.

The carroty-haired cook was sitting at the window in a state of shock. She said not a word, but stared out at the blowing dust.

A cheerful, large-limbed, broad-faced man whose leathery cheeks creased into deep gullies when he smiled, appeared at the compartment door.

"You the new A.I.M. Sisters?" he asked. "I was told you'd be on this

26

train and I've brought the buggy to meet you. Mounted Constable Jack McGuinnes. Welcome to the Springs."

He shook their hands. His grip was firm and strong.

"These your bags?"

They said yes, then indicated the English cook, who was sitting numbly looking out at a group of Aboriginal men in cast-off clothing standing on the far platform to watch the train come in.

"Oh, yes, they're expecting you at the pub, they'll be along in a minute," said Constable McGuinnes.

He led the two Sisters into what appeared to be the main, or only, street, a wide dusty expanse occupied by two goats. At the far end, outside the two-storied hotel with its upstairs balcony running right round, four camels attached to a cart were tethered and a blue dog slumbered in the dust.

The policeman's cart was two-camel power, a conventional buggy with special heavy-duty shafts and harness for the camels in front.

Alix and Mab looked askance at these large, rather supercilious creatures, who were chewing the cud and looking disdainfully over their heads. One gave a roaring cry, showing long yellow teeth. Alix started back nervously.

"Don't be scared," said Constable McGuinnes with a laugh. "I travel with camels all the time on my regular patrol, and I've become quite fond of 'em."

The Constable was a huge man, at least six feet two, Alix thought, and he must weigh about fifteen stone. He had strong black brows that almost met in the centre of his forehead.

"They get a bit cranky at times, but there's really no harm in them."

"You mean they won't bite?"

"Not usually. But it's wiser always to walk up to a strange camel with your hands behind your back, and let him 'kiss' your face, or at least sniff it." Just then the nearer camel turned its head toward her, opened its mouth to show a set of great ugly yellow teeth, and gave a complaining roar.

"No, thank you!" said Alix, and walked carefully round the beast.

Jack McGuinnes handed her up almost reverently. He was already smitten by her cornflower-blue eyes and the soft brown curls showing under the grey, wide-brimmed washing hat. It was part of her travelling uniform, worn with a long-skirted dress of plain grey linen, now sadly crumpled. Mab was dressed exactly the same, but with her small grey eyes with their sandy lashes and her ruddy cheeks she did not appeal to him like the other one. Alix was so slim, so fresh-looking in this rough outpost of few white women: the mailman's wife, thin and wiry, her hair like dry straw; old Mrs. Allison the storekeeper, seventy years old if she was a day. . . .

27

Alix and Mab stared about them. Here and there a stunted shrub outside a house struggled along on a diet of washing-up water; or a few hardy native trees, too dusty for greenness and too thin for shade, survived inside fences.

"I am determined to grow a garden!" announced Mab.

It seemed a wild idea. Most of the houses lined up facing the railway line had no fences, and goats had eaten everything. The Constable explained that the artesian water that was pumped to the town from the springs half a mile away was not fit to drink, though it was all right for stock.

"It's not really hot here, not like further into the Artesian Basin. But vegetables won't thrive on bore water. You save your washing-up water and any other scrap of tank water, and use that," he said.

He pulled up the camel-buggy opposite the hostel. An old building of local stone rebuilt by the A.I.M., it had only two rooms for patients, then a living-room and bedroom for the Sisters, a dispensary, and a big kitchen. The roof was of galvanized iron, the new iron glittering in the sun with an unbearable glare. And along the front was a veranda enclosed with fly-wire.

"Oodoo," said Jack McGuinnes to his camels. "Hey, Potwalloper, Rocket!" He helped the two girls to the bare ground. "I've just got in from a short patrol, and they've been on their feet all night," he said. The camels chewed the cud and looked disdainfully into the distance.

"I'll get a fire alight in the kitchen for you, and take your bags in." He picked up a clothing trunk and a cane travelling basket in each huge fist, and led the way. Mab and Alix looked at each other in unspoken dismay. Not a tree, not a green leaf, just some dirty papers caught in a sagging wire-netting fence in the midst of the orange dust. Beyond, across the wide bare road, the railway lines gleamed into the distance. This was their new home.

It was Mab who discovered the cellar, and the mesh safe full of good things—corned beef, goats' milk, eggs, home-made bread—which the townspeople had put there to welcome the new Sisters. In the kitchen was a Coolgardie safe, which they proceeded to make operable by filling its troughs with cold water. Mab had been used to one of these ingenious coolers at home. Strips of hessian hung over the mesh sides of the safe into a tray of water, and continuous evaporation made the contents cool.

The cupboards were filled with necessities, tea, coffee, sugar, flour, and the woodbox was full. Jack McGuinnes regretfully refused a cup of tea. The girls took theirs in the living-room, where there were cane chairs with floral cushions which gave an air of comfort.

They saluted each other solemnly with tea with goats' milk.

"To us!" said Mab.

"To us!"

*　　*　　*

28

In the next few days most of the townspeople dropped in to "have a geek at" the new Sisters. The mailman's wife, Mrs. Crombie, brought a home-made chocolate cake, and invited them over for afternoon tea.

The hotel proprietor brought a crate of soft drinks, lemonade and soda-water, a gift for the hostel. Others called on various excuses, were given a cup of tea, and remarked on how wonderful it would be to have two trained nurses at hand, instead of the nearest being two hundred miles away at Port Augusta.

Alix and Mab decided to divide their duties by taking turn-abouts to be cook. Alix was nurse for two weeks while Mab did the cooking; then they changed over and Mab became nurse. It gave them a break, and worked out very well.

Their very first casualty turned out to be a youth with a nasty camel-bite on his hand. He was the woodman's "offsider", Joe; they had to go farther and farther afield for their load of mulga and dead-finish, as the sparse timber around the town was eaten out by goats or cut down for firewood. There was a ten-mile radius of common where anyone could run goats or camels, but little was to be found there but sand, clay, and gibbers. The strings of camels which used to do all the carting of stores had eaten it out, but there were fewer of them now, as the original camel-men grew too old, and the younger men left for larger towns or the southern city.

The camel-bite, which had started to turn septic, looked nasty. Mab bathed it in boiled water with antiseptic, and made a bread poultice with one of the fresh loaves delivered from the train to "draw" the poison.

"Don't use all our bread ration," said Alix. "Remember there'll be no more for a week."

"I expect we can borrow a loaf from the pub. At least we know the cook." Mab expertly twisted the cloth wrung out of boiling water by the ends, so that the bread was squeezed almost dry. She reassured the thin, scared-looking boy (was he part Aboriginal?—she thought not, though he was burnt a deep tan by the inland sun) that she was not going to hurt him. "I won't put this on till it's cool enough not to burn you. But it must be hot. You tell me when you can bear it."

He winced, but bravely let her wrap the hot poultice round his hand, followed by a strip of flannel and an oil-cloth cover. Alf the woodman called in his four-camel cart to see how the boy was doing.

"Joe can go home, but he'll have to come in to have his hand dressed every day," Mab told him. "And he mustn't use it—lucky it's the left. I'm going to put the arm in a sling."

"Silly young codger. I told 'im not to put 'is 'and out, like you would to an 'orse. The camel didn't know 'im, see, and it was nervous-like . . ."

"I think I'd be 'nervous-like' if I had to work around camels," said Mab.

Joe gave her a shy smile and thanked her as he left. He had told her he had no family in Hergott Springs but boarded at the hotel. He had come north looking for adventure and to work outdoors. He couldn't save any money because the hotel took all his pay for board. But the meals were good.

"The cook's all right, is she?" said Alix, when Mab told her this. "You can never tell by appearances. We should go over on Sunday for a treat. Might be a roast dinner."

"Yes, I bet they have a roast, even in this heat. And a steamed pudding with custard to follow."

So as there were no in-patients and they had time on their hands, they took off their uniforms on Sunday. Alix put on a light muslin gown, Mab a tusser skirt and white pleated blouse.

They were dusty and perspiring by the time they had walked to the hotel, the biggest building in the town apart from the old Overland Telegraph Station.

"Roast mutton and veges., two," sang the young part-Aboriginal waitress through the hatchway into the kitchen. When carrying orders in both hands she pushed the swing door open with an expert thrust of her rounded hip.

She set down two steaming plates of meat, roast pumpkin, potato and gravy in front of the Sisters. "Would they have got mutton off the train, and how would they keep it for a week?" asked Alix doubtfully.

"I've seen no sheep about here."

As Mab took her first mouthful of meat she looked thoughtful. "H'm. Roast goat, I would say. But it tastes rather like mutton, if a bit dryer."

"Y'having dessert?" asked the girl from the other side of the table.

"Oh—er—, yes, I think so."

"Both of youse?"

"Both."

"Pudding two," yelled the waitress at the window.

She soon came back with two white bowls of steamed yellow pudding with custard. "I told you!" said Mab triumphantly. "Good plain English cooking, never mind the temperature."

"Just think what the temperature must be in the kitchen, with the wood stove going."

They had been going to call in and say hallo to the cook, but on second thoughts decided that she would hardly be feeling sociable at such a time. The dining room held several other guests, including Joe, to whom they waved, and the Constable, who evidently hadn't a wife in the town.

He had nodded and smiled when they first came in, and now he came across to their table and asked, "Mind if I bring my cup of tea over and

30

have it with you two? It's not often I get a chance to sit at a table with ladies."

"No, please do."

"By all means."

He dropped his wide-brimmed hat on the floor beside his chair and sat down.

A cup of tea followed dinner as night follows day. The waitress brought theirs without even asking.

They exchanged some small talk, the Constable's brown face showing his delight in this unexpected socializing. Then Mab remarked, "We don't see many Aborigines about the town, yet there was quite a group on the railway station, when we first arrived."

"No, the blacks live over the railway line—east of the town. So do the Afghans."

"Afghans?"

"Yes, the remaining camel-men; some of them travelled with explorers like McKinley and Larry Wells; some of them are hawkers, or descendants of hawkers, and some still take stores out along the Strzelecki Track, to Innamincka."

"We haven't seen *them,* either."

"I'll take you over to meet Abdul Dervish if you like. He's Muhammadan, of course—they hold their Sunday on a Friday. They're most law-abiding people, I never have any trouble with the men."

"But you do with the Aborigines?"

"Only minor things usually—cattle spearing or sheep stealing. Drunkenness, occasionally. Sometimes there's a fight and someone gets killed. Or a couple of white men get on the rum in a lonely camp, and one kills the other in a drunken brawl. I hardly ever see any real crime."

"And where do you go on your regular beat?" asked Alix.

"South almost to the Flinders Ranges, north to the Diamantina, and east to the border fence. My district covers about four thousand square miles."

He laughed at their dropped jaws.

"I go on month-long patrols, with two native police."

"In that camel-buggy we rode in?"

"Yair. Only way to travel up here, or by riding camel. Camels can live off the land, bushes and shrubs and trees, where a horse would starve; and there's no fodder, except in a good season when the kangaroo-grass grows. It's too expensive to bring it up from the south."

He entertained them with stories of his lonely patrols, of the perishers he had been sent out to find, usually too late to find them alive. "You know, you'd be interested in this, as nurses," he said earnestly, wrinkling his brow under the rough dark-brown hair. "When a man perishes in the desert, after a few weeks the flesh parts from the bones as it dries, quite cleanly. It's a strange sight."

31

"I'm sure," said Alix, glancing at Mab and pushing her pudding plate farther away. "I'm glad you didn't give us the gruesome details before we ate our dehydrated goat."

"Hell, I mean, heck, I'm sorry, ladies. I didn't think. Not used to dinner-table conversation."

"That's all right, Constable. It's just that we're new chums," said Mab. "We realize that this is a hard country."

"It's a wide open country, and that's why I like it. Couldn't stand being hemmed in by trees and hills. Give me the desert and a wide horizon. I wouldn't want to live anywhere else. Except perhaps Innamincka, on Cooper's Creek, where there's a permanent waterhole."

"We've seen nothing yet, except from the train."

"Haven't seen the Springs? I'll take you later on this afternoon when it gets a bit cooler."

The Constable was without his tunic—sensible man! thought Mab— and the sleeves of his khaki shirt were rolled up, showing his brown forearms. When he smiled, his grey-green eyes disappeared in a fan of wrinkles. Not young; in his late thirties or early forties, perhaps. But it was hard to tell; everyone who had been up here for long had aged, weather-beaten skin.

"Well, shall we go?"

They stood up, Alix turned towards the door—and stood in the middle of his official hat.

"Oh, I'm so sorry!" she said, trying not to laugh, her blue eyes dancing. "But it is rather a *large* hat."

"Think nothing of it," said Jack McGuinnes gallantly. "I shall treasure this hat now," he added, punching the crown out again and putting it on his head for safety.

Out in the wide dusty expanse of street, bordered by houses on one side and the railway line on the other, a willy-willy danced, whirling up dust and debris into the pale-blue sky. A flat-topped tent hill seemed to float in the distance, beneath it a beautiful sheet of blue, shimmering water. As they looked, the hill divided into three, became elongated, and appeared as three dark-blue towers on the horizon, wavering and changing.

"Mirage," said the Constable laconically. "That's how the first explorers thought Lake Torrens and Lake Frome were full of water. They still colour them blue on the map."

He called for them later and they walked out to the main spring. The water lay in a circular pool ringed by a wall of dark mineral deposits built up over the years. There was a windmill to raise the water to a gravity tank for the town supply and for the cattle-troughs for watering travelling stock.

Mab climbed the crusted ring of mineral deposits and scooped some of the clear green water into her hand. "It looks a lot more appetizing than that muddy stuff in the underground tanks," she said. She tasted it, then gave a good swallow. "It tastes all right too, if you hold your breath and don't smell it."

"Well, don't be misled by that. If you drink much of it you'll be sorry."

"But it isn't *poison*. Or the cattle couldn't drink it."

"No-o. It will just give you a bad case of the trots."

"Oh!"

He held out his big hand to help her down. Mab ignored it and jumped down by herself.

Away across the level plain, as they returned to the main street, the sun was setting in a crimson ball. It was like a sunset at sea—nothing to break the horizon's rim in any direction, except for a few low tent-hills like the hulls of ships. But away to the southwest the Willouran Range, just within the bounds of sight, glowed pink and purple in the last rays. To the east, a great gold full moon rose as the sun set. The west began to glow apricot, merging into a clear, cold after-sunset sky, more green than blue. The pure arch of sky descended all round them like the interior of a tinted glass bowl.

"I've never seen such a moon!" exclaimed Alix, who had been staring silently, her breath held in wonder. "It's clear as honey, and so huge and close you would think it was resting on the rim of the earth, that if you were over there you could reach up and touch it."

"Yair. Full moon's good for travellin', up here. It's cooler at night, and the moon's so bright you can see the red colour in the sand-hills. But wait till the dark of the moon, when you'll see the stars like you've never seen 'em before. One bloke swore he could read a newspaper by the light of the Milky Way."

"There are compensations, aren't there? I mean, for the heat and dust, the isolation—"

"I *like* isolation," said Jack McGuinnes with a grin.

CHAPTER FIVE

The mail travelled to and from Birdsville, just over the Queensland border, by a horse-drawn, four-wheeled, home-built buggy. Four sturdy horses pulled the Royal Mail over the sand-hills and through dry creek-beds, with a spare horse running beside. In drought or flood, the mail usually managed to get through. With a half-caste helper, Wal Crombie drove all the way, spelling the horses in turn. When the going was good they made up to fifty miles a day and reached Birdsville in a week; sometimes they travelled night and day to make up time when they were running late.

Jack McGuinnes called at the hostel to tell them that he was off with one of his black trackers to search for a foot-traveller who had gone missing on the Birdsville Track.

"He came through about three weeks ago on the train," said Constable McGuinnes, "and I warned him about the long waterless stretches. Even in winter, the air's so dry and the sun can be so hot that dehydration sets in very quickly. He wouldn't listen to me. Walter Crombie picked him up and gave him a lift to Kopperamanna, and advised him to come back to the Springs. He's not been seen since."

On his return trip from Birdsville the mailman had seen the stranger's footprints leaving the Track and heading for the dry bed of the Cooper. Wal had followed as far as he dared, but the tracks grew fainter and there was no sign of the man. As soon as he got home, Wal raised the alarm.

Nearly a week had passed, and strong winds in the last two days had probably covered all traces. Constable McGuinnes and Micky the tracker were now going out on two riding camels to search.

Unthinkingly, concerned for his safety, Alix put a hand on his brown forearm. She had grown fond of the big policeman, who had done all sorts of small services for them; she and Mab both now familiarly called him Jack.

"Be careful!" she said. "It must be dangerous, going off the Track into that empty sand-hill country, isn't it?"

"Not very, with two camels. One will be loaded up with tucker bags, and the other with canteens of water. You're far safer on a camel than on a horse in this country."

She had meant only natural concern for another human being, but now she realized that he had taken her gesture more personally. He put his big hand over hers. "And I'll be thinking about you all the way."

Confused, she drew her hand away and bent to straighten a bedcover and to hide the flush in her cheeks. Jack turned at the door to give her a long look with his green eyes, then, putting on his wide-brimmed hat, he patted the crown, waved, and was gone.

While Constable McGuinnes was still away, an exhausted stockman rode in from Etadunna Station, nearly a hundred miles north along the Birdsville Track. One of the small daughters of the station manager, Bob Rushton, had been badly burned when her dress caught fire, and the frantic mother had sent him for help.

Mab stayed in charge of the hostel, for she was attending the difficult birth of one of the part-Aboriginal girls—a girl of scarcely fifteen years.

Alix set off with the mailman, who was fortunately just leaving. She took with her anything that might be needed—disinfectants and soothing ointments, soft bandages, pain-killers—but from what she had learned from the stockman she was not hopeful; the burns were too extensive, the child too ill to be moved down the Track and sent to hospital in Adelaide in the train.

They set off at dawn over the stony gibber plain, on which, farther out, some sparse annual saltbush grew in tiny silver-grey tufts that looked as if they must be dead, but were in fact still growing. The saltbush survived except through the worse droughts by absorbing moisture from the air, not from rainfall. It was an excellent and nourishing stockfeed.

In spite of her grim errand, Alix was looking forward intensely to her first experience of really travelling beyond the town, on the fabled Birdsville Track, even though she would be seeing only its lower end, the first hundred miles. What surprised her, after they had traversed the stony desert and entered sand-hill country, was the sheer beauty and subtlety of the colours: a land bleached by heat, tinted to the delicate colours of potch opal, with vast lakes of pale-blue mirage above which floated pink-red and salmon-coloured sand-hills. They seemed almost transparent, like a water-colour wash against the pale blue of the sky. The sand-hills were real, but some of them floated like islands in the sky, with sheets of "water" showing beneath. Or they changed shape mysteriously, sometimes seeming to end in abrupt bluffs or breaking up into separate coloured blocks above their own reflections. It was a country of deception and illusion.

It was evening when they came to the Clayton River crossing, after passing over illimitable plains where the largest growing thing was a stunted bush and the empty horizon came down all around for 360 degrees. A line of timber, real trees, appeared. Now to this permanent waterhole in the dry river bed, made by the overflow of the artesian bore, had come all the wildlife, seemingly, for a thousand dry miles. Pink-breasted galahs rose from every tree, white cockatoos with sulphur crests flapped shrieking from one calm blue pool to another, and clouds of finches filled the air. A huge flock of budgerigars, slender as small green fish, veered in swift shoals above, their voices silver-shrill. The place was alive with birds: pigeons and wild ducks, plovers with their grating ratchet cry, ibis and egrets. As they stopped to change horses and boil the billy for tea, Alix watched entranced.

After the death-still plain they had traversed for most of the day, it was an affirmation of life, eager and vibrant, full of shrill fierce joy in being.

The hot, crusty damper baked in the ashes, the slices of salty corned beef that went with it, the sweet black tea tasted better than any meal she had eaten under a roof. She wished they could camp there and see the birds again in the dawn, but the mail must go on; she must get to her patient as soon as possible. She had ridden much of the way beside Wal, while Mervyn, the slow-moving, slow-speaking part-Aboriginal helper rode high on the load, spreading himself over the mailbags.

She woke to hear Wal saying, "Dulkaninna! We've got to spell the horses here and hobble 'em out, so we'll stop the rest of the night. Did you bring a swag, or d'you want to sleep in the buggy?"

"No, er, I didn't think of it. But I brought a warm coat."

Wal glanced at Mervyn with a long-suffering look which, Alix knew, meant "Women! They're always trouble."

"Here, you can have one of my blankets, and dig a hip-hole in the sand near the fire. You'll be more comfortable."

She protested but at length accepted, and spent a wakeful night, disturbed by the unfamiliar glare of a brilliant moon that had risen about ten o'clock. Yet though tired, she scarcely wanted to sleep. She wanted to savour the strangeness of camping out in the open in the middle of nowhere with only one white man and one black one for company, and the howling of dingoes in the distance. A stone-curlew cried, a lost and lonely call that seemed like the voice of the encircling desert. It sent a tingle up her spine. This strange, empty land! How could she sleep? And then at last she must have slept, for she woke to find the rim of the earth quickened with living gold, and Mervyn tending a small fire on which a quart-pot was already steaming.

"Breakfast, missus!" said Mervyn with a wide grin, unearthing the damper that had been left to bake in the ashes the night before. Wal was on his way back from a toilet stop at a group of small trees. With the bushman's unfailing courtesy he had gone to the trouble of walking some distance so as not to embarrass her if she should be awake.

They breakfasted as the sun rose over the cold windswept plain. Alix was glad of her coat. Looking back from the jolting buggy as they left, she saw the Dulkaninna bore-head smoking in the dawn. The cold morning air was turning to steam the hot water brought up from the bowels of the earth. They passed a deserted station, its walls crumbling, beginning to be buried in sand.

When the Birdsville Track was opened up as a stock-route, Wal told her, they were dependent upon natural waterholes and sometimes there were long dry stages of a hundred miles—the mail and stores then went by camel. Now there were government bores every thirty miles; but the natural waterholes had silted up.

The sand-hills had been running parallel with the Track, running roughly in a north-westerly direction with wide clay-pans between. Now, from Dulkaninna to Blazes Well, they became more tortuous and some-times crossed the Track at right angles. The horses would charge up the long slope, then at the sharp crest begin a wild slither downwards, the buggy held back by the brake. It was a nerve-racking ride, though Wal told her it was worse in the opposite direction where they had to climb the steep side first. The crests had been flattened by continuous traffic, but fresh sand kept drifting, each sand-hill smoking at the surface in the slightest wind. In a real dust-storm it became almost impossible to travel.

"But there's always some life and feed in the sand-hills, even when the gibber plains are bare. At the next one get out and walk, and you'll be surprised at the flowers and things growing in the bare sand.

"I dunno how they survive. After rain, of course, the sand-hills are like a garden—purple parakelya, yellow daisies and billy-buttons, scarlet desert pea. . . . But in the last drought I seen this country that bare you could flog a flea over it and never lose 'im. . . .

"O'course it was the rabbits that were the finish. Course there was overstocking to blazes, especially when they used to run sheep; and then about 1900 the rabbits arrived from the south. The gov'ment put in thousands of miles of rabbit fencing, but it got silted up so they hopped over the top, or they burrowed underneath. They ate every-thing."

He said they were like a plague. They had burrowed under the roots of the saltbush and bluebush, eaten out the grass, and all the plants binding the sand, so that it started to drift. They even ate the young shoots of the mulga trees, and ring-barked the saplings of ironwood and needlebush. "But the drought," he added, "was a blessing in a way; the rabbits died out, just about, but the damage was done."

Alix did get down at the next sand-hill crossing, ploughing up to the top in the yielding red sand. As Wal had said, there were delicate flowers, tiny shrubs, and a few larger casuarinas, and the flat silver leaves of saltbush which she nibbled and found tasty, salty though somewhat bitter.

She climbed aboard again at the summit, only a hundred feet or so above the depression below, but giving a view all round of a vast and empty land. There had been footprints in the soft sand, too, marks of lizards' feet, and the two paw-marks and long back feet of tiny marsupial mice—creatures that lived in holes during the heat of the day and came out at night to feed.

At Blazes Well there was no water, the well having fallen in and not been repaired. A hot wind blew across the scalded clay-flats between the sand-hills, strewn with the skeletons of cattle that had died in the last drought. It was a daunting, desolate place, and Alix was glad that they did not stop but made for Kanuwaulkinna Creek, where permanent water flowed from a bore and they could water the horses.

Suddenly the Track underwent a change: the green timber of the creek showed above the horizon, flocks of tiny emerald-green parrots filled the air, and all round there was good herbage, even grass.

"We are actually inside the boundary of Etadunna Station," Wal told Alix, "but it's still a long way off; there's no front fence, and the station covers three thousand square miles."

Alix welcomed the break for lunch in these pleasant surroundings. She was beginning to feel the journey would never end, although she had slept fitfully while Wal drove.

She was dozing again as they reached Etadunna homestead. She woke to the barking of dogs and gazed about her. The cluster of buildings surrounding the homestead included an abandoned wool-shed, for this cattle station had once run sheep in the days when the German Mission owned it.

Now the cattle ran free between each muster. The only fence, apart from a huge horse-paddock, was around the homestead building itself, to keep the stock out; and inside the fence was a green garden with stunted date-palms and native wattles in bloom.

As the buggy pulled up and Mervyn opened the gate for her, Alix was overwhelmed once more with the thought of the task ahead of her. She sent up a quick prayer that she would be able to help save the life of the little girl. Her heart was wrenched by the sight of the mother's face as she ran out to greet Alix: gaunt, weather-beaten, strained, with wisps of black hair falling untidily from her bun, looking as though she had slept in her dress.

"Thank God, Sister!" Mrs. Rushton grasped Alix's hand. "Thank God you're here! She's still alive."

"How—how old is she?"

"Lucy is only four."

Wal brought in the mail and Alix's bags, accepted a glass of cool well-water and was on his way. Stopping only to wash her hands, Alix went straight to the cot in a darkened room where the little patient lay between life and death.

CHAPTER SIX

Farther up the Birdsville Track another fight against death was taking place in the shifting sands and scalded clay-flats to the north-east of Kopperamanna.

As soon as the two men had reached the point where Wal Crombie had seen the tracks of the traveller heading out into the desert, Micky *hoosh-ta'd* his camel to its knees and dismounted. Leading it by the line attached to its nose-peg he began moving in wide circles. Jack McGuinnes searched farther up the Track in case the wanderer had doubled back. Then he saw Micky throw up his arm.

"Boss, I got 'im!" he called, setting off at a loping run with his eyes to the ground. He had picked up the faint imprint of an elastic-sided boot. Several times when he came to windblown sand or stone-hard clay-pan he lost the tracks and would circle patiently until he picked them up again. He was wearing his police tracker's red-banded cap, and a police inspector's discarded tunic over an old pair of trousers.

When night fell the trail was still leading indistinctly towards the dry beds of the Cooper. At least the man was not going in circles. At "piccaninny daylight" Micky was off again, eager as a hound upon the scent. There had been no wood for a proper camp-fire, but Micky had slept, blackfellow-fashion, curled about a tiny fire of smouldering sticks.

They must have covered fifty miles, with circling and doubling back, when the tireless Micky decided to ride again. He could see farther from the height of the camel's back, and the signs were now so clear that he could read them while mounted.

Now the tracks doubled back on themselves, a bad sign.

"Him sit down 'ere. Him tired." He pointed.

The tracks took their old direction. They crossed a bare gibber plain where Jack McGuinnes could not see any signs at all, towards a painted sand-hill lying along the skyline, a pale delicate salmon-red.

The tracks turned and went along its base towards the dry Cooper flood-plain.

After a while Micky said, "Him bin lie down 'ere. Then walk, walk. Him look for water."

"Well, at least he's still going. Apparently he didn't know that if he followed the Cooper down it would cut the Track."

They came to a dry sandy watercourse, its bed lined with the skeletons of dead trees. Here he had attempted to dig a soak with his hands, but if he had obtained any water, there was now no sign of it. He had thrown off his shirt and his walk had become a stagger. Then they found where he had thrown his empty water-bag away.

"Him close-up finish," said Micky.

And then, late on the second afternoon, he suddenly cried out and pointed ahead. His sharp eyes had seen a dark shape huddled under a dead tree.

There, crouched on his side in the dry creek-bed, was a man with his head in his hands. He looked up blearily at their shout, and attempted a croaking cry. His tongue was swollen and black, his lips were terribly fissured. But he was alive. Without Micky's skill and persistence, he would certainly have perished.

They gave him a piece of cloth soaked in water to suck, and gradually he was able to swallow. They put the stranger up on Micky's camel and began the long trek back to Kopperamanna, then Dulkaninna and Hergott Springs.

The child lay with her eyes open and glittering feverishly. Her hair and one side of her face were burned, and most of the rest of her body except the legs.

"Lucy! Can you hear me? Here's Nurse come to make you better."

Only the eyes moved in the charred face. "I tried to cut her dress off, but she screamed so, I couldn't bear it. I put olive oil—"

"She has to be bathed," said Alix, opening her medicine case. "I'm going to give her a shot of morphia so that it can be done without too much shock to her system."

"Lucy, I'm just going to give you a prick with this needle, so you'll be able to sleep."

When the child's eyes were closed and she was breathing more regularly, Alix cut away what she could of the charred and blackened clothes, then bathed the rest away with cold water. She knew that such extensive burns were always serious, and when they covered more than two-thirds of the body they were usually fatal. Shock and nephritis affecting the kidneys were the most dangerous complications.

Slowly and patiently she bathed away the scraps of cloth, strips of skin coming with them. When the trunk was clean she irrigated the surface with warm boric solution.

"I don't think I'll try to put on dressings," muttered Alix. "The burnt area is too extensive, and besides they will stick and be very painful to change. Open treatment might be best."

She was talking to herself as much as to Lucy's mother. She dusted the burns with sterile zinc powder, and rigged up a makeshift bed-cradle to keep the sheets from touching and pressing on the burns.

41

"I daren't give her any more morphia," she said, as Lucy began to show signs of returning restlessness. "Meanwhile I want *you* to go and lie down and try to rest. You haven't slept since this happened, have you? Next thing I'll have you for a patient."

Mrs. Rushton gave the ghost of a smile. "No, I haven't. But my husband will be in soon, and he'll give you any help you need. I might lie down for a bit. And I'll get the cook to make you some afternoon tea. You must be exhausted yourself by that trip."

"No, I'm all right."

While Alix was snatching a cup of tea on the veranda, Mr. Rushton rode in, left his horse with a black stockman and came striding up the steps.

"Sister! How wonderful that you got here!" He pressed her hand as she rose from her cane chair. "Is my wife with Lucy?"

"No, I just persuaded her to lie down. Lucy is still partly under from a morphia injection, and one of the black staff is watching her."

"God, what a dreadful business!" said Mr. Rushton. "It happened so quickly. She pulled over a lantern, the kerosene spilled on her dress, and she went up like a torch."

His lips were shaking. He was a short, solid, nuggety bushman with a nut-brown face and a fan of lighter wrinkles about the corner of each eye.

"What's the outlook, Sister? You can tell me. I won't tell my wife."

"Well . . . It's not good. She should be in hospital, really. What I fear is complications which I won't be able to treat. But we mustn't give up hope."

"No, of course not. I'll go and see her. Have you been shown to your room?"

"Not yet. I went straight to Lucy."

He showed her a door opening off the long veranda. Her bag had already been placed on the bed. "I expect you'd like to have a wash and change after that long trip. You must be tired out."

"That's what Mrs. Rushton said; but I'm not. I enjoy travel, and camping out, though it was a bit cold early this morning. And I had a wash and a cool drink when I arrived."

He turned away with a discouraged slump of his shoulders.

"Mr. Rushton! At least she has survived the initial shock. There is still hope."

"Yes, yes . . . I must go to my wife."

Alix bathed in the basin in her room and changed into a fresh uniform.

The other children, a fair little girl about six years, and a small boy, came and peered in the fly-wire door, but ran away giggling when she spoke to them. They were as wild as little bush creatures.

Next day Lucy's temperature was up. She had an unquenchable thirst, yet she passed very little water, a worrying sign. There was a lemon tree in the station enclosure, and though there were few lemons on it Alix had drinks with a squeeze of lemon made up from the cold water-bag on the veranda.

Lucy was in terrible pain from her burnt back pressing on the bed.

"I think I'll try immersion," said Alix. "Have you a small tub long enough for her to lie in? Fortunately it is warm enough in the daytime for her not to get a chill, and we'll keep the temperature of the water just tepid."

She added bicarbonate of soda to the water, and after dusting the burns with a sterile powder and rolling the child in a clean sheet, she lowered her into the bath with a support for her head.

"The water excludes the air, keeps the surface clean, and supports her weight," she explained to Mrs. Rushton, who had been talking quietly to Lucy throughout. The child had begun to cry weakly, but she drank a little milk and took some gruel from her mother's hands.

By the third day the burns were suppurating and forming sloughs. Lucy was put back in the cot and the surfaces irrigated with a solution of picric acid. But her temperature continued to rise. On the fourth day it reached 104 degrees. She was extremely restless, muttering in semi-delirium. Alix could not hide her foreboding. All the symptoms were there for nephritis: the scanty urine, with extreme thirst and vomiting. Alix gave Lucy a bromide, and tried to persuade her to drink some milk with lime-water, and lemonade with cream of tartar. She was snatching some sleep, sitting in a padded cane chair in the patient's room, when a scream from Mrs. Rushton woke her.

"Nurse! Nurse! She's unconscious!"

Little Lucy Rushton had passed into a final, fatal coma.

Lucy was buried on a sand-hill behind the homestead, joining a baby brother who had died at birth. The mail had returned to Hergott Springs while Alix was nursing the child, and had passed again on its way north; now it would have to come back from Birdsville before she could return to the hostel. Alix worried about Mab coping by herself, but was glad to be able to give a woman's sympathy to poor Mrs. Rushton, alone in a world of men apart from her children and the black staff—who had set up a terrible wailing at the death of the little girl. Alix gave Mrs. Rushton sedatives to help her sleep, and finally persuaded her to walk up the sand-hill with some petunias for the little grave, which at first she said she never wanted to see. Her hard, closed-up tearless face worried Alix. Now, at the sight of the new sandy mound, so pathetically small, she at last broke down and wept.

Alix felt numb herself. She had lost patients before, but this was such a little child, and she had fought so hard to save her. Perhaps she had eased Lucy's suffering a little. But why should innocent little ones suffer so?

What was God thinking of? She had always hated nursing in the children's ward when she was training.

She sat on the homestead veranda, going over in her mind all she had done, wondering if she had done right. Faintly, she thought she heard the sound of camel bells . . . and then, beyond the green garden enclosure, she saw two camels in single file.

Jack McGuinnes got down from his camel, and leaving Micky in charge, came through the gate and bounded up the steps.

"Oh, Jack!" Alix was on her feet, in a moment she had buried her weary face against his strong shoulder, and his arms went round her protectively. "Oh, Jack!" was all she could say. It was infinitely comforting to have a broad shoulder to weep on.

"There, there!" said Jack McGuinnes.

"I lost her. I did all I could."

"There, there. Yes, I heard from a stockman on the way in. In fact, after what I'd heard of the burns, I didn't expect you could save her. I can sign the death certificate, look after the formalities. I can't take you back to the Springs, but the mail will be here soon."

"Oh-h, Jack!" was all she could say again. And then, "Did you find your man?"

"Yes, and we found him alive, what's more. He's been doubling up on Micky's camel. Not in bad shape now, but you might have a look at him. Give him some ointment for his lips, they're badly cracked."

"All right. Oh, Jack, it's so good to see you back safe!"

At this he looked at her so tenderly that she withdrew herself from his arms. "I'm sorry. I don't usually cry. But it has been rather a strain."

The rescued man, still weak, sat on the veranda while she applied some soothing ointment to his lips and his sunburn. He seemed vague about why he had left the Track; had some idea that the Cooper was not far away, and he would be able to swim in a waterhole.

Bob Rushton shook his head in disbelief, and raised his eyes to the brush roof.

"The Cooper was about forty miles away, and he'd be lucky to find a waterhole before Innamincka that wasn't dry."

"Just as well Micky's a top-notch tracker," said the Constable.

When they had gone Alix sat and talked for a little with the station manager.

"Mrs. Rushton will take a long time to get over this, I'm afraid," she said. "You must give her all the help and companionship you can."

"Of course. Until mustering starts. But it has meant a great deal, having another woman here at this time. God bless you, Sister."

"I just wish I could have done more."

✳   ✳   ✳

When the mail buggy arrived from Birdsville Wal Crombie already knew the sad outcome. Somehow he had heard along the Track by the "bush telegraph." He took with him an order for a small tombstone to be sent up from Adelaide five hundred miles away.

Back at the hostel at last, Alix found that the wanderer had been admitted for a couple of days, and then packed off by the Constable on the next train south.

"Other men could have lost their lives looking for you," he said. "You should remember that, when you decide to go off the beaten track. This is a hard country."

"I know that now. You and Micky saved my life, Boss. And I've learned a lesson I won't forget in a hurry. Think I'll stick to the coast from now on."

Mab was delighted to see Alix back. She said it hadn't been a very busy time, but the Aboriginal girl had been in labour for three days, and nearly died of exhaustion. "She would have died, in the old days. Native women very rarely have complications, but when they do—say from some malformation of the pelvis—they usually die. So the characteristic isn't passed on to the next generation."

"And the baby?"

"Was born dead. The cord was around its neck."

"What if she gets pregnant again?"

"It shouldn't happen again. This was a breech presentation. How I wished you were here to help me!"

"Yes. And I didn't do much good by going all that way."

"Alix, from what you told me it must have been pretty hopeless from the start. And at least you were able to ease her pain a bit."

"Yes . . . I suppose so." But she was still depressed over her failure to save the child.

CHAPTER SEVEN

Alix strolled along to the only store, a small fenceless building set back from the road. Mrs. Allison greeted her warmly—a little woman with grey hair, spectacles, and a neat storekeeper's apron over her floral cotton dress.

She seemed a kindly soul, though her voice was rather harsh, like a crow's, as if the inland dust had got into her vocal cords.

The store was jammed to the roof with goods. There were hobble-chains and saddles, boots and camel-bells, blue blankets and canvas water-bags, ground-sheets and camp ovens, billy-cans, quart-pots (but no teapots), Bedourie ovens, tin plates, sheath knives, butchers' knives, buckets. . . . Mrs. Allison was a universal provider. She kept some bright cotton dresses ("gins' frocks") for the Aboriginal women in the town, and jodhpurs and leggings, drill trousers and hats, and elastic-sided boots for men, but in general, horses were catered for better than human beings. Groceries were stored on the floor and on shelves behind the counter.

"Well now, I was meanin' to call," said Mrs. Allison, leaning companionably on the counter. "I heard youse two had arrived, but I thought I'd give you time to settle in. I bet the whole town's been having a gander at the new Sisters."

"Yes, we have had a good few visitors. But everyone's been very kind. I wonder if you have any postcards?" said Alix doubtfully.

"Yair, sure to be here somewhere." Mrs. Allison began sweeping aside a pile of hessian sacking, and came up with four postcards showing the main street, with two camels.

"Yes, I like a bit of life, somethin' going on, like you get in town."

Alix looked out the door at the wide, empty street. There were no trains in, and the only sign of life was a lone blue-grey dog dozing outside the pub.

"I suppose there's plenty going on when a droving plant comes in?"

"You can say that again. Or a string of camels with wool. Wouldn't know the place then."

"Have you lived here long?"

"'Bout five years. Before that my late hubby and me, we kept a store out on the Birdsville Track. Never saw nobody except the trooper with his camels, or an Afghan hawker, or the mailman twice a fortnight. It

46

was the drovers kept us goin'. Not like the old days, before the waterholes all silted up."

"There are not many women in the town, then, besides yourself? The mailman's wife, and the cook up at the hotel—the publican's wife lives in Adelaide, I believe."

"Yair. Couldn't stand the climate," said Mrs. Allison scornfully. "Who'd want to live in the cold old south, with rain pourin' down, and sleet, and I dunnomany what-all. Up here, it's nilly always cool at night —can be real cold in the winter—and the sun shines all day."

She paused to give a deep, phlegmy cough.

Alix bought some soap, dried milk, and canned butter. They could sometimes get fresh goats' milk, but the supply was erratic. The Aboriginal woman who drove the goats with their tinkling bells out to where there was something, however dry and unappetizing, to eat, would sometimes fail to return at dusk, and would come back the next morning with the nannies bleating in pain at their swollen udders.

"Y'know what the black gins like to buy when they've got a few bob?" Mrs. Allison asked.

"Lolly-water?"

"No, soap. 'You got chope?' they say. They love soap, 'specially if it's scented or a pretty colour. The men never buy it. Men and women is different, no matter what their colour."

"Yes, I know what you mean. Not just biologically different, but— different."

Mrs. Allison coughed deeply in agreement.

"D'you do anything about that cough?"

"What cough, Sister?"

"I'd say you had a chronic cough—probably worse in winter."

"Oh, it doesn't worry me none. I'm used to it, like."

When Alix got back she found that Alf and young Joe had brought a full load of wood for them, and had not charged for it. Joe's hand had mended nicely and he was no longer an out-patient.

"The people in this town are very kind," said Alix, stoking the wood stove with the dry lengths of wood, for this was her fortnight for cooking.

"They couldn't be nicer," said Mab. "How was Mrs. Allison?"

"Oh, a bit of a character. She's got a nasty smoker's cough, but it doesn't seem to worry her. She's coming over one day soon to meet you."

"By then we'll have met everyone on this side of the line."

"But we still haven't met the Afghans on the other side. Remember Jack promised to take us to meet Abdul Dervish?"

The three of them crossed the rail the next afternoon, walking with their backs to the sun. They passed the kerosene-tin and corrugated-iron humpies of the blacks, who like the Afghans kept to "the other side of the

47

line," or the east. The humpies looked deserted, except for a group of ragged children playing at kicking an empty can about.

The Afghan residents, who were called 'Ghans, though most of them or their forebears had come from northern India rather than Afghanistan, had slightly better homes than the Aborigines. They were decorated with white or blue paint, peeling in the relentless heat. Some of them, said Jack McGuinnes, had married Aboriginal women, some had married whites. There was a school for their children where the boys studied the Koran, for all were devout Muslims.

Abdul had been a famous camel-man in his youth, travelling with early explorers and surveyors.

As they approached his house through a dusty yard, the girls recoiled slightly. A bunch of bloody entrails, pluck and liver and heart, hung in the porch, dripping blood on the floor.

At Jack McGuinnes' call a slim young girl came to the door, dark and sloe-eyed as an Eastern princess. She called her father, and Abdul Dervish welcomed them, immensely tall and brown in baggy white trousers, a European shirt worn outside them, and a grey silk turban on his head. He had a magnificent beard sprinkled with grey, and a strong, hooked nose. He smiled and welcomed them in with a graceful sweeping gesture.

The girl had swiftly retired from sight.

"Well, Abdul, I brought the new A.I.M. Sisters to meet you. So you'll know them if you ever have to go to hospital."

"I am never sick. Never, never." He clapped his hands twice, and soon the first girl and her sister, older but just as pretty, brought sickly sweet coffee in an elaborate metal jug, which they proceeded to pour into thick white cups without saucers.

The girls did not drink with them but stood submissively in the background. "These are Mira and Deneb," said Abdul, with one of his lordly gestures. "Named after stars by their mother, may Allah give her peace."

He proudly showed them his greatest treasures, including a beautiful sapphire ring made from a stone he had found himself. Then he accompanied them outside on the way home. Inside his fence a small irrigation channel flowed into a mineral-encrusted pool, and beside it grew two tall date-palms. Abdul gave the Sisters a lesson in elemental biology.

"This one," he said, slapping the trunk of one, "lady tree; and *this* one," slapping the other one, "gentleman tree. Without this one, no dates."

He promised to send them some dates when his meagre crop was ripe, but the trees were failing from a diet of too much salt. There had once been a big grove of date-palms at Hergott Springs, he said, now almost all dead. "Once, many of my people; now only few. Camels, not many.

The young men, all but one of my sons, go away, go to the south; and who in this town is there for my daughters to marry?"

His son was away on a camel trip up the Strzelecki Track, taking stores and goods to remote stations. Abdul was a mournful, dignified figure as he stood beneath the palms, with his turban making him look even taller, as they took their farewell.

"He's right, of course," said Jack McGuinnes reflectively. "Who is there for them to marry? The men sometimes find a white wife, but it rarely happens the other way around. Aborigines will marry them—but Abdul despises the Aborigines as uncivilized. It's a problem."

"They're beauties, too," said Alix. "What a pity they couldn't go to the city, where I believe people are less racist in their attitudes; or where they might meet men of their own race."

"They have no mother, and Abdul Dervish would never agree for them to go unchaperoned, or let them marry an Infidel."

Mab, struck by a thought, asked if one of the girls might like to work at the hostel?

"We haven't really enough·work for two," added Alix. "You see it's not really a hospital, just a tiny dressing-station."

Jack McGuinnes doubted if Abdul would agree, though he thought the girls would be delighted. They must be bored with their life. Perhaps it could be arranged for them to work week about, so that each had a job and one would not envy the other.

Next day a short, bearded bushman came limping in on makeshift crutches cut from two forked limbs of a mulga tree. He had tipped the boiling quart-pot off the fire over his foot, some of the scalding liquid had gone inside his boot, and he'd had to cut the leather from his swollen foot.

"If it turns septic we'll have to send him down to Adelaide on the train," said Alix. "Otherwise he risks losing his lower leg. And he's one of those independent types who'd rather be dead than crippled."

She tried compresses of the clear green bore-water, which contained so many dissolved minerals that surely some of them must be beneficial.

Mab had tried drinking it, but after two days she was making a beaten path to the earth dunny, and beginning to feel weak. She gave in and drank the brownish-muddy water from the underground tanks. The rain-water tank attached to the hostel roof was dry.

She had coaxed some tomato seedlings to come up, and they seemed to be flourishing, when there came a dust-storm from the north-east— more flying sand and big particles than dust—and completely buried her vegetable garden. When unearthed the small plants were burnt and withered. The hot wind and flying debris had the same effect as a severe frost down south.

Yet the next morning dawned clear and still. The pale golden sunlight spilled from a pure blue, cloudless sky. Alix, busy sweeping dust out the front door while Mab muttered over her buried garden, leaned on the broom to watch the galahs. A great flock of the rose-breasted cockatoos was arrayed on the Overland Telegraph Line, which they used as an elongated perch. They were clowning among themselves, turning somersaults, hanging upside-down by claw or beak and swinging, pretending to fall and swooping up again to the crowded wire. All the while they kept up a shrill chatter and squawk.

"To think that people keep them in cages, down south!" said Alix. "Why, they're as tame as house-sparrows."

The birds ignored her as she stepped out into the dusty stony road. Then as she turned to go in they decided to take off, as one bird, for their morning drink at the railway-station tank's overflow. The pale grey mass swept into the air, then turned, banking slightly, to reveal one sudden flash of rose-pink against the blue.

Yes, it has its compensations, thought Alix.

CHAPTER EIGHT

Some unusual overcast nights—though no rain fell—made the air hot and stifling after the sun had set. There was only one patient, in the women's ward, and she was thoroughly enjoying herself. It was Mrs. Allison from the store—as there was so little to do in the hospital, the Sisters let her borrow Mira to keep an eye on it for her. Abdul's daughter Mira was now on the staff, but her older sister preferred to remain at home to look after their father.

Mrs. A. had fallen over a piece of old iron in the yard and broken both bones in her leg just below the knee. It was a clean break and she would soon be able to get around on crutches. Meanwhile, after a long hard life with few luxuries, she appreciated afternoon tea on a tray, and three meals a day that she did not have to cook herself.

She told them stories of the bush, some funny, some grim. Her late husband had once rescued a man who'd fallen off his horse and broken his upper arm, the splintered bone protruding through the flesh. He was not far from a waterhole and managed to keep alive, but when by chance Mr. Allison found him the arm had turned black.

"It had to be amputated in the end. It took a week to get him to a doctor, and by then gangrene had set in."

When a droving plant arrived in town she was distressed. "Just my luck!" she moaned. "Just when there'd be a bit of business, I'm laid up. Can't I get up, Sister Mab?"

"Not for at least a week. We have to make sure the bones have begun to knit, and you might be tempted to put your foot on the floor if I let you up on crutches."

Stan Reilly, the boss drover, came in to get some drops for his eyes. They were red and inflamed with the dust of the track, after following behind a thousand head of cattle.

He was a sturdy-looking man in his early thirties, dark-haired with a shadow of dark stubble on his chin and upper lip. He wore leather leggings, a khaki shirt with the sleeves rolled up, tight gabardines, and a high-crowned, wide-brimmed hat.

"It was a hell of a trip from Queensland," he said. "An unlucky plant —it was jinxed from the start, I reckon. First one of my men died, and then the others deserted—rode off back the way we had come. I was left with one black stockboy and a lad driving the cart. One man alone, tailing a thousand head! Had no sleep for about a week. We could only make seven miles a day."

Mab bathed his eyes with a weak boracic solution, and suggested he should lie down for a while with cold compresses on his inflamed eyes.

"Can't," said Reilly laconically. "Have to get the beasts ready for the train. The copper has to inspect them before they go. And it takes time to water a thousand head."

She gave him a cup of tea, and told him that weak black tea would make a good eye-lotion when on the track.

"Thanks, Sister!" And he left, squashing his dusty felt hat down on his dark hair.

The cattle, having been watered at the mound spring where the water was allowed to flow into a series of open troughs, were driven into the holding yards near the railhead. Alix and Mab heard the bellowing, blended notes from a thousand throats, the sound rising and swelling as they came nearer, the crack of stockwhips and the shouts of the drover and the Aboriginal stockman. They went out on the veranda to look. "He's one of the most *masculine* men I've ever met," said Mab, watching the drover.

"Curse it! Can't you let me out of here?" wailed Mrs. Allison from her bed.

"There won't be all that much business at the store, there's only one drover with the plant, Mrs. A."

A sea of red-brown backs and tossing horns was moving beside the road towards the stockyards. The drover rode his horse easily, keeping the tail-enders up to the mob, his whip circling in the air, and helped by a blue cattle-dog; while Billy, his offsider, rode on the flank on a lean brown horse that could turn in its own length. The shouts of the men, lowing of cattle, and crack of stockwhips blended in an outback symphony.

They watched, fascinated. The cattle-train was due from the south in two days, and would leave the following morning for Port Augusta and Adelaide, and for the fattening-paddocks where the cattle would put on condition before being sold for beef.

When the mob was safely penned, the drover went off to the pub for a well-earned beer. Under the laws of the land his helper, being Aboriginal, was not allowed to drink alcohol. He went round the back and Reilly handed him a bottle out the window. He made camp that night near the yards, while the boss drover "dossed down" at the hotel. Earlier, he had sent Billy over with a choice piece of rump for the hostel larder.

The next night was so hot and airless that the Sisters left the hostel door open, with just a swinging wire door between them and the night. They went to bed early, and around ten o'clock were awakened by a dreadful din. It sounded like clattering hoofs, crashes of crockery, an army careering round the wards.

"Sister! Sister!" shrieked Mrs. Allison.

Had the cattle broken out and invaded the hostel? Alix and Mab put on wraps and lit a lamp. A ghostly shape cantered along the passageway. They followed it to the kitchen. There was a white goat on the table, eating the rice custard from under a net cover.

Two other goats dashed into the women's ward, dancing across the beds. "Get them out of here!" shrieked Mrs. Allison, fearful for her leg.

But that was easier said than done. After ten minutes of chasing and shouting, the goats were still in occupation.

Mab sat down, gasping and laughing. "I've heard of a bull in a china-shop, but never a goat in a hospital!"

"*Three* goats," said Alix.

"I'm going to get the drover and his 'boy.' They'll get them out," said Mab. She slipped into a dress, took a lantern and walked to the hotel.

The hotel bar was lit, and looking in the window she saw Stan Reilly leaning on the bar with a pint mug of beer in his hand. She had to steel herself to face the tight little circle of men, but she went to the door and called, "Mr. Reilly!" She had not stopped to put on her uniform, and Reilly, who had seen her only in her apron and white cap, did not recognize her.

"Sister Kingston, from the hostel," she explained. "There's—a mob of goats inside, and we can't get them out. They're wrecking the place. If you could round them up—"

"Sister! Of course. I never recognized you in clothes."

There was a shout of laughter. Stan Reilly detached himself from the bar. "Er—I mean in mufti, out of your uniform." He grinned. Mab looked furious. "Come on, we'll pick up Billy on the way, and a stockwhip."

At the hostel the goats were still enjoying themselves, munching at the thin curtains and chasing each other round the wards.

"Just leave it to us," said the drover, and uncoiled his whip. But there was no room to swing it properly. After minutes they had caught one goat with a running tackle, and evicted it. The other two were loose in the women's ward, and Mrs. Allison, enjoying herself hugely, was cheering them on and shaking with laughter.

"Call yerselves drovers!" she jeered. "Can't round up a couple o' goats. Why, if I could get out of this bed . . ."

Reilly set his jaw, made a lunge at a goat and missed. Then the animals took it into their heads to run down the corridor towards the back door. It was shut, but in the narrow space the two men collared the goats and thrust them outside. Panting and covered in sweat, they came back to find Mab and Alix helpless with laughter.

53

"I'm sorry!" said Alix. "You did a great job evicting them."

"It was good as a circus!" said Mrs. Allison.

"I think a cup of tea all round?" said Mab. "I'm afraid we've no beer."

When the tea was brewed they sat drinking it on the two empty beds in the women's ward. Billy was very quiet and shy and said little, but every now and then he broke into a wide reminiscent grin. "By cripes, Boss, I'd rather drove cattle 'n goats," he said.

Mrs. Allison said afterwards that it had been as good as a tonic. She hadn't laughed so much for a long time, she told Mab, who was collecting cups to take to the kitchen. Mrs. Allison sat with her good leg hanging over the side of the bed, her night-dress rucked up round her waist. "I'll never get to sleep again. Better give me an aspirin or something, Sister."

Mab brought a tablet and a glass of water. Mrs. Allison took the glass in one hand and the pill in the other, but somehow she dropped it. She scrabbled anxiously between her legs, then came up with the pill and swallowed it.

"Help, I thought for a moment it had fallen into the letter-box."

Afterwards, in the kitchen, Mab said, "It's certainly a term I've never come across before; at first I didn't know what she meant. But I had to laugh."

After the goat episode, they had an adventure with camels. They were having dinner once more at the pub, and this time managed to see the carroty-haired cook. She had lost weight and her face was thin, but she said that the job was "not so bad", as most nights there were only the few "permanents" to feed—two railway staff, Joe the woodman's assistant, the hotelkeeper, and the barman. "I'm gettin' used to the heat," she said, "but you never told me how cold it gets. When that wind comes up it goes right through yer. I been colder here than I ever was in London."

Jack McGuinnes, back from a patrol out to the dingo fence, had come over to their table and asked them if they would like to try camel-riding.

Alix looked nervous, but Mab said at once, "We'd love to! Wouldn't we, Alix."

"Er—well . . ."

"Of course we would! When?"

"This afternoon, if you like."

He helped them up onto Rocket, Mab in the double saddle and Alix "donkeying" behind. It was not so bad while the camel was kneeling, but when with an unnerving roar he lurched to his feet in three bone-jerking movements as his long legs unfolded, it was like sitting on top of an earthquake. From his full height it seemed a very long way to the ground. Alix nervously tucked in her gossamer fly-veil which, tied under the chin, held her shady hat in place. The Constable led them round for a while at a walk. Then he handed Mab the noseline. "When you want him to get going," he said, "you have to say *'Ibna!'* They don't understand English."

But at the word for "Go!" Rocket emulated his namesake and set off at a sudden gallop, striding with first two legs on one side, then two on the other. The girls, precariously seated side-saddle on top, clung to the saddle and each other as the Ship of the Desert rolled from side to side. Jack ran after them, as well as he could for laughing, while Mab pulled at the noseline, which was supposed to convey instructions to the beast through its sensitive nostrils. It did not seem to get the message. Then Jack shouted *"Oodoo!"* (Stop!)

The camel stopped as suddenly as it had begun. Its stomach rumbled, and it gave a loud belch.

"I think," said Alix, "that that was a comment on our riding ability!"

They asked Jack to lead them back at a walk, and he complied.

"I think I'd prefer an elephant," said Mab. "It has such a broad back, it would be harder to fall off."

"But farther to the ground."

Outside the hostel they tried saying *"Hoosh-ta"* and were rather surprised when Rocket obediently folded his knees half-way, then his back legs, then tucked the front ones under, tipping the riders back and forwards as he did so. Mab slid down quickly, but Alix's long poplin skirt was caught in the back of the saddle. As she tried to descend it rode up and revealed a pair of white boots and slim legs in white stockings.

"Here, let me." Jack McGuinnes unhitched the skirt, and lifted her to the ground. Alix, a little flushed, thanked him and escaped inside. Not that he had *looked*, exactly, but she had felt the tremor in his hands as he held her waist.

A few days later he called to tell them he was off on a patrol to the west of Lake Eyre, the desolate region between the west shore of the lake and the railway to Oodnadatta. Word had come down the line that there had been a brawl in the fettlers' camp, and a man had been killed.

"It will be an easy trip," he said. "At least I can't get lost, with the railway line on one side and the lake on the other. In fact I think I might go by train; the 'Ghan is due in tomorrow."

They gave him afternoon tea in the cool-looking living room with its cane furniture and the cushions that Alix had covered with some sea-green material her mother had sent her for a dress. (She didn't like sewing and she didn't need another dress.)

He laughed over their story of the goat invasion. "Pity I was away. I should have been called to arrest them for breaking and entering."

"Not to mention stealing—a bowl of rice custard!"

A few days later a dust-storm blew up. It started as just a few swirls of sand; then the sky to the north-east took on a reddish-yellow tinge, as though from the smoke of a bushfire; but there was no thick bush for many hundreds of miles.

Out of doors, the infinitesimal specks, each separate grain of sand, stung the flesh and gathered in the corners of eyes. Only one advantage came from the dust-storm: the all-pervading flies were blown away, or sheltered somewhere out of the wind.

The yellowish-red cloud came nearer, dimmed the sun, and turned it a livid blue. It went on for two days, days in which they had to light the lamps at two in the afternoon.

Sand and grit came through the fly-wire and silted up the veranda, seeped under the doors; even the meals tasted of grit. Mrs. Allison had gone home, and mercifully there were no patients. Mira had not come to work.

They sat listening to the roof-iron flapping in the fierce wind, and wondered if the roof would blow away. An empty water-tank came bowling along the street, banging and booming like a giant drum.

"I just hope," said Alix nervously, "that Jack went by train. I wouldn't like to be out in this in an open camel-buggy."

"He couldn't travel in this dust. He'd have to camp somewhere and sit it out."

It was stifling with all the windows closed, for the wind was hot as the breath of Hell. Mab tried opening a window on the lee side, but an eddy swirled a choking cloud into the room, making in no time a miniature sand-hill on the linoleum.

The roar of the wind dropped to a wavering, high-pitched whine through windows not properly sealed, and it was just barely possible to make out the other side of the street. The sun was almost without light, as pale and ghostly as a daylight moon. Alix looked through the front windows and gave a cry.

"The front fence is *buried!*" she called. A smooth orange sand-hill had taken its place.

"And we don't even own a wheelbarrow!"

"We'll be able to get one at the store. Mrs. Allison stocks everything."

When the wind finally dropped they went out into a silent world. All the birds had disappeared, even the flies had not come back. Hillocks of sand were piled against every obstruction. Not even a dog or a goat was to be seen in the empty street.

"Well, it's no use crying over spilt milk," said Mab practically. "We'd better start sweeping up inside."

Even the curtains seemed to be impregnated with the finer particles of dust, and would all have to be washed. They shook the bedspreads, beat the dust out of the green cushions, and then started to sweep.

"Jack would have come and given us a hand, if he was in town," said

Mab. They sat side by side on a bed and stared despondently at the gritty floors.

"What about Wal Crombie? Is he on the way to Birdsville?"

"I hope not."

But just then there came a cheerful hail from the veranda, and in walked Wal with his eldest son. "We've got a wheelbarrow outside, and a couple of shovels," he said. "We'll just clear your front gate for you. It's no job for a woman."

Gratefully the Sisters watched as the men shovelled sand in a kind of parody of men shovelling snow in a cold climate. Except that the fine dust and sand flowed like water, trickling through a hole in the wheelbarrow, and it was not white but orange and yellow.

Mab's herb garden, which she had started again, had entirely disappeared. "I'm going to grow them indoors in pots this time," she said indomitably. "As soon as I can get some seed."

Chapter Nine

Mira had a "follower," a part-Aboriginal boy who hung about the hospital waiting to escort her home, for she did not live in. Alix had taught her to make a creditable egg custard, but jellies, except in winter, were out of the question; they would never set.

The Sisters had found that in summer they had to keep even the thermometer in the cool-safe, or patients would seem to record horrifying temperatures. It was frequently 110 degrees inside the building by late afternoon. But in the clear dry air the heat quickly dissipated after sunset and the nights were usually cool.

Mira wore an embroidered blouse over a white cotton skirt down to her ankles to work. She usually added a bright-coloured scarf thrown loosely about her neck, or tied round her thick black braids. She was gentle, quiet, unassuming and willing, but was inclined to go into a day-dream in the midst of dusting or sweeping. Leaning on the broom she would gaze unseeingly out at the empty main street with her liquid dark eyes.

"A penny for your thoughts, Mira," said Alix, finding her mooning about, an unused duster in her hand.

"They not worth much. I just wishing I been born a boy. Men can travel, do things. I never bin outside the Springs."

"Perhaps you'll get married, go and live on your husband's place, somewhere different."

Mira shrugged. "Who I to marry? Our men, they marry white women sometime, but white man no marry us. Only Abos want us, they just rubbish peoples. And they have to turn Muslim, or Father not let us marry. Never."

Alix said nothing, as Mira began desultorily to dust the furniture. Alix knew that it was true. But Abdul was a travelled man, he had been down to the city and visited the Mosque there—the one in Hergott Springs was little more than a corrugated iron shed. He must have some money stored away, and his son was still travelling to the outer stations with his, Abdul's, camels laden with store goods, Indian silks and cottons such as Mrs. Allison never stocked; blouses and scarves and kitchen gadgets all calculated to catch the eye of lonely white women hundreds of miles from the nearest big store.

58

She resolved to suggest strongly to Abdul when she saw him again that he should take the girls for a holiday to Adelaide. Mira was saving her salary, for there was little to spend it on in the town. She would soon have enough for her fare.

Constable McGuinnes came back without a prisoner. He'd travelled by train after all, but the dust-storm had caught them on the way to Oodnadatta, and sand drifting over the line stopped the wheels from turning.

"We all had to get out and shovel sand," he said, telling Alix about it. (Mab was in the kitchen, supervising Mira in the setting up of two trays.) "And then when we finally got going, there was still some sand on the track, and the wheels screamed and slipped over it—enough to put your teeth on edge."

"What happened at the fettlers' camp?"

"I didn't get my man. He'd hopped on the train to Oodnadatta, and when I wired there they said he had left by camel for the Alice. He could travel across country, well away from the usual track. But I telegraphed the Constable at Alice Springs to arrest him on suspicion of murder as soon as he gets there. Unless he perishes on the way."

He said this so impersonally that Alix gave a little shiver.

"He bashed his mate's head in with a shovel," said Jack grimly. "Might be better to disappear in the desert than be brought back to hang for murder."

"I suppose so . . . D'you want to stop for lunch?" she asked rather coldly.

"No—no, I've got loads of paperwork to catch up. But I want you to come over tonight when you can get away—towards sunset, if you can."

"We're rather busy at present—"

"Just for half an hour. I've got a present for you. There's only one of them, so I can't ask Sister Mab."

"A present!" She was intrigued. What could he have brought back from the "abomination of desolation" about Lake Eyre? Perhaps a polished pebble, or a collection of garnets, "Centralian rubies," which could be picked up in dry creek-beds. "Why didn't you bring it? Is it heavy?"

"No—light as a feather." He laughed. "But I want to give it just to you, no one else. See you tonight."

After the patients had been fed at five-thirty, Alix washed her face and changed into a cool tusser silk blouse and skirt. She told Mab she was just going across to the police station to get something and would be back soon.

Her heart beat a little faster as she crossed the dusty space, lifting her long skirt above sand-drifts and heaps of dry roly-poly bushes. She knew that Jack McGuinnes was attracted, she had even flirted with him a little, and now she was worried.

What could his present be? Surely—surely not a ring? At that thought she almost panicked. Then she scolded herself for vanity. He must be at least thirty-five, and no doubt was a confirmed bachelor. And he had never even tried to kiss her.

At the sound of her high-heeled boots on the two wooden steps of the little police station, the Mounted Constable came to the door to greet her, a huge grin on his sun-bronzed face.

"Come in, come in! I was afraid you wouldn't be able to get away."

"I can't stay. I've left Mab getting our tea."

He led her into his tiny office, lifted his report ledger from the desk and opened it. Then, going to the window where the last yellow rays of the level sun shone in, he held up something coloured like a jewel. A feather!

"It's for you," he said, handing the foot-long feather to her. "It's from the tail of a red-barred black cockatoo—I found it in a dry creek-bed, caught in a dead bush."

Alix's mouth was open in an "O-oh!" of delight. It was beautiful, like a painted sunset—red shading down to orange, edged with palest yellow, and, sketched across it like a flight of dark birds against the sky, wavering lines of black to dark-brown. The tip was a glossy jet-black.

"Jack! It's beautiful. I saw those cockatoos near Etadunna, but they don't seem to come down this far. O-oh! Can you bear to part with it?"

"Of course. I'll probably find another. Anyway I'd give you anything, you know that."

"Thank you. Thank you. Thank you very much."

He came close, loomed above her. Such a large man! Although she was tall, she felt frail and vulnerable before him.

"Is it worth a kiss?"

"I—I suppose so."

She was crushed against him in a moment, her feet almost leaving the floor. She had been kissed before at parties, by various medical students and young doctors a little elevated with drink, but never so thoroughly as this. Her heart beat faster, but she disengaged herself from his bearlike embrace.

"I've wanted to do that for a long time," he said with satisfaction. "Ever since you trod on my hat."

She said breathlessly, "And now I must go. Thank you again for the feather. I shall treasure it."

"Don't go! Sit down a moment, please! I wanted to talk to you alone, that's why I asked you to come over."

The sun had set, with the effect of a great lamp being extinguished, as it disappeared abruptly below the flat horizon. Already the office was growing dim. Given courage by the fading light, Jack McGuinnes made his proposal.

"I want you to know, Alix, that I don't kiss girls lightly, unless I really care for them, I mean. And if you could care for me . . . I would be honoured if you would be my wife."

He took her hands and gazed into her face, but she dropped her eyes and pulled away from him.

"Jack, you know I'm fond of you, but that is all. I don't love you, and I really don't want to get married, not for a long time."

"Unfortunately, I have fallen in love with you."

"Oh, Jack!" (That's all I ever seem to say to him, she thought fleetingly.) "But I'm afraid I don't feel that way about you."

"I thought—I thought you liked me a little."

"I do! I like you a lot . . . and you're a good friend. But—but I don't want to get married, or even engaged. And I don't love you in that way."

She had been looking down at her hands, clasped together in front of her. As she looked up into his face she saw that it had become greyish, the healthy ruddy tan had faded and changed. She saw the pain in his eyes, but what other answer could she have given? It was not fair to raise false hopes, when she knew she would not change her mind.

"Well, what was the big surprise? Did he bring you a fabulous opal?" asked Mab when she returned to the hostel.

Alix held up the cockatoo's feather silently.

"A feather! But it's beautiful. You don't look very happy, however. Were you disappointed?"

"No, of course not. . . . Only, Mab, he has asked me to marry him."

"Good heavens! Though I did think he was a bit smitten. And what did you say?"

"I told him it was impossible."

"And he took it badly?"

"Yes. I hope it won't spoil our friendship."

"Oh dear! Well, it's your own fault for being so attractive."

"But it *is* my fault, at least. . . . I *did* flirt with him a little. I mean, he's the only man near our age group about the place."

"Oh, MacFarlane! I hope you have learned a lesson."

That night, for the first time in many months, Alix thought about Dr. Hamilton. She had loved that man with a sort of idolizing emotion, from a distance. He had never so much as touched her hand. Yet she had almost fainted with excitement if she saw him coming towards her down a corridor. She would gaze across the ward when he was on his rounds, seeing his calm, kindly face bent above this patient or that, and her heart would swell with love. Of course, she had told herself impatiently, nurses always fell in love with senior surgeons. But it did not alter the fact that when he spoke to her she became breathless and pink in the face, quite unable to control her pulse. If her feelings were obvious, he did not seem to have noticed.

She thought perhaps she would dream of him, as she put out the lamp and settled down to sleep. Instead she had a horrid dream about a ten-foot snake that had somehow got into the kitchen, and which she eventually killed by cutting off its head with a meat-cleaver. It had been so real that she lit the lamp and looked round anxiously, while Mab slept on, unconcerned.

Alix lay awake, thinking, quite unable to get back to sleep. It was Jack's proposal that had unsettled her. She liked him, she hated to hurt his feelings. . . . If only he had fallen for Mab! She wondered how she would feel if Mab went and got married, perhaps to someone like that manly drover she had been rather taken with. She couldn't imagine carrying on without Mab's companionship. They complemented each other, they had the same sense of humour, they simply "got on"; and they had years of shared experience behind them. There was something like love between them, though neither would have admitted it.

No, she couldn't get married, not even if Jack McGuinnes were the most attractive man in the world.

She punched her pillow irritably and turned out the lamp. She got back to sleep, and had no more nightmares about snakes.

The very next day as she was going into the kitchen she saw a movement by the Coolgardie safe, and gave a scream of horror. But it wasn't a snake, it was a huge Perentie lizard that had got in when Mab left the outer wire door open while she went round the side of the building to water her tomatoes. The lizard had evidently smelt the eggs which were stored in the safe.

Alix, not feeling at all brave, took a straw broom and waved it threateningly at the creature. It opened its ugly mouth at her and stood firm. She jabbed with the broom, and suddenly it took off, with a ridiculous undignified waddle, and disappeared out the door. Mab found her sitting in a kitchen chair clutching the broom, for her knees had turned to jelly. Mab promised that she would not leave the wire door open again.

"Remember the goats!" said Alix. "And this time it might have been a snake."

* * *

62

Hergott Springs in winter was unexpectedly cold, but at least it was not wet. The small isolated hills, flat-topped or pointed like a pyramid, showed grey beyond the wide gibber plain, where the desert-hardened, sand-polished boulders appeared dark purple as you looked towards the sun; but when you looked back, the sun-struck surfaces were every shade from maroon to rose-madder to orange-red. The beautiful blue mirages had disappeared.

A cold dry wind came down from the direction of the Simpson Desert to the northward. The wind whistled mournfully through the wires of the Overland Telegraph Line and stirred up feathers of pale-orange dust in the road. It flapped the old sheets of iron and piled up the dirty papers against the fences. A veranda blind made out of a garish painted canvas from some former advertising sign waved like an untidy flag.

And old Uley, last member of the Dieri tribe which once flourished north of here, was brought into the hostel suffering from bronchitis.

He was the first full-blood Aborigine they had treated, and they were advised by his relatives to make up a small fire for him.

"Him gotter have a fire. Old blackfeller bugger-up pinish, sposem no got fire where him bin schleep."

The Sisters showed them the fairly primitive heating arrangements, which consisted of a kerosene drum with holes punched in it and a fire burning inside.

No, that wouldn't do at all, the retinue of followers who had brought the old man explained. He had to have a *little* fire, a blackfellow fire, to sleep beside. In the end Mab came up with a solution: a sheet of iron was placed on bricks on the floor, and a small fire built on top of this.

The old man was too sick to take part in this discussion, but lay groaning and coughing in his ragged shirt and trousers while his relatives argued. Alix and Mab suspected that he would never have agreed to be brought in for treatment unless he was in a pretty bad state.

He was their only patient at the time, and between them they managed to get him into a clean pair of pyjamas borrowed from the mailman. Uley struggled feebly against being bathed, but even this was accomplished by dint of much patience, and a warm poultice, placed on his hairy grey chest with its tribal scars, seemed to give him relief.

It was hard to get him to eat, but though he had little appetite he loved bread and butter and tea with plenty of sugar. He had been brought up on "whitefeller tucker," for his tribe had been taken in by the German Lutheran missionaries at Kopperamanna, after the massacres by early white settlers in the Coongie sand-hills, where it was said up to two hundred men, women, and children had been shot. The Dieri fought fiercely for their land and their precious water, but after a few white stockmen had been speared, the revenge was swift and terrible.

Having failed to persuade him to let her trim his big grey beard, which got in the way of the hot poultices, Alix sat down to talk to Uley and gain his confidence.

"Where you born, Old Man?" she asked. "This not your country?"

She knew the importance of "place" to the blackfellow—that it held a spiritual meaning for him, "me-country"; also that "Old Man" was a title of respect, among a race where age gave status and the old men of the tribe used to rule.

"On t' Cooper, that where I born, out Kilalpaninna way. Then I bin brought into Mission. Father Vogelsang, he grow me up."

"There were many of your people in those days?"

"Big mob. Around Lake Kopperamanna there was hundreds of the dark people. They laugh. They sing. They dance. Now all gone. I lie here, I think about them old times."

Uley coughed painfully. There were tears in his dark, bloodshot eyes.

To distract him, Alix pretended to have trouble with the tongue-twisting native names. "Kopperamanna, Kilal-paninna . . . My word, those plenty long names. What the longest you know, Uley?"

He thought for a moment. "Out by Ooriwilannie," he said, "dry lake by name Noodlawandracooracooratarraninna."

"You gammon—that a real true name?"

"True!"

Soon she had him laughing at her attempts at pronouncing, or even remembering all the syllables of this extraordinary word, which he told her was the native name for the kangaroo-rats that bred there, which the blackfellows killed with a quick throw of the boomerang.

He said that at Kilalpaninna where there was once a second Mission station some twenty-five miles down the Cooper, there had been a big lake, now silted up and turned to desert, where they had fished for bream.

"But there's water at Kopperamanna now," he added. "Big gub'mint bore, bring water from undergroun'." Alix realized that this was the same water which at Hergott Springs flowed to the surface, for the town was at the edge of the Great Artesian Basin.

In another week he was fit to be discharged. His whole family came to pick him up, bringing a stretcher, but he insisted he was well enough to walk.

"T'ank you, Chister," he said to the two girls. "Ol' Uley not ready kick t' bucket yet, eh?"

They laughed; the colloquialism sounded quaint from the lips of the dignified old man, last of his tribe. His relations were all of mixed blood, some lighter-skinned than others, but all descended in part from white men who had travelled or worked in this area for almost fifty years.

Uley took home a bottle of the "coughin' medchin" to which he had become rather addicted.

CHAPTER TEN

Whenever one of the Afghans from across the railway line had to be admitted to the hospital there were all sorts of problems. They would not come in until they were desperately sick, not liking the idea of being touched by an Infidel woman. They would not eat meat unless it had been killed in the prescribed way. And they often refused at first to remove their clothes; they never removed their turbans.

When Akbar, a hawker with a string of camels, was admitted with a nasty ulcer on his leg that had eaten almost into the shin-bone, he clung to his long blue tunic and white pantaloons but consented to roll them up above the knee. He had brought a beautiful hand-woven prayer-mat with him, so that he could pray towards Mecca at the appointed times during the day. Mab warned him sternly against kneeling on the bad leg, but he still got up and bowed himself over the stretcher, touching with his forehead the mat spread upon it instead of the floor.

Mahomet Ali, a wizened old Afghan, came to Alix to have two teeth out. Dental patients usually visited the pub first to fortify themselves with a couple of strong rums or whiskies; Mahomet Ali, being Muslim, did not have the benefits of numbing alcohol. Alix painted his gums with oil of cloves to deaden the pain. When the operation was over he thanked her with a bow, and took her hand in farewell. As he did so, Alix felt something hard pressed into her palm. She looked down and found two glowing pieces of opal.

"A gift," said the old man.

"Oh, but there's no need—"

"For you," he said, and departed with a graceful wave of his brown hand.

Alix was often called on to show her dental skills, though all she could do were extractions. Her hands were slender and her patients sometimes looked doubtful, but she had very strong wrists.

A traveller came in one afternoon, rather the worse for drink, asking to have two teeth out.

"They've been giving me hell, Sister, if you'll excoose the expression," he said, weaving his way along the veranda.

"Come in and sit down in that chair," said Alix firmly. "Now, open!"

The teeth were fairly loose, and soon both were lying in a dish with their bloody roots exposed. Only one of them was a double tooth. She plugged the sockets with cotton wool.

"By jingo, you're a top-notch dentist," said the man admiringly. He wavered off towards the pub, holding a handkerchief to his jaw.

Some time later a second patient arrived. He was completely drunk, scarcely able to stagger.

"Me cobber tells me you're a great dentist," he muttered. "'Little thing, looks as if a puff of wind'd blow her away, but she's all right.' Thatsh what he said. Had—had a coupler drinks for Dutsh courage, yer know. Want you to take out this tooth."

He opened his mouth and Alix peered in, recoiling slightly from his whisky-laden breath. He had not a tooth in his head.

"I don't think you need my ministrations," she said, escorting him firmly off the premises.

"But the toothache, somethin' crool it is—"

"Well, it must be imaginary. You don't have any teeth left to ache."

For the next fortnight Alix was cook and Mab took over the nursing. She was having a worrying time with a maternity case. The wife of a dingo trapper had been brought in by her husband from his camp near Lake Harry. Mrs. Bates was near her time. She was overweight and far from healthy. Her legs were swollen and she had high blood pressure.

On testing a sample of her urine, Mab found that it was almost pure albumen; after heating the specimen and adding a drop of nitric acid, a dense white cloud formed and coagulated into a solid precipitate.

"Nurse, I can't see properly," moaned the woman.

"All right, Mrs. Bates. Just keep calm."

She asked Mira to call Alix from the kitchen to help. She expected complications, and as Mrs. Bates went into labour she developed eclampsia. The fits were frightening, she frothed at the mouth and went rigid, her eyes rolled up in her head. They held her during the convulsions that followed, put a peg between her teeth to stop her biting her tongue. Then she became comatose. Her contractions had ceased.

"We'll have to bring on the birth as quickly as possible," said Mab, preparing an injection and an infusion of quinine.

Mira was looking rather green. Mab sent her away to the kitchen.

After yet another eclamptic fit, as she entered the second stage of labour, the woman became comatose again. Mab tried vaginal dilation with a Sims' speculum. The water had broken, and peering into the cavity, Mab said, "I can see its hair!" Then, "I'll have to use forceps, I'm afraid. The mother will die if she goes on like this much longer."

Mrs. Bates woke up. "Try to bear down," said Mab urgently. "I'll help you." As soon as dilation of the cervix was complete, Mab gently inserted the instrument and gripped, careful not to use too much force and crush the vulnerable skull. She had been present when a doctor did an instrumental delivery, but had never had to try it herself.

Soon a dark head appeared, a purplish face, and then the small body slid out, covered in blood and mucus. Mab held it up triumphantly. "It's a girl, Mrs. Bates."

She bathed the infant in oil and wrapped her up well before placing it in a basket by the bed. Mrs. Bates was pale and exhausted, but her eyes were clear. "Can I see her?" she asked.

"Just for a moment," said Mab, holding out the yelling baby for her to see. "I want you to relax now." Her fear was that Mrs. Bates would go into another fit before the placenta was passed. She waited anxiously, kneading the patient's abdomen gently until the afterbirth was expelled, sliding out so much more easily than the round skull of the baby. Surely, she thought, Nature has made a mistake in creating such large heads on new-born infants. She had seen so much suffering in her midwifery course and since, that she had decided she never wanted to have a baby. And the only way to be sure of that was not to get married.

She gave Mrs. Bates a double dose of potassium bromide and hoped for the best. The fits did not recur, but the patient was exhausted. She would need a couple of weeks' bed rest.

"Certainly she can't go back to that camp," said Mab decisively. "We must make sure she has milk for the infant first, and also try to get her weight down. Her blood pressure has improved since the birth, however."

She was up half the night with the baby, giving it boiled water. Alix thought she was over-anxious and should let the baby yell. But Mab said the important thing was for Mrs. Bates to rest, and she would never do so while she heard her infant crying. After two days the baby, though only six pounds in weight, was sucking vigorously and the milk had begun to flow.

Mab took over as cook as Alix went back to nursing.

She was up at night a lot with the baby, who was underweight and rarely slept more than three hours at a time. One night, walking about the silent ward when the infant had gone back to sleep, she felt wide awake, and she went out onto the veranda to stare up at the sky, which seemed to overflow with brilliant stars. Looking east across the railway line, she watched a star, flaring in blue and red fire, rise over the horizon and slowly climb the sky beside the dark shape of the water-tower. She could feel the turning earth, the great solid ball of it beneath her feet.

A terrible yearning overcame her, a longing for she knew not what. . . .

Well, what *do* you want? she asked herself crossly. Here you are in the outback, doing what you want to do, dealing with life and death. But still that divine discontent troubled her. It was the night sky in this place, its great gold moon and glittering stars, the thin cry of the dingo uttering his desire, the stone-curlew with his eerie call, sounding so lost and lonely.

Alone! That was it. She wanted someone to share her feelings, some soul-mate, some man. Not good, worthy Jack McGuinnes, salt of the earth though he might be. But there must be someone, somewhere who felt this terrible unrest too, who shared her longing and would make her life complete.

The baby gave an irritable cough and started a half-hearted cry. She went inside and felt normality close round her, with the safe and friendly roof overhead.

Scattered thunderstorms had fallen farther up the Birdsville Track towards Mungerannie, and "you could almost see the feed growing," according to Wal Crombie. With the amazing recuperative power of the sand-hill country, the soil was covered with purple parakelya, bluebush and annual saltbush, daisies, and even some Mitchell grass. Stock were beginning to be moved down the Track to the railhead, from beyond Birdsville. Mab and Alix no longer rushed outside to see a mob of cattle arrive; it had become almost commonplace.

Even the dreaded Strzelecki Track was in use, for though Cooper's Creek was still dry for almost its whole length, there had been other falls in the area, where rain had not fallen for years. The Strzelecki Creek, if not flowing, was at least reputed to have some water in it.

One afternoon when Mab, having cooked a midday meal for two hungry men patients and baked a silver cake and some scones for tea, was lying down taking a rest, Alix heard a step on the veranda and to her confusion saw that it was Jack McGuinnes. She had not seen him alone since the night he'd proposed, and she felt shy in his company; while he had adopted an almost offhand manner towards her, evidently still suffering from hurt pride.

"Are you there, Sister?"

He bent his head through the doorway, at the same time removing his wide-brimmed khaki hat.

"Oh—Sister Alix!" he said formally. "I came to borrow a stretcher for an urgent case. The man must be superhuman, he's just ridden in with this great gash in his stomach, cobbled together with a hair from his horse's tail."

"Horsehair is still used for sutures sometimes. But how did it happen?"

"He was coming down the Birdsville Track, and then after leaving Mungerannie he had a fall, or his horse threw him, while he was rounding up a runaway bullock. The bullock went for him on the ground and ripped him up. There's an Abo horse-tailer with him, who'll help me carry him over. He's a bit exhausted. They came to the police station first because it was nearer."

"I'll prepare a sterile cot at once," said Alix, all embarrassment forgotten in this emergency. "I'll put some water on to boil. I suppose I'll have to

69

try and sew him up. I wish there was a doctor in this town! I'll just have to do my best."

"I'm sure you'll manage."

Before long her patient arrived on the stretcher. He even managed a smile, with very even white teeth in a brown face. "G'day, Sister! I hope you're handy with a needle. I stitched myself up with a needle I had in my kit. But as soon as I tried to ride, the horsehair busted. This is the second patch-up."

Alix compressed her lips as she opened his shirt and saw the wound. It looked deep, nearly a foot long, and an angry red where it was puckered around the clumsy black stitches. She sent up a quick prayer. Then she proceeded to undress the patient and get him into a clean cotton gown. Constable McGuinnes and the Aborigine faded away.

"They're big long-horned fellers back there," said the drover. "You've got to be quick, they'll go for you as soon as look at you."

Mab got up and came to help. She took down his particulars. He was Jim Manning, aged twenty-nine, of Cappamerri Station on the Diamantina beyond the Queensland border. He had been bringing his father's eight hundred head of cattle down to the railway at Hergott Springs, but after the accident he had left the cattle and ridden on ahead. It was nearer to come on to the Springs than to go back to Birdsville, and he had heard there were nurses here. He had rested a little at Etadunna and Dulkaninna and then come on, riding slowly and in pain. He had just missed the mailman.

"We'll have to give him a whiff of ether while I clean the wound and stitch it up," said Alix.

"I didn't have any ether the last two times," muttered the drover.

"Nevertheless, I don't want you moving while I'm operating, Mr. Manning," said Alix grandly.

"Call me Jim."

They had arranged a table in the office and covered it with a clean sheet. The patient lay on this, with another draped table alongside for the instruments, clamps and needles, tweezers and scissors. Mab held the ether bottle over the pad on his face and shook out a few drops.

"Right!" said Alix. "Is he under?"

She cut the horrid-looking puckered stitches of horsehair and removed them with tweezers. The wound was inflamed, but not as deep as she had feared, and there was no pus. She cleaned and irrigated the wound, then took up a needle threaded with surgical silk. She saw that she would have to draw together a partly severed muscle as well as the outer flesh. For this she would use catgut, which would be reabsorbed.

Noticing that her hands were shaking slightly, she took a deep breath to calm her nerves and began drawing the opening together. The man breathed stertorously, but his colour remained good and his pulse steady.

When all was finished they rolled him onto another sheet and carried him between them to the men's ward, where he woke up and vomited.

He asked to see "what sort of a job you girls have done." Alix told him she had a dressing over the wound for the present. "It was slightly infected, and no wonder," she said. "In fact you're very lucky."

"I did boil the needle and the horsehair."

"Yes, but the wound wasn't fully closed—"

"And it is now?"

"Yes. I'm afraid I was never much good at sewing, and it's not very neat, but I think the sutures will hold. As long as you rest quietly; no getting out of bed till the infection is controlled."

"Hell! I can't stay in bed! And what about when I want to go— You know."

He looked so embarrassed that Mab reassured him. "Don't worry, we have a bedpan. Nothing to it."

Jim Manning looked resigned. He was feeling rather sick and not inclined to argue.

Alix, lying wakeful in her bed that night, heard the weird, lost cry of a curlew out on the stony plain. She was thinking about her patient. He was exactly her idea of the Australian bushman—lean brown face, sun-bleached hair, pale-blue eyes like chips of glass between slitted lids used to screwing up against the glare of the outback sun, which had left a fan of pale wrinkles at the corner of each eye. There was no spare flesh on him. He was wiry but not thin, well-muscled and very fit. And game, to have ridden his horse for days with that wound in his stomach.

All their troubles seemed to be coming at once.

Next, Mr. Bennet, the station-master, was brought in with pain in his abdomen, which was tight and hard. It looked like an acute appendicitis.

"I'm not attempting an appendectomy!" said Alix.

"Me either," Mab said. "We'll have to get him down to Port Augusta on the next train. It's due today, back from Oodnadatta."

"What if peritonitis sets in?"

"He'll have to take his chance. We *can't* operate. But one of us had better travel down with him."

When the train came in from the north, they asked the Constable to inquire whether there was a doctor among the passengers. Fortunately there was one on his way back from Oodnadatta and the Alice with a scientific party; two geologists and an ethnologist from the Adelaide Museum.

Dr. Brown, appealed to, agreed to leave the train and try to operate, but he said he was out of practice as he had been semi-retired for some years.

The driver of the 'Ghan was never in a hurry, sometimes stopping in

71

the middle of nowhere to brew a billy of tea with the guard or to shoot a tasty plains turkey for the larder. He decided that he could wait for the doctor.

The men passengers all got down and visited the hotel for some bottles of beer which they carried back to the train for the next dry stage to Farina. This was almost a ritual at the few stops where there was a liquor store. The railway line from Port Augusta to Oodnadatta was strewn on each side with brown glass bottles, indestructible artifacts glittering in the sun.

Once more the office table was draped in white, with a second table for the instruments. They hadn't all the correct items, but a breech hook was used as a retractor, and a pair of angular forceps. The doctor, who did not look young, remained unflustered while he made his incision. Mab assisted him and Alix gave the anaesthetic.

All went well until, as he was tying the purse string, the catgut broke and the stump had to be found again and oversewn. The doctor gave vent to a mild expletive. Eventually the operation was over successfully, and the patient transported to the men's ward.

Mab and Alix were pleased that they had made a correct diagnosis.

"Just got it in time," said Dr. Brown cheerfully. "Another day and it would have ruptured."

Alix and Mab then asked the doctor to look at their other surgical patient, and he congratulated Alix on her sutures.

"Should be no further trouble," he said. "But I'd advise bed-rest for the present."

Jim Manning groaned. "Fair go, Doc. I'm sick of this bed."

"And if you get up too early you'll be back there for even longer."

Alix, thinking about her patient, reflected that almost all the men she had met in the north were of solid build—the Constable, the mailman, the drovers who passed through. The publican was positively fat, and the station-master looked well fed. But Jim Manning was different, with his rather hawklike profile and clean-boned face. She decided that she liked him.

It was just chance, or fate, that it was her fortnight for nursing duty when he came in, or Mab would have cared for him while Alix looked after the meals. As it was, she rather enjoyed bossing him about, making him lie still while she changed the dressing and examined the stitches. He had been very shy when she brought him a urine bottle and still more so over the bedpan. I hope I don't have to give him an enema, she thought. He'd never forgive the insult to his dignity. But soon he was able to get out on the commode.

When after ten days the stitches were ready to come out, the wound looked clean and healed. She snipped and tweezered while he wriggled and complained that it tickled.

"Lie still!" she said sternly. "Or you'll get another puncture from these scissors."

He stayed quiet, but as she worked he surveyed her with a quizzical expression and a lurking smile in his eyes that made her self-conscious. When she had done, she picked up the surgical tray to remove it. A lean brown hand stretched out and held her other wrist.

"Sit down, Sister. Come on, I won't bite. Talk to me for a while."

Alix felt a moment of panic. Her breathing was uneven, and she did not meet his eyes.

I fear thee, ancient Mariner!
I fear thy skinny hand!
For thou art long, and lank, and brown,
As is the ribbed sea-sand . . .

The lines popped into her head, though they were not at all apt for a place hundreds of miles from the nearest ocean; nor did the patient have a "long grey beard and glittering eye" like Coleridge's Ancient Mariner. But he had those far-gazing eyes of explorers and sailors, accustomed to looking away to the rim of the world.

She sat primly on the foot of the bed.

"What shall I talk about?" she asked defensively.

"First of all—can I get up now?"

"Yes, you can go to the bathroom and the toilet. Tomorrow you can get dressed."

"Well, thank the Lord for small mercies. I can't stand being helpless like this."

"Tell me about your home and family . . . Jim."

"We-ell. . . . There's my dad, Big Jim Manning, and my mum—her name's Olive . . . I'm the only son, and my two sisters are married and left home."

"Is Big Jim bigger than you?"

"Not really. Same height, but more solid."

"And you run cattle at Cappamerri?"

"Yair, we had to get rid of the sheep. The dingoes got most of them, and the fleece was always sanded. Still, mutton made a nice change from everlasting steak. Which reminds me—Sister Mab is a great cook."

"You're lucky you're about ready to be discharged. I'm the cook next week, and the meals won't be as good."

"Well, you can't do much with corned beef and tinned dog. I'll get you some fresh beef when the mob arrives. They should be here in a day or two."

"Thank you. Now, I do have other patients—"

"But you haven't told me about you!"

"Another time. Morning tea's at eleven, after out-patients. I'll see you then. You don't really need any more nursing, but you might as well stay till the plant arrives."

Chapter Eleven

"I don't know!" said Mab despondently. Her straight, sandy, wiry hair was electric with the heat, and falling in long wisps from her bun. Her cheeks were burnt to a ruddy hue.

She looked over the veranda rail at the spindly tomato plants struggling to grow in the sandy soil. "I don't know why we bother. And I don't know why we drink boiling hot tea in this heat."

"The theory is that it makes you perspire, and that makes you feel cooler . . . Evaporation."

"Like a Coolgardie safe!" said Mab.

Alix had decided to serve morning tea on the veranda on Jim Manning's first day up. She had it all set out when a thick dust-storm blew up, and within minutes the milk was covered with a skin of sand, the bread and butter looked as if spread with brown sugar, and Mab's white cloth was filthy.

They had to remove everything inside, shake out the cloth, and reset the table. They dreaded a full-scale dust-storm, but in the early afternoon clouds appeared, and there was actually a sprinkle of rain—the first rain they had seen since arriving in Hergott Springs more than a year ago. The air was filled with that sweet scent of rain on dry earth, which Alix remembered after summer storms at home.

The droving plant from Cappamerri arrived next day. Though Alix warned him against riding as yet, Jim insisted on walking over to talk to his men.

"They were a bit surprised to see me walking about," he said on his return. "I rather think they expected me to have conked it, or at least been very crook. But you can't keep a good man down."

"Of course, good nursing *could* have had something to do with it."

He grinned. "Yair. Could be."

He had brought a haunch of fresh beef with him. She thanked him and hung it down the cellar in a muslin bag.

That afternoon the temperature reached 115 degrees in the shade. The rain had not made it any cooler, and the thin film of moisture was soon baked out of the dusty road.

The present drought had lasted since 1910, and it was now 1913, with one of the worst years yet to come. No one had yet realized that drought was the normal condition for the far north of South Australia and far western Queensland.

The relieving station-master from the city was the only man in the town who regularly looked spruce and tidy, wearing his official uniform. But Jim Manning was resplendent this morning in checked shirt, well-fitting moleskin trousers, and high-heeled riding boots with spurs. He looked a real cattleman, Alix thought admiringly. The effect was rather spoiled by the high-crowned, battered, sweat-stained felt hat he wore.

He had collected his swag from the wagon travelling with the plant when it came in, and appeared in his clean change of clothes. He asked Alix to walk over with him to see the eight hundred beasts penned in the railway stockyards.

Alix and Jim leaned companionably on the stockyard rail, while Jim pointed out the good and bad points of various beasts.

"One thing, they've all got our brand on 'em—CM—not a cleanskin among them."

"Isn't that usual?"

"Well, most droving plants pick up a few stray beasts on the way—it's a big country with very few fences, and some unbranded cattle get mixed in with the mob, and you just sort of incorporate them."

"And what if they carried another station's brand?"

"Some blokes would try and alter the brand—for instance ours could be changed to OM fairly easy—but I wouldn't come at that caper." He grinned disarmingly. "But if someone else's bullock wandered by when you were about to kill a beast for tucker, well, he might just get in the way of a bullet."

"Isn't that illegal?"

"Yair. But there's no brand on raw beef."

"Which reminds me, I'd better go and get the dinner on. Roast beef. As you're still officially a patient, you'd better come and have some." As she was now cook, Alix had looked forward to baking a succulent roast, with plenty of cold roast beef left over for meals.

"Right-oh. Thanks."

He had asked to be discharged the next day so that he could supervise loading of the mob on the cattle-train in the morning.

He came back riding a brown horse as if he were part of it, and hitched it to the front fence.

"I'm not sure if you should be riding yet," said Alix. "What do you think, Mab?"

"Oh, he's tough. If he could ride with a bit of horsehair holding him together—"

"And riding has given me an appetite." He sat down to do justice to a meal of his own beef.

"This is good-oh!" he said appreciatively as he cleaned his plate. "I thought you said you couldn't cook, Sister Alix."

"I didn't say I couldn't cook. Only that Mab is better at it."

"Anyway, this'll do me. We don't get anything but steak mostly on the track, and boiled corned beef. I just hope this is the beast that opened me up. Serve the bu—, er, the beggar right."

He lingered on the veranda, looking down at Alix with those light-blue eyes with their clear whites against his brown skin.

"Eh, what about coming up to the pub with me tonight, Sister?"

"We don't usually go to the hotel, except sometimes for midday dinner on a Sunday."

"Well, come for a ride in the moonlight, then. I suppose you can ride?"

"Yes. But I'm not an expert."

"Like you're not an expert cook? Well, you can donkey up behind me, then. My mare can canter like a rocking-horse when she wants to."

Alix had an impulse to say no, to make some excuse, but then she thought, He'll be gone in a couple of days and I'll probably never see him again. Why not go?

"All right," she said faintly. "I'll be ready after I've cleared up the kitchen after tea."

Jim came early and helped her wash up while Mab was giving the patients their night medication. He dried while Alix washed, polishing the glasses and cutlery with care.

"See, I'm real domesticated," he said, draping the tea-towel over his shoulder.

She put the things away and prepared a supper tray for the patients— only two of them, including the station-master, who was also making a good recovery. His wife called in with a home-made cake.

She brought it out to the kitchen. Alix thanked her, and cut a few slices while Mrs. Bennet looked at the young cattleman with interest.

"Oh—this is Jim Manning. We had to sew him up, you know."

"Yes, of course, you were in the ward with my husband. I didn't recognize you at first. How's the wound?"

"Right as rain, thanks to Sister Alix here. She's a dab hand with the needle."

Mrs. Bennet's thin face did its best to look arch. "Well, it's quite romantic, isn't it? I bet you've never been sewn up by a slip of a girl before."

"No-o," drawled Jim. "Only by an Abo. Would you like to see my scar?"

He made to pull the shirt out of his trousers, but Mrs. Bennet backed away. "Oh, no, no, thank you! I'm sure it's very interesting, but I must go and see my husband. . . ."

"He'll be able to go home in a few days," said Alix. "But not back on duty for another week."

She and Jim exchanged a smile as the station-master's wife hurried away. Mrs. Bennet, perhaps seeking to bring some colour into her drab life, ordered romantic novels from the south every month, and had read most of the books in the small A.I.M. library.

Jim stepped out onto the veranda. Alix went to tell Mab she was going out for a while, and that the supper was ready in the kitchen.

As she came out through the wire door, Jim Manning took her hand and led her into the street. They came out into brilliant moonlight—the moon, close to full, showed every detail and threw deep black shadows. Alix had never got used to its brilliance in this clear inland air.

Once in the saddle, he instructed her to place her left foot on top of his in the stirrup, and swung her up behind him.

"Now, put your arms around me."

"There's really no need—"

He jerked the rein and the mare started off with a bound. Alix gasped and held on to him with both arms. She was seated sideways and felt none too secure.

Jim calmed the mare with his voice, walked her to the end of the street, then put her into a rocking canter. Alix began to enjoy herself, as the lighted hotel and Mrs. Allison's store, the post office and the water-tower fell behind. The moonlit plain stretched before them as they rode out towards the Springs. She felt his supple trunk in its thin shirt, the firm muscles of his diaphragm. She had bathed this man all over and knew the wiry length and strength of him.

The tall shape of the windmill rose ahead, and then they came to the pool of the mound spring, the water sparkling in moonlight as it overflowed into the troughs. There was so much artesian water, it flowed so unendingly that no one thought of conserving it, and millions of gallons flowed away and soaked into the sand.

He pulled up and dismounted, putting the reins back over the head of the mare, who stood quietly.

"Is she the one that threw you?" asked Alix to tease him.

"No, it was my night horse, and he didn't throw me, he fell and I went down with him." He put up his arms and lifted her down, but slowly, so that she slid the length of his body before her feet touched the ground. He did not release her at once but held her close against him, while Alix trembled, too breathless to speak.

At last, "Let me go!" she said faintly.

"Are you sure you want me to?"

"Yes! . . . No."

When he kissed her it was quite different from anything else she had experienced. She seemed to float above the ground. Time ceased to exist,

78

the moon stood still in the sky, she was not aware even of the splashing of the bore-water. After an eternity he raised his head and looked deep into her moonlit face. He put up a hand and caressed the soft curls falling from the neat bun.

"Such soft, fine hair," he murmured. "It's really light brown rather than fair, but I think I'll call you Sandy. Alix doesn't suit you, it sounds efficient and masculine. I've no doubt you're efficient, but you're also very feminine."

"I'm also a dedicated nurse who doesn't have affairs with her patients."

"I'm not your patient any more. I've been discharged. I'll bet the men patients keep falling in love with you, but."

She thought of the men she had treated since coming to the Springs —podgy Mr. Bennet, two Afghans, a part-Aboriginal boy, a drunken swagman . . . She laughed. "Not really."

"I'm sure I'm not the first."

"The first what?"

"The first patient to fall in love with his nurse."

"And have you?"

"Yes! From the first moment I saw you, I thought, There's the girl for me! You liked me kissing you, didn't you?"

"Y-es."

He kissed her again, then leaned back against the frame of the windmill and cradled her in his arms. Alix felt a great flooding peace. She laid her head upon his shoulder. The vast silent night stretched round them, the wide moonlit plain, the sky full of silvery light and a few pale stars. The scratchy cry of a plover woke her as from a trance.

"The blackfellows call him the Death Bird," said Jim. "They fly over the camp to bring news that someone has died."

Alix shivered, and he held her close. "I'd never seen anyone die until I went nursing. There was a young girl who was badly burnt—" She found herself telling him about Lucy, and how she herself had lost some of her faith after that tragic death. "If only we could have got her to a proper hospital!"

"Yair. You soon learn out here that life is not always pretty. Nature can be cruel; the country itself is hard. In a drought you watch the cattle slowly starving until they drop."

"I had lived all my life in the city, in Adelaide, before. Have you ever been down to Adelaide?"

"Yair. . . . Went to school there."

"You did! I nursed at the North Adelaide Hospital."

"I was a boarder at Prince Alfred College. Only for a couple of years. Before that it was home lessons, but I got out of them whenever I could. Mum made me work at them, but Dad would say he needed me out on the run, and of course I preferred riding to schoolbooks any day."

"But you live in Queensland?"

"Birdsville is our nearest town, and everyone, everything, even our mail, comes up by way of the Birdsville Track from Adelaide. Brisbane's too far away. There's nothing beyond us in Queensland except a little place called Betoota, and the Stony Desert in between. So South Australia is regarded as our home state. There's nothing to mark the border out there anyway, except a broken-down fence."

"How big is Cappamerri?"

"Oh, about five thousand square miles. Only part of that is of any use, except when there's rain, or water in the Diamantina apart from the homestead waterhole. We haven't had a good year since 1910; we're just hanging on. Those thunderstorms let us move some of our stock out, they were too weak to travel before."

"*You* should be too weak to travel for a while."

"Is that your professional advice?"

"Yes. Besides—"

"Besides, I don't want to leave Hergott Springs, and you, when I've only just found you."

"This is ridiculous! We scarcely know each other."

He said seriously, "I've known you long enough to admire you, and like being with you, and want you as a woman. And it seems to me that adds up to love."

"Jim—"

"I'm not the romantic type, I can't make flowery speeches, but—you've just bowled me over."

"Oh, Jim!"

They stared at each other solemnly.

"I suppose you always kiss the girls when you come to town," she said with an attempt at lightness.

"Well, yes . . . . But none of them was a patch on you."

When they reluctantly turned towards the town, the moon was at its zenith and shadows were at their smallest. This time she sat in front of the saddle and he held her in his arms, while they moved to the dreamy rhythm of the mare's effortless canter, the tattoo of her hooves on the dusty road.

He tied the mare to the corner of the front fence and led Alix into the black shadow of the veranda.

"Alix—Sandy dearest—let me come in with you? Don't you want me to? Please, darling. I've never wanted anyone so much—" He was whispering urgently, his hands running up and down her thighs. But she stiffened in his arms and pushed herself away.

"You just want to get me into bed. And anyway, I share a room with Mab. It's not possible, even if—"

"There's a bed on the veranda," said Jim with a flash of white teeth in the darkness.

"There's also a patient on the veranda. No, Jim. No, I mean it! You must go, we'll be waking everyone up."

She slipped away with a whispered "Good night," and cursed the wire door as it creaked on its hinges.

She did not light the lamp but began to get undressed in the dark. If Mab should wake she didn't want her to see her flushed cheeks and somewhat tousled hair. She felt that the kisses they had exchanged must show on her mouth like bruises.

But Mab was wide awake.

"Well?" she said. "Did you have an interesting time?"

Alix, her mouth full of the hairpins she was taking out of her bun, mumbled, "Quite interesting, yes."

"You were long enough. Where have you been all this time?"

"We just rode out to the Springs."

"Just out to the Springs. Mm. What have you two been up to?"

"Oh, shut up, Kingston!" snapped Alix, flinging herself into bed. She didn't want to talk, she wanted to savour every moment of the experience, the feel of his lean, hard body, that hard part of him pressing into her groin through their intervening clothes, making her faint with desire. Was it possible to fall in love in a single night?

CHAPTER TWELVE

Alix mooned about the hostel like Mira, forgetting what she was doing and taking every opportunity to leave her cooking and look out for a glimpse of Jim on his brown mare. A great swelling bubble of happiness kept rising inside her, as if she would burst. She felt herself at the centre of some sweet mystery, only half-guessed before, as if she had been admitted to the secret society of lovers, and could only feel sorry for those who did not love.

Mab regarded her quizzically but said nothing. Somehow she did not quite trust the cattleman.

When the cattle had been safely dispatched, the Cappamerri men wanted time to sample the fleshpots of Hergott Springs, such as they were. By the time they were ready to leave, Jim and Alix had got to know each other, and the more she knew him the more he surprised and intrigued her, and the more deeply she was in love. They spent the last evening together on her first night back on nursing duty. She would not ask Mab to take over for her—for Mab had shown her disapproval of the affair in various subtle ways—so instead of going out they sat in the little living-room on the cane chairs till Mab went to bed, and then occupied one chair between them.

He kissed her deeply, his tongue searching her mouth. He pulled out his shirt and she kissed the scar on his muscular belly, the wound that had brought them together. Fortunately the nights had become cooler, but she was aware of the scent of male sweat, and burying her face in his hair as he nuzzled her breast, she found that it smelled sweet and clean as a baby's.

His hand was under her skirt, tugging impatiently at her pants as she sat with her legs across his lap.

"Jim—I don't want—"

"No, darling, no, I won't do anything to hurt you, I promise. I wouldn't want you to be worried. I'll stay outside, if you'll just help me . . . like that . . . ah! Oh, Alix, oh, darling, oh, God, you're so sweet, my sweetheart, my darling, I love you, love you . . ."

His body arched beneath her. With a great sigh he slid to the floor and knelt against the chair. He undid the buttons of her shirtwaist and took a hard nipple in his mouth. The great baby! She yearned over him like a mother.

Then his searching fingers found her centre, and with practised skill began to caress her. She became a mindless mass of longing, a core of pure sensation. It left her tingling and quivering, flung back in the chair, flooded with a new joy and understanding.

"Oh, Nurse! Nurse! Are you there, Sister?"

Alix hastily pulled down her damp skirt and pushed some loose hairpins into her hair.

"What beaut timing!" said Jim wryly.

"Yes. She probably wants a bedpan. Romantic, isn't it?"

She got up to go to the ward, but her legs felt weak. There was pleasure even in walking as her thighs brushed together. Sister MacFarlane on duty! Smelling of semen, still throbbing from that marvellous experience. And yet she was technically still a virgin. Only she did not feel like one.

Next morning Jim Manning came in to say goodbye. He shook hands with Mab in the kitchen, said "So long, and thanks"; bid goodbye to Mira, washing vegetables at the sink; then sought Alix in the dispensary. She had a dropper in one hand and a medicine bottle in the other, and as he grabbed her in his arms she tried distractedly to brush the curling strands from her brow with the back of her wrist. He bent and kissed her forehead and wound a soft curl around his finger.

"I have to go, dearest," he said. "Now don't cry, Sandy, or you'll have me blubbing too. It's not forever, you know. I'll come back for you one day—"

"When? Mab and I are here for only another ten months. Then I don't know where we'll be. Write to me, Jim!"

"Of course. The mails are pretty slow, but they always get through, barring a major flood. And there's not much chance of that, worse luck."

She was not listening to him, she was gazing at his face, the clean line of his jaw, the taut brown skin and sun-bleached eyebrows, memorizing every detail. He stroked her hair and held her head against his chest, against the blue poplin shirt that was exactly the colour of his eyes. Then he kissed her long and hard, his hands running up and down her back, pressing her to him. When he let her go she staggered against the bench, feeling almost too shaken to stand.

"I'll come and see you off." She recovered herself, put down the bottle, and followed him out to the road. He mounted the mare in one easy, fluid movement. Then, heedless of onlookers, he bent and kissed her full on the mouth.

He looked down at her with a smile, but his brow was troubled.

"D'you ever read Henry Lawson?" he asked unexpectedly.

"Why—yes. We have a copy of his poems here somewhere. I always thought they were a bit jingly."

"There's one of his I rather like—'The Sliprails and the Spur.' You should read it."

"I'll remember."

"And I'll remember you. Goodbye, love."

He lifted his battered felt hat for a moment, the mare turned in her own length, and, with a scattering of pebbles, he galloped off down the street, after the small cloud of dust in the distance that marked the passage of the horse plant and the returning stockmen.

Alix stared along the empty street until the dust settled. A flock of pink and grey galahs was busy sliding down the corrugated iron roof, like a pack of kids on a slippery-dip, squawking and fluttering when they reached the edge. She looked at them unseeingly.

A cold foreboding gripped her. "I'll remember you . . . Goodbye." It had sounded so final. He was going four hundred miles away—would she ever see him again? She rushed inside and flung herself on her bed, curled into a foetal position, biting her knuckles. What had Henry Lawson said? "There's many a good mate in the Bush called Jim."

Jim. Dear Jim. But would he make a good mate?

She had to go to out-patients now. But as soon as she could she would find the copy of Henry Lawson—was it his *Bush Ballads*?—and look up "The Sliprails and the Spur." She hoped it was a love poem.

There was a small box of books supplied by the A.I.M. for the use of patients and for anyone in town who liked to borrow them, as well as a pile of well-thumbed magazines. In the afternoon Alix went and searched in the box, feverishly throwing aside *Benbonuna* and *Paving the Way* and the songs of Banjo Patterson. Where was Henry Lawson? She reached the bottom of the box and sat back on the floor, defeated. It was not there.

At tea she asked Mab casually, "Have you seen that volume of Henry Lawson poems we had here?"

"Not *While the Billy Boils*?"

"No, that's short stories. I mean a book of ballads."

"Oh—I think Mr. Bennet was reading that. He must've taken it home with him."

"There's something I want to look up. Jim and I had an argument over a quotation."

"So Jim Manning reads poetry? I wouldn't have thought he read anything but the stock and station reports."

"That shows how little you know him." Alix had been aware that her friend did not like Jim, that there was a certain antagonism, almost jealousy, which Mab had never shown over Jack McGuinnes. "I'll go over after tea and get it back from old Bennet. His wife never reads anything but romantic novels."

"Yes, she had you and Jim practically at the altar."

Alix pretended a non-committal smile, but her throat was constricted.

When she had extracted the missing book from the station-master's house (which was overfilled with furniture and knick-knacks) she hurried back to her room. Mrs. Bennet, who just happened to be looking out the window when Jim was saying goodbye, had handed it to her with a bright query. "That young man has left for home, then, has he?"

"Our other male patient? Yes, he left this morning."

She fled from the woman's avid eyes.

Sitting on her bed, she turned the pages feverishly. "The Sliprails and the Spur." There it was. She couldn't remember having read it before. Yes, it was about two lovers, he a horseman named Jim. Now they were saying farewell by the sliprails before he rode away. . . . with their "Goodbye, Mary!" "Goodbye, Jim." And then—

Oh, he rides hard to race the pain
Who rides from love, who rides from home;
But he rides slowly back again
Whose heart has learnt to love and roam.

Oh! So that was his message! She smiled bitterly. His heart had "learned to love and roam."

She read to the end, where poor forsaken Mary kept stealing out to the sliprails in the dusk, waiting for the sound of his hoofbeats returning, waiting for the sight of faithless, footloose Jim.

Alix groaned. Why had he pretended to love her, pretended that this was something different, special, unique in his experience? What a fool she had been! She flung the book violently to the floor, breaking its spine.

Mab was aware that her companion was out of sorts, scarcely eating and moping about the place. Mira on the other hand had become quite lively, for her, and went about the cleaning of the wards and peeling the vegetables with a cheerful smile, at times humming a monotonous tune. Mab noticed these phenomena with interest, but kept her own counsel. If they wanted to confide in her, they would.

But Mira, who had been so unusually cheerful, suddenly turned despondent; Mab could hardly get a word out of her. Alix, too, was snappish and uncommunicative. If this is love, thought Mab, preserve me from it!

She waited for Alix to confide what was troubling her.

Mira became so forgetful, and so often stood motionless by the window with big tears rolling from her great dark eyes, that at last Mab spoke to her one day in the kitchen.

"Mira, is something wrong?" she asked kindly.

"Nuthin' wrong."

"Then why are you so sad? You can tell me." A thought came to her, and she studied the girl's figure as she stood by the sink. Was she rather larger round the middle? "You can talk to me, Mira. I'm a nurse, and nurses are never shocked. Aren't you feeling well?"

"I . . . sick, early morning. Bring up my breakfast twice."

"H'm. Any other symptoms?"

"No-o. On'y— Oh, Sister, my monthlies? They have stop . . . I so scared!"

She began to cry, mopping her eyes with the tea-towel.

Mab sat down by the kitchen table. "Now come and sit down, child." (Mab was twenty-six, but felt older.) "How many periods have you missed?"

"Two. One was due last week."

"Oh dear. I suppose you realize that you've got yourself into trouble. And what will your father say?"

"I couldn't tell him. He kill me!"

"What about the boy who's responsible for your condition? Is it Reuben?"

"Yair." She sniffed and gulped. "Said he marry me, but my father'd never—"

"Would you like me to speak to him?"

"No, don't tell him, please, Sister!"

"Well, we needn't tell him yet, until you begin to show. Cheer up, it's not the end of the world. Perhaps Reuben might turn Muslim, and then—"

"Father not like Abos."

"Reuben is only part-Aboriginal, and Mission-bred. And Abdul Dervish might prefer him as a son-in-law to having a grandchild without a father. I'll have a talk to Reuben—have you told him?"

"Yair. You think I having baby then? Maybe I could lose it—"

"Don't talk like that!" said Mab sternly. "You'll have your baby, and you'll find you love him, and if it's a boy Abdul might even be pleased at having a grandson. I'll tell him, but later, when we're absolutely sure. Would it be three months yet?"

"Could be."

"I'll give you an examination next week when I'm on duty. You can come to my room and no one else need know."

"Not Sister MacFarlane?"

"Well, yes, she'll have to know. But no one outside the hostel."

She told Alix about Mira's predicament that night as they were getting ready for bed. They were having an easy time, no patients for once, only out-patients coming in for dressings, and one whom Alix was visiting at home.

"I suppose it was to be expected," said Mab charitably. "You can't blame the poor girl, with no mother to advise her and nothing much else to do after work. But I'm afraid her father will blame us."

86

"We can't be responsible for what happens between here and home. But I suppose we should have got Abdul to call for her after work. Poor kid!"

The news had shocked her. Watching the dispirited droop of Mira's shoulders and her stricken face as she went about her work, she realized how lucky she herself had been. There, but for the grace of God, go I, she thought. Or rather by the restraint of Jim Manning, who hadn't wanted her "to be worried." And how she would have worried! Yet she knew that if he had insisted she would have let him do anything, reckless of the consequences.

Of course, he hadn't wanted to feel tied down or responsible; no doubt that was why he had been so careful. She felt grateful to him all the same, though she had told herself that he was no good, a philanderer with a girl in every town the way sailors were supposed to have a girl in every port. But it didn't stop her thinking of him continually, with a painful longing to see him again.

CHAPTER THIRTEEN

Alix waited in suspense for the mailman's buggy each fortnight as it returned from Birdsville. Jim had not written. He had never meant to write. She would not be the first to write, pride forbade it, but she longed for some word. He might at least have sent a note to say he'd arrived home safely, that his wound was completely healed. She would not write to ask. It would be too shattering if he didn't bother to reply.

Mab had examined Mira and there was no doubt about her condition; but she had not told her father. They sent Mira home with a message for him to come over to afternoon tea. She hadn't even told her sister Deneb; she was too ashamed.

Abdul came stalking onto the veranda, his blue turban meticulously folded, his loose shirt hanging outside his white trousers. They gave him tea and home-made biscuits while he sat in one of the cane chairs. Alix had a vision of herself and Jim struggling in that same chair. . . . She was no better than Mira, only luckier.

"Abdul Dervish," said Mab formally, "we think you should know that Mira may have to give up work soon."

"She not work well? I soon see to that!"

"Yes, she's a very good worker, on the whole . . . but . . ."

"She's . . . unfortunately . . . not well," said Alix desperately. "I mean . . ."

"Not well? She sick?"

"I'm afraid," said Mab firmly, "that Mira has got into trouble. She was scared to tell you. The baby is due in about six months."

There was a suffocating silence; then Abdul Dervish sprang to his feet, the teacup rolling on the floor.

"You—telling—me," he shouted, "my daughter! My daughter been with some dirty Infidel! What man has done this thing? I kill him!"

"Mira will tell you who the father is. The young man wants to marry her. But they thought you wouldn't agree."

"Bah! He is not Muslim?"

"No," said Mab reluctantly. "But he loves Mira, and would be willing to change his religion. If you would give your permission—"

"I will not! I kill him! And you—you white Sisters! You take my daughter away from her father's house, and this what happen! Allah be thanked her mother not live to see our shame!"

"We are very sorry, Abdul," said Alix. "But we couldn't have prevented it. Mira is young, don't be too hard on her."

"She not work in hostel no more! Finish!"

"Very well. She has saved her wages, enough to go to Adelaide. She could go down there while the baby is born. But I think you should let them marry."

But Abdul only said "Bah!" again, and strode outside and across the railway line. The girls looked at each other anxiously. They expected he would beat her. But perhaps he might come round later.

Mab made an effort to get a replacement for Mira from among old Uley's half-white descendants who lived in the town. Mab and Alix interviewed several girls, finding them shy and uncertain of their own abilities; but at last they found one, Elvie, who said she'd like to try. She had clean, wavy brown hair and smiled with very large white teeth.

"Well, Elvie, you must ask your father and mother, and we will put it to the Hostel Committee."

To Mab's and Alix's surprise, what they had regarded as a mere formality resulted in a veto from the committee, which helped to raise funds for the hostel and conferred with the Sisters and the A.I.M. about the need for any new equipment, or repairs to the building.

Mr. Bennet, chairman of the committee, gave a cough.

"I scarcely think an Aboriginal girl would be suitable," he said.

"Why not?" asked Mab.

"Well, really, Sister, I thought that would be obvious."

"In what way obvious?"

He said impatiently, "That patients would prefer not to be treated by black gins."

Mab's cheeks were flaming. Alix said mildly, "Elvie is not black. Her father was white."

"Well, half-castes then. And we all know what they're like. Mixed blood never leads to any good."

"And if you're objecting to her mixed blood," said Mab indignantly, "you might remember that it was a European man like yourself who was responsible. It wasn't a case of immaculate conception, you know."

Mr. Bennet bristled, and Mrs. Bennet bridled. "Well, really, Nurse Kingston! There's no need to be blasphemous."

"Quite!" said the third member of the committee, the postmaster.

Unfortunately the fourth member, Constable McGuinnes, was away, and Mab and Alix were outvoted. They had to tell Elvie that she had not been accepted. Yet they felt it would have been excellent for the girl, and given her a sense of belonging to the community.

Instead of training her as a ward-maid and nurse's aid, they could only offer her a job helping in the kitchen and with the weekly wash. She agreed, but did not last long at these uninteresting chores.

Two months had gone by and not a word had come from Jim Manning. Alix had given up waiting with terrible suspense for the mail to come in. She began to hate the monotonous cry of the plover, flying through the moonlit nights with its grating call.

"Those blasted birds!" she burst out one night, turning her pillow over and thumping it.

"The plovers? I don't mind them," said Mab mildly.

"I hate the damn things!" She lay staring at the moonlit square of the window.

Mab said with apparent inconsequence, "You haven't heard from Jim since he left?"

"No." She turned over and hunched her shoulders against further questions. She would have liked to unburden herself to Mab, to admit how she had been hurt, but she could not bring herself to speak of it.

They had seen nothing of Mira since Abdul's visit, but one day Mab met Deneb in the store.

"How is your sister?" she asked anxiously. "We haven't seen her . . ."

"Father not let her out of the house. Poor Mira! Reuben come to see her, but Father chase him with a knife. Now he frightened to come. She is very sad."

"But she is well, physically?"

"She all right."

Alix and Mab decided there was nothing they could do. Mira was under age, and anyway Muslim women had few rights, and were trained to be subservient to the male. Alix and Mab could only hope that Abdul would come round and let her marry.

It was Mab who went to collect the mail from the post office when the postcard came. Wal had come in that morning from Birdsville, and the train arrived from the south in the afternoon, so it was a big day for the local post office. Mab came back with three letters, one for her, one for Alix from her mother—and a square envelope with a Birdsville postmark.

"For you," said Mab with a smile. "I think it's from Jim."

Alix snatched her letters and hurried to the bedroom. With shaking fingers she opened the Birdsville envelope, tearing it jaggedly in her haste. Inside was a postcard: "Pelicans. Diamantina River, Birdsville." A black-and-white photograph.

90

On the back were two lines of handwriting in bright-blue ink: "Dear Sandy, Still thinking of you. Love, Jim."

Two lines! Two lines, after nearly three months of silence!

Her first impulse was to tear it across. But she paused. At least he was thinking of her, he hadn't utterly forgotten her existence as she had feared. But he might have written a proper letter, one page even!

She got up and put the postcard in her top drawer, under her handkerchiefs. Then she sat down to read one of her mother's complaining letters. It seemed that her father had not been very well, had been told by the doctor to slow up and take things easy. He had appointed a new manager and no longer supervised the flour mills himself. He hasn't done anything for years, thought Alix, who knew that the old manager had done most of the work and Major MacFarlane, though "the Boss," had been little more than a figurehead. Still, it was worrying; he was no longer young. At least her mother had not suggested that she ought to come home. Alix realized that she did not want to leave Hergott Springs. Up here, four hundred miles seemed almost close. But in the city she would be nearly a thousand miles away from Cappamerri.

"Was it from Jim?" asked Mab as they ate their tea of cold corned beef and mashed potatoes.

"Um." Alix had her mouth full and did not feel she had to say more.

"Well! What did he say? Has he quite recovered?"

"I don't know." Alix gulped a mouthful without tasting it. "He—it wasn't a letter. Just a postcard. O-oh Mab, he sent me *two lines!* And a picture of some pelicans."

She dropped her knife and fork with a clatter, and covered her face with her hands.

"H'm, obviously not one of the world's best correspondents. Cheer up, Alix. It's probably the longest missive he's written for years."

Alix removed her hands from her face. Her cornflower-blue eyes were swimming with tears.

"I'm sorry, Mabs. I haven't been much of a companion these last few months, have I? You guessed why, but I couldn't talk about it, it was hurt pride, I suppose. But now—now I'm going to forget him."

"Will you answer the postcard?"

"No! At least I might. If I can think of an even shorter message." She pushed her plate away. "I'm afraid I'm not hungry."

"I must say I had some reservations about that young man. Too much charm. And almost *too* handsome."

"I know you did. But unfortunately I fell for the charm, head over heels. Oh, God! I've tried to forget him. But I can't."

"Never mind, old girl. You'll get over it when we've left this place behind us. You'll find someone else."

91

"Never!"

"I'm willing to bet on it."

"Anyway, I'm not going to think of him any more. From now on he's just a memory."

Brave words! But on moonlit nights when the plover called, she tossed restlessly on the hot bed, going over in her mind every precious moment they'd had together, afraid that she'd forget. She composed several replies to the postcard:

Thanks for nothing!

Not thinking of you.

No more ink?

Message received.

Commendable brevity, congratulations.

But none of them was enough to convey her hurt and anger.

I hate you. Alix.

No, that wasn't true. She couldn't pretend to hate him. At last she came up with a message somewhat longer than his, and addressed it to "Mr. Jim Manning, Jnr., Cappamerri Station, via Birdsville." She chose a postcard from among the limited stock at Mrs. Allison's store: a rather blotchy view of the overflow at the Springs. On the back she wrote:

"How is your wound? Mine is now healed. Alix."

She enclosed the postcard in an envelope, as he had done. At least he had not sent an unenclosed postcard for the mailman, the postmaster, and everyone else to read. She did not expect a reply. Her message was clear enough: *It's over, finished, as far as I'm concerned.*

Fortunately she was kept busy. It was her turn on nursing duty and they had several patients, including Wal Crombie's son with bronchitis. One of the men was admitted with boils, and there were two cases of conjunctivitis calling at out-patients, besides a man with a septic finger. Constable Jack McGuinnes had hurt his shoulder and elbow in a fall from a camel—although he insisted he hadn't fallen; he'd "just dismounted awkwardly." The elbow was painful and very swollen and blue. Alix treated it with hot and cold compresses, striving to be brisk and efficient while Jack gazed at her tip-tilted profile and heaved a sentimental sigh. She made a sling out of one of her spare nurse's caps, for the loose type that fitted round the forehead and hung down the back was now in fashion, instead of the little starched caps they had worn in hospital training. But her soft curls still escaped at the front.

"There you are," she said, patting his upper arm. "Just as well it's your left arm. You're lucky you didn't break a bone. But you'll have to rest it till the swelling goes down."

"You mean I don't need any more treatment?" The big man looked like a small boy denied an outing.

92

"If it's very painful, come in again and I'll put a cold compress on it. Next week Sister Mab will be on duty, she's good at sprains."

"I'd rather have you," he murmured.

"Now, Jack!" she said warningly.

He took her hand with his good right one. "Alix, is there no hope for me? I still think of you."

(Oh no, thought Alix. *Still thinking of you!*)

"I'm afraid not, Jack," she said firmly. "What I said before still goes. I'm not thinking of marrying, and I'm not in love with you."

"I thought you were a bit keen on that drover fellow," he said. "But he's been gone for months. I thought I might still have a chance."

She patted his arm again. "Sorry, Jack. I'm really sorry." But she felt a tenderness towards him. He was not a fly-by-night like that Jim; he really loved her.

She heated some Antiphlogistine in its tin, and spread the clayey mass on a piece of white cotton cloth, cut to fit round the neck and over the chest of Wal's son, young Ken Crombie.

"Tell me if it's too hot," she said, holding the plaster just away from the skin. She touched one corner to his chest.

"Ow!"

"All right, I'll let it cool a bit. The heat will stop your chest hurting." The smell was antiseptic, the texture as she had spread it on the cloth with a knife like that of soft butter.

Mrs. Bates came in with her baby in her husband's light spring-cart, pulled by a skinny horse. The baby was dehydrated and suffering from dysentery—the dreaded "summer diarrhoea" which carried off so many infants. Alix consulted with Mab and they moved the cot down to the cellar, the only cool place. It had windows, though half underground. They draped damp cloths over the sides of the cot to cool the baby, and gave as many fluids as she would take.

Young Ken, much improved, was about ready to be discharged, and the Bates baby was out of danger (Mrs. Bates had offered to do the washing if she could stay in the hostel with her infant) when an exhausted rider came in from a station out towards Lake Eyre, about halfway between the railway to Oodnadatta and the track to Birdsville. At Mutoorinna the station manager's wife was in desperate straits, too ill to travel; she had been in labour for nearly two days and was growing weaker every hour.

"It's only about sixty miles away," said the young stockman who had ridden for aid. "The Boss wondered if you could come out and help his wife."

"If it's only sixty miles, why didn't he bring her in to the hostel for the birth?" asked Mab with some asperity.

"Well, it's not a first, see, and she'd had no trouble before."

Mab and Alix looked at each other.

"Could you ride on horseback sixty miles?" asked Alix.

"I very much doubt it."

"Nor could I. The camel-buggy? We could ask Jack McGuinnes—but it would be terribly slow, and this is urgent."

"Anyway, Jack is out of action with a sprained shoulder and badly contused elbow."

Mrs. Bates, who was listening with interest to this exchange, now spoke up. "Youse can have the spring-cart and the 'orse I brought in," she said. "If yer can drive, that is. It's a nice light vehicle, will go over the sand all right. I'll stay and mind the fort here, if y' like."

"I'll pilot you along the track," said the young man eagerly. "Not that you can miss it really, you more or less follow the bed of the Frome River."

"Is there water in it?"

"Not at present, no. You'd have to carry water. There's a good well at the station, though. The bore-water out there is that salt you can't hardly drink it."

"Well," said Mab briskly, "we'd better pack a medicine kit at once. Just as well there are no in-patients. Mrs. Bates can look after her baby here as well as we could. Let's see—we'll need morphia—chloroform—hyascine hydrobromide; and I suppose I'd better take the forceps and dilators, though I hate the things."

"I'll get the horse and harness it up to the cart," said the young man, whose name was Luke. "We'll start as soon as you're ready."

When Constable McGuinnes was told of their journey he looked anxious. "I wish I could come with you," he said. "You'll be right off the usual tracks out there, you could easily get bushed and it's still very hot. Promise me, if you have any trouble that you'll stay with the vehicle. Don't try to walk for help. You'll get dehydrated in no time."

"We'll have a guide all the way to Mutoorinna, and then we only have to follow our own tracks back again," said Alix. "Stop worrying, Jack."

"How long will you be?"

"There's no telling with an obstetric case," said Mab. "If there is fever or haemorrhage we'll have to stay; it could be a week or more."

"If you're not back in ten days I'll organize a search. There'll be water at the bore at Lake Letty, so you should be all right. But don't drink it unless you have to; it's very saline."

"We'll remember."

They set off in the early morning before the day had heated up. Alix drove the light cart, her slim hands with their strong wrists firm on the reins. She had often taken her mother driving in their buggy at home.

94

The young man rode ahead, waiting for them to catch up, lingering to watch them through a patch of sand. But mostly the track was stony, filled with those strange polished pebbles that lie about Lake Eyre, rose-madder to purple in colour. The track was narrow, having been made by strings of pack-camels in single file bringing Mutoorinna wool down to the railway.

The thin horse which they called Horace trotted bravely over this rough terrain. As the sun grew high and the day hotter, Mab and Alix had frequent recourse to the canvas water-bag hanging under the front step of the cart. Then suddenly it was empty. They had to stop and get out one of the four two-gallon tins which Jack had insisted they carry. They happened to be near a stand of needlebush and dead-finish, though much of the way had been bare of vegetation, so they allowed the horse a brief rest. Now the little black flies descended on them in a sticky cloud, crawling into lips and eyes. They hurriedly urged the horse on, to where the station hand was waiting for them up ahead, waving one hand in front of his face in "the outback salute" to disturb the flies.

He had made the trip from Mutoorinna in one day and night, but in spite of the urgency Mab and Alix had to stop at sunset when they reached Lake Letty bore, to water the horse and eat some damper and corned beef, which made them thirstier than ever. They gave the horse a nosebag of chaff.

They were still barely half-way, and by midnight they were up again and on their way in the cool of the desert night. There was no moon, but they followed the shadowy shape of the horseman (for the track was invisible) by the light of the stars reflected from the pale earth and polished gibbers. The stars were a blaze of ghostly blue-white light, the Milky Way a river of radiance curving across the sky.

By morning they were in sand-hill country. Rows of red and pink sand-hills, tending almost in the same direction—north of west—that they were following to the station, rose on either side; the distant ones floating like pale islands on a sea of tranquil blue mirage.

The sand-hills were long and low, nowhere more than about two hundred feet high; but when one cut across their track, they found it was better to do a detour round its long axis than to attempt a crossing of the crest, which was often sharply sculpted by the wind.

Warned by the speed with which they had got through the drinking water yesterday—though they'd had a wash in the warm, salty waters of the Lake Letty bore—they spared only enough water at breakfast to clean their teeth and wipe their hands and faces with a damp cloth. The second-to-last tin was broached to make a billy of tea. They were already within the boundary of Mutoorinna Station, their guide told them. They'd make the homestead, about twenty miles from where the front fence would have been if there'd been a fence, by midday. Mutoorinna carried

95

sheep, not cattle, but so far they had seen none. By now, Mab thought worriedly, the poor woman would have been in labour for over three days —if she was still alive.

CHAPTER FOURTEEN

There was an ominous silence at the homestead, no sign of life or activity. The white, low-roofed house was set in a fenced garden with a few green shrubs and palms, and even a vegetable garden watered from an overhead spray. But beyond the fence all was bare, an eaten-out desert of clay, dust, and stones.

About a hundred yards outside the fence some low rounded humpies, made of old bags and tin, were clustered together. A dark figure came crawling out of the side opening in one of these. She stood up, a plump lubra in a bright cotton gina-gina.

"Missus sick-feller prop'ly," she said, strolling over and holding the horse's bridle. "Me an' ol' Molly, we try to help 'er. Baby no come."

Another dark figure appeared from the outbuildings at the back, and a part-Aboriginal in shirt and tight-fitting trousers opened the gate and took the horse to unharness him. Mab got her medicine case out of the buckboard, and Alix and the dark woman carried their bags inside.

They found the woman in a dim bedroom, with her husband beside her bathing her face with a damp cloth. Her straight brown hair was plastered to her forehead with sweat, and her eyes looked enormous, dark-shadowed with pain. A low moan came from her throat.

With a professional glance at the poor woman's swollen belly and pale, exhausted face, Mab knew what a difficult case she had on her hands.

"Mrs. Jackson—we're here to help you," she said brightly. "This is Sister MacFarlane, and I am Sister Kingston."

The woman moved her head fretfully on the damp pillow. Mr. Jackson stood up. He was tall, dark, and broad-shouldered, with a blue-black stubble on his upper lip and chin.

"Her pains seem to have stopped," he murmured, shaking hands with them both. "Nothing's happening."

"If you could show us where we can wash and change," said Alix, "we'll do what we can."

In the dim bedroom, shuttered against the heat, where Mr. Jackson brought a can of hot water and a jug of cold for the flowered china basin on the wash-stand, Mab looked at Alix grimly. "I expect the baby's already dead," she said. "Contractions have ceased, and if it's not expelled or

97

removed, it will putrefy in the uterus. Then septicaemia for the mother is almost inevitable."

The five Jackson children, ranging from three to eleven, were playing on the veranda in a subdued fashion, knowing that Mum was ill. Alix looked out and saw that the eldest, a little girl, was carrying the toddler. They all had bleached, wispy straw-coloured hair and skinny legs and arms.

"A caesarean section would be the answer, I suppose. If she could get to a hospital," she said over her shoulder.

"Yes; but as it is—"

Mab was getting into a clean white uniform that had been packed in an oilcloth bag for the journey and did not seem to be contaminated with dust. After they had scrubbed up she set her jaw and straightened her back. "Well, here goes!" she said.

During the long struggle that followed, Alix stood by with sterilized instruments, fetched boiling water from the kitchen and clean cloths from a trunk of spotless linen. When Mab tried pressing down on the swollen stomach, the woman came out of her lethargy and screamed. She had given up and made up her mind to die.

"Mrs. Jackson, you must help me. Try to push, just once more—"

"No! The pain will start again." She began to cry weakly.

"Just for a little. And if it does get bad, we'll give you chloroform." She kneaded the taut belly.

"Ahhr! O-oh! Blessed Mary Mother of God—"

A weak contraction was followed by two stronger ones. Mrs. Jackson screamed. "God, help me!"

Mab nodded, and Alix administered a pad of chloroform, but only briefly.

"She's exhausted. We must get it over with," said Mab.

There were no more contractions. Mab, having passed the speculum, inserted the polished Heger's cervix dilators, and then took up the forceps with a steady hand. Alix moved in with the chloroform, but Mrs. Jackson had fainted. Mab prepared to make an entirely instrumental delivery, thankful for the practice she'd had on Mrs. Bates at Hergott Springs.

As soon as she could see part of the baby's head and face, she knew there was no more need to be careful. It was cyanosed, almost black. She grasped with the instrument and pulled. The head was too large.

"I'll have to slit the perineum," she said. "She's going to need stitches. . . ."

When it was over, they kept Mrs. Jackson under with chloroform until Alix—who was more experienced in the skill—had inserted a few stitches of catgut. Mab called Mr. Jackson and handed him the dark, wizened form of his latest son, wrapped in a cloth.

"Dead, Sister?"

"Yes. And I suggest you bury him before your wife asks to see him. He has been dead for some time."

"But my wife . . .?"

"Will be all right."

The woman's muscles were so weak that Mab had had to express the placenta manually; but now there was nothing more to do than to clean up. Then came the moment she had dreaded. Mrs. Jackson opened her eyes and asked to see the baby.

"I'm sorry, my dear. He didn't live. The labour was too prolonged."

"He? It was a boy, then. You know, I'm just too tired to care." She closed her eyes again.

Alix bathed her face and hands. They rolled her expertly out of the way while they put fresh sheets on the bed, and changed her blood-stained nightgown. Then it was time to call Mr. Jackson to see his wife. Apart from her pale face and dark-ringed eyes, there was nothing to show that the bedroom had been a bloody battlefield, with one dead and one wounded.

They had dinner with Mr. Jackson that night, a boiled leg of salted mutton, cooked and served up by Judy, the Aboriginal woman who had greeted them on their arrival. They noticed that their host had still not shaved his bristly chin.

After she had brought the second course, Judy faded away towards the humpies, carrying a billy of stewed tea and some scraps from the kitchen.

"Those little humpies must be terribly hot," said Alix musingly. "Is there room to stand up inside?"

"I shouldn't think so. I've never been inside one. Of course they wouldn't be happy in a house."

"And do the girls get a wage?"

"Not a fixed one. They get tea and sugar and tobacco, food for themselves and all their family, a cake of soap and a couple of gina-ginas a year. It's all they want."

"What about the men?" asked Mab. "I suppose you pay the men working as stockmen."

"The same. They get shirts and trousers, riding boots, tobacco, tucker, a bit of mutton when we kill. What they really like is the innards best. We feed all their relatives as well!"

"But they make very good stockmen?"

"Yeah . . . seem to have a natural seat on a horse. The half-castes are all right, but you can't trust a nigger. They're likely to go off on walkabout and leave the stock."

Alix noticed Mab's face growing red as she put down her knife and fork with a clatter. She started to change the subject, but Mab said in a dangerously quiet voice, "That term should not be used in Australia, Mr. Jackson!"

"What? Walkabout?"

"Nigger. I believe the Australian Aborigine is not Negroid. And even if they were—"

"I dunno. But they're not white, are they?"

Alix interposed tactfully.

"How many sheep can you carry to the acre?" she asked.

"Not more than ten acres to a sheep," said Mr. Jackson with a dry laugh. "You don't even have one sheep to the acre up here. And not even that with the present conditions. We're just hanging on, waiting for rain. It's the worst drought since 1902."

He lapsed into a morose silence and Alix and Mab said no more, but sat quietly eating their canned fruit and custard. They finished the meal and the washing-up was left for the lubras in the morning.

"I'm glad we came," said Mab the next day as they drank their morning tea brought on a tray by Molly, a shy, very fat Aboriginal maid in an orange dress. "But I wish—"

"You saved her life," said Alix. "And you couldn't have saved the baby. It was too late when we got here."

"Yes—but all that suffering for nothing. I'm *never* going to get married!" she said vehemently.

"I expect you'll change your mind when the time comes. Anyway, there are ways and means of preventing conception these days. I've half a mind to mention it to Mr. Jackson."

"But they're never absolutely certain. And I don't think you'd better—"

"Well, I'll talk to *her* about it then."

She did have a word in private with the patient. Mrs. Jackson, still weary after her ordeal, gave a wan smile.

"Yes, I know there are such things. I did suggest to my husband once . . . but he said it wasn't natural, and besides, it is against our religion."

"It's not natural for you to kill yourself with child-bearing, when it isn't necessary, and you already have a family. He can order something from an Adelaide chemist, and they'll send it under plain wrapper. He needn't be embarrassed."

"Well, I'll speak to him. But we only get a mail about once a month, when someone goes in to Hergott, or Finniss Springs."

"That will be quite soon enough. You're going to be an invalid for some time, even after the stitches have healed."

"Yes, Sister. And I want to thank you and Sister Kingston for coming all this way. I thought I was going to die."

"You can thank Sister Kingston that you didn't. She's a very skilled midwife."

"Yes . . . I'd like to give her a little present. In that top drawer there —the handkerchief case."

Alix fetched the linen case with its drawn-thread work, and put it on the bed. Mrs. Jackson took out an exquisitely embroidered handkerchief of finest lawn, with tiny rosebuds and blue forget-me-nots in the corners.

"Would you give this to her? And for you—"

"No, I don't want anything. I always lose handkerchiefs, anyway. But Sister Kingston will appreciate this. She's feeling a bit tired, and I told her to lie in for a while. We'll be leaving early tomorrow morning, before the heat."

But when they rose before dawn the next day, it was already hot, with a breeze from the north-east that conveyed nothing of coolness though it did help by evaporating perspiration on the skin.

Mr. Jackson had their water-bag and tins filled with sweet well-water, and he sent his man Luke with them to guide them on their way. Alix and Mab thought he meant to travel with them as far as Lake Letty bore; but Luke, who had ridden twice over that dreary track in the past week, was not keen on traversing it again.

"Will you be all right now?" asked the stockman casually, reining in his horse after they were through the front boundary of Mutoorinna and within sight of the Frome channel. Pink sand-hills rose on either side of the now well-marked track, but did not pose any difficulty as they ran roughly in the same direction.

"Just follow your tracks back," he said as they were silent. "Your way is south-east. Keep the Frome on your right hand, but don't go off along any of its channels; you might get bogged in sand, and if you try to come back you'll find the channels branching off in all directions."

"Well, I suppose . . ." said Alix doubtfully.

"We can hardly get lost," said Mab.

"Hardly. Just let the horse take you back; he'll know the way. And if you're at all worried, climb the nearest little jump-up and look for Lake Letty bore-head. That's right on your line for the Hergott."

Mab and Alix looked at each other. They both wanted to prove that a woman is just as capable in the bush as a man.

"We'll do that," said Alix.

"You'll be right," said Luke, turning his horse's head back the way he had come. "So long, then."

Alix picked up the reins and urged Horace on. He seemed reluctant to go, though he'd had a good rest at the station. He put his ears back and tossed his head, looking back at the other horse receding into the distance. Alix had to urge him on.

Mab was still tired after her night-long vigil, so they camped among the pink and yellow sand-hill country as the day reached its hottest in the afternoon. There was little shade and feed for the horse, but they felt they had to share some of the water with him, as they had not made it as far as the bore.

They made a simple meal of cold mutton with some of the station's home-made bread and a few ripe tomatoes. There was no question of carrying even tinned butter in that heat.

"I know real bushmen always boil the billy," said Mab, "but I vote we just drink water. I reckon it's too hot to light a fire."

"I agree."

"I wonder what the temperature is?"

"About 115 degrees in the shade, probably. In the sun—I hate to think."

As they spread their swags they noticed small holes everywhere in the sand, probably made by kangaroo rats, hopping mice, or lizards; but they couldn't help wondering if some of them held a snake, like the deadly Fierce Snake.

"We must make a really early start," said Alix. "It's going to be a scorcher tomorrow."

She watched the sun set in an orange glow over towards the dry bed of Lake Eyre South. The sky was pure and clear, shading up from apricot to peacock blue to pale blue and grey at the zenith. The first stars appeared, the brilliant pointers among them.

"We could travel at night and find our way by the Southern Cross," said Alix. "My father showed me how to find true south: you prolong the long axis of the Cross, bisect the pointers and produce a line at right angles, and where the two lines meet is the South Celestial Pole."

And then, as they settled down on their ground-sheets, the enormous night sky arching over them, she said, "It's exciting, isn't it? Being away out here in the middle of nowhere, on our own."

"H'm, yes. But I'll be happier when we're in sight of the bright lights of home."

"Come, where is your sense of adventure?" Alix asked.

"I don't know . . . I feel uneasy, somehow."

Horace the horse stamped and whinnied. They had unharnessed him, but having no hobbles, had tethered him to a myall where he could munch at the leaves if he wanted to.

In the night the dry wind rose, and by morning the tops of the sand-hills were "smoking," blowing loosely in the direction they were going, east of south.

"At least we'll have the wind behind us," said Mab, helping Alix to harness up and load the cart with their things. They had a drink of water and wiped the dust from their faces with a piece of damp cloth. Alix wanted to give the horse a drink from the second tin, but Mab thought it would be wiser to wait, in case they did not make the bore or the Springs by tonight.

"Just think! We can have a swim in warm water when we get there—won't need to wear anything, either."

By mid-morning the sand was blowing in a stinging cloud, and looking behind them they saw an ominous sight—a huge, rolling dust-cloud reaching up into the sky, billowing like smoke, and moving rapidly towards them.

"Hell! A sandstorm!"

They stared at each other with reddened eyes. The horse continued to plod along the track, his head hanging. Then suddenly there was no track; it had been blotted out completely in a choking orange cloud. The horse stopped.

"We'll just have to camp and wait for it to blow over," said Alix. "You can't see a thing through this."

She groped around the back and lifted down a water-tin and refilled the canvas bag. They both had a raging thirst, their mouths gummed with dust.

"We'll have to give poor old Horace the horse one gallon. We're dependent on him to get us back."

"Well—I suppose so. Shall we unharness him?"

"There's nothing to tether him to—at least I can't see a tree or anything else."

"He's not likely to go anywhere in this. Better let him out of the shafts, and loop the reins over the footplate or something. Then he can lie down to get out of the wind if he wants to."

They managed to rig up a ground-sheet under the back of the cart to break the flying, stinging sand. Immediately swarms of little black flies came from somewhere to share their shelter.

"Blasted flies!" said Mab. "It's almost worth while going out into the storm to get rid of them."

But they didn't talk much. Their mouths were too dry and sticky, and as soon as they opened them the flies crawled in.

"This can't last," said Alix at last. "Or can it? If only we had reached the bore!"

Mab said nothing. But her face looked grim.

Chapter Fifteen

They slept fitfully that night. The hot, stifling wind ceased about midnight, and there was a lull in the flapping of the ground-sheet. The air seemed suddenly more breathable. Mab got up and fetched them each an enamel mug of water. The moisture seemed to disappear in their dust-choked throats, leaving them still thirsty. The wind rose again.

Horace smelt the water and whinnied. He was thirsty, too. But a mug of water would go nowhere with him; he would have to wait.

"We'll be able to move on in the morning," said Alix, "and he can drink all he likes at Lake Letty."

An uncanny silence woke them. The air was still, but smelt of dust. At first they thought the sun had not risen, but peering out from under the cart, Alix saw it floating in the east—a pale ghost of a sun, paler than the moon, shrouded in a veil of fine colloidal dust. Then she looked towards the front where Horace had been tethered.

"Mab!" she squeaked, her throat made dryer with fear and shock. "The horse is gone!"

They leaped out from the shelter, staring wildly about. There was no doubt about it. Horace's tracks showed in the soft new sand, which had drifted up around the wheels of the vehicle, leading away along the track toward Lake Letty. In places the track was completely covered by a new sand-drift. "He must have broken the reins," said Mab, "and has made his way to the bore, where he remembers having watered on the way out. I wonder how far it is."

They sat down, their legs suddenly turned to jelly as the full danger of their situation struck them. Little more than a tin of water left, which they would have to carry with them while they walked to the bore, however far that might be.

They made a meagre breakfast, scarcely able to chew the bread, the crust of which now resembled wood in texture and hardness. Before they had finished, the wind rose. Soon they were once again enveloped in a blinding cloud of sand and dust. They crawled under the cart with the last tin of water, and curled their backs against the stinging blast. The air was like a furnace breath, the temperature must already be over a hundred, and it was only morning!

"Horace will make his way back to Hergott, and someone will come looking for us," said Mab.

"Yes . . . Jack said whatever happened, to stay with the vehicle. At least it gives us some shade."

"I wish he could see you now! Your hair looks like red wire, there's a rim of mud round your mouth, your eyes are bunged up and your face covered in dirt—"

"I never thought I'd long to see him, but I do. If he turned up now, I —I'd even kiss his camel!"

Mab's mask of red dust cracked in a smile. They were trying to cheer each other up, trying not to panic. After a while, Alix said in a small voice, "Horace will never travel in this. Suppose he just stays at the bore? There's a bit of feed around there."

"Then we'll have to walk. As soon as this stops."

They moistened their lips and wiped their faces with a corner of a wet cloth. Their skin felt dry as paper, their hair electric. Mab's face was bright red, her grey eyes were bloodshot. Alix's soft lips were beginning to crack.

The wind blew all that night and half the next day. By rationing themselves to one small drink night and morning, they had managed to keep about a quart of water. Two pints. Four cups.

In the afternoon they moved their cramped limbs and crawled out into the sun. The sky was clearing to a pale, dusty blue. The horse's hoof-prints had been obliterated, in fact a sand-drift covered the whole track. But the sun gave them direction; they only had to keep east of south, pick up the dry channels of the Frome and follow them down. But how far was it? By night they might lose their way. But how could they travel in this searing heat?

"Jack said to stay with the vehicle."

"Jack wasn't going to send out a search party for ten days after we left."

"But if Horace turns up—"

"And if he doesn't? We'll perish here without water."

They stared at each other, admitting to themselves the dread both were feeling. Nothing on the horizon but empty plain, some half-dead trees with their wind-eroded roots standing above the ground, and long pink sand-hills, one of them floating in a cruel, cool-blue mirage.

To the westward was an isolated flat-topped hill, a "tent-hill" or "jump-up" as they called it out here—a remnant of the ancient plateau now worn down everywhere else to the present level of the plain, somewhere near sea-level.

"Luke back there said to climb a jump-up and get the direction of the bore," said Mab. "At least we'd know how far we had to go. You stay here while I climb that hill. I'll have to go before sunset if I'm to pick up the borehead."

"We'll both go," said Alix, suddenly afraid of being left alone in this empty, hostile place. No, not hostile. Just supremely indifferent. Man was an insect crawling over its surface; whether he lived or died was of no moment. The earth would remain, unchanged, unchanging.

"No. You stay here in case the sand gets up again, and you can coo-ee to give me direction."

She drank half a mug of water, used a little to dampen the silk scarf around her throat, and set out. Within a few minutes the scarf was dry.

Alix watched her figure with its long skirt and straw hat as she ploughed through sand-drifts, then made better time over a scoured clay-pan, till she reached the foot of the small hill. She began to climb. Half-way up she faltered, sat down on a rock. The sides were not steep, they sloped out all round the flat summit like a skirt. Mab must be exhausted by climbing in this heat. They should have waited till morning. But every day was critical now. They would have to start walking tonight, navigating by the stars if they couldn't see the track.

At last the small figure reached the top and stood there, gazing to the south and east. Alix saw her wave. On the way down she stopped again to rest, her face in her hands. She came on slowly, stumblingly, reached the level, and began crossing the clay-pan. Their enemy the sun was dipping to the horizon, but the heat was no less.

It must have been about a hundred and twenty today, thought Alix. Wish we had a thermometer.

She was tormented with thirst, but would wait to celebrate Mab's return with what she hoped was good news, in their third-to-last cup of water.

Mab had crossed the clay-pan and was floundering through the soft sand. Suddenly she pitched forward on her face and lay still.

"Mab!" croaked Alix, starting to run. She went back and got the water-tin, now frighteningly light.

She reached Mab's prostrate figure and lifted her head from the sand. Her eyes were staring, her face was bright red, her open mouth filled with sand. Alix splashed some of the precious water over her face, into her mouth. Mab shuddered, and comprehension came back into her eyes.

She tried to lift one arm to point, but it fell back. "Bore—not too far." Her eyes glazed again.

Alix felt her pulse. It was rapid but weak, and her skin was dry, burning like fire. "Heat hyperpyrexia." The words came back to her from some forgotten textbook. *In this condition the body temperature may rise to 107 to 110 degrees. . . . A complete cessation of sweating; at 95 degrees sweating becomes the sole means of heat loss in the body. . . . In severe cases, death often . . .*

"Oh God, don't let her die!"

She lifted Mab's head on to her lap. "Kingsy, say something, speak to me. Can you hear me?"

106

At temperatures over 100 degrees physical activity should be limited. . . .
Of course! She should never have let Mab make that climb.

Mab lay inert, breathing rapidly and noisily. Her eyes were open but unseeing. She was muttering something. It sounded like "Headache . . ."

"Mabs, can you stand if I hold you? I must try to get you back." The sand was still giving off the day's heat as the sun dipped below the flat horizon. "A bit cooler under the cart."

She got her arms under Mab's shoulders and dragged her to a kneeling position. But her legs would not straighten, her arms swung lifelessly. Alix swallowed a mouthful of water from the tin, then sat down in despair. She could not move her.

She might drag her a little way, but not as far as the track. And in the morning the blazing sun would rise.

Alix went back to the cart and collected their ground-sheets. At least the flies had gone. Rooting in the back of the cart for something to prop up a shelter for Mab, she found a tomato from Mrs. Jackson's garden that must have rolled out of the tucker-box the day before. Without thinking she wolfed it down, feeling the warm juice delicious in her dry throat. It gave her new strength. Heat exhaustion—salt deficiency—dehydration. She knew all the stages. But Mab seemed to be suffering from heat-stroke.

She went back to the hot sand, dragging the ground-sheets after her, and a piece of wood she had pulled from the seat. She rigged up a shelter, took off her blouse and rolled it up for a support for Mab's head. Mab did not speak again. Her eyes were open, but she seemed to have sunk into a coma.

Ironically, the wind which had caused their predicament had completely dropped. There was not a breath of air to dispel the heat being given off by the sand, even though the sky was growing dark. Alix lay down beside her friend and must have dropped into a doze of exhaustion. She woke and saw the splendid stars overhead—remote, uncaring. Then she became aware of the silence. Mab's laboured breathing had ceased.

"No!" she screamed. She knelt up and listened for a heartbeat. Nothing. The air had grown cooler, and Mab's hands were already cold. She felt her wrist. There was no pulse. She gave a wail, and bowed her head to the sand. Now she was alone, alone in this dreadful desolation. Her friend of so many years was dead. Dead. She could not believe it. She had always thought of Mab as the strong one. She caressed the cold face, and closed the lids over the sightless eyes.

She did not think to sleep, but when the desert chill woke her before dawn she knew she must have. She took a few sips of water, now cool and refreshing. In the east a line of livid gold showed between two long banks of grey cloud. Cloud! Could it be going to rain, now when it was too late for Mab? As the light grew she felt a reluctance to look at the still figure beside her.

She would have to walk on, try to reach the bore. But she could not leave Mab here in the sun, for the flies and the dingoes . . .

Using the piece of flat wood she began scooping a grave in the loose sand. It seemed to flow back again as fast as she dug. She knelt and dug frantically with her hands, throwing the sand behind her like a dog.

At last she had scooped out a shallow grave. But she couldn't put Mab in the sand, cover her face with it. She wrapped her in a ground-sheet and, sobbing and gasping, rolled her into the hole. She stuck the piece of wood upright in the sand. Not a cross, but at least a marker. If she could get back to Hergott, they would come and get Mab and bury her properly. How far to the bore? Not far, Mab had said with nearly her last breath.

Alix backed away from the pathetic mound, then turned and hurried back to the spring-cart. She tied her hat on firmly with her veil, picked up the water-tin now holding a little over half a pint. She thought of damping her blouse before she put it on, but knew she must keep every drop for drinking. The sun, which had been beaming through the gap in the clouds, now went dim.

The enemy which had clubbed them with its rays was relenting, though the thin, motionless clouds did not look like rain. The landscape lost its colour, seemed grey and menacing. Alix trudged on along the sand-drifted track. On her right she could see a line of dead trees, one of the channels of the Frome, but she knew there was no water there. She was now walking in a sort of daze, one foot in front of the other, drag the back leg forward, then the other. Her lips were gummed together; she had to stop and drink half of the remaining water, already growing warm. With the sun veiled, though the air was stifling it was not as hot as yesterday. But she could not risk the loss by evaporation if she put the water in the cooling canvas bag. With half of her mind she realized that with Mab gone, she had twice the chance of surviving on what was left.

She knew that if another sandstorm blew up, she was finished. The air remained calm, the veiled sun enabled her to walk on; otherwise she would have had to stay in the shade of the cart until the water ran out and she perished. It was all very well for Jack to tell her to "stay with the vehicle." To reach Lake Letty bore was her only hope.

Dehydrated, her skin burning through the chiffon veil covering her face, she had to sit down and rest in the meagre shade of a dead tree. She drank the last of the water, not enough to satisfy her thirst, and threw the tin away. At least she would not have to carry the awkward thing any further.

The track ahead looked level. It was level, she felt sure. Yet she began to hallucinate that she was making her way down a long, steep slope. It seemed to make walking easier. In fact the track had been climbing slightly, and now as she topped a low, sandy ridge she saw ahead of her the shape of the bore-head. Elation gripped her. There would be cool water in the bore overflow. The lake, she knew, was dry and silted.

She trudged on, too weak to hurry though her goal was in sight. She came to the bank of the bore-drain. Water! Pale-green, milky water. . . . She staggered along the slope and fell full-length in the blessed moisture, seeming to drink through her skin like a desert lizard. Along the drain, the water had had time to cool by evaporation of its surface, though it had come hot from deep in the earth. She opened her mouth and swallowed. It was horrible, warm and mineralized. But it was wet! If cattle could survive on it, so could she. She crawled back to the edge for the shoulder-bag in which she had carried her only provisions, a piece of the rock-hard bread from Mutoorinna. She dunked it in the bore-water and forced the softened mass between her sun-cracked lips.

Then a thought struck her. There was no sign of Horace, except for some horse-dung about the bore-drain, fresher than what he'd left on the trip out. It was possible he had returned to Hergott Springs and help might be on the way. Exhausted, she crept under the shelter of a needlebush, sparse and prickly, not even green, but some comfort in the vast surrounding emptiness.

Chapter Sixteen

Alix slept, and dreamed about the sea. She had not consciously missed it, though they had lived fifteen miles from the coast in Adelaide. In her dream she was a child again, wading in the glass-clear shallows at Semaphore Beach, where Mrs. MacFarlane had taken a cottage for the summer. Her companion was the English maid, Rachel, straight out from Liverpool, who could hardly believe the sun-drenched white sand beach, the miles of blue sea under the cloudless skies of summer.

They built a backrest from the heaps of dry seaweed that lay along the beach like stranded brown whales. Then they were wading in the wide pools left by the tide. Alix kicked up a shower of crystal drops. The sand under her feet was firm, ridged with a pattern of ripples. The water looked so inviting, she bent and scooped up a mouthful and swallowed it.

"You mustn't drink seawater!" shrieked Rachel. "If you do you'll go mad."

Alix screamed. She had swallowed the seawater, and now she would go mad, and be locked up in Parkside Asylum behind the high grey walls where they kept the lunatics. . . .

She woke with the salty taste still in her mouth and a sense that the experiences of the past week were unreal. But then she was struck by the simple, stark fact of Mab's absence. She had to admit Mab was gone.

It was now the eighth day since they had left Hergott Springs. The sky had cleared to a pitiless, cloudless blue. Alix was beginning to feel weak from lack of food, and from the dysentery that plagued her due to the mineralized bore-water. She was not delirious, but she was subject to strange fancies, while knowing that they were only fancies. At one stage as she stepped into the shallow green water she fancied herself back on the beach at Semaphore, paddling in the zircon-clear shallows left by the retreating tide. Then she was arguing with her mother about whether they should have gone to Mutoorinna at all—Mrs. MacFarlane insisting that it had been "foolhardy, typically thoughtless, dangerous and stupid."

"But Mother! The woman would have died in agony."

"So Mab Kingston died instead."

"Ye-es."

Mrs. MacFarlane was gone. Alix stared at the pale-blue, heat-hazed, empty sky and remembered that she had not once prayed in their extremity, except for that one involuntary, "O God, don't let her die!" as she sat beside Mab in the sand.

But Mad *had* died; and Alix felt that she probably would never pray again.

As soon as she moved to go down for a drink she began to feel weak and giddy. A warm breeze sprang up, but did not cool the hot water coming out of the pipe, and she had to go a long way down the bore-drain till it was cool enough to wash in, let alone drink. The taste of it sickened her. Her throat had become sore.

There were birds at morning and sunset, flights of green budgerigars moving in shrill-voiced clouds, and little waxbills with their bright-orange beaks and creaking, whispering voices. No doubt if she could trap a bird she could eat it, though the thought revolted her. Or perhaps a lizard . . .

Then she remembered what Jack McGuinnes had said. "If you're not back in ten days I'll start a search party."

The tenth day was tomorrow, or was it today? It was then she began to hope. She had been dozing under the bush when a shout woke her. She sat up, believing that she was hallucinating again. But it was real: there was Jack perched on the two-camel buggy, and beside him Micky on another camel, water-bags hanging from each side of its neck.

Her throat slaked with sweet fresh water, her hunger by a rather dried-up cheese sandwich, she told them croakingly of how Horace had got away, and that Mab was lying back there in a shallow grave. "We can't leave her there," she said urgently. "Out there in that dreadful emptiness!"

"No, no," said Jack soothingly. "We must get you back for now, then I'll take a party out with a coffin, and the horse to pick up the Bates's cart, and we'll bring her back to Hergott Springs for a proper burial."

Alix began to cry weakly. "What did happen to Horace?" she asked at last.

"He turned up at the Springs yesterday, not much the worse for wear. He must have stayed here for a while where there was water, until the feed cut out. I was already preparing to set off, because I'd been worried ever since that big dust-storm. But everyone said you'd have stayed at the station till it was over."

"No . . . we were in the thick of it. And Mab climbed a hill in the heat, to look for the bore . . . and—and—"

He held her hand and stroked it. "Don't go over it now, dear." She put her other hand over his big brown one. Dear Jack! So solid, so dependable! As she watched his large figure coming towards her, to rescue her, she had felt a surge of something like love.

Now she was back at Hergott Springs, the nightmare behind her, recovering in her own hospital. But whenever she closed her eyes, Mab's

111

face rose before her with staring, sightless gaze and open mouth filled with sand. (Years later, digging idly on an Adelaide beach where she was staying, she felt the sand jammed beneath her fingernails and turned faint and sick at the memory it brought back.)

A telephone message had been sent down the line to Adelaide to inform the A.I.M. headquarters of the tragedy. Alix did not want a replacement nurse for Sister Kingston; she would carry on alone until the two new appointees, due next month, had time to get there.

Back came a message that the Reverend John Flynn, the originator and moving spirit behind the A.I.M. hostels, was about to leave on the northern train for Hergott Springs and Oodnadatta, whence he would go on to Alice Springs to examine the possibility of a hostel there. One was already built at Oodnadatta, and he was going to dedicate it. From there he would have to travel from the railhead by mail coach to Horseshoe Bend, and then another hundred and twenty miles by camel to the Alice, with Tex of the camel mail.

When she heard that he was coming, Alix began to hope that he would be there in time to conduct the burial service. Mab would have liked that. . . . Alix looked forward to meeting this extraordinary man whose vision had led to the first bush nurses' going to the outback, and the first hostels being built by the A.I.M. of which he had become director in 1912.

When he arrived on the train, she found an unassuming, gently spoken man in his thirties, the hair already receding from his high forehead, with a quirk of humour about the mouth and eyes in his rather long face. She liked him at once. Jack was not yet back from his mission, but she asked John Flynn if he would mind conducting the burial service.

"Of course, my dear. It's the least I can do for that brave girl. Can I go to see her parents when I return to Adelaide?"

"Only her father is alive. I wrote to him about it. But I'm sure he'd like to hear from you."

She also told him about Mira's problem. He was a Presbyterian, but the least bigoted of churchmen, and he offered to talk to Abdul Dervish.

He came back to tell her that the father had agreed; Mira was to be allowed to marry Reuben, in a Muhammadan ceremony. "He was a Mission boy, so we've lost a Christian to the Muslims," said Flynn with a wry smile. "But I'm sure God won't hold it against him. He can still be a Christian at heart."

As the men's ward was empty, Flynn had a bed there. He liked to talk, and after tea would outline for her his dreams of a "Mantle of Safety" to cover the whole of outback Australia, the small towns without doctor or hospital, the outlying stations and lonely camps. He planned hostels at strategic points in Western Australia, the Northern Territory, Queens-

112

land, as well as South Australia, where it had all begun: and he dreamed of aeroplanes and the new wireless to connect them.

Alix would get sleepy about ten o'clock and go off to bed, but getting up one night towards midnight she saw the light on in the sitting-room. John Flynn was sitting over a notebook, writing. He told her that he rarely went to bed before 1 or 2 A.M. but didn't like getting up early in the morning. In the evenings he wore his jacket; by day, his only concession to the heat was to remove the jacket, though he still kept on the waistcoat of his dark suit over a long-sleeved shirt, his gold watch-chain looped in front.

Mrs. Bates had taken her baby and gone back to her husband's camp out towards Lake Harry, for Alix was feeling quite strong again. She was thankful for a quiet time in the hospital, having feared that patients would be banked up and waiting after the Sisters' ten days' absence. She had only a child with a septic throat, and an old prospector who had wandered in with an infected toe, who came to out-patients for treatment each morning.

When the cortège arrived with Mab in the coffin, Jack left the cart standing in the street and came to find Alix. "The burial should be straight away," he said, "for obvious reasons. . . . I've sent two men out to dig a grave in the cemetery."

Alix swayed on her feet, feeling faintness come over her. Jack Mc-Guinnes put an arm round her to steady her.

"Bear up, old girl. At least we have her safe from the dingoes. They'll often dig up a shallow grave, you know."

"I—didn't know."

"You'll want to come, I suppose. I'll have a shot at the burial service, but—"

"It's all right, Jack. The Reverend John Flynn, the Presbyterian minister, is here on an inspection for the Inland Mission. He's agreed to take the service."

Jack was relieved. He had to be everything at once out here: coroner, registrar of births and deaths, signer of death certificates, burier of the dead, stock inspector, besides arbiter of the law and protector of Aborigines. . . .

He and the minister shook hands and sat down to a cup of tea provided by Alix, who left them to go round the town collecting people for the service.

Almost the whole town turned up—except Wal Crombie, who was away with the mail, and the postmaster and station-master because there was a train due in. The little crowd, both men and women wearing hats against the burning sun, stood about the open hole that had been dug with crowbars in the iron-hard soil.

John Flynn spoke simply and movingly about sacrifice and service.

113

"This is the first such loss we have had in our new venture," he said. "A tragic loss . . . but without the dedication of Sister Kingston and others like her, many others would have died."

He then read the burial service, and at the words "ashes to ashes, dust to dust," Alix thought, how appropriate, she has been dug out of sand to be interred in dust. . . .

But John Flynn had opened the service with the beautiful passage from Isaiah:

The wilderness and the solitary place shall be glad for them; and the desert shall rejoice, and blossom as the rose . . .
It shall blossom and rejoice, even with joy and singing . . .
Strengthen ye the weak hands, and confirm the feeble knees.
Say to them that are of fearful heart, Be strong, Fear not;
The eyes of the blind shall be opened, and the ears of the deaf shall be unstopped;
Then shall the lame man leap as an hart, and the tongue of the dumb sing; for in the wilderness shall waters break out, and streams in the desert.
And the parched ground shall become a pool, and the thirsty land springs of water; in the habitation of dragons . . . shall be grass with reeds and rushes.

As there were no flowers in the town—if there had been, the dust-storm would have buried them—Alix had brought a handful of white everlasting daisies, dry as paper, which used to decorate the table in their sitting-room.

In place of fresh flowers she carried the small white handkerchief that Mrs. Jackson had given Mab, with its embroidered roses and forget-me-nots. She spread it on the coffin before it was lowered into the grave, and turned away, her eyes blinded by tears.

John Flynn put a steady hand under her elbow, tucking the Bible and prayer-book under his left arm. Big Jack McGuinnes, his eyes moist, came up and silently wrung her hand. There was nothing to be said.

CHAPTER SEVENTEEN

Alix missed Mab at every turn, not just in the daily running of the hostel. In the last weeks the place had become hateful to her. She could not leave soon enough, when the two new Sisters should have arrived. She threw herself into the work and into giving the whole place a spring-clean, though it was nearly autumn. The seasons did not vary much up here; all equally dry and clear, though colder at some times than others.

She asked Jack McGuinnes over for a meal because she couldn't stand the emptiness of the other place at table. He came several times, when he was not away on duty, and though he was circumspect and did not importune her in any way, she knew that he was hoping she would turn to him in her loneliness and grief.

"I feel so guilty!" she had told him. "Not just because I am alive and she is dead. But I'm a trained nurse, I should have thought of the possibility of heat-stroke in those awful conditions. Mab was always so strong. . . . I just didn't think of such a thing."

"You mustn't blame yourself, Alix." He had dropped the semi-formal "Sister" before her name.

"But I do! I want to get away from this desolate place, which reminds me all the time of how she perished. I'm going back to Adelaide."

A shadow crossed his face. "You mean you're going to give up outback nursing—stay in the city?"

"No. I don't think I could stand that. But perhaps I could get a posting to somewhere with permanent water, and green trees. Even then I'd have to find a new partner. They always appoint nurses in pairs."

Jack said, "I'm thinking of asking for a transfer to Alice Springs. Bloke up there is resigning, I heard."

"Alice Springs! I've always wanted to go there."

He stared at her under his square black brows, then took her hand across the table.

"Alix, would you come with me, as my wife? Will you just think about it? It's even more isolated than here, but it does have water and trees, and a reasonably cool climate for much of the year."

"Oh, Jack! I don't know. I haven't really thought about marriage."

"Well, just promise me you will think about it. I don't mind waiting.

Have a holiday at home first. Then if I get my transfer I'll come down to Adelaide and find you."

"I'll give you my address. But I can't make any promises."

She was packing up her things, and Mab's, to take down to Mr. Kingston in Adelaide, when Wal Crombie came in from Birdsville with the last mail before her train left. With him came a note from Jim Manning at Cappamerri. When she saw his handwriting, and the Birdsville postmark, she hurried home and opened the envelope with trembling fingers.

There was half a page of writing, neat and well-spaced, in very blue ink.

My darling Sandy, I am so very sorry to hear about the tragedy that has overtaken you. Word has just come about Sister Kingston. I was planning to come down with a mob of bullocks anyway, to see you before you leave—next month, isn't it? I find that I can't forget you. From your last message I know what you think of me now. But I must see you again. Jim.

Well! She felt winded, as if all the breath had been knocked out of her body. So Jim Manning had not forgotten her! Fighting down a surge of joy, she called up her reserves of pride and anger. He thought he could just drift back into her life after months of absence and silence. But she was leaving on the train in a few days and he would not find her waiting by the sliprails when he returned,

"Her face grown pale—
Ah, quivering lips and eyes that brim!"

She wrote a formal note of thanks for his condolences, and informed him that she was leaving immediately for the south, and would not be coming back. "I never want to see this place again!" (Or you either, she implied.) She signed it grandly, spurning his pet-name, as "Alexandra MacFarlane."

And that was the end of that chapter in her life, she told herself firmly. Yet she did not feel any elation at thus slamming the door in his face. However, the letter was written. She sealed it doubly with glue, for in that small community everyone had been aware of her brief affair with Jim, and she did not quite trust the postmaster not to look. She walked along the dusty road to post it before she could change her mind.

Returning over the barren landscape, past the splendid Flinders Ranges in the narrow-gauge, rocking train, she was reminded poignantly of the journey in the opposite direction with Mab, the excitement and enthusiasm of their first trip to the north. Who would have thought that she would be returning alone? Mab lay in the barren cemetery at the Springs, under the simple stone monument her father had sent up in the train from Adelaide.

Alix changed into the bigger train at Port Augusta, watching the delphinium blue of the Mount Lofty Ranges beginning to lift along the horizon. At the Adelaide Railway Station her parents were waiting. She stepped down onto the platform and into her mother's arms. So much had happened, she seemed to have been away so long, that she was amazed to see her mother unchanged, perhaps a little plumper, with no grey threads in her black hair and her sharp blue eyes as bright as ever. Her father enfolded her in a loving hug, and bent to brush her cheek with his whiskers. Her parents were still the same, incredibly the same, yet she felt herself to be a different person, older and more cynical than the young woman who had left the city just over two years ago.

They spoke briefly on the way home in the car, of the tragedy of Mab's end. "We couldn't help thinking, that it might have been our daughter!" Mrs. MacFarlane said tremulously. Alix replied shortly that she didn't want to talk about it.

"I'm dreading having to go and see her father, and take him her things, but I have to do it," she said at home, setting aside the bundle of Mab's few possessions. It hadn't seemed worth while to bring her clothes back, and she had given them to the Aboriginal girls in the town, leaving the white uniforms and caps to the relieving Mission Sisters, one of whom was about Mab's size.

She remembered how, when going through Mab's things, she had come across her mutilated fine wool dressing-gown: a great three-cornered piece had been cut from the skirt to make a shawl for a baby whose mother was too poor to provide one. Typical of Mab, who had given Mira, to cheer her, the pretty coloured ribbon she sometimes wore round her hair when off duty.

Sitting on the side of her daughter's bed, Frances MacFarlane tried to imagine what it had been like, to see another perish in the desert, and then dig her grave with one's bare hands. . . .

She shuddered, and said, "Never mind about that now, you need to rest and recover from your journey . . . and everything."

"I don't want to rest! I want to be busy so that I can't think, and so tired at night that I can sleep. For a while I thought I would never sleep again, because I kept seeing her face in nightmares."

"There, there." Alix suffered herself to be rocked in maternal arms. "My poor, dear baby," said Frances, stroking Alexandra's soft curls. Absence seemed to have made her mother's heart grow fonder. "What you have gone through, up there in the heat and dust! Indeed, your complexion is a little brown and coarsened, and do I detect a few lines around your eyes? Just tiny ones, of course, and if you put cold cream on them regularly we'll soon have you quite presentable—"

"But I shall be going back to work just as soon as I find something suitable."

"What? Go off again into the back of beyond, where you will never find a suitable husband—"

"I am not looking for a husband. I just want to work at my profession."

Frances compressed her lips but said no more.

Alix unpacked her things. Beyond the window were the old familiar rounded shapes of the Adelaide hills, Mount Osmond where she had dedicated herself to nursing . . . it seemed like fifty years ago. She came to the orange-and-black feather.

"Where did you get it?" asked her mother. "It's beautiful!"

"The feather? Oh—it was a gift. From the local policeman. It's a tail-feather of a black cockatoo."

"A gift! Was he an admirer of yours?"

Trust mother! thought Alix irritably, to nose out your secrets. Well, she was not letting on about Jim Manning and the suffering he had caused her. Nor about Jack McGuinnes either.

"Just a friend."

The very next week came a letter with a Hergott Springs postmark.

Feeling her mother's eyes boring into her as she handed over the envelope with its rather untidy scrawl – for Jack hated filling in reports and had formed the habit of dashing off his words as fast as possible— Alix bolted for her room and shut the door.

"Dearest Alix," it began. He was hopeful of the Alice Springs posting, but the trouble was to find a replacement for the huge Hergott Springs beat. No inexperienced city policeman would be able to take it on. And whoever came, he would have to stay and "show him the ropes" before leaving.

"However, I'm due for some leave soon, when I'll be coming down to Adelaide. I hope by then you will be able to give me an answer, dear girl."

She felt close to him because he was the only one who really knew what she had been through, not just because he had been her rescuer and she owed her life to him. He was honest, dependable, and kind, and she felt she ought to love him. She would have to wait and see how she felt when he arrived. Alice Springs would be new and different, and as the policeman's wife she might be able to go on patrols with him and use her nursing skills where they were most needed. Yet somehow, at the back of her mind, was a feeling of doubt, of unease.

She wrote back non-committally.

*　　*　　*

118

Enjoying the mild and sunny autumn, with windless days and crisp nights, she began to feel better. She wandered in the suburban garden, picking overripe muscatel grapes from the vine that grew over a trellis. They were golden-brown rather than green, and had a taste of sultanas. Many of the bunches were composed of withered skins, emptied by the birds and the bees. That was how she'd felt when she first came back— empty and dehydrated, both mentally and physically.

She heard the front gate click, a step on the gravel path, and turned to bolt for the back door. She had a morbid dread of visitors offering sympathy.

Then a well-remembered voice said, "Sandy!"

She whirled round. Jim Manning, the last person she would have expected to see here.

"You!" she gasped.

"Yes, it's me. I didn't write, or ring up, in case you refused to see me. When I got to the Springs and found you gone, I took the first train down. I had to see you."

She stood rigid with shock, unable to move. Unconsciously she spat out a chewed grape-skin. Then she was in his arms, pressed to that hard muscular frame. One quick, fierce kiss and she relaxed against him, all her defences down.

He led her to a wooden garden seat in the shelter of the front hedge. If her mother looked out the window . . . but she didn't care. She was filled with joy such as she had thought she would never feel again.

As a concession to the city, Jim wore no spurs, but he was unconventionally dressed in a leather jacket and light drill trousers. And he seemed to have bought a new wide-brimmed hat.

Mrs. MacFarlane was enchanted by the handsome bushman, with his tall figure and engaging smile; and when she discovered that his father owned a cattle-station, it made him in her eyes almost a member of the aristocracy.

"I suppose your property is a large one, Mr. Manning?" she asked, pouring tea. Jim's hat was safely stowed beneath his chair. His legs were too long to tuck underneath, but stretched out in front of him.

"A fair size. Just under five thousand square miles."

"Square *miles!* And how much stock do you carry?"

"Normally around thirty thousand head of cattle, but we've been getting rid of them because of the drought. Now they're too weak to be moved, what's left of them. You see, I wasn't really coming down with a mob, droving," he said to Alix, realizing that he'd given himself away. "Just taking a wagon-load of hides down to the train."

"Do you run sheep as well?"

"Not any more. We lost fifty thousand in the last big Dry. But at least the drought killed the rabbits."

"Cappamerri is in the gibber and sand-hill country, Mother," said Alix. "They need a lot of acres to feed one beast. You have no idea what desolation is, till you've seen the Channel Country. . . . And they say this is the worst drought since the 1902 one."

"Ah, but wait till you see it after rain! Talk about 'the desert blossoming as the rose'! In three days, at most four, the new growth is up, and there are flowers everywhere on the sand-hills—red and pink and yellow and purple . . . And all the gibbers covered in saltbush and daisies."

"But it hasn't rained for three years."

"Except for a few thunderstorms, no. But Cappamerri is on the Cooningbeera waterhole in the Diamantina—permanent water. So there are plenty of trees—coolabah and silver box, and birds by the thousands. The homestead is on a knoll above flood-level."

"And what happens when the Diamantina comes down?"

"When she comes down we're cut off from Birdsville, though we can usually get through to Betoota. The water runs away fast, but."

Alix knew that all this picturesque detail was for her benefit. She had noticed that strange way of ending a sentence with "but." It seemed to be a Queensland phenomenon.

"And how long are you in the city for, Mr. Manning?"

"Jim, please. Just as long as it takes to persuade Alix to marry me."

Alix glared at him, but she could see he had won her mother over; Mrs. MacFarlane was already seeing him as the son she'd never had.

"A most suitable match," she told her husband privately. (He had been away on business, and had not yet met his daughter's suitor.) "I always said," she added mendaciously, "that the outback was the place for Alexandra to find a husband. Nice girls are few and far between out there."

"H'm. I'll reserve my judgment until I've met the feller."

Alix at first refused Jim's offer of marriage. She hadn't forgiven him, and it was only after a great many recriminations, and expressions of regret on his part, that she began to soften. But he knew that cruel country which yet held such strange beauty, and he understood what she had been through on that dreadful journey.

She wondered what would have happened if, instead of finding her in the garden, he'd been admitted by her mother and they had met on formal terms in the drawing-room. She'd have had time to steel herself against him.

"You took a lot for granted," she said. "How did you know I wasn't married already?"

"Oh, I asked around. I got the impression from the locals that the copper had his eye on you. So I didn't waste any time."

"You wasted a lot of time in the last year."

"I know. I was crazy. You see, I'd always had this horror of a woman putting a leg-rope on me, and her brand on me for life. I like girls, but I didn't want to be tied down."

"That was obvious."

"After your card came back I thought it was no good anyway. Yet I couldn't get you out of my mind. I thought of writing again, but I'm not much of a correspondent."

"*That* was also obvious."

"And then I heard the news. Everyone was shocked. And I thought, What if she had died too? I knew then how much you meant to me. . . . Sandy? Please say yes."

"We-ell . . ."

"That's near enough. Dear darling girl, you won't be sorry, I promise."

He sealed her lips with a kiss, so she never did get round to saying "Yes."

Her father approved, her mother was delighted. She began planning a large wedding and reception.

Alix said firmly, "Mother, I intend getting married in a cream linen suit and an ordinary hat. I doubt if Jim owns a formal suit. We don't want a lot of fuss. Just a family reception, if you like."

The hardest thing for Alix was not leaving her family, but breaking the news to Jack McGuinnes. She began, "Dear Jack," and then could not go on. Dear Jack! And he *was* dear, a sterling friend, and she was terribly sorry to have to hurt him. Resolutely she dipped her pen in the ink and began to write.

CHAPTER EIGHTEEN

"The old man is a bit of a rough diamond," said Jim Manning as they travelled northward in the 'Ghan after a honeymoon at the beach, "but I think you'll like him. He doesn't have any small talk—the strong, silent type. How he and my mother came to marry is a mystery. She was a city girl. She's looking forward to having another woman to mag with."

"What about the cook?"

"The cook's a man. With the nickname of Leavin' Soon. When anyone criticizes his cooking, he says, 'That's all right, you can cook for yerself, I'll be leavin' soon.' He doesn't leave, but he's always threatening to."

"There are black women helpers too, I suppose?"

"Yes, but Mum gets very frustrated having only gins to talk to. You have to talk to them in pidgin, which is a bit limiting."

"Perhaps if they were taught proper English from childhood—"

"Yair, perhaps. But who's going to teach them? It's hard enough for a white kid to get an education out here."

"So the black children never learn to read?"

"They can read cattle brands, and the letters on the kerosene cases."

Alix saw herself bringing the light of learning to these wild children of nature. For of course they could be taught.

They were to travel north from Hergott Springs with Wal Crombie and the Birdsville mail. Alix was nervous about a possible meeting with Jack McGuinnes, who had not replied to her last letter. She was relieved to find that he was out on a month-long patrol when they arrived. She knew her happiness and fulfilment showed in her face. It would have been like twisting the knife in a wound. . . .

During the time between the train's arrival and Wal's departure, she visited the Sisters at the hostel, even though it was full of painful as well as happy memories for her. She called on Mrs. Allison at the store, leaving Jim drinking with some mates from the train. She knew that women never, never entered the bar, except to serve drinks to the men. The English cook had left, replaced by a thin, dark, sour-faced woman who looked as if she lived on pickles.

Alix walked out to the cemetery, wearing a wide hat against the sun's rays, in the later hours of the afternoon. Dry-eyed, she stood and looked at Mab's last resting place. The raw mound in the bare dusty cemetery was marked by a carved stone:

Sacred to the Memory of Mabel Alice Kingston, only daughter of James and the late Alice Kingston, of Adelaide. D. February 22, 1914, aged 26 years.

She smoothed the hard dry mound with her hands, and placed some white shells she had brought from the coast in a pattern on the grave. No plants would ever survive there.

She looked up at the pitiless blue of the sky and round at the desolate peneplain. Then she left, closing the gate, for the cemetery was fenced against marauding goats. She was closing the gate on her past life and turning towards the new life with Jim. She began to hurry, already longing to see him after so short a separation. They'd had to share their compartments with strangers, she with two women and he with three other men at night.

Nearing the big stone hotel with its encircling balcony, she hesitated. How well did she really know her husband? What if he stayed in the bar for hours, and came to her hopelessly drunk? She went cold at the thought.

In the comparatively cool parlour, she glanced through the bar window and saw him leaning on the counter with one elbow, the sleeves of his blue shirt rolled up, the neck open. He held a narrow-waisted glass of beer in the other hand, as he talked with two rugged-looking types. He glanced up and waved.

"I'll be with you in a jiff, darling," he called. "Just let me finish m'beer."

"I'll go on up to the room," she said, feeling irked that she could not join him in the bar. She could do with a long, cold beer. It was a man's country all right! She climbed the stairs, visited the Ladies', and walked along the high-ceilinged corridor. She went through their dim, shuttered room with its double iron bedstead, its shiny linoleum floor, and out onto the wide balcony above the street. A single horse was tied to a downstairs post, and a dog dozed in the shade of a galvanized iron water-tank.

Would he come? She might have to go down to dinner alone. The sun was still above the horizon, but this side of the hotel was shaded in the afternoon, and there was a slight easterly breeze. A light step on the boards behind her, and a pair of brown arms circled her waist. He kissed the back of her neck. She turned to him hungrily, and they stood locked in a long embrace.

"Ker-ist, it's been a long time," said Jim. "Two whole nights since we shared a bed! Let's not waste any more time." He took her hand and led her inside.

He had brought her a bottle of soda-pop and pushed the glass marble stopper in and poured her a drink.

"Actually, I'd have liked a beer," said Alix.

"What! I didn't know you drank beer."

"I don't usually, but that amber glassful in your hand looked inviting. Besides, your breath smells of it."

"Oh, sorry! We'll have a bottle of beer with our dinner."

He began to undo the buttons of her white cambric blouse.

Wal made a leisurely trip, camping out three times where there was water along the way. Some of the pale sand-hills had drifted across the road, and the horses made heavy going. The passengers had to get down and walk; Jim helped to dig sand from round the buggy's wheels. The weather was cooler than when Alix had left for the south, and travelling with two experienced bushmen she did not feel the terror of the wide, flat, empty landscape that she had thought might return.

At Etadunna she was welcomed like a long-lost friend, when they stopped to deliver mail and to have some cool lemon syrup and water. Mrs. Rushton, mother of the poor, burned Lucy, was thinner, but she seemed to have come to terms with her loss.

Kopperamanna, Ooroowillannie, Mungerannie, Mirra Mitta—the euphonious native names chimed in her ears like bells. Now that she was not afraid of it, the vast bleached landscape with its painted sand-hills and blue mirages began to exert its old fascination. There was something about this country, even in a drought, something in its emptiness and wide horizons, that she had missed in cosy Adelaide with its friendly grassed hills. Instead of feeling dwarfed and threatened, she felt her spirit expand.

For the whole of the next day they drove across the enormous expanse of Clifton Hills Station, leaving mail for the homestead, which was off the track, at the makeshift mailbox by the road.

In the afternoon, while crossing a plain paved with small stones that had been swirled into "crab-holes" by some long-ago flood, they were treated to a magnificent mirage. The plain ahead was transformed into a cobalt, almost purple lake, fringed with dark-blue trees that seemed to float above the "water," and backed by tall crimson cliffs which wavered and changed as they approached. Then the whole thing disappeared, as if a magic lantern had been switched off, leaving only burning sand.

At Goyder's Lagoon, dry now and filled with a tangle of lignum bush, they took the track to the east to avoid the uneven bed of the swamp; but this brought them to the edge of Sturt's Stony Desert. The horses picked their way along the ill-defined track among great purple-red gibbers that gleamed like polished iron in the glare of the sun. It was slow going.

They camped beside the track at the foot of one of the sand-hills which trended almost north and south, the direction they were going. They were now within striking distance of Birdsville: only thirty miles to go.

Next day they passed through a gate in a drunken-looking wire-netting fence. "The border between S.A. and Queensland," said Jim. "It's supposed to be rabbit-proof."

Then they were at Birdsville, fabled end of the notorious Birdsville Track. The horses dashed over the dry sandy bed of the Diamantina in fine style. Lower down, the overflow from the town bore filled part of the channel in a permanent waterhole.

The township seemed even smaller and barer than Hergott, to which the railway and the Overland Telegraph Line had lent a certain importance.

A long sand-hill blocked the view to the west. Beyond it lay the endless sand-hills of the Simpson Desert. In all other directions stretched the flat gibber-plain, great expanses of broken stone among which a few dried-up stalks of saltbush barely survived. The only street was deep in dust. But there was a school provided by the Queensland Government.

Their first stop was the post office, a single-room building with windows at the front and back that could open to catch any breeze that was blowing, or be shut against dust-storms. The small sheltered porch was full of townspeople waiting for the mail to be sorted—some receiving nothing, others no more than a packet of patent medicine ordered from faraway Adelaide by post. There were a few precious postcards and letters, and larger parcels of necessities transported over eight hundred miles. At the words "Wal's coming!" or "Mail-buggy's in!" the dead-looking town sprang to life. Jim was greeted on all sides, and congratulated on bringing back a bride.

Everyone then adjourned to the Royal Hotel, a single-storey building of the local stone, with a curved iron roof to its front veranda, which ran the length of the building. It was not nearly as imposing as the Hergott Springs Hotel. The bedrooms were small and dark, the dining room long and narrow like a railway carriage. But they were to stay there only one night while Jim collected the buggy he had left behind the pub, along with the two horses which had been expensively fed on hay transported by train and mail van from Quorn in the south.

Wandering about the town in the late afternoon, Alix came upon an inviting-looking green pool, the first cooling-pond into which the bore discharged. She thought she would like to paddle, and took off her white kid boots and stockings. She dipped a bare toe in—fortunately not her whole foot. The water was near boiling, though the air temperature was so high that it was not steaming, but looked deceptively clear and cool. Her toe turned bright red like a cooked prawn.

Then the blended cries of water-birds, the raucous calls of cockatoos coming in for their evening drink, drew her on to the long blue-green

125

waterhole. She stood entranced. Red clay banks and crimson floating duckweed contrasted with turquoise shallows and white-boled paperbarks. Green bullock-bush and coolabah grew on small islands, and the bank was fringed with reeds and canegrass.

An oasis, alive with sailing pelicans and wading white egrets, ibis and cranes and herons: the cacophony of birds' cries, even the croaking of frogs! It seemed miraculously beautiful after the long dry stage they had just passed through. Now she knew why this town on the edge of the desert was called Birdsville. The town of birds.

They left early in the morning, after a hilarious and uncomfortable night during which Jim fell out of the narrow stretcher into which they had crammed themselves, and Alix sank almost out of sight in the sagging middle of the mattress. He had to give up and transfer to the other stretcher. A Royal Hotel did not necessarily live up to its grand title.

Leaving Birdsville they recrossed the dry bed "to the Cappamerri side of the river," and set off across the gibber plains. Alix was excited and nervous, wondering what her new home would be like, wondering what her in-laws would think of her, and she of them. But with Jim at her side, she felt she could face anything.

They camped that night beside the track. They were following the trend of the Diamantina to the north of east, and the dead trees marking one of its channels were on their left. There was plenty of good dry firewood. Jim made a bright, dancing fire and hung the billy-can on a metal tripod, mixed a damper of flour, salt, and cold water with a pinch of self-raising powder. Alix decided that she would have to learn to like strong bush tea; it was certainly a refreshing drink, black and sweet, after a long dry day. With the damper they ate cold corned beef with lumps of yellow fat, which she found to her surprise she relished as a substitute for butter.

Then they made love under the stars. There was no moon, and the inland sky was a blaze of blue-white radiance. "What bliss!" murmured Alix, but in fact there were several small stones underneath the sleeping bag on which she lay, which pressed into her back. There was no doubt the man on top had the best of it out in the bush, she thought.

But she was too shy and too new a bride to complain.

The horse-bells sounded sweetly as the hobbled horses foraged for dried-out feed. One horse travelled in the shafts, the other was a "spare" which ran alongside, ready to take over pulling the buggy when the first horse tired.

It was eighty miles from Birdsville to their destination; first along the dirt "road" that led towards the little settlement of Betoota, and then turning north along the stock route to Cappamerri.

There was no change in the iron-hard gibber plain, in the brilliant orange sand-hills rising against the blue sky, when on the second day Jim

126

said, "We're inside the borders of Cappamerri now. See that skull propped up on the empty drum? That's the marker for our mail."

She looked around. Beside the track lay the bleached bones of dead bullocks; a little farther on, in an utterly bare and eaten-out patch around a bore, were whole carcasses reduced by heat and exposure to mere mummies of hide over bone, with dreadful eyeless sockets staring at nothing. She thought of Mab, and began to feel sick.

"Jim, could you stop for a minute? I think I'm going to be ill."

"I'm sorry, darling. Is it the heat?"

With the wind of their movement it had not been unbearably hot, but she murmured, "Yes . . . I think so."

He pulled on the reins, and the horse, which had come twenty miles that day, with a break at lunch-time, stopped thankfully for a rest. There was a red sand-hill beside the track, shimmering in the heat, but out of the burning sand grew a desert oak with dark trunk and thin pine-like leaves, almost black in colour against the brilliant orange-red of the sand, and throwing a dense shadow like a pool of coolness.

She staggered towards this and Jim followed with a handkerchief he had moistened in water from the water-bag under the cart—crusted now with red dust, but still cooling the water by evaporation. She sat with her arms between her knees, head hanging. He tenderly wiped the sweat from her brow. She had not been sick after all and was beginning to feel better.

"Would you like a drink?"

"No, thank you. I doubt if I could keep it down."

"You'd better rest for a bit in the shade. I was pushing on because the sooner we get to Cappamerri the sooner you'll be able to have a bath and a rest."

Her light-brown curls were sticking to her forehead as she pushed the wide panama hat with its filmy veil to the back of her head.

"You still manage to look beautiful with a sunburnt nose and a dusty face," said Jim.

She smiled wanly.

"Those poor cattle!" she said. "It's a cruel country, all right."

"Yes. It's damned hard to be religious in this country. When you see a bogged bullock, still alive, with its eyes picked out by crows—"

"Don't tell me about it!" she begged. And then asked, "A great many must have died in this drought?"

"Yes. They have to stay within reach of water, and gradually eat out all the fodder round the bore. Then they get too weak to walk to feed and back to the water, so they die of starvation."

"I never knew, when I enjoyed roast beef at home."

"Of course this is one of the worst droughts we've had. And my old man is a confirmed optimist, who tends to overstock in the good years, and then when drought strikes he's caught with cattle he can't feed and

127

can't unload. Yet recurring droughts are inevitable. The old-timers say they are getting worse, that the waterholes are drying up, silting over."

"Mr. Jackson said it was caused by the rabbits."

"Yair, partly. The government spent thousands putting up the rabbit-proof fence, but there were soon as many rabbits on one side as the other. But the dingoes come down from the other direction—I reckon they breed in the Simpson Desert in the good years, and spread out into the sheep country in a drought."

Alix pushed the damp hair back from her forehead and stood up. "I'm all right now, really."

"Really?"

"Yes. Let's go."

He gave her a quick kiss and helped her up into the buggy. His lips tasted salty from sweat.

CHAPTER NINETEEN

That morning they passed through the first gate for many miles. The wire fence stretched into the distance to left and right.

"The horse-paddock," said Jim. It looked as big as a coastal farm.

The track now came nearer to the eastern channel of the Diamantina, which here ran roughly north and south. They passed through a group of white-faced steers, which stood immobile, dully staring, too listless to bound away in fright. The river course was marked with a line of green trees.

"That's the Warrawarra waterhole," said Jim. "At least that's what we call it. The blacks told Grand-dad when he first came here that its proper name is Warrawarrapirralellyalullamalulullacoopalannie."

"I believe you," said Alix, laughing. "But I don't know how you get your tongue round it."

"Dad used to make it a game, see if we could say it without leaving out any syllables. My young sister always cried when she couldn't pronounce it."

"Well, here we are at 'Government House,'" said Jim a little later. There ahead stood a cluster of iron-roofed buildings about a central homestead. As they came nearer Alix stared silently. She had dreaded some barren, rocky terrain, but they approached through a series of sand-hills rising like waves. The wide, low stone homestead was situated between two delicately crimson sand-hills, beyond which lay a blue waterhole screened by coolabahs and paperbarks.

Alix sat entranced. "Oh, Jim!" she murmured. "It's beautiful!"

There was a stock-proof fence around the main building, and inside this all was green. Tall sunflowers stood against the walls. Flowering bushes of oleander made a splash of pink.

Dogs barked, and small children and their mothers came pouring out of the canegrass shelters of the blacks' camp to welcome the "Young Boss" and his bride. A plump lubra came out on the wide, grass-thatched veranda of the homestead and then dashed inside, arms and legs waving in frantic excitement. Someone opened the gate of the garden enclosure for them; someone else took charge of the horses. Jim picked up their bags and carried them in.

Mrs. Manning was waiting on the front veranda to greet them. Alix,

129

conscious of her own sunburnt face and grubby dress, saw a tall thin woman with a sallow face and clear light-blue eyes like Jim's. The hem of her pastel-coloured dress, with fine pleats on the bodice, reached to her instep. This was not the tough outback type Alix had expected to find on this isolated station.

"Mother, this is Alix," said Jim, dropping the bags and kissing her. "Where's Dad?"

"He and most of the men are out on the run, there are some cattle bogged in the Coppambara waterhole. . . . Welcome, my dear."

She took Alix's hand and deposited a cool kiss on her cheek. She might have welcomed a new daughter-in-law every day of the week. Her voice was neutral, neither warm nor hostile. In spite of the heat, Alix felt a little chilled.

"You must come and have a cup of tea," she added.

"I think Alix would like a bath and a change before anything else. We've had two dry camps on the way."

"Of course. Follow me." She said over her shoulder to Jim, "I've made up your room at the far end of the veranda."

She led the way along to the last pair of fly-wire doors opening on to an airy room with a double bed and marble-topped wash-stand. Alix noted the white honeycomb quilt and the white mosquito net above the bed.

"Mosquitoes! I didn't think you'd have to worry about them in a drought."

"Yes, they breed in the billabong. It's only in flood time when the larvae are washed away that we're really free of them in the hot months."

There was a kerosene lamp on the bedside table, and a couple of books lay beside it.

"I thought you might like something to read. Now come and I'll show you the bathroom."

Alix took off her hat and laid it on a cane-bottomed chair. She glanced in the mirror over the duchess-chest and saw that her hair looked terrible, wispy and falling down and far from clean.

"I really am longing for a bath," she said with a rueful smile, unpacking a clean if crumpled muslin dress.

"Of course. The bathroom's a bit primitive, but there is fresh water laid on. I must ask you to be sparing with it, though. We usually bathe in bore-water, when the river's not flowing."

"I'm used to bore-water, from living at Hergott."

"Yes, I forgot you were used to the bush. . . . I have *never* grown used to it," she murmured.

She handed Alix a brownish-white towel, no doubt washed in muddy river water, and a small coloured hand towel.

"There's fresh water in the wash-jug in your room, by the way. This is the bore-water tap, this the fresh, which you will want for your hair. I'll leave you to it."

Alix was relieved to see a commode in the corner.

There were a face-washer and a cake of yellow soap on the side of the tin tub. A round tin basin stood on a tripod. Alix filled this with fresh water, then ran a bath, and lay luxuriating in the warm, soapy-feeling bore-water. She dipped her head right under.

She washed her hair in the basin, rinsed it, and vigorously towelled the water out of it. She noticed guiltily that she had splashed a lot of water over the linoleum floor—lino probably brought all this way on the back of a camel—and she hastened to mop it up with one towel while she wrapped the other round her damp curls. It was wonderful to feel fresh and clean again. The bath when she emptied it had been half an inch deep in red silt.

Dressing in clean underwear and the white muslin frock, which was short enough to show her ankles, she hesitated whether to put on stockings or not. It was so hot . . . but then, first impressions! She realized that she was rather intimidated by her mother-in-law. She couldn't imagine addressing her as "Mother." Yet she could hardly call her "Mrs. Manning."

She found Jim in the bedroom, dressed in a clean poplin shirt and with his elastic-sided boots polished to a sherry-coloured shine. He opened his arms.

"You look lovely, dearest."

"What, with my hair in a towel?"

"Let me dry it for you."

She sat on the side of the bed while he rubbed her scalp and wet hair, then spread out the long strands and rolled them in a fold of towel, pausing to kiss the back of her neck. As the curls dried in the warm breeze coming off the veranda, they sprang up and turned a lighter golden-brown.

"So fine!" he said, feeling a silken strand between his fingers. She turned and buried her face against his throat. This was true intimacy, she felt, to have him dry her hair for her as if she were a child. He fetched a brush from her dressing-case, which had been sealed against dust, and began brushing her curls until they shone. Then he dropped the brush on the floor and pushed her back on the white counterpane, and stretched himself upon her.

She kept him nervously at arm's length. "When did you have a bath?"

"Just now, in the outside shower. It's a bit difficult—you have to fill the kerosene bucket and then pull it up with a rope, and then when you've soaped yourself you pull another rope and the water spills over you. Very refreshing."

"Mm . . . You smell fresh."

His hand was exploring under her muslin skirt, her lace-edged petticoat.

131

"No, Jim, no!" She rolled her eyes towards the fly-wire door to the veranda. "Your mother might come—and she's expecting me to appear to drink tea. Jim! You're crushing my dress!"

"It was crushed already," he said sulkily, rolling off her. "I say—you're not frightened of Ma, are you?"

"I am a bit."

"It's just her manner. She's very reserved; she'll be all right when she gets used to you. Since the governess left and the two girls got married, she's hardly had another woman to talk to."

"Perhaps she will see me as a rival!"

"Nonsense. Come on, put your hair up, then."

Before they left the room she glanced at the two books. *The Story of an African Farm*, by Olive Schreiner. H'm, interesting. She'd heard of it but had not read it. The other was a Meredith novel, *The Ordeal of Richard Feverel*. This she did know. The story of a youthful marriage ruined by a dominating father and a too-strict upbringing. . . .

They gathered in the central room, the living-room, which was open to the veranda at each end, for it ran the depth of the house. The veranda was closed in with louvers, which could be shut against a dust-storm but were now open to catch the breeze. The kitchen and its wood range were in a separate building connected to the house by a covered way.

There was home-made bread and butter, the slices cut rather thickly, and some kind of bought biscuit that tasted slightly rancid.

"I'm afraid I'm no cake-maker, Alix," said Olive Manning, pouring tea. "The cook will bake it when he's in a good mood, but I daren't ask him at present."

"I suppose he said, '*I'll be leavin' soon*,' when he heard there was to be an extra one for meals."

Olive Manning smiled faintly. "Something like that. We don't have many visitors here, and he gets spoilt. But he's a good cook, and they are hard to come by." She handed Alix a delicate china cup. "Now, tell me all about yourself. . . . Where did you train?"

After they'd taken tea, Mrs. Manning excused herself—"I always have a lie-down before dinner"—and Jim took Alix's hand and showed her round. The veranda ran on three sides of the house, shading the northern, eastern, and western walls. The back veranda, strewn with comfortable cane chairs and long cretonne-covered couches, looked out over the blue waterhole with its pink sand-hills, shady gums, and white-boled paperbarks.

"There are water-lilies there in spring," said Jim. "And there's a beaut swimming-hole with a sandy bottom."

"Any fish?"

"Yes, the blacks catch fish and bring them up to us in exchange for some extra 'bacca. But Leavin' Soon will have cooked a roast of beef in your honour."

Thinking of the starving cattle, Alix thought she would rather have eaten fish.

Jim showed her the office, where his father reluctantly worked at times. The desk was untidy and covered in a film of pink sand, an ashtray held a blackened pipe. "Things are so tight we've had to let the bookkeeper go," he said. "I help out with the bookwork. But Dad won't let anyone touch his desk to tidy it. He's warned old Lucy she's not to set foot in the office."

There came a loud squawking from overhead, and a raucous voice demanded, "What're you doing, y'bloody ole bastard?"

"George!" said Jim warningly. "There are ladies present."

Alix looked around and up, and saw through a hole in the corner of the ceiling a snowy-feathered head, softly flushed with pink, a hooked beak, and an alert dark eye looking down at them.

"Meet George," said Jim. "He follows me around and thinks he owns me. He gradually pecked a hole in the ceiling, after making his way in along the canegrass thatch of the veranda, so that he can keep an eye on me. I can't think where he learned such language," he added virtuously.

"Is it a cockatoo?"

"Yes, a Major Mitchell; he lives down at the river but comes up to visit."

Just then George, peering down at Alix, nearly fell through the hole. He gave a squawk of alarm and his crest rose—a gorgeous sunset-hued crown of feathers, yellow, orange, and white.

"He knows Mum won't let him inside. Come out and I'll introduce you properly."

They walked down the steps, Jim gave a whistle, and the immaculate bird came flying from the roof, his delicate rose-flushed underwings showing. He landed on Jim's shoulder and began nibbling his ear.

"He's beautiful!" said Alix. "Hallo, George."

"Hallo, George," said cocky.

"Put your hand out—as though it were a bough—hold your arm still. . . ." He lifted the cockatoo down onto his wrist, and transferred him to Alix's forearm. George walked up her arm to her shoulder, while Alix rolled her eyes at the proximity of his strong beak to her soft cheek.

"It's all right; George is a gentleman."

"You take him," said Alix. "He's gorgeous, but I'd rather look at him from a distance."

George travelled on Jim's shoulder while he showed Alix the cool-room, a hut built of dry canegrass and roly-poly packed thickly between chicken-wire frames, and kept damp by overhead water pumped by the windmill.

"It's just like a giant Coolgardie safe!"

"Yes, we use it to keep perishables in, and when it's really hot we sit in it. The meat-house over there is the same. That's the store, the men's quarters, the tool-shed and blacksmith's shop . . ."

"Shut yer gob! Shut yer gob!" said George rudely.

"Now, George, that's enough." Jim brought a couple of nuts out of his pocket and George ate them daintily, first shelling every bit of the brown skin from each almond. "Now off you go, back to the river." He launched the bird into the air, and after circling once it flew straight to the coolabahs in the waterhole.

"He's never been in a cage, but he's quite tame," said Jim.

All the outbuildings stood on the bare sand beyond the green confines of the garden enclosure. "Mother will show you the garden tomorrow. She loves her garden."

"I hope she will learn to love *me*. Or at least like me."

He looked at her in concern. "What makes you think she doesn't like you?"

"I don't know . . . she seems so cool, almost aloof. You said she was looking forward to another woman's company."

"So she was, but she has to get used to you, and the fact that her only son is old enough to get married. She's actually shy of you."

"That wasn't my impression. I would say rather . . . withdrawn."

"She's had a difficult life. I'll tell you the story someday."

As they turned the corner into the north veranda he put his finger to his lips. "That's Mum's room," he said, indicating the second door. "Dad's is along here."

"They don't share a room, then?"

"No. Haven't for many years."

Outside the door of their room he kissed her and said, "I must go and see that the horses have been watered and fed. You have a bit of a rest before dinner."

"All right. I *am* tired. I'll have a look at the books your mother left for me."

Before dinner that night she met "Big Jim" Manning, and he was as typical of the country as his wife was not. Tall and broad, with the slightly bandy gait of a man used to long hours in the saddle, he had a deeply sunburnt red-brown complexion and a stiff, brushlike moustache. His hair was still dark but beginning to recede from his tanned forehead. A life spent battling with the elements, with drought and flood and burning sand, had etched his face like an eroded inland plain. His eyes, which seemed to have retreated under his brows and between screwed-up lids away from the glare, gave him a hard, calculating expression; his mouth in repose was straight and firmly closed. This was a characteristic she had noticed among men in the bush, where a carelessly open mouth would soon be filled with the sticky little bush flies.

But when he smiled, laughter-lines joined the wrinkles about his eyes, his mouth relaxed to show teeth as strong and white as young Jim's, and he looked less formidable. Alix smiled back. He grasped her hand and shook it, or rather crushed it between his hard leathery fingers and thumb.

"Well, so this is young Jim's girl? You certainly know how to pick a good-looker, son. She's got pretty hair, eh, Mother?"

His slow drawl was answered by Olive Manning's precise tones. (I bet she came from Melbourne, Alix thought.)

"Yes, Jim. I had noticed."

"I should hope so! Well, girlie, I hope you'll settle in all right. What's she like on a horse, Jimmy?"

"She can ride."

"But not well," put in Alix. "And the only time I rode a camel, it bolted with me. Actually I'm a bit nervous with horses."

"Ah, you'll soon get over that."

The meal was roast beef, as Jim had predicted, and it was the best and tenderest beef Alix had ever tasted.

When she commented on it, Jim said, "Wait till you taste the steak at breakfast."

Olive explained that there were no eggs at present, as it had been too hot for the hens to lay.

The plates were cleared away by the plump lubra they had seen running with the news of their arrival at the station.

"Lucy, this the new young Missus," said Olive Manning.

"Hallo, Lucy," said Alix.

"Lucy has been with us for years, she could just about run the house on her own . . . eh, Lucy?" said Big Jim Manning.

Lucy's smile grew broader. "No-more, Boss." She took the plates and went back to the kitchen, to scrape the scraps of beef and potato into a big tin pannikin—not for the fowls, but for the camp blacks. Another container was filled with stewed tea, which had been brewing on the side of the stove since afternoon tea-time. When she had finished in the kitchen, she and the kitchen lubra, Jenny, would take the food down to the camp, together with two loaves of bread baked that morning in the big stone oven kept just for bread-making. There were also handouts of flour, corned beef, and tea and sugar from the store each Monday morning.

Mr. Manning explained that Lucy's husband, Billy, was one of his best stockmen. "A half-caste, and a fine horseman."

Alix had noticed that her father-in-law had not changed out of his dusty boots and moleskins, but had put on a clean shirt for dinner.

He and Jim talked about the bogged cattle, the state of feed, or rather lack of it, on the Birdsville Track, and the price of stock in Adelaide. Jim had brought his mother a silver brooch for a present, which she now wore on the pleated bodice of her gown.

"You've had no thunderstorms while I've been away?" asked young Jim.

"Yes, a couple reported over at the outstation, enough to bring up a bit of feed. But no real rain." He added for Alix's benefit, "The Meteorological blokes have installed a rain-gauge on the property, and I'm supposed to send in the readings every couple of weeks. I haven't had to look at the thing for three years."

As they were separating to go to their rooms about nine o'clock, Alix said to her mother-in-law, "Thank you for the books. I've read the Meredith, but I'm looking forward to Olive Schreiner."

"I expect you prefer modern novels."

"Not really—except for Arnold Bennett. I've brought some of his with me."

"I think I like Thomas Hardy best of all. I have *Tess*. But many of my books were left behind in Melbourne . . . transport problems."

"Well, you're welcome to borrow any of mine."

Chapter Twenty

Lying in bed reading *The Story of an African Farm*, Alix kept listening for Jim's step. He was sitting on the front veranda talking to his father; she could hear Big Jim's slow drawl and her husband's lighter, quicker tones. She was impatient. This was their first night in what was to be their home together, and she felt a sense of strangeness and excitement.

Of course, he hadn't seen his father for some time and they must have a lot to talk about. She liked listening to men's talk about practical things, and felt dismissed by Jim's "Run along to bed now; I'll be there soon." But nearly an hour had passed. She began to think that Jim was punishing her for her primness this afternoon.

She was getting sleepy when at last he came to bed. By now she was feeling perversely antagonistic to his arrival. She pretended to be engrossed in the book, though her heart was beating painfully. He dropped his clothes on the floor, after pulling off his elastic-sided boots, and slipped in beside her. He put his head down on her shoulder and threw one bare leg across hers, demurely shrouded in a new nightdress. The page blurred before her eyes. He took the book from her unresisting hands and blew out the lamp.

The light of a half moon filtered in through the veranda shutters beyond the doorway, making the mosquito net a shimmering white curtain about them. They were close, cocooned, enveloped; without words they conducted the mysterious dialogue of the flesh: question and reply, demand and answer.

Then they talked quietly for a while, until a wandering plover flew over the homestead with its grating, urgent cry.

She said drowsily, "How I used to hate those birds! Because they reminded me of you . . . and your desertion."

"Did I desert you? I must have been mad."

"I was going to get married to someone else, just to show you I didn't care."

"But you did care—thank God!"

"Jim, the other day you said 'Christ' as a swear-word. I'm not religious, but it shocked me somehow. You're not a Christian, are you?"

"I don't know what I am. I believe in *something*, a kind of pattern, 'a destiny that shapes our ends, Rough-hew them how we may.' But I

137

certainly can't believe in Gentle Jesus meek and mild, and virgin birth and all that. Of course the Church wanted it both ways, a Mother-figure and a pure maiden, so it invented the Immaculate Conception. No, it's a religion for children and old women of both sexes."

"Yet we got married in the Church."

"Just imagine your mother's reaction if we hadn't! But I like the marriage service, all those sonorous phrases and the symbol of the ring sliding over the finger—very suggestive."

"Jim!" But she snuggled into his shoulder, feeling that he had expressed something she had been groping towards ever since Mab's death. She remembered Mab's crack about Immaculate Conception at the Hostel Committee meeting.

Alix gave a reminiscent chuckle. "Mab said once that she would be surprised if you read anything but the Stock and Station journal."

"Well, I read that too. She should have heard me reciting Banjo Patterson or Victor Daley. But my favourite is Will Ogilvie. You know his 'Fair Girls and Grey Horses'? No? He was a Scot, and he worked as a horse-breaker and a station hand, and went droving too: *Store-cattle from Nelanjie! The mob goes feeding past, with half-a-mile of sand-hill 'twixt the leader and the last.*"

He went on reciting while she drifted into sleep, lulled by his steady voice.

She woke as sunlight streamed in through the shutters, and turned into his arms.

Jim was out on the run, visiting distant bores and outstations, all the next week, sometimes camping out with the men, sometimes returning, dusty and sweaty, just in time for the evening meal.

Then a heavy thunderstorm came up from the north-west. The dark-bellied clouds, riven by fierce lightning, with purple skirts of rain drifting from them, could be seen far out on the run.

A few days later the men prepared to move cattle from the eaten-out bore to the area where there had been rain.

Big Jim had pin-pointed the direction and estimated the distance at about twenty to thirty miles.

"I know it doesn't seem possible," said Jim, "but the feed will be already up, and by the time we get the bullocks to it there will be enough to keep them going, enough to save their lives. There will be water lying in the clay-pans for them to drink. And if the rain has fallen over sand-hill country, the wild flowers will be blooming in a day or two; the annual saltbush will be starting to cover the gibber plains; the buckbush will recover and the bullock-bush will be green."

"I'd love to see it!" said Alix. "Oh, Jim! Couldn't I come with you? It's not such a very long ride, is it?"

"No-o. If you're sure you can stick on a horse. But you realize we might have to stay overnight out there, and a woman in a cattle-camp will be regarded as a damn nuisance."

"I don't care! It mightn't rain again for months, or a year."

"Don't say that," said Jim. "It's unlucky."

At dinner on the night of the thunderstorm, Big Jim Manning told Alix, "You know there are kids in the dry country who've never seen rain. When Jim was a little tacker, about three or four, it started to rain while he was playing outside. He came rushing in, crying, 'Water fallin' out the sky!' Remember, Mother?"

Olive Manning's response to this anecdote was to draw her rather long upper-lip down farther, and shake her head with a quick frown.

"Don't you remember? It was in 1895, when . . . Oh."

"When Jim was nearly nine years old. It wasn't *Jim* who said that. It was—"

Her face froze, and she put down her spoon and left the room.

There was an uncomfortable silence while the others spooned up their tinned fruit and custard, then Big Jim gave a strained laugh and said, "Of course, you would have seen rain before that, young Jim." He turned to Alix. "That's the sweetest music on earth, the raindrops on the tin! It means money in your pocket, but it's more than that: it's a blessing, and an assurance that this spot is not a God-forsaken corner of the continent after all."

"Here's something you won't believe," said young Jim. "I've actually seen it raining fish! They were only little fish, but they were kicking, still alive. Some blokes reckon that pelicans drop them when flying between waterholes, and they get caught in the updraught of thunderclouds. But it seems more likely that they're sucked up by big willy-willies and then come down again in the rain."

"I've seen whirlwinds picking up boxes and tins and whirling them into the air, but . . . you wouldn't be pulling my leg, by any chance?"

"No, Scout's honour! It's true, isn't it, Dad?"

"Yes, I've seen 'em. One feller is supposed to have eaten them raw when he was perishing from hunger out on the plains. Saved his life."

"The miracle of the loaves and fishes!" said Alix.

"Yair. No bread came down, but."

Olive Manning came back as Lucy brought in the pot of tea, and she poured it with a steady hand. No comment was made on her sudden departure, but Alix wondered what had upset her.

"Alix wants to ride out with us on the run, when we shift the cattle to the new feed," said young Jim.

Olive raised her eyebrows but said nothing. Big Jim stared, laughed, rubbed his hand across his mouth, and drawled, "We-ell, I don't see why not, if she can ride."

"I'll find her something nice and quiet."

"Don't you ever go out riding?" asked Alix, looking at her mother-in-law. She was embarrassed still about what to call her; the word "Mother" stuck in her throat.

Olive's face became even longer; her lips turned down. "I never go riding these days," she said distantly.

"She has a good seat in the saddle, all the same," said her husband.

Alix had brought a tailored divided skirt with her; she certainly didn't intend to ride side-saddle in the bush. She brought it out in the bedroom and brushed it lovingly, and chose a plain cotton shirtwaist with long sleeves to go with it.

"A dress rehearsal, eh?" said Jim, giving her a kiss.

"Why does your mother never go out on the run? If she's a good horsewoman?"

Jim's face clouded. "Oh, it's a long story. I said I'd tell you one day. . . ." He pulled her down on the bed beside him, and caressed her arm as he spoke. "It was years ago—my young brother was only four at the time. Dad was going to one of the outstations and Mum went with him, leaving us with the governess, a city type who didn't like station life at all. We were working in the schoolroom, but young Dan wriggled and sighed until Miss Wadsworth told him to run along and play, since he was only distracting his brother. Dan wandered off outside. He didn't come in for lunch, and the black gins were sent to look for him. Most of them had gone on the muster, gins as well as stockmen, and there were only a couple of old women at the camp. After a while they came up to the house, wailing and crying. They'd found Dan in the home waterhole, and floating beside him was the little toy boat Dad had made him out of scraps of wood. He could swim a little, but the boat must have sailed away from him with a gust of wind, and he'd have gone after it into deep water farther than he meant to, and found he couldn't get back."

"*Oh*—!" said Alix, appalled.

"Yes, Mother came home to find her favourite, the younger one of us boys, was dead. She shut herself in her room for days. Apparently she felt terribly guilty, felt it was her fault for going off enjoying herself, while. . . Anyway, she never went riding again."

"And I suppose she doesn't even like swimming in the waterhole, since."

"No, she never goes swimming." He was silent for a while. "She became quite strange for a time, used to hear Dan's voice calling her. Then one day when the men were away she filled her pockets with heavy bits of iron from the blacksmith's shop, and walked into the waterhole. It was old Lucy who saved her."

"The poor thing! What a sad, sad story."

"She apparently blamed herself, rather than the governess for not

140

keeping an eye on him. Every year, on the anniversary of his death, she stays in bed and doesn't leave her room."

"Does she ever speak of it?"

"Never. His name is never mentioned. Which is why she was so upset tonight when Dad confused him with me over the rain incident. She doesn't even visit his grave any more."

"I haven't seen a grave."

"It's quite small, naturally. It's over behind the second sand-hill. Dad thought it was morbid of her to want him buried in sight of her window. I don't think she's ever forgiven him."

"But they had more children?"

"Only one, my younger sister. My older sister was away when Dan died, staying with friends on another property. Mum became withdrawn, almost as if she wasn't here; I think that's why my sisters were glad to get away. Meredith married young, she was only seventeen."

"So now you're the only one left."

"Yair. Except that in her opinion the wrong one survived."

"Poor Jim! A tragedy like that—it must have had an awful impact on you at that age."

"Mm. When you're young you know about death, but you don't believe it happens to children, to people younger than yourself. It made me grow up very fast. I played up in lessons; the governess couldn't cope and Mum tried in a half-hearted way to teach me, till they sent me away to boarding-school."

"And you hated it?"

"Only at first. I made friends, found I actually enjoyed some subjects, like geology and chemistry, and did quite well without being brilliant. One thing Mum did for me—she got me to read the Australian balladists, to learn them off by heart. At school we only got Wordsworth and Shakespeare."

"Me too. But Mother had a few Australian books, a novel by Henry Kingsley, and Victor Daley and Adam Lindsay Gordon in fancy editions. I don't know that she ever read them."

"My mum's a great reader."

For the next week the men were away mustering, collecting the beasts to be driven to the new feed. They were not hard to find, as there was no water except in one or two waterholes and the bore-drain, and no fodder except for the few bushes left on the sand-hills, and the green mulga which the men cut for them every second day. They would eat this seemingly dry-leaved plant, and the myall, another desert-hardy acacia, when there was nothing else.

The cattle were kept in a holding-paddock ready to leave at first light in the morning, before the heat of the day.

There was only the faintest light in the sky beyond the veranda when Jim rolled out of bed, calling on Alix to "rise and shine." She leaped up, awake at once, her heart beating high with excitement. This would be her very first cattle-camp. Swags and provisions for the trip had all been packed the night before.

After a scratch breakfast of tea and toast they went out into the cool, clear morning where the last stars were still fading from the night sky. Along the eastern rim the light was steely bright, and down in the river coolabahs the birds were already stirring. The lowing of cattle, uneasy at the disturbance to their routine, came from the mob which was already stringing round over the first sand-hill, ahead of several stockmen riding on their tail and cracking long stockwhips.

Alix was mounted on a roan mare which Jim said was the quietest of the horses, though Alix thought the animal looked at her askance as it rolled the whites of its eyes towards her. But feeling smart in her divided skirt of khaki drill, long-sleeved shirt, and blue scarf, she mounted bravely and followed behind Jim on his brown horse. Her wide-brimmed hat hung by an elastic round her neck, ready for when the sun rose. From habit more than because she expected to need it, she had packed her first-aid kit in her saddle-bag.

Jim turned in his saddle. "All right, little 'un?" he asked.

"Don't call me that," she said painfully, acutely reminded of Mab and her pet-name when they first went nursing.

"Well, Sandy then. Do you want me to put you on a lead until you get used to her? Not that Cleo should give you any trouble."

"Certainly not!" said Alix, sounding braver than she felt. She cantered round in a circle just to show him. Cleo behaved perfectly.

"If something frightens the cattle, and there's a rush, don't attempt to join in the chase. Get behind the nearest tree and stay there."

"If I can find a tree." She looked about at the sparse, sticklike mulga and needlebush growing on the flats between the sand-hills. The creak of saddle-leather, the sweetish smell of horse-sweat, the crisp morning air, and the lowing cattle, strung out in a red-brown stream that flowed ahead of them, combined to fill her with exhilaration. She touched her heels to Cleo's flanks and trotted up beside Jim.

"This is fun!" she said, her cheeks flushed, her blue eyes alight. "Thank you for letting me come."

"H'm, wait till tonight when you're saddle-sore and weary. You mightn't thank me then."

They stopped to boil the billy at mid-morning, the two coloured stockmen lighting their own little fire and sitting apart. The dry gidgee wood burnt brightly, with scarcely any smoke and a hot flame—yet another of the ubiquitous acacias, which flourished in apparently dry clay-pans.

Big Jim Manning leaned over and picked up a glowing coal in his gnarled fingers to light his pipe. He was calm and relaxed as always, but today he radiated contentment. Alix realized that he was really happy only when out on the run. He was not one to manage his station from his office.

"Y'know," he said, puffing reflectively on his pipe, "the 1902 drought was the worst we'd ever seen, nearly half the stocks of cattle in the west were wiped out; but it broke eventually. It started earlier than that, about 1900, but that was the worst year; and in 1903 the rains came, and the country was in great heart again. We only have to hang on—with the help of a few well-spaced thunderstorms—till the good seasons come again."

Alix knew that the conversation, though centring on the ever-popular themes of weather and rainfall, was meant to exclude her by referring to the past. She felt that her father-in-law disapproved of girls in cattle-camps, and had not accepted her. She kept very quiet, gnawing at a bit of brownie that the cook, Leavin' Soon, had sent out with them.

Young Jim gave a snort, a noise half disagreement and half derision. He lifted the quart-pot with a piece of wire and after tapping the sides to make the leaves settle, poured the clear black tea into their enamel mugs. It was nearly boiling, and Alix put hers in the shade to cool.

"What you don't seem to realize, Dad," he said, "is that drought is the *normal* condition out here. It's the good seasons that are the exception. There was a crippling drought in 1880, and again in '86. About every five or six years. And you still go on building up stock when it rains, and losing half your beasts in the next drought."

"Aw, I dunno," drawled the head stockman, Milton Gibbs. He was a short, solid half-caste with the bow-legs of one who has lived in the saddle from an early age. He reminded Alix of the boss drover who had come down to Hergott Springs when Mab was alive. "I reckon this drought will break next year, or in 1916 at the latest. We haven't had a really good year since 1911, stands to reason it can't last much longer."

Jim looked unconvinced.

When they went on into a section of barren gibber country, bare purple and red stones reflecting the sun with an unbearable glare from their polished surfaces, Alix wondered how such a stony desert could ever come to life.

They stopped for lunch where a sand-hill, long and low, spread over the plain, as isolated as if it had been dropped there by some mighty willy-willy. There were a few desert oaks, dense and dark, to give shade, and some stunted saltbush which the cattle browsed on, though it looked too dry and withered to be nourishing.

About three in the afternoon, the cattle which had been crawling reluctantly along suddenly livened up, lifted their heads and began to hurry, bellowing as they went.

"They've smelt water!" said Jim. "I hope to God there's plenty of feed as well, or we'll have to drove them back again."

Less than an hour later they topped an almost imperceptible rise, and there in the hollow beyond lay the miracle of greenness—blue-green annual saltbush, bullock-bush, grass in clumps beginning to cover the ground, and flowers everywhere—yellow billy-buttons, white and blue daisies, purple parakelya, scarlet desert pea covering the sand-hills in a waving mass. And the gibber plain was clothed with perennial saltbush, pale blue-grey and already a foot high.

Water lay in sheets in the clay-pans that covered the hollows between. They let the cattle spread out contentedly, and went on to make camp at the foot of a large sand-hill. No longer following behind the slow-moving cattle, they could give the horses their heads: they galloped down to some fresh water lying in a "crab-hole" and drank greedily, Cleo nearly pulling the reins out of Alix's hands as she stretched her neck to the water.

"Well, how do you feel?" asked Jim, as she dismounted stiffly.

"Not too bad—a bit chafed," she said, aware that the inside of her thighs hurt when she moved.

"That's nothing, wait till you wake up tomorrow."

"I'll be all right."

The sun was setting in an orange glow as they unsaddled and hobbled the horses. The pack-horses were already unloaded and a fire was being lit on which to cook damper. With tea and salt beef, this was the standard fare in a cattle-camp.

CHAPTER TWENTY-ONE

Alix had slept in her clothes and only had to pull on her boots to be dressed; but the dawn wind was chilly and she snuggled a moment longer in her blankets, listening to the sounds of morning. One of the Aborigines had gone out after the hobbled horses, and the man who had ridden round the mob at night, making sure that they were settled down, came in on his night-horse and dismounted by the fire, rubbing his chilled limbs.

Alix saw a dusty boot beside her face, and heard a soft voice, "Young Missus—you 'wake?"

She sat up to find a black man standing beside her, holding a quart-pot by its wire handle, and smiling.

"Yes, Micky. What is it?"

"Old Boss bin tellem me bring you 'ot water. Maybe you wantem wash."

Alix was touched. Maybe it was a hint to her to get up and not lie in her sleeping bag, but it was a kindly gesture all the same.

Sitting up had been painful, but now as she crawled out of her bag and tried to stand, every muscle in her back and legs cried out in protest. Though they had ridden slowly, she had been eight hours in the saddle yesterday, using unaccustomed muscles, and now she could feel every one. Groaning, she washed her face and hands and dried them on a handkerchief. It was all she could do to get her arms up to her hair to put in some pins and tidy it a little. Then she tottered away to look for a tree—there were no trees! Not even the flimsiest bush to squat behind.

She compromised by sinking down among a profusion of wild flowers that reached to her waist when she was sitting. Her head and upper body were of course perfectly visible, and everyone must know what she was doing—but the bushmen looked elaborately in the opposite direction.

She came back, rinsed her hands again and tossed out the water. Walking to the sand-hill had loosened her muscles a little, but she still walked stiffly and in pain.

After breakfast Jim informed her that they were going over to the nearest bore to check that it was flowing and to clear the bore-drain, as the cattle would be dependent on it when the water in the clay-pans dried up.

"Not all of us," he said. "Two men will stay to keep an eye on the cattle, and the blackfellows want to do a bit of hunting for their larder. Nothing big—kangaroo mice, lizards, and so on—they like to get out and have some bush tucker. You'll want to stay and have a rest, eh?"

After her muscles had loosened up a bit, Alix decided to climb to the top of the sand-hill, only about a hundred and fifty feet high, which rose from the stony, greyish clay-pan in a smooth orange-red wave. Every hollow was like a flower-garden: pale purple marshmallows, white and golden everlastings, little blue sweet peas, and the brilliant cerise-purple of parakelya.

She ploughed upward through the soft, shifting sand, marvelling how it held such nourishment and such a wealth of seeds in such unpromising-looking soil.

"I wish we had more sand-hill country," Jim had told her. "There's always some feed in the sand-hills, even when the gibbers are bare. Though it looks desolate, the flat stony country doesn't erode like the blacksoil plains in a flood; the stones just get washed into crab-hole depressions but are not carried away. Cappamerri can carry a lot more stock than we have at present. The trouble is, the Old Man gambles on good seasons, with the beasts as the living stakes. Then overstocking eats out the perennials, mulga and myall are cut down for feed, sand starts to drift—he's like a man living on his capital, gradually using up all his assets. He blames the rabbit plagues of early this century, but I say it's bad management."

"Have you told him so?"

"Often. But he won't listen to me. He's convinced the land will always recover. But it's the long-lived woody plants, the myall and old-man saltbush and small acacias, which aren't regenerating. Their seed takes a long time to germinate, and stock eat the seedlings before they've had a chance to set more seed. It's a slow process of degeneration, and I'm afraid it's irreversible."

Alix thought about this now as she reached the steep, bare crest of the dune, which stretched away for half a mile, running roughly north and south. She looked out over miles of country, clumps of gidgee in the hollows, dark desert oaks in the sand, saltbush covering the gibbers with a soft grey mantle. There was not much spinifex in this region, though they had passed through a patch of the pincushion-like clumps on the way. "Like velvet porcupines," she'd said, pointing at the rounded shapes with their spiny fronds, looking as if they were ready to burrow into the earth and disappear.

146

The mob of cattle was feeding peacefully, watched by one white stockman mounted and riding a wide circle; cattle were inclined to wander when water and feed were plentiful. If there was new growth at the bore, they would be driven on there tomorrow, so that when the surface water dried out they would make their way back to the sand-hill country to feed and return to water at the bore.

As she came plunging down the slope, forgetting her stiffness in the exhilaration of the climb, she noticed that the black stockmen were busy about their small fire. The gidgee burned palely in the clear sunlight. Though the sun was getting hot, the air was so clear and dry under the pure blue canopy of sky that the heat was not enervating. There was enough breeze to keep away the bush flies that could make life a misery.

As she came past she saw that the stockmen were roasting a big Perentie lizard, skin and all.

"Him good-feller tucker?" she asked.

"You-eye. Number-one tucker, this one."

One of the men had a neckcloth bound roughly round his left hand.

"You bin hurt-im?"

The man grinned shyly, seeming to retreat under his large, floppy hat, trying to make himself invisible.

"Go on, 'Arry," said the other, pushing him. "Show Missus."

Unwillingly he pulled off the blood-stained cloth and showed a nasty jagged wound across the back of his hand.

"Perentie bin catch-im," said Micky, grinning.

With difficulty she persuaded the injured man to follow her to the "whitefeller camp," where she unpacked her first-aid box: scissors and sterile bandages, iodine and tweezers, cotton wool and a small enamel bowl. She should use boiled water, but there was still a little in the water-tins brought from the station, so she used some of that, and the iodine would disinfect the wound. She wondered if lizard bites were poisonous.

Preparing to use the stinging iodine dressing once the wound was clean, she said to distract him: "Your name Harry?"

"Yair, Jarry."

"Is it Harry or Jarry?"

"Yair, thass right."

She left it at that. He did not even flinch at the iodine.

He thanked her sheepishly, not meeting her eyes, and went back to his companion, holding the white-bandaged hand up in front of him like a trophy.

Alix found herself singing as she washed her hands and packed away her kit. Why was she feeling so light-hearted? She realized that it was because she had enjoyed using her nursing skills, even on such a minor injury. She missed her work.

That night they had a singsong round the camp fire, the men singing some old drovers' songs. One of them, known only as Bob the Bastard, recited a ballad by "Breaker" Morant:

". . . Then over sand and spinifex and on, o'er ridge and plain!
The nags are fresh—besides, they know they're westward-bound
   again . . .
The brand upon old Darkie's thigh is that upon the hide
Of bullocks we must muster on the Diamantina side . . ."

Alix sat on her swag and stared about her. The night was cool, dark, and still. There were no flies, no mosquitoes, and the young moon was just setting, with a bright planet beside its yellow sickle. The fire danced, its flickering red and yellow lighting the faces of the men grouped around it. From the darkness beyond came the *tinkle! tonkle! tong!* of the horse-bells. This was the life!

During a moment of silence, a dingo howled somewhere near at hand, to be answered by another and another. Alix felt the hair stir on her nape. The thin wailing seemed to rise clear to the glittering stars: a howl of longing, of untamed desire, the authentic voice of the wild.

Jim began to quote softly,

"Out in the wastes of the Never Never,
That's where the dead men lie!
There where the heat-waves dance forever—
That's where the dead men lie!

Out where the grinning skulls bleach whitely
Under the saltbush sparkling brightly;
Out where the wild dogs chorus nightly—
That's where the dead men lie!"

"Who wrote that?" asked Alix.

"Barcroft Boake. He went droving in western Queensland last century."

"Well, he may have been a good poet, but he wouldn't get an A for observation. I mean, saltbush! It's a sort of dull, powdery grey—"

"Ah, but you haven't seen it on a night of frost in mid-winter, when the moon is shining. The frost-silvered leaves seem to be coated in diamonds. It's quite beautiful."

"Oh!" Alix was mortified. She had shown herself up as a new-chum.

Jim reached over and squeezed her hand reassuringly.

148

"Poor bloke killed himself, didn't he?" said the head stockman.

"Yes. He hung himself with his stockwhip."

"How old was he?"

"Only twenty-six."

In the darkness beyond the firelight's ring, the dingoes howled again. More than one man gave a shiver. Seated at a distance at their own small fire, the blackfellows now began a low chant, ending with a sharp "Yakkai!"

"It's a song about their good day's hunting," said Milton, the head stockman. He had a foot in both camps; but he had been "brought up white" by a station-owner's wife who had no children and took him in as a little fellow when his mother died.

The dingoes howled again at midnight, and all night long the stone-curlew sent up his weird cry: "Weerloo! Weerloo!"

"We might see some kangaroos and emus today," said Jim as he helped Alix saddle up in the morning. "They're often around a bore where a bit of green tucker grows along the bore-drain. We didn't see any yesterday, but we were there in broad daylight. They usually feed in the morning and evening, and lie up during the heat of the day."

"I thought we would have seen a lot more about."

"The drought has driven them into the more closely settled areas. They'll come back when we get a good season."

The whole party would be tailing the cattle to the bore, and then they would return by a direct route to the station. Cleo was rather skittish after a whole day on the luxuriant feed, but she soon settled down and Alix felt her confidence increasing, her muscles less stiff. She was looking forward to the ride home, which would be much less slow than the journey out with the mob. She had enjoyed camping out, but she had slept in her clothes for two nights and began to long for a bath. If the men weren't there she'd take a dip in the bore-drain where the water cools down enough for stock to drink it.

They had started at dawn, and it was still early when they arrived at the bore. Jim led her out wide of the mob of cattle and they cantered on ahead of the party till he moved up and put a hand on her rein.

"Quiet!" he murmured. "Look—down there drinking—a mob of kangaroos."

Alix held her breath as she saw a group of magnificent big red kangaroos at the water's edge. As soon as she moved to get nearer they were off, their powerful hind legs thumping the earth, their tails balancing like a rudder. One big fellow stopped, sat up and looked back at the horses, his head held proudly as though he questioned their intrusion on his domain. Then he too was off in effortless bounds.

"That's a fatal habit they have—they take off fast, and then have to stop and look back inquiringly—and that's when they get shot."

149

"Fancy shooting such beautiful—"

"Don't worry, Dad would have had a shot at them if he'd been here. He reckons they eat too much feed. But I like to see them around the place."

As soon as the cattle had settled down on the new feed around the bore, the whole party set off for the head station. Before they left Alix had put a clean dressing on the Aboriginal stockman's hand.

As they rode fetlock-deep in the saltbush and waving grasses, a solitary plain turkey showed its head above the growth. Big Jim quickly loaded his rifle and from the saddle shot the bird neatly through the head. One of the men picked it up, and the Boss tied it by its feet to the pommel, its bloodied head hanging limply down. It was a large plump bird, nothing like a domestic turkey, with soft grey feathers on the breast and black-and-white patterned wings. Alix was sorry to see it shot, but Jim said it would make a tasty addition to the larder.

They came to the foot of a long red sand-ridge. The horse-riders fanned out to take it at different angles. Big Jim was ahead and to the right. As they came over the ridge they saw a small mob of brumbies, led by a black stallion, moving along the lower slope.

The black horse smelt the strangers, and stood arrested, mane and tail flowing, in a statuesque pose against the sculptured sand. Then he whinnied a warning to his mares. There were five with heavy dark-brown coats, and one handsome chestnut mare with a yearling colt at foot. The stallion turned to lead them away at a gallop, down to the smooth clay-pan below, where they could move at speed. Big Jim Manning already had pulled up, with his rifle at his shoulder. He fired once, and the horse faltered in his stride; tried to gallop on, then his legs crumpled under him and he lay still. The mares ran on without him.

Alix, who had been watching the magnificent free movement of the wild horses over the red sand, sat rigid, staring in horror and unbelief. She turned to Jim, who had pulled up near her, and saw that his jaw was set so hard that lumps of muscle had come up in his cheeks.

"How could he?" she muttered.

"It was a brumby," he said. "There are thousands of them in this country in a good season. The Old Man shoots them because they eat out the feed."

"It was a beautiful animal!"

"Yes."

They rode on in silence, Alix averting her face from the stricken body. A pool of blood was spreading from the stallion's open mouth to stain the sand a darker red. She thought of the widowed mares, without a mate or a leader now. For the time she hated her father-in-law.

*   *   *

Tired after the long ride home, and still feeling sick from the death of the brumby, Alix went straight to bed on their return. She was asleep when Jim came to ask if she wanted some tea and toast.

CHAPTER TWENTY-TWO

After living on salt beef that became tougher as it aged, Alix found the roast turkey delicious. Then it was time to kill a beast for the larder. A bullock was singled out and shot, the carcass hauled up on the gallows, bled, and gutted. Some of the meat would be kept fresh—rump for steaks, sirloin for roasts—but even in the meat-house it would not keep for long. The rest would be salted, some in casks, some thrown on top of the bough shed to season and cure in the sun.

There was great excitement in the camp at the kill. Women and children came flocking up, the women yelling to their men to get the best parts, liver and lights and sweetbread. Nothing was wasted, not even the intestines, for the offal was regarded as a great delicacy. Everything would be eaten, right down to the hoofs, only the bones being left for the dogs.

Alix kept inside during the actual killing. Like many city-bred people who like beef, she preferred not to think about the fact that her meal meant the death of a fellow-creature. But hearing the excited cries of the women, she put on a hat and went out to look. There in the dusty yard the people were helping themselves to the parts unwanted by the whites. Jenny, who looked so neat usually in her clean gina-gina as she waited at table, her damp hair combed and sleek, was sitting in the dirt passing a long rope of intestines through her fingers, expelling its contents. She was covered in blood and filth.

Alix went back to the veranda and the unfinished letter to her mother. She imagined Mrs. MacFarlane's shudders of horror if she described to her the scene she had just witnessed.

There was no fresh beef for dinner that night, as the meat had to be hung before it was ready to be cut up. Lucy brought the main course, a sort of shepherd's pie which Leavin' Soon had cooked up from minced salt beef and mashed potatoes. He had pointed out that this was almost the last of the potatoes until the next lot of stores came in.

Jenny followed with an egg custard—for the hens were laying again, and a milker had been brought in and was giving a little milk twice a day. Kitty, an old gin from the camp, had the job for a while, as she was skilled in getting the cow to let down her milk. But one morning the Boss, going the rounds early in the morning, found Kitty with her feet in the bucket, warming them in fresh milk.

Olive Manning must have noticed the scene about the bullock carcass, for she looked sharply at Jenny, whose hair was tousled, though she had put on a clean dress.

"Jenny—why you no washem-hair?"

A shrug from Jenny.

"And you not have a bath."

"Did have bath, morning-time."

"You go now, bathe properly and washem-hair."

Jenny drew up her lithe figure and scowled under her heavy brows. She went out sulkily, dragging her bare feet.

"I'm always giving that girl soap," complained Olive. "What she does with it beats me. Trades it with the other gins, probably."

Within little more than five minutes Jenny was back, bearing the teapot. She was dripping water—her hair, her dress were soaked, her feet left damp footprints on the stone-flagged floor. "Now me bin clean-feller prop'ly," she said cheekily.

Olive sent her away to dry herself, and Lucy could be heard in the kitchen across the covered way, loudly berating her.

That night the station blacks, happy and full-bellied, staged a "little-bit corroboree." There were no real corroborees any more, with mime and stamping and painted bodies decked with cockatoo feathers and bunches of leaves, the click of music-sticks and clapping of the women in time. They still went walkabout occasionally, liked to hunt for bush tucker for a change; but the easy life of station handouts, the "flash" clothes of the black stockmen with their felt hats and coloured neckerchiefs, trousers and "chirts," had led them to give up the old ways. The youngsters were not interested, and the old men had lost their authority.

Sitting on the veranda, the whites heard singing coming from round the fire on which the people had cooked their feast.

A new song—really an old song that had made its way from Wellshot Station to the east, carried by shearers and drovers from station to station —was being sung in English:

White man wash in old tin tub,
    Black man wash much cleaner,
Black man wash in waterhole
    And in t' Diamantina . . .

Oliver drew down her upper lip, but the others laughed. There was no doubt Jenny had had the last word.

After her successful treatment of Jarry, or Harry, whose injured hand had healed nicely, Alix thought that she might find some more patients among the Aboriginal residents of the camp. Hesitantly, she walked down to the collection of bark wurleys and cane-grass shelters grouped near the water. Though the morning was hot, a small fire burned in front of nearly every hut, its thin smoke rising straight into the still air.

She had been told that it was bad manners, in Aboriginal custom, to walk into a camp uninvited; you waited at some distance until you were noticed, and an "ambassador" came to inquire your business. So she sat down on a dead tree a little distance away. Soon an old man in shapeless trousers and a threadbare shirt ambled over and asked, "What-name, Missus?"

"Er—anyone in camp sick-feller? I'm a nurse—all-a-same doctor. You ask Jarry—I treatem hand, makim better. Good-feller medicine."

"You gottim ashpin?"

"Er—ashpin?" she asked uncertainly.

"Yer—all-a-same little-feller white stone." He brought out a dingy rag and unwrapped it, handing her a small black circular stone—a tektite, one of those mysterious fragments thought to have entered the earth's atmosphere in a molten state: flat as a button, with a small depression in the centre, like the mark of a raindrop in mud.

"Him good medchin," said the old man, taking it back and polishing it on the sleeve of his shirt. "But ashpin more better."

"Ah—aspirin! Yes, I gottim."

"Old woman belong me, she sick longa chest. You see her?"

"Yes, if you'll take me to her."

They passed along a line of huts, gathering an audience of giggling children who accompanied them in a circle. It was unheard of for a white missus to visit the camp.

An old woman with white hair and a single garment of worn and dirty cotton lay on a grey blanket at the door of her hut. She looked eighty, but the gins led a hard life and she might well be no more than sixty. She looked up apathetically and started to cough.

"You tellim I make sick peoples better," said Alix.

"Orright. Merna, this one Missus clever-feller doctor, got good medchin. She makin Jarry's 'and better."

Merna gave a weak smile.

Alix knelt in the dust and leaned close to listen to the old woman's wheezing chest—holding her own breath, for Merna's unwashed body had a distinct smell. She felt Merna's brow and noted that she was feverish. Opening her first-aid box and dressing-case, she took out a thermometer and shook it down, watched with fascinated attention by the old woman and her husband and the children gathered round.

"Now, I put this-feller under your arm," she said firmly. "This one magic stick, tell me what wrong." She didn't dare put it in the woman's mouth in case she bit on it with her still-strong teeth.

She took out two aspirin tablets and held them in her palm.

"Ah, ashpin!" said the old man.

"Get her some water to swallow them with," she instructed, and he leaned inside the wurley and brought out a small tin—it had been a jam-tin from the station store—filled with water. Merna rose on her elbow and swallowed the pills.

"Now, you takim two-feller more aspirin sundown, and tomorrow I bring coughing-medicine."

Alix knew that if she left the whole packet with her, Merna would take the lot at once, believing that if two were good for her, a handful must be better.

Alix took a lint pad from her dressing-case, dipped it in the water-tin and bathed Merna's burning face and brow. It was not possible with a dark skin to see the flush of fever, but she knew before she retrieved the thermometer and read the figure that it would be well over a hundred. A hundred and two.

"Now, what-name you?" she asked the old man.

"Me—Johnnie."

"Well, Johnnie, Merna very sick-feller, I want you give-im plenty water, cold tea, anything—she must drink plenty. Tomorrow I bringim milk, medchin, more aspirin—all right?"

"Orright."

Turning towards the children, a cheerful well-fed-looking lot, though their eyes crawled with little bush flies, which tumbled among their long, curling lashes, she wished she had some sweets in her pocket, even a few biscuits, to gain their confidence. Two bigger girls pushed forward a small boy whose hair was matted on one side with dried blood. He stood shyly in front of her, a finger in his mouth, staring unblinkingly.

"Silly-feller Tony walk into tree-bough. Down in waterhole."

Alix guessed that he had dived, or jumped, too near a snag, for the water was full of old dead trees.

"Well, who's going to get me some water for bathe-im?"

The children dashed away in a body, two of them came back lugging a quart-pot full of water. Alix dipped some in a beaker and added some permanganate of potash. As the water turned pinkish-lilac, there was a chorus of in-drawn breaths.

"Him good magic, that-one."

"Him pretty!"

She took some cotton-wool and gently bathed little Tony's head. He stood stoically while she took out her surgical scissors and clipped some hair away from round the wound. It was a deep cut, but did not appear to be infected. With some ointment to stop it from sticking, she wound a gauze bandage around the youngster's head. His hair was inclined to be wavy, but was stiff with dust.

There were murmurs of admiration. Tony smiled proudly.

"Now, I come look-at him tomorrow. No swimming till then. Head belong-you must keep dry. No more water."

Tony's grin grew even wider. His huge eyes were shining and black between their fringe of long lashes. The women had held aloof, but Alix was a great hit with the children. Two of them took her hands, and the whole mob escorted her back to the fence of the garden enclosure. Some, like Tony, were pure Aboriginal, but she noticed among them a number with lighter skins, some with fair, bleached hair.

Mrs. Manning was on the veranda.

"I don't think you should bring the black children up here, Alix," she said. "The house and garden are strictly forbidden to them, except when I let them have a 'playabout' watering the lawn. Otherwise they will be stealing what little vegetables we have."

"I didn't bring them, exactly," said Alix. "They sort of escorted me back. I'm treating an old woman who's on the verge of pneumonia, and I'd like some fresh milk for her in the morning. And there's a small boy with a nasty gash on his head."

"They won't thank you, you know. You might as well save your energy. And if the old woman dies, you will be blamed for killing her."

"Oh! I didn't think of that. But she won't die, now she's getting some treatment. Is there a lemon tree?"

"Yes, but it's not bearing."

Olive had taken her daughter-in-law round the garden enclosure, where Alix dutifully admired the flowering pink oleanders, the enormous sunflowers, and some Christmas lilies just poking green shoots through the red soil. There was a palm tree, rather sickly-looking and with no dates. An athol tree, a tamarisk, and a big old pepper-tree with pink berries, gave some welcome shade.

There were even a few vegetables, spinach and fat hen and some healthy-looking tomatoes.

They'd had fresh tomatoes with their corned beef several times lately. Thinking of this now, Alix asked, "Are there any tomatoes left?"

"Only a few. The rest are still green. And you realize that when the hot winds come in January and February, all the vegetables will be withered and burnt up. They are a great luxury. Why do you ask?"

Alix had been going to beg one tomato for the sick Merna, but seeing her mother-in-law's mouth closed like a trap, she thought better of it. She changed the subject.

The men had been out on the run all day, but that night in bed when she had him to herself, Alix told Jim about her visit to the camp. She was quite wound-up, excited at finding some outlet for her nursing skills. To her surprise he frowned, his thick fair brows coming down over those ice-blue eyes.

"I wouldn't be going down to the camp if I were you," he said. "If someone's sick, tell them to come up to the house. Now they know you've got medicine, they'll be pestering you all the time, and you might pick up something in the camp—"

"Such as?"

"Oh, I don't know. Scabies, head-lice, Barcoo spew . . ."

"I've treated Aboriginal people before, you know. I do take precautions. And I assure you I've had a shower since returning, and washed my hair."

"Yes, but I still don't like you going down there."

"Why ever not?"

"Because I don't. Isn't that enough?"

"No, it is not enough! Don't you or your parents take *any* interest in the health of the station people?"

"Of course. If they ask for help, they get it. They can come up to the store for Robinson's Pills and Perry Davis' Painkiller. Those and Goanna Salve are the favourites."

"But you know they won't ask for help unless they're desperately ill. You know how stoical they are. Today I found an old woman with a bad attack of bronchitis, and a little boy with a nasty head wound."

"They've always got head wounds. The gins quarrel and bash each other with nulla-nullas. Their skulls are thick, and they don't mind the sight of a bit of blood."

"Nevertheless, I am going to take some milk down to old Merna in the morning."

"You give it to Lucy to take down to her."

"No. I want to take her temperature, see if the aspirin has brought her fever down."

"I forbid you to set foot in the camp."

"Good God, you're like those racist residents of Hergott. Worse. You have some responsibility for the blacks on Cappamerri. And I am going to treat Merna until she is on the mend."

"I'm warning you. You'll be sorry."

"Oh!" Alix was seething. She turned her back on him and hunched the sheet around her shoulders. Treating her like a child, ordering her about! She, who had been an independent woman, earning her own keep, responsible for running her own hospital. It was beyond belief. She had said those words, "to love, honour, and obey" in the marriage service. But blind obedience was for slaves. She set her jaw firmly and glared at the mosquito net. When he put a tentative hand on her shoulder she shrugged it off and wound the sheet more tightly around her.

As soon as it was getting light, before the sound of the triangle being beaten over at the men's quarters woke everyone up, she slipped out of bed and into her clothes without waking him.

She unlatched the gate to the garden enclosure and set off for the

157

nearest pink-red sand-hill, just beginning to take colour in the growing light. She would watch the sunrise behind the homestead from that vantage point.

She heard the sound of the wake-up gong just as she reached the summit, and turning saw the eastern sky flushed with gold. Soon the blinding, brilliant yellow orb of the sun appeared over the ocean-flat plain to the eastward. Long shadows streaked out across the flats from house and shed and windmill, and behind her the boles of the paperbarks shone white-gold above the green reeds of the river.

The two sand-hills and the station waterholes were fenced off from stock, as they would always break back from the bore to natural water and would soon have eaten the sand-hills bare and muddied the waterholes. Alix felt safer when she was through the fence; she had no wish to confront one of the half-wild, long-horned bullocks while on foot.

She had slept badly, and had woken still angry with Jim, though she worried about their first real quarrel. Now all her tension fell away, her spirit seemed to expand and float over the endless plains; a sky of tender blue spread without a flaw above, and the air was still fresh with morning. Yes, she loved this country. They talked about the "dead heart" of Australia, but its immense red vibrant presence was not dead; and that the desert could flower as the rose, as in the Reverend John Flynn's favourite passage from the Bible, she had seen with her own eyes. She wished a flood would come down the Diamantina and fertilize the barren-looking gibber plain.

The crest of the sand-hill was bare, patterned with wind-ripples and the tracks of little nocturnal creatures that were never seen in the heat of the day. She traced a hopping-mouse to a clump of silver-grey eremophylla, but there was no sign of the animal itself.

Alix began to plunge down the steep side of the sand-hill towards the river channel. Suddenly she pulled up. Where the dune levelled out there was a stout fence surrounding a small grave. She leaned on the fence with tears pricking her eyes. A cairn of small stones was heaped on the grave—of course, to keep out dingoes—and there was a carved wooden headboard that wind and sandstorms had eroded till it was like pitted stone. She just made out the words "son, Daniel . . . aged four . . . sadly missed." What a wealth of suffering lay behind those simple words!

She went on to the bank of the waterhole above the reach where the blacks' camp spread. Flocks of green budgerigars were coming in to drink, a cloud of white corellas flew screeching from tree to tree. There were even galahs, the birds that had been almost tame in Hergott Springs, with their sunrise-pink breasts and ash-grey backs. The bank was shaded by leaning coolabahs, the water partly covered with red floating duckweed. She did not venture farther, worried about snakes, which were often found near water.

Half-way down the other side of the dune she met Lucy toiling upward, eyes on the ground following her tracks. "Young Boss tellim-me go findem Missus."

"But I wasn't lost, Lucy."

When they got back to the homestead the men were gone and there was no one in sight but Jenny, in a yellow gina-gina which suited her brown skin and dark hair, making up their bed. Jenny flashed her a smile with her big white teeth.

"Breakfiss been pinish," she said.

"That's all right, I'm not hungry." (She was, all the same.)

"That Tony, him happy you fix-im bandage longa head."

"He had a bad cut. You see old Merna, morning-time?"

"Nah. She bin sick long-time."

"Well, I'm going down the camp, see her, take medicine."

Alix went to the kitchen where Leavin' Soon was banging heavy iron pots about, cleaning up after breakfast. As she stood in the doorway he gave her a sour look.

"Breakfast's finished."

"I know, I just wanted a pannikin of milk for a sick lubra."

"Milk? There ain't enough milk for the table, let alone for the blacks. Not enough feed—the cow's goin' dry."

"I just want a cupful. The Boss said I could have some," she added on the spur of the moment. The cook scowled, but took up a small pannikin by its wire handle and went to the Coolgardie safe. While his back was turned, Alix swept a broken piece of damper from a bench into her pocket. She did not dare ask him for anything else. Going back to the house, munching her piece of damper, she searched the bathroom and found a bottle of cough-medicine, smelling strongly of aniseed, in a cupboard. Thank goodness! She didn't want to have to face the storekeeper as well as the cook.

Jenny had finished tidying the bedroom. Alix went back and changed into her divided skirt and boots and a high-necked, long-sleeved white blouse. Though she did not admit it, Jim's list of possible skin conditions had worried her. Old Merna clasping her arm, the sticky little fingers of the children . . .

As it happened there were only a few smaller children about the camp. From the shrieks and splashings coming from the waterhole she guessed they were all having a swim. Would Tony keep his bandage out of the water? She doubted it.

She found Merna lying just inside the shade of her wurley, on the same dirty grey blanket. The old woman looked better and gave Alix a gap-toothed smile. "Good-day, Missus."

"Hullo, Merna. I bin bring you some milk."

"Millik!" She took the pannikin and drank thirstily.

"You feeling better, Merna?"

"You-eye. Tchest belong-me no more cough, cough all-a-time."

"That's good." Her eyes were clear, her temperature was nearly normal. Alix produced the small jar into which she had tipped some cough-medicine. She instructed Merna to take a sip morning and night, but if she liked the taste no doubt she would drink it all in one go.

Merna's old man came back, and Alix asked him would he get Tony up from the waterhole, or wherever he might be.

"Orright, Missus. Me bin fetch-im."

Tony arrived dripping wet, wearing nothing but a tattered pair of shorts. There was no sign of the bandage.

"Him come off in water," he explained with an innocent smile.

"Oh, Tony! You not get it wet, me bin tellim-you."

She took another clean bandage out of her dressing-case, dabbed the wound, which didn't look any worse, with iodine—which made Tony yell—and bound his head once more.

"You can bogey, but no put head under, see? You understand?"

"Yer, Missus. Me unnerstand."

"Otherwise, more of stinging-medicine tomorrow."

He ran off. Old Johnnie fumbled in the pocket of his shirt, and held out in his palm half a dozen small black tektites.

"You take-im, Missus. Me no want-em."

"But Johnnie! You say they number-one blackfeller medicine?"

"No-more. Ashpin more better."

She left a few more aspirin and packed her dressings-case and first-aid box. After thanking him, she made her way towards the homestead, but a tall, thin man plucked at her sleeve.

"Missus, Missus. You doctor-lady? Me got headache longa eye."

She looked and saw that his eyes were almost closed with sandy blight; they would need bathing with warm saline solution and treatment with eye-drops or ointment. She could do nothing here. She looked around despairingly.

"What-name, Missus?" Johnnie was at her elbow. He seemed to have authority in the camp.

"Johnnie, I want you get all the men with sore eyes, all come up to house tomorrow. Wait by gate. 'Bout midday . . . I make-im better. All right?"

"Orright, Missus. Me bring-em."

She wondered what Olive would have to say about her first eye-clinic. Jim was rarely in for lunch, and she hoped he would not be there.

160

CHAPTER TWENTY-THREE

Alix had learned her lesson. That night she did not tell Jim eagerly about her day's activities, and it seemed his mother had not noticed or mentioned her absence at the camp. She was rather surprised at this. Surely if Olive were jealous of her—as she had suspected—she would have made sure to tell him. But perhaps she was indifferent to Jim too, as she seemed to be to everything and everyone.

"Where did you get to this morning? I woke up and you were gone. I told Lucy to look-out for you, I knew she would track you if you were lost. You should never go off alone like that without telling me. I was worried."

"I'm sorry. I wanted to watch the sunrise. I climbed the big sand-hill."

"Well, you can always see the homestead from there. But never go off in the other direction, over the plain. What if a dust-storm came up?" He was conciliatory, but she did not respond. After a silence, she said: "Jim—I came across the little grave, over the other side. Just a wooden headboard, I was surprised—"

"Stone doesn't last much better than wood in this country. Any inscription would soon be polished away by the wind and driving sand. That memorial is made out of iron-hard wood from the waddy-tree. It's a fairly rare tree, and the blacks always used it to make their fighting waddies with. Old Tommy, who's dead now, brought it in and one of the station hands carved it."

"It made me think of Mab's grave in Hergott. Jim, I feel so sorry for your mother. Yet I can't get through to her somehow."

"No. She's shut herself off from all of us."

He put an arm under her head. "Darling—I'm sorry about last night . . . but I'd really rather you didn't go down to the camp. If they are sick they can always come up and ask for medicine."

"Yes, but they often don't. And I'd like to keep on, now they've got to know me."

"I know you must get bored sitting about the place all day. I'm riding in for the mail tomorrow morning, would you like to come? The mailbox is on the Betoota Track, remember—only about twenty miles away."

"That's forty miles there and back."

161

"We'll take it slowly, go across to the river for a picnic on the way back."

"No, Jim, I don't think so. I need more riding practice, but not so far. You could take me out riding after sunset, when it's not so hot."

Jim made a grimace. After being in the saddle most of the day he didn't feel much like going out again at night. He said, "Tell you what. I'll take you swimming in the waterhole. One evening next week."

She did not answer.

"You're not still cross with me?" he asked.

"Yes, I am. I don't like being bossed about."

"No, but you like being made love to," he said, tightening his arms about her.

"Actually, I'm rather tired."

But she said it without too much conviction.

Alix lay awake for some time after Jim was asleep. She was feeling a bit guilty at deceiving him, but she couldn't be away tomorrow morning and let down those old men who were expecting her to treat their eyes, perhaps stop them from going blind. She would have liked going off alone with Jim, but . . .

Big Jim Manning and Young Jim had ridden off early in opposite directions, and Alix found herself alone with her mother-in-law at breakfast on the veranda. The hens had stopped laying again as the weather warmed up once more and there was no fresh beef left, but Leavin' Soon had cooked up some corned beef in batter.

As they drank their tea, looking out at the green-blue waterhole framed between the coloured sand-hills, Alix was tempted to mention that she had seen the little grave; but she thought better of it, seeing Olive Manning's closed face. Instead she said, "Jim has promised to take me swimming one evening." She said impulsively, "Wouldn't you like to come with us? It's so hot."

The other woman's mouth closed tightly, and she shook her head decisively. "No. I never go swimming. I shall sit in the cool-house today and read one of your books. I'm enjoying *Anna of the Five Towns*."

"Well . . . you may notice some of the older men from the camp are coming up to the house so I can treat their eyes. I'm afraid it is trachoma, and they could go blind."

"What? Up to the *house!*"

"Yes," said Alix, setting her chin firmly, though she quailed inwardly. She added, "Not to the house, exactly. They'll come as far as the gate, and I'll take my first-aid things out to them. What I need is a little dispensary and casualty station."

"This is not a hospital," said Olive Manning disapprovingly. "You say they could go blind? You'd better get Lucy to help you put up a table in the shade, and hold your 'clinic' there. I don't want them on my veranda."

Surprised and grateful—she hadn't thought they'd be allowed in the garden—she said, "I'll do that," and went to check her supplies of cotton-wool swabs and clean enamel basins. She had one bottle of eye-drops and some Golden Eye ointment.

When she thought Lucy had finished the washing-up Alix went over to the kitchen and asked her to help with the table. "The Missus say it all right," she explained.

Between them they carried a light folding table down the two steps from the eastern veranda, and set it up near the fence in the shade of an athol tree. Alix fetched a clean sheet to spread over it, feeling excitement rise in her as she put out her few instruments, including an orange-stick for rolling back upper lids. Then she explained to Lucy that she must have a kettle of boiled, not boiling, water, and a jar of salt.

Lucy stared. "You put salt in him eye, Missus? Mmm!" she said, screwing up her own eyes as if in pain.

"Only little-bit salt, in plenty water. Make-im eye better."

She asked Lucy about her patient, Merna, and Lucy said she was on the mend and had spread the word that the Young Missus was a "clever-feller doctor." Little Tony's head was healing, though he'd lost the second bandage.

Alix realized that she would need a chair, not for herself but so that she could reach the eyes of the men, who were often six feet tall. She fetched a cane chair from the veranda and set it up by the table. When all was ready she forced herself to go to her bedroom and relax, putting her feet up and breathing deeply. She must have steady hands for her task.

Four men turned up, led by Johnnie, full of importance. All were elderly, with white beards and eyebrows, which somehow made them look more European than the younger, clean-shaven men. Two of them were in a bad way and she would have liked to bandage their eyes, but this was clearly impossible, and anyway, the bandages would not last much longer than young Tony's.

They were shy about approaching the "tchair," till Johnnie showed them the way, sitting down and leaning back his head. The first man did not flinch when Alix turned back the lids of each eye and irrigated them with saline solution, then applied drops and a soothing eye ointment. (This form of trachoma was known as "sandy blight" because the lids of sufferers felt as if lined with grains of sand.)

When she had finished she said, "Now I want all you-fellers come up for treat-em eye again Monday morning. Same day store opens. Orright?"

"Orright, Missus. Tchank-you, Missus."

She was pleased with her patients and her morning's work. If it saved the sight of only one man, it was worth it. She went and changed her clothes and scrubbed her hands. She would leave the basins till she could get some boiling water to sterilize them. Just now it was lunch-time.

At lunch, Olive Manning did not ask about the clinic, or comment on it.

Alix was resting in her room, while waiting for Lucy to clean up in the kitchen and help her with the folding table. She must have fallen asleep. She woke to hear dogs barking and realized that Jim must be home already. He had left before dawn this morning.

Jim had gone to the kitchen with a letter addressed to "Harold Jensen, care Cappamerri Station, via Birdsville." It was so long since anyone had used the cook's real name that at first Jim couldn't think who it was for. Then he took it to Leavin' Soon together with some small parcels of patent medicine and other mail-order items for him to distribute to the men.

Meanwhile Alix had slipped out to the garden and guiltily removed the basins and the chair. She could not manage the table by herself.

When she came back there was a letter on the bed, addressed in her mother's handwriting. She picked it up, feeling a curious reluctance to read it.

She sat on the bed and skimmed through it. One of Frances's usual epistles, she thought, reading that the latest housemaid had had to be dismissed for "getting into trouble" with a man. But the next page made Alix sit up and stare at the letter in her hand.

Your father believes that we will be at war with Germany before the end of the year. They have been building up their Navy, and are envious of British trade all over the world. He says it is only a matter of waiting for an excuse, and the Kaiser will invade Belgium and France. Of course Britain will have to come to their defence, and Australia to the aid of the Mother Country and the Empire. It should all be over in a year, he thinks, when Germany will have learned their lesson.

Alix was disturbed by this news. They saw no newspapers in the outback, and did not know what was going on in the world. War! She remembered the Boer War, the hysterical patriotism, the shock when the son of someone in their street was killed in South Africa.

Of course it would not affect them here. A few of the white station hands, looking for adventure, might volunteer to go overseas. But Jim couldn't leave the station, he would not think of going.

Jim came in, threw his hat on the bed beside her, and went to the jug and basin to have a wash. He did not speak to her or attempt to kiss her. She waited for him to say something, but he walked past her to the door, remarking only that his mother was waiting for them to come to afternoon tea.

"Jim—!"

"I don't want to talk about it now."

She followed him along the veranda, tucking the letter into her skirt-band.

"A letter from Marjory!" said Olive Manning, looking quite animated. "It seems we can expect a grandchild next year. She asks would I like to come and stay."

"Well, why don't you?" said Jim, buttering a slice of bread and taking a hefty bite with his strong teeth. "Do you good."

"Oh, I don't know . . . It's so long since I've been to Brisbane."

"Nonsense. You write and tell Marj you'll be coming in the autumn, when it's not so hot for travelling. I'll drive you up to Windorah to get the mail to Longreach."

"My mother says we will soon be at war with Germany!" Alix burst out. She took the letter from her belt.

"It's just the newspapers scaremongering," said Jim.

"No, I don't think so. Apparently my father is convinced."

"And of course the Major would know, wouldn't he?"

At his sarcastic tone Alix flushed. She knew he was angry with her, he had seen the signs of her "clinic" in the garden, had perhaps questioned his mother about it.

"Well, my parents are more in touch with world affairs than we are, out here in the back of beyond," she said defensively.

"Marjory doesn't mention anything about it," said Olive. "I suppose she is too full of her own exciting news. I've been so hoping for a grandchild. I had thought by now you and Jim—"

"Fair go, Mum!" said Jim uncomfortably.

Alix coloured again, and looked down at her plate.

"It's all right, Jim," she said quietly. She had been hoping for the same thing. Now, noticing her mother-in-law more interested in what was going on around her than Alix had ever seen her, she realized that what Olive Manning wanted was to hold a baby in her arms again, a new little Daniel. If she, Alix, could only produce a grandson, it might break through the wall of glass that Olive kept between them.

"Where've you been, you old devil?" asked a raucous voice from up near the ceiling. George the cockatoo had poked his head through his peep-hole and was looking down at Jim with one bright eye, his head on one side.

"You wait, I'll bring you a biscuit in a minute."

"Ouf, ouf, ouf!" said George, barking like a dog, and raising his beautiful crest.

When Jenny came in with a new pot of tea Jim asked her to get a dry biscuit from the cook for him.

165

"He not there," said Jenny. "Cookie, him read-im letter, bin leave-im kitchen soon."

"Well! He must have had some news. I hope he's not really leaving this time, eh, Jenny?"

"No-more. Me get-im you bishkit."

"And you better get Lucy to help you bring that table inside before it gets dark."

Jenny shot a sidelong glance at Alix. "Orright, Boss."

"A war won't affect us here, at any rate," said Olive.

This had been Alix's reaction. Jim looked thoughtful. He remarked that if it came to war, and troops had to be supplied with bully-beef, it might put up the price of beef and consequently the price of cattle.

"If we could only get them down to market," he added. "But with the back country in the state it's in, the stock-routes eaten out, you can't overland beasts to the railhead."

Olive said as though she had not heard, "The baby is due early next year, about March. I hope it's a boy."

Jenny came out to the veranda with some fresh hot water and a dry oatmeal biscuit from the kitchen. Jim went down to the garden and could be heard talking to George as the bird flew down to his shoulder, held the biscuit in one claw and nibbled at its edges.

"All right, don't drop crumbs all over me! You're wasting as much as you're eating."

"Sqwark!"

"Well, you're not getting another one."

Jim did not come back to the table and Alix did not see him until they met at the dinner table that night. Big Jim was told the news about the war, which didn't seem to interest him much, and then the good news about the grandchild. "Good!" he said, and glanced at Jim. "Time you had a son to carry on the name, eh?"

"There's plenty of time," said Jim stiffly. Alix said nothing.

They did not linger over the meal, which was one of Leavin' Soon's poorer efforts. It consisted of cold corned beef with boiled onions, which Jim sprinkled liberally with the tomato sauce that always stood on the table. They ordered tomato sauce by the case at Cappamerri.

Before the second course came Jim announced that he'd had a long ride, was dog-tired, and thought he would have a bath and an early night. Alix, nervous about being alone with him, stayed on at the table till Jenny had cleared away the sweets dishes. Then she took a second cup of tea out on the west veranda and watched the clear orange light drain away behind the trees, their leaves in a black lacy silhouette against the glow. Venus was following the sun as the evening star, a great silver lamp above the horizon. Alix saw it expand and send out silver spears as her eyes filled, and hot tears fell on the hand holding the cup and saucer.

Jim would probably never forgive her, and the family felt she had let them down by not producing any sign of an heir in four months of marriage. The one thing she could do well and was trained to do—nursing—she was not allowed to practise. She and Jim had been so happy at first. Now she began to feel he was a stranger.

She set the cup down with a crash and made her way round the veranda to their room.

CHAPTER TWENTY-FOUR

As Jim was still in the bath, Alix hastily got undressed and into bed, hoping he might think her asleep when he joined her. He came in wearing a pair of pyjama pants and towelling his wet hair, which looked dark, almost brown, while damp.

The one lamp was burning on the table on his side of the bed. He did not turn it out but climbed under the mosquito net and lay on his back, his hands behind his head, staring at the ceiling. Alix looked at him from under her closed lids. She tried to breathe naturally and slowly, without success.

"All right," he said at last. "I know you're awake."

"Jim, I—"

"Don't talk to me. I can't believe a word you say any more. So you couldn't spend the day with me, because you preferred to give your time to some dirty, diseased old blacks from the camp. I know, Mother told me when I came in: I asked her about the table set up in the garden."

"Jim, it wasn't like that. I really did think it was too long a ride for me. And I'd already promised the old men to treat their eyes today. I didn't want to let them down."

"You could at least have ridden out to meet me along the track."

"I—I didn't think of it."

"No, you didn't think of me at all. If all you want is to be a nurse, why did you marry me? You gave up nursing to come and live with me."

"I know." She touched his brown arm timidly. "I should have told you about today, but I was scared you'd stop me. I've arranged for them to come up for treatment every Monday morning till I've cured their sandy blight."

"Really! It's kind of you to tell me."

"I didn't go down to the camp since you asked me not to. I'm sure there are others needing my help, but I'll wait for them to come to me. Since I am able to do something for the sick, it seems wrong not to make the effort."

"It's your deceiving me that I can't stomach."

"But you would have stopped me, wouldn't you? And yet without treatment at least two of those old men would go blind."

"I think you exaggerate."

"I do not exaggerate! I'm familiar with trachoma from nursing in Hergott Springs."

"Let's drop the subject, shall we? I want to go to sleep."

He put out the lamp and turned his back on her.

"Jim . . . ?"

"What is it?"

"Will you still take me swimming?" she asked humbly.

"I don't know. I'll think about it."

They were awakened by loud wails and shrieks from the direction of the kitchen. It was just getting light. Bare feet came pounding along the veranda, and Lucy was shrieking, "Boss! Missus! Ai-eee! Cookie bin dead-feller properly. Him bugger-up pinish."

Lucy, finding the kitchen dark and no fire alight in the stove or the bread oven, and no bread set to rise from the night before, had gone to Leavin' Soon's room in a lean-to thatched with cane-grass adjoining the kitchen, but found it empty. In the dim light she searched about outside for tracks, which led behind the building.

At first she thought he was lying there asleep; but putting a hand on his shoulder to shake him, she felt it sticky with blood. Lying by his right hand she saw the gleam of the carving knife on the ground.

Jim dashed out in his pyjama trousers and met his father just emerging from his room in nothing but a pair of shorts. His mother was calling querulously to know what was happening.

Lucy was almost incoherent, wailing and throwing her arms in the air, one hand and wrist covered in blood.

"Now calm down, Lucy!" said Big Jim in his slow, deep voice. "Where you bin find him?"

"Jus' now. I go wake-im, but him no wake no more. Ehh! Ohh! Be'ind cookhouse—"

"All right, you go and get the fire alight, make yourself a cup of tea and one for the Missus. We'll see to it. Come, Jim."

They stepped out into the morning and looked behind the kitchen building. In the growing light they saw a grim tableau. Leavin' Soon had cut his throat, a great gash that gaped open like an obscene mouth. Blood had poured over his chest and over the ground. In his left hand, clenched on his chest, was a blood-stained letter.

Big Jim edged it out of the stiff fingers and attempted to arrange the arms tidily on the man's breast. There was no question but it was suicide. Nor was there any question of a doctor or a doctor's certificate, as the nearest doctor was at Winton, four hundred miles away. The man would have to be buried, and a message would have to be taken through to the police at Birdsville, and to his next of kin.

"Poor cow had a wife, it seems," his father said to Jim as they went

169

back into the house. Jim looked rather sick. The cook had bled like a stuck pig, or a slaughtered bullock.

They leaned on the veranda rail while Big Jim held the blood-stained missive in his big fingers. "Dear Harry," he read, "As your cobber I think you should know that your wife is playing up with the publican at Winton. She took a job in the bar there, but if you arsk me she as taken up with him as well. A word to the wise. A friend."

"A bloody anonymous letter!" said Big Jim savagely.

Alix came along the veranda in the cherry silk dressing-gown from her trousseau, tying the sash as she came. She saw the blood-stained letter, and looked an inquiry.

"The cook has killed himself. Cut his throat," said Jim tersely. "Apparently he had news that his wife was living with another man."

"How awful! You're sure he is dead? Perhaps I should—"

"You should keep away," said Jim. "It's no sight for a woman—"

"Jim!" Her voice had a dangerous edge to it. "You forget that I am a trained nurse, used to dealing with accidents and dead bodies. Someone will have to clean him up, lay out the body decently for burial. I'll just get dressed. Meanwhile I suggest you cover him with a mosquito net, before the flies get busy, and set up a trestle-table to lay him out on."

She turned on her heel, leaving the two men looking rather dazedly after her.

Lucy brought a cup of tea, her eyes still moist, her usually cheerful smile missing. "Me bin find-im, Missus! Oo-er. . . !"

"That's enough, Lucy. Now I want you find-em me plenty cloth, old sheet, towel. You ask Missus. And two-feller bucket water, one warm, one cold. Understand? And bring-em to Cookie's room."

"No-more. Me not go there."

"Well, leave them at the door. And I want two men for lift-im. You go over to men's quarters and get-im." She dismissed Lucy and drank her tea before getting dressed. She wished she had one of her full-length starched aprons to wear. She would tie a cloth over her old grey twill skirt and white blouse.

As she went across the covered way she found Olive in the kitchen, distractedly organizing Jenny in cutting some of yesterday's bread. The fire was alight in the stove, with a pot of oatmeal porridge bubbling on top.

"Oh, Alix!" wailed Olive Manning. "What a thing to have happened! Do you realize we might not be able to get another cook for *months!* I don't know how we shall manage!"

"Well, we'll just have to, won't we? Did Lucy ask you for some old cloths?"

"Yes, she took them. Jenny, no cut-im so thick! It's for toast, not for building-bricks."

170

A trestle-table had been set up in the cook's room, and when Lucy brought the water and clean rags, Alix put a basin on the small table by the bed. Two men came in, carrying the cook, now draped with a net, and with a cloth over his head and face.

"You'll have to lift him on to the trestle," said Alix briskly. The blood had congealed and no more had flowed when he was moved. The men picked him up, one at the feet and one at the shoulders.

"Poor ole Leavin' Soon," said one, removing the hat that was almost a part of his head. "He wasn't a bad old bastard. A bit moody sometimes."

"A lousy cook, but," said the other. "Well, he won't be leavin' this place, that's for sure."

"We'll leave 'im to you, Missus. Rather you than me," said the first man, as they stepped outside. A few flies were beginning to buzz round the room.

After she had bathed away most of the blood, Alix bound a strip of cloth like a muffler around the gaping wound. She cut off the blood-stained shirt and bathed the upper body. The trousers and boots she decided to leave intact. She found a clean cotton shirt in a tin box on the floor, and managed to get it on him. She brushed his staring eyes shut and weighted the lids with two pennies. "Harold Jensen, you look fit for burial now," she said, emptying the first bucket out the door and dropping the blood-stained cloths into it. She was about to empty the second bucket on the bare ground, but thinking better of it took it round the corner of the house and poured the contents on the struggling Christmas lilies. She had learned the hard way to conserve water.

Coming back, she found Jim in the doorway. He looked at her admiringly. "You've done a great job," he said. "I don't know, most women would have screamed and fainted, been completely useless—"

"Jim, you keep forgetting that I'm a nurse. I once had to lay out a man after he'd been run over by a train. You learn to deal with such things, even if you never get used to it. And I stitched *you* up, remember? 'Most women' would probably have fainted at the sight of that horrid-looking wound, cobbled together with horsehair."

"Yes, of course. I'd forgotten that's why I first fell in love with you."

He went to kiss her, but she drew back. She had rinsed her hands and arms in a bowl, but her shirtwaist and the front of her skirt were stained. "I'm going to take a shower," she said, "if you'll fill the tip-bucket for me."

"Right. I'll do it now."

"This old skirt can be burnt, it's not worth washing."

Jim said they would burn the rags too, and the cook's old shirt.

"By the way, you won't get Lucy and Jenny into this room again. They're very superstitious. And you must never mention the cook's name to them. He'll be just 'that poor-feller,' or 'that-one cook.'"

171

"I'll remember," Alix promised.

After Harold Jensen, alias Leavin' Soon, had been decently buried in the small graveyard half a mile away from the homestead buildings, Big Jim wrote to the police officer in Winton to let his widow know the news, and enclosed a cheque for the cook's wages made out to the end of the next month.

He wrote a report of the fatality for the Birdsville police, and made up a parcel of the cook's few possessions—a pearl-handled pen-knife, a silver fob watch, a battered wallet holding some photographs and papers, and a few pound notes in a cigarette tin. Leavin' Soon's spare clothes were in the tin box, but it didn't seem worth while forwarding them all that way. Everything would eventually have to go by a long roundabout route to Winton. The letter and parcel had to be taken down to the mailbox on the Betoota-Birdsville road.

"The mailman won't be there for another week, on his way back," said Jim. "Would you like to come with me this time? I'll take the buggy."

"Can I drive part of the way?"

"If you want to."

Also in the mail went an advertisement for a new cook. It would probably be months before there was a reply, and few itinerant workers turned up at this isolated station.

Alix explained that she was not much good at cooking, except invalid cookery, which would hardly appeal to the tough cattlemen, but she was willing to learn to make bread and damper. She found there was a certain satisfaction in kneading the great lumps of dough, and setting them to rise in covered pans by the warm stove. The bread was like a living thing, growing and expanding. Her first efforts were heavy and tough, but when she turned out a respectable loaf at last, she felt a great sense of achievement. With damper it was only a matter of mixing cold water and flour to the right consistency, with some baking powder and a pinch of salt. The main thing was not to over-cook it till it became hard. And to remember the rising—Alix made one batch without, and it came out like millstones, flat and rocklike. Like her first disastrous bread, she buried it darkly at dead of night.

She enjoyed the long drive to the mailbox and back with Jim, taking over the reins for part of the way. They left before the sun was up, the back of the buggy weighed down with water-tins and more water in a canvas bag hanging underneath. Most of the way they would not be far from the many channels of the Diamantina; but as Jim pointed out, the majority of these were now dry.

Jim's tame brolga accompanied them part of the way. The great crane with his soft grey plumage and long neck and legs would sometimes fly after Jim when he rode round the property, landing wherever he stopped, and finally giving up and going back to his companions on the waterhole.

"I don't know whether he mistakes me for another brolga, or what," said Jim. "They call them 'native companions.'"

"Perhaps 'he' is a female, and is trying to woo you."

"I never thought of that."

Mail was waiting at the empty drum marked with the bleached skull of a steer.

On the way back Jim pulled off the track and turned towards the river channels, where a few trees gave some shade, to rest the two horses.

As Jim broke some dry wood to light a fire and boil the billy, the brittle branches cracked like a rifle-shot. Instantly a cloud of black cockatoos rose from the dead timber along the channel. They screamed like demons, flying heavily and clumsily, with their red-barred tail feathers spread against the sun. Strange, barbaric, harsh-voiced creatures, they seemed less like birds than the dark spirits of the land, the red heart of Australia, belonging as the Aborigines belonged to a dream-time thousands of years old. Alix felt a shiver, part delight, part superstitious fear, run down her spine.

As they sat in the shade drinking black tea, she said thoughtfully, "You know, I realize now that sending and receiving letters at Cappamerri is no simple matter. I have forgiven you for not writing for months after you first left Hergott Springs."

"It *is* a long way to the mailbox. But I might have written a decent letter while I was about it. I bought the postcard in Birdsville on the way up—should have posted it from there. Then I let two mails go by, wondering what to say."

"You could have said, 'I miss you.'"

"Yair. Well, I've made up for it since, haven't I?"

They lingered in the shade for the hottest part of the day, then Alix said she must get back in time to help get the evening meal. "Poor Olive is doing most of the cooking, and she hates it. Lucy can do simple things like boiling eggs, making toast, and grilling steak, but your mother is doing the rest."

"At least you're making bread for the men and the house. Six loaves a day is not bad going. But I hope the stores come through soon. The flour won't last much longer."

Jim told her that the six-monthly store supply was due before Christmas. It would come the long way round from Brisbane, by rail and then by coach to Windorah, and from there by camel train to the stations between the Barcoo and the Diamantina.

"We have to order jam by the crate, flour by the hundredweight, tinned butter by the case, kerosene in four-gallon tins. It takes a string of a dozen camels to freight them in.

"Dad has put a special order through for things like nuts and dried fruit and shortbread for Christmas. And we're fattening up the hens that aren't laying."

"It will be our first Christmas," said Alix, kissing him.

Chapter Twenty-five

In spite of Jim's objections and Olive's disapproval, Alix had expanded her work as several mothers brought their children to her Monday-morning clinic, held just inside the gate of the garden enclosure. Sometimes it was a baby with dysentery, or a small boy with a cut foot; occasionally a lubra came with a horrifying gash in her head from some women's fight.

Alix had asked her mother to send her a new box of bandages with ointments and lotions. She felt she was doing some good. Her old idea of teaching the children their letters had been dropped; obviously she would not be allowed to take a class on the veranda. Unfortunately the children nearly all had running noses, caused by an unhealthy diet with little vitamin C; and though their eyes were large and lustrous, the little bush flies crawled in them continually. Olive preferred them at a distance.

A small boy was carried up from the camp one morning with terrible burns to his feet and lower legs. It seemed he had been jumping over a fire in some camp playabout and had landed short, among the burning hot coals.

Alix did not hesitate. She told the two men to bring the lad up to the veranda, where she let down a canvas chair till it was almost flat and folded a blanket, with a clean sheet doubled over it, for a mattress. She sent Jenny for boiled water from the kitchen stove, and set out a tray with basins, surgical gauze, scissors, and dressings. Both feet were so badly burned that he would not be able to walk for some time. It was important to keep the wounds clean, to change the dressings once or twice a day, to keep them bandaged against flies and dust. She certainly wasn't going to let him go back to the camp.

The little boy was a full-blood with the tribal name of Wondan. He did not have parents or even close relatives in the camp; as a toddler he had been left behind by a wandering family of blacks when his mother died. He had been brought up by "aunties" and "uncles" of the Cappa-merri people.

Alix judged that he was about ten. She placed a small table beside him to hold a jug for water and a cup, and her tray of surgical dressings. She gave him aspirin and codeine, as big a dose as she dared, for he must be in terrible pain though he did not cry out or complain, just compressed his wide mouth and breathed quickly. With Jenny's help she rigged a mosquito net over him like a tent.

She had put Wondan on the side veranda, as the other two verandas were really extensions of the living rooms. Walking round from her bedroom for lunch, Olive Manning saw this apparition on her veranda and stopped dead, then walked on quickly to confront Alix.

"What is going on? There appears to be a black child on the veranda, asleep!"

"Yes. I'm sorry, I didn't want to disturb you, but I couldn't send him back to the camp. Both his feet are badly burned, he can't walk. Also he's still in a state of shock."

"But he can't stay *here!* Even the house lubras don't sleep here. I certainly can't allow him—"

"You'll just have to, for the time being. As soon as he's well enough I'll make up a bed for him down at the camp, and visit him there to change the dressings."

"Jim won't approve of that."

Alix went on eating her fried rice without replying.

While Wondan slept she had been out to the kitchen and made some thin porridge. After lunch she put some in a bowl, added golden syrup and a little goats' milk, and took it to Wondan. He had just awakened, and looked frightened. She decided to ask Lucy to feed him, for he was used to her and Jenny, who would help ease the strangeness for him. He was going to miss the other children as soon as he felt a bit better.

"Wondan, I want you drink plenty water," she said, holding the cup to his lips, which had relaxed a little though a frown of pain pleated his heavy brows. "Plenty, plenty water, from china cup. See? Him pretty, eh?"

But Wondan, she noticed later, always drank direct from the wide-mouthed jug.

She also found a glass jar and showed him how to use it. He seemed to find this operation intriguing; but solid motions were more of a problem. She found an old baking-dish in the kitchen, and showed Lucy how to slip it under the boy's backside. But old Lucy preferred to hold the boy out over the edge of the veranda. Alix prayed that her mother-in-law would not see this operation. She would go round with a spade and cover the evidence later.

When the men came home Olive was waiting on the veranda with her complaints.

"Jim! Your wife has a dirty black child from the camp sleeping on my veranda. Will you please speak to her?"

Jim looked harassed, and said only that it could wait till he'd had a wash. Big Jim asked what was wrong with the child. Alix popped out from where she had been listening, and said, "It's only a ten-year-old boy. His

176

feet have been so badly burnt that he can't walk. I need to have him close for a while, to change his dressings and watch for infection."

Big Jim scratched his ear. "Well, Mother, I suppose it won't hurt for a little while to—"

"It's against all the rules!" cried Olive. "Next thing I'll have those children in the garden, rampaging over my plants, leaving the gate open."

"I assure you that won't happen." Alix spoke quietly, but the blood was pounding in her ears. She was determined to fight for her patient, whatever the opposition.

She turned on her heel and went to the bedroom where Jim was changing his shirt for dinner.

"You've really got Mum's back up now, haven't you?" he said, it seemed to her accusingly.

"You might wait till you've heard *why* the child is there." She told him what she had told Big Jim.

"And he really can't walk?"

"No."

Jim rubbed the back of his head, an irritable gesture. "I don't know! She was starting to accept the garden clinic, but this—!"

"There was nothing else I could do. Would you like to see him?"

She led him along to the side veranda, and saw the deck-chair was empty. There was a white bundle on the floor beyond. He had managed to slide off, with the sheet and net, and was rolled up like a possum on the wooden floor.

"Wondan!" She touched the bundle gently. Matted dark hair and a single large brown eye appeared over the edge of the sheet.

"Wondan, this the Young Boss. I show-im feet belong-you."

She uncovered the large white bandages under which a piece of angry red scorched skin disappeared at the ankle. Wondan made no sound. His huge unblinking eyes stared up at them.

"Well, little feller, your feet sore-feller prop'ly, eh?" Jim squatted on his heels beside the little boy and spoke reassuringly. "Nemmind. You soon all better, go back to camp." He patted the bundle and stood up, in one fluid, easy movement.

As they went back to their room Alix slipped her hand into Jim's and gave it a squeeze. His support was important to her. Now she felt she could face Olive and her displeasure.

"Leave him on the floor," said Jim. "He's used to sleeping on the ground, and he'll be more comfortable."

It was not so comfortable for Alix, having to sit on a cushion on the veranda boards to treat her patient. When she came with her tray of surgical gauze, scissors, and swabs, he would look up from big, liquid brown eyes with those incredibly long curling lashes, and bite his full

177

lips; but he never cried out or made a sound of pain. She was amazed at his stoicism, and the rapidity with which the burns healed.

She had washed his hair, which was wavy and shiny. He was now an attractive child, but she could not persuade Olive to visit him.

"Wondan, your feet better now," she told him one day, unwinding the bandages and lifting the dressings, which no longer stuck to the raw tissue and had to be bathed away. "See—new skin here, and here."

"You-i, Missus."

"Soon all better, eh?"

For the first time she saw him smile fully, a wide, white smile in his brown face. Yet she had heard him laughing with Jenny in the mornings when the young lubra joked with him as she swept the veranda.

The atmosphere in the house, meanwhile, was strained. Alix noticed that Olive never spoke to her at the meal-table, or said so much as "good morning" when they met. Jim was worried, because he did not like taking sides between his mother and his wife, and was still a little in awe of his mother.

Only Big Jim Manning was unaffected, taking no notice of the situation but occasionally asking Alix casually, "How's the patient?"

Olive spoke only once during the first day or two after Wondan's appearance, to say frostily, "Alix, I trust you have washed thoroughly before coming to the table?"

Alix flushed and muttered that she had, naturally. This was at lunch-time when the men were out. Alix took her plate out on the veranda and ate there.

One of the men made some crutches from two forked myall branches padded with flour sacks. As soon as the less badly burned foot, though still bandaged, was sufficiently healed to take his weight, she let the men patients on her next Monday clinic carry Wondan back to camp.

She threatened and warned him about no swimming, and keeping the bandages dry till she came to take them off. "No bogeying in the river, mind! Or I'll be prop'ly cross."

When the stores arrived, there was great excitement. The people came up from the camp to watch as men shouldered heavy bags and crates into the store. The two Afghans had hoosh'd their strings of laden pack-camels down in the dust. As they came swaying along in single file, they looked like some Eastern caravan.

Perched on one of the loads was a small fat man with slanting eyes and a pigtail. He was a Chinese cook, Wing Lee by name, who was looking for work on a station.

This was the best Christmas present Olive could ask for. She engaged him at once, not even asking why he had left his last employ.

The Afghan drivers brought the news that England and Germany were at war, and the Federal Parliament had voted to send Australian troops to help the British Empire. The camel train had been on the track for two months, visiting other stations on the way. It was now the first week in November; news of the outbreak of hostilities had reached Longreach only the week before they left.

The storekeeper was busy taking an inventory and checking the flour for weevils, the potatoes for mould. He sniffed doubtfully at a forty-pound bag of sugar, which smelt strongly of camel. A large tin of biscuits, taken up to the house by Olive and opened with great expectations, was found, after two months of swaying on a camel's back, to be nothing but crumbs.

The next excitement was an Indian hawker arriving on a riding camel, with one pack-camel, from the other direction: he had come down the Georgina from Boulia and Bedourie. He put up a tent and unpacked a bale of treasures: coloured scarves, bright ribbons, combs and mirrors, cheap bangles and beads. The station hands bought presents for their girl-friends, or their future possible sweethearts when they hit town again. The black stockmen and the kitchen lubras who had saved their tiny wages bought freely.

That night, while the white people discussed the implications of war on the other side of the world, Jenny waited at table with her hair shining clean and a bright pink ribbon tied round it. Two glass bangles tinkled on her wrist. She had an air of coquetry and self-satisfaction worthy of a Frenchwoman in a new creation from a leading fashion house.

Alix could not sleep. Although she knew, in theory, that the war could not affect them in this outpost, she yet felt a sense of dread. Away across the sea, young men were marching out to kill each other; women no doubt were dancing in the streets and cheering with patriotic fervour.

And what if it wasn't over in a year, or even two? It occurred to her that nurses would be needed at the front, like Florence Nightingale. Travel overseas, companionship, work—. What nonsense! Married women would certainly not be expected to volunteer, even if Jim—. But what if Jim decided to go? No, he would never leave Cappamerri.

She slipped quietly out of bed and through the wire door on to the veranda, walking silently on her bare feet. The waning moon was setting, but there was enough light to see the garden trees, the pale blobs of oleander blossom. A curlew cried out on the plain, was answered by another: *Wer-looo-oo! Wer-looo-oo!* That eerie, mournful, wailing cry . . .

A savage place! as holy and enchanted
As e'er beneath a waning moon was haunted
By woman wailing for her demon-lover!

As the lines from Coleridge came into her head, a dark shape seemed to move silently in the shadows of the veranda, by the door of the Boss's room. Alix froze with superstitious dread. What had she called up out of the darkness and the sallow moonlight?

The dark shape moved towards the front steps, and there came the tinkle of glass bangles. Staring unbelievingly, Alix saw Jenny step out into the moonlight and turn towards the gate. She was naked, carrying her gina-gina carelessly by one hand over her shoulder.

Alix felt winded. She sat down in one of the cane chairs to think about what she had seen. There was no doubt about it, Jenny had been visiting the Boss in his bedroom. Perhaps it was a regular arrangement. She remembered the half-caste children down at the camp—might some of them be Jim's half-brothers? Of course she had realized that such things happened in the outback, were accepted though not publicly acknowledged. Perhaps even Olive turned a blind eye . . .

And Jim? Were some of those dark children his? "Yeller-fellers" they were called out here, because of their creamy complexions, neither white nor brown. But it was an expression of contempt. Surely not Jim! And yet, when not travelling with cattle, he must have spent long months here without a woman. Probably even fat old Lucy had been lithe and attractive not so long ago. She wanted to ask Jim—in fact, she wanted him to deny it —but she would not. Any such liaison must have been over before she came here, and anyway perhaps it was not so; perhaps Jim even despised his father for his weakness. For he must know about it. Everyone in the camp would certainly know; Jenny would have great status there as the Big Boss's woman.

Alix felt constrained with her father-in-law at meals, and found herself watching for any covert understanding between him and Jenny. But he seemed to treat both black women the same, with a kind of jesting familiarity born of long acquaintance. Perhaps Lucy had once occupied Jenny's place as favourite!

The embarrassment she felt with her father-in-law was relieved when the men went off on a ten-day trip to the outer bores, to clean out the bore-drains, muster what cattle were left alive, and burn the carcasses of those which had died. Any young calves which had been born were knocked on the head, to give their mothers a chance to survive until it rained. They cut boughs of mulga and myall for the miserably thin and apathetic beasts.

In the area where rain had fallen and the cattle were still in good nick, they cut out the cleanskin calves and brought them back to the stockyards for branding and castrating. Alix, wearing her divided skirt, climbed up and sat on the top rail to watch. The first calf was brought down, *thud!* on its side; one man held its horns and sat on its head, while another was heating the branding-iron and a third was ready with a knife to cut off the testicles. Alix felt sick at the stench of burning hair and hide. Bellowing, the calf was let up and blundered away, while its companions milled about in terror at the smell of blood.

180

She noticed the men carefully picking up the limp balls from the dust and setting them on the rail, and remembered having heard that they were regarded as a great delicacy, grilled over the coals. She climbed down and went back to the homestead, the bellows of pain following her all the way. She walked swiftly, trying to leave them behind.

The calves would have hung around the homestead bore, where the ground was eaten out to bare dust, until they starved. Another thunderstorm had brought feed up on the Jalata Bore, half-way to where the main mob was fattening, so they were driven there. Jim said that the cattle in the thunderstorm area were in such good condition they could be sold as "fats," if only the stock-routes were open.

"Things are getting pretty desperate," he said. "We can hang on if we get a few more thunderstorms, then if a big Wet comes down from the north it will give us a chance to move them down to market."

"And if it doesn't?"

"We'll be finished. Another year like the last three, and we'll have to walk off the property and leave it to the bank that holds the mortgage."

"How long have the Mannings been out here?"

"Since the 1870s. Away back. You should get the Old Man talking— he'll tell you about the first family of Mannings to take up land on the Diamantina. It's quite a saga."

One night after dinner when they were all sitting on the eastern veranda watching the moon rise, Alix asked Big Jim about his family history. "Jim tells me they were real pioneers."

"Aw . . . yair, I suppose so. Came out here pretty early, only about ten years after the explorers, McKinlay and Landsborough." He stopped and re-lit his pipe.

"They were your grandparents?"

"No, parents. I was born in 1864; I was only a kid when I came out here with the family. After the homestead was built, sometimes I'd be left in charge of the cattle at night. I daren't sleep because I was that scared of the dingoes howling round the camp. Before it got dark I'd pile up plenty of wood, and keep building the fire up to keep them away. I was only nine years old at the time. My father, Bill Manning, was a very stern family man, and his word was law. He had a big beard and these thick bushy eyebrows and bright blue eyes. . . .

"When the family set out from the coast, there were my parents and their children, and Mum's younger sister and her husband. We travelled in bullock-drays, about fifteen miles a day, carting water and food, and sometimes having to live on bush rats while we were droving a mob of cattle that were too valuable to eat. We were away out on the western plains beyond Winton, when a big Wet set in. All the creeks were flooded, and we couldn't go forward or back.

181

"My Aunt Annie thought she had plenty of time to get to our destination on the Diamantina, but we were still held up, completely out of flour and tea and living in makeshift tents that let in the rain, when the baby arrived. My mother did all she could, but Annie and the baby both died."

"It's a cruel country," said Olive Manning hollowly.

"Yes, well, there was hardly enough wood even to boil water in that treeless country—we'd carried some firewood with us—and there was nothing to build a coffin out of. So they broke up one of the drays and used that, with a piece to make a cross to mark the grave. The ground dried out and they had to go on and leave her."

"Terrible for your mother!" said Alix.

"And for my Uncle Tom. They'd only been married a year."

"How old was she?"

"Just nineteen."

Big Jim leaned back and puffed on his pipe. Alix stared out at the brightening yards beyond the shadowed garden, the shiny tin roofs of the outbuildings reflecting the moon as it rose.

"I had to attend a birth on an isolated station once," she murmured. "The mother lived, but the baby died. If there'd been a doctor, or a hospital near enough, it would have lived. That's what John Flynn is fighting for—hospitals and medical services for outback families—what he calls the Mantle of Safety over the inland."

"The distances are too great," said Jim. "And half the time the tracks are impassable!"

"He has some idea of using aeroplanes—yes, I know it sounds crazy, but the man's a visionary."

"Crazy, all right. Unless they had a telephone, how would the doctor know when someone was sick? And where would the plane land? Anyway, aeroplanes are too unsafe."

"Yes, I suppose it's just a dream."

"Back in those early days," said Big Jim reflectively in his slow, deep drawl, "there was trouble with the blacks. They didn't like their waterholes being taken over—naturally enough—and they couldn't see why they shouldn't spear cattle for food.

"It got so bad that a couple of stockmen at an outstation were speared. My father sent a rider with a message for the Native Police, and a party of them came out from Winton with their carbines. There was no trouble with the local blacks after that."

"In fact, they were shot?" said Alix in disgust.

"It was called 'dispersing the natives.' The tribes were broken, those who were left camped around the stations and became dependent on hand-outs, and the men turned out to be excellent horsemen and cattle-men.

"As for the black police, they'd been recruited from Victoria, and had no compunction about shooting wild Aborigines in Queensland. They had a white officer in charge. Later he was speared by the blacks up near Dajarra. His grave is somewhere out there in the north-west."

"Along with the bones of hundreds of slaughtered Aborigines."

"Yes, Alix. But you must remember that it was a case of survival. The pioneers had gone through tremendous hardships to bring their cattle overland and establish a station in the middle of nowhere. The Abos didn't use the land for anything except to wander over. The settlers couldn't see why they should be driven off by a lot of myalls."

Alix said nothing more, but she told Jim afterwards that she had read something about the Queensland Native Police—a bloodthirsty lot, who notched up their "kills" on the stocks of their carbines. "I suppose it was the same in South Australia and the far north—I know the Dieri were all but wiped out, up near Lake Callabonna; I nursed the last full-blood of the tribe down at Hergott. If one or two white men were speared, it was called a 'massacre' or a 'treacherous murder,' and men, women, and children were shot in reprisal. Apparently this was called 'dispersal,' not murder."

"It wasn't just one or two white men," said Jim. "At Pelican Water-holes, four men were swimming one afternoon when they were all speared and left in the water. And at one station, nineteen of the Wills Family —women and children too—were clubbed to death in 1861. People today don't realize how dangerous and daring they were in defending their land. It was war, just as much as the Maori Wars in New Zealand."

"A pretty unequal war—Stone Age spears against modern guns."

"Well, dear, you've married into a family of squatters. My grandparents took up this land; they worked hard to create a pastoral property out of what was near-desert, with an average five-inch rainfall—"

"*Five inches!* Is that all?"

"That's all. But of course the artesian bores have made a terrific difference. And then floods can come down through the Channel Country without any rain actually falling here. Wait till you see the place in a good season. Sometimes the water even reaches Lake Eyre."

Chapter Twenty-six

On Christmas Day the thermometer hanging under the shade of the front veranda registered 115 degrees. Olive had made lemon syrup, using crystallized lemon rind boiled with water and citric acid. This was kept down the cellar until needed, then mixed with cool water from the big canvas water-bag. There was even some soda-pop that had come in with the supplies, but no alcohol except for the "medicinal" brandy in the store, which was rationed out to the Chinese cook to put in the boiled plum pudding. The huge pudding was mixed in one of the bread-pans and boiled in a cloth in the outdoors copper. A vealer had been killed for the men's table, and the Boss went out and shot two plain turkeys for the house and a kangaroo for the camp, and several hens were sacrificed.

Olive had picked the three red Christmas lilies that still survived to decorate the dining-room table, with a few grey-green branches of athol tree. They exchanged presents in the morning, things ordered months before from catalogues. The last mail had brought parcels from Jim's sisters and from Alix's parents, which one of the black stockmen riding down with a pack-horse had brought back.

Before midday on Christmas Day, the blacks came up from the camp by invitation to where "lolly-water" and boiled sweets had been set out on the trestle-table for the children; and little parcels of bright ribbons and beads for the women and tobacco and gay neckerchiefs for the men were handed out. Lucy and Jenny each received a small bottle of perfume, violet and lavender. Alix had sewn them each a dilly-bag of coloured cotton with a draw-string at the top in which to carry their treasures, like the "pretty smell belonga me," as Lucy referred to her scent bottle.

Old Johnnie was there with Merna, quite recovered. She had brought Alix a necklace made of seeds from the quondong, or native peach, seeds as naturally round as a bead. The old men she had treated came up to Alix and pressed her hand. Wondan, without crutches but hobbling a little, gave her a small black-and-white-striped tail-feather from a zebra finch.

Rather to Alix's surprise, her mother-in-law gave her a beautiful scarf of Indian silk—perhaps bought from the Indian hawkers who had called here earlier.

"I've had a lovely Christmas!" said Alix that night, and Jim said, "Tomorrow I'll take you for that swim I promised you."

She read him Frances MacFarlane's Christmas letter, which informed Alix that her father was very busy as he was in charge of the recruiting office in Adelaide. "There is no conscription," she wrote. "Young men are anxious to serve their King and country, and go to the help of little Belgium." But the Major added a note that it would be all over in a few months.

Big Jim's Christmas present was a litter of six cattle-pups one of the blue heeler bitches had produced. She was given a box with straw in the harness-room, where she lay panting with the heat while the pups clambered over her. The Boss, going in to have a look how they were progressing, was surprised to find only four pups. Could she have eaten the other two? Poor old Tess couldn't count; she didn't seem to miss them. The four were growing apace, their little bellies tight as drums with milk.

Wing Lee, who was a great improvement on the dour Leavin' Soon, surpassed himself with some delectable meat pies with light pastry made from the new stores of flour; he was also a wizard at suet dumplings. The pies appeared a second time—he must have kept some left-over veal from the men's Christmas dinner.

When no more were forthcoming, Olive thought she would compliment him by asking when they might expect some more of "those delicious pies—very good, very tasty."

Wing Lee turned from kneading the bread dough, and said with a smile:

"Ah, Missee! Wing Lee no can make more pie. Yesterday there plenty puppy—now the puppy he all gone!"

Olive gave a shriek and rushed out to the harness-room. Tess was anxiously licking a solitary pup; the rest were indeed "all gone."

"We'll have to get a new cook!" she wailed that night, after toying with her dinner and eating little but bread and jam and some stewed dried apricots. She had not told the others the story of the puppies until after they had eaten. But Big Jim was not worried about that—his family, after all, had eaten bush-rats and he had tried both goanna and snake when travelling in the bush. But he was angry with the cook for turning potentially valuable cattle-dogs into meat pies. Three of them had been bitches, but the other three were males, of which only one was left. "He'd better not touch that last pup," growled Big Jim.

"He won't. I gave him a talking-to he won't forget," said Olive grimly.

Indeed, she had handed out a tongue-lashing in pidgin-English while the kitchen lubras listened with wide eyes, their hands over their mouths to suppress their giggles.

"My cli'," the cook was heard to remark to them afterwards, "Missee talkee muchee, allee time, Missee talkee muchee when closs."

*　　*　　*

Jim and Alix rode over to the station waterhole for a swim in mid-afternoon, when everyone else was asleep. Jim was wearing shorts, Alix her demure neck-to-knee navy-blue swimming costume with white trim round the neck and sleeves, under a divided skirt of grey linen.

The milky turquoise of the water looked inviting between its banks of red sand and patches of floating duckweed. There were water-lily leaves on the surface, but Jim said the flowers would not be out till the next fresh came down: frail blue cups with gold stamens, spread over the water like a floral carpet.

It was an ideal swimming place, shaded by drooping coolabahs, with a sloping sandy bottom that had been cleared of snags. Alix wondered why she had not come for a swim on her own before this; she would, now that Jim had shown her the way to skirt the big sand-hill instead of climbing over the top.

She was better at swimming than she was at riding. She showed off a little, striking out strongly across the deepest part, daring Jim to follow her. He caught up with her and kissed her, and as they sank together kissed her under water. Alix surfaced, laughing, and began racing him to the bank.

He caught her in the shallows. "You don't need this silly costume," he said, pulling off the navy pants and then the top with its short sleeves. The wet jersey material clung like a second skin.

"Just like skinning a rabbit," said Jim.

"Thanks very much!"

"But the result is different. Whoever saw a rabbit with these beautiful pointed breasts?"

They made love in the shallows, half in and half out of the water, a perfect union that left them flooded with peace and well-being.

"Like a water-lubra," he murmured, sliding down to nuzzle between her wet thighs. "If only you had long dark hair, I would think I'd caught a water-lubra."

"What's that?" she asked drowsily.

"I think they're daughters of the Rainbow Serpent, or something. It's very dangerous to catch one. And if you take her anywhere near water, she'll slip away and dive in and you'll never see her again."

"I wouldn't. I'd never want to leave you."

They rode back to the homestead as the sun was setting, sending their shadows stretching like giants' across the sand. Alix felt in love all over again. And she had a strange feeling, almost a certainty, that she'd just conceived a son on the banks of the Diamantina.

In the new year the whole camp went walkabout. This meant the house lubras too, Jenny and Lucy, and all the Aboriginal stockmen. They would come back in two or three weeks, refreshed by their sojourn in the bush, but reminded too of how pleasant it was to have meat and bread provided, without the long process of food-gathering, hunting, digging for yams, and winnowing the nardoo seeds to grind up for flour between two stones. But the freedom, the change of place, and the bush tucker did them good.

"It's very inconvenient," sighed Olive, "but we have to put up with it. They have this need to wander sometimes, and it's only once or twice a year."

CHAPTER TWENTY-SEVEN

Since she would soon be going away, and she could not very well go and leave the station without a cook, Olive decided to overlook the unfortunate business of the puppy pies. Wing Lee was a good cook, with a light hand in bread-making, dumplings, and johnny-cakes. (Johnny-cakes were a variation on damper, but the dough was fried in small pieces instead of being baked. They made a pleasant change for breakfast.)

The station hands, who always grumbled on principle about the standard of cooking, were more content. Their old joke, "Who called the cook a bastard?" the reply being "Who called the bastard a cook?" was laid to rest.

In late March, with the weather noticeably cooler in the evenings, young Jim left in the buggy with two horses to drive his mother over the mail-route, covered by a mailman with pack-horse every two weeks, to Windorah. From there she would take the mail coach to Longreach, and then go by rail to Rockhampton and Brisbane. In case of sudden rains, or a dozen other possibilities, the buggy was stocked up with food and plenty of drinking water. The horses would have to be spelled at Betoota, where there was a hotel of sorts. At Windorah on Cooper's Creek, Jim would spell the horses again before making the long journey back by easy stages to Cappamerri.

Alix felt a lightening in the atmosphere at her mother-in-law's departure. Since Big Jim's tongue had been unloosed in telling her about his pioneer family, she found it easier to talk to him. She sometimes discussed dinner menus with Wing Lee; although his English left much to be desired, he was always affable and smiling, and did not intimidate her as the late cook had done.

Wing Lee was a moon-faced, cheerful little man whose eyes almost disappeared in his fat cheeks when he smiled. He got on well with the kitchen lubra and the housemaid. But with the Missus gone, Jenny began to put on airs, and was often cheeky. Alix longed to give her a piece of her mind, but refrained; the household was not hers, and Big Jim Manning might back Jenny if it came to a show-down. It was she, Alix, who was the newcomer.

She missed Jim. He was away for more than two weeks, and as the full

188

moon returned, flooding the sky with yellow light as it rose, she sat on the veranda thinking of him.

One reason why Alix longed to see Jim was that she believed she had some good news for him. She had missed one period, and when the next one failed to make its appearance she felt fairly certain that she was pregnant. She stopped riding over to the waterhole for a swim. She must look after herself and the heir of the Mannings. As Jim was the only boy, her son would surely inherit the station. That is, she thought, if the drought breaks and it isn't taken over by the bank. For the first time she felt a personal involvement with Cappamerri. Mannings had been here for three generations! Her children and Jim's would be the fourth.

"Gosh, darling! Are you sure?" Jim held his left arm round her as they sat on the bed. He tentatively felt her belly with the other hand.

"There's nothing there to feel yet. But I'm as sure as I can be without a medical examination. Already my skirts are getting tight around the waist. And I've been feeling a bit nauseated in the mornings."

"Well! Won't Dad be delighted. He's been wanting a grandson to carry on his name."

"And if it's a girl?"

"Well, we can have a boy next time."

"I'd rather not tell your father yet, if you don't mind."

"No, that's fine. I'm going to be walking round with a big grin on my face, but. You'll have to go south in plenty of time to have it. How long before it's due?"

"Oh, ages yet. Probably about next October, the first week."

"We'll make a trip down to Adelaide."

Long before then, and while Olive Manning was still away, there occurred a crisis that called for all of Alix's nursing skills.

Big Jim had ridden out on his own one morning, taking the rifle and saying he was going to get a kangaroo and perhaps a couple of turkeys for the larder.

"I'll probably camp over at Wiluna Bore," he told Jim, "and get a shot when they come in to drink this evening, or early tomorrow morning."

When he had not returned by the following evening, young Jim looked a little worried. "The Old Man has probably stopped to shoot and burn some bogged cattle. He'll be back tomorrow," he reassured himself.

But when there was no sign of Big Jim the next day, Jim sought out the best black trackers, Micky and Quartpot, and three of the men to help him search—a party of six, the Aborigines on foot. It was fifteen miles to the bore. The trackers indicated that the Boss had ridden this way, but there were no tracks coming back. After several more miles Micky stopped and called to Quartpot, meanwhile scratching his head and pointing to the ground.

189

"What name?" he asked.

"Might-it dead kangaroo—Boss pull-im along?"

"No-more. This one"—he pointed to a smaller indentation beside the large one—"boot-heel. This one might-be stick."

The men followed the trackers back the way they had come, but deviating off to the left from the old tracks. Then in the softer sand they too could see the drag-marks of a large body being pulled over the ground.

Micky and Quartpot started running, following the well-marked trail, and suddenly threw up their arms with a loud "Yakkai!" Under the meagre shade of a straggling mulga, they had seen the figure of the Boss, supine on the sand.

His leg was broken above the knee, and he had strapped his rifle along it with his belt as a makeshift splint. The leg was swollen and contused, and Big Jim was feverish and dehydrated. Jim lifted his head and gave him a drink from the canvas water-bag. He swallowed with difficulty through his cracked and blackened lips.

"Came off . . . Pilot," he muttered. "Broke m' leg. No water. About ten miles back." He waved a feeble arm towards the direction of the bore.

He had dragged himself on his backside, over stones and through sand and prickles, pushing himself along with the rifle, and then when the leg became too painful, using it as a splint.

"Don't try to talk any more," said Jim, holding his father tenderly. "We'll get you home as soon as we can. Wonder Pilot didn't come back, and we'd have known you were in trouble."

"P'raps—he's hurt. Or gone off with the mob of brumbies."

"He might be at the bore. Did he toss you?"

"He fell . . . and I banged . . . leg on rock."

"It's a nasty fracture, bone's come through the skin. Alix will know what to do."

Jim had sent two men home for a stretcher; it would be too painful for Big Jim to be carried on horseback. They were not five miles from the station. Big Jim had dragged himself two-thirds of the way. "I'd have come on at night, after a rest," he said later, "and got back under my own steam. You can't keep a good man down."

Alix was horrified at the state of the leg, with puffy, purple flesh, and blackened blood around the wound where the bone had come through the flesh. She could get the fever down with aspirin and sponging, and the dehydration was responding to frequent small drinks. But she had no ether, no anaesthetic to give the patient while she set the bone.

Then she remembered the small ampoule of morphia which she had taken out of the hostel stores and carried with her on her journeys off the beaten track, in case of just such an emergency as this. It was still packed at the bottom of her first-aid kit.

190

After she had cut away the moleskin trousers and irrigated the wound, she fetched a syringe and injected the morphia. Big Jim's features relaxed, the lines of pain went out of his forehead, and he stopped clenching his teeth.

Jim had fashioned a splint of wood and torn up a sheet for bandages. Alix clenched her own teeth as she straightened the leg, and heard bone grate against bone. Big Jim bit his lip, but said steadily, "It's all right, Alix. I can take it."

"If there's any plaster of Paris, I'll make you a cast later on," she said. "For now you will have to stay in bed and keep still. As the skin is broken, the leg is likely to be infected; I'll have to put clean dressings on it."

"You're a good lass," he said, his voice far away as he floated on the wave of morphia.

"You should have a doctor, but I've done what I can. Now see if you can get some sleep. You're still suffering from shock."

Big Jim Manning, who had an iron constitution, made a good recovery, "thanks to Alix's good nursing," as he said. But it was to be a frustrating four months before he could walk or ride.

Olive came home, looking almost happy. She announced that Marjory had a son and she was calling him James Manning Bristow, her married name. Olive could not stop singing the praises of her new grandson. He was, apparently, the most handsome, the cleverest, most adorable baby that ever was born. She showed restrained pleasure at Alix's news—by now her condition was becoming obvious—but Big Jim was delighted that the next grandchild would bear his surname. He treated Alix like a heroine. No one thought it might be a girl.

Jim felt he could not leave the property for long until his father had fully recovered. This meant that Alix would have to go to Adelaide alone to have the baby. He would drive her to Birdsville to catch the mail-run with Wal Crombie.

Alix did not want to go away from Jim, on the long journey of nearly a thousand miles and a separation of months; but though she might have had her lying-in at Birdsville or Hergott Springs, she had seen too much of what could go wrong in childbirth to take the risk of not having a doctor handy. If John Flynn's Mantle of Safety had been spread over the inland, she might have had the baby at home without any qualms. She was young and healthy and there was no reason to expect complications, but she was taking no chances. Her mother was delighted that Alix was coming down to Adelaide for the birth. Alix feared she would be mother-smothered by Frances, but she would spend the first ten days in hospital after the birth of the baby. Then she would have two months with her parents before setting off on the journey north. If the baby was delicate—well, it might be necessary to wait over December and January, perhaps stay till March, when the hottest season would be over.

She knew they would want her to spend Christmas in her old home.

Late in July, before the hot summer dust-storms returned, Alix set off on the eight-hundred-mile journey to the southern capital. Jim took the buggy in easy stages, and fussed about seeing that she rested properly and didn't get overtired. They camped out on two nights, then spent a night in the Birdsville Hotel while waiting for Wal to be ready to leave.

"You'd better write to me, or else!" she said mock-threateningly on the last morning.

"Of course I will, darling! Every mail. Well, every other mail, perhaps."

"You rat! You know I'll write to you. And I don't want any three-line postcards, either."

She sat in front of the buggy with Wal, under a canopy to keep off the sun. He treated her with exaggerated care, helping her up into the buggy and down again whenever they stopped.

"If you want a rest, just let me know," said Wal. "Won't matter if the mail's a bit late for once."

"I'm all right; I'm fine."

He spoke, diffidently, of Mab's end and said how sorry he was to have missed the funeral.

"You know, Jack McGuinnes went out to Mutoorinna. They'd heard from a camel-man what had happened, and they were terribly shocked. He wanted to confront this Luke, give him a reprimand from the Law he wouldn't forget; but it turned out the bloke had shot through—whether he had a guilty conscience, because it seems he camped out a night on the run and didn't tell the Jacksons how early he'd returned—or whether he just got itchy feet; he took his horse and a pack-horse, and said he was going to make for Coward Springs. A terrible dry track. He may've perished on the way. Serve him right if he did."

But Alix, who had come near to perishing herself, could not wish such a terrible end for anyone.

"He was young and thoughtless," she said. "It was just incomprehensible to him that anyone could come to grief in less than fifty miles on a well-marked track."

"You know, the irony of it was," said Wal, "that the dust-storm apparently came from out Strzelecki way, and missed Mutoorinna. They had no idea."

In Hergott Springs, Alix was amazed to see a motor car—a brand-new Model T Ford—parked outside the hotel.

"Who's your new police constable?" she asked as Wal threw down her swag on the hotel veranda.

"Jack's still here," he said. "He didn't get his transfer after all. He took his long-service leave, and then came back here."

"Oh!" said Alix.

When she had washed away the dust and sweat of the track, and had had a good night's sleep, her first visit in the morning was to the hostel. The same two Sisters were there and gave her a warm welcome. They sat in the little living-room with the cane chairs and the cool green cushions.

"Have you seen Jack?" asked Sister Adams.

"No, he doesn't know I'm passing through."

"But we must tell him you're here!"

And the part-Aboriginal girl who came in to do the hospital laundry was sent over to the police station with a message.

Alix tried to swallow some now-tasteless cake, and gulped some tea. Then there was a heavy step on the veranda, and in came Jack McGuinnes, ducking his tall frame through the door and removing his khaki hat as he did so.

Alix, in spite of her heavy body, got to her feet.

"Jack!"

"Well, Alix. This is a surprise." She saw his eyes take in her condition, and the sudden constriction of his smile. Impulsively she went up to him and kissed him on the cheek.

"I didn't know you were still here, or I'd have let you know."

"Yes, I didn't go to the Alice after all. Seemed no point, really. And it meant transferring to the Commonwealth Police."

He sat down and accepted a cup of tea. As he drank and set the cup down, it rattled slightly in the saucer. He got up and set cup and saucer down carefully on the small bamboo table.

"I see you haven't got one of these new automobiles yet," said Alix brightly. "Have you driven one?"

"Yes, for short runs. But camels are best for the sand-hill country. Wal still swears by his horse-team, but I bet he'll end up with a motor-truck." He added, "Are you catching today's 'Ghan? I'll drive you to the station if you like. The pub-keeper will lend me his car."

"That would be a help."

Before the train went, he drove her out to visit Mab's grave. The bare, lonely cemetery, well outside the town, was depressing; she felt it was not much better to have brought Mab to this desolate spot than to have left her out among the sand-hills of the Frome. How she would have loved telling Mab about the baby! But her friend was gone into an eternal silence.

On the way back to town, Jack said, "I don't need to ask you if you're happy. . . . When's the baby due?"

"End of September or early October. I'm going down to my parents for the birth. Jim wouldn't let me risk having it up here." (Indeed, she didn't want to risk it herself.) "Did you get to Adelaide on leave?"

"Yes, but I'd already had your letter."

She put her hand over his on the wheel. "Jack, I'm sorry."

"It's all right. I'll get over it."

Jack drove her to the station to put her aboard the 'Ghan at midday, with many admonitions about looking after herself and not trying to lift heavy bags. She had a sleeping berth to herself all the way to Port Augusta.

It was time for the train to leave. He still sat beside her holding her hand.

"You must get down, you'll be carried away," said Alix, as doors slammed and the guard's whistle sounded. Jack smiled crookedly, as if to say he wouldn't mind if he were. The train started to move. He kissed her on the lips, then opened the compartment door and jumped out, running a few steps along the platform to keep his balance. He went on waving his big hat until he was out of sight.

Chapter Twenty-eight

Alix was surprised to be called for at the Adelaide Railway Station by Major MacFarlane driving a gleaming new Hupmobile.

"Everyone's getting motor cars now," said her father, looking self-satisfied. Indeed, there were almost as many automobiles in the city as horse-drawn vehicles, many of them Model T Fords, reliable, if not much to look at.

"Can I learn to drive the car?" asked Alix.

"I've no doubt you *can*. I'm not sure that you should, in your condition."

"Certainly she should not," said Frances firmly.

"But Mother! It's another six weeks, at least. It couldn't possibly hurt the baby."

"Nevertheless, motor-cars are not entirely safe."

Frances wore a wide-brimmed straw hat swathed in a chiffon veil that tied beneath the chin, both to keep the hat on her head in the supposedly fast-flowing air of their motion, and to protect her complexion. "It is called a motoring-veil," she explained.

"You are looking well," she added grudgingly, "in spite of the conditions under which you've been living—"

"The station homestead is very comfortable, Mother. We have a cook, a housemaid, and a kitchen maid. I had to learn to bake bread at one stage, when we were without a cook, but I enjoyed it. And you know I am used to the heat."

The war news dominated everything else, as Alix found in the next weeks. At Cappamerri they had been insulated from the daily bulletins from the front, the endless lists of casualties, dead or wounded or missing.

Some of the men she had known in what she now thought of as her youth would never return. The Great War suddenly had become real.

Her father was deeply involved with recruiting of volunteers and her mother in what was known as "the War effort"; she had joined the Red Cross organization and rolled bandages and made up comfort parcels for the troops. Though she was no knitter, she managed to turn out some rather shapeless hand-knitted socks in khaki wool. She organized fund-raising teas. Frances, in fact, was rather enjoying the war. And her

195

husband, safely preserved by his age, was enthusiastically sending young men into the carnage.

The disastrous attempt by Australian and New Zealand infantry to storm the heights of the Gallipoli Peninsula had failed a second time on August 8. Terrible reports were still coming through of the Anzacs, who were cut to pieces by the crossfire from entrenched Turkish troops at Lone Pine and Hill 60. Patriotic feeling ran high, for stories of great bravery and daring skirmishes were being published every day. And still the casualty lists grew. Alix found herself rolling bandages and writing little notes of encouragement to go in the Red Cross parcels.

In Rundle Street one day she was looking in Balfour's cake-shop window, when she saw some Berlin buns. She suddenly had a craving to taste them again. She went in and said, "Two Berlin buns, please."

"Eh?" said the girl behind the counter, staring. "They're not called that any more. You mean Kitchener buns."

They tasted just as delicious as Alix remembered them, whatever they might be called. She supposed it would rather stick in the throat of a patriotic Australian to eat a bun named after the enemy capital. How Lord Kitchener might react to being commemorated by a doughnut was another matter.

Caroline MacFarlane Manning was born on the last day of September 1915, at a small private hospital that specialized in midwifery cases. It was a normal birth in every way; though Alix, knowing how many things could go wrong, had worried right up to the time when her labour pains began. Then suddenly she felt nothing but excitement, and curiosity to see the infant she had been carrying for so long, the mysterious stranger fed by her blood.

When they brought her the little bundle with a wizened face and a wisp of dark hair at one end, she unwrapped it reverently and counted the perfect little toes and fingers, the frail pink shells of the nails. As she touched a tiny furled hand, it unclenched and closed around her finger. My daughter! she thought with emotion. It was only later that she thought, "Our daughter." She had felt like the initiate of some old order to which only women were admitted: Caroline was one more link in the chain of life that went back to Eve and the birth of the first girl-baby. She forgot she had wanted a son.

Her father sent a wire via Hergott Springs, though by the time it had travelled up the Birdsville Track and been taken by the mailman to the Cappamerri mailbox, and called for by a station hand, it would be hardly any quicker than a letter would have been. Alix wrote from hospital to Jim. They had discussed names before she left; she had agreed to the name of James, if a boy, and had had some arguments with Jim over the name Caroline for a girl.

"It was my grandmother's name on my father's side," she had explained.

"I've always liked it, though I believe Gran was called 'Carrie.' I don't like that very much."

"Neither do I." Jim had thought for a while, and then suggested, "We could call her 'Caro' for short; I like the sound of it."

So they had agreed, and as soon as she went home from hospital Alix began instructing her mother not to call the baby Carrie or Caroline, but Caro. But she was christened Caroline. Alix knew that Jim did not mind if it was a boy or a girl, but no doubt his parents would be disappointed. If Caro eventually married, her sons would not be Mannings.

A letter came from Jim at last, a whole page of exclamations and endearments and congratulations. Olive had enclosed a few lines in Jim's letter. Mr. Manning had slipped a ten-pound note inside the envelope, with the words: "Good girl, buy something for yourself and baby."

Her own parents doted on Caro, their first grandchild. And of course she was a most beautiful baby, thought Alix, as the dark wisps of hair fell out, to be replaced by a fine cap of fair hair, soft as thistle-down.

Jim wrote again at Christmas, to say that they were having an unusual summer, grey skies and numerous thunderstorms. There was said to be some feed coming up on the Birdsville Track, and things were looking up at Cappamerri.

He might bring 500 head of cattle down to the railway at Hergott, and travel home with her in February. She must let him know in plenty of time when she was leaving.

"I can't wait to see you again, not to mention meeting our daughter. If she's anything like you, she must be lovely."

Laden with gifts for the baby, Alix set off in early February—almost six months after she had left the station—when Caro was just over four months old. She was a bonny, healthy baby and Alix felt no fears about the trip. Her mother was full of dire forebodings: the baby would be dehydrated by the heat, or drowned in a flood; either way it was madness to take so young a child on such a trip to the back of beyond.

Alix had met these objections with firmness: the child was going home to her father; she had been away too long already.

She took a bassinet and a pile of clean napkins in the train, and fed Caro from the breast every few hours. They both slept well as the little 'Ghan swayed and rocked its way north. Four years since she had travelled this way with Mab! She remembered their youthful excitement as they set off on the new adventure together.

When the train pulled in at the open platform at Hergott Springs, there was Jim waiting, lean and brown and with his light-blue eyes dancing with joy at her return. He folded them both in a great hug. But Caro screwed up her face and thrust out her pink bottom lip at this stranger. It was some time before she accepted that Jim was part of the family.

The Sisters at the hostel, nearing the end of their two-year stint, which had begun when Alix left for the south, made much of the baby Caro. The younger, Sister Henley, her complexion sallow from the heat but her hair pretty and abundant beneath her cap, told Alix shyly that she was engaged to be married when her term finished.

"She's engaged to the Constable, Jack McGuinnes," said Sister Adams with a smile.

"Oh! I do hope you'll be very happy. He's a fine man."

"Yes, I know."

"What a pity! He's out on patrol at present," said Sister Adams. "He'll be sorry he missed you. He is getting a transfer to Innamincka, on Cooper's Creek."

"We-ell . . . Give him my very best wishes for his happiness."

Alix felt a slight pang that her faithful admirer had consoled himself with someone else. Of course she was glad for him, she told herself sharply. And his wife-to-be was a pleasant, sensible girl.

She hadn't told Jim of her meeting with Jack four or five months ago, when he'd shown that he still cared. Now there seemed no point in telling him. It was over and done with.

Jim had already watered and hand-fed his stock at the Springs, had them checked by the Police Constable before he left, and sent them south in a cattle-train. He told her they had not been exactly "fats" after their trip down the Birdsville Track, but they were "in quite good nick."

Jim had brought the buggy along beside the dray, getting one of the station hands to drive while he rode behind the cattle with the men. Now Jim transferred to the buggy, lifting Alix and the baby in with exaggerated care. Alix greeted the two Aboriginal stockmen, Micky and Jarry, and the two drovers, Paddy the Gob and Bob the Bushrat, who were always addressed by the others by their nicknames.

So it was in convoy that they travelled up the Track and through the Channel Country, introducing Caro to her new home. She slept a great deal in her bassinet on the buggy floor, and though the days were hot, the nights were cool. There was saltbush and bright-flowering parakilya, even some grass along the Track, although it was patchy, following the scattered thunderstorms of the last months. The men had a last fling at the Birdsville Hotel, where Alix and Jim and the baby stayed for the night "in *comparative* comfort," as Jim put it.

"You know, I believe I prefer camping out," said Alix, in their dark little room at the hotel. "There's nothing like sleeping under the stars, even with dingoes howling all round."

"Ah, we'll make a bushwoman of you yet," said Jim. "I was going to suggest that you ride all the way, but then I remembered Caro. We'll have to teach her to ride as soon as she can walk."

"Jim—do you wish we'd had a son?"

"Not a bit. I think she's absolutely beautiful. Mum will think so too."

Once they were across the channel of the Diamantina, Alix asked to be allowed to drive. Jim thankfully went back to his horse, a stock-horse which he said was "as clever as paint", and unrivalled in cutting out a beast from a mob.

Within the borders of Cappamerri, though the Diamantina was not flowing, there was evidence of scattered rainfall in several areas.

"But the drought hasn't broken yet," said Jim. "Of course the Old Man wants to stock up at once, while cattle prices are still low, but I persuaded him to wait. The bit of feed that's come up will keep our present stock going, but if that's eaten out they'll be starving again."

At the homestead there was a great welcome from the blacks, who had been missing Alix's ministrations. Children and old people came streaming up from the camp as soon as they saw the dust of the party approaching, to see the "new-feller piccaninny belong Young Missus."

Jim had driven the last few miles, as Caro was awake and Alix held her in her arms. It was too hot for a shawl. The baby wore nothing but a napkin and a short dress of lace-trimmed white madapollam, and a little lace bonnet to match. There were exclamations of wonder and admiration from the assembled blacks. Jim took the baby from Alix and held her high to be admired. Then they went through the gate of the garden enclosure and up the two steps to the front veranda, where Olive was waiting.

Mrs. Manning kissed Alix and accepted the baby into her arms, but her welcome was lukewarm. The reason was obvious—Caro was not a boy. At least, thought Alix, she wouldn't have to worry about Grandma spoiling her—which had led to some sharp words between Alix and her mother in Adelaide.

Caro was a bit unsure of all these strange people; there had been so many changes in her young life. But she suffered her grandfather to take her on his knee and bounce her up and down in an expert way. Alix thanked him for his generous gift, and brought out the hand-crocheted cream silk shawl, with an intricate pattern and a long silk fringe, which she had bought for Caro with the ten pounds. By now Caro accepted Jim as her father, and would put her arms up to him when she caught sight of him. He was a doting father. Between them, he and her father-in-law made Alix feel like someone special in producing a little Manning. She had plenty of milk—she would have had enough for twins—and Caro thrived and grew fat.

Totally absorbed with the baby, Alix rather neglected her clinic. Even though Caro slept a good deal, her mother hovered about the crib, moving it to the shady side of the house, making sure the mosquito- and fly-net was secure, and draping wet cloths over it when the temperature was high. There were no more thunderstorms; the sun burned from a clear

199

blue sky or was hazed with the dust of hot north winds. Wearing nothing but a napkin pinned around her chubby bottom, Caro crawled everywhere on the polished floors. By barricading the front and back steps, Alix made a big play-pen from the wide verandas. But she kept an eye on the baby at all times. The price of safety, she knew, was eternal vigilance.

CHAPTER TWENTY-NINE

Soon after Alix's return, the long drought broke in the far north. The first they knew of it on Cappamerri was when a swirling red flood came down the channels of the Diamantina. Some cattle farther down the river would probably be drowned, but most of them were on higher ground, in the sand-hills and gibber plains of the back country.

The Boss and Jim were jubilant, though Big Jim said, "I told you so! We should have stocked up earlier. Now the price of cattle will go sky-high."

The flood, bearing dead trees and brushwood on its crest, rose steadily; the waterholes disappeared in the swollen river. Still there was no rain. From far up beyond Kynuna, in north-west Queensland, the rain that had fallen over a vast area of the north came flowing down towards the basin of Lake Eyre, which was lower than sea-level.

A last trip down to the mailbox was made before the track became impassable. There was a note from the mailman saying that the track at Betoota was already cut, and he was hurrying back to get over the Diamantina at Birdsville.

"So we are completely cut off, then? No mail, no stores . . ." said Alix.

"That's right. Just as well we're self-sufficient, eh? It won't get as far as Lake Eyre, but. The country's so dry, even the river beds are so parched, that half the water will just soak into the ground. And of course there's a great rate of evaporation out here."

Leaving Caro with Lucy, Alix rode over to the highest sand-hill, her horse up to its fetlocks in muddy water, to see the extent of the flood. The river had overflowed the shallow banks of its many channels, and spread over miles of flat low-lying gibber plains.

Alix gasped at the great sea of shallow water over the run, with the sand-hills sticking up like long, low islands. The cattle had all made for higher ground; though in the first week some bloated bodies came floating down with the current—beasts that had been grazing in one of the river channels and had been caught by the sudden rising of the water.

It took weeks for the floodwaters to go down, till the river was flowing once more within its banks, clearing debris from the waterholes and washing away the floating duckweed, which was beginning to choke the swimming-hole. Since no rain had fallen to replenish the underground rain-water tank, the rather muddy river water was pumped to the house —dead cattle notwithstanding. Alix, who had come to like billy tea, now drank tea with every meal like the others. She did not fancy the murky liquid in the water-bag, and she boiled all Caro's drinking water.

As soon as the water went down, a green film of new growth spread in all the depressions; perennial saltbush flourished among the gibbers, covering the bare stony plain till it looked like a field under crops. The new river silt made long, waving grass grow in the clay-pans, and yellow and white daisies began to flower, living their full life cycle in a few weeks so that they might set seed for the next generation of plants. Their seeds could lie dormant for years, till water returned to the soil.

A busy time followed for the Boss, young Jim, and the men. With plenty of feed the cattle no longer congregated round the bores. As there were no fences, they spread over hundreds of miles of open country; mustering and counting stock meant weeks out on the run, at distant outstations and cattle-camps. Beasts that had become hopelessly bogged in the drying depressions, some with their eyes picked out by crows, had to be shot.

Before the country had completely dried out, a low-pressure system, blocked by a high to the east of Australia, was held up over the centre; clouds built up, the atmosphere became unstable, and the result was five inches of rain. Rain! They all rushed outside to bathe in it, raising their faces to the warm drops, laughing with exultation. It was the first real rain in five years.

George, the pet cockatoo, became excited by the rain and danced up and down, flapping his wings, in a puddle just outside the garden enclosure. His pale-rose breast was soon covered in red mud. Then he flew up on the roof and let the rain wash him clean again, while uttering loud self-satisfied squawks.

"Looks as if I'll have to send some rainfall reports in at last," said Big Jim, beaming as he came back from checking the rain gauge. "I knew the drought had to end before long."

Within a week the whole countryside had changed its colour from red to green. The lower slopes of the sand-hills were first veiled with a wash of green; a few days more and the growth was dense and several inches high.

With the rain came hordes of flies and mosquitoes. Alix, worried about the spread of dysentery by the flies, lectured Lucy on how the food should be kept covered: the milk-jug with a mosquito-net circle edged with beads to hold it down; cooked meat and custards to be covered at once with fly-wire meat-covers or cloths.

"Now, fly properly cheeky-feller," she told Lucy. "Make-em all-about sick longa stomach. That one fly sit down longa dung-heap or might-be another dirty place, then come inside, sit-down longa tucker. Suppose people eat-em tucker, they get properly sick. Might-be close-up finish altogether. Understand?"

"Yair, Missus. Fly prop'ly dirty-bugger. Me kill-em dead."

"All right; but see you cover custard soon as him cooked."

Spiders and centipedes swarmed after the rain, and big black and yellow wasps preyed on the spiders, paralyzing them, then walling them up in mud-houses under the veranda roofs in which the wasps laid their eggs: a living larder for when the eggs should hatch.

Sand-hills burgeoning with flowers, and orange-and-black butterflies, were a more welcome result of the rain. There were clumps of bluebells the colour of the sky, floating on hairlike stems; wild geraniums and tufts of creamy-white candytuft and pale-pink convolvulus, which Olive called blushing bindweed. The depressions in the sand-hills were like flower-bowls filled with white-and-gold everlasting daisies and yellow soldier's buttons. The bushes of acacia and tecoma and neddlewood bloomed in varying shades of yellow all the brighter for the contrast of the deep-blue sky. Alix wished she could paint it, capture all that beauty and colour before it faded.

"I'm glad you've seen the place in a good season," said Jim. "You're seeing it at its best. If only we could count on a good season coming more often!"

With the return of herbage and the refilling of waterholes, wildlife multiplied. Big mobs of kangaroos, and parties of seven or eight emus were seen close to the homestead. Many of the does carried joeys in their pouches, from which a head or a leg might protrude as the mother hopped along, feeding. Big Jim complained that the kangaroos would eat out all the new feed; they bred with great rapidity after the rain because the does had the ability to store fertilized eggs during a drought, and release them one by one into the uterus after rain. The black men went hunting, and the camp ate well.

Great flocks of budgerigars flew overhead in green clouds, black swans and pelicans arrived at the home waterholes as soon as the floods subsided, black duck flew in and the trees flowered with Major Mitchell cockatoos and white corellas.

The drought that had depleted the herds had created a demand for fat cattle, with prices soaring. So as soon as they had put on condition, a mob was rounded up and sent off to the railway at Hergott Springs. A few days were spent going over camp gear, mending and making hobbles and plaiting greenhide into long whips. Then the droving party set off for two months "on the track."

Since Alix and Caro had returned from Adelaide, Major MacFarlane, horrified at Alix's ignorance of the Great War, had begun sending newspapers every fortnight full of patriotic fervour and gloomy dispatches from the front. Jim read these and became increasingly thoughtful. Major MacFarlane wrote that enlistments had fallen off to such an extent in 1916 that the government was thinking of introducing conscription. (A referendum was put to the people later, but conscription was voted out.)

News came through of the terrible blood-baths on the Somme, for the Australian Imperial Force was now fighting in France. It was another Gallipoli—a blunder by the British generals, and the loss of 5,500 Australian soldiers and officers in one night. Recruits were needed urgently to fill the depleted ranks.

"I don't know; a man ought to be in it," said Jim.

Alix looked at him in horror. "But not you," she said. "You're a primary producer, and someone has to stay home to produce the meat for the bully-beef to send the troops. You're doing your bit."

"I suppose so," said Jim with a sigh. "All the same—a free trip overseas, no worries or decisions, just taking orders . . ."

"Yes, orders to march into a hail of machine-gun bullets and get yourself killed. I don't want to be the widow of a war hero."

She became so uneasy that she tried to hide the papers that came with the mail if Jim was out on the run at the time. Another mob of fifteen hundred head was being readied for a drove down the Birdsville Track. Jim would be away for about eight or nine weeks. Alix said goodbye to him with a feeling of foreboding.

He returned looking sun-browned and fit. The rain had laid the dust and the journey had been "like a picnic", he claimed. He brought with him a recent magazine given him by the new Sisters at the hostel.

He showed Alix the pictures, some blurred like amateur snapshots, of men casually clad in flannel shirts and riding trousers, sitting about drinking tea in the desert; of a long line of mounted soldiers moving along a desolate track; and a close-up of four men smartly dressed in riding trousers, leather leggings, belted tunics, and felt hats turned up at the side with a bunch of emu feathers.

"The Australian Light Horse!" said Jim proudly. "I didn't realize they were over there, fighting the Turk in Egypt. Apparently they're nearly all from the bush, could all ride before they joined up. Some even took their own horses with them."

"And their horses will probably be shot, or blown up. It's not fair to animals to take them into war."

"There have always been horses in warfare," said Jim impatiently. "What about the Charge of the Light Brigade?"

"And that was a piece of folly and needless sacrifice."

"But what a great feeling to have been in it! Listen to this." And he read out an account of the approach to Romani, where the Seventh Light Horse had successfully routed the Turks:

"Dawn came with a crimson sky. From a ridge we gazed behind at a grand sight all lit up in pink and grey and khaki, stretching right back past the redoubts of Dueidar, a winding column of New Zealand and Australian mounted troops.

"We laughed with the exhilaration that disciplined comradeship brings, then rode towards the boom of guns. . . .

"We watered our horses at an oasis and moved off again, whistling and singing, laughing and joking, the horses pulling at their bits, seemingly careless of the fierce desert heat. . . . All in our shirt sleeves except the officers, all hardy, eager, fighting men. . . ."

"It must be a grand feeling," said Jim wistfully.

"I would say that was written by a very young man. I wonder if he is still alive."

She had tried to keep the hostility out of her voice, but Jim put the magazine away and did not refer to the article again.

CHAPTER THIRTY

By September of 1916, with stock being depleted not by drought but by sales at good prices, Cappamerri Station was out of the red. Big Jim wanted to attend the sales in the south, hoping to pick up some year-lings and rail them up to Hergott. The droving teams could take advant-age of the unusually good season to take them north along the Birdsville Track.

Jim volunteered to make the trip for him, since Alix wanted to take the baby down to Adelaide for the hot summer months, and her parents wished to see Caro before she grew too much older. He would stay a couple of months himself, as things were so much better that the station could afford to employ a bookkeeper and some more station hands, making the workload less for his father.

Alix had been conscious of her mother-in-law's irritation when Caro cried or played up at meals; this made Alix over-anxious for her to be good, and the baby sensed it and played up even more. She had started to walk, with a determined plodding gait, but every few steps ended in a sudden thump on to her bottom. Unless she happened to hit her head as well, on door or table-leg, Caro never cried when she fell over.

She had begun to discover gravity; she threw her drinking-cup on the floor and watched with interest as it shattered on the stone flags; she pulled Olive's vases and knick-knacks out of the shelves, laughed when she pushed a tower of blocks and watched them fall. Jim would patiently build the tower again, over and over, and Caro never tired of this game, which gave her a sense of power.

Alix couldn't help being a doting mother. Caro was so beautiful, with her rosy cheeks and straight, silky fair hair, her large grey eyes with their wide black pupils and curling lashes, her brows like a fine brush-mark above them. By temperament she seemed to be good-natured but deter-mined on her own way; usually with a sunny smile, but occasionally with rages, when she screamed with frustration and her little face went scarlet to the roots of her hair.

Jim doted on her too, except when she woke him after a long day's work. Alix had made a habit of giving her the breast to keep her quiet, but when she was weaned this had to stop; Alix wasn't going to warm milk mixtures in the middle of the night. After a while Caro settled down to the new routine and slept through till 6 A.M., when everyone was awake anyway.

Alix remembered how she had quarrelled with her mother for picking Caro up from her pram whenever she cried. She had to admit that she had done a bit of spoiling herself for the sake of peace. Lucy adored the baby. She would carry "Little Missie" round on her ample hip; Caro appreciated the comfort after her mother's rather bony frame.

Lucy was the only one who cried when they left. Olive kissed the baby goodbye with more enthusiasm than she had shown on her arrival.

Back in Adelaide Alix rather enjoyed being fussed over by her mother, and having a willing baby-sitter at all hours. She and Jim were able to go out to dinner and to the pictures, a rare treat. They laughed at the Keystone Cops, and a new comic actor called Charlie Chaplin. But what Jim liked best was the enormous *The Birth of a Nation*, a long, vivid film of the American Civil War. There had never been a film quite like it before. Australians, deeply involved in the war in Europe, flocked to see it.

Major MacFarlane was gloomy about the war. The news from France was devastating. In August and September there were 43,000 Australian casualties on the Somme, on what was called "the Western Front." The entire population of Australia was less than five million.

Many were invalided out with gas gangrene or "trench feet" from the unending filthy mud in the trenches and in no man's land, over which the contending armies fought back and forth after intense bombardments that cut up the soil into water-filled craters.

Recruits were needed to replace the missing troops. Everywhere round the city of Adelaide were large posters with a portrait of Lord Kitchener pointing accusingly and the words "Britain needs YOU!"; others shouted, "THINK! Are you content to let him fight for YOU? Won't you do your bit? JOIN TODAY!"

When they saw a uniformed digger in the street, a hard-bitten soldier who had been invalided home, Jim stared at him almost enviously. Alix tried to hurry him past the posters, but Jim would stand rooted in front of them. Major MacFarlane began dropping hints about how the country needed "every able-bodied man to fight for the British Empire against the Hun."

"It's all very well for you," said Alix, furious, as Jim looked discomfited. "You know there's no danger that *you* will have to go. And Jim's doing important work at home, growing beef for the troops."

"There's nothing I'd like better," said Major MacFarlane with dignity, stroking back his military moustache, "than to be able to have a crack at the fighting; but I'm too old, alas." Alix thought that he looked rather splendid in his officer's uniform, with his polished Sam Browne belt and leather leggings and smart peaked cap.

Jim said quietly, "I'd like to have a go. But there's Alix, and the baby . . . and my father carrying on the station on his own. . . ."

"Everyone is making sacrifices," said the Major. "The more men we have, the sooner the war will be over." He unfolded the paper and showed a cartoon covering half the page: a civilian with a guilty expression, sitting with a little girl on his knee who asked innocently, "Daddy, what did *you* do in the Great War?"

Jim purchased fifteen hundred head of cattle at the saleyards north of Adelaide. He arranged to travel with them on the train as far as Hergott Springs, where the drovers would be waiting to drove them up to Cappa-merri. Then he returned to the city at the beginning of December to pick up another thousand head.

But he did not travel back with them to the north. By December the Australians had 87,000 casualties, and some battalions were down to quarter strength.

In Egypt, the Australian Light Horse under General Henry Chauvel were faring somewhat better. The winter desert was cold but there was no mud, and the men were mounted, so that they did not have fatiguing route marches between battles. They had routed the Turks and saved the Suez Canal.

On New Year's Eve, Jim came home and broke the news. He had joined up. He was to be sent to the Middle East to join the Australian Light Horse. Because he could ride and shoot, he was accepted gladly at the recruiting office. He would receive his training in desert warfare after his arrival in Egypt.

"Congratulations, my boy!" said the Major. "This calls for a celebration. Some of that French champagne left over from Caro's christening last year, eh?"

Alix got up and rushed from the room.

"How could you? How could you, Jim?" she wept when he followed her to their bedroom. She was face-down on the bed, her tears flowing into the damp pillowcase.

Jim sat beside her and patted her back.

"Dearest, the war can't last much longer. If I missed it, I'd be kicking myself for the rest of my life. Do you know," he added enthusiastically, "that the Light Horse is the largest body of mounted troops the modern world has known? We don't carry swords, like British cavalry, but rifles, bayonets, and bandoleers."

"Oh, yes?" She noticed that "we." He had begun to identify himself with the Army already.

"And the fighting's not so bad in the desert. In France a man has every chance of being killed, but not in Palestine. I promise to come back to you."

Alix was not reconciled. She picked Caro up and held her against her breast, rocking back and forth in her grief. Caro began to cry in sympathy.

After a week, Jim was sent to the Mitcham Light Horse Camp to commence drilling. The volunteers had to ride round the grounds without stirrups, arms folded, without touching the reins, then jump a three-foot hurdle. Nearly every man came through the test.

After a while even Alix was affected by the fervour, the surge of patriotism that gripped young and old. The Australians were fighting towards the Hindenburg Line in Europe, and chasing the Turks towards Gaza. Jim came home in his new uniform. She had to admit to a thrill of pride as she looked at him wearing the turned-up felt hat with the bunch of emu feathers which was the badge of the Light Horse. His riding-trousers and tunic fitted his slim height; his leather leggings were polished till they gleamed. She saw him off in the troop-ship from the Outer Harbour with a brave smile, then went home and shut herself in her room.

He had promised to write, of course, but she did not expect much, knowing his aversion to putting pen to paper.

The Australian and the combined Anzac mounted troops, known as "the Desert Column," had fought their way across Egypt and the Sinai Peninsula through parching deserts where the dead were unearthed again by the searing winds, or dug up by Bedouin raiders who stole their clothes and left the naked bodies for the jackals.

The battle of Rafa had been won, fought half in Sinai and half in Palestine. Jim and the rest of the relief troops knew when they were passing the battlefield in the dark by the smell of dead men. One of the returning troops told him that when they entered Palestine, they didn't think much of the Promised Land: "They ought to give it back to the bloke they promised it to," was their opinion.

Jim had written home from Egypt, a cheerful note saying that the fiery desert wind, the khamsin, and the blowing sand made him feel at home. They were training with Australian horses, stout-hearted "Walers" who were both strong and game. "There is real affection between each man and his horse," he wrote. "Often they are only used for transport of the troops; the men spring off and fight as infantry, with a mounted horse-holder minding every four horses, ready for the men to remount and make a quick get-away."

At the first battle of Gaza the Australian Light Horsemen had stayed in their saddles and charged straight into the city, and actually reached the suburbs, when the message came from the British generals to retire. Men swore unbelievingly as they "gave the city back to the Turk."

209

The Turkish Army brought up reinforcements, and were soon pouring troops and guns into Gaza.

Our men just can't understand why the Heads made them retire. Two Brigades were actually in the city [wrote Jim]. It seems that the Turk is a brave soldier, but is terrified of the bayonets attached to our rifle barrels. . . . They just surrendered, terrified by the "mad Australians." Our General, Sir Harry Chauvel, made a strong protest when the Big Heads ordered him to retire his men; but he was over-ruled. . . . The Turkish defences now stretch right across Palestine from the sea coast at Gaza to Beersheba inland.

Jim was sorry he'd missed the Gaza battle. His next letter, which reached Alix in June, surprised her with its fluency and depth of feeling. Jim had been taken out of himself, his emotions sharpened, by the heady excitement of danger and the approach of his first big engagement.

I have your photo in my hand, and as I gaze at our little daughter looking at me with her darling little face, I think I have been a brute to leave you for this life and all its danger, but I don't know, I can't explain, the only thing I can say is that if I hadn't come I wouldn't be worthy of my name. Dearest, I am about to go into action for the first time. I must say goodbye to you now, my darling. I trust that after my return we will live a long and happy life together. . . .Bless you, love, and my darling little Caro.

Your loving husband,
Jim.

Alix tried to forget that Jim was fighting, perhaps for his life, on the other side of the world. She had never seen a Turk, but from the photographs of prisoners of war in the paper, they looked a villainous lot.

There was no forgetting the war. Her mother held teas in aid of the Red Cross, and if they went out to a concert there would be wartime songs, "Australia Will Be There," "Pack Up Your Troubles," and "There's a Long Trail A-Winding."

A sentimental ditty to a heart-rending tune was heard everywhere, and Alix joined in singing with a lump in her throat:

Keep the home fires burning
For our lads re-turning,
Though they still are far away
They dream of home.
There's a silver lin-ing
Through the dark clouds shining,

Turn the dark clouds inside out
Till the boys come home!

News from the Western Front dominated the pages of the press. Almost a million men from both sides died in the mud of Flanders in the third battle of Ypres. Australian troops spearheaded five of the attacks, with heavy losses. By comparison the losses in Palestine were slight. Alix began to hope that Jim would come through the war.

Jim's first engagement had been to back up the Anzac Mounted Division in a successful raid on the Turkish railway line.

. . . Our 80,000 horses, camels, and mules have churned the plains into finest dust [he wrote]. It hangs all day in the air, stirred up by the sea-wind or by a scorcher coming from the other way, from the desert. We were sorry our brigade was not in the actual blowing-up of the line, we just guarded the flank and cleared the country of snipers. We galloped right down on a Turkish outpost fronting us with rifle- and machine-gun fire. . . . Very rarely, in these mad gallops of ours, does any good Australian horse go down. When it does happen, well, the rider is picked up by a mate on another horse. . . .

It was not until a month later that those at home heard the details of the Light Horsemen's greatest feat. On October 31, the Fourth Light Horse made the magnificent cavalry attack that took the wells of Beersheba. It was crucial that Beersheba should fall that day, so that they could get water for the horses.

General Chauvel had decided, after a day's fighting by the Australians without dislodging the Turks, to send in the cavalry with bayonets fixed.

The Turkish gunners saw them coming and opened fire with shrapnel and machine guns, but could not get the range as the horsemen came on at a hard gallop. As they neared the trenches the rifles opened fire, but still the horsemen swept on. They leaped the trenches, dismounted, and turned on the Turks from the rear with rifle and bayonet. The garrison surrendered. Parties of bewildered Turks in the rear trenches threw down their arms as another squadron galloped through them and on into the town, just before the sun set over the wells. Beersheba had fallen.

Jim had been in that mad, exhilarating ride. The German engineers who built the redoubts and fortresses of Gaza and Beersheba had claimed that they were impregnable. The Turks never dreamt that mounted troops would be madmen enough to attempt rushing infantry redoubts protected by machine guns and artillery. The thunder of a thousand hoofs, the loud shouts of the mounted men in that last berserk half-mile as they came on at a frightening speed, paralyzed and terrified the defenders so

211

that their firing was wild. Within a week the whole Turkish front, including Gaza, collapsed.

That was at the end of October and the first week in November. No more letters came from Jim. Alix waited in dread, even going into the city and studying the casualty lists posted up each day on public buildings.

Then came the cold, official telegram.

MANNING, J., 4TH LIGHT HORSE, WOUNDED 9 NOVEMBER NEAR GAZA, PALESTINE.

Alix rushed to her room, picked up Caro, who was having her morning sleep, and cradled her in her arms as she rocked to and fro. She had feared, had expected this news. They did not say how seriously he was hurt. . . . Would it mean that he would be coming home? But most wounded men were invalided out to hospitals in Britain.

When a second official telegram came she would not at first open it. She knew what it contained. Later came a letter from a man she had never met. He had been with Jim when he was wounded; now he wrote:

It is with a sad heart that I write to tell you of the death of Jim, who was my mate. He was wounded about 3 P.M. on 9th November during an attack on a Turkish outpost about fifteen miles east of Gaza. All through the day he had fought splendidly, taking all sorts of risks. . . . In the early afternoon the squadron moved forward and carried a ridge occupied by the enemy. Jim and his troops were advancing along the ridge and all firing had practically ceased. I was only a few yards away when he was hit. He was very cheerful and suffering no pain. I remained with him till the ambulance took him. We shared a last cigarette.

Now I hear that he died at the Light Horse Field Ambulance Station. I feel poor Jim's death, and I feel for you. We shared many dangers on the battlefields. Never again can I have such a mate.

He and I made an arrangement before the battle started, that in the event of either of us "going under" the other was to fix up his effects. . . . I will see to this, and send them on to you.

His effects . . . thought Alix dully. They would include the photograph of herself and baby Caro. He would not yet have received the photograph she had sent with her last letter, of Caro at her second birthday party, blowing out the candles on the cake.

Now his light was blown out. He would never read that letter. He would never be coming home.

In the first terrible weeks Alix was upheld by anger. Anger at fate, which let him be shot when the engagement was almost over. Anger that *he* had to die, rather than the mate who was close by. She even felt angry

212

with Jim, who had "taken all sorts of risks." She wanted a warm, living man, not a dead hero.

She was angry with her father and all the recruiting officers, still safe at home; and the bird-brained women who sent white feathers in the post, and sang, "We don't want to lose you, But we think you ought to go."

She turned coldly away from her mother's tears and sympathy, from Major MacFarlane's gruff attempts to justify Jim's death as "a hero of Empire."

"I will never forgive you," she had told her father in the first wild paroxysm of her grief. But it was not just her father; it was the whole system of glorifying war. Would the fighting never end? It was supposed to be "the war to end all wars," and she hoped that it was true. She had to write to Jim's parents and tell them that their only remaining son was dead.

As anger gave place to dull misery, it was Caro's needs that kept her going, the feeling that she, as a mother, had to take the place of both parents. And Caro was a part of Jim that was still alive.

When Armistice Day came towards the end of 1918 Alix felt her bitterness come back. But as the returned men, some still sick from their wounds, some with terrible disfigurements, came off the troop-ships— on stretchers, on crutches, or with the remote dead eyes of the badly shell-shocked—she volunteered as a Red Cross nurse in a repatriation hospital. She was able to sleep at home, and Caro at three could be left with her doting grandmother. Alix began to feel once more a purpose in life.

There were legless and armless men in the streets; the big, cheerful "follower" of the MacFarlanes' housemaid Mary came home blinded, with the empty sockets weeping about his new glass eyes. Mary gave her notice and married him, to spend all her time nursing him while he adjusted to his blindness.

Alix wondered how it would have been if Jim had come home disabled —crippled, unable to ride a horse ever again, perhaps confined to a wheelchair. How he would have hated it! He would have preferred to die in battle.

In 1919 nearly all the troops came home, but with them came the deadly Spanish influenza. It was like a plague that spread over the world, killing almost as many as the war. By the end of the year, ten thousand Australians had died of it. Public gatherings were forbidden, and people wore gauze antiseptic masks in the street.

Alix was terrified that Caro might catch the flu, as children and old people had little resistance. Worried she might unwittingly bring the deadly germs home from the hospital, Alix resigned from her job and prepared to take Caro back home to Cappamerri.

Her mother wept when she saw them off at the station, but she admitted

213

that the child would be safer away from infection. Big Jim Manning wrote to say how much they looked forward to her return, and he would meet her in Birdsville.

Alix found that Hergott Springs, like the Kitchener buns, had been renamed in the anti-German fervour; for the springs had been discovered by a German explorer in 1859. The town was now called Marree, an Aboriginal name.

Otherwise the town looked much the same, as hot and bare-looking as ever; but there were motor cars parked outside the pub instead of camels, and she found that Wal Crombie's horse-team had been replaced by a Commer truck.

Wal carried rolls of wire netting and lengths of iron sheeting to put under the wheels in the soft sand.

"I've never had to get a horse to pull me out yet," he said. "The trouble is the iron gets nearly red-hot in the sun, sometimes it's too hot to handle."

It was a quicker trip, not having to stop to spell the horses and change over the leaders, but not much more comfortable: the vehicle jumped like a kangaroo over obstacles, hung frighteningly over sheer drops of undercut sand-hills, and slithered over clay-pans in a zigzag course.

But the greatest surprise for Alix was the crossing of the Cooper. Across the Track spread a wide green waterway, not flowing but obviously deep and semi-permanent. "Yes, the Cooper came down in a great flood," said Wal. "It came down the Thomson and the Barcoo from Queensland. First time for about fifty years, they say, Lake Eyre is full—or it's got water in it, anyways."

There was a barge tied up at the bank, and a dinghy. Boats in central Australia! Alix was bemused. Wal and his new young helper began to offload the truck on to the barge. On the other side another vehicle was waiting, and everything had to be loaded up again. Caro had a lovely time paddling and splashing in the shallow green water under the coolabahs.

"It happened last year," said Wal. "It's certainly made a difference to the Track. She's been dry ever since, but."

Alix realized with a feeling of guilt that she had not kept in touch with her in-laws. All her interest had been centred in Jim and their baby. When the mail-car arrived at Birdsville there was Big Jim waiting, his red-brown face shaded by a wide felt hat, his checked bushman's shirt open at the neck, the sleeves rolled up above his brawny arms. He folded Alix and Caro in a bear-hug. His eyes were wet as he lifted Caro on to his shoulder and picked up Alix's bag.

After Caro was asleep in the hotel bedroom they talked about Jim, in a way Alix had never been able to talk to her own parents.

"How is his mother taking it?" she asked.

Big Jim sighed. "She's taken it badly, I'm afraid. I think she realizes now that she was unfair to Jim, all those years after Dan died. Now she has lost him, she regrets that she didn't appreciate Jim while he was alive."

"She did send me a note, but it didn't say much."

"No. She's withdrawn almost completely into herself. You know, how she used to be, but worse. I'm hoping young Caro may help to pull her out of it."

Alix had wondered how she would be able to bear coming back to Cappamerri when Jim was not there. But as they followed the sandy and stony track from Birdsville and she saw that the country was "in good heart," as they said up here, her spirits rose. Within the boundaries of Cappamerri they passed mobs of sleek cattle which shied wildly away from the buggy.

"You haven't gone in for one of these new automobiles, then?" she had asked when they set off.

"No way. Horses are best, if you ask me. Can't stand these new contraptions, noisy stinking things they are."

They crossed two long red sand-hills green with bullock-bush, and flats covered in flowering mulga with its yellow spikes. As the delicate salmon-red of the homestead sand-hills rose on their left, and the green-blue reach came in sight beyond with its shady coolabahs and white-trunked paperbarks, the dusty blacks' camp down by the river, and the station buildings with their iron roofs glittering under a limitless blue sky; as she saw all this again, Alix heaved a great sigh, half joy, half sorrow. She knew she had been right to come back to Cappamerri.

The barking of dogs brought the people streaming up from the camp —old Johnnie and his lubra, the men she had treated for trachoma, the children and their mothers, to welcome "Young Missus" and her little one. Caro waved delightedly from the buggy at the smiling dark faces. Then they were at the gate of the garden enclosure and old Lucy came down to take Alix's bags inside.

"You go ahead. I'll just have a word with the head stockman," said Big Jim.

The only thing worrying Alix was her mother-in-law's attitude. Would she somehow blame her for Jim's death? And how would she be with Caro? When Olive was not waiting on the veranda to greet them, Alix's heart sank. They found her sitting in a cane chair in the dimmest corner of the living-room. The outer shutters were closed against the heat. She rose slowly and gave Alix her hand and kissed her cheek; but little Caro, now an engaging four-year-old, slipped her hand into her grandmother's and looked up confidingly. In her small world she had not known anyone fail to respond to her sunny smile.

Olive stooped suddenly and picked up the little girl, who put her arms round her grandmother's neck and nestled into her shoulder. Olive's face began to crumple from its calm severity, and in a moment she was weeping. Alix had never seen her cry.

"Don't cry, Ganma," said Caro sympathetically. Olive managed to smile and kissed her. She put her free hand out to Alix, and said, "I'm so glad you brought her home. She reminds me of Jim, with that straight fair hair, though her eyes are not so blue." She heaved a sigh. "Poor Jim! The foolish, foolish boy. Why did he have to go out and get himself killed?"

Alix, who had often asked herself the same question, gave a helpless shrug.

"Now Caro, Grandma will get you some nice cool lemonade. And Alix? Would you rather have tea?"

"No, a cool drink will be fine."

So the homecoming was rather different from what she had expected. It seemed that the ice had melted around Olive's heart, and she was to give Jim's daughter the affection she had withheld from him when he was alive.

Life at the station went on as before. The Chinese cook, still smiling and good-tempered, reigned in the kitchen building. Jenny was a little plumper and Lucy a little older. Alix's Aboriginal patients drifted up from the camp with their various ailments. She felt that she had come home.

The vast inland to which John Flynn had introduced her all those years ago had laid its spell on her. Wherever she might travel, her heart was here in the red centre of Australia, and Jim's child would grow up in this pure dry atmosphere, far from the teeming cities of the coast.

CHAPTER THIRTY-ONE

Yet Caro stayed on Cappamerri only for another three years. What finally decided Alix to leave the station was her mother-in-law's departure for Brisbane, as well as Caro's need for further schooling.

For some time Olive Manning had been in poor health, though mentally she seemed better since accepting Jim's child. Caro and Olive got on well, and it was Olive who taught her to read and helped with her education till she was in her eighth year.

Olive had decided to leave the inland and live with her married daughter in Brisbane, where she could be near a doctor. Alix stayed on for a while, but after his wife's departure, Big Jim became quite open in his liaison with Jenny. Lucy still ran the house, but the younger lubra began putting on airs and became sullen when Alix gave her orders. Big Jim did not seem to notice. Since his second son had been killed, he seemed to care about nothing; he even neglected the property, where the delicately balanced ground cover of native pastures and shrubs was deteriorating each year. He had no sons to inherit, and had never seen his city-born grandson, who did not carry the name of Manning.

Alix regretted leaving for only one reason: she would have to leave her Aboriginal patients to take their chance with sickness and injury. In 1923 a new Australian Inland Mission Hostel was to open at Birdsville. Alix applied for a position when there should be a vacancy, and took Caro down to Adelaide for her eighth birthday.

Big Jim drove them down to the mailbox on the Betoota road, so they could pick up the mail-truck for Birdsville. The mail was now carried by a Ford buckboard instead of packhorse and mounted mailman.

"I'll write, and send you some pictures of Caro," called Alix as she waved goodbye.

At Birdsville she visited the A.I.M. hostel and was a bit taken aback to find that, far from being in a new building, the hostel had been converted from an old deserted hotel. The women's ward was in what had once been the bar. But at least the building was of stone, with a curved galvanized iron veranda roof to keep out the western sun. The two Sisters had been appointed together.

There had once been three hotels in the town, which had quite a big school at the turn of the century. But now with the silting of waterholes and the great droughts of 1902 and 1910–1916, the town was a shadow of its former self. There were no great droves any more, except in unusually good seasons. With grass and saltbush cover uncertain, and the woody desert perennials killed by rabbits and travelling stock, there was not enough feed along the famous Track. The school was now run by one teacher with less than a dozen pupils.

Although she had enjoyed station life, and would miss her pony which she had ridden every day, Caro was looking forward to a real school. She wanted playmates of her own age. Grandma had always discouraged her attempts to fraternize with the black children who came to Alix's clinic.

She could scarcely remember her other grandparents in the city. But it was fun to be travelling with Mum through the desert, though terribly hot.

On the way down the Birdsville Track Alix yarned with Wal Crombie and his helper, known as the Lyrebird, or simply as Billy the Liar.

Billy was a great teller of tall yarns, and he claimed that he could kill a snake by breaking its back after cracking it like a stockwhip.

At their first camp, Wal caught a six-foot mulga snake. He handed the wriggling reptile to Billy, holding it well at arm's length. Billy gave a yell, swung it round once, and threw it as far away as he could.

"Curses, the bloody thing slipped," he muttered. "It weren't much of a snake, anyways. Why, there was a king brown I killed up in the Channel Country; it was eleven foot long if it was an ounce."

He reckoned that the mixture they were serving one Christmas at the Betoota pub, based on overproof rum and port wine, was "that potent that after two drops of it a little willy-wagtail come down out of his tree and wanted to box with an emu."

They didn't dare give the pet emu any, he said, in case it got dangerous.

"Was the emu scared of the willy-wag?" asked Caro.

"My oath! Went for his life. We didn't see 'im again till Boxing Day. By then Willy was sittin' on a dead bough with his eyes sorta closed. Musta had a beaut hangover."

As they set off next morning, Wal held forth about the state of the Channel Country and the sand-hill country in the triangle between Innamincka, Birdsville, and Marree.

"There's no doubt the country's going back," said Wal, changing gear and grinding up a small sand-hill. "They've had to close the Strzelecki Track, it's that bad; and things have silted up something terrible between here and Marree.

"The old blokes say there wasn't any Cobbler in the old days, there was water in the Strzelecki and good waterholes all the way. O' course, there's been a bad drought every ten years.

"It's not just a question of drought, though; there must always've been drought in this country. But the sand-hills used ter carry a lot more cover in the early days. Overstocking has stripped the perennial saltbush, so it'll never grow again. Spinifex and cane-grass used ter be thick, and they stopped the sand from drifting. Today the sand's blowing, and it's silted up the waterholes that used ter be permanent. Even the needlebush and mulga's been killed, by cattlemen lopping the boughs for feed in drought-time, and drovers have been cutting 'em down for firewood for about forty years. No wonder it's going back. It's gone back a long way since I first come up here."

"Jim always said his father would ruin the place with overstocking," said Alix.

"Yair—Big Jim was always an optimist. But you can't go on flogging it year after year. In the Channel Country, the grasses and annuals that come up after a flood don't last long; they dry up and blow away before the next summer. There's plenty of permanent waterholes along the upper Diamantina. But the feed isn't coming up like it did, and the topsoil's blowing away."

"Is it too late for something to be done?"

"Well, what the country needs is a good long spell. But how . . . ? There's no fences; and if you try to spell one area, the stock'll find their way to it as long as there's feed on it. The stations need to be fenced, and subdivided into different paddocks, so they can be rested. But no one can afford to do it, the values are too low; when you can only run about one beast to a square mile, you need an awful lot of land." He paused to negotiate a sand-drift. "Ah well, I won't be around to see it; but I reckon the sand'll take over eventually, and the homesteads will all be deserted."

Alix gave a shiver. There was something prophetic about his mood. She wondered if that would be the fate of Cappamerri.

She and Caro, after leaving Marree in the train, had a fairly restful trip to Adelaide.

At the station they were met, to Alix's surprise, by her mother driving a new Essex. "Your father doesn't drive any more," she explained. "You'll find him aged a lot, Alix. Do you remember Grandpa, pet?" she asked, her arms around Caro as she stooped to her level.

"Yes, he drove us to the mailbox," said Caro.

"No, dear, I mean your other Grandpa—Mummy's father."

Caro looked uncertain.

"She was only four," said Alix.

"Yes!" Frances gave her a reproachful look. Her little mouth with its pearly teeth had grown thin, her blue eyes sharp. "Four years you've been away in the bush. She's grown such a big girl! Grandma hardly knew you."

"I merember *you*, though," said Caro, and Frances hugged her.

Alix had noticed the grey threads in her mother's dark hair, but she

219

was unprepared to find her father completely grey. Major MacFarlane was sixty-five, and looked more than his age. His military bearing, his upright carriage had sagged, so that he seemed shorter, and his manner had become rather vague. Since the excitement of the war was over, when he had felt important and useful, he had become an old man, querulous and partly deaf. Alix could no longer feel any animosity towards him over Jim's death. At least Jim would never know the indignity of growing old.

She enrolled Caro at the local State School for the remainder of the year, and in the new year of 1924 received her call to Birdsville. Alix knew she was fortunate to get the appointment, for the Sisters usually worked in pairs. The ill health of one of them had caused the vacancy before their two-year term was over. In February Alix and Caro left once again for the north, in spite of protests from Frances.

A flight of pelicans had arrived from somewhere over the horizon, perhaps all the way from the distant coast. Caro watched them flying in formation on their splendid wings, rising and falling with the waves of air. There would be several slow beats of the wings, and then a glide—but always in unison, as if one brain informed the whole flock. The majestic birds circled and came in to land on the Birdsville reach of the Diamantina, planing down one behind the other. They braked with their wings as they spread their webbed feet on the surface of the water, sending up a spray of white foam like a fast-moving boat.

It must be a wonderful feeling to fly, thought nine-year-old Caro. Sometimes she dreamt she was flying, floating effortlessly over the landscape, rising and falling over hills and valleys. She had seen an aeroplane: the little single-engined biplane of Ross and Keith Smith, which came to Adelaide from Darwin after they'd completed the first flight ever from England in 1919. Grandma MacFarlane had made a flag for her to wave at the small humming object as it came over the Adelaide hills from the direction of Sydney. It looked like a toy, and Caro did not believe that there were big grown men inside it. Then Mummy took her to the aerodrome where it was on display, and she touched its fuselage and walked under the big letters painted below the wing: G.E.A.O.U., which the papers said stood for "God 'Elp All Of Us." Caro had been four then, and just learning her capital letters. It *was* big enough for two men, after all.

They had quickly settled in at Birdsville, and Caro was now going to the local school. Caro liked to come down to the waterhole after school. She loved to see the white-trunked trees reflected in the blue-green water from the bore. There was another drought beginning and the Diamantina's bed was once more dry except for the bore overflow. She stopped on her way back beside the first cooling pond, where the water came almost boiling out of the ground. The pool, about fifteen feet across, looked pale-green and inviting, but she knew better than to dip her bare foot into it.

One of the boys from school was squatting by the hot-water pond, poking under the surface with a stick. Billy Flannigan was part-Aboriginal in spite of his Irish name. His feet, too, were bare. Most of the children ran about without shoes except in summer, when the sand was hot enough to burn the feet.

"'Lo, Care-oh," said Billy. The children insisted on calling her Care-oh, however often she told them her name was Car-o, which her mother had told her was Italian for "dear." And it was, of course, short for Caroline.

"Bet you daren't put your hand in it," said Billy, squinting up under his heavy brows.

"You're damn right!" said Caro. "I wouldn't be that stupid."

Billy grinned up at her with his big white teeth.

"Not if you knew there was a whole shillin' in there?"

"Eh?" Caro came and squatted down beside him. He pointed with the stick at something round and shiny, glinting under the surface. Ripples made by the light breeze distorted the image, but there was certainly something small and silvery on the bottom.

"Can't you get it out with the stick?"

"Na; it keeps slidin' back."

"Here; give us a go." She tried to pull the object towards her up the slope of the pond, but it evaded the end of the stick each time.

"We could use a magnet."

"Magnets don't attract silver, silly."

Since she was a year older and Billy was a boy, Caro felt superior. "I'll get a flatter stick, and try to dig it out."

"Bags we go halves."

"What? If I get it out, it'll be my shilling."

"I saw it first, but."

"Well . . . I suppose so."

She scouted around and found a flat piece of deal long enough to reach the bottom. But though the coin moved tantalizingly nearer, it began to dig into the silt on the bottom. Billy tried with the pointy stick, and unearthed it again.

After ten minutes of futile dabbing, Caro's forearm ached and the coin was still under a foot of hot water. She lost her temper and threw the piece of wood across the pond.

"I don't care!" she shouted. "I *will* get it!"

And without giving herself time to think, she plunged her hand above the wrist into the near-boiling water, and grasped the object. Her hand

221

turned red as a cooked lobster, but the metal lay in her palm. It was only a silver button, after all.

"You stupid boy!" She turned unreasonably on Billy, blaming him for the smarting of her hand and wrist, for the disappointing find. "It's all your fault!" And she threw the button at his feet. She ran home to her mother.

Alix scolded Caro when she came into the hostel holding the smarting hand in front of her. "Why did you do such a silly thing?"

"Billy made me," said Caro, biting her bottom lip.

Alix had just given afternoon tea to two patients, so she used the dregs of the teapot to bathe Caro's hand in tannic acid, and dusted it with bicarbonate of soda before binding it expertly in a clean gauze bandage. She remembered how she had scalded her own foot in the same hot pool when she first visited Birdsville.

Alix tucked in the bandage end and gave Caro's arm a pat.

"There you are. Your hand will be too sore to hold a pen tomorrow, so you might as well miss school."

"Aw, Mum! I don't want to miss—"

"You will just have to miss one day." She tied a scarf round Caro's neck for a sling, lifting her long, shining fair plaits out of the way. "You can help me sort bandages with your good hand."

Alix was happy to be nursing again after eight years of being a lone parent to Caro. There was no resident doctor in the town, which was hundreds of miles from the nearest railway. Alix and the other nurse—Sister Kinross—had to deal with medical emergencies on their own.

Sister Kinross was a pleasant Scotswoman, an experienced outback nurse, and a surrogate aunt for Caro. The three of them got on well, though Alix knew that Janet Kinross missed her nursing companion of years, now sent south with suspected tuberculosis; just as she herself had missed Mab after she died.

During that summer there was a heat wave in Birdsville, when the thermometer stood above 110 degrees nearly every day, and dropped to 100 degrees at night. On the day the temperature reached 120 degrees in the shade, the school closed down and the whole population of the town gathered at the big waterhole. One old man had died of the heat, and had to be buried at night in the burning-hot sand.

The few sparse trees were full of birds; there were budgerigars like a swarm of bees, their beaks open and gasping; the ground beneath the trees was carpeted with dead birds. Every building had a solid mass of birds sitting in its shade.

For the rest of the week the school opened only from 6 to 8 A.M., after which, the teacher declared, it was too hot to work.

"Aye, and if it's too hot for yon teacher-laddie, it's too hot for us," said

222

Janet Kinross. "Eh, Alix? I vote we take the bairn and go for a picnic by the water."

"Ooh, yes, Auntie Janet," said Caro. Her little face was scarlet with the heat, and her long fair plaits were pinned on top of her head for coolness.

As there were no seriously ill patients in the hostel, each day they donned their bathing costumes of navy-blue cotton jersey, and with parasols, towels, and a water-bag they walked down to the river over the bare burning ground where some stunted grey saltbush still survived here and there, on the very edge of extinction.

By the waterhole there were green reeds and shady trees, though the water was far from cool and had to be cleared of dead birds. But without this oasis on the outskirts of the barren little town, Alix thought, it would have been unbearable.

CHAPTER THIRTY-TWO

The older bushmen were nervous of strange women coming to their country, taking their "brands and descriptions" when they fell ill. They didn't want females fussing over them, keeping them helpless and probably not allowing them to smoke.

Harry Hays was a pioneer cattleman of the Channel Country who years before had opposed the building of the hostel.

"They'd have to put a head-rope on me and skull-drag me into that place," he'd said when the hostel opened. Now, nearly five years later, he had fallen from a borehead at Duthie Station and been brought in for treatment of a fractured femur.

Alix knew he would need to be in traction, but the problem was to know what weights to use and where to procure them. She was able to contact a doctor in Quorn by radio for advice. Then she borrowed some weights from the post office, measured an equivalent weight of stones and odd pieces of metal into a bucket, and weighed both bucket and contents.

With the help of the local carpenter she built a Hodgen's splint, which held the leg from below the hip to the knee. Cords and pulleys were fixed to the sides of the splint to keep the leg elevated. Following the drawings in her invaluable *Modern Methods of Nursing*, the carpenter was able to make a Buck's extension with the whole apparatus attached to a stout cord run over a pulley wheel fixed to the high end of the bed. Alix raised the foot of the bed, hung the weighted bucket from the cord, and Harry Hays was in traction—as helpless as a trussed turkey.

"You girls like to get a man helpless," he growled, submitting with bad grace to the indignities of the bedpan and the urine bottle. But his hands were free, and after a while he began to enjoy the home-cooked meals and dainty afternoon teas. Caro liked to sit by his bed when she came home from school and listen to his stories of cattle-droves and "rushes."

"I mind the time the cattle rushed, out on the Ranken Plain," he would begin. "Me night-horse fell, and I was lying right in their path . . ."

Caro found that he and her grandpa, Big Jim Manning, had been mates on the track years before.

When he asked one day for "a piece of wood to whittle," Caro brought out the pictures of Sopwith Camels and Puss Moths she had copied from Mr. Ryan's books. She asked him if he could carve her a model aeroplane.

"Well, I'll have a try. I saw one of those buggers in Longreach once. I'm walking all round it when the pilot asks, 'Do you like the look of it?' "'Like the look of it!' I says. 'How the hell would I know? I've never seen one of the buggers before.' Then he asks if I'd like to go up for a spin, three guineas for a joy-ride."

"And did you?" asked Caro. "Did you go up?"

"Go up? What, and have the bugger fall to pieces? Not for a hundred quid I wouldn't. She was just like a bloody big hawk with engines. 'So long, mate!' I says. 'I'm going for a beer.'"

He soon had the fuselage carved from a solid piece of deal, the cockpit hollowed out, and a single wooden propeller attached to the front. Wings proved more difficult, but Alix came up with an old thin silk scarf which he glued over a plywood frame with struts of match-sticks to hold the double wings apart, and wires made from cotton.

Caro was thrilled. With the other children she had followed the development of flight and knew famous fliers, such as Kingsford-Smith. "Smithy" was a hero. She had a newspaper picture of him pinned on the wall above her bed.

Far to the north, half-way between the east coast and the Northern Territory border, the aeroplane was already established. Young pilots who had returned from the Great War were eager to keep on flying. Kingsford-Smith joined a Western Australian company, and Hudson Fysh helped establish Qantas—the Queensland and Northern Territory Aerial Service—at Longreach in central Queensland. Backed by wealthy graziers, an air service was begun that would one day send huge passenger jets around the world. In 1922 they carried the first airmail from Charleville to Winton.

Pilots lived by giving demonstrations of stunting, and offering joy-flights in country towns in their little biplanes, saving their money to start small commercial operations. They had to overcome the prejudice of people who were suspicious of aeroplanes and reluctant to trust their lives to such flimsy contraptions.

Though John Flynn's dream of a "flying doctor" was still unrealized, suitable planes were now available and all he needed was a viable form of radio communication from isolated stations to a flying doctor base in some central position.

He had already started building his brain-child, the air-cooled hospital at Alice Springs in what was known as central Australia.

Soon after Alix settled at Birdsville, John Flynn came through on one of his "padre patrols" of the inland stations. He was welcome among the station people, for he did not preach, but would sit on a stockyard rail to yarn (though always wearing his dark suit-trousers and a dark waistcoat with gold watch-chain over his shirt). He would conduct a funeral or a wedding, listen to problems, and mend any clocks or watches that had stopped, for clocks were a passion with him. And everywhere he went he spoke of the need for the Alice Springs hospital, and for a mantle of safety over the outback that could be provided only by a flying doctor.

Alix had not seen him since he conducted the burial service for Mab at Marree ten years before. He looked older, if anything a little thinner, and he was wearing glasses. As usual he talked far into the night, telling Alix of his unique design for the Alice Springs building, on which he had an expert stone mason working.

"It will have a sort of in-built air-cooling system," he said. "Here— where's a sheet of paper—I'll sketch it for you roughly. The air comes in below here, through two ducts with damp cloths hanging across them, to the cellar, then it circulates through the building."

He had brought an open Dodge tourer on the trip. It was loaded down with spare tyres, tube-mending gear, rolls of wire netting and sheets of iron for getting through the sand-hills and across the wide sandy beds of the Finke and the Alberga. He was travelling with a young wireless amateur from Sydney, who was making an experimental tour of the back country to test the possibility of a portable wireless.

"It has to work," said John Flynn as he took a cup of tea on the hostel veranda and enjoyed a piece of Sister Kinross' Dundee cake. He explained that they could set an electric generator on the running-board of the car, jack up the back wheel, and run the engine to drive the generator by a drive belt to get power for broadcasting.

"We've been experimenting with messages in Morse code from the most isolated places, just setting up the equipment in the desert. We'll try again from the Birdsville Track on the way down to Marree, and then between Oodnadatta and Alice Springs on our way north again. We keep hopefully sending messages that no one may ever hear."

Months later, Alix read in a copy of *The Inlander*, the A.I.M. journal, that a message had actually been picked up three hundred miles away across the Simpson Desert, by an amateur radio buff at Oodnadatta. At last the dumb inland had a voice, the lonely outposts far from telegraph lines or railways.

Flynn had seen the desperate need for this means of communication —for what use was a flying doctor who had no way of knowing where he was needed?

Some months after Flynn had departed, this was demonstrated in a tragic manner at the Birdsville hostel.

Ironically, it was the son of the manager of Clifton Hills, who had been very sceptical of the wireless experiments, who badly needed assistance. Billy Williams had taken a somersault with his horse, which then rolled on him, at a station nearly a hundred miles south of Birdsville. Jimmy Naylor, the part-Aboriginal stockboy mustering with him, left Billy alone in the waste of sand with his water-bag beside him and a

226

supply of damper and corned beef in the tucker-box. He rode into Clifton Hills, but Mr. Williams was away. Jimmy took a change of horses and set off up the track for Birdsville, where he arrived two days later.

"He's broken somepin and it's bad," he said, rolling exhausted off his horse at the hostel door. "I never tried t'move 'im case I made 'im worse."

Sister Kinross was attending an obstetric case, so it was Alix who packed her first-aid kit, morphia and splints, and set off down the track with Constable Wills in his uncomfortable Ford T Utility. They had rigged a stretcher over the back tray with a canopy over it.

They found the injured man lying where he had been left. Big meat ants had come swarming after the beef, and he'd been forced to throw it as far away as possible.

"I couldn't help thinking how they'd make a meal of me, if you didn't turn up," he said wryly.

"I'm afraid you have a broken pelvis," said Alix after a careful examination. "I'll give you a sedative and we'll get you into the car; you mustn't attempt to stand. Let's hope the spine is all right."

They left before dawn the next morning and were back at Birdsville by that night. He was in a state of shock, so that his eyes were unnaturally bright and he was unable to lie still, though firmly kept in a prone position by Alix. He kept talking about the things that had gone through his mind as he lay there for three days unable to move, in the vast loneliness of the sand-hill country.

"One thing I've decided," he said. "That John Flynn fellow has the right idea; if we'd had wireless at Clifton Hills, you'd have got the message two days earlier."

"And if there'd been a flying doctor at Cloncurry, as Flynn is planning, you could have been flown back for expert care by now."

"I'm grateful to have *your* care," said Billy Williams.

She did not tell him what she feared, that there was some internal bleeding, which could turn septic and dangerous. After a few days the patient became delirious, and though she sponged him to get his temperature down, the outside temperature was 110 degrees in the shade, and even the water from the water-bag was not really cold.

His pulse was rapid and irregular, and his breath shallow and sighing. Alix consulted with Janet Kinross, who could suggest only pillows under the patient's knees to make him more comfortable, and cold compresses over the injury. She put her hand over Alix's and gave a slight shake of the head. The prognosis was not good. "Och, the poor wee laddie!" she sighed.

At 4 A.M. the next day, as Alix got up to check her patient's condition, she heard him gasping and fighting for breath. Raising the lamp at his bedside she saw that he was blue about the lips.

"Bill! Billy!" She took his wrist in her hand and felt only a faint flutter of a pulse.

"Sis-ter . . . I'm a goner," he sighed, and became unconscious. It was a final collapse.

He had been young and strong; there was no doubt that if there had been an aerial ambulance and he could have been transported quickly to hospital, he would have survived. But the hostel was not equipped for either blood transfusions or surgery. This was the battle John Flynn was fighting for the people in the far-out places.

Charley Williams, the boy's father, had been away at an outstation on the huge property when the accident happened. He wrote to thank Sister Manning for her help, and enclosed a cheque for £500 for John Flynn and his Inland Mission.

In the years they had been in Birdsville, Caro had mothered a baby kid, feeding it with dissolved powdered milk from a baby's bottle.

Unfortunately he had grown into a large, aggressive billy-goat, full of strength and cunning. Alix was wary of him, but visitors were his special target. When the postmaster's wife came over with a gift of a baked pudding in a bowl for the Sisters, Billy waited till she had her back to him and then charged, head down. With a hefty butt he knocked Mrs. Harris over in the dust, the pudding bowl went flying out of her hand and landed some distance away, and the pudding sailed on to the veranda.

Mrs. Harris, though knocked nearly breathless, rescued the bowl and aimed it at Billy, who was about to sample the pudding. It hit him on the horns.

He bounded away, while the postmaster's wife shrieked after him, "You blasted goat! I'll kill you if I get my hands on you! My lovely golden pudding . . ."

Fortunately the veranda was not too dusty, so she scraped the broken pudding back into the bowl and carried it through to the kitchen, where it was Alix's turn to be cook.

"Oh, lovely! A pudding for dessert!" said Alix.

"'Fraid it's a bit broken. I had a bit of a go-in with that goat of Caro's. But it should taste all right." She poked at the pieces doubtfully and picked out a bit of dry straw.

"It'll be fine. Caro's favourite!"

"You can tell her it's the last one she'll get from me, unless she ties up that goat or gets rid of it."

"Oh dear! Did he butt you?"

"My oath he did."

When Caro came home from school Alix told her that Billy would have to go. He was too big and strong, and he might end up hurting someone, perhaps an old, infirm person coming in for treatment.

Caro stuck out her pink bottom lip. "Billy's my pet!"

"I know, dear, but he's getting too much of a menace."

"But—"

"Do you want some golden pudding for dessert?"

"Ooh, yum!"

"Well, Mrs. Harris brought it over, and Billy nearly got the lot. She said she'll never bring another one till that goat goes."

"Well . . ."

"We'll give him to Billyjim's lubra, who can put him with her milking herd. It's time Billy had a nanny of his own and some little kids. He's grown up now."

"All right," said Caro.

She tossed a shining plait back over her shoulder and began to run along the veranda, her arms outspread like wings.

"Mummy, I'm a pelican. Flap, flap, flap, glide. Flap, flap, flap, gli-i-ide. I wish I could truly fly like a bird."

CHAPTER THIRTY-THREE

In November 1926, John Flynn and Alf Traeger, the Adelaide inventor who had been working on a portable wireless, made the first transmission of a telegram by field radio in Australia. Traeger had invented a light transceiver, which could both send and receive. One of their messages was picked up in Adelaide, a thousand miles away. But the equipment was still too heavy and complicated.

Traeger, a lean, keen, eager young man who was fascinated with wireless, thought hard about the problem. What he wanted was a simple, hand-operated electric generator. But turning by hand while sending Morse was too hard. So he put bicycle pedals on a small manual bench-grinder and screwed it to the floor, where it could be operated by someone sitting in a chair and pedalling while transmitting.

It was a unique invention, the first pedal-wireless in the world. The set would transmit, under good conditions, up to three hundred miles. It had taken him two years to perfect. But there was no voice transmission; the whole of the outback would have to learn Morse code.

In isolated Birdsville, though it had been gazetted a "town" for about sixty years, they had never had telephone or radio communication. Messages brought by a blackfellow on a piece of folded paper in a cleft stick, or the fortnightly mail from Marree or Windorah, were their only contact with the outside world. Alf Traeger arrived at the hostel with one of his little pedal-radios, and it took a fortnight to install it and teach the Sisters Morse and a running knowledge of radio science and upkeep.

The whole set, with its two-valve receiver and one-valve transmitter, only cost £32. But to the residents of Birdsville, and of the far-out stations with transceiver sets, it was worth its weight in gold.

"I expect I'll grow old and grey, still travelling about the country, installing and servicing sets and teaching Morse," said young Alf Traeger ruefully. "But John Flynn is such an enthusiast, and so utterly determined, that you just have to go along with him."

"I always knew he'd do it in the end," said Alix.

Traeger said, "I wanted him to wait until I devised some method of voice transmission. I mean, imagine trying to send symptoms and receive instructions from the doctor three hundred miles away, all in Morse."

"Aye!" said Sister Kinross, who had been pedalling and trying to transmit, without success. "I canna work my feet at the same time as my hands; they willna agree."

"No, Morse won't do, though it's better than nothing. I'll think of something."

When he went back to his workshop in Adelaide he spent some months on the problem, and came up with another invention: a Morse typewriter. It was incorporated in the pedal-wireless—and Alf Traeger and John Flynn had to travel all over central Australia again to add this refinement. All the operator had to do was press down a letter on the keyboard, not forgetting to pedal, and an automatic disc caused the transmitter to flash out the Morse signal for that letter.

More and more stations were added to the network, until there were thirty, with technical improvements that gave a range of six hundred miles.

Cappamerri was one of the stations next to be equipped with a pedal-wireless, and Alix found its call-sign and pedalled a message to her father-in-law.

"Lovely to hear from you," came back the message in reply. "Drought bad here. Stock very low. Am just holding on. If rivers don't come down this year will be finished."

What could she say to comfort him? Alix typed, "Sorry to hear bad news. Caro sends her love." And Caro typed, while her mother pedalled, "Dear Granpa how are you I am well," and Alix signed off, for there could be urgent medical messages waiting to come in. Janet Kinross had mastered the machine at last, but she preferred to let Alix do the transmitting.

Sister Kinross wanted to return to Melbourne when their term of office, already extended, was over in December. Alix offered to stay on, and a relieving nurse was sent up from Melbourne by way of Broken Hill, Tibooburra, Arrabury Station, and Betoota—a vast circle through some of the most inhospitable country in the continent.

She arrived in an exhausted and dehydrated state with the mailman from Betoota; Alix had to nurse her for the first week.

"I didn't know it would be like this!" she wailed. "I don't think I can stand it. I knew it was hot and dry, but the air is like a furnace blast, it seems to dry out the inside of my lungs and I can't breathe—"

"You'll be all right when you get acclimatized, Sister Bowen," said Alix soothingly. "The nights can be quite cold, even frosty, at Birdsville. But that's in the winter, July and August. You've come in time for the very hottest months."

Sister Bowen seemed very young to Alix. It was her first appointment since her training; she was in her early twenties. Alix, who was thirty-six, felt old and wise beside her. She did not spend much time looking in the mirror, but she knew there were as yet no grey threads among her

231

pale-brown hair; though it had perhaps lost some of its shine, it was curly and abundant as ever. She dallied with the idea of having it bobbed when she went down to Adelaide. Because she had the sort of skin that freckles rather than tans, she had always worn hats and veils in the worst of the outback sun. But her face was lined with fine wrinkles, especially about the eyes and mouth.

Caro, on the other hand, had her father's smooth golden-brown tan, contrasting with her fair hair, which bleached lighter under the inland sun. The top layer was a pale gold, over straw-colour and deeper tones, almost brown, so that it was particoloured rather than just blonde. The fine strands were dead straight, except when the two long plaits in which she wore it were undone, showing a pattern of waves where it had been braided.

Caro studied the prostrate Nurse Bowen.

"Why don't you come down to the waterhole for a swim, Sister?" she asked. "That's the best thing in hot weather."

"Waterhole? I thought it was just dust and gibbers and saltbush round here," said Sister Bowen in a faint voice.

"No, there's a beaut permanent waterhole in the bed of the Diamantina —kept going by the bore overflow. Want to come?"

"I'm afraid I'm too weak to do anything at present. Perhaps later . . . tomorrow."

With some slightly cooler weather, Sister Bowen rallied and took her share of the duties. She also managed to walk down to the Diamantina with Caro, borrowing Alix's swimming costume, for she had not dreamt of swimming in the arid centre.

"But you said it was just a waterhole!" she said, stopping short and staring at the long sheet of blue-green water with its white-boled paperbarks and green reeds, crimson floating duckweed and far bank of red sand. "Why, it's a lagoon—it's beautiful!"

"That's what we call a waterhole up here. On the station, at Cappa-merri, the homestead waterhole is about twelve miles long, with a sandbank in the middle dividing it into two. And that's in drought time."

"Well!" Exclaiming at the green grass underfoot, Sister Bowen made her way to the shallows and dipped a toe in. The water was warm, of course, after the prolonged heat wave of the past two weeks, but as the dust washed from her ankles she realized that it was also liquid and refreshing. A flock of quarrions, small crested parrots with pale delicate colouring of grey-brown and yellow, decorated one of the dead trees, uttering their melodious rolling calls: "Quarrion, quarrion." Five peli-cans, quite unalarmed by the arrival of human beings, continued to fish in convoy in the deeper water. They were as graceful afloat as in the air, sailing like stately galleons above the invisible thrust of their large webbed feet.

Flynn of the inland came through Birdsville again with Alf Traeger, very satisfied with his design for Adelaide House at the Alice, which was now the most comfortable of all the A.I.M. hostels, though one of the most remote.

"Not that it's as hot there on an average as Birdsville; it's two thousand feet above sea-level, and can be cold in winter," he said. "Fewer dust-storms, too. The Macdonnell Ranges are like a great rocky wall lying across the land from west to east. It's beautiful country up there. The real centre of Australia."

"I've always wanted to go to Alice Springs," said Alix. "Perhaps if I applied for the next vacancy? There's nothing to keep me here once Caro finishes her primary schooling."

"They often need a relieving Sister at the Alice," said Flynn. "The fettlers working on the railway bring a lot of extra patients. The train-line should reach there by 1929."

Because there were only eight children in the school, the bright ones were able to go at their own pace. Caro, just turned twelve, passed her Qualifying Certificate along with the one fourteen-year-old, a boy.

"You know, you should really go to secondary school in Adelaide," said her mother. "If I go to Alice Springs, there will be correspondence lessons, but they can't take you much further. Wouldn't you like to do some science subjects, chemistry and botany, physiology—"

"And aerodynamics."

Alix blinked. "What's that?"

"It's part of physics—the study of bodies moving against the resistance of air. Mr. Ryan is interested in aeroplanes and what makes them fly although they're heavier than air. He says that one day people will travel from England to Australia, and all round the world, in big passenger planes."

"But they'd have to weigh tons!"

"Yes, it's all a matter of power-weight ratio and the right design of the fuselage and wings, he says."

"Fuselage! Power-weight ratio! Whatever next will you come out with?"

"Mr. Ryan has lots of books on flying; he lets me look at them after school, but he won't let me bring them home because he says he couldn't replace them."

"I don't suppose he could, up here. But when you go to school in Adelaide there'll be plenty of reference books. I'd like to spend Christmas at home this year."

"Could we go to Cappamerri first?"

"I don't think so, dear. We'll see."

233

CHAPTER THIRTY-FOUR

Frances had written that Major MacFarlane was failing in health, and wanted to see his daughter and granddaughter, so they would leave for Adelaide as soon as the relieving Sister arrived and had been shown the ropes.

Before they left, Big Jim came down from Cappamerri with a truckload of hides for Marree, with his head stockman, Milton, driving the truck. By the time they had been railed to Adelaide, the freight would not leave much profit, but the beasts had been too weak to walk the distance and had to be slaughtered anyway. He was, he said, "cutting his losses," but he doubted if he would ever be able to stock up again in any quantity.

He told Alix that his wife, Olive, had died of cancer in Brisbane.

"I'm sorry! I didn't know . . ."

"It's all right. We haven't even kept in touch by letter for years. My daughter writes occasionally."

Alix felt a twinge of pity for her unhappy mother-in-law.

"So you've bought a truck after all," she said, looking from the hostel veranda to the vehicle parked outside the hotel, piled high with skins.

"Yes—have to move with the times, I suppose. Still prefer horses myself, but when there's no feed, motor vehicles come in handy. And they don't eat petrol when they're not working. Even the mail comes from Windorah by motor-car now."

"Next thing it'll be by aeroplane."

"Whatever next! I've never seen one of those contraptions, except in pictures."

"Come in and see my model aeroplane, Grandpa," said Caro, tugging at his hand.

"Guess who made it," said Alix. "Your old mate Harry Hays from Duthie."

"Old Harry, eh? Fat lot *he* would know about aeroplanes. Horses were more in his line."

"Yes; he told us he was nearly killed when his night-horse fell during a rush at—at—where was it?"

"The Ranken Plain. Yes, that's one of his favourite yarns."

Alix could not get home for Christmas; it was February before they arrived back in Adelaide. She was shocked to see her father so weak and breathless.

He'd had one heart attack, and had to take things very quietly. He'd even had to give up lawn bowls, his only exercise. Frances belonged to a croquet club and played in the parklands once a week.

Caro did not find her "other grandpa" as entertaining as Grandpa Manning. He could walk only very slowly in the garden, and when she asked him if he could make her another model aeroplane, he said he was no good at carving things. Instead he sent Frances in to the shops to buy her a model aeroplane, which gave her immense pleasure.

In Adelaide, living at home with her mother and her bridge parties, Alix found the time dragging. Frances dropped many hints that after more than ten years as a widow, Alix should be thinking about marrying again.

"You're still young enough to start another family. Don't you think Caro should have a brother or sister?"

Alix tried to explain that nursing and her career were still important to her and she did not intend to tie herself down. She was only marking time before taking up another position with the A.I.M., somewhere in the outback.

In May 1928 the *Inlander* announced the opening of the first Flying Doctor base at Cloncurry in western Queensland. A small single-engined DH50 Moth was on lease from Qantas, who also lent a pilot, and the Commonwealth Government promised a subsidy for every mile flown.

"I knew the service would come," John Flynn had said. "My faith in it never wavered."

The Cloncurry base could cover eventually a huge area from the Gulf of Carpentaria to well over the South Australian border. The town had an airfield and hangar and a public hospital with a resident medical officer, apart from the Flying Doctor.

The same issue contained the news that one of the Sisters at Alice Springs had to go on sick leave for an indefinite time, and a single nurse was needed to take over till she returned. Alix sent off her application. With her qualifications she expected no trouble in getting the position.

When the reply came, asking her to proceed to the Alice in the following autumn, she told her mother rather diffidently, feeling she might be expected to stay and help look after Caro. But Frances seemed pleased, though she and Alix had been getting on better of late.

In Adelaide Caro missed the swimming-hole—for they were ten miles from the sea—just as she had missed her pony when they first left the station. In Birdsville there were few horses in town except during the Picnic Races once a year, when riders came in from all the stations round. There was not enough feed for them in most seasons, and the cost of transporting fodder was too high.

Alix took Caro for an interview with the headmistress of a girls' school in the farther foothills, at Brown Hill Creek. The grounds were spacious;

it turned out that they included a stable so that day-girls could ride to school.

Caro hated the thought of boarding-school. Her grandmother backed her in asking that she should live at home with her grandparents when Alix went back to the bush. Caro begged for a horse so that she could ride to school; there was a large vacant paddock just across the road from Grandma's where a horse could be kept on agistment during the week.

Alix objected that she could not afford to buy and feed a horse. But her father said he would be happy to get a pony for Caro so that she could ride to school every day, and save boarding fees. It was three against one, and Alix gave in.

Major MacFarlane did not believe in half-measures. He brought for Caro a pedigreed white Arab mare, with a beautiful head and flowing silver tail. So it was that Caro appeared to her less fortunate schoolmates, all of whom without exception were horse-mad, to be a kind of princess, traditionally blonde and mounted on a milk-white steed. And Caro did not stint on her descriptions of Grandfather Manning's cattle-station and the size of the homestead at Cappamerri, which began to sound like a palace.

Alix said goodbye to her father at home, before Frances drove with her to the station.

"Well, my girl," he said gruffly. "I probably won't be here next time you come back—"

"Don't say that, Father!"

"It's true, though. I could pop off any time, doctor tells me. Not that I care much, now I'm not fit for anything, not even bowls." He brushed his white moustache back with the old military gesture, and straightened his shoulders. "Well, goodbye, dear."

He hugged her tightly, and she kissed his slack old man's cheek and brushed away a tear as she turned to get into the car.

While she had been home Alix had learned to drive the car, and got her driving-licence. Now she slid behind the wheel, with her mother in the passenger seat. The hood of the convertible was down, and they both wore close-fitting hats that would not blow off. "Did he tell you he hasn't got long?" asked Frances, seeing that Alix was upset. "It has done him good, having you home, and young Caro will keep us both young. That's why I'm so glad she's going to live with us. It will stop me being so lonely when . . . when . . ."

Alix pressed her hand. She put the car into gear, starting off smoothly in bottom and then changing up without any grating of teeth.

As it was a schoolday, she had said goodbye to Caro in the morning. With all her new interests, she did not seem to feel the parting as much as her mother. Alix hated to leave her behind, but she wanted Caro to

236

have two or three years' secondary education before she decided what she wanted to do with her life.

"I expect I might do nursing, like you," Caro had said, but at thirteen she could not be sure.

The trip to Alice Springs, which she had dreamt about for so long, did not disappoint Alix. After leaving Oodnadatta the train toiled north over the wide sandy beds of dry rivers, then the orange Depot sand-hills and the empty Finke River. Beyond rose a pale-blue wave: the Ooraminna Range, and then a flat peneplain with low tent-hills on the horizon; wandering wild camels and donkeys along the track, and finally the splendid, bare Macdonnells, which seemed to lie right across their route.

Then two rocky masses moved apart like shifting stage scenery, and an opening appeared in the mountain wall—and as they came through Heavitree Gap, there quite suddenly was the town, with its few white roofs nestling beneath the green gum-trees that lined the Todd River. Though the river was dry, the trees on its banks and growing right in the channel were flourishing. Others grew in the middle of the few streets, giving the whole town a pleasant park-like air. The sky that arched above was a pure pale blue, darkening to almost purple above the ranges.

Here she was, thought Alix, in the most central town in the heart of Australia. The springs themselves and the telegraph station were farther north. The town was still officially named Stuart, and had less than a hundred residents.

There was one hotel, the Stuart Arms, a police station, two stores, and the imposing stone building of Adelaide House. After Marree and Oodnadatta the place looked cool and inviting. With nearly every house having a fresh-water well, good vegetable gardens abounded, and even a few flowers. There was also a new railway station. Alix and the final extension of the railway from Oodnadatta had arrived in Alice Springs together.

The lone Sister was being helped by a retired A.I.M. nurse married to the local police constable. Hearing this, Alix scarcely dared ask if it was a Mrs. McGuinnes. But she found she did not know the policeman.

The pedal wireless now linked women all over the outback in gossip and comradeship for a time each morning, known unflatteringly as the "galah session." Alix found that Jack and his wife were at Innamincka in South Australia; she had a brief chat with the former Sister Henley from Marree. Jack was out on patrol, she said. The Cooper had long ceased to run, and even the big waterhole was almost dry.

Because of the springs, because of the fresh water lying ready to be tapped just under the sand, Alice Springs was a true oasis in the red, burning heart of the continent. There was sweet water lying in pools in the ranges at places like Emily Gap, which held the blue sky, red and orange rocks, and some enigmatic Aboriginal ochre designs in calm reflection.

Then there was the blue in the atmosphere. This was something intangible, yet all-pervading. It veiled the distances in shimmering colour, so that red hills became mauve or softest blue; the closer rocks turned more purple than red and the shadows in their clefts a deep and vibrant cobalt. Against them the trunks of the ghost-gums, as pure and pale as if they had been whitewashed, stood out in clear contrast.

There was no Aboriginal Ward, she noticed; the cool, comfortable building of Adelaide House was for whites only.

"I expected to see more natives around the town," she said to Sister Plomer on her second day.

"A lot of them, the Arunta people, are out at Hermannsburg, the Lutheran mission—about eighty miles away. Those who still stay round the Alice live outside the Gap, to the south where the Police Constable has his house."

"What about a clinic for the children?"

"We don't have a regular clinic, but they are brought in if they're really ill. They don't like going into hospital. We use the clubroom in the grounds for a Black Ward when necessary."

Alix liked to walk out, when she was not on duty, to watch the dawn on Mount Gillen, the nearest peak of the Macdonnells. It was painted with the marvellous haze of blue, through which the red rock burned as the sun picked up the peak and outlined the folded strata sloping steeply down to the plateau beneath. The range rose straight out of the flat, without any intervening foothills.

An old black man was ambling along in the sand, dressed in shapeless cast-offs of shirt and trousers, his feet bare, his chin bearded. Alix caught up with him. "Good-day," she said, the universal greeting of the bush. "How y' going?"

"Orright." He glanced at her once from his bloodshot dark eyes, then kept his eyes before his feet. His voice was low, almost a whisper. What have we done to these people? she thought. Was it the dazzling technology of the white man, was it the guns, the vehicles, their sheer numbers?

Yet whites were not numerous in the far inland. This man and most other members of his race seemed to be overwhelmed, subdued, unable to assert themselves or even to speak up, to look "the bosses" in the eye. They were—yes, the word was cowed. Once their land, their ancient waterholes, had been taken from them, it was almost as if they had ceased to exist.

There was a good reason why the natives of the centre should be quiet and inoffensive: fear. The older ones would remember, as children, seeing their parents shot down like kangaroos for trying to protect their precious waterholes and native wells, their land to which they "belonged" in a mystical relationship with every rock, with every hill and gully.

And not only the older ones; only last year, in 1928, the murder of Fred Brook at Brooks' Soak, 150 miles to the north-west near Coniston Station, had led to much ill-feeling, for his body had been dismembered. A punitive party under Constable Murray had set out from Alice Springs, and rumours of wholesale slaughter filtered back to the cities on the distant coast.

"What-name that feller?" asked Alix in a friendly voice, indicating the sharp edge of Mount Gillen outlined against the pale morning sky.

"That one belong Dingo-dreaming," murmured the old man. "Long time ago, Dingo-men come along t' ranges, come out of t' desert, come along 'ere; and this feller, big Old-Man of Dingo tribe, he stop 'ere an' look aroun', he sniff aroun'. Him turn to rock. You see 'im sniff the air, that dingo snout up there? Him still sit-down; that place belong him."

"Thank you," said Alix with feeling. Of course! Now she looked at it, the peak of the mount *was* a dingo snout, the head of a giant dog who ranged the country in the dream-time. And to the old man, though all else was changed and his tribal life was no more, the Dingo ancestor was still real and present.

CHAPTER THIRTY-FIVE

For the long Christmas holidays Alix had hoped Caro would come up in the train, travelling in the care of the guard, but a diphtheria epidemic broke out in the Alice, and Alix sent a wire by way of the Overland Telegraph telling Caro not to come. One of the retired, married Sisters living in the town came to live in, so there would not have been room for her anyway. Already the extra nurse occupied a bed on the screened veranda. Watching their patients night and day, and visiting others at their homes, the small band of nurses became exhausted.

One night Sister Plomer performed an emergency tracheotomy on a little girl choking to death from the false membrane growing across her throat. Intubation was performed at once so that the child could breathe through the tube, but she had to be watched continuously. She gradually recovered. But three others had died.

"And we might have saved them all if we'd been called in earlier," said Sister Plomer crossly.

She was plump and good-natured, but lack of sleep and strain were beginning to tell on her.

Alix's skill and practice in stitching wounds was called on when a young man, driving a rusty old truck, turned it over in a washaway and badly gashed his foot.

"He should have a shot of tetanus antitoxin," said Alix, consulting the senior Sister.

"We are very low in antitoxin," said Sister Plomer. "Are you sure it's necessary? The wound was a clean one, wasn't it?"

"Yes, but road-dirt—he's a definite risk. I'd like to give him as much as we've got."

The wound was already healing when Tom Greaves, the young truck-driver, came in complaining of "tight" gums and a stiff neck. Alix admitted him at once. "We must get some more antitoxin," she said. "It must be a bad infection; the small dose hasn't stopped the symptoms beginning."

She pedalled a message to the Flying Doctor base at Cloncurry. "Please bring anti-tetanus vaccine urgent. Alice Springs Hostel."

A message came back that the Flying Doctor was out on a call over the Territory border.

He would get in touch as soon as he returned. Their own supply was low, but they'd get some more flown up from Brisbane.

"Damn!" said Alix, and went back to her patient. The dreadful tetanic cramps were beginning; teeth clenched, back arched, he fought through them with sweating brow and emerged from each attack exhausted.

"I want absolute quiet in the hospital," said Alix. "Not even a dropped saucepan, and no noisy feet in the corridors. The slightest sound can send him into a convulsion."

Everyone tiptoed about the two wards. Young Tom was the only patient in Men's, fortunately, and on the second day came a wire from Cloncurry: the doctor would fly down tomorrow with the antitoxin, arriving probably after sunset.

All was quiet when the young man's boss, the owner of the truck, arrived at the hospital demanding to see the patient.

"I'm sorry, Mr. Roberts, no one can see him. He needs absolute rest and quiet."

"Rubbish! I only want to see if he's all right, wants me to bring any-thing—"

He pushed past Sister Plomer and arrived at the door to the Men's Ward. Here Sister Alix stood on guard; she had heard the argument and was furious at the disturbance.

"Get back!" she said, barring the entrance with an arm across the opening.

"Out of my way!" said the man rudely. Alix whipped the other arm from behind her back. She brandished a syringe filled with liquid.

"Look out! Unless you want an injection that will make you very sick," she said quietly. "Now kindly get out—quickly!"

"And if you attempt to come back I will fetch Constable Rycroft to deal with you," said Sister Plomer behind him.

He went, muttering, but a few days later the Secretary of the Hospital Committee came in to report that Roberts was spreading a story round the town that young Tom would have been all right, but his foot became infected through dirty sheets at the hospital.

Sister Plomer laughed grimly. "That is *nonsense!* The tetanus bacillus entered at the time of the wound, with road-dirt driven into the flesh. It usually takes some time for symptoms to manifest themselves, and we were watching for them."

Because the Flying Doctor's plane would be arriving after dark, the Constable organized all the owners of vehicles in the town to go out to the airstrip, park all round it, and shine their lights towards the centre as soon as they heard the drone of the little aeroplane.

About two hours after sunset, the plane was heard approaching from the north-east. The pilot had to battle a south-easterly, almost a head-wind, and had needed to refuel on the way. A small fire with white smoke, lit by the nearest headlights, showed him the wind direction for coming in to land. He circled twice and put down, bumping over the rough runway that was rarely used.

Constable Rycroft was there to meet the doctor. He climbed down carrying his doctor's bag in which lay the precious serum. The people gathered round in the darkness cheered.

The hostel, because of its generator, was one of the few well-lit buildings after dark. The policeman dropped the doctor there.

"Hallo, Sister, I've brought you a parcel," said the man casually.

"Oh, thank you! And you are?"

"I'm the doctor. Dr. Vickers."

"I'm sorry! Of course, Dr. Vickers! Come through."

The doctor quickly washed his hands in a basin provided by Alix, and unpacked his bag.

"Good nursing, next to the antitoxin, is the most important thing in tetanus cases," he said. He cast an appreciative eye over the ward and the nurse in charge. Alix gave a restrained smile. "I've been specialling him, day and night," she said. "He is holding his own; but beginning to get exhausted with the spasms. I've given him barbiturates regularly."

"Well, Tom," said the doctor quietly, lifting the young man's arm and sponging it with methylated spirits. "I'm just going to give you an injection of antitoxin, a much bigger dose than you had before, which will help you fight the infection, and beat it."

The young man's mouth was clamped shut, his dark eyes looked frightened. He made no sign that he felt the needle, but almost imperceptibly he began to relax, reassured by the mere fact of the doctor's presence.

Dr. Vickers talked to Sister Manning just outside the door of the ward. "I think we've got it to him in time," he said. "Thank God! With that head wind, and being afraid we'd miss the town in the dark, I was worried."

"You are doing a marvellous job," said Alix warmly. She had taken an instant liking to the slender young doctor with his thick, dark hair and strong dark brows. How old was he? Hard to tell, but he might be thirty at the most. "We hear stories of the Flying Doctor all the time, and I get the *Inlander*. You are very game, flying in all weathers."

"Don't worry, the pilot won't fly if he thinks the weather is too bad. I've had many an argument with Arthur about taking off on an urgent flight when he said it was impossible. He's right, of course; no sense losing the plane, the pilot, and the doctor through being foolhardy."

Dr. Vickers kindly offered to stay with the patient while Alix had a break. She had tea with Sister Plomer and Arthur Affleck, the first Flying Doctor pilot.

"Your aeroplane looks very small," said Sister Plomer, pouring tea.

Alix noted that the pilot had a big nose and a long, humorous face. He looked as if he enjoyed his work.

"Yes—but Moths are easy to fly, and you can land almost anywhere. In Normanton you land in the main street—it's wide enough and empty enough—and taxi up to the pub."

"Normanton—that's on the Gulf, isn't it?" asked Alix.

"Near enough. It's about twenty miles up the estuary of the Norman River. Full of big salt-water crocs, too. I saw some of the local blacks swimming the river, back to their camp on the far side. They all swam in a bunch, sending an old lubra on ahead, and with an old dog following behind. They reckoned if there were any crocodiles around they would get them first."

He told them about "Bedourie showers," dust-storms so thick that you could not see ahead through the dusky red curtain, but had to look behind for landmarks. "Like they say, the crows out there fly backwards to keep the dust out of their eyes.

"It's real bad country out between Cloncurry and Mount Isa," he said. "There are all these sharp rocky hills and the flat land is all trees or spinifex. But landing in a smooth paddock is just as bad if it's too small. I once managed to get down in a tiny paddock in an emergency, but the question was how to get out again? I backed the craft into a corner, with six men from the town holding on to each wing and the tail-skid roped to a corner post. Revved her up, and shouted 'Let go!' Someone cut the rope, and we were up and away.

"But we didn't have enough height to clear the telegraph lines just ahead. So I flew under them."

Sister Plomer shook her head unbelievingly. "Now, Sister," she said, "I think you should take a little rest while you have the chance. I'll take over while Dr. Vickers has his tea."

"But I don't feel tired," said Alix, who hoped for another talk with Dr. Vickers, though her head was swimming with weariness.

"Off you go," said Sister Plomer. "I'll call you a bit later."

The little DH50 *Victory* took off at dawn next morning for a six-hundred-mile flight to Croydon, in northern Queensland, to pick up a child with meningitis. But thanks to the doctor's visit, and the extra serum, Alix's patient recovered. He was to be an ardent supporter of the Flying Doctor Service for the rest of his life.

Chapter Thirty-six

Major MacFarlane died in the new year. In February there was a prolonged heat wave when the city temperatures finally reached 112 degrees in the shade. Many city-dwellers went down to the beach or into the parklands to sleep. Caro and Frances took mattresses out on the front lawn, inside the prickly hedge, and slept under the stars. The clear starry sky, once the street lights had been turned out at midnight, reminded Caro of camping out in the Inland.

Was Grandpa somewhere up there, among or beyond those thousands upon thousands of stars? It was very confusing. They told you he had died; that was all they knew for certain. One day he was there, the next he had disappeared forever. (Frances had sent her to stay with a school-friend until the funeral was over. She was glad she was not expected to attend.) Or they said, "He has passed away." Yes, but where? Where did he go?

She had seen animals die, to be left where they fell, until in the burning air of the Inland the skin and dried flesh fell away, leaving only whitened bones. It would be more simple to think that people just went to bones, like dogs and cattle.

Frances said simply that Grandpa had "gone to Heaven." She took Caro each week to the local Church of England service, where Caro found the old clergyman's dull sermon unutterably boring, and the prayers went over her head. They sang about "Peace in Thy Heaven." But where was Heaven now that the sky was traversed by noisy aeroplanes that sometimes flew above the clouds?

Frances wrote to Alix to tell her of her father's death. She did not use the phrase "blessed release," but she implied that he had been glad to go.

It is such a help to me to have Caro here [she wrote]. Of course Robert was older than me, and I knew I'd probably be left a widow one day, but after forty years of marriage, it is very strange to be alone. . . .

Your father has left everything to me, apart from a small bequest to Caro when she shall have reached the age of 21. He knew that the house and all I have will be yours when I go. I shall of course continue to pay Caro's school fees and look after her needs. . . . I suggested she take dancing classes with some of the other girls, but she doesn't seem interested. All her spare time is spent with that horse.

Alix was a little surprised and hurt that her father had left her nothing, not even a token hundred pounds. Of course she had her war widow's pension, and there was nothing to spend money on in Alice Springs. She was saving most of her small salary. Perhaps her father had thought that she should have stayed at home and nursed him in his last illness?

At least all the expense of Caro's schooling and clothing was taken off her hands.

Alice Springs was growing rapidly since the railway had arrived, and soon no doubt would have its own doctor and school. Yet old-timers still sat in the sun outside the Stuart Arms, or perched on saddles and packs at Charley Myers' saddlery, when the day was cold. They puffed on their pipes, nested among nicotine-stained whiskers, and yarned the time away.

"John Flynn's done a wonderful thing," one of them said. "He's the right sort of parson for out here—and he chooses the right men, like Skipper Partridge."

Apart from the roving Presbyterian ministers such as Kingsley Partridge —known affectionately throughout the centre as Skipper—and the Anglican Bush Brotherhood farther north, there was also a Methodist Mission at Tennant Creek.

Skipper Partridge arrived in the Alice on his way back from one of his patrols for the A.I.M. He brought the story of the young Methodist parson who had recently disappeared from Tennant Creek. The news had just come through on the radio.

The young man, fresh from Melbourne and knowing nothing about the bush, had arrived in town with his wife and their little dog. The Church provided a car for him to visit the mines and the more accessible parts of his parish.

Hearing that the wife of the manager at Rockhampton Downs was something of an invalid, who could not travel into town to church, the young man decided to pay her a visit and at the same time show his wife something of the country. The station homestead was only sixty miles away over a well-used track, to the east of the Overland Telegraph line. The minister was warned of the dangers of leaving the north-south road, and of the need to carry water; but he had good mechanical knowledge, and was confident of his ability to get through.

They set out by car, taking the little dog with them. At Number 3 Bore the dusty road was, as usual, obliterated by cattle-tracks from beasts coming in to drink and fanning out to get feed. The thing to do was to make a wide circle round the bore, until the unobliterated track was cut. But they did not know this. They followed the best-marked cattle-track, which led out into an area of sand and gilgai bush, with no road at all. After about four miles the tracks began to disperse out into the bush. The car bogged down in sand. Although the temperature was fierce, above 115 degrees in the shade, they set out to walk for help.

When they failed to arrive at the station, which they had informed by radio of their intention, the manager set out to look for them; but it grew dark, and he went back to the station and radioed the police in Tennant Creek. The party from town, including the Constable and Skipper Partridge, set out at first light and found the car tracks diverging from the bore.

"We'd been joined by the men from the station, and we found the bodies about ten in the morning," said Skipper. "They had only walked about five miles but it was very hot, and they must have become dehydrated before long. We found the little dog first; and I couldn't help thinking how that kind-hearted young woman probably gave the last of the water to the dog, which would've become distressed first—not realizing the deadly danger they were in themselves.

"When we found the two bodies we put them on the back of the Constable's truck and took them back to Tennant. It was rough and we had no rope. They kept sliding off. In the end I had to sit in the back and hold them."

He closed his eyes a moment as if to shut out the memory. "They would never have thought," he added, "that anyone could perish on a trip of only sixty miles on a well-used station track. Who would dream . . ."

"I would," said Alix, reminded once more of Mab's end.

"Oh—! Of course. Sorry, Sister Alix. I'd forgotten."

Alix was shaken. She remembered someone in Hergott Springs—Jack McGuinnes?—warning them: "This is an unforgiving country. You only have to make one mistake, and that mistake can be fatal." Yes, it was a cruel country. And though its harsh conditions created great "characters," its centres of settlement contained some narrow-minded and prejudiced people.

She had seen how the Aborigines who once owned all this beautiful area had been pushed outside the new town, and away from the springs, to a settlement south of Heavitree Gap. They had become fringe-dwellers, hangers-on, except those given the status of black tracker for the police. The others had no respect and little consideration from the white invaders.

Their money was as good as anyone's, yet she had seen them forced to wait in the shop to buy their bottle of "lolly-water," their loaf of white bread, while all the other customers, even later comers, were served first. And she remembered the ill-natured gossip over the tetanus case, when the hostel was accused of causing the infection through dirty sheets.

Alix began to feel that Alice Springs, in spite of its physical beauty,

246

was not for her. Since the railway had arrived, it was becoming too big. She would like a smaller place again, or a bigger place, like Cloncurry, the centre of the Flying Doctor network. Meanwhile, once her time was up, she would go back to Adelaide to see Caro, who had not come before because of the diphtheria epidemic.

She felt a longing for the trim little city on its coastal plain, with the rounded hills behind and the blue waters of the Gulf St. Vincent in front, and no blacks with a lost darkness in their eyes to trouble her conscience.

She would go home for a while, and get to know her daughter again.

And then she thought of that attractive Flying Doctor, the amusing pilot who flew him into the Alice. Perhaps she might go to Cloncurry in western Queensland, the base from which all those wonderful mercy flights set out, and where at times she might become a Flying Nurse.

Alix sent a wire to her mother and began packing her things. She was looking forward to her trip on the 'Ghan, which now had not only sleeping berths but a dining car. A few tourists were beginning to discover the red centre.

The train made a long stop in Oodnadatta on the way down. She went to call on the Sisters in the little bush hostel that had been one of the first to be built. With its low iron roof and veranda and water-tanks to catch the infrequent rains, it reminded her of the Hergott Springs hostel where she and Mab had nursed together. But in front of this building was a well-grown palm tree, and a garden of established shrubs sheltered by a neat picket fence, which made it look much less bare and hot than the Hergott building on its stony plain.

Alix had a cup of tea with the Sisters, who were young and enthusiastic, as she had been once. It was almost twenty years since she had qualified as a nurse. Would she like to be starting again at Oodnadatta, or somewhere similar? No; she envied them but she did not wish to go back.

BOOK TWO

CHAPTER ONE

Caro Manning thought she'd had a wonderfully interesting childhood, except that she'd never had a father, as far as she could remember. She went to the morning service in the city on Armistice Day and thought about him, so dashing and handsome in his turned-up hat with the emu feathers in the photograph Mummy took with her everywhere in its beaten-silver frame. A lump came into Caro's throat during the two minutes' silence. At the stroke of eleven the whole city stopped: trams and traffic and pedestrians with blood-red silk poppies pinned to their coats in memory of the dead. Then came the long-drawn quivering notes of the bugle, so heart-rendingly sad: the Last Post. Then the traffic started up, and life went on as before.

Caro's grandmother had settled down in her role as the widow of a distinguished man. No longer insecure in her social position, Frances had become more relaxed and less prejudiced. Of course, she still believed that Aborigines and Chinamen were dirty, and that "nice" women did not get divorced; and she did not approve of these new beach pyjamas, or even of riding trousers. But she had to admit that Caro was a trim figure, with her long legs and small waist, in the jodhpurs Alix had sent her with a pair of short riding boots. If Caro liked horse-riding and climbing trees, and absolutely refused to learn to play bridge, Frances blamed her granddaughter's tomboyish ways on the years she had spent on the cattle-station when she was little.

In 1930, when Caro was fourteen years old, an event occurred which she was to remember for the rest of her life: Amy Johnson came to Adelaide at the end of her record-breaking flight from England.

The Great Depression had touched Caro very lightly. Her life was bounded by school, and as she rarely went to the city, she did not see the misery of the unemployed, the queues for sustenance, the peaceful marches of the hungry demanding work. As a change from the gloomy financial news, the newspapers were suddenly full of stories about Amy Johnson, the adventurous young Englishwoman in her tiny Moth biplane.

By the time she touched down in Darwin after crossing the Timor Sea on the last leg of her journey, the press was delighted; for Amy was slender and photogenic, with an English-rose complexion. This slip of a girl on her "epic flight" had become a heroine.

251

Wherever she stopped the crowds became ecstatic, the adulation almost hysterical. In Adelaide a welcoming reception was organized.

Frances took Caro into town for the public meeting in the old Exhibition Building. They parked some way up North Terrace, and as they neared the building the crowd thickened. Soon they were jammed in an immovable mass of people waiting to welcome the young aviatrix.

Caro began to feel panicky.

She had never been caught in a crowd before, forced to stand still, forced to move when it moved, to sway forward when the official cars arrived and people tried frantically to get a glimpse of their heroine. Caro saw nothing; she closed her eyes and clung desperately to her grandmother's plump arm, fearing she would faint or suffocate among the taller adults.

Then at last there was space and air. The crowd thinned as Amy Johnson passed into the building, and those who had tickets moved up the steps. Frances resolutely pushed forward and found two seats not too far from the front. The crowd was conducted in singing, "When Johnnie comes flying home again, hurrah, hurrah!" and there were official welcome speeches; then Amy was speaking.

Caro listened entranced to the soft, girlish voice, stared at the slight figure in a long fur coat, at the wavy brown hair and pink cheeks of what had become her idol. At last it was over. There were some questions from the body of the hall, some friendly Australian chi-acking, then she was coming down from the dais and along the aisle towards the front door.

Caro held her breath. As the young woman came opposite her seat on the aisle, Caro put out a tremulous hand and touched the soft fur coat. "Amy Johnson, Amy Johnson, I love you!" she chanted under her breath.

She went home in a daze of emotion.

"I think I'd like to be an airwoman," Caro announced next morning. "I'd like to learn to fly."

"Out of the question!" said her grandmother. "That is not a career for women, dear."

"What about Amy Johnson?"

"That is quite different. She is an *English* aviatrix. There may be openings for women flyers over there, but a young lady could never make a career of flying in Australia."

At fifteen Caro went through a period of adolescent gloom, brooding upon death and tortured by religious doubts and guilt about sex. Sex was everywhere, and she was obsessed with it. She watched the pigeons mating on the roof, the little gilded flies jumping on each other in a beam of sunlight, a rooster treading the hens in the chook-yard at the bottom of Grandma's garden. She climbed a smooth-limbed wattle-tree, its crown a mass of silver leaves and golden puffballs, and pressed a rounded bough between her thighs.

Since her mother was a nurse, it should have been possible to talk to her about such things, but the thought made Caro go hot all over. In developing she had grown away from Alix, who had prepared her sensibly for menstruation but not for sexual maturity. And as for asking Grandma, the very idea was unthinkable.

On her return from Alice Springs Alix had found her daughter changed, more mature, though she still wore her hair in long fair plaits; her breasts were starting to develop and she was starting to take an interest in boys.

Alix decided to do a midwifery course at her old hospital. She was able to live at home and travel to work each day. When Alix came off duty wearing her nurse's uniform, Caro looked at her admiringly. She had watched films set in the First World War, which she was too young to remember. The Army nurses were shown as Sisters of Mercy, their flowing veils a symbol of succour and self-sacrifice. But there were films, too, about gallant airmen in caps and goggles, engaging enemy flyers in desperate dogfights in their flimsy aircraft of wood and cloth.

When her mother asked her what she wanted to do when she left school, Caro wasn't sure if she wanted to be a nurse or a pilot.

"Of course, Grandma would want me to be a nurse," she said. "She thinks flying is unladylike. Yet she took me to see Amy Johnson."

"Grandma thought nursing unladylike when I wanted to take it up more than twenty years ago. Her attitudes have changed a bit since the war. If you take up nursing, you must be sure it's what you really want to do. Would you like to come bush nursing with me? I'm thinking of asking for a post in Cloncurry—that's the Flying Doctor base in far western Queensland. Perhaps you could do part of your training there."

"I don't know. Anyway, I'd like a holiday on Cappamerri first. Grandpa must be terribly lonely. And he might leave me some money when he dies," she added naively.

Alix did not take that up. "Yes . . . well, we'll see." She presumed that Big Jim would leave his property to his grandson in Brisbane. If there was anything left to leave.

By the time Alix had finished midwifery, a letter confirming her appointment for the coming year arrived from Cloncurry Hospital. Her old friend John Flynn, "Flynn of the Inland" as he was now known, had written her a reference.

She and Caro looked up the town on the map of Queensland. Caro pointed out that to go from Adelaide to Cloncurry in a straight line was only about eight hundred miles. To go round the coast and then north-west by train was almost three times as far.

"If I had an aeroplane," she said, "I could fly you there in three hops."

"I'll enjoy the sea voyage," said her mother. It was possible to fly from

Brisbane to Cloncurry these days in one of the little Qantas mail planes; but in truth she was rather afraid of flying.

Alix went by boat and train, and rocking westward over the endless grassy plains she thought once more what an enormous country this was: the thousands of miles between Sydney and Perth, between Adelaide and Darwin, the empty deserts of the interior and these lonely plains that seemed to be inhabited only by sheep and cattle. Flynn was right. This was a land that cried out for the aeroplane.

After the treeless downs they came to open savannah where the trunks of the iron-bark trees were black against the tawny grass, and their leaves a silvery blue, a most unlikely combination.

That night, alone in her compartment, Alix switched off the overhead light and watched the brilliant stars go reeling past, yet keeping pace with the train. Venus as the evening star dived behind a small hill and reappeared like a silver lamp almost ahead. Alix was leaning out the window, smelling the grass with dew on it under the scent of coal-smoke coming from the engine. A thrilling whistle streamed back across the night, the wheels clacked rhythmically over the track, the carriage rocked. Flying above the earth could not be as exciting as this! They seemed to be boring a tunnel through the night, the powerful headlamp piercing the darkness ahead.

She slept at last, outstretched on the padded seat with her head towards the window. Her last waking sight was of the Southern Cross, low to the horizon and about to dip below it, as it never did in the south.

Next day there were patches of spinifex and red sand, the spiky spinifex flowering with tall yellow fronds and waving like a wheat-field. Here there were small but shapely eucalyptus with slender white trunks and green leaves among the dry creeks and jump-ups. Then Black Mountain and the mine workings appeared and the train pulled in to Cloncurry, only two hundred miles from the Gulf of Carpentaria, where the sea takes a great bite into the north of the continent. The soil was still red, but she was no longer in the centre.

CHAPTER TWO

"It's quite all right, Grandma," said Caro impatiently, "you get the very best training at the Adelaide Public Hospital."

"Your mother trained at North Adelaide, and I'm sure it is nicer."

"Grandma! She did her midwifery at the Queen Victoria Maternity Home, which is a free hospital. We used to knit babies' vests at school for them."

Frances set her lips in the thin, down-turned line they had taken since Major MacFarlane died. "Well! Please yourself, then."

"I intend to."

Caro enrolled for the three-and-a-half year course, including midwifery, on her seventeenth birthday; but stayed on at school till after the final exams in November. Then she sold her mare, not without some tears at parting, and opened a bank account. She was saving up to buy a second-hand motor-car. Although Caro had her driving-licence and loved to drive her grandmother's car, Frances would rarely let her take it out on her own.

The dilemma facing Caro was that she needed a car to get out to Parafield Aerodrome, but then she would have no money left for flying lessons. Since it seemed that it was impossible for a woman to make a career as a commercial pilot, except perhaps in the Flying Doctor service, she would make nursing her career and somehow combine it with flying. She knew now with absolute certainty that she wanted to fly. And when she came into Grandpa MacFarlane's money, she would buy her own little plane.

She celebrated her first week at the hospital, which provided accommodation in a separate building for a Nurses' Home, by getting her schoolgirl plaits cut off. Then she went defiantly to see her grandmother, wearing a hat so as not to give her too much of a shock at first. The salon shampoo had made her straight hair shine in all its gold and silvery-brown strands.

"Well! I don't know what your mother will say," said Frances when she saw the plaits were gone.

"It's my hair, and I'm not a schoolgirl any more, Grandma."

"Alas, no," said Frances with a sigh.

Caro put her arms round her. "Cheer up, you'll get used to it after you've seen it a few times."

255

Caro rather neglected her grandmother in the freedom of having her own quarters. It was a long tram ride out to the suburb where Frances lived, and a long walk from the tram. So much time was spent in travelling that she would make the effort not more than once every two weeks, when she was invited to midday dinner. Trams did not run on Sunday morning, so she had an excuse not to arrive in time for church.

Alix sent her blessings on the nursing career, and a postcard of the hangar with the Flying Doctor plane outside it, a red cross painted on the side. It was a small plane with one engine, but it had an enclosed cabin. Caro pinned the postcard on the wall of her cell-like room, half underground, which she shared with a thin, cheerful nurse called Betty.

There followed a long letter from Alix describing the town of Cloncurry and its surroundings:

This is the centre of a mining district, a fading "copper town" because of the fall in the price of copper.

Round Cloncurry are low craggy hills which radiate the heat in summer so that even the nights are often hot; it can be 103 degrees at 8 P.M. You know what dust-storms can be like, and there are willy-willies which one of the pilots told me can reach up to two thousand feet.

But winter here is beautiful . . . cold and clear and sunny. Just after daylight the ground is covered with frost, the native cypress-pines white-frosted like Christmas trees and the air wonderfully clear and fragrant. All the rivers here flow north, which seems strange to me. That is, when they flow at all.

The hospital is old but well-equipped, with cases being brought in from all round the map by the Flying Doctor Service—it covers an area of 300,000 square miles! I get on well with Matron, partly because of my being so long in the tooth. She hasn't much patience with young probationers, so perhaps it's just as well you're not training here.

Please write and tell me all your news, and give my love to Grandma. She must be missing you now that you're living away. You must make time to go and see her on your days off.

Betty had a friend who was a photographer on the evening newspaper. She asked Caro to make a foursome with them on their evening off, as her friend, Barry Muirden, was bringing a journalist from the same paper along. They were going to have dinner at a little pub in the hills.

Caro was excited. This was her first date with someone older, not one of her school-friends' brothers. They called for her in the photographer's Buick, which belonged to his paper, the *Standard*. The other man was a blur in the back seat; she only caught the gleam of glasses and a flash of white teeth as they were introduced.

On the way round the hairpin bends to Clarendon, she was thrown against this stranger who obligingly put his arm round her to steady her. She was nervous and talked in a continuous stream to Betty in the front seat. In the light of the hotel veranda, when they arrived, she found that Malcolm was not tall, rather stocky, with a lot of short wavy dark hair and a humorous mouth that was wide and curly to match his hair; the upper lip long, Irish, and deeply indented. Then as they took their seats in the dining room, which was empty of other guests, and he sat opposite her, she saw that he had the most amazing dark-blue eyes. They were enlarged by his horn-rimmed spectacles, and shone with a lively intelligence. She found them hypnotic.

With their steaks they had a good local red wine; and Caro, unused to alcohol, became a little elevated.

Both sides of the table talked shop a little, Caro and Betty telling stories of the horrid, arrogant honorary surgeon who thought he was God; and Malcolm of the insensitive sub-editors who ruined his best opening paragraphs.

Half-way through the second bottle of red, Barry sang a little ditty while Malcolm beat time with two spoons:

Caviar comes from virgin sturgeon,
Virgin sturgeon is a fish,
Virgin sturgeon needs no urgin',
That's why it's my favourite dish.

I had a sweetheart kind and gentle
She was a virgin tried and true,
But since I fed my love on caviar
There is nothing she won't do.

Then Caro recited a verse from "The Bastard from the Bush," beginning:

"Would you let a woman work and slave, to
keep you if she could?"
The Bastard from the Bush replied,
"My bloody oath I would!"

But when Barry started to sing "The Hole in the Elephant's Bottom," the others shushed him, being aware of the disapproving looks of the proprietor.

When the meal was over, Caro danced out of the hotel on feet that did not seem to touch the floor. Malcolm caught her in his arms as she stumbled over a loose brick in the paved path, and helped her into the car.

Barry drove them to the Clarendon weir. The still water above the weir

257

spread black and glassy under a nearly full moon. Caro noticed approvingly that the men did not feel a compulsion to lob rocks in the water to mar the perfect reflection of moon and downward-pointing trees. She was very conscious of Malcolm's sturdy figure beside her.

"We're going to walk down to the weir," said Barry, with his arm round Betty.

"Then we'll take the high road." Malcolm took Caro's hand and led her over small rocks embedded in the grass. She expected he would kiss her now. At a level spot above the shining water, he took off his raincoat and spread it on the grass beneath a gum-tree with dark leaves glistening in the moonlight.

"Are you cold?" he asked solicitously.

She was wearing her best apricot silk knitted suit, with a white pullover under the jacket, and was quite warm.

"Y-Yes," she said. Her teeth were chattering, but not with cold.

He put his arms round her and kissed her deeply. His mouth was soft, warm, demanding, wonderful. They staggered slightly. He drew her down beside him on the coat spread over the tough, springy grass. In a moment she was lying beneath him, everything forgotten but his weight upon her, his mouth on hers. The pulsating sound of frogs, the hollow call of a wild duck, the scent of moonlit grass, the pain of a small intrusive rock beneath her back: they ceased to exist. There was only his mouth, his caressing hands, and oh, she wanted him, and oh, this was beautiful, and this was how she wanted it to be. . . . To her intense surprise he rolled away from her and stood up, turning to look over the water, putting on his glasses.

"Malcolm . . . ? What . . . what is it?"

She stared up at him, dazed, unconsciously pulling her skirt down. She was still wearing her suspender belt, her artificial silk stockings, her flimsy scanties; in fact she was fully clothed.

"Stay there. I'm just going for a leak."

So that was it. But when he came back . . .

When he came back he put out a hand and helped her to her feet. He kissed her forehead and led her back up the slight slope towards the road and the car. She stumbled after him, trying not to cry. Before they got there he stopped and held her close, putting his face down against her neck.

"I'm sorry, Caro. I had no right. . . You're only a kid."

"I'm seventeen," she said defensively. "I mean eighteen. And I have a birthday in September."

"Eighteen!" He lifted his head and laughed ruefully. "Do you know how old I am, child? Thirty-two. But I got carried away a bit there . . ."

"Malcolm! I didn't mind. What are you sorry about?"

"Because I nearly . . . I know nurses are supposed to know all about these things, but . . . I'm older than you, and I had to think for both of us. You're only a kid, really."

"I am *not* a kid! Stop saying that!"

"Look, I've really enjoyed this evening, and I like you very much, but—"

There came a coo-ee from down-river.

"Hey, you two," called Barry. "Is Betty with you?"

"I thought she was with you."

"No, she said she was just going behind a bush, and she didn't come back."

They called up and down the bank, but there was no answer. The black water holding the floating moon suddenly looked sinister. Caro saw in her imagination the police dragging the deep pond above the weir, saw Betty laid out on the bank, streaming with water, blue-faced and motionless. . . .

"I'll go and get the torch from the glove-box," said Barry. "You keep looking."

He hurried up the slope, and soon they heard the car horn sound. "She's here!" he called. "In the car."

Betty was seated in the front, her arms folded, staring straight ahead.

"Why didn't you answer us, you silly bitch?" asked Barry, anxiety turning to anger. "You must have heard us calling."

"I thought I'd let you sweat for a bit."

"That wasn't funny, Bet," said Caro reprovingly. "We were really worried."

"Sorry. It was for his benefit, not yours."

Malcolm said nothing. He put his arm round Caro in the back seat, and she laid her head on his shoulder. In the front-bench seat, Betty sat as far away as possible from Barry. They did not speak.

"We'll have a meal in town one day," said Malcolm, kissing Caro before the car pulled up at the hospital nurses' quarters. "I'll tell you the story of my life."

In their room, Betty flung her handbag on the floor and kicked it.

"What's up, Bet?"

"That bastard Barry. Soon as we got away on our own he put the hard word on me. Wouldn't take no for an answer. I fought him off, and then said I wanted to go for a pee. I did, too, after all that wine. So then I quietly went back to the car and sat there. Sorry I gave you such a fright."

She tore off her jumper and pleated skirt, and scrubbed cold cream into her face. "I mean, I don't like him in that way. How was it with Malcolm?"

"He's a beaut bloke. I think I'm in love with him."

"Well! Tell Aunt Betty all about it. Did he . . . ?"

259

"No. I don't want to talk about it. And I simply must go— I'm bursting."

Sitting on the toilet seat, feeling the utter relief of emptying her full bladder, she began to dream of Malcolm, of his boyish, wavy hair, his dark-blue eyes. She sat there until Betty called out to know if she'd gone to sleep.

Caro waited in suspense for a week, then Malcolm called and asked her out.

"Well, if you can't be good, be careful," said Betty anxiously.

Malcolm took her to the Black Bull, the journalists' pub in Hindley Street, for a beer before dinner.

"But I don't like beer!" protested Caro.

"Have to learn to drink beer. You can't go out with a journalist otherwise."

"Well . . . can I have lemonade in it?"

"Just a dash."

Then they went to a fish café in Gouger Street—Caro had never been to that end of town before, except to pass through it in a tram. There they had the most perfect fresh whiting.

"The fish is always good here, but the coffee's lousy," said Malcolm.

"We could have tea . . ."

"*Tea!*" Malcolm was affronted.

"We always had tea with meals in the bush. Billy tea if you were travelling and camping out."

She had been talking her head off, and he had encouraged her, intrigued by her stories of Birdsville and Cappamerri, the mysterious inland that he knew only by hearsay. Now she realized that far from telling her the story of his life, he had told her nothing.

"We could," he said hesitantly, "go back to my rooms while I make us some real coffee."

Caro, who was in a state of euphoria and couldn't have cared less about coffee, agreed eagerly. She was in love. Her brain kept returning to a recent popular song:

. . . Lovely to look at, delightful to know,
And heaven to kiss:
A combination like this
Would make my
Most impossible dreams come true . . .

His room, a bed-sitting-room up two flights of stairs, was lined with books. She had never seen so many books except in the Public Library. She was enchanted, examining them while he put on the percolator in the adjoining kitchen.

"Oh! You've got *Ulysses!*"

"It's only been lent to me by a friend. You can't buy it, you know."

"I know, it's banned. And the *Decameron!*"

"That isn't banned. What the authorities consider the worst stories are printed in Italian. It's a great incentive to learn Italian."

"And Tolstoy! May I borrow *War and Peace?*"

"It's in three volumes. You can only have one at a time."

"Good! Then you'll have to ask me back."

He brought the coffee. They sat on cushions on the floor, leaning back against the divan, which was covered with some sort of Mexican rug.

"Would you like a drink? Port? Muscat?"

"I don't mind."

There were bottles and glasses on the low table. He poured her a glass of muscat.

"I wrote you a letter," she said. She drained her glass, seeking for courage. "And then I didn't post it. It—I told you I'd fallen in love with you."

He gently removed the glass from her hand, and kissed her muscat-sticky, sweet-tasting lips.

"Did you?" he murmured. "Did you really say that?"

"Yes. I do love you, Malcolm. I'll never love anyone else."

He kissed her again, and she pressed herself against him. Now, she thought, he will lift me on to the divan, and he will be my lover.

But he put her gently aside and went to the gramophone and his stack of records.

"What sort of music do you like?"

"Oh—!" She was too dazed and disappointed to think. "I don't know. Opera."

"Opera!" he said disapprovingly. "You mean Mozart?"

She didn't know any Mozart operas. "No, Puccini."

"See if you like this." He put on a record. "Schumann," he said. "'Träumerei,' or Reverie."

But she soon began to talk again, telling him how she thought of him all the time, even when she was on duty, how she had been reproved for absent-mindedness by the Matron, a tall, daunting woman with a nose like the Duke of Wellington's . . .

When the record was finished he got up and turned off the machine. "You probably like music," he said tolerantly, "but you've never learned to listen to it."

"You mean I talk too much."

"Well, dear, it isn't necessary to talk *all* the time."

She said resentfully, "You know how to stop me."

261

It was true. One kiss could reduce her to quivering silence.

But he said lightly that it was time he sent her home.

She had to be in by midnight, and on duty at six-thirty in the morning. He called a taxi and put her in it, paying the driver. Caro sat in the back seat with tears rolling down her cheeks, clutching the first volume of *War and Peace*, while the cab crossed to the other side of the city. She had planned to rely on an antiseptic douche as soon as she got back, though Betty said that journalists and medical students were always prepared, like Boy Scouts. But anyway nothing had happened.

CHAPTER THREE

By the time she was up to the third volume of *War and Peace*, Caro was still a reluctant virgin. She had been much moved by the romance of Natasha and Prince Andrew; but when she read that Natasha, after her marriage with Pierre, had become the plump, matronly mother of four, whose greatest interest was whether baby's dirty napkins were a healthy yellow; when she read this, Caro shouted "No!" She almost threw the book on the floor. Natasha, that lovely, lively, fascinating girl, with all her spiritual qualities, to be reduced almost to the level of a cow!

When she returned the book she told Malcolm of her disgust, but he only laughed at her and said that was how life was. He had cooked some spaghetti and they ate it in the kitchen, with a bottle of claret. Caro did not dare tell him that she preferred claret with lemonade.

She was feeling rather quiet and depressed.

"You're a bit down in the mouth," said Malcolm. "What is it?"

She fingered her glass and said, "I had to deal with my first dead man today. Matron sent me into his room to cut the tapes and remove the nasal feeding-tube. But—he didn't look peaceful or as if he was asleep. He just looked . . . lifeless. As if he was only a model made of wax."

"Yes. The dead do look very dead. You said your grandfather died . . . didn't you see his body?"

"No, my grandmother sent me away."

"I think Victorian children were much better prepared for death—of course nearly every family lost one or more children—and they learned to cope with the sight, and the fact of death for those close to them more easily."

"Children don't die in such numbers now, but they still die. My room-mate Betty started at the Children's Hospital, but she had to give it up. They put her in the cancer ward. Quite small children get cancer. There was a little boy with cancer of the hip, they'd operated on his leg twice, removing more and more, and finally it reached his hip. It became inoperable. And the pain . . ."

"Suffer the little children. . . ."

"Yes, but not just the child suffers. Think what its mother must go

263

through. Betty said it was terrible to see. So she resigned and took up general nursing instead. Seeing old people dying of pneumonia, and young people with broken legs, is somehow not as bad."

"You have to be tough to be a nurse."

"Yes. I thought I was tough. I suppose I'll become so."

"I doubt it."

In keeping with her mood he put a record on the gramophone, the Dead March in "Saul." But she threw off her melancholy and, balancing a small cushion on her head, walked round the room with slow and stately strides in time to the music.

He put on "Liebestraum" and drew her down on the cushions.

She found she could listen quietly to any amount of music while his arms were round her. But he still sent her home early.

Caro took some flowers which a discharged patient had left behind when she went to see Frances. It was early spring, the hills that made a backdrop for the city were a brilliant green after the winter rains, and the almond groves seemed to be drifted with snow as the pale blossoms fell and strewed the ground. The empty paddock where the mare had been stabled was bright with yellow sour-sops. Caro no longer missed her horse. She had sixty pounds towards a car, and it seemed she would need another twenty or thirty to buy anything reliable.

Frances was delighted with the flowers, a bunch of spring bulbs, for though she had daffodils and hyacinths in the most shaded part of her garden, she hated to pick them. Caro led up to the subject of her eighteenth birthday at the end of the month, and mentioned how much she longed for a little motor car, and how she didn't have quite enough money and couldn't save much on a nurse's salary. "If you could just lend me enough, Grandma, say twenty-five pounds, I'd be able to get a reliable second-hand one. And then I could pop out and see you so much more easily, and I could come more often."

A week before her birthday a parcel arrived from her mother, and a card from Frances. She opened the card first, and out fell a cheque for thirty-five pounds. "I want you to get a *reliable* vehicle, and a safe one. You don't have to pay this back, it's a birthday present."

Caro danced round the room, kicking up her heels. Then she opened the parcel from her mother, and found in a padded box a piece of polished malachite, deep green with white lines through it, and a large piece of Queensland opal, like blue butterfly wings with flashes of fire, still in the rough setting of brown rock in which it had been found. It was beautiful, but the car money was more exciting. She rang her grandmother to thank her, and arranged to come to dinner on her birthday, driving the new car.

Caro had seen what she wanted, a smart little red Morris Cowley with a folding canvas roof. It was ninety-five pounds, but when she showed the dealer the cash in her hand he let her have it for ninety.

She drove out to her grandmother's in daylight so that Frances could admire the car, and took her for a spin around the block. Caro had the roof folded down so that it looked more sporting, and Frances found a short ride quite enough. The little car had a straight-out exhaust that made a satisfying throaty sound. Caro had nick-named her Matilda.

She could not wait to show her acquisition to Malcolm. He had to admit she was an adult now, a trainee nurse with her own car and a driving-licence, and he thought she had turned nineteen. She wore her hair in a straight long bob, hoping to look like Greta Garbo.

He took her to see Garbo and John Barrymore in *Mata Hari*, and they held hands all through the film. The next time they had dinner and went back to his place, he kept her mouth well occupied while they sat on cushions listening to a Chopin nocturne. He said, "Do you know you have a very sensuous mouth, eminently kissable," and kissed her again. Garbo had a rather thin mouth, though beautifully cut. . . . Perhaps, Caro thought, she should try to look like Katharine Hepburn?

She wrenched her lips away and, fingering his tie, not looking in his face, she murmured, "Why won't you make love to me? You know I want you to."

He hesitated, smoothing the straight fair hair back behind one of her ears. At last he said, "Caro, there's something I have to tell you." And then, "Oh, hell! Sometimes it's easier to talk in bed."

He lifted her on to the divan and slowly began to undress her, kissing each part as it was revealed. "You have a lovely figure," he said, "like a beautiful boy's—such long legs and narrow hips, and all these warm womanly attributes as well. . . . Lie there, I just have to go to the bathroom for a tick."

Afterwards, looking back on it, Caro had to admit that the experience hadn't been quite up to her expectations, had, in fact, been rather painful. But she loved him, and was happy to have made him happy. It was the shared intimacy she valued, the exchange of more than bodily contacts, the drowsy talk as they lay twined together among the tumbled sheets.

"You know," said Malcolm, chuckling, "that most girls of your generation have their first experience in the back seat of a car. And here you are in a real bed."

"We *could* try my car, but you'd have to be a contortionist and very determined. . . . By the way, Betty helped me with a contraceptive, just in case. . . I was always hoping. Why did it take you so long to get me here?"

"I was wearing something, too, but . . . these things are not always effective. That's partly what worries me, and then, your being so young."

"I'm a woman now."

"Yes, my darling; and I have something to tell you."

He fitted her head under his chin and stroked her hair, staring at the ceiling while he talked.

"You see, I have a wife in Melbourne."

He felt her stiffen, but he went on, "We're separated, but just about the time I met you, she wrote and said she'd like me to come home, she doesn't want a divorce. So you see . . . I have a sort of vested interest in her, six years of my life. As soon as I get a transfer to the Melbourne *Herald*, I'm going back to her. It may not work out, but I have to try."

"Oh," she said flatly.

"And then we may go to London. I have the chance of a job over there."

She asked stonily, "What is her name?" and when he said "Julia," she announced, "I'll be leaving now."

"No! Don't go! Not now we've just found each other. I've wanted you ever since that first night in the hills."

He held her arms and pinned her down with his weight. She struggled feebly, but she didn't really want to leave; his eyes without their glasses had a blind, defenceless look, intensely blue. She closed her own and sighed.

It was more pleasurable the second time, and it was he who had to remind her, happily dozing, that it was nearly midnight: "Come, Cinderella!" and she who clung to him and did not wish to leave.

A blowfly, the first of the summer, was buzzing about the ceiling and bumping into walls. When it came down low Malcolm stalked it with a rolled-up copy of the *Standard*, leaping about the room and swiping at it with the paper, wearing nothing but his glasses. He stunned the fly and tossed the *Standard* into a corner. "It's a better fly-swat than a newspaper," he said.

The romantic Caro thought wryly that instead of a nightingale—or even a little willy-wagtail—singing outside the window, she had woken to the sound of a blowfly, the pest of the Australian bush.

When he took her down to her car he said, "Perhaps we shouldn't see so much of each other, darling."

"Yes, yes! You'll be going away forever; I must see you, I must."

"Well, I'll get in touch."

"When, Malcolm? When shall I see you?"

He said with a sudden flash of irritation, "I don't know! Don't nail me, Caro."

She shrank back and climbed into the car and drove off. So! she thought bitterly. He's got me into bed and already he's tired of me! Back at the Nurses' Home she crept into bed without waking Betty, and quietly cried herself to sleep. But in the morning, finding blood on her pyjamas, she

266

felt a surge of happiness. He was hers, her first man. He would forget about going to Melbourne. He would not be able to leave her, after all. . . .

It was two weeks before she saw him again. She longed to ring him at the *Standard* office, but dared not. She took detours past the front of the building, but never saw him emerging. Then one day she saw Barry with his bulky press camera slung over his shoulder, and tooted and waved. He came over to the car.

Longing for news of Malcolm, she said brightly, "Can I give you a lift?"

"No, thanks, love, I'm just going round to get the car. Are you looking for Malcolm? He's up at the courts."

"Oh."

"I'm just on my way to Parafield to meet a pilot and take a picture of his aeroplane. The same one he flew out from England, it's a Klemm Falcon or something."

"Not Ray Butler? Is he in Adelaide?"

"Yes, there's to be a story in the *Standard* tomorrow. He'll be pleased you've heard of him."

"I'd love to meet him."

"Come on then. He might take you up for a short spin if you smile at him nicely. Do you know the way? I'll go ahead."

Caro had never seen a plane with only one set of wings, apart from Kingsford-Smith's *Southern Cross*, which everyone knew from photographs and newsreels. The stark, streamlined shape of the low-winged monoplane looked strange to her. The airman, dressed in slacks and a leather jacket, was tinkering with a wheel-strut when they came up. He straightened and flashed Caro a smile, and shook hands as Barry introduced her.

Ray was not her idea of the dashing pilot; he was short, with straight dark hair plastered flat on his head, and thick dark brows. The plane was quite small, with two open cockpits, one for the pilot and one for the passenger.

Caro told him of how she had always wanted to fly, and that she had read about his solo flight from England last year, and how she hoped later to get her pilot's licence. She had no ambitions to break records like Amy Johnson, but wanted to work with one of the aerial ambulance services in the outback.

"Caro is training as a nurse first," said Barry.

"Good for you!"

"I've never been up in an aeroplane," said Caro wistfully.

"Well, there's no time like the present. I was just going to take her up. Want to come for the ride?"

Caro jumped at the chance.

"But you'll need something warmer to put on."

Barry offered the coat of his dark suit, which she put on over her yellow linen summer dress. Ray helped her up to the forward cockpit and handed her helmet and goggles.

"Before we take off," he said, "strap yourself in. Tell me if you want an exciting ride or not."

"Oh yes! Please!"

"Right-oh. If it gets a bit too exciting, just put your hand up, like this."

Caro tightened the strap of her helmet, put on her goggles, and fastened her harness.

The plane taxied out on to the runway and turned into the wind. A pause while the pilot revved the engine and checked the controls. Then a roar and vibration and they were away. Caro felt a great bubble of elation forming in her chest. A short, bumpy run over the earth runway, then the smoothness of flight. They were in the air. The earth fell away. The gold paddocks of summer tilted sideways as they banked and turned, and as they climbed, the blue waters of the Gulf widened out, the far coast showed as a low dark line beyond.

The little plane seemed to hang motionless in the air, droning to itself, while the landscape moved slowly beneath. Then they were climbing steeply, the nose pointing into the blue. There followed a steep dive, down, down, the earth rushing up to meet them. Caro held her breath. They were over a poultry farm; she saw the startled hens streaking for cover.

At the last moment Ray pulled her out of the dive, and they went swooping up again. Up, up, up, in a stomach-fluttering climb to the point where the engine stalled and the plane seemed to hang in the sky by its propeller. . . . Then they were over, the sky beneath, the earth far above. They came right way up again, and as they began a silent plunge the engine coughed and roared once more into life. Caro's heart beat high. She was flying, and they had looped the loop!

Ray zoomed down to hedge-hop over farms and paddocks of grazing cattle. Suddenly the feeling of speed was very real, as fence-posts flashed by beneath at a hundred miles an hour. Up again in a glorious sweeping curve, at the top of which he pulled the joystick back and brought the nose right up till the engine stalled. They came down in a controlled spin, the nose pointed straight at the earth, which revolved like a coloured wheel. Then he pulled out of the spin and they were diving, then swooping up again. Caro felt a wild surge of joy.

All too soon they were circling the aerodrome, seeing the wind-sock stretched out from the south-west, and coming in on a long glide to a perfect three-point landing. They taxied towards one of the hangars and stopped.

Caro climbed down with glowing pink cheeks and shining eyes.

"Oh, Mr. Butler!"

"Call me Ray."

"Oh, Ray! It was wonderful! Thank you for taking me up."

"I noticed you didn't put up your hand."

"No. I wasn't scared. And I knew I wouldn't be airsick." She didn't tell him that during the first mad dive, certain that they must plough into the ground, she'd had to sit hard on her hands.

Barry was waiting by the hangar for his coat.

"She'll make an airwoman yet," said Ray. "What about next weekend, Caro? Care to go up again?"

"I'd love to, but I won't be able to get Sunday off. I'm supposed to be on duty."

"Well, the week after then."

Driving down the straight bitumen road to the city, she pushed Matilda to her maximum speed of 55 miles per hour. The canvas top was down, and Caro's pale straight hair fluttered in the wind of movement. But it was not nearly as exciting as flying.

She could not wait to start her flying lessons. Yet at present she had less than ten pounds in the bank, enough for only two lessons. It was hardly worth starting. Back in town, she ate frugally at the kiosk in the Botanic Gardens, resolving to save every penny she could. Anyway, as it was Sunday, everything else in Adelaide was shut. Even the children's playgrounds in the parklands were closed, the swings chained together so that they could not be used on the Sabbath. It was a very Methodist city.

She lingered over her pie with peas and tomato sauce, wanting to relive in her mind the exhilarating experience of her first flight.

CHAPTER FOUR

A message came for Caro at lunch-time at the hospital.

"Telephone for Nurse Manning." She flew along the hall and heard Malcolm's voice.

"Caro? What about dinner tonight?"

"Oh! I'm on duty tonight."

"Tomorrow, then?"

"Yes. Yes!"

"Right. Pick me up at the office just before six."

It was such a warm evening that Caro suggested driving to the beach. Even if he was too wary to take her back to his apartment, they might make love on the sand, she thought.

They parked above a deserted beach twenty miles from the city, where the tame waters of the Gulf began to build into surf. After eating salty fish and chips from a newspaper parcel, they wiped their greasy fingers on a new afternoon copy of the *Standard*.

"What sacrilege!" said Caro.

"Yes, some of my immortal prose is contained in that journal. Makes even a better table-napkin than a fly-swat."

Caro chattered about her outing to Parafield and her first flight, and the excitement of stunting in a small plane.

"Sounds mighty dangerous to me," said Malcolm.

"If you won't have me, I don't care what happens."

She turned into his arms, her heart beating high. And heard above the crash and sigh of waves beyond the dunes, the first heavy drops of rain on the stretched canvas roof.

It was not just a thunder shower; the rain set in steadily. A smell of damp sand came up from the beach, the rain drummed on the roof of the silent car. Caro asked herself why she hadn't bought a large car with a wide back seat.

It was some time before they spoke, and then he told her that he had received his transfer and would be leaving for Melbourne at the end of next week. Caro made him promise he would see her again before he left.

But he left it till his last night to call her, and then she had to be on duty till nine-thirty. By the time they met there were only snack-bars still open, so they went to the pie-stall outside the Town Hall.

She was near enough to feel the contact of his solid shoulder as they stood beneath the canvas awning with their elbows on the wooden counter. One drunk and two men who looked as if they slept in the parklands were the only other customers.

Though choking with misery, she ate her way through a soggy meat pie in a plate of thick pea soup, known as a "floater." The soup was a yellow-green colour, rather like vomit, but it was quite a good pie, with plenty of gravy and no gristle.

"Coffee, love?" asked the pie-cart man.

Malcolm shook one hand in a definite negative, and her spirits rose. They were going back to his place for coffee!

But he said no, he was going back to the office to finish cleaning out his desk.

"Then I'll drive you to the office."

Instead she drove straight down to the Botanic Park and flung herself in his arms, sobbing.

"Caro! For God's sake! You knew this had to happen."

"Yes, but I can't b-bear it."

She groped in her handbag for her handkerchief, and felt the little parcel she had forgotten to give him—a gold fountain pen in a folding case.

He was touched and grateful. "But I should be giving you presents, not the other way round."

"Will you write to me, with this?"

"No, darling. It must be a clean break."

A clean break! When she felt a torn, jagged place where he was tearing himself away from her side.

She dropped him at last at the *Standard* building where lights showed on several floors as the army of office cleaners worked their night shift. Then she drove round aimlessly, wondering whether to drive into an electric light pole and end it all. But what if she was just paralyzed, not killed? And she hated to think of poor Matilda the Morris mangled and bent.

A stupid rhyme went round in her head, like the words of a popular song:

After a pie,
We said goodbye.

Melbourne was 500 miles away, and might as well be at the ends of the earth. And then he would probably go to London. . . . She groaned aloud and beat her hands on the steering wheel. After a pie, we said goodbye. She would never see him again.

"Well, did you see Malcolm?" asked Betty. "What did he say?"

"He's going to Melbourne."

271

"Well, old girl, you knew there was no future there."

"Yes. But—it's so final."

While she had Betty's sympathy Caro asked her if she would mind swapping her next Sunday off, as Ray had asked her to go up with him again. But Betty had an arrangement with a medical student to go sailing. There was no way she could change it.

Sunday dawned sunny, and clear, perfect flying weather. Caro was getting herself a cup of tea in the pantry during a lull in the afternoon (on Sundays the wards were full of visitors bearing flowers) when she was called to the telephone. It was Barry Muirden.

"Caro? Listen, there's been an accident. I didn't want you to read about it in tomorrow's paper—"

"Not Betty?"

"No. It's Ray Butler. He was stunting somewhere north of Parafield, when a wing came off his plane. They were both killed instantly when it crashed."

"Both?"

"He and his passenger. He took another girl up this Sunday."

Caro was silent, shocked.

"Caro? Are you there?"

"Yes . . . I heard you, Barry. Thank you for letting me know. I suppose you've just taken a picture of the wreck for tomorrow's paper?"

"Yes. It's just a tangled mess."

"God! I can't believe it. Poor Ray. He was so young."

"The girl was younger. I suppose this will put you off flying for life. I mean, it could have been you."

"On the contrary, I feel it's Fate saying to me, 'You are not destined to die young.' I'm still going to get my pilot's licence."

She went back and drank her cold tea without tasting it. A terrible thing to have happened! But underlying that thought was another: I would have been killed, if Betty had changed her day off. I might have been killed two weeks before. But I am alive.

At Cloncurry the local newspaper had brought out a feature commemorating the tenth anniversary of the first Qantas flight. In her next letter Alix sent Caro a copy, with the "Regulations for Operation of Aircraft" issued in 1920. Alix wrote:

Arthur Affleck has left the Aerial Medical Service, and the new pilot is Eric Donaldson, a happy-go-lucky chap. Dr. Vickers has flown fifty thousand miles on calls from here in two years. He doesn't normally take a nurse with him, but I had one exciting flight to Kynuna, where he operated on a man at the station for an urgent appendicitis, while I performed the anaesthesia and Eric Donaldson held the lamp. We

272

couldn't have the lamp too near because ether is inflammable, and flying beetles kept falling into the wound, but the op was successful.

The patient was taken to Kynuna Hospital, a tiny place with a Matron and one Sister but no doctor: population about twelve.

They usually fly in the mornings up here, because the currents of heated air make the bumps worse in the afternoons. But as it was an emergency we had to leave after lunch, and it was very rough, and the noise and vibration gave me a headache. I was glad to get back to Cloncurry in one piece.

Be careful driving your new car—no, I know it's not new, but you are a fairly new driver. Give my love to Grandma, and tell her I will be writing to her soon. She complains that even now you have a car she doesn't see you very often.

With some amusement Caro read the "Regulations." Many were still valid where the smaller Moths were concerned, with their frail fuselages of wood and wings of doped cloth; all made by De Havilland and all single-engined, though remarkably stable.

The Regulations said crisply:

1. Do not take the machine into the air unless you are satisfied it will fly.
2. Pilots should carry hankies in a handy position to wipe goggles.
3. Riding on steps, wings or tail of a machine is prohibited.
4. Learn to gauge altitude. Do not trust altitude instruments.
5. Pilots will not wear spurs when flying.
6. If the engine fails on take-off, land at once regardless of obstacles.
7. No spins or tail-slides will be indulged in as they unnecessarily strain the engine.

Perhaps, she thought, Ray had strained his machine by too much stunting. Driving out to her grandmother's a couple of weeks later, she stopped the car to watch a little training Moth, high up in the blue, flying towards the hills. It circled and came back, shot upwards, and did a perfect loop-the-loop. In sympathy, her heart seemed to stop as the engine stalled on the top of the loop, then started again as the following dive spun the propeller and the pilot opened the throttle. The plane zoomed away towards Parafield. Certainly it looked more like a moth than a bird, with its double matching wings. She felt they were safer than the single span of the monoplane.

She dashed away again soon after midday dinner, as she wanted to go to the Public Library in town and read up about flying.

"I don't know; you rush in, and rush out again almost before I know you're here," said Frances.

273

"Sorry, Grandma, but I'm a working girl. I can't spend all my Sundays visiting. And petrol costs money."

(It had used three times as much petrol to go to the aerodrome as it did to this outer suburb in the foothills.)

At the Library she became absorbed in a manual on flying:

"There is safety in height; and there is safety in speed. . . . Flying is easy, provided everything goes right; but it takes an experienced pilot and some care to see everything does go right."

All the illustrations were of training planes with double wings, like the DH 6 and the Avro 4J.

The book said that after a minimum of ten hours flying with an instructor, the learner could fly solo "circuits and bumps." He then had to do twenty-five hours solo flying before getting his "A" class licence. The "Advanced A" licence was needed to carry non-paying passengers.

Caro wrote to her mother:

> Now that you have been on a flight in a small plane, you will know how fascinating and exciting it is. I have been up for a short flight and I am *passionately* determined to learn to fly.
>
> But it will cost perhaps £150 to £200 for lessons. If necessary I will sell Matilda, but then I'll have no way of getting out to Parafield when I have a few hours off at the hospital.
>
> I have passed my First-Year exams in theory and practical. I don't mean to give up nursing, just to take up flying as well.
>
> If you could lend me the money, Mum, I would pay you back as soon as I get Grandpa's thousand. It's no use asking Grandma, I haven't even told her that I've been out to Parafield. Please let me know soon. I am longing to get my wings.

Alix replied that as far as she was concerned she never wanted to go up in a small aircraft again.

> I was terrified! Some of the flight was very rough, and there was no toilet in the plane so that I had to use an open tin in flight. I didn't get airsick, but I felt woozy for days afterwards.
>
> But if you're sure that is what you want, I'll send you a cheque for what I can spare, about £180. I suppose you'll need a flying-suit and helmet. The Flying Doctor plane has a cabin, at least.
>
> And *please* don't take risks! Remember you're my only chick.

Caro rang Frances to explain that she couldn't come out that Sunday, as she was on duty. It was nearly true, she had to be on duty at five-thirty in the afternoon. Instead she drove to Parafield Aerodrome, twelve miles north of the city. She wandered among the hangars, in one of which was the Vickers-Vimy which she remembered as a child, flying over the Adelaide hills. It was to be set up as a memorial to the brothers Ross and Keith Smith and their record-breaking flight from London. Ross Smith had been killed when his plane crashed soon after take-off for another world flight in 1922.

As she came out into the sun, she saw the lanky figure of Barry Muirden with a press camera slung from a strap over his shoulder. Anyone remotely connected with Malcolm was an object of painful interest to her. She hailed him enthusiastically.

"Why, hallo, Caro. How have you been keeping? I haven't seen anything of Betty for ages."

"Have you heard anything of Malcolm since he left?"

"I believe he's gone back to his wife, and landed a job with the Australian Press Bureau in London—lucky bastard."

Caro, who had been nourishing a faint hope of seeing him again, saw the hope wither and die upon its frail stem.

"Yes, I knew he'd gone to Melbourne."

"Still mad about aeroplanes, eh? Have you joined the Aero Club?"

"I haven't got a plane yet. But I mean to join."

Back at the hospital, she told Betty that Malcolm had left for London.

"Barry told me about Malcolm. He asked after you."

"Oh?" said Betty indifferently. She was having a torrid affair with her medical student.

Caro applied to join the South Australian Aero Club, which helped organize aerial pageants, air races, and receptions for pioneer aviators when they landed in Australia. It was also a social club, and provided flying lessons for a fee which at present Caro could not afford. What Barry had not told her was that the joining fee alone was £25, of which £10 would be refunded when a licence was issued.

The fees were £4 an hour with an instructor, and £2 an hour flying solo. She had just enough for two lessons, until her mother's cheque arrived.

In a second-hand bookstore Caro bought a copy of Swoffer's *Learning to Fly*, a manual that detailed all the mistakes a pupil was likely to make, and all the alarming things that can happen to a craft in the air. But Caro was not daunted. She read the book from cover to cover, kept it on her bedside table and studied it in her time off. Betty called it her bible.

She also studied the advertisements in aircraft magazines that showed drawings of smart young women in the latest flying gear: suede or calfskin jacket with map pocket, £4 10s.; calfskin cap, lined throughout, 2s. 6d. Goggles and gloves would be extra. Her jodhpurs and boots

275

she had long grown out of. But she was determined to look the part, whatever it cost, and though it might be years before she had her own plane.

CHAPTER FIVE

On a cool grey day in early April, Caro set out for the aerodrome, wearing long suede trousers and leather jacket, and carrying her goggles and helmet. She was to have her first lesson with the senior Aero Club instructor. When she made the booking he had looked at her doubtfully and said, "Aren't you rather *young*, my dear?"

Caro, who would not be nineteen till September, had said airily that she only looked young, she would in fact soon be twenty.

Now she was actually climbing into the back cockpit of the Tiger Moth which waited on the runway, nose pointed up as if eager to be in the air. She was in the pilot's seat, the instructor sat in front, speaking to her to make sure she could hear through the intercom.

She felt no fear, only elation, as the aircraft rolled forward with increasing speed, the runway blurring past, and lifted sweetly into the wide embrace of air. Then they were banking steeply, and climbing to three thousand feet. She had been told not to watch the instruments, but to feel the movement of the plane by the seat of her pants. She held the stick loosely while the instructor demonstrated turns with the dual controls in the front cockpit. Then he let her try for herself.

Soon she was nervously making turns, correcting, trying to keep the plane's nose dead on the horizon seen through the translucent circle that marked the place of the turning propeller. It seemed no time before her twenty-minute lesson was over. The instructor took over the controls and brought the machine down in a long controlled glide, ending in a perfect three-point landing—two wheels and tail-skid touching the ground together—known as the Angel's Kiss.

She had to wait two weeks for her next lesson, when she began to get the feel of the aircraft, with the instructor's steady voice in her ears: "Don't lose speed on your turns. . . . a little more to the left, left, ease her back, a little to the right, that's it . . . hold her, hold her!"

There came the day when she felt the aircraft responding correctly to her every touch on the controls, and at last she was allowed to make a landing: climb, turn, throttle back, and come in on a long glide, with a bit of a bump at the end, but the instructor said, "Not bad for a first try. You'll learn."

When at last the great day came and she was to go solo to do "circuits

277

and bumps"—practice taking off and landing—she was trembling with excitement as the instructor climbed out and said casually, "All right, you're on your own now." She had been flying well, making her turns smoothly, getting her gliding angles right and touching down almost perfectly. But now that head in the front cockpit had disappeared, the insistent voice of the instructor was gone; he had always been there to get her out of trouble. Now it all rested entirely with herself.

As she was about to take off, he said, "Remember, if your approach is wrong, don't try to land; open up the throttle and go round again. You can make as many approaches as you like."

Her feet were shaking on the rudder-bar as she taxied on to the runway. Climb, turn, turn again, close the throttle, and glide in; judge the height, bring the stick right back at three feet above the earth, then let her settle gently down. . . . She had made it! Without even a bump!

Her instruction was still not finished when she had won her "A" licence. To have it endorsed "Advanced A" she had to practise side-slips and spins, and landing on a closed throttle from fifteen hundred feet within so many feet of a small mark.

Her instructors stressed that the pilot's job was to stay with his aircraft till it was safely on the ground—not that they had any choice, having no parachutes. They said you could bring an aeroplane in to land on almost anything, even if it involved shearing off a wing or two on a tree; it was usually possible to control a crash. Moths could land at 50 miles an hour, so they did not need large cleared areas for landing.

The only instruments in the cockpit were the air-speed indicator, the altimeter, the rev counter, a spirit level for an inclinometer, a fuel gauge, and oil gauge. In clouds you had to keep your head, trust your instruments, and make no sudden corrections. It was easy to become disorientated, and come out of the cloud in a steep dive or a spin.

Every hour that she flew was entered in a log-book and signed as she came in. As part of her "Advanced A" requirements she had to fly cross-country for fifty miles, so she flew to Murray Bridge, over the lowest part of the Mount Lofty Ranges, and had her log-book signed by an official before flying back again. It was the first time she had seen the Murray River from the air, winding and twisting upon itself like a great green serpent.

Since in country towns pilots were still looked on as some sort of heroes, the locals rushed out in their cars to the football field where she landed. When they found the pilot to be a woman, it was so unusual that she was photographed and interviewed by the local newspaper.

Caro had not ceased to think about Malcolm, but she went out sometimes with a medical student called Andrew, a likeable fellow with a rather round, pale face. He was an amusing companion and shared her interest in engines, about which she was determined to learn all she could. So under Andrew's instruction she pulled Matilda's engine down and put it together again. She ground valves in his workshop in the garage at his parents' home, cleaned spark-plugs, fitted piston-rings and new gaskets, learned to check tappet clearances and to clean a carburettor and adjust the mixture. She had trouble cleaning grease from under her fingernails before going on duty at the hospital.

Andrew owned a large second-hand Bentley, an aristocrat of a car in which he sometimes took her for spins to the beach or the hills. It had no roof and the windscreen folded flat. The low-slung body gave a wonderful feeling of speed; it was the next best thing to flying.

They went swimming on lonely beaches, where Andrew kissed her with increasing ardour and eventually she let him make love to her, more from sheer persistence on his part than desire on hers. Flying was her only love.

On her second cross-country flight, she flew north along the flank of the Mount Lofty Ranges and went up to six thousand feet. It was strangely lonely up there in the empty blue sky, with the earth a mile below; but how soft and beautiful the ground looked with its coloured paddocks, green and gold and purple-brown, its vineyard-clad slopes, and a few white clouds far below looking as if pasted to the earth. She tipped the nose down and went zooming earthward in a long, thrilling dive: "Caro Manning, here I come!" she chanted. It was as the details of houses and roads and railway lines came clear that she felt the first hesitation in the engine. Her heart gave a responsive flutter.

She opened the throttle and climbed again: "There's safety in speed, and safety in height," she remembered. But something was wrong with the engine; it was missing badly. The fuel gauge showed half-full, but it sounded as if the tank were empty. She looked around anxiously for somewhere to land. She heard the instructor's voice: "Always watch your country, know where you can put her down if something goes wrong." And now she was too high to see what the surface was like down there. She had neglected that wise precaution.

She would simply have to go down for a look, and pray that something turned up. There were green patches that were probably vineyards, and dark patches which would be ploughed paddocks—possible for landing, but probably impossible to take off again. With the engine coughing ominously she dropped, using her dive to keep the propeller turning. The engine picked up again, and she saw the township of Clare ahead—all telephone wires and electricity poles—and then a pale square opened out, a stubble paddock just large enough for her to put down. . . . It was on a slope of a low hill, so she landed uphill so as not to roll too far.

If there were any hidden stumps, it was too bad. She glided in over a four-strand wire fence, ready to open the throttle if the next fence loomed

279

up too soon. . . . But the soil was firm, and the plane was safely down, while the slip-stream threw up a cloud of dust and straw like a threshing machine. She stopped two plane-lengths from the next fence.

Now to try to locate the trouble. She took the petrol filters off to clean them, but they were all right; checked the points and spark-plug gaps; still nothing wrong. Then she removed the plugs and found two of them badly oiled up. This was the answer.

A farmer and his lad now arrived, full of curiosity and amazement at finding a woman flyer in their field.

She got them to help her swing the tail round so that she could take off downhill for extra speed; and as the Moth had no brakes, to hang on to the wings and hold her back as long as they could while she revved up the engine.

"Shut your eyes—you're going to be covered in dust," Caro called, as she switched on, climbed down to swing the propeller, and climbed back again. She opened the throttle, the engine gave a roar, then suddenly the plane leaped forward and she was racing downhill towards the fence; she pulled her up, up—and over!

She circled once and dipped a wing to acknowledge the help of the two men waving their hats at the edge of the paddock. She felt sure she had made their day, and the farmer would be telling the story in the pub for weeks to come.

Now Caro was licensed to carry passengers, but she did not have a machine in which to take them up. She hung about the aerodrome whenever she had time off, hoping to be asked to go up with someone; buying—when she could afford it—half an hour solo. There was only one other woman regular at the Aero Club, so the two of them would lunch in the little Club dining room, sitting at a table in the far corner of this room devoted to men and male pursuits.

One day she drove straight from the aerodrome to her grandmother's, wearing her flying kit and helmet. Frances, who was in the garden cutting roses, nearly fainted.

"Caro! What on earth—"

"Hallo, Grandma," said Caro, kissing her and taking off the helmet. "I thought you'd like to know that I'm now a qualified pilot."

"What!" Frances clasped the roses to her with a pained gesture. "A pilot! Whatever next!"

"Next I want to get my own aeroplane. Then I'll be able to take you up. I am licensed to carry passengers."

"You'll do nothing of the sort. I don't intend to go up in an aeroplane, least of all one piloted by a mere girl."

"But you know I'll be twenty-one in two years. Then . . ." She opened her arms wide and smiled at the sky.

280

"By then, I hope, you'll be married and settled down," said Frances tartly.

"I very much doubt it."

"Does your mother know about this—this—"

"She lent me the money for my flying lessons. Come on, what about afternoon tea? Some of your almond biscuits," she said, taking the roses and carrying them inside.

She had received the ten pounds back from her joining fee at the Aero Club, but still had to wait to get in enough flying hours for her "B" class licence. She had studied for the theoretical examination, and had learned all about thrust and drag, lift-drag ratio, wing-loading and lift coefficient, all the mysteries of aerodynamics that kept a heavier-than-air machine flying. She copied out her lecture notes at night when off-duty, sometimes five or ten times over, to fix them in her mind.

Caro spent no money on clothes and ate at her grandmother's or at the hospital. Andrew sometimes took her for a meal or to the movies, so her only expenses were for uniform stockings, petrol for Matilda, and flying lessons. At two pounds per hour she had enough for an hour's flying time a week, and gradually built up her flying hours.

She spent her one and a half days off a week, and some of her days when she should have been sleeping after night duty, at the aerodrome. She had less time for Andrew, who sometimes drove her out to Parafield, but complained that he hardly ever saw her alone.

There had been a coolness between them after Caro told him about one of her patients, a young woman whose oesophagus had been badly burned by caustic soda when she was a child. The girl's condition necessitated periodical returns to hospital after food-particles got through the damaged food-pipe and became lost in the chest cavity.

On their next meeting Andrew produced a neatly written page of verse, which he handed to her and then waited expectantly.

She read:

Emily's oesophagus
Is no longer worth a cuss.
Her infant eyes mistook for beer
A bottle of what was, I fear,
Caustic soda deleterious;
With consequences rather serious.
For ever since, if she incline
To gorge above the water-line
The choicest morsels go astray,
And lodge among her vertebrae.

"Well?" he asked smugly.

She handed back the paper with a slight frown.

"It's clever—and completely heartless," she said. "I thought you knew how I felt about that girl. She must have suffered hell as a child. And will never be able to eat normally again."

"Of course; we see tragic cases every day. But you have to laugh, or you'd go mad."

"I still don't like it."

"Very well; I thought it might amuse you."

He took the paper sulkily, and scrunched it into his pocket.

"Doctors are terribly cynical," said Betty when Caro told her. "They say nurses get hard, but doctors. . . !"

Inevitably, Caro's nursing studies had suffered. At the end of third year, Betty passed her final exams with a credit, while Caro just scraped through. In the same month the devastating news came through that "Smithy"—her hero, Kingsford-Smith—had disappeared somewhere near Burma on a flight from England. Neither he nor his plane nor his co-pilot were ever seen again.

Caro took her certificate home to show her grandmother: certifying that she was "received as a probationer on the 9th day of December 1932, and had completed her full term of three years' training in the Medical & Surgical Wards of the Hospital, both on day and night duty. Dated this 9th day of December 1935."

Frances was pleased that she had persevered, and Alix sent her congratulations and a little gold-and-blue enamel locket on a fine gold chain.

Betty went off to do relieving work at other hospitals, and Caro took four months off before going to the Queen Victoria Maternity Hospital to enrol in midwifery. By the time she was through she would be twenty-one and able to buy her own plane. Meanwhile she could also study for her aircraft engineer's ticket, although that, too, could not be attained before she was twenty-one.

She pawned the gold locket to pay for flying lessons, for she had to log sixty hours' solo flying to get her "B" class licence, which would entitle her to take paying passengers, or to work for a commercial airline—if anyone would employ her.

She also had to spend half an hour at six thousand feet. The instructor used to say, "Don't be a fair-weather pilot. Remember, above the clouds the sun is shining." So she took off on an afternoon when large blue-shadowed thunder-clouds were building up over the hills.

The clouds were enormous, towering to possibly thirty thousand feet; there was no way she could get above them. Instead she flew in the narrow spaces of clear sky between, with the great rolling solid-looking masses almost near enough to touch. She knew that in their centres was turbulence strong enough to tear off her wings. It was like flying past snowy alpine mountains, exquisitely beautiful but also a little frightening.

It was so exciting that the half-hour passed too quickly and it was time to return to earth. As she made her approach into the wind and throttled down for landing, she knew the recurring joy of feeling the aircraft responding to her every touch; then the exultation of the long glissade down through the shining air, like a bird returning to its nest on the ground.

It was an experience she never forgot in all her years of flying.

Now she had to do half an hour's night flying; this was exciting, coming in to land along the flare path at Parafield, judging with difficulty the height of the craft above the ground. But the most frightening part of the course was flying blind.

The instructor travelled with her at the dual controls for this exercise. A canopy was placed over her head and shoulders so that she could see nothing outside the cockpit and the instruments in front: compass, air-speed indicator, rev counter, inclinometer, and altimeter. She had been warned to keep a close eye on her instruments, or she would lose all sense of balance and direction in a few seconds; and any misdirection of the aircraft could send it into a dangerous spin.

"Remember what to do in a spin," she counselled herself. "Centralize all controls, stick right forward, and out she comes."

She breathed slowly and tried to relax as the instructor handed over the controls to her, his calm voice reassuring her from the other cockpit. His voice in the earphones was her only guide as she groped her way through the air, feeling little sensation of movement as all outside visual reference points were gone.

Her mouth was still dry with fear and excitement when they landed, but the instructor said, "Congratulations; you came through that very well. Now you'll feel safe if you suddenly find yourself flying in cloud."

Chapter Six

Caro was now a fully qualified commercial pilot.

Andrew, who was still an undergraduate, took her out to celebrate.

They danced to the music of a small band, against a background of dark-blue velvet curtains. Andrew was a good dancer, and Caro, who was not, enjoyed following his guiding steps. They went back to their table, his arm still around her, and over a supper of asparagus omelettes he asked her to marry him.

"Oh, Andrew!" It was her first proposal, and she was touched. She was truly sorry, she told him, but she couldn't possibly get married—even if she loved him enough—when her new career as a flying nurse was almost about to begin. He poured her another glass of champagne with a hand that shook slightly.

"I didn't mean right away, darling. I mean, I won't be through Medicine for another two years. But we could just get engaged."

She had a moment of panic, beginning to feel trapped. She didn't want to be tied down. She looked at him, with his round, pale face and anxious eyebrows.

"I'm sorry," she murmured again, touching his hand. "It's just impossible." His hand was white and smooth, hers roughened and skinned about the knuckles.

It was true she wanted to be free, but also she had not yet got over Malcolm.

Amy Johnson, her schoolgirl heroine, had been the first woman to qualify as an aircraft engineer in England. Caro determined to be the first woman to do the same in Australia. She already knew something about petrol combustion engines, both theory and practice.

It was not a difficult course, she found; the difficulty was in being the only woman in a class of men at the Institute of Technology, a class that led up to an exam by the Department of Civil Aviation. She wished she had been better at mathematics. Inevitably she came in for some teasing from her class-mates.

When they had to make notes and drawings of "a male-and-female joint"—a term she had never before encountered—she felt afraid that she might begin to blush, and of course the very fear made her do so. No doubt all the jargon had been invented by men, beginning with the obvious origin of "joystick" for the main control lever in the floor of the cockpit.

Oh, it was ridiculous—but, aware of sly grins from the students on either side, she hung her head and let her straight fair hair fall forward to hide her burning cheeks.

Working on actual aircraft was better. She enjoyed all the detail of servicing a plane and making sure that it was safe to fly. She wore workmanlike overalls and a scarf tied round her hair, and did not mind how dirty her hands got or that there were smudges of grease on her cheeks. Just to be able to tinker with an aircraft was the next best thing to flying.

She was so busy that she saw much less of Andrew. Indeed, he was less attentive since she had refused his proposal, and seemed to have given up any hope of making her change her mind.

It was with a sense of shock that she read how a woman pilot had been killed at Mascot Aerodrome in Sydney. And Qantas had had their first bad crash when a DH 86 went into a flat spin near Longreach and killed all four on board. Caro was undeterred, but her mother wrote from Cloncurry that she hoped, now that Caro was fully licensed as a pilot, she would be content to fly only for pleasure, hiring a plane occasionally.

"Not a hope," wrote Caro cheerfully. "As soon as I'm a triple-certificated nurse, and get my inheritance, I shall buy a little plane and take off for the north. So expect me at the end of the year!"

Having finished her basic training, Caro found midwifery less exacting. She was no longer a junior probationer who could be bossed and harassed by senior Sisters. And she could sleep at home when she was not on night duty.

Caro didn't really like babies much. They were incredibly messy creatures, at both ends. The sheer volume of noise from the nursery was the worst on early-morning duty, when forty or fifty babies, all screaming with hunger that sounded like rage, had to be distributed to their mothers for the 6 A.M. feed.

Caro put her foot wrong in the first two weeks, when one young mother pointed out worriedly that there were white patches on her baby's inner cheeks and tongue. "Could it be thrush?" she asked.

Caro unwisely offered to mention it to the Matron, who swelled like a turkeycock and exclaimed "THRUSH? There is no thrush in my hospital, Sister. *Thrush* comes from dirty conditions. You will find that it is just a clot of half-digested milk. Kindly inform the mother so."

However, the mother remained unconvinced, and Caro swabbed the baby's tongue with gentian violet just in case, so that the infant looked like an outsize blue-tongued lizard.

Instead of books on test-feeds and baby weight gain, Caro studied motor manuals, reading up on airlocks and carburettors, valve-seats and piston-rings, wing-nuts and Whitworth bolts.

But she was nothing if not determined, and she could apply herself with great concentration when she tried. Just before her final exam she swotted up on theory, and she had proved herself in the labour ward as conscientious and unflappable, though some young mothers found her unsympathetic.

She finished her course in midwifery and received her certificate.

Caro gained her aircraft engineer's certificate on her twenty-first birthday, and celebrated with lunch at her grandmother's. She fretted while a firm of lawyers finalized the details of her inheritance, but at last she had her thousand pounds in the bank.

She had been looking round for some time for a suitable and not too expensive aircraft and now was able to buy, in Adelaide, a second-hand DH 60 Gypsy Moth for seven hundred pounds.

She spent weeks doing long and short hops to familiarize herself with the plane, but it was very similar to the ones she had done her training in: they were all different types of the De Havilland Moth. But before setting off across Australia from south to north, she needed more experience of long-range flying. The Brisbane-Adelaide Air Race in December gave her an opportunity, and she entered without telling her mother. (Caro had written to tell her she was a triple-certificated nurse at last.)

A group from the Aero Club flew in leisurely convoy, with plenty of stops on the way, to Brisbane. When the field was assembled at the Brisbane airport, it was found that they had to wait for a Qantas overseas airmail flight to take off for Darwin before they could start. There were several women pilots among the starters.

They had to fly to Coffs Harbour on the coast, then to Sydney for an overnight stop; then left Mascot aerodrome for Cootamundra on the western plains, and spent the night in Melbourne. The next day was the hop to Adelaide, with a stop near the South Australian border to refuel. The winner was a young man called Reg Ansett. Caro did not get a place, though she came a creditable fifth.

She was well pleased with her effort, and greatly enjoyed the comradeship of other flyers at the stops en route. She had flown over mountains and through cloud, hazards she would not be encountering on her way north—unless they were clouds of dust.

Caro was off on her great adventure. She had bought almonds, raisins, and barley sugar to chew on the way, and some canned sardines and a ground-sheet in case she should be forced down; besides some screw-top cans of water, a bottle of soft drink, and two square four-gallon tins of petrol, enough for about eighty miles. She was assured that she would

286

have no trouble obtaining fuel at the big stations on the way, but it would be expensive because of freight charges.

Everything had to be kept to a minimum in the Moth's cramped space. She had to find room for tools and tying-down gear for anchoring the plane in the open, for it could easily be blown away in a high wind or a willy-willy.

Frances, horrified at her making such a journey from Adelaide alone, had asked why she didn't take a companion; but as Caro pointed out, the space occupied by a passenger or second pilot would leave nowhere to carry things but for the slip pockets on the inside of the two cockpits. These would be used for carrying such things as maps, a torch, matches, a comb and lipstick, a drinking flask, and a cloth for cleaning her goggles and windscreen.

Frances still insisted that she take the tin of biscuits she had baked. Caro did not argue; the tin would be useful later. She asked for some empty jam-tins as well, without explaining to her grandmother the rather lowly use to which they would be put, on the longer stages of the journey to Cloncurry. For the same reason she wore wide-legged shorts instead of her trousers, even though it would be cold if she had to ascend to any height.

Betty and Andrew were at the airport to see her off, as were her grandmother, keeping a brave face though she evidently never expected to see her again in this world, and some of her Aero Club friends. They waved until the little blue-and-silver craft, which she had christened *Circe*, had dwindled away in the empty blue sky to the north.

Caro felt a sense of exultation as the neat square paddocks below gave way to plains covered in mallee, looking as dark as cinders against the earth, then to grey saltbush and the beginning of the painted desert. She left the rugged Flinders Ranges on her right and headed for Port Augusta, two hundred miles north, at the top of Spencer Gulf, which penetrated like a blue spear into the dry centre of South Australia.

Caro landed briefly to top up her fuel tank; from here she set a compass course due north over Lake Torrens, 120 miles of dry salt-pan. It was fascinating to trace its shores from the air, indented by water that no longer existed, the surface apparently of pink clay with white salty patches. Towards the northern end, where the lake bent away to the west, were some small islands.

Animal tracks leading out to these from the shore showed where the animal had broken through the pink-and-white surface into the dark damp clay below. It did not look at all safe to land on. She had no detailed route maps, and she had not been required to lodge a flight plan before leaving, so no one would know where she was if she was forced down.

But she could hardly get lost between Lake Torrens and the north-south railway line. She planned to stop at Marree, then briefly at a station on the way to Birdsville, with a short hop from there to Cappamerri to see her grandfather. Leaving the dead lake, she made north-east for the railway and followed it over the desolate dead-flat plains to Marree. She came in on a line between the dry bed of the Frome River and the railway line, to land on what she thought was an airstrip, but was in fact the racecourse.

Her arrival by air did not cause much excitement in the town—hadn't they seen Smithy himself land here in his *Lady Southern Cross*? And sometimes the Flying Doctor plane took an urgent case down to hospital at Port Augusta or Adelaide. But the townspeople were rather intrigued when they found the pilot was a woman.

The Sisters at the hostel were new, but they had heard of Sister MacFarlane and her companion Sister Kingston who had perished. When Caro told them she was Alix MacFarlane's daughter they made much of her and invited her to stay the night on the wire-screened veranda, and call Cappamerri on the pedal wireless early in the morning, before the day's schedule of medical calls began on the Flying Doctor network at 6 A.M.

It was much easier these days with a microphone instead of having to tap out messages in Morse code. They showed her how to work the pedals, and the switch, and gave her the two call-signs:

"8YM to 8TG, 8YM to 8TG," she called, pedalling vigorously.

"Not too hard, dear," said Sister Walsh. "You have to get the rhythm of it; otherwise you'll get out of breath."

Caro slowed down her pedalling. "8YM to 8TG," she called. "8TG, it's 8YM calling, 8YM from Marree. Come in, 8TG."

It seemed ages before an answer came in: a faint and croaking voice, "8TG, 8TG to 8YM. Cappamerri Station. Over."

"8YM to 8TG . . . Grandpa, this is Caro here. Yes, I'm flying up the Track. See you late this afternoon. Well before sunset. Over to you. Over."

There was a crackling silence over the air-waves. Then a blurred voice. "8TG calling 8YM. Caro? Is that really you? Did you say you're flying? Over to you."

"8YM to 8TG. Yes, I'm flying all the way. In my own plane, what's more. I'll land on the clay-pan near the house. See you soon. Over and out."

She switched off and beamed at Sister Walsh. "He doesn't really believe me. He sounded half asleep. But he'll believe it when he sees me land."

She felt sure he *had* been asleep when she called. Grandpa, still in bed after sunrise! Big Jim Manning must have changed his habits since she last saw him nine years ago.

She refuelled at Marree, saving the tins of petrol stashed in the front seat with the jerry-cans of water. As long as she did not lose the often-obliterated track in a dust-storm, she could scarcely go wrong. Cappamerri was less than an hour's flying time from Birdsville.

As she took off and circled for height, the shadow of her plane slipped over the bare ground in the shape of a perfect cross, and for a moment rested on a white headstone in the cemetery. Although she did not know if the grave was Mab Kingston's, it could well have been, and moved by the little touch of symbolism she decided to tell her mother it was so.

She was tempted to fly west towards Lake Eyre where Alix had nearly perished with Mab. At the Clayton Crossing she turned and followed its wooded channel north-west from the bore-drain. But as the river bed became dry and the stony desolation about Lake Eyre appeared below, she realized that she was doing a very foolish thing. The Sisters at Marree would have warned Mungerannie Station that she was on her way; but if she failed to arrive no one would be looking for her in this empty area west of the Birdsville Track. There was nothing to the west and north but the salty expanse of Lake Eyre and the dry bed of the Cooper. She turned east-north-east and made for the Birdsville Track.

It was not nearly as easy to follow as the railway line, but she picked it up at Dulkaninna, where the homestead had its name painted in large letters on the roof; the aeroplane had well and truly arrived in the outback, Caro thought. There were a group of people waving from near the homestead. Caro flew down and "buzzed" the station roof and waved a scarf in acknowledgement.

Even though mail-trucks used the Track regularly, it was necessary to come low over the Oorowillanie sand-hills to pick out the winding wheel-tracks through the maze of sand. She had seen no water anywhere except at the government bores; and where she crossed the Cooper with its lines of dead trees at Kopperamanna, she saw the old homestead, once part of the Lutheran Mission to the Aborigines, almost buried in sand. The sand was moving north-west along the longitudinal axis of the sand-dunes towards the Simpson Desert, leaving behind silted waterholes and bare clay-pans in which nothing would grow again.

It was depressing to see. She was relieved to arrive at Mungerannie homestead, to a green oasis inside the garden enclosure, a bath in the bore-water, and a meal of fresh beef. She had asked Marree to tell them to light a small fire, or "smoke," to give her wind direction, and Caro landed bumpily on a sand-drifted airstrip, to the squashing and popping of green paddy-melons. The station people, a new family since her mother's day, showed her the usual outback hospitality, and told her that the best place to land at Birdsville was on the racecourse.

"I remember the racecourse," said Caro. "I went to school at Birdsville."

It was noticeable how the Boss and the Missus warmed towards her when she told them this, and that she had spent her early childhood on Cappamerri and that Big Jim Manning was her grandfather. She was

289

"one of them"—the battlers, "We of the Never-Never" types, not some city girl visiting the country like a tourist. Though pressed to stay the night, she said she must get on as her grandfather was expecting her.

"We'll give him a call and tell him you've left here," they promised. "Good luck, lass. You're game to be flying up here on your own."

"It's nothing," said Caro carelessly. "I'm on my way to Cloncurry, to see my mother."

"Goodness! That's another three or four hundred miles further. The Flying Doctor base."

"Yes; my mother is nursing at the Cloncurry Hospital. And I might be the new Flying Doctor pilot—who knows?"

CHAPTER SEVEN

Caro made only a brief stop at Birdsville to take on fuel; also she wanted to see the town again for old times' sake. The river bed was dry except for the bore-fed waterhole, and the new punt installed in 1930 lay unused.

"Hasn't rained in Birdsville for five years," the Shell gasoline man told her. He had driven out to the racecourse as soon as he saw her land. "It has to break soon, or so we keep saying. . . . The school's closed down, so has the Royal Hotel. The A.I.M. hostel burnt down, but it's been rebuilt since. The town's not what it used ter be."

He offered to run her into the town in his truck and drive her back again.

"No, I don't think I want to see it. It's too depressing. I lived here at the hostel until I was twelve, but it's all changed."

The old hostel was gone, the school closed, the waterhole was invisible in the flat and stony expanse, among the few wisps of half-dead saltbush and dead roly-poly blown into depressions. She did not want to see any more. And then, above the hidden waterhole, a flock of eight pelicans rose and circled against the blue. With wide wings held motionless, they climbed an invisible spiral of heated air, higher and higher. Gazing at them, she remembered how she used to watch the pelicans and wish she could fly. It seemed a good omen.

She took off into the dry south-easterly and circled back over the low scattered roofs of the town. To the west stretched the Simpson Desert, streaked with pink and orange, long sand-hills as regular as the waves of the sea; to the east were the bare plains of Sturt's Stony Desert, with the dry channel of the Diamantina meandering through it. She set off for Cappamerri, following the river's course but cutting off the bends.

She passed by several permanent waterholes, shrunken but not yet empty. She saw no sign of cattle, and no green anywhere except on the banks of the river. And then the long red sand-hills, the twelve-mile waterhole and the iron and cane-grass roofs of the station. . . . The sand-hills had encroached until only the garden enclosure was clear.

She had travelled in less than an hour the route which had taken the station buggy two and a half days. Caro dived towards the homestead roof and then zoomed up again to make sure they heard her, then circled the clay-pan as dark figures began to run out of the campsite wurlies, and someone in a white shirt came out of the house and got into a truck to come and meet her. As she made her last turn and began to glide in to the landing, she saw two blackfellows industriously sweeping the bare polished surface of the clay-pan with a yard broom! She could only hope they would get out of the way in time.

She made a perfect landing, cut the throttle and watched the propeller falter and stop, while her ears adjusted to the silence after the steady roar of the engine in flight. She began unbuckling her harness and helmet as her grandfather's utility truck came bouncing over the rocks, raising a cloud of red dust.

The big man, with brick-red face and white hair showing under his broad-brimmed cattleman's hat, lifted her down from the steps, hugged her, and set her on her feet. Others were waiting with outstretched black arms to shake her hand, those who remembered young Jim's wife and daughter—the little girl with her pony and her friendly ways, the Young Missus with her clinic for the children and old men with trachoma. One old man had tears in his eyes as he welcomed her. "Young Missus save me goin' blind," he said. "Mumma belong-you, before you born."

He must have been about eighty, Caro thought.

Big Jim put his arm around her shoulders.

"So you're a full-blown pilot, eh?" he asked admiringly. "You always had plenty of spirit, like your mother."

He smiled, and the tiny slits of blue that were his eyes disappeared entirely in the folds of his cheeks.

The sun was close to setting as they went up the shallow steps to the veranda. The sand-hills glowed with pure colour, and the waterhole beyond gleamed blue-green in contrast. The sound of water-birds came up from the river, and a mosquito whined past. Yes, it was the same place she vaguely remembered. Her grandfather, Caro noted professionally, was overweight and did not appear to be in good condition. He had left one of the men (or "boys," as he persisted in calling them) to carry Caro's small bag, but he wheezed and was short of breath just from climbing the steps.

But Jim Manning's deterioration was nothing to that of the homestead since Olive's day. No white woman had been there for years, and old Lucy, who had run the place so well, was probably dead. On the veranda they stumbled over wisps of dead leaves and sticks, and little heaps of sand deep enough to grow vegetables. Caro felt sand grit under her feet on the flagged floor of the living-room . . . well, perhaps they'd had a sandstorm recently. But the curtains were ragged and hung crookedly from missing rings, and the table was apparently kept half-set with sauce-bottles, salt and sugar, and some uncleared plates from the last meal. Caro thought it might be wiser not to venture out to check on the condition of the kitchen—after all, she had to eat here.

Outside, the nearest sand-hill had encroached on the station outbuildings, half-burying the meat-house and cool-room, and was already up to the garden fence. The garden itself was withered and neglected.

There used to be a black girl who helped to water the garden, and who worked in the kitchen—Jenny, was it? As if in answer to her thought, Big Jim went to the door opening towards the kitchen annex, and called, "Jenny! Drinks for Young Missus, you lazy bitch!"

There was some delay before Jenny arrived with two glasses on a tray, filled with lemon cordial and water—and actually two blocks of ice!

"Yes, we've got a kero fridge now," said Jim Manning.

Meanwhile Caro was trying not to stare. This fat and shapeless figure in a dirty gina-gina—could this be Jenny? She had evidently made some attempt to do her hair, but it was still like a rats' nest.

"Hallo, Jenny. Remember me?"

"You-i, Missus. You bin growed up; one-time you little tacker. Might-be seven, eight year old."

"That's right; more than ten years ago. You see me land my aeroplane?"

"No-more. Me bin schleep."

In the old days, Jenny would not have been sleeping in the late afternoon, with guests coming. Things had indeed changed. The evening meal consisted of tinned meat and tinned beans, with some thick hunks of bread and no butter.

"I've seen no cattle about, Grandpa," said Caro as they sat on the western veranda after dinner. The clear inland sky shaded down from palest turquoise to glowing apricot behind the dark frieze of river gums.

"All dead," he said laconically. "I can't afford to stock up again when this drought breaks—if it ever does—and the place is eaten out. Don't even own a riding horse any more." He slowly filled his pipe. "I'll end up in this old-timers' home I hear they're going to build in the Alice. As for the station—I'll give it back to the crows and the kites."

"What about staff?"

"Don't even have a cook, let alone a bookkeeper. Place has gone to pot since old Lucy died, as you can see. The blacks will hang about the waterhole, catching their own tucker like they used to, or drift into Birdsville as fringe-dwellers."

"And Jenny?"

"She's been a loyal helpmate." He looked defiant. "I know you don't approve, but—"

"I didn't say I didn't approve. But—if she has sons . . ."

He shrugged. "They can have the place, for what it's worth. Even a good season won't help now. And she can have the house, and whatever I can leave her."

In the morning, Caro found that Jenny had washed her dress and smartened herself up, and had even swept the floor. But she was guarded, watchful, and unsmiling. Caro realized that she dreaded a white woman coming here to live, where she had ruled the roost for so long. She had a room in the cook's quarters adjoining the kitchen, but it was evident she was used to being free of the house.

Caro saw her sullen mouth relax when she told Jenny that this visit was a short one, she was on her way to north Queensland and would not be coming back.

"You look after the Old Boss now, Jenny. I know you his woman. He say those boys belong-you can have this place when him gone."

Jenny's fat, dark face broke into a smile. "Me got girl, too. She wan' to be nurse at Ho'pital, longa Birdsville, like-it you Mumma."

Jenny said her daughter had once been taken down to the hostel with a poisoned foot, and she had never forgotten the clean white building and the kind Sisters.

Caro explained that she could be a ward-maid at the hostel, but it took a long time to learn to be a nurse.

"I'm a nurse, and it took me four years."

"You nurse too, Missus? Mine tink-it you bin Bird-lady."

"So I am. A sort of flying nurse."

Caro spent another two days at the station, enduring the terrible meals. She could have offered to cook, but the idea of the wood stove in the increasing heat of early summer did not appeal, and she felt sure she would not be welcome in the kitchen building. She had looked forward to riding again, but there were no horses. She talked to Alix at Cloncurry and told her to expect her within a week, so that her mother would not worry if she was delayed for some reason. So far the flight had gone like a dream.

Her greatest danger lay in getting lost. Poring over the map with Big Jim, she agreed that "the longest way round was the best way home." In that trackless country, and with no railway lines as guides, the safest path was to follow the beds of the great dry rivers, along which station properties were strung and waterholes could be found. But to take the direct route north to Cloncurry, she would have to cross a hundred and twenty miles of empty sand-hills on the very borders of the unexplored Simpson Desert to the westward. If she missed her way and flew into the desert, she would eventually run out of fuel and perish there.

Big Jim's idea was that she should follow the Diamantina all the way up to Kynuna, and then use the main road to Cloncurry as her guide. Caro wanted to see Boulia and the legendary Bedourie, where the Bedourie oven came from, and the dust-storms known as Bedourie Showers. But the whole route was desolate and dangerous.

She decided instead to fly north-east along the Diamantina to Diamantina Lakes Station, then north-west by compass to the Hamilton River, pausing at Springvale Station on the way. This would be the most difficult part of her route, and her first major change of direction. She would then follow the Hamilton northward through the Selwyn Range, and so to the town of McKinlay and the mail-route to Cloncurry.

The whole camp came out to see her leave, the Bird Lady who was the Boss's granddaughter. The sky was light in the east but the sun had not yet risen. She would get a good start before air currents from the heated earth made flying uncomfortable. With luck there would be no bad dust-storms before the hottest months, February and March. The sky as she lifted into it was clear from horizon to horizon.

As the sun rose, the earth revealed the ethereal beauty of dawn from the air. Even the endless sand-dunes took on a softness and charm in the diffuse golden glow along their summits; and shadowed with palest blue were the clay-pans between them, while the harsh, forbidding gibber plains to the east looked soft as a water-colour. From three thousand feet all was level as the sea.

Following the mile-wide dry channels of the river, Caro settled comfortably into her pilot's seat, relaxed and content. This was the best sort of flying: when human wits and nerves were pitted, alone, against mechanical weakness or elemental forces. Though nursing to her had been incidental to her great commitment to flying, she saw now that there were points of similarity between them, and perhaps one training had helped the other. In both one must be constantly alert, aware, and foresighted, ready to tackle an emergency without giving way to anxiety or alarm.

Duthie Station was coming up on the starboard side of the river, a few cattle just visible, moving along the radiating tracks round each bore. Sand-drifts showed around the homestead buildings, but Duthie did not seem to be in as bad a state as Cappamerri. There was still a blue-grey sifting of growth on the slopes of the sand-hills, though the gibber plains were bare. Caro wondered if Grandpa's old mate Harry Hays was home.

Climbing for safety to four thousand feet, she levelled out and gazed round for signs of dust or cloud. But the whole horizon was clear, merging into the blue of distance all round.

A line of trees marked the main channel of the river, but sometimes there were three or four, parting and meeting again. She passed over Monkira Station, seeing a gleam of water in a long reach, and the white specks of water-birds or cockatoos rising above the trees. It was fascinating to see the country spread out like a map below, a map that seemed to be unrolling slowly backwards beneath her. The engine droned sweetly, without a miss, the wire stays vibrated gently in the wind of movement. The air up here was pleasantly cool.

She dropped down to a thousand feet for a good look at Monkira.

She made a wide circle round the homestead, banking and turning, seeing no very inviting landing ground. It was too early to refuel, so she waggled her wings in acknowledgement to the few people waving from the ground, and flew away up the river bed. She felt sure her passing would be recorded in the "galah session" during the morning, so her whereabouts would be known.

From three thousand feet she could see the braided channels of the river disappearing to north and south, but now they began to widen into a confusing pattern, three or four channels joining and meeting again, sometimes ten miles apart. At last the channel she was following, with an occasional permanent waterhole in it, suddenly disappeared into the desert. There was nothing ahead, no landmark, no river bed, not a hill; just the endless empty plains. Was she west or east of the main channel? If she kept taking wrong turnings she would run out of fuel. It was daunting to think of landing in the midst of this emptiness to refuel from her tins, even if she could find a suitable place to put down. Her watch had stopped, and she did not know how long she had been flying since Monkira.

The safest course was to retrace her track to where the tributary had branched off, and then follow what seemed to be the main channel again. She had lost all faith in the river as a guide but it was the only point of reference in this vast, flat land. She had come at least fifty miles along the false channel. This would mean a hundred miles before she was back on course, if she returned. Forcing herself to breathe slowly and deeply, refusing to panic, she made a swift decision and turned due east. She climbed for a wider view, but the day was advanced towards noon and the sky was becoming hazy. She wiped her goggles and peered ahead, her eyes smarting with the strain.

Chapter Eight

After an anxious quarter of an hour Caro saw ahead a dark line of trees trending north and south. But was this the main channel, or another tributary leading off to the north? She flew on until she could see a second channel beyond the first. From the map, Diamantina Lakes was on the easterly one of two channels. Then, on the second channel but slightly to the south, she saw the roofs and outbuildings of a station, and a large waterhole beyond. She had nearly missed it! This was her turning-point for flying west towards Springvale.

Feeling her knees begin to shake from the reaction to tension, she thankfully circled lower, looking for a possible landing ground. The wind, she was sure, would still be a steady south-easter. A sudden bump and a lurch as a heated air pocket caught the plane, and figures like small black ants appeared below. As she came lower she was able to see that they were pointing southward to where a faint track crossed the dry river bed and led to a scoured clay-pan. She side-slipped, throttled back and glided —there was still time to pull up again if the clay-pan was strewn with large boulders—as a motor vehicle came tearing along the track leaving a plume of red dust.

"Are you Caro Manning?" asked the station manager as she climbed stiffly out of the cockpit.

"Yes. Is this Diamantina Lakes?"

"No, this is Davenport Downs. The Lakes is twenty miles on."

Caro felt a chill of retrospective fear. If she hadn't needed fuel, if she'd gone on without descending to ask her way, she'd have flown out into a hundred miles of nothing between the Diamantina and the Hamilton. She could have missed Springvale altogether.

"We heard on the pedal radio that you were flying up the river towards Cloncurry. Come in to the homestead and have a drink. Or still better, stay the night."

Caro squinted at the sun. She estimated that she still had five or six hours of daylight left.

"No, I think I'll keep going. But if I could have a bite to eat—and get you to draw me a local map? The channels are so confusing. Is Diamantina Lakes on a single channel?"

"No, the channels are eight or ten miles apart there. But you've no need to follow the river any further."

More than food, Caro craved a visit to the station's outside lavatory. She had left early in the morning, with a selection of empty tins which she threw out when they were full. And though she was thirsty, she had limited her drinking as much as possible. Now she needed more than a tin.

After lunch, Mr. Brooks drew a map, with accurate distances marked, among the clutter of papers on his office table.

"See, you're in the heart of the Channel Country here. You go north-west till you pick up the Mangeroo Knobs, a group of ironstone jump-ups, and they will lead you to Spring Creek. Go up Spring Creek to Springvale and just before its source you come to the track leading to the Hamilton Hotel on the Hamilton River; whenever you strike the river, go north, and it will lead you through the Selwyn Range to the McKinlay River, which you follow into McKinlay and the main road to Cloncurry. As soon as you see the rivers start flowing north instead of south, you're nearly there."

Refreshed, and with the plane refuelled, she set a compass course north-west. The manager would send a pedal-radio message ahead to Springvale that she was on her way. She picked up the group of small knobby hills and the green-looking course of Spring Creek, and kept at less than a thousand feet to be sure of not losing her landmarks, till the white roofs of a large station showed ahead. She circled Springvale once, waved to the people on the ground, and flew on for the Hamilton River.

Bare stony plains stretched as far as she could see on all sides. Not a single habitation anywhere. She strained her eyes ahead until at last she picked up a winding line of black cinders, as it appeared, strewn on the red-brown earth. This was the line of trees marking the river bed. She came down to only five hundred feet and skimmed along above the trees, looking for the Hamilton Hotel. No sign of it. Well, perhaps she had cut the river too far north. But there was no doubt she was on the right track; the dry bed of the river was tending steadily north-east.

After that, as the manager of Davenport Downs had mapped for her, she followed the river through the lowest part of the rugged Selwyn Range and looked for a river flowing north. It was strange to fly over the "backbone" of the land where the rivers flowed off in opposite directions. But she had little time to study the landscape. She was being flung up and down in a series of heat-bumps, and feared going the whole way down on to those inhospitable-looking rocky ridges. The Hamilton petered out in a mountain creek, and ahead was the beginning of the McKinlay, flowing north. Soon she was over McKinlay, and turning north-west along the main road and with a tail-wind to help her, she was in Cloncurry in little more than half an hour, with two hours of daylight left.

298

She had made it! It was an anxious business flying alone over unknown territory, and without a watch. It was not till she landed on the Cloncurry airfield, seeing the Qantas hangar, that she realized how tense she had been for the last three hundred miles. But she had made it.

That night Alix was not on duty. She and Caro stayed up till near midnight talking, though Caro was physically exhausted by the long, hot flight from Cappamerri. She had a bath and went to bed in the second bed in her mother's room, then Alix came and sat on her bed and they talked some more, catching up on five years.

"By the way, I'm the sub-Matron now," said Alix. "I could probably get you a job on the staff."

"No, thanks," said Caro. "I want to fly. If they won't take me in the Flying Doctor Service—"

"The Aerial Medical Service, it is called."

"In the Aerial Medical Service, I'll take my plane to some little country town and offer it to the local doctor for visiting his patients."

"What! You'd set up in competition to the A.M.S.?"

"Why not, if they're silly enough not to employ me? By the way, I've got your hundred and eighty pounds, Mum. Two hundred pounds with interest."

"I don't want interest, child."

"I'm glad you didn't get your hair cut, like everyone else," said Caro, looking at her mother's soft curly hair with scarcely a grey thread, which was falling about her shoulders as she took out her hairpins.

"I like yours short, after all." Alix stroked Caro's long bob, falling as straight as straw on each side of her face, and with straw's silvery-gold sheen. "Did you bring your nurse's uniform? I've never seen you since you became a nurse."

"You've never seen me since I became a pilot, for that matter."

"No—you were still at school! I felt a bit guilty, leaving you with your grandmother, but you were a great companion for her after Grandpa died. Frances and I couldn't live in the same house for long. Has she aged much?"

"After Grandpa died she looked a lot older. But she doesn't seem to have aged any more since. Like you, not a grey hair—but I think she tints it. You know that sort of dead black?"

"Yes. She'll never let herself go grey. And Grandpa Manning? How is Big Jim?"

Caro sighed. "He—he's going downhill. So is the station. He admits he will have to walk off and leave it eventually. There's no feed left, and the sand-hills are encroaching on the homestead."

"He has someone to cook his meals?"

"To open cans, more likely. Yes, Jenny seems to have taken over the house."

"Ah—Jenny!"

"I was only a kid when I was there before. Was she—was she already established then?"

"Yes. Even in Olive's time. She was what the Bible calls a concubine."

"He's going to leave the station to her boys. What's left of it. There are no cattle any more, just a few goats. Not even a riding horse!"

"So he won't be leaving you anything?" said Alix with gentle irony.

Caro laughed unselfconsciously. "Not a hope!" She added seriously, "Poor old Grandpa! He says he'll end up in an old men's home."

"I hope for his sake that he dies before that happens."

In the next few days Caro gave her plane a thorough overhaul. She was very pleased with the performance of the engine; it had not given her a moment's worry, and she had averaged almost ten miles to the gallon of fuel. . . . She was leaning on a wing, testing the wing-struts, when she noticed the hangar was open, and two men were wheeling an aircraft out into the sunlight where the red cross gleamed on its side. She guessed it was the Qantas ground engineer, who serviced the medical-service plane as well as the Qantas mail-planes, and the pilot, Eric Donaldson.

It was too hot for overalls, so Caro was wearing shorts and sandals and an open-necked shirt, the shorts revealing a length of slender leg.

She climbed down and strolled over. The mechanic nudged the pilot.

"This is the A.M.S. plane, isn't it?" she asked with interest. "And you're Eric Donaldson? I'm Caro Manning, Sister Alix's daughter."

"Ah! We've heard of you from your mother—she's very proud of you. And I hear you've just flown solo all the way from Adelaide—quite a trip for a little crate."

"Don't you mean, 'Quite a trip for a girl'?" she asked mockingly.

He smiled disarmingly. "Well—it *is* unusual."

She smiled loftily, "Amy Johnson flew solo all the way from England when I was a child."

"Yes—well—she was unusual, too."

"And let me tell you I'm a commercial pilot, with a "B" licence, and a certified aircraft engineer as well."

He whistled. "That really *is* unusual for a girl. Thommo, meet Caro Manning, who will be able to help you out when you've got two planes in for servicing at the same time. Thommo Thompson is the Qantas engineer," he explained.

Thommo grinned and sketched a salute.

She allowed herself to smile. "What's the problem?"

"It was a blown valve. All fixed now."

"I've been checking my engine, and it seems okay. I was worried by the oil overheating on the last leg."

"In mid-summer you have to watch for vapour-locks. The temperature is often 115 degrees on the ground. Shade temperature, that is. It's all right once you've got a few thousand feet on the clock."

"I had to hug the ground so as not to lose the rivers and the roads I was following," said Caro. "You should have seen me hedge-hopping up the Diamantina. And even then I got lost."

Eric Donaldson looked at Thommo and shook his head admiringly. "I still say she was game to take it on."

Caro was used to being around flying men and talking shop, and when tall, laconic Eric asked her to come and have lunch with them at the pub she agreed readily.

"The only thing," said Eric hesitantly, "is that they're a bit old-fashioned out here, and a lady in shorts—however attractive she looks—might not be accepted in the hotel dining-room."

"Not that *we* object, of course," said Thommo with a grin.

Caro, who had driven Alix's Baby Austin Seven out to the aerodrome, said she would pop back to the hospital for a skirt, and join them later.

Over lunch in the Leichhardt Hotel Eric suggested that they ought to organize a party to welcome her to the town. "Everyone wants to meet you, especially the unattached males; they're always delighted when some new talent arrives."

"Such as a new nurse at the hospital? Well, I'm a trained nurse too."

"You are amazing. There is a doctor in the Northern Territory Service who flies his own plane, but there are no pilot-nurses!"

Caro was immediately interested. "Who is he—this doctor who flies himself?"

"Dr. Trenowith. You must have read of his exploits—he's always getting lost and having hairbreadth escapes from death. But John Flynn won't have him in the A.I.M. Service. His idea is one man, one job, and a doctor must be able to concentrate on his patient without flying the ambulance plane as well."

"So, does this Dr. Trenowith have his own practice?"

"He works for the Northern Territory Medical Service, out of Darwin. There's no Flying Doctor base in the Territory as yet, though we often fly across the border to attend urgent cases. But Flynn intends to make the Alice a Flying Doctor base eventually."

"My mother was at the A.I.M. hostel there about eight years ago. Perhaps I might get a job with the new service when it opens. Meanwhile, I'm looking for charter work."

"We really need a back-up plane when *Victory* is out of action—as it has been the last couple of days," said Thommo. "Qantas has to scratch round and lend a plane in an emergency."

"And what are my chances of getting *your* job?" she asked, looking at Eric.

301

"You've got Buckley's chance, I should say. Wouldn't you, Thommo? The doctor's a bit conservative. You'll meet him—Dr. Avery. He and the Medical Superintendent of the Cloncurry Hospital don't get on. He's supposed to be Honorary Surgeon, but complains they never consult him."

As they were finishing off the bottle of beer they had ordered with lunch Eric said, "Dr. Avery will be a bit nervous when he finds he has a woman pilot. He'll be expecting you to crash."

"I've never had a crash," said Caro, crossing her fingers. "I suppose it's a bit like falling off a horse—you go up again straightaway to make sure you haven't lost your nerve."

"That's about right. My worst crash was in December 1930, when the engine failed: a vapour-lock in the fuel system. The temperature in the shade was 115 degrees that day. The plane was a wreck, but I walked away from it."

"He was born lucky," said Thommo. "You know what he does when he's lost? Flies low over the first traveller he sees, shuts off the engine and shouts, 'Where's Camooweal?' or wherever."

"Yes, one bloke was wild because I made his pack-horses bolt."

Caro laughed. "I'll try that next time I'm bushed."

CHAPTER NINE

In the next week Caro managed to get some charter work with local graziers from the cattle-stations to the north when they came into town and saw her advertisement. Some of them looked very doubtful when they found that "C. Manning, Pilot" was a young woman. But as soon as one had been brave enough to take the plunge—or rather the ascent —he encouraged others to do the same.

It was amusing to hear one sturdy, sun-browned cattleman urging his friend over a beer in the Leichhardt Hotel: "Go on, George, you really must go up, you've no idea how it gives you a complete view of your run in only twenty minutes or less."

The same man, Caro had noticed, closed his eyes as she banked steeply and he saw his property tilting alarmingly; he had gripped the sides of the cockpit throughout the flight.

The party suggested by Eric was duly held, people coming in from properties around. It was also a pre-Christmas party and the local hall was booked and decorated with tinsel and red bunting. A bush band which was passing through was commandeered.

Since everyone plied the orchestra with beer during breaks, as the night wore on the fiddler became more and more frenetic, playing in faster tempo, until at last his belt broke and his trousers fell down about his knees. He kept on playing in his undershorts in the dim light, for the petrol-lamps were running short of fuel.

All the men wanted to dance with Caro because she was new, an unknown quantity. Her mother danced with the Medical Superintendent from the Hospital, but Matron did not put in an appearance, pointing out that "someone must hold the fort," for of course all her young nurses wanted to be at the party.

Eric introduced Caro briefly to Dr. Avery, who did not dance, and his wife, a local girl who had married the Flying Doctor.

"He's a fine surgeon," Eric told her as they danced. "Has rather a regal manner which frightens some of his patients, but he has a kind heart and will go anywhere at any time if he's needed. He knows that sometimes a man who's been too long alone on an outstation may be imagining his symptoms, but his policy is 'When in doubt, fly.'"

As he took her back to her seat—all the women sat together round the edge of the dance floor, while the men congregated round the door of the hall—Eric said, "I want to ask you something, Caro. I'm trying to wangle leave so I can go down to Sydney for Christmas, and I wondered if. . . ."

For a moment she looked startled, thinking he was asking if she would like to accompany him on such short acquaintance. "I wondered if you could help. I might be getting married, at least I want to go and see my girl, but they keep telling me there are no relief pilots available. And this is where you come in."

"Me?"

"Yes, I want a few weeks off, and I'm sure you could carry on here. I'll claim that I'm jaded and need a break. Your mother knows John Flynn, perhaps she can pull some strings with the A.I.M. in Sydney. Are you game?"

"What do you think?" said Caro with a broad grin.

"Good girl!"

Caro's appointment as temporary relief pilot with the Aerial Medical Service came through in time for Eric to leave for Sydney before Christmas. To her disappointment her first medical flight was to be a short one, back over the route she had flown on her way to Cloncurry. It was to Kynuna, on the upper reaches of the Diamantina River. This was the same flight which Alix had written about with such drama.

Caro was in her workmanlike long pants and boots, with a white shirt, as she waited for Dr. Avery to arrive at the airstrip. She wanted to check everything herself before take-off. Eric had briefed her and gone up with her on a short flight but a Fox Moth's controls were not new to her though a cabin-type was. The pilot still had his head out in the air in the cockpit, with the usual inadequate little windscreen curved in front of him.

Hearing the doctor's car approaching, Caro quickly put on her flying-helmet with the goggles pushed up on her forehead, her blonde hair out of sight. She wasn't sure if he knew who the temporary pilot was. Dr. Avery, carrying his black bag, stepped briskly up to the open door of the cabin and placed the bag within. He then turned to say "Good morning," and his eyes became fixed on Caro's smooth brown arms emerging from the rolled-up sleeves of her shirt, and the way the front of that shirt fitted her figure. A keen glance at her face, and he turned, reached into the cabin for his bag, and began walking back to his car.

"Dr. Avery! Aren't you ready to take off?" she called.

He stopped and looked back. "Not with a woman pilot, thank you!"

Caro shrugged and looked at Thommo, who was trying to stifle his laughter with an oily rag, out of sight on the other side of the plane. "Thommo. . . !" she appealed.

He came out from behind the plane and addressed the doctor. "It's quite all right, Doc. I'd trust my life with her, any day. Eric says she's good, and he'd know. She's just flown solo all the way from Adelaide."

"Another Dolores Bonney, eh?" growled Dr. Avery. (Mrs. Bonney, the year before, had flown around Australia alone.)

"And I came fifth in the Brisbane-Adelaide air race, *and* I won the Ladies' Trophy." Even as she said it Caro had a feeling of dismay. What if he knew that wasn't true? Actually, a young red-headed, bright-eyed woman called Nancy Bird had won the trophy—what a wonderful name for a woman pilot! It wasn't that she told lies, Caro reasoned, she was just a bit prone to exaggeration. . . .

"Well, we'd better get on, I suppose," said Dr. Avery, putting his bag into the cabin once more and climbing in after it. Caro closed the cabin door and smiled at him. Thommo swung the propeller.

"Switch off."

"Suck in."

"Switch on."

"Contact."

"Contact!" And the single engine sprang into life.

She taxied out and faced into the wind, after giving the engine a thirty-second burst before the chocks were knocked away. She would show this doubting doctor she could fly!

There was no trouble with navigating: she followed the road south-east to McKinlay, the way she had come, then on over the dead-flat plains to Kynuna. Here the river bed was flat and sandy, with some small water-holes among the sand. There was obviously not much fresh water to be had; the only sign of green was a tiny lawn at the hospital, looking no bigger than a pocket handkerchief. (After they landed, out of curiosity she measured it; it was exactly fifteen feet square.) The hospital had two Sisters under the Bush Nursing Scheme, so Caro's assistance was not needed during the operation on a child with a foreign body in the oesophagus.

Kynuna township was small and bare. There was no bridge, and there was no water in the river. Only a few stunted trees, and beyond, the baked earth of the empty plains. Goats nibbled at empty tins and old papers in the dusty street.

Caro was glad to accept an invitation to lunch at the tiny hospital. She had chocked the wheels of the plane. The sky was clear, and though she had brought her tying-down gear she did not use it.

They sat down to a late lunch of cold roast goat and tomatoes. "I had

305

only two tomatoes, so I shared them among the four of us," said the younger nurse.

The doctor was in a good mood after a successful operation. Caro had taken only a few mouthfuls when there came a shout from the road, then someone was hammering on the front door. "Eh, Sister, Sister!" he cried. "You better tell the pilot of that there doctor's plane—"

Caro rushed to the door. "There's a bloody big willy-willy heading this way," said the man, whose short sandy hair seemed to stand on end as he pointed behind him. The sky was clear, but moving towards them over the plain was a giant willy-willy, a spiral of red dust twisting hundreds of feet into the blue.

"Quick! Come and help me hold her," shouted Caro, making at a run for the large open paddock where they had landed. The little plane stood alone and unprotected. No time to tie her down now. The first man collected a bystander, and they sprinted after her. "Grab the wings!" said Caro, watching as the towering red dust-cloud, tapering at the base, came wavering towards them. Old papers, roly-poly bushes, a sheet of loose iron were swept up by the whirlwind. Caro was desperate. She could see in her mind the Moth snatched up and bashed down again, perhaps impaled on a post—and she would have lost the Flying Doctor plane on her first flight.

She gripped a strut between the wings till her knuckles were white. The man who had called her held on to the opposite wing and the third man grasped the tail-plane and rudder. Then the willy-willy was upon them, whirling and dragging. Fortunately there were no trees or fences to obstruct them as they went dancing along, with longer and longer strides, every now and then taking twenty-foot leaps as the plane tried to fly. Their eyes blinded by dust and debris, they closed them tight and hung on.

As suddenly as it had caught them, the whirlwind let go its grip, and the sand and dust subsided. Dazed and half-blinded, Caro saw the red column dancing away over the plain. The aircraft was very dirty, but did not appear to be damaged. Caro bent and kissed a gritty wing. Then for safety she drove in the pegs and fixed a guy-rope.

When she made her way back to the hospital after giving each of the men ten bob to spend at the pub, the others looked at her with worried faces. "We kept your lunch," they said, and "You'll need a wash." They pointed her towards a wall-mirror. Caro took one look and burst into near-hysterical laughter. Her face was painted red with dust, her mouth and eyes showing as three white patches, and her hair was full of grit and straw.

"Well, that has taught me a lesson," said Caro to Dr. Avery as they went back to the plane to fly home. "In this country, never leave your aircraft untethered."

"Not in summer, anyway," he gravely agreed. "We could have lost the plane."

She rather liked that "we."

In the next two weeks Caro flew the doctor more than a thousand miles, and on each trip he grew more relaxed. She had her first glimpse of the unfriendly flying territory to the west when they flew to Mount Isa to pick up a miner with a broken pelvis. At Cloncurry the Great Australian mine was still producing copper and some gold and iron from the dark peak called Black Mountain; while at Mount Isa a great lode of silver-lead had been opened up. The mineralized area was about a hundred miles across, and from the air showed as quite distinct from the pastoral lands around it.

But good mining areas meant dangerous flying conditions, mile after mile of jagged, barren hill and gully; scorching hillsides of a dull red-brown, topped with rocky backbones like the plates on the back of a dinosaur; great tumbled masses of broken rock; scrub and spinifex, and a few stunted trees along the dry watercourses.

Caro found that under the regulations Qantas planes (and the Aerial Medical Service plane was one) were not supposed to fly direct to the Isa, but must take the long way round by following the railway line south to Duchess through a gap in the hills, and then northwest again. It was exactly twice as far.

She flew the safe way going out, but coming back with an injured man in pain, she flew the direct route, going up to six thousand feet to give her time to glide over the worst country in an emergency. The doctor did not complain.

Much as she was enjoying being the Medical Service pilot, Caro had to refuse to take off in a severe dust-storm that blew up from the south a few days later at Cloncurry. Dr. Avery knew that a road trip to Julia Creek would not only be uncomfortable, but it would take six or seven hours, whereas they could fly there in one and a half hours. "What use is an aeroplane if we can't use it in an emergency?" grumbled the doctor.

"I'm sorry," said Caro firmly. "I daren't risk the aircraft, not to mention your life and my own. If we wait till tomorrow morning, the dust may have cleared."

"It can't wait. The matter is urgent, gunshot wounds to the chest and internal haemorrhage. I have to go and operate as soon as possible. There's only a Bush Nursing Sister at Julia Creek."

"I'm sorry," said Caro again. He turned away impatiently and went to see about a car and driver.

Distressed, Caro went to see her mother. "I honestly couldn't fly in this weather," she said. "We'd be sure to get lost. Eric told me that the

307

view ahead is almost nil, looking into the propeller and the haze; you have to fly along looking backwards, and I don't know the routes well enough for that."

"You were quite right, dear," said Alix soothingly. "You mustn't let Doctor bully you into acting against your own judgment."

Later that morning a wireless message came for the Qantas agent to say that owing to the widespread dust the mail-plane could not leave Longreach, as it would not be possible to find its way to Cloncurry. Caro felt justified, but she also felt that the doctor might hold it against her. Did he think she was afraid? It occurred to her afterwards that she might have taken a risk with her own plane, but she could not be responsible for jeopardizing the Medical Service craft.

That evening a call came from Julia Creek to ask her, if the weather had cleared sufficiently, to fly out and pick up him and the patient next day. She gathered that he'd had a fairly hot and unpleasant drive. Fortunately the sky did clear.

As the summer heat increased, so did the frequency of dust-storms. The visibility was reduced to a hundred yards, and the dust-clouds reached thousands of feet into the air. Even at midday the sun appeared like a pale Aspro tablet suspended in the orange sky.

On December 30, Caro had to fly to McKinlay yet again on the way to take the doctor to El Rita Station, about forty miles south of the town.

"Better stop at McKinlay for directions," said Dr. Avery before they took off, but Caro explained that she had flown that way on the trip from Adelaide, had passed almost over El Rita near the source of the Hamilton, and she could remember the route quite well. "After I lost the Hamilton I followed a stock-route all the way north to the main road. I must have passed the station on the way."

The report had said that an old man making a fifty-mile cross-country ride had broken his leg away out in the range. He was delirious and blood poisoning was feared.

A car was waiting at El Rita and the manager drove them ten miles into the hills; the patient was being carried nine miles on a stretcher from where he had fallen.

Caro and Dr. Avery sat down in the river bed to wait. He had asked her to come with him (after tying down the plane securely) to help ease the patient's journey back to the plane

The sun beat down into the dry river bed and radiated from the heated rocks. They waited and waited. Mr. Chalmers from the station drew some water up from a soak dug in the river bed, and they quenched their thirst with black tea—far better than plain water. It was now 2 P.M. and they'd had no lunch, but it was too hot to think of eating.

As Mr. Chalmers handed Caro her mug of tea, a fly fell in and drowned in the hot liquid. Unconcerned, he hooked it out with a horny-skinned finger. "If you can't drink tea with seven flies in it, out here," he said, "you have to do without tea."

It was nearly 6 P.M. and the blazing sun had gone behind the shoulder of the cliffs when they heard horses' hoofs stumbling on rocks, and the party appeared—four men carrying a stretcher made from a camp-bed and leading their pack-horses. A large old man, about seventeen stone, lay on the stretcher with his eyes closed. His leg was held in an improvised splint of bark; his long white beard was spread on his chest.

The four men, quite worn out, lay on the sand to sleep till daylight, while the doctor and nurse attended to the patient. He still had ten miles to travel over a rough track in the station car, for there was no way the plane could land anywhere in this rocky gorge.

There was nothing to eat—though fortunately someone had brought sugar as well as tea—but Caro did not complain. After Dr. Avery had given the old man an injection, she bathed the dust from his face, and then sat with him and fanned the last flies of the day from his eyes and mouth.

Before his eyes closed again he stared up at her blonde hair and trim figure, and muttered "Cripes! An angel!" And then, with a weak smile, "I'm ready to go." The men said he had been raving on the way out of the hills, calling for his dead wife.

His injuries were worse than just a broken leg. His horse had fallen back on him, and he had lain with a broken leg, collar-bone, and ribs, from late in the afternoon till his mates reached him at midday the following day.

Dr. Avery fixed a proper splint for the leg, and gave him something to bring the fever down. As the rocks cooled and the camp-fire died down it became quite cool. Caro covered the old man with a blanket they had brought. When he was restless in the night she gave him two aspirins and a drink of water, without calling the doctor. She went back to her sleeping place where she had dug a hip-hole in the sand, but a brilliant moon, a quarter past the full, rose over the cliffs and turned even the spinifex to silver; it was so unbearably bright in that clear dry atmosphere that she could not sleep. Here she was, sleeping out in a creek-bed in the middle of nowhere with half a dozen men for companions, and accepted naturally as one of them. She was content.

At "piccaninny daylight," well before sunrise, they heard another vehicle approaching—this time a Ford van. They lifted the stretcher into the back. The patient looked at Caro and put out his uninjured arm to take her hand. "I'll travel with him," she said and crawled in the back without waiting for the doctor's reply. She held the patient's hand over the ten miles of dreadful bumps and jolts, and he did not complain once.

Dr. Avery rode in front with the driver. There was a car from the station waiting by the plane, with coffee, and fresh scones with jam—a hurried but most welcome breakfast before they took off.

CHAPTER TEN

In the last hundred miles over the now-familiar route from McKinlay, Caro felt her eyes grow heavy from lack of sleep. She fought the urge to close them and landed safely at Cloncurry, where the ambulance they had radioed ahead for was waiting. Tired and dirty, she said goodbye to Dr. Avery at the hospital, had lunch and a bath, and went to bed.

Alix listened half-enviously to her tale of adventure. "It must be interesting," she said, "but I can't stand flying." Caro said she thought their shared mercy flight had made Dr. Avery think better of her. "He looked quite vulnerable, covered in dust and sweat. And as we parted he actually smiled and said, 'Thank you, Sister.'"

She was glad to be able to demonstrate her nerve and ability as a pilot as well as a nurse on a short but exciting flight to the little mining town of Selwyn in the heart of the Selwyn Range. The landing ground was small and tucked away in a gully where winds were funnelled in a direction to make landings awkward. Caro made her way in cautiously, side-slipping neatly to lose height, and made a perfect landing. A waiting car drove them in to the half-deserted settlement to pick up a sick child.

The child, who had never been away from home, was most unwilling to come. It was Caro, with a piece of barley sugar from her pocket, who persuaded her into the car and then into the plane. On the way out Caro had to weave her way up a gully to clear the hills that crowded round the small airstrip. As she cleared the rim of the hills the craft hit an air pocket with a great bump. Dr. Avery, who was not strapped in, was thrown forward out of his seat, but the patient was safe on her stretcher.

When they landed, Dr. Avery said to Caro, "For a moment there I thought we were going all the way down. My heart was in my mouth."

"Is that a medically accurate statement, sir?"

He laughed. "Well, no. To put it accurately, I was scared stiff."

Caro took a personal interest in the patients she had brought in from points all round the compass. She visited the little girl, Margaret, and the white-bearded old man, Mike Dunne, pleased to see that he was keeping cheerful and was apparently on the mend. Alix had asked her to wear a white dress when she came out of visiting hours, and preferably a cap over her hair.

"Sister Alix tells me you're her daughter, eh?" said Mike. "And a nurse, too? I thought you was some kind of angel when I come to, and that I was dead for sure. I *was* a bit surprised to see an angel in riding trousers, but."

Caro laughed. "Not an angel, just a flying nurse."

"Well, I say you're an angel."

On the next flight they were called to Normanton, on the Norman River Estuary, and to the Lorraine homestead on the Leichhardt River.

Fortunately the wet season had not set in, or they would have found landing-grounds too boggy or completely under water.

First they flew north along the dry course of the Cloncurry River, over miles of fertile red soil lightly timbered with white-trunked eucalyptus, with a ground cover of spinifex and Mitchell grass, good cattle country. The plain was intersected by more and more tributaries and watercourses, and forty miles away they saw the first glimpse of the sea, a suggestion of deeper blue on the northern horizon. Over the plains there was often an illusion of being ringed by distant seas, as the horizon on a clear day was always veiled in soft blue.

As the vegetation became denser they could see the cleared line for the telephone, and followed it up to Normanton. Along the Norman River great flocks of corellas flew against the green, and as they came low and coursed down the river at little more than a hundred feet, crocodiles basking on the banks slid hastily into the water.

Normanton, with its great wide empty streets, two pubs, bank, gaol, and police station, and the large Burns, Philp store, had once been a thriving town of three thousand people when the Croydon gold-fields were in full production. Yet it had not the melancholy of a ghost town. The little hospital, painted white, was situated on a red gravel hill overlooking the town. It was built in an open design with wide verandas and high roof, so that every breeze could flow through the open louver windows.

While Dr. Avery was assisting with an operation at the hospital, Caro wandered about the town. She saw several groups of Aborigines on the river bank. They told her shyly that their camp was on the other side of the crocodile-infested river; they had to wait for the ferry to take them home. (In fact, they were not allowed to stay in the town overnight.)

There were acacias growing down the middle of the main street, and bright bougainvillaeas. The place was neat and cared-for; the pubs with their first-floor balconies and wooden pillars freshly painted. Normanton lacked the deadly indifference to appearances that made the smaller inland towns so depressing.

Burketown was their next stop. Dr. Avery had heard that the resident doctor was seeking help with a puzzling case.

312

As they took off from Normanton, Caro could see the wide tidal river meeting the bright blue waters of the Gulf of Carpentaria twenty miles away; she turned north before heading west to Burketown. She thought of the explorers Burke and Wills, reaching the Gulf near here after struggling across the continent, only to die on the return journey. Now, if they'd only waited till the aeroplane was invented. . . .

Burketown seemed even more deserted than Normanton. A few black and part-Aboriginal children came out to wave at the plane as they landed. They knew the hospital; a regular clinic was held here each week for them. They took Caro's hand and led her along. Once more the barley sugar, very sticky now, came out from her pocket.

Another small plane, marked "N.T.M.S.," was already parked at the airstrip. It turned out that the Northern Territory Flying Doctor, visiting the Doomadgee Mission, had heard the call from Burketown and flown the extra miles.

So there were three doctors at the little hospital to confer over the mysterious illness of one man, and his symptoms; intermittent fever, ague-like pains in the bones, and fluid in the peritoneal cavity. It seemed to be some sort of infection, perhaps carried by mosquitoes or drinking water, and had so far proved intractable. Perhaps a new virus was involved. Dr. Fennell of Burketown was naturally alarmed. They had lost a large proportion of the population in the last typhoid epidemic.

After giving the medical men time for their conference, Caro walked up to the little hospital and made herself known to the only Sister. When they all met for a cup of tea in her sitting-room, Caro was introduced to the Northern Territory doctor. He was casually dressed even by Territory standards—no socks, just sand-shoes, shorts, and an open-necked shirt.

"Dr. Trenowith!" she exclaimed. "I've heard of you. Isn't that your own plane out there?"

"No, alas!" he smiled, and his lean cheeks folded into deep grooves as white teeth flashed in a brown face. "My plane was burned to cinders. I got out just in time. This one is borrowed until I can get a replacement."

"I know; you're always having hairbreadth escapes and getting lost and found again—"

"Oh, please!" He looked embarrassed. "The press never mentions all the flights where no drama happens at all."

"Dr. Trenowith's exploits are good publicity for the Medical Service, anyway," said the hospital Sister.

"You always fly yourself?" asked Caro.

"I prefer to; that's why the Flynn organization won't have me. And you—I believe you're the Flying Doctor's pilot?"

"Sister Manning is a jolly good nurse, too!" put in Dr. Avery.

"Really?" Dr. Trenowith gave his engaging grin, a smile that involved his whole face: even his blue eyes smiled. His thick dark hair was wild

313

and uncared-for-looking, as though it might have been cut some time ago with a pair of sheep-shears.

"I'm only a temporary pilot," said Caro, "while Eric Donaldson is on leave. They couldn't get anyone else!"

"Are you a Queenslander—from Brisbane, perhaps?"

"No—I got my licence in Adelaide, and flew up to Cloncurry in my own plane. . . . Poor *Circe* is grounded, with nothing to do."

"*Circe!* Wasn't she a wicked witch, who turned men into beasts?" asked Dr. Fennell.

"She was an enchantress," said Caro.

After tea there was to be a clinic for Aboriginal children. Dr. Trenowith left for the Territory on his way back to Darwin. Caro drove him to the airstrip in the hospital vehicle—half utility truck, half ambulance.

"Is it true," she asked with a smile as they bumped over the corrugations, "that you once buzzed the open-air cinema at Darwin during a programme —you were actually between the projector and the screen?"

"Oh, you've heard of that? Yes, I was coming back late into town and saw the screen all lit up—it was only just after sunset—so I thought I'd have a look at the programme. Some of the patrons got a bit upset and called the police. Then the Civil Aviation Department took away my licence for a while. I had to apply for special permission to fly to urgent cases."

"Yes, the Department can be a bit stuffy at times."

"Of course they're a Canberra mob. Darwin is an easygoing place. The proprietor didn't mind a bit, he thought it was a joke. But he said I should have bought a ticket for the peformance."

She pulled up at the airstrip. They sat and talked for a while.

"Have you ever landed upside-down?" he asked. "It's a queer feeling."

"Never, touch wood," said Caro, patting the dashboard.

"I did once. At least I landed right-way up, and then flipped over. I was flying a Qantas kite, a small biplane with a cabin, and I had a passenger for Katherine. I was forced down and landed, as I thought, on a nice flat clay-pan—but the plane somersaulted on to its back. My seat-belt had given way, and as the noise died away I found myself upside-down, on the back of my neck, under the instrument panel. I couldn't move a muscle because of what was piled on me—all the medical kit had fallen through the cockpit door and landed on top of me. My passenger was a large muscular pearler from Broome, and he had dropped on top of me too. All I could hear was the shattering silence.

"'Greg,' I said, 'are you all right?'

"No answer. Cripes, I thought, I've killed him.

"'Are you okay, Greg?'

"'No, I'm not bloody okay,' came from behind me. 'What the hell happened?'

"'I don't know, but if you can get off me I might be able to untangle myself and have a look,' I said.

"There was a bit of an upheaval behind me, a foot trod on my stomach and I was free to move—if I could. At last I managed to lever myself out of the cockpit and got to the cabin door, treading on the ceiling.

"Well, I found both landing wheels had broken through the thin crust —what I thought to be a clay-pan turned out to be a salt-pan, with soft mud underneath. So be warned."

"I've had some lucky escapes," said Caro, trying to think of one to impress him, "but I've never wrecked an aircraft."

"Well, I suppose I'd better get on my way," he said at last, shaking her hand warmly.

"Happy landings."

"Perhaps we'll meet again, Sister Manning—I certainly hope so. The distances are enormous, but the people are few."

She watched his tall, lean figure as he walked to his machine with long strides, buckling on his leather helmet. He was not strictly handsome, his face was too long and his nose too big; still, she hoped that they might meet again.

After a clinic lasting an hour, to which several Aboriginal children came, they took off again. Caro turned south along the Leichhardt River, avoiding the first fifty miles of tidal channel, which twisted like a demented snake, and flew on to Lorraine. Dr. Avery wasn't sure of the landing ground. Circling low over the homestead, Caro dropped a note wrapped in a handkerchief. Someone waved a white sheet, and then three sheets were placed to form an arrow pointing to a cleared airstrip about five miles away.

A station vehicle met them there to take them back to the homestead, crossing two creeks on the way. With typical outback hospitality the manager and his wife invited them to stay the night after Dr. Avery had seen the patient, the station cook. One of the men had taken over baking the bread, he said, since "the cook's crook," but he advised them not to go too near the centre of the loaf as it was "a bit boggy."

In the morning Caro went down for a swim in the Leichhardt, in one of the small pools in the shallow brown river. "Don't be frightened if you see a croc," she was told; "they're only harmless freshwater ones . . . never grow very big." She was still a little nervous, all the same.

"Him not cheeky-feller," the Aboriginal children who accompanied her assured her, as she sat nervously on the bank and pointed to a swirl in the water. She plucked up courage to go in and had a refreshing swim.

At an early lunch, before they set off back to Cloncurry, she was told that everyone was not aware of the safe limits, in fact they varied at different times of the year. Two friends of the station people had gone for

315

a swim in a waterhole farther down the Leichhardt, in what was supposed to be a safe area, when a stockman rode up and told them he had seen "an alligator" take the shoulder off a horse in the same waterhole only a few days earlier.

Leaving Lorraine soon after lunch, Caro headed south for Cloncurry. It had been a most satisfactory flight of some six hundred miles. She had now flown from Spencer Gulf in southern Australia to Carpentaria in the north.

There were only two days left before Eric returned from his leave. Caro hoped they would get some urgent calls from somewhere far away, perhaps in the Northern Territory.

She would have gone up for a flight in her own plane, but she had to be on call and available in case she was wanted.

"You know, Mum, you haven't once been up with me," she said, having lunch with Alix in the nurses' quarters at the hospital.

"I don't know that I want to all that much."

"But, Mum! You have to. Why, even the doctor has got used to being flown by me."

"I'm sure you're a good pilot; I just don't like little planes. With my head out in the wind. . . ."

"That's all right. I've got a spare cap and goggles."

"Later, then. When there's not so much thundery weather about."

CHAPTER ELEVEN

A most interesting part of flying the Aerial Medical Service network was the contrast from day to day as they travelled three hundred miles north or four hundred miles south. One day they might be among the crocodile rivers and lily lagoons of the north, green with paperbark and palm; the next flying above the burning deserts of sand and spinifex, the thin grey vegetation of the centre; and each had its own beauty. Caro actually preferred the red sand-hills and the plains of purple stone to the lush green of the far north. Perhaps it was bred in her, a feeling for wide, bare spaces and the subtle opalescent colours of the inland.

Her last trip as pilot with Dr. Avery was to Innamincka in the heart of the desert country. The A.I.M. hostel had been built on a bend of Cooper's Creek near where the explorers Burke and Wills perished.

After flying along the Qantas airmail route to Winton, she stopped there to refuel. It was a flat town with trees down the centre of the wide main street, and the level black-soil plains stretching all round it. Because she did not know the way to the Cooper, she had to fly on over the waving Mitchell grass plains to Longreach. Then she turned south along the Thomson River. Flying low over billabongs full of gold-white water-lilies, she followed it until it became Cooper's Creek.

The long lagoon at Innamincka Station was full and fringed with drooping coolabahs and white-boled gums. The station was three miles upstream from the hostel, on the opposite bank.

The wife of the local Mounted Constable was seriously ill in the hostel with pleurisy. Dr. Avery drained some fluid from the chest cavity, and soon made the patient comfortable. He then found that another case had been brought in—an Aboriginal man with a broken-off spear-point embedded in his chest.

Constable McGuinnes, a big man with grizzled dark hair and the deeply weathered face of one who has lived long under central Australian suns, explained that he was supposed to charge the assailant with attempted murder. "But really," he told the doctor, "it was a tribal matter, some woman-trouble, and the law according to the blacks said this man had to be speared. I certainly don't want to drag the avenger in chains all the way to the nearest court-house. I'm grateful to you for operating, Doctor.

If he'd died I'd have had to arrest someone for murder—though in the eyes of the blacks it isn't murder, it's justice."

The policeman's residence was a comfortable double-fronted galvanized iron building with a wide veranda and high roof, set just across the road from the nursing home. A wire fence enclosed a garden bright with flowering oleanders and green with tamarisks, but everywhere beyond the fence spread the red-purple gibbers of the Stony Desert.

As there were two Sisters at Innamincka, Caro's help was not needed with the operation. Constable McGuinnes asked her to come across to his house for afternoon tea. He made the tea efficiently and brought it out to the enclosed veranda, where he had even laid a tea-cloth on the little table.

As he handed her the teacup his brown hand shook a little. He looked searchingly under his square dark brows at Caro's face.

"Sister Manning," he said, "was your mother Sister MacFarlane of the A.I.M.? I used to be stationed at Marree."

"Of course! You're the one who brought my mother in from Lake Letty bore, after Sister Kingston died. She used to speak of you."

"Yes . . . Alix MacFarlane. And she married young Jim Manning from Cappamerri. I last saw her in Marree when she was carrying you."

"My father was killed in the war, you know."

"Yes. . . . What a long time ago it seems! You must be at least twenty?"

"Twenty-one."

He continued to stare at her intently over the rim of his cup. "Yes," he said, setting it down. "I can see a likeness to your mother about the eyes. But you don't take after her, do you?"

"No, I suppose not. I didn't get her curly hair."

He said after a silence, "I was in love with your mother, you know. Did she ever tell you I asked her to marry me?"

"No!" Caro was intrigued. To think that she might have been this man's daughter, growing up in a town with about five inhabitants. . . ! But of course she would not be herself, Caro Manning, with a different father.

"She must have been very pretty as a young woman."

"She was lovely," he said sincerely.

"And do you have any daughters?"

"One, about your age, and two boys. My younger lad is working as a jackaroo on Innamincka Station."

After tea he offered to escort her back to the hostel, as he wanted to visit his wife. And does she know about your lost love, I wonder? thought Caro. "No, I think I'll walk over to the river and have a paddle," she said.

When she came back the doctor was having tea with the two Sisters, who had come to the back of beyond straight from Melbourne.

The Innamincka Hostel, built in 1924, was an imposing two-storey building set on a stony rise, with wide fly-screened verandas and thick concrete walls. With plenty of rain-water stores in underground tanks, and a waterhole that never dried up about three miles away, they had better conditions than in some less isolated posts.

The hostel had floors of polished hardwood, a kitchen with an underground cellar, and two bathrooms with white porcelain baths and wood-chip heaters.

But the Aboriginal patient would not be sleeping there. He was conveyed on a stretcher to a cane-grass hut built in the police-station grounds, where, the Sisters explained, he would feel more at home than in a hospital ward.

Out of curiosity Caro put her head in the ward and said hello to Mrs. McGuinnes, now out of danger. She was dark-haired, with a plump and pleasant face, and bore no resemblance to Alix MacFarlane.

The very day Eric returned, an urgent medical call came from Monkira Station, away down the Diamantina. They didn't have wireless, and had driven seventy miles to Davenport Downs to send the message. Caro, hanging about the airport, half-hoping she might be asked to go along as a nurse, spoke to Eric as he was going over the plane with Thommo. When she heard the destination she exclaimed, "But I flew by way of Monkira Station and Davenport Downs coming up here! I could pilot you straight there," she added hopefully.

"No, Caro; you've had your go at being pilot," said Eric. "But you can come as a passenger, if Doc Avery agrees."

She drove to the doctor's and found him just ready to get into his car. "I can give you a lift to the airport, Doctor," she said. "I'm going back there right away."

"H'm, all right, if you're as good with a car as you are with an aeroplane."

"Is it a serious case?" she asked.

"Yes; sounds like a strangulated hernia. I'll probably have to operate at the station, as soon as we get there. He's in a bad way."

"Would you—would you like a surgery sister to go with you? I'd love to come."

He frowned quickly and her heart sank. Then his brow cleared. "Yes, I don't see why not. I'll probably need some help."

Caro called at the hospital for her uniform and a warm jacket just in case.

They called at Boulia to let the hospital know they might be bringing a patient, then flew on for the Diamantina, Caro staring ahead to catch a glimpse of that wide mass of channels that marked its course. For 120 miles they had seen no living thing, nor sign of habitation, except for one lonely station homestead. There was not a tree or shrub or sign of water, just the desolate red-brown earth. It was no place for a forced landing.

They came to the river and turned south, and soon saw the roofs of Monkira. Two sheets were laid out in front of the homestead to indicate the landing-ground. They landed and taxied across the dry and sandy paddock to the house.

The manager's wife, Mrs. Wilson, apologized for the sand over everything. After a recent storm they'd taken five barrow-loads out of the house.

"Thank God you've come, Doctor," she said, her lips trembling. "He's very sick, and in great pain."

After a brief examination Dr. Avery turned to Caro and said, "I'll have to operate at once. He's already bringing up faecal matter from the lower bowel."

Dr. Avery was always neatly dressed in white shirt and long white trousers. Caro slipped into the crumpled uniform she had stuffed into her bag, and put on her white cap. The sight of her looking so professional seemed to calm the patient, who was very distressed.

A scrubbed deal table from the kitchen was brought in and covered with a newly laundered sheet that had been shut in an airtight linen cupboard away from the dust. Caro, having prepared the patient, administered the anaesthetic. Dr. Avery went in to the bowel, cut the constricting band, and straightened a twisted loop. Caro passed instruments and counted swabs as if she were in a proper operating theatre.

As the patient regained consciousness, his condition after the operation monitored by Caro, Mrs. Wilson hovered anxiously.

"Your husband will be all right, but he'll have to go in to hospital," said Dr. Avery. "Will you prepare the stretcher, Sister?"

They took off again about 4 P.M., and in another two hours the patient was in a comfortable hospital bed in Boulia. The hospital building was tiny, so the three of them went to the Boulia Hotel for the night, as it was too late to get back to Cloncurry. Night flying was frowned upon by Qantas.

At dinner in the hotel dining room, where they had only tinned meat and tinned vegetables to eat, Caro told them how the day's flight had made her feel quite nostalgic. "You see, I was born on the Diamantina," she said, "on Cappamerri Station, not far downstream from Monkira."

"So you are a Queenslander!" said Dr. Avery. "You told David Trenowith the other day that you were a South Australian."

"Well, I was actually born in Adelaide—Alix went down there for the birth. But I lived on Cappamerri until I was about eight."

"I was born on a cattle station too," said Eric. "Out from Winton. I joined Qantas when I came back from France."

"You must have been very young when you joined the Air Force," Caro said.

320

"Seventeen. But I passed as eighteen."

He told them some hilarious tales of the early days of Qantas passenger flights, when there were no toilets and sometimes no paper-bags for sick passengers. "We did provide free chewing gum, though.

"I was flying a Puss Moth with one passenger who was very sick, and desperate for a receptacle; he let fly into my new felt hat which I'd thrown into the front.

"Another time I was flying 'Derby' Hawkins, a big hefty cattleman whose favourite drink was overproof rum taken neat by the half-tumblerful. I was coming from Longreach and had to deliver the mail. All the passengers were aboard when I heard this plaintive voice from the rear, 'Eric, where can I have a leak?'

"Every minute was precious if I was to get to Cloncurry before dark. 'Sorry, Derby,' I said, as I shut the cabin door and hurried through to the cockpit. 'No time—you'll just have to hang on till Winton.'

"When we arrived at Winton I saw Derby still seated near the back. 'Come on, Derby, I thought you were in a hurry!'

"No answer. Then he burst out, 'Okay, Eric, I'll get out. But what do I do with these?'

"And he handed me two elastic-sided riding boots, both brim-full."

Tired after the long day, Caro retired early. She went to the ladies' bathroom and found that the bath taps would not turn on, so she stood in the bath under the shower rose.

The highly mineralized bore-water had a strange chemical smell; Boulia water was said to rust iron in an hour. On the way back to her room she passed the Gents, and as she did so Eric Donaldson popped out of the men's bathroom door.

He was fully clothed, and he beckoned to her and pointed to the door.

"Just have a look at this," he begged, bubbling with laughter. "Go on, there's no one in there."

Curious, she pushed open the door. A red cement floor, a small opaque window, a large tin bath set on metal feet. Over the bath was a hand-printed notice on a piece of white cardboard:

Gents are requested please not to pee in the bath, as it causes fever.
By order,
Mrs. Jackson, Proprietress.

Caro giggled. "Well, that's telling them," she said.

CHAPTER TWELVE

Caro was not an A.I.M. nurse and she received no salary as assistant to the Medical Officer. Her temporary appointment as a pilot had ended, and she had no official position. She was still occupying a bed in her mother's room at the hospital, as the Matron accepted her offer to act as a relieving nurse on night duty.

Caro took a flight up to the Gulf and back just to pass the time. Alix refused to come with her. When Caro called at the Normanton Hospital and had tea with the Matron, at the back of her mind was the idea that the attractive flying doctor David Trenowith might be there.

He was not; but two weeks later a telegram came to Cloncurry Base asking for Caro Manning to get in touch with him at Katherine in the Northern Territory, with a view to leasing or chartering her plane to the Northern Territory Medical Service for at least a month.

It seemed that his little Moth had been grounded for some weeks for repairs, and the N.T. Medical Service was without a plane for emergencies.

Caro wired back: OK FOR CHARTER BUT INSIST FLY HER MYSELF.

She realized that this would not be possible where the doctor had to pick up hospital cases and fly them back; anyway there was no room for a stretcher so they would have to be well enough to sit up.

She said her farewells to the hospital staff and the Qantas staff, to Dr. Avery and his pilot, and learned that Eric was leaving the service for good.

"I won't be here when you get back," he said.

"So they'll be appointing a new pilot?" Her eyes flared with hope.

"Yes, my dear. In fact, they've already appointed him, from Sydney."

"A 'him,' of course."

"I'm afraid so."

Alix didn't like to see her go so far away, when they'd only just got together again. "You won't be coming back after a month, I feel it in my bones," she said.

"I'd come like a shot if they'd give me the pilot's job permanently."

"Alas, it seems that they want another man."

"It's not fair! I've proved I can do it; and Dr. Avery would recommend me, I'm sure. But no! They're too hidebound, the Board and your

322

precious John Flynn. He won't even let a good pilot like Dr. Trenowith fly his own plane, though he'd be a great asset to the A.I.M."

"Flynn has certain fixed principles, to which he sticks. And one of them is 'one man, one job.' He's a bit conservative—"

"A *bit* conservative!" cried Caro. "Do you remember when he arrived in Birdsville in the middle of summer, still wearing his dark suit and waistcoat with its gold watch-chain? I bet he never takes them off even when he's digging the car wheels out of the sand in the middle of the desert."

"He does take the coat off. But the waistcoat is to cover his trouser braces when he's in shirt-sleeves. I suppose he feels braces are undignified for a man of God."

Eric gave Caro the benefit of his experience of flying to the Northern Territory, as he had been a Qantas pilot before joining the Aerial Medical Service. She would have to fly over about five hundred miles of new territory, but the whole trip was not as far as her journey from Adelaide.

She set off at dawn direct for Mount Isa, taking the more dangerous route over the ironstone hills; then made north-west along the stock-route to Camooweal. She saw the southward-flowing feeders of the Georgina appearing on her left, while the Gregory and its tributaries made northward for the Gulf. Once more she was flying over a divide. It was a wonderful lesson in geography to cross the continent in this fashion. In a few months she had flown from the Southern Ocean to the north coast; now she was travelling from east to west.

After landing for fuel at the bare and dusty little town of Camooweal with its temporary-looking galvanized iron buildings, she took off again and crossed the dry bed of the Georgina. In five minutes she was crossing the Northern Territory border, marked by the straight, endless line of the rabbit-proof fence.

Below stretched the red-brown earth, flat and unbroken by even a dry watercourse, mile after mile as featureless as the sea. Sometimes she passed an earth-dam and a windmill of some outstation, for this was the Barkly Tableland, famed cattle country. Above and all round spread a cloudless sky, and below the flat land was ringed with the aerial blue of distance.

The road she was following was the only guide. She came to the Ranken River and the plain where Grandpa Manning's friend Harry had his marvellous escape from the stampeding cattle—a rush, as it was called.

After two hundred miles of unchanging landscape, she was over the huge cattle-station of Brunette Downs. In a good season they stocked forty thousand head, and nearly all the work of herding, mustering, and branding was done by Aboriginal stockmen—natural riders, and inured to heat and flies. And cheap, because they came under no award.

As she came in to land, a station truck set out to meet her. It was crowded with black children clinging on everywhere, who tumbled off and inspected the machine as she tied it down. They had seen aeroplanes before, flyers on their way from Darwin after crossing the seas from England, and the Flying Doctor plane from Cloncurry: but a lady pilot was different.

Caro was pressed to stay the night by the hospitable manager and his wife. After dinner, sitting on the veranda in the warm peaceful evening, tired but relaxed, Caro was filled with content. She walked out into the inland night and listened to the silence, broken by the cry of a water-bird down at the lagoon. She looked up at the splendid summer constellations, blue-white and glittering like chips of ice. There was no city within hundreds of miles in any direction.

She attended two sick Aboriginal children in the morning, one with sore eyes that were so gummed with matter that they would not open, and another with a sharp sliver of wood embedded in the sole of her foot. Caro had brought a first-aid kit with her, but though it included a small scalpel she had great trouble extracting the wood from the leather-like skin of the ten-year-old girl, used to going without shoes from infancy. She had no anti-tetanus serum, but hoped for the best.

The next part of the journey was easy. As Eric had told her, there was a well-marked road made by cars and trucks heading for Darwin.

Farther north the landscape began to change, with a few low hills to break the monotony of the plain, and a cover of timber of some density. Then on her left, she saw an open laneway tending south through the trees: the clearing cut for the Overland Telegraph line. Approaching the O.T. line, she flew low enough to see the bottle trees and magnetic mounds of the white-ant nests, standing like roughly sculptured red monuments among the dry grass.

She had come two hundred miles from Brunette Downs, and decided to fly on to Daly Waters where there was a good airstrip and a store for petrol. Following the excellent guide of the O.T. line, she was able to get some height as the day warmed up and the bumps began. There was grey cloud ahead, and after an hour's flying she had to come down low to get under it in case she missed Daly Waters altogether. The beginning of the wet season? The Wet was late this year, or she would have been in trouble on her flight to Normanton. The engine was overheating, making the oil thin, and was running ragged when to her relief she saw a few white roofs ahead and a cleared landing ground with even a wind-sock! She was now less than four hundred miles south of Darwin, and her next stop would be Katherine.

On the ground, as she stepped out of the cockpit, the heat enveloped her like a hot, damp blanket. Here she was only about fifteen degrees from the equator, and much farther north than Normanton.

After a short break to stretch her legs, and a welcome cool drink with her late lunch at the store, she asked the storekeeper about the weather as he filled *Circe* with petrol and oil.

"She's due to break any day now," he said, with a glance at the rolling clouds ahead. "The Wet is late this year, but I reckon you've only just made it in time."

"The air feels full of moisture," said Caro. "D'you think I'll get to Katherine before it starts to rain?"

"I reckon so. We've had a buildup of cloud like this every afternoon for weeks, and a lot of thunder, but only dry storms so far."

"Perhaps I should wait, and fly on tomorrow morning?" The store had a tiny hotel attached to it. "No, I'll get on. Dr. Trenowith probably has some emergency waiting for my arrival. I can hardly get lost with the Telegraph line to follow. But it doesn't look too good for a forced landing," she said, gazing at the open forest timber and the red anthills.

She sent a wire up the line to Katherine: ARRIVING THIS AFTERNOON D.V.W.P. wondering if indeed weather would permit. There were only 170 miles left to do: she intended to follow the road all the way and not take any short cuts. And if cloud threatened to close in, there was Birdum, where no doubt she could find a place to land.

She took off into the wind, which was north-west so that she would have a head wind all the way; it would take her at least another two hours to her destination. She felt hot and sweaty and promised herself a swim in the Katherine River—for the town was far enough inland to be free of salt-water crocs.

The little settlement of Birdum passed by on her left and the beginning of the railway line to Darwin. Now the line bent north-west, a forty-five-degree change of direction, and led straight to Katherine.

She had flown about half-way along this section when wisps of cloud began to flip past the wings. Looking ahead, she could see no break in a towering mass of cumulus. It was useless to try to climb above it, as these clouds were known to build up as high as twenty thousand feet, and anyway she had to keep in visual touch with the ground if possible. She looked at her watch; only twenty minutes to go. Just then the ground below was blotted out completely. She was flying blind in the heart of a white woolly mass.

Her first reaction was one of panic. Then her training came to her aid. She fixed her eyes on her instruments and concentrated on keeping an even keel, now that the horizon was lost. The little plane buzzed steadily on. She had her compass bearing for Katherine, and told herself sturdily that there were no mountains anywhere round, that she was flying over a level plateau intersected with river gorges, and until she had to land she was perfectly safe.

Caro began to feel as if she and the machine were a small blowfly

325

caught in a huge white web: buzzing uselessly but unable to get out. She must watch the time, and her ground-speed indicator, and work out exactly how far she had come before trying to descend. It was possible that the air was clear at five hundred feet, but what if she came down that low and found herself skimming the rugged walls of the Katherine Gorge?

She swallowed down the fear constricting her throat. After so much fair-weather flying—apart from dust-storms—she had forgotten what it was like to fly in cloud.

The trapped fly buzzed in the heart of the white web. She strained her eyes downward, looking for the smallest break. After eighteen minutes she tilted the nose down. One thousand . . . eight hundred—how high above sea-level was the plateau? About four hundred feet, she thought. She braced herself for the jarring crash as they ploughed into a tree or a rocky jump-up. Her hand was on the joystick, ready to pull up and back the moment she saw some obstacle ahead. Then, like a miracle, an avenue opened in the cloud and there below was the Katherine River, a blue ribbon in its rocky gorge. She banked and turned, praying that the sky would not close in again—there seemed to be plenty of cleared space below, and the buildings of a cattle-station right on the river bank, where the gorge flattened out and the river spread between bush-clad banks. She shot over the town and turned.

Then she saw it, a hangar and a wind-sock like a pale elephant's trunk, beckoning her to safety on the ground. Thank God! She came in too fast, bounced slightly, and came down again with a bump. She turned in a wide arc and taxied towards the hangar. There was a tall figure standing by the runway in khaki shorts and shirt, dark tangled hair blowing in the warm wind. Chagrined, she realized that David Trenowith had witnessed her botched landing, the first time he had ever seen her fly.

CHAPTER THIRTEEN

Caro tore off her helmet and met him with outstretched hand. She was a tall girl, five feet nine in her shoes, and he was half a head taller. He must be well over six feet; but his broad shoulders were slightly hunched, as though he were trying to disguise his height. His blue eyes smiled at her.

"Hallo! You were a brick to come at once. I was worried for you when I saw the cloud closing in—"

"*You* were worried! I was scared stiff for the last thirty miles." And unexpectedly she felt her lips and chin tremble; it was reaction to the tension she had been under. "I haven't had much practice in flying blind."

"I'm sorry!" He patted her shoulder in a fatherly manner. "We've had almost no cloud till the last week or two. You'd better come and have a drink."

They tied down the plane and he carried her bag to the waiting vehicle, an ancient utility truck. He had to start it manually with a starting-handle —"Starter-motor's had it," he explained. There was no door on the passenger side—"Well, you didn't expect to be met by a Rolls-Royce, did you?" He seemed to use the lowest gear, by changing down when he came to corners, in lieu of brakes.

"Your wire went to the Telegraph Station," he said, "but I could have heard a voice message from Cloncurry. I live upstairs above the radio installation, which is under the house. I can give advice to patients by radio from here."

"I thought your headquarters were in Darwin?"

"I was Honorary Surgeon at the Darwin Hospital, which has its own Medical Superintendent. But this place is more central, and it normally has a hospital—a tiny place run by one Sister—but closed down at present. Sister's health broke down and they're having trouble getting a replacement, apparently."

His house, just round the corner from the one main street, was a typical Territory building set on high stumps, with the radio room underneath. Caro looked askance at the sixty-foot radio mast. Perhaps she really hadn't been that low, but it had felt like it.

"Billy!" he yelled, and a very dark, full-blood Aborigine appeared. "This

327

Sister Manning, berry-good, number-one pilot. She thirsty properly. You gottim ice longa box?"

"You-i, Boss."

"How about a Scotch to settle your nerves and celebrate your arrival? We'll arrange your accommodation later," said the doctor, leading her upstairs.

"I'd just like to see the lavatory first." (There was actually an indoor toilet in the building—no shortage of water here.)

"Then I'd like a swim in the river. No crocodiles?"

"Only little ones—freshwater crocs."

After a stiff whisky she began to unwind, and happily talked shop, giving him a run-down on her plane's idiosyncrasies: "She lists to the right a bit on take-off, you learn to make allowances for that—"

"Don't you think," he said seriously, "that you'd better let me fly the thing for a while? You can come with me and get an idea of the country. It's a bit different to the western plains."

"We-ell . . ." Her experience in the cloud had shaken her. "I suppose it would be sensible. Do you have any immediate emergencies?"

"Yes, unfortunately. An Aboriginal girl has been brought into the Bathurst Island Mission who's apparently gone way over term. She had some contractions a month ago, but they stopped again. The child must be dead by now. Her relatives brought her in. I'll have to fly up there first thing in the morning."

"I'll come with you. I've done midwifery."

"There's a trained nurse at the Mission. You'd better have a rest tomorrow, after that long flight."

She explained that she'd broken her journey at Brunette Downs. "But I hadn't time for a swim in the lagoon. I used to go swimming in the Diamantina waterholes when I was little—"

"I thought you were a South Australian."

"No, I was born on the Diamantina," she said, deciding not to go into details. "On Cappamerri Station in Queensland."

"So I suppose you like riding?"

"Love it."

"I'm sure one of the stations round here will lend you a horse. Meanwhile I've booked you in at the hotel. You'd better have a sleep-in tomorrow; I suppose you left Cloncurry at dawn, or before it, and you must have started pretty early this morning."

"Not really. I held a little clinic for the black children on Brunette before I left. But I think I *will* rest tomorrow, and unpack, and wash my shirt and so on."

He explained that he held a clinic of the air each morning unless he was away on a call. "When I'm not here, the Telegraph Station monitors calls for me."

328

He hoped she wouldn't mind the hotel; they could find a better arrangement later, perhaps.

"I suppose," he said hesitantly, "that I could ask the N.T. Medical Service to let me open the hospital building for you, but—"

"No, thank you!" said Caro. "I'm here as a pilot, not a nurse, remember? And as soon as it was known there was a Sister at the Hospital, people would start coming in. I'm not really keen on cooking, either. The hotel will be fine."

He looked at her with respect tinged with disapproval. "You certainly know your own mind, don't you?"

"Yes. No doubt you'd like to get me involved at the hospital, and fly yourself around as usual. But it won't work. And now, where's the river?"

"I'll show you the best swimming place. The ford is quite shallow at present. The famous Katherine Gorge is miles upstream."

After showing her the nearest swimming place, where there was a rocky bar and a sandy bottom, he took her to the hotel. Mr. Tim O'Shay, the proprietor, was standing on the veranda with his lanky pet brolga, a handsome pale-grey bird with a red patch on his head. David introduced Caro. "Look after Sister Manning and see that she gets a good night's rest; she's just flown all the way from Queensland."

"Shure and I didn't know a plane was due today."

"She flew herself here in a little Moth."

"She did?" The proprietor's roughly shaven jaw dropped open. "Whativer next, I wondther?"

"I'll see you here later," said the doctor as he handed Caro over. "I'll pop in for dinner tonight."

After a refreshing swim near the ford in the clear, shallow river, shaded thickly by paperbarks and pandanus palms on the river bank, Caro returned to her balcony room at the pub and washed her hair under the shower. She dried it with a towel, but the air was humid and it was still damp when the dinner-bell sounded. All she could do was comb its straight strands into a smooth cap, though its colour was darkened by water. She put on a fresh pale-green blouse and a gathered skirt with stripes of white, pink, and green. The water had dampened and darkened her lashes and washed her eyes a clear grey-green. (When she wore green, they looked more green than grey.)

As she came downstairs and moved through the dark little parlour towards the dining-room, she saw David Trenowith standing by the hatchway to the bar with a beer in his hand.

"Sister Manning! Like a beer with your dinner?"

"Thank you. I'm acquiring a taste for beer. It's the most thirst-quenching drink next to black tea that I know."

They carried their drinks into the dining-room and were shown to a

329

table by a part-Aboriginal girl with pretty wavy dark hair and a complexion of pale yellow-brown.

Over dinner they discussed business. The charter fee, he told her, would be paid by the Commonwealth Government, which administrated the Northern Territory, and would be based on mileage flown. The costs were shared by the Department of Civil Aviation and the Northern Territory Medical Service.

"I was a bit taken aback when I had your message about doing all the flying yourself," he said. "I suppose I'd counted on getting the plane without the pilot. I'm so used to flying myself around—"

"You sure it's not my sex that's worrying you? Do I have to cite Amy Johnson and Lores Bonney and Nancy Bird to show that women pilots have proved themselves?"

"No, no, I assure you. I thought when I met you up at Burketown that you looked efficient, and you wouldn't have had the job if you weren't."

"Was that your first impression of me—brisk efficiency?"

"No. As a matter of fact, the first thing I thought was, She looks nice."

He smiled, and his whole face crinkled the way she remembered into deep-grooved laughter lines. He must be good-natured, she thought, for his face to show the permanent marks like this. She smiled into his eyes. "I thought something the same about you," she said.

A subtle current passed between them. She had to admit that she had set out to attract him. Her youthful ego had been badly bruised by Malcolm's rejection, and she felt a need to prove that she could be attractive to a mature man. Not that she meant to get too deeply involved. She did not intend to lay herself open to being hurt like that again.

After the meal they walked out of the noisy pub, where the bar was doing a roaring trade, into the still and humid night. Sheet-lightning, too far away for thunder, flickered along the horizon.

Flying-ants danced in filmy clouds about every lamp, in a mad mating flight about their queen.

"Do you know," Caro said musingly, "that after the nuptial flight the queen bites off her own wings and crawls into a crack in the ground to start a new colony? And then her whole life is devoted to laying eggs. It's appalling!"

"Not perhaps for an ant. You are carrying the analogy into human behaviour—"

"Exactly! I've *seen* women give up interesting careers to get married. They have three or four babies, and their whole life revolves round the cradle and the nursery, until the children grow up and don't need them any more, and then they feel lost."

"I gather you don't intend to get married?"

"Never! I'm not giving up my freedom to fly for anyone. I'm wedded to my aircraft."

"Then I suppose you'll give birth to a row of little blonde spark-plugs."

They walked to the railway station and saw the once-a-week train come in from Darwin, hissing and breathing steam into the hot night. A few passengers got off.

"You know, it's ridiculous," said Dr. Trenowith, "that the rail from Darwin ends at Birdum, and the rail from Adelaide at Alice Springs, with seven hundred miles between them. There is a railway right across the continent from Sydney to Perth, but none from north to south. In the event of an invasion—"

"You don't think that's likely, do you?"

"It's a possibility. New Guinea is very close, and if the Dutch were to lose their half of it, say to the Japanese, we could be in trouble. Troops and tanks and so on couldn't be transported up here by air, and there's no road. Heaven knows I don't want to see another war; I was in right at the end of the last one—"

"You don't mean you joined up? How old were you?"

"I was only sixteen, but being so tall I bluffed my way in. It was 1918 by the time I got to France, and by then it was nearly over. I saw our planes in the air, they seemed to me like eagles. And I resolved to learn to fly if I didn't get killed."

"My father was killed in 1917, soon after Beersheba. He was in the Light Horse."

"Hard on your mother!"

"Yes; I was too little to understand much about it."

"I can see you as a little girl: straight bobbed hair, big grey eyes, and firm little chin emerging from the baby fat."

"Actually, I wore my hair in plaits."

They had walked to the end of the one street and back. At the hotel he asked, "Would you like a nightcap?"

She said no, she was ready for bed after her long day.

"I may not get back before dark tomorrow. In fact, I'll probably stay the night in Darwin. My wife complains that she never sees me."

Caro hoped that her jaw did not drop visibly. He was married! Well, of course. He was thirty-five years old and very masculine, why wouldn't he be? It just had not occurred to her.

"Of course you must visit her, Darwin is right on your route to Bathurst Island. I'll expect you the day after tomorrow. Good night."

She turned on her heel, suddenly seething with anger. What cheek! She had flown almost non-stop to bring the flying doctor an aircraft, and he was using it to visit his wife! *Her* aeroplane. . . No doubt the Mission call was authentic, but was it urgent? He had cleverly arranged to leave her behind. Or did he think the patient might need evacuating to hospital? If she was not too ill, he could fly her across to Darwin.

After a morning spent washing clothes, swimming in the river, and

331

resting in her room with the door to the balcony and the door to the corridor wide open in an attempt to get some breeze, Caro was fretting for her aeroplane. She hated to be separated from *Circe*; it was like being without an arm or a leg.

Then she had an idea. The doctor had left the utility truck for her to use, saying she could get Billy to turn the starting-handle for her. She went round to the house and asked Billy if the Boss had any tools. There were none in the tray of the truck.

"You-i, Chister," he said with a broad grin. He dived beneath the house and came out with a collection of screw-wrenches, screwdrivers, chisels, and pliers.

She did not know how to work the radio receiving set, but she drove to the Telegraph Station to see if they had monitored any calls for the Flying Doctor; there were none. He flew the two hundred miles back from Darwin the next morning, and arrived in time for lunch, having got a lift round to the hotel.

"You don't have to be polite and eat with me, you know," she said coldly. He replied that he'd felt lonely since the Sister left: she often gave him a meal. "Besides, I thought you'd like to know how *Circe* and I got on."

"Well? How did you?"

"She's a lovely little craft! Better than my old crate."

Caro's heart warmed towards him.

"And how was your patient?"

"She's alive. I'd rather not talk about it till after we've had lunch, if you don't mind."

There were cold thinly sliced corned beef and mashed potatoes, and actually a fresh salad! Caro hoped there might even be fresh fruit to follow, but it was baked bread-and-butter pudding.

They talked about the plane, and flying conditions in the Wet: "In Darwin, for instance, you can count on it raining every afternoon, then the sun will come out as hot as ever; the mornings are muggy but dry; there will be no rain at all between April and November, and about sixty inches between December and March. So in the Wet you try to fly in the mornings."

"In Cloncurry you also fly in the mornings in summer, to avoid the dust-storms and the air pockets."

Striving to keep her voice level, Caro asked after his wife.

"Well as ever, but she's still nagging me to come back to the Darwin base. We have a nice house and garden, and she doesn't want to leave it for a rented place down here. And I suppose she has her friends, and a social life of a sort. I can do without that."

"They say that women transplant less easily than men. Are more attached to places, houses, society. I get attached to *things*, like my car and my aircraft. I think Smith must have loved his lumbering old *Southern Cross*. 'The Old Bus,' he called her."

When they had finished their lunch, rounded off with the inevitable cup of tea, she asked him about the patient he had gone to see.

He gave a quick frown. "It was worse than I expected. The girl was very sick, and the baby was very dead. I had to remove it piecemeal from the uterus, with forceps. And the smell—Gah! I can't get it out of my mouth."

Caro made a face in sympathy. "Will she live?"

"I hope so. She didn't want to go to hospital in Darwin. I washed her out as well as I could with warm douches. But I can't understand that Sister at the Mission, not calling me earlier. 'Oh, you can never get any accurate dates out of the black girls. I just thought she'd made a mistake, or the baby was a little bit late, until she started to get distressed, and we sent for you.' A little bit late! I reckon it was six weeks over term."

"You'd have been there earlier but for your damaged crate. Wasn't your fault."

"No. And then I was able to operate on a blackfellow with a broken jaw, back at Darwin Hospital. He loved the flight."

Caro felt that she knew him much better since their talk over lunch. His leased aircraft had been seriously damaged in a crash that had made the headlines, for he had a Commonwealth Government official on board. He admitted to her with embarrassment that it was his own fault, he had lost his way over the maze of winding streams and timbered ridges in the head-waters of the Victoria River, and run out of fuel. Just before he ran out, he glimpsed an outstation of Victoria River Downs, and knew where they were. He tried to land, without power, among the trees. One of the wing-tips clipped a tree, and they nose-dived into the ground. The plane was a wreck.

"Yes, I read about that in Cloncurry," said Caro. "And when you were rescued after four days, all you said was, 'I'm damned hungry.'"

"What I said in fact was, 'I'm bloody hungry,' and I was. We lived on some malted-milk tablets I had with me; 'two tablets twice a day, without meals.'"

"And your own little plane, *The Flying Carpet*, what was she, an Avro Baby? What happened—you said she was burnt?"

"Yes, she went up in flames. I made a pancake landing in a squall on a twenty-five-foot landing-ground. The sparks from the friction ignited the petrol-tank."

"Where was that?"

"At the Mission on Bathurst Island."

"What? And I trusted you in your first flight in my precious *Circe* to the same landing-ground?"

"Lightning never strikes twice in the same place," he said blithely.

"I'll drive you home," she said, getting up. The old utility truck had no keys; it was perfectly safe in the main street. She sat behind the wheel, while he went round the front to turn the handle. She waved him away. Then, as she pushed the self-starter, the engine rumbled into life.

"It's all right, I fixed it yesterday," she said. "The brakes will need some spare parts."

He stared at her as he climbed through the side with the missing door. She smiled smugly.

"Well, there's no doubt about you!" he said. "I suppose you can fix aircraft engines as well."

"Yes, as a matter of fact, I can."

CHAPTER FOURTEEN

The first call they attended together, the Flying Doctor and Nurse Manning answered an urgent message from a cattle-station on the edge of nowhere, near the maze of rivers flowing into the Gulf east of Daly Waters. The wife of the owner, a woman in her sixties, had been gored by a scrub bull. Mrs. Ronson had been born in the Territory and had ridden ever since she could walk; she had helped to work cattle with her husband for years.

"My mother," said Caro as they drove to the airstrip in Katherine, "once had to operate on a cattleman who had been gored in the stomach. He rode into Marree with his wound cobbled together with horsehair. He'd sewn it up himself."

"Ah, they breed 'em tough in Queensland. But I thought your mother was an A.I.M. Sister, not a doctor."

"She was. But there was no doctor nearer than three hundred miles away, you see. She ended up marrying the cattleman."

"So! You get your courage from both sides."

"And I think it's my turn to be pilot, Doctor."

He did not argue. The route was fairly straightforward: down the railway line to Daly Waters, then east to the McArthur River where they would turn and follow the stream upriver to the station.

The last half-hour was worrisome, as the sun set and the light was fading, but at least the sky was clear. Coming in low over a small fire marking the cleared airstrip, Caro set down in a perfect three-point landing. The tail-skid bit into the loose dry soil and pulled them up after a short run. That will show him, she thought, pleased.

The doctor decided to operate at once. Caro assisted at the operation on the scrubbed kitchen table, while Mr. Ronson held the lamp in a hand that trembled. When he looked as if he might faint, Caro gently took the lamp and sent him out to get some fresh air. "Mrs. Ronson has lost a lot of blood but fortunately there is no serious infection," the doctor told him, after the wound was sewn up and the patient, watched by Caro, was recovering consciousness. "You'll have to nurse her for a while; keep her in bed for at least a week—"

"I'll have to sit on her, then. She's a terror for work. Do you know she bakes twelve loaves of bread a day for the men, as the lazy bugger of a

335

cook won't have anything to do with breadmaking; and she works on the run as well, good as a man."

Mrs. Ronson was a thin, dried-up little woman with straggly grey hair. When she woke up the first thing she said was, "I never had a bull get me before in me life. Must be getting old and slow."

"Maybe he was just a very quick bull," said Caro.

"Oh, they're quick, all right, those wild scrubbers. They'll go you as soon as look at you."

They had an indifferent meal with Mr. Ronson, cooked by the kitchen lubra, and some excellent bread left over from Mrs. Ronson's last batch. They stayed the night, Caro keeping an eye on the patient, for she was not young and there was a chance of delayed shock. But in the morning Mrs. Ronson was perfectly alert and complaining because she was not allowed up to get their breakfast. The breadmaking, she said, was easy: there were two large stone ovens set into the outer walls of the kitchen building. Fires were lit in these till the stones were heated through, and then raked out. The risen dough was placed inside, and cooked perfectly without any fear of burning.

Doctor and nurse were now at ease together. There was a bond between them from the shared duty of the operation. She had also felt a difference in her relationship with the crusty Dr. Avery after their flight to Monkira for the hernia operation. But they had never been on first-name terms.

After checking and re-dressing the wound, Dr. Trenowith impressed on Mrs. Ronson the importance of resting and not disturbing the stitches while the wound healed.

"Now, do you think you can remove the stitches after ten days?" he asked her husband.

"I dunno, Doc; I'll try."

"He could never even remove a splinter without turning sick," said his wife. "I'll prob'ly have to do it meself."

"If you have any problems, let us know at once, and one of us will come back."

"A thousand thanks for coming, anyway."

After a good breakfast of thick steaks so tender that even the station cook couldn't ruin them, they set off for Daly Waters and Katherine, checking first that there were no new calls.

"Let me fly the first leg?" asked David Trenowith.

"What, to Daly Waters?"

"No, to Mataranka. I know a beaut swimming-hole. I thought we'd stop on the way back."

The day was already heating up. Caro looked at the clear sky.

"All right. If it's on the way home."

They came down at Daly Waters to refuel and buy some sandwiches from the store for a picnic. When Caro asked about the purchase of a swimming costume, the storekeeper, Mr. Pierce, said there was not much call for them. Towels? Yes, he could let them have a couple of towels. They took off again and flew the 150 miles to Mataranka without incident, landing in a tiny clearing near the deserted station.

The walk to the thermal pools he had promised her was extremely hot. They threaded their way through dry grass and thin gum-tree shade, where flying-foxes in great colonies hung upside down in the tree-tops, fanning themselves with their leathery wings.

They came to a green grove of feathery palms and tall paperbarks, and there was the first pool, clear and inviting.

Caro stopped entranced.

"No, come on to the next pool, it's better."

An underground stream connected the pools. The water was a clear mineral-green, and reflected the bright yellow-green of palms as well. The second pool was longer, sparkling in sunlight. Every pebble and grain of sand on the shallow bottom showed through the glass-clear water.

Caro kicked off her shoes and tested the water with a toe. It was warm, about blood-heat, but not hot. She slipped off her navy linen skirt and white blouse and waded in, wearing her panties and brassiere. She swam a few strokes upstream, and then let herself drift back with the current. Putting her face under water, she stared down at the netted sunbeams patterning the bottom with gold.

David Trenowith made a shallow dive, his body brown against his white cotton underpants. The pool was long, but only a few yards across.

"Taste the water," he said. "It looks good to drink, doesn't it?"

The taste was bitter, the water highly mineralized.

"Where does this water flow eventually?"

"Along the Roper, and all the way to the Gulf of Carpentaria, due east from here. This bit of river dives underground a bit further down, and reappears later. The blacks say it was made by Kunapipi, or one of their mother figures, in the form of a black snake."

She swam against the current as far as she could go, then floated lazily down towards him.

His chest was almost hairless, she noted with approval, smooth and brown with just a few hairs sprouting about the nipples. He swam with long lazy effortless strokes.

Eventually she came out and sat on the mossy bank in a patch of sunlight, squinting up at the flying-foxes squabbling in the trees. Her body felt relaxed and refreshed from the mineral-spring water. He sat beside her and they munched companionably on the rather dry sandwiches.

"That water is exactly the right temperature," she said.

"Yes. I told you you'd have a beaut swim. Now we can go back to

Katherine and say we've had a bath together; that should set the tongues wagging."

"I believe you like to be talked about."

He considered a moment, his head on one side. Then his face folded into one big smile. "I suppose I do, really."

He looked so like a cocky small boy that she had to laugh. "I'm going to get dressed," she said, and taking her skirt and blouse she went along the bank and into the bush, took off her wet things and had a pee. She dressed and walked back carrying her damp underwear. Brushing against a tree growing close to the water, she felt something fall on her bare neck.

In a moment several red-hot needles seemed to pierce her flesh. She gave a scream and beat frantically at her neck and back.

David, dressed once more, came towards her along the bank. He grabbed her, tore off the blouse and began brushing at something.

"Green tree ants!" he said. "They are buggers to bite if they fall on you."

She slowly buttoned up the blouse again, twisting her shoulders in pain. "I'll get some lotion out of the first-aid kit as soon as we get back to the plane," he said. "You've only got three bites, luckily."

"Ow! They're burning."

"Well, at least they're not poisonous, like scorpion-bites. Just painful."

He thought she looked childlike and appealing, with her straight wet hair flattened against her head and her grey-green eyes filled with tears. He took her hand. "Come on. Let's hurry."

Back at the clearing he got out a bottle of soothing lotion with a dash of ammonia in it. She loosened the top buttons and let the blouse fall from her shoulders.

"Turn around."

She turned obediently. He dabbed the lotion on with his fingers and smeared it a little round each bite. It felt like a caress. His hand slid round under her arm and caressed her breast. She closed her eyes and swayed back against him.

In a moment he was kissing the back of her neck. Slowly she turned her head till he was able to reach her lips. And so they stood locked together, while *Circe* waited beside them like a patient beast, her nose pointing towards the sky.

He released her abruptly and turned away.

"Oh God, Caro! I didn't mean to do that. I'm sorry. Now you'll take your little craft and fly away forever, and I don't blame you."

She did up her blouse with fingers that trembled. That one kiss had told her that she wanted him, she loved him. And he was married. It was like Malcolm over again. She took a deep breath, striving to keep her voice stern and calm.

"David, it's all right. But this must never happen again, if we are going

338

to work together. I came here to work with you, not to have an affair with you. Is that clear?"

"Yes, of course. You fly us home, will you?"

He repacked the first-aid kit and climbed into the front cockpit. As she climbed into the rear seat she realized that somewhere in the excitement she had dropped her blue panties; the damp brassiere was looped over one arm.

There were no calls waiting when they got back. Caro was still hungry after their lunch of sandwiches, so after he had dropped her at the hotel, she had a shower and washed her hair, then walked along to the bakery for some little cakes for afternoon tea. She had noticed it earlier, a tiny corrugated iron building with its front decorated by signs in large print:

WEIRD PIES   STRANGE PASTIES
ROCK CAKES FOR ROADMAKING   LOVE BUNS FOR LOST VITALITY

while round the back the baker claimed:

IN THE DOUGH FOR THIRTY YEARS, AND STILL A LOAFER.

She bought some rock cakes and took them back to her room. There was a canvas chair on the balcony where she could sit in whatever breeze was moving. The air was steamy and oppressive.

He did not come in to dinner that night.

She felt churned up and restless, sad and happy, wanting to see him again yet fearing that she would let her feelings show. The main thing was, they had to work together, important work that must not suffer. She could let him fly himself to all his calls, as he did normally; but she would be terribly bored sitting around in this little town for a month with nothing to do. But wait—what had he said about getting a horse for her to ride? That might be the answer. Then she could explore out to the Katherine Gorge and the country round. It was a change to be in such well-watered country; for even in the Dry the Katherine did not entirely cease to flow.

A telephone call came for her early in the morning. She had to grope her way down the dim stairs to answer it. "Dr. Trenowith wants to speak to Sister Manning," the girl told her.

"Yes? Caro Manning here."

"Caro, I've had an urgent call to Brock's Creek up the Line—four men injured in a fall of earth. I don't know how serious it is—may have to fly one of them in to Darwin Hospital. Can I take the plane?"

"Of course. You don't need to ask—she's yours for the month."

"Thanks. See you tomorrow." And then he added in a rush, "I didn't sleep very well."

"Nor did I."

There was a speaking silence. The line hummed between them.

"I behaved badly. But I want you to know I didn't plan it."

"Let's just forget the whole thing, shall we?"

"That's the trouble. I keep remembering. . . ."

So do I, she thought. Aloud she said clearly, "Goodbye, David."

After his return from Darwin the next day, there followed three days without any emergencies, apart from a ganger on the railway at Pine Creek with a crushed thumb. It was only a few stops up the line, and he could have waited for the weekly train. But Dr. Trenowith flew up and put a splint on the hand and gave him something for the pain. It did not have to be a matter of life and death for the Flying Doctor to come. He gave a tetanus antitoxin injection as well.

Since there were no calls, David suggested that they might take the afternoon off and drive over the river and see about a horse for her to ride.

He went across the shallow ford to Lovegrove Station. Lovegrove, the Grove of Love, thought Caro, her imagination running in one direction. She met Mrs. Dixon, the manager's wife, and took tea in the cool enclosed veranda of the old stone homestead. Then a lanky booted and spurred roustabout was sent to the horse-paddock to get her a horse to ride.

He came back with a neat black gelding, saddled and bridled, which stood quietly but showed the whites of its eyes in a way Caro did not quite like.

"He's got no real bad habits, doesn't pig-root or buck," said the young man. "Just watch, though, if he puts his ears back; he'll nip your arm or shoulder if he's in the mood."

While the others sat on the veranda, Caro, with a nervous eye on the horse's ears and the wicked white of his eye, hastily mounted and gathered up the reins.

The others watched while she put him through his paces in the yard. She found that he had a lovely gait: a brisk, even trot and a rocking-horse canter, and a soft mouth that responded to the lightest touch on the reins. "What's his name?" she called.

"Satan!"

The roustabout opened the yard gate for her. She held him at a walk for a while to establish who was boss, then gave him his head. They galloped along a well-marked track that followed the river bank. Satan seemed to want to go down to the water, so she let him make his way down the steep bank where there was a break in the dense green growth. She let him walk in till the stirrups were just above the water. He pulled at the reins and drank deeply. She sat idly with loose reins, absorbing the peace of leaning trees and calm reflections. The water was not as clear as the Mataranka pools.

There came a sudden clap of thunder, and Satan started nervously.

340

Looking up, she found the sky half-covered with blue-black clouds rolling down from the north, though here the sun still shone from a blue sky. She gathered up the reins and turned for the homestead.

Satan put his ears back at the next thunder-clap, and bolted for home. But Caro kept her seat and gradually slowed him down. At the yard gate she dismounted and led him through.

"What, did he toss you?" drawled the roustabout, strolling over from the shade of a tree. "I forgot to mention, he gets a bit skittish in a thunderstorm."

Caro suspected that the lapse of memory was deliberate; her horse-riding ability was being tested.

"He did not. He behaved like a perfect gentleman, and hasn't even tried to bite."

David drove her back to the hotel in pouring rain.

"I see you have a good seat on a horse, apart from your other accomplishments," he said. "I'm a bit scared of the things, especially ones that bite. And you drive a car like a veteran, too."

"Well—I've been driving since I was seventeen. I had my own little car in Adelaide."

"You must use mine whenever you want, to drive over to the station or out to the Gorge. They've given you an open invitation. They like you," he said.

CHAPTER FIFTEEN

Late in the afternoon of the next day an urgent call came for the doctor from Daly Waters: a drover on the stock-route from Nutwood Downs Station had been kicked by his horse and had his ear torn off. He couldn't leave the cattle, but he'd sent a blackfellow thirty miles back to the homestead with the message, and the ear wrapped in a clean handkerchief. It was now in the kerosene refrigerator at the Downs.

Dr. Trenowith set off into the gathering storm, after telling Caro that he would need the passenger seat to fly the drover back to the homestead to be reunited with his ear.

"Don't worry, the storm won't extend as far south as there," he said. "But I must leave at once if I'm to make it before dark."

He arrived back at lunch-time next day, his mission accomplished. The ear had been sewn back in place, covered with a dressing, and the drover had been flown back to his mob of cattle to continue the drove the very next morning.

"He'd never been up before, and he gripped the edges of his seat all the way there and all the way back. We caught the edge of the storm taking off, and it was pretty rough.

"'By cripes', Doc,' he said when we landed, 'she's quick, I'll give you that, but she's a beggar to buck.'"

"That reminds me," said Caro, "I had another ride on Satan this morning. Mrs. Dixon has asked me to drive out to the Katherine Gorge with them tomorrow, if I'm not needed."

"It's spectacular, but you really need a boat to see it properly. You'll see plenty of crocs, but they're the small freshwater ones."

"I don't really like them, any size."

While David took his morning clinic of the air, Caro went for a delightful picnic out to the gorge with Mrs. Dixon and the station bookkeeper, an Englishman with the unbelievable name of Wigglesworth.

On a trailer they towed a small boat with an outboard motor. Soon they were cruising slowly along the waterway under vertical yellow cliffs. Where there was a level bank below the cliffs, crocodiles sunned themselves or slipped into the water, leaving only their prominent eyes showing. On one low outcrop, Aboriginal designs in red ochre had been painted. The bare, jagged edges of yellow and orange rock at the

342

top of the cliffs contrasted with an almost purple sky at the zenith. Caro felt her neck growing stiff from holding her head back, as she stared and stared.

Here the gorge was wide and deep, with calm water reflecting the blue of the sky. They returned to where the bank flattened out and picnicked on cold chicken and hard-boiled eggs under the shady pandanus palms. Only two hundred miles to the south-west, a man could perish in the sand-hill country.

When she arrived back in Katherine a message was waiting at the hotel: "Called to Anthony Lagoon; will pick you up at 2 P.M."

It was nearly a quarter to two. Caro flung off her damp swimsuit and shorts and put on her skirt and blouse with a linen hat. Fortunately her hair had dried on the way back. She powdered her nose and dashed on some lipstick, grabbed her helmet and goggles and leather flying-jacket, and she was ready.

He pulled up at the door as she was telling Mr. O'Shay not to expect her back that night; it would be dark or nearly so by the time they reached their destination.

"Good. I thought I'd have to go without you," said David with a big smile. "I'll need you to do some nursing out there; no hospital, just a police station and a store. But you'll find the people interesting."

Anthony Lagoon had radioed Cloncurry first, but the doctor was away. One of the few inhabitants had been seriously injured in a road accident. He was unconscious and had some severe lacerations.

The usual afternoon storm was building up as they took off on the three-hundred-mile flight. David was in the pilot's seat, and for once Caro was glad; pelting rain began, and though they were flying below the cloud, visibility was restricted, and he knew the way better than she did. It was nearly four in the afternoon when they landed at Newcastle Waters, having flown out of the rain. He arranged for a wireless message to Anthony Lagoon to park a car with lighted headlights beaming along the runway if they should not be in before dark.

"You take her in," said Caro when he looked a question at her. "I'll fly on the way home." Her helmet and the shoulders of her calfskin jacket were darkened with rain.

They were still about fifty miles from their destination when the engine began missing. It could not be a vapour-lock, the temperature at two thousand feet was not high enough for that. David tapped her on the shoulder and passed a note. "Will try landing at Eva Downs." She looked back and nodded, as he pointed downwards. They were following the stock-route to Anthony Lagoon, and below and to the left appeared a small cluster of white roofs. David dived steeply to make the engine turn over faster, and it picked up, then faltered again. He circled the homestead, looking for a cleared space. The horse-paddock, dotted with trees, looked the only possibility. He skipped over the roofs of the outbuildings, then the high fence, banked sharply to get between two trees, landed on an even keel and pulled up just in front of another tree. A truck, its tray covered with black children hanging on anyhow, came tearing over the bumps and through the trees towards them.

In half an hour they were ready to take off again. Caro had diagnosed oiled-up spark-plugs, and so it proved.

"My fault," she said. "I should have been giving the engine an overhaul instead of going on a picnic."

"I could have done it for that matter," said David. "I haven't got a ground engineer's ticket like you, but I've had to learn to service my own bus."

Resisting the urging of the hospitable station people to come in for a cup of tea, they took off again in failing light.

A vast Himalaya of cloud spread along the western horizon, its snowy peaks back-lit by the declining sun. Keeping low to make sure of not losing the stock-route, which was their only guide, after an anxious hour of flying they picked up the wide, level gleam of water, and then the few scattered buildings of the tiny township of Anthony Lagoon. But there was no sign of a headlight or a burning smoke to indicate the landing place. As they circled lower, they saw something moving below—the roof of a van. They kept it in sight till it stopped and the headlights flashed on.

David skimmed the roof of the van and landed in the beam of the lights on what was a fairly good airstrip. They were taken at once to see the patient, who had come in from a nearby outstation of Anthony Lagoon Station for a celebration of the storekeeper's birthday. They had celebrated all too well, and on driving home afterwards, he was thrown off the back of the truck when the driver cornered too fast. They'd taken him to the police station where Mrs. Simmons, the Constable's wife, had put him on a couch and placed a cold compress on the great swelling bruise on his head, before calling the Flying Doctor. The radio tower and transceiver were at the police station.

The doctor administered a stimulant but said he could not assess the damage until the patient recovered consciousness. Meanwhile Caro bathed and dressed his lacerations, and the doctor gave him a tetanus shot just in case. They spent the night on folding canvas stretchers, borrowed from the store, in the little sitting-room.

Before turning in they visited Count Belyondi's home, which was attached to the store, at the request of a plump middle-aged lubra, who came to the police station with the message.

"That's the Count's wife," said the Constable. "He lives in dread of his brother and sister-in-law finding out he's married to a black gin. His brother is something important in the Italian Consulate in Sydney, I believe."

"At least he's married her," said Caro. "This sort of thing goes on all over the north, as you know; or there wouldn't be so many half-castes. But up here it seems to be regarded as more respectable *not* to marry the woman concerned. It's an upside-down morality, if you ask me." She thought of Grandpa Manning and Jenny, who was his faithful wife in all but name and status.

Maria, the black woman, had informed them, "Him cut bad longa him head. Him fall off tchair larse night, we bin celebratin'."

"It must have been some celebration," said David as they walked to the store. "Two wounded, one seriously, and I would say several bad hangovers."

The Count, a small dark man with greying curls and a luxuriant black moustache, stood up to greet them and bowed low over Caro's hand. His bright eyes flashed from one to the other as he smiled.

"This is my nurse, Sister Manning," said David firmly. "She is assisting the Flying Doctor this month; that is her plane we flew in from Katherine."

"Ahh! *Un'aviatrice, sì? È bellissima, non è vero?* A signorina both brave and beautiful!"

"You'd better let me look at this cut, if you want us to treat it."

The Count was wearing a bright handkerchief tied round his head, which gave him a rather piratical air. Maria, in a clean print dress, hovered in the doorway but did not enter. David untied the handkerchief and revealed a nasty gash over the right eye, filled with dried and blackened blood.

"You bin bathe-im?" he asked over his shoulder.

"No-more. Jus bin tie-im up."

"I no want-a spoil the *festa del mio compleanno,* you onderstan'? So I hold a cushion to my head till the bleeding stop."

He indicated a cushion on the couch where he had been sitting, which was soaked with darkened blood.

"Not the most aseptic dressing, a cushion," David muttered to Caro as they washed their hands with yellow soap in the kitchen. "I'll clean out the wound and put a couple of stitches in, and then you can show off your bandaging."

"Yes, Doctor," she said submissively. Her heart was beating high at having him stand so close beside her.

"This won't need an anaesthetic," he told Count Belyondi. "But perhaps a hair of the dog—"

"Ah, sì! Maria! Fetcha me the whisky."

He swigged down a neat tumblerful, sighed, and closed his eyes.

"*Bene, Signor Dottore.* I am ready. *Avanti!*"

As soon as the operation was over, Maria brought coffee, three cups on a tray.

"And where is your cup, Mrs. Belyondi?" asked Caro as she took hers and sat down.

Maria shook her head and smiled. "No-more!" she said.

"She has not learn-a to drink the coffee," said the Count. "But the red vino—ah, *sì!*"

All the same, Maria did not sit down with them but faded away. "Just like a servant!" Caro said indignantly to David afterwards. "Afraid to sit down in her own house as an equal."

"You were the trouble, my dear. She wouldn't have been shy of me, but a young, smart white woman was too much."

Before they left, Count Belyondi offered to sing for them in gratitude. His head did not ache in the least, he said. Accompanying himself on the guitar, he began to sing "*O Soave Fanciulla*" in a tenor voice full of Italian *bel canto.*

"What about some more Puccini?" asked David. "'*Che Gelida Manina'* —your tiny hand is frozen? I know that one."

And to Caro's delight he joined in, singing the Italian words in a light but sweet tenor.

"You amaze me," said Caro as they walked back to the police station with the tin of biscuits the Count insisted on their taking from the store. "I suppose you'll tell me next that you play the piano?"

"I do, as a matter of fact. That's one thing I miss in Katherine. Must ask Tim O'Shay if he wouldn't like to get one for the pub."

"I suppose it's the Cornishman in you," she mused. "Cornish people are supposed to be musical, aren't they? And with a name like Trenowith—"

"Yes, my grandfather was a Trenowith and my grandmother was a Pascoe, from Truro."

"They're also great Methodists, I believe."

"Not me!" he said fervently. "The war knocked all that religion out of me. I saw too many young men die; now I say 'Take no heed of the morrow,' and 'Sufficient unto the day is the evil thereof.'"

"You see! You're quoting the Bible."

"Oh yes, it was church twice a day and Sunday school in the middle when I was little."

"I know the Presbyterian hymn-book off by heart, from my schooldays. But my mother was not a church-goer, though my grandmother used to try and drag me there."

Back at the police station they found their other patient conscious, but complaining of a headache. The doctor tested his reflexes and his vision, and diagnosed concussion.

"Keep him in bed for a couple of days, on a light diet," he told Mrs. Simmons. "The lump has started to go down. I don't know why he was blacked out for so long, but I think partly he'd passed out from a large amount of alcohol. Would that be right?"

346

"That'd be right," said the Constable. "They'd been celebrating all day and half the night, on wine, whisky, and home brew."

"I'm glad it didn't happen when Bill was away," said Mrs. Simmons. "Sometimes I'm here on my own for weeks on end when he's out on patrol."

"You're only a radio call away from help, don't forget. You can call us or Cloncurry, whichever has a doctor available."

He told Caro afterwards that Bill Simmons, together with Constable Muldoon of Newcastle Waters, had made the round-trip journey of a thousand miles in twenty-five days to Darwin, taking two prisoners for trial.

"I knew Constable Jack McGuinnes at Marree," said Caro who had, in fact, met him only a few weeks before at Innamincka. "He used to patrol the desert with camels. He saved my mother from perishing out near Lake Eyre."

"Yes, they're remarkable men. Like the Canadian Mounties, I suppose, who 'always get their man.'"

Flying back along the same course they had come, Caro was studying the map when her eyes lighted on Lake Woods, a large blue expanse south of Newcastle Waters and to the west of the O.T. line. Dry salt-pans were often marked in blue on maps, misleadingly; yet it might be full of water.

By making a slight detour, she would come out over Lake Woods, and have a look at it from the air. As the Line disappeared beneath them, David turned inquiringly. She held up the map inside her windscreen, drew a circle in the air, and pointed downwards, jabbing her finger at the edge of the lake, now coming into sight as a sun-reflecting sheet of blue against the red-brown earth.

He nodded comprehension. Starting to circle downwards, she thought what fun it would be to have a plane with floats, and be able to land on the water like a pelican. She swooped low across the lake and back again. The shores were lightly wooded, mostly stunted trees and low shrubs. Perhaps the water was salt after all? She longed to go down and explore, but did not dare. It would look as though she were suggesting another swim together; and the consequence of that last swim was still vivid in her mind.

Reluctantly she turned, banking steeply with one wing pointing down at the water, then turned north and began following the track of the O.T. line towards Katherine. A peculiarity of the motor-track as it threaded in and out below the wires was that it twisted like a snake in a loop around each post. This was because the track had been made by camel teams carting the first posts (now replaced with metal poles because of white ants) which dropped a pole off the load first on one side, then on the other.

When they landed at Daly Waters to refuel David said, "I thought for a moment there that you were going to try a landing at the lake."

"No, I just wanted to look at it."

"It's hard to find a clear space to set down. You weren't thinking of another swim, then?" he asked, looking into her eyes. There was a smile lurking in his.

"Certainly not!"

"Because I wouldn't advise it. The mosquitoes there are like swarms of bees, and almost as big. They're starving for blood. I once tried camping there in an emergency. The mossies were like a grey fluff over my arms and the backs of my hands—standing room only, and they were standing on their heads to bite me."

"I thought it might be a freshwater lake."

"Brackish. And it often dries up with evaporation. There'd be settlements all round if there were that much permanent fresh water in this country."

Back at Katherine he drove her to the hotel and stayed to dinner. They had been greeted on the veranda by the tame brolga and Mr. Tim O'Shay himself, who said "Shure and it's glad I am to see ye safely back. For we had the father and mother of a storm afther ye left in that flimsy machine."

Caro was pleasantly tired after the four-hundred-mile flight home. Her last thought before drifting off to sleep was of David Trenowith and his smiling blue eyes. She felt that their friendship ripened with each flight they made together.

CHAPTER SIXTEEN

Milingimbi Mission, set on an island off the Arnhem Land coast about 250 miles east of Darwin, had sent an urgent message to the N.T.M.S. at Darwin, relayed to Katherine for the Flying Doctor.

8YW to VID. I have an urgent medical to C.M.O. Darwin. Native female age ten years. Fall from tree, fracture of both forearms. Some deformity. Much pain. Have immobilized forearms in splints, aspirin and codeine for pain. Please advise.

Dr. Trenowith wired back that the message was received, and he would leave first thing in the morning. He asked them to light a small smoke-fire to give wind direction.

David and Caro were on their way at first light. The morning was fine, a heavy downpour and thunderstorm the afternoon before having cleared the air. David was the pilot, as he explained that he knew the way; it was near two other missions on the same coast where he had called before.

"The kids for some reason loved canned sardines. I gave them a couple of tins of rations I had on board, and they wolfed them. There was only half a tiny fish each. We'll take two dozen tins with us to Milingimbi."

They flew up the railway line and then headed east of north. They had refuelled at Pine Creek but carried a can of petrol just in case. They crossed Deaf Adder Creek, and as they came to the East Alligator River they flew low along the channel so that they could see the crocodiles. Big salt-water ones, though they looked small from the air, basked on the banks or slid into the tidal river. They flew over green swamps which never burned brown, not even at the end of the dry season. Water buffaloes looked like grey slugs, and white birds, ibis and egret and corella cockatoos, flew up from the billabongs. Oenpelli Mission passed beneath, set on one of these. The rugged scarps and deep ravines of the Arnhem Land plateau they crossed at its narrowest tip, then headed for the north coast, which they would follow round to the Crocodile Islands, passing Maningrida Mission on the way.

By now David was giving anxious looks at the horizon ahead, which appeared to be blotted out by a thick grey curtain of cloud and rain. He set a compass course north-east to cut the coast well west of their goal.

After fifty miles, peering down through occasional breaks in the low grey cloud, he made out a curving yellow beach fringed with dense green. Then a blinding rain squall blotted it out. They still had almost a hundred miles to fly to their destination.

David scribbled a note and passed it to Caro: "Will have to land. Visibility soon nil." He jabbed his finger downwards at the swirling mist, now thinning to show another crescent of dull yellow beach. There was no clear space except on the sand, and in places mangroves came right down to the water.

Caro closed her eyes and came close to praying. She would have liked to have been at the controls of her plane, but knew she couldn't be in better or more skilled hands. David had a light but sure touch on the controls, and the machine responded almost like a horse to the hands of a skilled rider.

He circled down to a thousand feet. He knew the land was perfectly flat here, but wanted to keep some height and possibly glide in, engine throttled right down. There was not much room between water and jungle edge. To land on the beach would probably mean getting bogged. The blinding rain closed in again.

He circled twice more till the rain thinned. Seeing an open patch in the cloud below, he dived through it, and turning over the sea, came back to land with nose pointing up the slope of the beach. There was a thump, a jolt, then they were upside down.

Caro hung in her harness while medicine bottles, luggage, and cans of sardines showered over her. There was a deep silence and a feeling of suspended time. She felt disinclined to move; yet the can of petrol might have broken and it was imperative to get out quickly.

There was a scrambling noise ahead of her, and David dropped to the sand. He should have been behind; but the plane had gone completely over, nose first, and the tail now pointed up the beach. In a moment he had her harness unbuckled and she slid head-first into his arms.

"Caro! Dearest! Are you all right? You look so pale."

"Really? I thought all the blood was running into my head."

"No, you're white as a sheet. And there's a bruise on your cheek—"

"I think I'm bruised all over."

He set her gently on the warm, damp sand well away from the plane and went back to examine it. Not badly damaged, except for the prop. The wheels had dug into soft dry sand above the high-tide level, and locked immediately, flipping them over.

He brought back the square can of petrol, only slightly dented, and from the back of the beach collected driftwood. It was saturated, but with the help of petrol he was able to get a fire going under the shelter of the big tamarind trees, grown from seed brought to this coast centuries before by Macassar seamen looking for *bêche-de-mer*.

350

The rain poured down again. Caro, who in the heat had not been wearing her flying jacket but some new white overalls, was already soaked to the skin; but it was not cold. Her shoulders and underarms were bruised from the harness; besides, she had several grazes where things had fallen on her. She moved stiffly towards the fire through the soft, yielding yellow sand. At least they were alive, she reflected, even if they had only a vague idea of where they were. And *Circe* was not badly damaged, though undoubtedly grounded until help came.

Because of course a search would be mounted as soon as their disappearance was known.

While David tended the fire, she peeled the foil top from two tins of sardines. It hurt to use her right arm.

"Of course they'll find us before long," said David, reading her thought. "We were on course for Milingimbi, and Maningrida can't be far ahead—"

"Unless we passed it in the rain."

"That's possible, but anyway we're still on the coast. What worries me is that poor kid at the Mission with two broken arms, waiting for me to come. No doubt they'll radio Cloncurry for a doctor if we don't turn up."

Cloncurry! Caro suddenly realized what their disappearance would mean to her mother. Alix always worried when Caro was in the air.

She lifted an oily sardine from its tin and bit into it without tasting it.

The news of the missing doctor and his flying nurse was soon spread by radio all over the north and was relayed to Cloncurry, which flew a doctor out to treat the injured girl. The plane went on to search the coast between Milingimbi and Maningrida, but did not go far enough west to find the lost pair. It was supposed rather that in poor visibility they had overshot the mark and were now somewhere east of their destination, among the maze of bays and waterways on the Arnhem coast. They might have run out of fuel, or landed to wait for better weather. Dr. Trenowith had always turned up unharmed from groundings and accidents, and the mood was optimistic.

But Alix feared the worst. She could not sleep until she dosed herself with sleeping tablets, and would wake woolly-brained and depressed. She asked to go on the roster for night duty. She might as well be in the wards as lying in bed worrying.

The young Aboriginal girl was brought in to hospital for treatment, as the A.M.S. doctor had a plane equipped to take a stretcher. On the way back to Cloncurry they followed the coast eastward as far as the Goyder River, but there was no sign of the little Moth.

When Alix heard this she became convinced that Caro and the doctor had crashed into the sea.

Within days there were four planes out searching, one from Qantas,

351

one from the A.M.S., and two from the R.A.A.F. base at Darwin, and all missions and pearling luggers in the area with wireless had been alerted. It was such a wild, deserted, deeply indented coastline, the only settlements those of Aboriginal missions, that it would take weeks to search every bay and river mouth. But the missing pair were unlikely to stay near a river mouth because of crocodiles. And as for drinking water, even after rain the tidal rivers would be salt.

David Trenowith had wrenched off a curving piece of engine cover and set it to catch rain-water. "There will be water in those rocks at the other end of the beach," he said, pointing. "Even if it doesn't rain any more."

"Shouldn't we walk till we find a river mouth?"

"No."

"Why not?"

"Because river mouths are muddy, with mangroves. And salt-water crocs love them."

"Oh!"

Caro had enjoyed her first meal of sardines. The fish were oily and not dry. (By the time they had consumed half the tins, she never wanted to see a sardine again.)

Since she had been sitting by the fire, her bruises and bumps had stiffened up. She said she would go down to the point and have a swim, for the sun had come out, and let her clothes dry on the rocks.

"No, you won't!" said David. "At least not unless I come with you and keep a look-out for crocodiles."

"Are they really as bad as that?"

"They are very, very dangerous."

Caro looked about discontentedly at the curve of deep yellow sand backed with green trees, the clear sea of turquoise water breaking in small waves. It was such a lovely beach, the water was so inviting. . . .

"I don't care," she said, getting to her feet.

He brought a water-container and followed after her, both walking in the firm wet sand at the water's edge.

"You don't have to come."

"Oh yes, I do. I don't want to be a lone survivor."

She had a delightful swim; she didn't believe crocs really liked lovely clear water like this. But when he called her peremptorily to keep closer to shore, she obeyed. In her underthings she sunbathed while her overalls dried on the rocks. It was early afternoon and the tropic sun was at its warmest. They were only twelve degrees from the equator. At the far end of the beach a dark clump of mangroves clothed the point.

As they walked back to the plane, a decorous distance between them, the sand was so hot that she walked right at its edge, where the tide was fast running out. He still had his shoes on, and moved up to the jungle edge to collect firewood.

Suddenly he stopped, peered at the sand, and walked back towards high-water mark. "Come and look at this!"

She was carrying the still-damp overalls across her shoulder. By treading on this garment, then picking it up and throwing it ahead and jumping on to it again, she made her way over the burning sand to him.

He gripped her arm so hard that he nearly made another bruise. "D'you see that?"

Distinct above the high-water mark were the tracks of a crocodile: its clawed feet, the groove made by its tail. The tracks led up into the greenery. She looked at him wide-eyed.

"Yes; a big one, too."

She stared and shivered.

"Let's get back, and get plenty of firewood. We'd better keep the fire going all night. He'll probably go back into the sea before morning."

Caro kept very close to him, on the seaward side, for the rest of the walk.

Back at the camp he had rigged a tarpaulin, only six feet square, sloping from the wooded edge to the beach, to deflect the large drops. Rain-clouds were massing out to sea again. The fire was lit under a tree where a downpour would not extinguish it. They made a swag from their spare clothes and after another meal of sardines huddled under the tarpaulin as the rain came down again and doused the last embers of the western sun. Caro had gone a little way down the beach for a pee rather than trust herself among the dark trees.

It would seem romantic if there were stars, and a moon, and a silver sea, thought Caro. She was not cold, for her clothes were dry, but she shivered slightly. But rain, and c-crocodiles, and sand-flies—! The irritating specks had begun biting at sunset, but now the rain seemed to have subdued them.

David had a big pile of firewood handy, some damp so that it made a smoke to ward off mosquitoes, and a heap of dry underbark to keep it going. They sat on their swags, huddling closer together as the rain poured down again.

"You know, you'd be more comfortable if you'd lean on me," he said, and they sat almost back to back while she leaned against his broad shoulder, and talked. It was too early to go to sleep. But both were tired after their long flight, and bruised from the crash. He gave her a chaste kiss on the cheek and said, "Good night, dear girl. Go to sleep. I'm just going to stoke the fire up."

She lay and listened to the groaning croaks of tree-frogs and the sharp cry of some nocturnal creature, bat or bird. What sort of noise did crocodiles make, apart from the snapping of their jaws? She shuddered, and curled into a foetal position, hands and feet drawn up close. She was glad when David returned and lay beside her on the other swag. Did she want him to hold her in his arms and make love to her? Of course she did. But he was evidently determined not to "take advantage" of her, or to be faithful to his wife or something. She was not going to make the first move. Her heartbeat and breathing slowed, and soon she was asleep, in spite of the odd sensation of lying up- and down-hill, due to the steep slope of the beach. But the sand beneath was soft and warm. Her last thought was of David's words, in the first shock of their crash: *Caro, dearest!*

Some time later she woke. The rain had stopped, the tree-frogs were silent, there was just the drip, drip of water from the trees on to the canvas roof. Something had awakened her, in spite of the quiet. She lay rigid, straining her ears.

Ah, there it was! A *scrunch, scrunch, scrunch* in the coarse sand. A crocodile's footsteps? And then something took hold of a strand of her hair, and pulled. She sat up with a scream.

"David!"

He was instantly awake, and groping for the torch he had brought from the plane. He flashed on the beam and swung it in a semi-circle. There was a papery rustle, and a small army of ghost-crabs with eyes on stalks sidled away. They were pale, stilt-legged, and about the size of a hand: obscene-looking creatures that fixed their little black eyes on the light until they melted into the ring of blackness beyond.

"It's all right—just crabs looking for a feed."

"They actually pulled at my hair!"

"Testing to see if you were dead or not. They don't have the courage to attack living creatures."

"They are revolting!"

"Queer-looking, I agree." He got up and put some more wood on the dying fire. Low over the ocean a few stars showed, glowing with a steady yellow light, quite different from the diamond sparkle of the frosty inland nights.

"It may be fine tomorrow. More chance of our being seen from the air," he said.

"You think they'll be looking for us, then."

For the first time she felt a twinge of doubt about whether they would be rescued; not when, but whether.

It was long before she slept, for under her ear she could hear the ghost crabs digging, *scrunch, scrunch!* to undermine her.

Cloncurry kept in touch by voice with Darwin, Elcho Island, Milingimbi, and Maningrida. Darwin had made contact with luggers in the Arafura Sea. They would search for wreckage between Elcho Island and Cape

Arnhem. Milingimbi had sent out the small Mission launch, and from Maningrida black trackers were moving along the east bank of the Mann River and the beaches of Boucaut Bay. None of them was looking far enough to the westward; yet neither Mission had heard an aircraft overhead during the thick weather when the plane went missing.

Alix, on duty during the night, spent most of the day haunting the radio base for scraps of news. Her distrust of small aeroplanes had been reinforced. In spite of her fear she even offered to go as an observer in one of the search planes, but was gently told that an experienced navigator would be of more use. Also most of the passenger space was taken up with rolls of mosquito nets, bedding, and food, cream for insect bites and citronella repellent, and waterproof sheets. The missing pair were unlikely to be in need of water at this time of the year. If their plane was more or less intact they would have plenty of medical and first-aid equipment. If it was not—this alternative was not spelled out, but if the plane should be sunk or burnt there were unlikely to be any survivors.

Alix wished she could pray, but she no longer had her childhood faith in the efficacy of prayer. After Mab died she had decided that either God was not aware of the terrible things that happened to people; or that he knew, but was unable to stop them. Either he was unknowing and uncaring, or omniscient but impotent.

Not long before Caro disappeared a child had been brought in from a station suffering from tetanus, too late for the antitoxin to take effect. The little girl died from exhaustion after a few days, but not before Alix had seen her suffer the terrible spasms, as her jaws clenched and her head curled back towards her heels; and fully conscious all the time in spite of strong barbiturates.

Alix, sitting beside her, had clenched her own teeth in sympathetic agony. She tried singing old Presbyterian hymns to herself to calm her mind. She came to "All Things Bright and Beautiful. . ." He made them one and all. Yes, but he also made the bird-eating spider and the deadly stonefish, the bacteria of diphtheria and cholera, and the tiny viruses that caused such misery in the world. It was the conundrum which had puzzled William Blake about the tiger:

Did he smile his work to see?
Did he who made the Lamb make thee?

No, Alix thought, she would not pray for Caro's safety. But with all her strength she willed that her daughter might be alive.

Chapter Seventeen

Caro woke sweating. The air was close and humid, but no rain was falling. Her first thought was of a swim in that beautiful clear sea, crocodiles or no crocodiles. She felt much safer in daylight. Her second thought was breakfast, till she remembered there were only sardines. If only they had a bit of flour to make a damper! David appeared and dropped an armful of wood near the fire.

"Good morning!" he called cheerfully.

She sat up, rubbing her eyes, and looked down the beach. The sea was gone. In its place spread acres of grey, glistening mud almost to the horizon, where there was a thin silver streak.

"The sea!" she squeaked.

"Is gone until the tide comes in. They have twenty-foot tides up here!"

"Blast it! I was looking forward to a swim."

"What about breakfast instead? There are sardines *au naturel*, sardines in oil, or sardines without toast."

"Erkh! I'm losing my taste for sardines."

Her youthful appetite was strong enough to overcome her distaste, however. There was a roll of toilet paper, something she had always carried in the plane since her first long flight, so she rolled them in paper and removed most of the oil.

After breakfast they walked a little way out in the mud and found some whelks, but most of the shells were empty ones, appearing to be walking about on the surface but actually home to tiny hermit crabs. They had thin, spidery legs and Caro did not fancy them to eat even if they'd been bigger. But the live whelks they took back and cooked in the ashes till the operculum opened, and Caro provided a bobby-pin from her hair to extract the mouthful of shell-meat.

"We'll have to keep a small fire going as a signal to a boat or a plane," said David. "I'll have some oil-soaked rags handy, which will make black smoke. They wouldn't see a small fire through the tree-tops. We might have to burn the propeller, nice dry wood."

Caro sat on the sand under the shadow of a wing while he smashed off pieces of the splintered wood. She was wearing her uniform of white cotton, buttoned up the front, but not the white starched apron

356

and cuffs that completed it, and nothing underneath for coolness. In her white cotton hat she felt like a lady bowler, dressed for a tournament.

David set aside a long piece of broken wood with a sharp point. After carrying the rest up to the fire, he said, "I'm going to walk along to the mangroves and see if I can get a mud-crab or two. They're number-one tucker." And barefooted, in his shorts and shirt, he began walking down to the firmer sand at the beach's edge.

Caro stared in disbelief. "Wait! Don't leave me!" She ran, stumbling in the soft sand, after him.

He stopped. "You can't come with me. Someone has to be here to build up the fire if a plane comes over. And to be seen near the wreck. I might be hidden in the mangroves."

"But a crocodile will get you!"

"Not in daylight, I hope. And I've got a weapon" (a piece of brittle wood that a croc's jaws would snap like matchwood). "Go on back. I won't be long."

In the pocket of his shorts was some twine for binding the formidable claws of the "muddie" for carrying. He was getting as heartily sick of sardines as Caro, and wished there were enough length of twine to make a fishing-line. Crab-meat would make good bait.

His tall figure with its broad, hunched shoulders dwindled away into the distance as Caro watched, till it was swallowed entirely by the mangroves. She felt suddenly intensely alone, somewhere on the top of Australia, on the shores of the lovely-sounding Arafura Sea.

Caro pottered along the muddy edge, looking for more whelks, then took them up to the camp. She sat down in the shade and gazed towards the mangrove point. Nothing moved there. If there were any passing boats, they would be out of sight, where the sea had gone. Her watch was still working, hanging on a twig for safety. An hour passed with incredible slowness. . . . She was too scared to walk along to the red rocks at the other point, where she could have washed her panties in the water David had found among the rocks. There was more than one hollow, he said, with a good supply.

Out of boredom she was becoming drowsy in spite of her worry about David, when a rustling and a breaking of twigs in the thick bush behind her made her leap to her feet. She glared in terror, but could see nothing. As soon as she could force her petrified limbs to move, she ran down the beach to the machine and climbed up, sitting on the bottom of the fuselage between the wheels. Would a crocodile, if hungry enough, tear at the wings and fuselage with its great jaws? The plane was only of fabric and wood construction, but she felt safer sitting up here with a good view of the empty beach. The silver streak of water along the horizon had widened. The tide was coming in.

She stared along the yellow sand towards the mangroves. Nothing moved but a shimmer of heat. Oh God, what if he never came back? She forced herself to look away, to watch the slow advance of the tide. She counted a hundred slowly, and scanned the back of the beach for crocodile footprints. If he wasn't back before dark, could she sleep up here without falling off? If only the plane had been right way up!

She looked once more towards the wooded point. A dark shape detached itself from the dark trees, was moving along the edge of the glistening mud towards her. . . .

It was him, he, it was David! She tumbled to the ground and ran towards him along the damp sand at the edge of the mud. The soft sand by the plane had burnt her feet, but she did not notice it.

In the wide, flat perspective of tidal flats he looked impossibly tall, a god, a hero of some marine legend. . . .

As she came nearer he waved his stick, and she saw something large, a silver fish, impaled on it. Then she saw that he was carrying another object in his other hand—a trussed crab.

"Oh, darling David!" She began to sob with relief. By the time she reached him her face was wet with tears. She flung her arms round his waist and buried her face in his shirt.

"Dear, what is it? I thought you'd be so happy to see I'd caught some real food."

"I am, I am, but oh! I thought you were dead, and I heard a cro-crocodile in the scrub just behind the camp, and I've been frightened—"

"Darling!" He dropped the fish and the crab to the sand, and folded her in his arms, rocking her. "Darling, darling, darling, I'm sorry! But I bet it was only a wallaby, or a big cassowary or something."

He kissed her tear-wet eyes, her cheeks, her throat, and then her lips, a series of light butterfly kisses, until she reached up and drew his head fiercely against hers, and they were lost in a long kiss, lips, tongues, and teeth all mixed up together. He stood with his feet wide-braced and she clung to him.

She felt him harden against her thigh. But even in the grip of desire the successful hunter remembers his catch. After a few moments he released her and picked up the fearsome-looking crab, still making restricted movements of its huge claws.

He handed her the pointed stick with the silver fish impaled on it, and with his arm round her trotted up the beach, half-carrying her over the red-hot sand nearer the trees. He broke some green branches and laid his catch on them in the shade. Then he drew her down on the swag spread under the canopy and began undoing the buttons down the front of her single garment, kissing each breast as it was exposed.

"Oh God, Caro," he muttered, "I was mad not to do this earlier. I've held myself back, and held myself back, when I wanted you so much—"

"Don't talk," she whispered. Quivering, molten, receptive, she had not felt this way since Malcolm. And even with him she had not known the complete union, the intense and perfect climax at the same moment, which she was to reach so easily with David. It was, no doubt, due to some physical characteristic, some natural compatibility of their organisms, but at the moment she put it down entirely to love. And the tide came flooding in towards the yellow sand.

He stayed within her and they fell into a light sleep still joined, arms and legs intertwined. It was as though two seeking halves had met and made a perfect whole. When they woke they were bathed in sweat. As they drew apart their torsos separated with a loud thwacking noise.

"The middle of the day's too hot for love-making," he laughed, rubbing his chest with his discarded shirt. "The next priority is—food!"

There was plenty of water, as he had placed the container so that any rain ran off the tarpaulin into it. But he went down to clean the fish in the sea, using his pocket-knife. He built up the fire and let it die down to coals to grill the fish.

"We'll have the crab cold for tea," he said. "I don't fancy eating them when they've been alive minutes before."

The fish had been trapped in a tidal pool, by the greatest good luck. Grilled on green sticks, it was rather dry, but a great improvement on canned sardines.

But when he would have put the crab, still sluggishly moving, on the coals to cook, Caro objected.

"You can't cook it alive!"

"But we have to—there's no container deep enough to boil it in. Besides, you know, a crab's nervous system is fairly primitive, you can't compare it with a human being's suffering in the same—"

"I won't eat any!"

He shrugged. "All right." He put the crab down, fetched a piece of wood, and bashed in the shell about its head. He complained that it would let out the juices and the crab-meat would be dry. "You're inconsistent," he said coldly. "You put the whelks to cook, still living."

"Y-es. But. . ."

It was a small rift between them.

She knew that doctors could not indulge in too much empathy with a suffering subject; some nurses too—she remembered how she had begun to be impatient with screaming women in the labour ward. She had said to Betty that doctors were hard, and here she was madly in love with one!

And the cold crab was delicious after all.

That night she cared not for crocodiles or ghost-crabs. It was too hot for sleeping in each other's arms, they lay apart with feet touching and hands clasped. She said, "If it weren't for my mother, who will be worrying herself sick, I would wish them not to find us yet. It will never be quite like this again."

"I know. It's a kind of enchanted place, outside of ordinary life."

"I believe time can expand to an extraordinary degree in extraordinary circumstances. How long do the minutes seem to a man while he's drowning, or plunging towards the earth with an unopened parachute? They can't be measured. And if we can cram enough living and loving and joy and excitement into a few days, they will expand into a month of ordinary time."

"Yes, I believe it's a matter of heightened awareness. We felt it in the war, knowing we had to leave on a dangerous patrol at dawn; and during the attack all sense of passing time was suspended. Let's cram in a bit more loving while we can," he said, reaching out his arms for her.

It couldn't last, of course. David Trenowith, who had been several times lost with his little plane in the bush, without wireless, confidently expected their rescue. Caro was not so sure. She knew their disappearance together would by now be in the newspapers throughout the land. It had not occurred to her that not only Alix, but her grandmother in Adelaide must be worrying about their safety. And David's wife. . .

On the fourth day after their forced landing, a Darwin-based plane, brought in by the Medical Service of the Northern Territory as a replacement for the Flying Doctor since he had gone missing, saw the wreck on the beach in one of the scallops of Junction Bay. The plane was on its way back, taking a more northerly course than usual, from a search between Maningrida and Elcho Island. Circling lower, the pilot saw two figures run out from under a shelter at the back of the beach, and a plume of smoke rising from among the trees. He waved, dropped parcels of food and mosquito-nets, pointed in the direction of Darwin, and waggled his wings in farewell. With radio on board, he sent the welcome message: "Plane found. Both safe", which was soon to be relayed round Australia.

Alix heard it at the Cloncurry wireless base and clasped her hands in gratitude to Fate, or whatever controlled the destinies of human beings.

As the days stretched on with no word, she had found herself wringing her hands together in anguish as she paced up and down, unable to sleep. Then came the news that a Mission lugger from Maningrida would sail round to pick them up tomorrow and take them back to the Mission, where there was an airstrip from which they could be lifted to Darwin.

David and Caro had waved to the plane with muted enthusiasm. Rescue meant the end of their beach idyll, albeit an idyll somewhat marred by ghost-crabs, mosquitoes, and sand-flies. But as the parcels fell, burying themselves in the soft sand, they ran to retrieve them like children welcoming gifts from Father Christmas.

The mosquito-nets would make their nights more comfortable, but it was the bread they welcomed most. They each tore open a loaf and munched it eagerly, before they had even found the canned butter with (thoughtfully) a can-opener fastened to it.

"I've noticed," said David with his mouth full, "that it's not the exotic things to eat that you dream of when you're stranded. Not roast turkey and smoked salmon, but good old bread and butter."

There was a small bag of self-raising flour as well, perhaps in case the bread package fell into the sea. David proceeded to make a damper and set it to cook in the hot ashes. When it was done he tapped it on the bottom and it gave out the authentic hollow sound of a well-cooked round of soda-bread. They broke off pieces of crisp crust and ate them with butter, but not before they had wolfed some fresh bananas and juicy mangoes, which their systems had been craving for the last four days.

It was early afternoon, and the once-daily tide was getting later each day.

"If they send a lugger for us," said David, "by the time they get here and wait for the tide, it will take until late afternoon or early evening for us to board her."

"So we have another day?"

"Yes; one more day together."

He interlocked the fingers of his right hand with hers and drew her close for a kiss.

"Your lips taste of butter and they don't smell of sardine oil. It's a pleasant change."

They finished that most satisfying meal with a big enamel mug of tea with sugar, brewed in the quart-pot that had been included in the pack of grey blankets and mosquito-nets. Then they lay under the trees, replete, and watched the tide come in.

"Tomorrow," said David lazily, "we will have to get all the things left in the plane, and stack them ready on the beach. If they get here late, there won't be much time. You've seen how fast the water can drop."

In the time since they'd come together on the second day, they had talked and talked, exploring each other's past and hopes for the future, their ideas about life and time, tastes and dislikes, prejudices and beliefs and memories. She had told him about Malcolm, and also that he was the first man who could make her forget that unhappy first love. Then she asked him, diffidently, about Margaret, his wife.

"Do you still love her?" she asked painfully.

"No, and haven't for some time. I'd been thinking about you ever since the time I met you in Burketown."

"Really?" She was pleased. "You made an impression on me, too. I even flew up to Normanton, hoping I might run into you. Remembering what you said: 'The area is immense but the people are few.' It seemed a non sequitur at the time, but I see now what you meant. Sydney is much smaller in area, but you'd be more unlikely to run into someone you knew in the street there than you would in the Territory—because you know most of the inhabitants here."

"Something like that."

He told her he'd been married ten years. His wife didn't want children and was addicted to playing bridge, which he found boring. She always kept herself looking nice, even in the heat; but at night the ritual of getting ready for bed took half an hour or more. She had to wash out some panties in the bathroom, brush her teeth, roll her hair in two curlers in front, rub cold cream into her face, then skin freshener, then a moisturizer, put on hand cream, push back the cuticles of her nails with an orange stick, and brush the back of her hair, which she wore long below her shoulders. Then, clean and shining, smelling of face-cream and toothpaste, she would at last climb into bed.

"I still wanted her," he confessed. "Love and sex are two branches of the same tree, but not necessarily the same thing. There's affection, and gratitude, and habit, and shared experience; all help to keep a marriage afloat. But since this happened—this has knocked me completely off the rails, and I don't think I can go back to calm domesticity. I've been hit by a hurricane."

"A few mixed metaphors there," said Caro judiciously. "Trees and branches and railway lines (branch lines. . . ?) and boats and hurricanes. But I take your meaning."

He grinned and gave her a kiss. "Don't be so pedantic. In short, I love you, and I want to be with you always."

CHAPTER EIGHTEEN

The lugger crew had managed to get the aircraft righted, then covered it with tarpaulins, tied it down well, and left it there. Caro hated to see poor *Circe* crippled and abandoned, but David said that when a new propeller had been obtained, a pilot and mechanic would be brought by boat with spare fuel and rolls of matting for a temporary runway. The pilot would be able to take off along the beach, it was hoped, and return the Moth to Darwin for overhaul. When that had been done, he promised that he would personally ferry it to her in Queensland.

Meanwhile the castaways were taken back to the airstrip at Maningrida, from where they were flown to Darwin to be met by the local press with cameras. David's wife was not there, but he rang her at once. The Medical Service car would take him straight home. He asked Caro if she would like to come to his house for lunch, but she did not want to meet his wife, and he looked relieved. A mail-plane was leaving shortly for Cloncurry, so Caro booked a seat with Qantas. She and David were forced to say goodbye in public without even a last kiss.

David would send a radio message direct to Cloncurry Hospital to let Alix know what flight she would be on.

Alix waited at the airport, scarcely convinced even yet that her daughter was coming back. After all her anxious imaginings, even after the tremendous news of the pair being found safe and well, she could not quite believe it.

As the Qantas flight came in and the plane taxied towards the little waiting-room, and stopped, Alix broke all the rules and ran out to meet it. Down the steps came a slender girl in white overalls, her straw-gold hair fluttering in the breeze.

"Caro! Darling! Dear child." Her arms were around the warm, living flesh she had feared never to hold again. "Let me look at you! You're all right?" Tears ran down her face.

"Perfectly all right, Mum," said Caro, returning her kisses but a little embarrassed. "You shouldn't be out here, you know."

It occurred to her that David's wife had not even bothered to come to the airport, let alone greet him with open arms.

Grounded in Cloncurry without a plane, Caro fretted and moped for that lost enchanted beach, for her damaged craft, and above all for David —now presumably back living with his wife. She did not tell her mother why she was so depressed, but Alix guessed, seeing the change in her face when a letter arrived with a Darwin postmark. She wanted Caro to be happy but also she did not believe in divorce; and she knew that Dr. Trenowith was married. She could only hope the child would get over it without too much pain (the "child" being nearly twenty-two years old).

Matron had recently retired, and Alix had been appointed Matron of the Cloncurry Hospital, a position of responsibility that she enjoyed. The former Matron had been rather old-fashioned in her ideas, and now Alix began instituting a few reforms. The first of these was that nurses did not have to stand at attention with hands behind their backs when addressed by a Sister. They were even encouraged to express opinions.

Loose white flowing caps had to be worn, but uniforms were much freer and more suitable to a hot climate than when she had trained: gone were the scratchy starched collars and cuffs, and she allowed nurse's aides to wear a light-blue uniform with short sleeves. She enrolled one bright Aboriginal girl as an aide, which scandalized some of the older patients.

On her days off Alix and Caro sometimes went on picnics, to the permanent waterhole in the Cloncurry, or even farther afield to the upper Leichhardt River; but in winter the rivers were dry, and in summer the blacksoil became impassable and the roads a quagmire.

She made friends with some station people and sometimes spent a weekend on their property. The daughter had been a patient for a long time with poliomyelitis—she had recovered, fortunately without any paralysis. Their station was set on a mixture of red loam and blacksoil country about fifty miles north, covered with small but shapely white-trunked gums and acacias, or with stunted spinifex; and after rain the Mitchell grass made splendid cattle feed.

Alix enjoyed her work and did not think she would marry again.

She'd had one proposal, from an elderly grazier who was a patient for a time. He was a widower in poor health, looking for a nurse in his declining years.

Then there was a doctor relieving at the hospital who had pursued her with some tenacity. She had a mild flirtation with him, but did not really find him attractive and was glad when he departed. Sometimes the three years of her marriage seemed like a dream. But Caro was the living proof that Jim had existed. Sometimes she looked at his photograph in the Light Horse uniform, and it seemed unreal to her. What she remembered most was their first meeting at Hergott, and the first year of their marriage, on Cappamerri Station.

Caro wrote to the Queensland section of the Aerial Medical Services Council, suggesting the provision of a Flying Nurse to supplement the work of the Flying Doctor, one with her own aircraft who could visit lonely women on isolated stations, act as a midwife, and inaugurate a regular clinic for both white and Aboriginal children for immunization against diphtheria and tetanus. She would also be available to fly with the doctor and to pilot the A.M.S. plane, as well as to help with seriously ill patients being operated on in the field or transported back to base hospital.

The branch had recently received a substantial bequest. John Flynn had already been planning to establish a sub-base at Normanton, to service Cape York Peninsula and the little inland towns of Croydon and Georgetown, former gold-mining centres set among rocky hills about a hundred miles inland from the Gulf. Qantas did not like its chartered planes to fly there from Cloncurry because of the rugged and mountainous country.

As it happened, when the Committee sent Caro's application on to John Flynn, he was travelling west of Alice Springs with "Skipper" Partridge, who had roamed the outback for years as a "patrol padre" for the A.I.M. Skipper had seen how his wife, who usually travelled with him, brought comfort to lonely station wives who had not seen a white woman for years; and she was not a nurse. He urged Flynn to give Caro the job.

"I feel inclined to," said Flynn. "She's Sister Manning's daughter, you know, at Cloncurry; used to be at Birdsville and Marree in the early days. I know the daughter is a strong, resourceful and independent person, as well as being a good nurse and a good pilot. And she's young and has a sense of humour."

"Sounds ideal," said Skipper. So instead of them advertising for a pilot for the new Flying Doctor base at Normanton, Caro was appointed. She would also be on call to transport the resident Flying Doctor, who would be a part-time resident at Croydon. There would be a mileage allowance for her plane as well as her salary. When not needed to answer emergency calls, she would conduct regular clinics at the larger cattle-stations and the Aboriginal missions scattered about the north.

Elated, she radioed Darwin base to ask when her aircraft would be delivered. The reply was, as soon as Dr. Trenowith's plane was back in circulation; it was nearly repaired, but meanwhile he was using hers for urgent cases.

Caro was speechless. So *Circe* was already back in the air, and he was risking her over heaven knew what dangerous territory in the Wet; and without even consulting her! And instead of flying immediately to see her while delivering her machine as he had promised, he was using it to carry on his practice! She wired grimly:

KINDLY INFORM DOCTOR TRENOWITH MY AIRCRAFT NEEDED CLONCURRY IMMEDIATELY. IT IS NO LONGER UNDER LICENCE TO THE N.T.M.S.

How devious! He had never mentioned in his passionate, longing letters that *Circe* had been repaired and was safely back in Darwin, and that there was nothing to stop him taking off tomorrow for a reunion, however brief. No, because he wanted to use the plane himself! He could not bear to be without one, and the Northern Territory Medical Service had none to spare.

When a letter arrived giving a post-office box number in Darwin, but no mention of returning her plane—for it had been written before she sent the wire—she wrote a blistering letter accusing him of deviousness, selfishness, thoughtlessness, male arrogance. . . . "You obviously believe your work is more important than that of a mere woman. But as I now have a permanent appointment—well, for a year anyway—with the Queensland branch of the Australian Aerial Medical Services, I will thank you to return my craft as you should have done as soon as it was ready. And to think. . ." And so on and so on.

No reply came in the next week, and Caro began to panic. She had not read over what she wrote in the heat of her anger, and now she wondered if she had said something unforgivable. What if he never got in touch with her again?

When a message came at last it made her almost as angry as relieved.

DARLING I AM TRULY SORRY ARRIVING WEDNESDAY AFTERNOON WITH CIRCE IN GOOD CONDITION. LOVE DAVID.

How could he be so thoughtless as to send an intimate message by telegram? Did he think telegrams were private in a small place like Cloncurry, where she knew the radio operator, and the man who typed the message out, and the man who delivered it to the hospital? Now everyone would know that she was having an affair with the glamorous and much-publicized flying doctor from the Northern Territory, with whom she had been marooned for five days on a lonely part of the coast. For of course the story had appeared even in the southern papers.

She happened to be on duty on Wednesday, but Alix offered to stand in for her.

"Thanks, Mum," said Caro, hugging her. "You know how it is—I'm longing to see *Circe* again, and perhaps take her up for a quick flip around the district. . ."

"Yes, I know how it is," murmured Alix with an inward smile. "You can take my car out to the aerodrome if you like. I won't be needing it."

So on Wednesday afternoon Caro was waiting at the airport, hair washed and shining, wearing a fitted white linen dress with a black patent-leather belt—something between a nurse's uniform and a smart day-dress. They were having an extremely hot late summer, with such strange weather that pilots reported flying between rain on one side and a dust-storm on the other. Instead of being humid, the heat was dry and burning, the temperature standing at over 110 degrees Fahrenheit day after day.

When rain did come down from the north to cool the air, the flies appeared in swarms. That was one advantage about the north coast, thought Caro: sand-flies and mosquitoes, yes, but at least there were few flies.

Today it was hot and dry. A dust haze was beginning to spread over the town, and Caro watched it anxiously. Should it get worse, David might not be able to land; but if a dust-storm was going to be bad it had usually reached its greatest intensity by now, at two in the afternoon. That was why the doctors preferred to make early-morning flights in summer when possible.

The drone of a small aeroplane sounded from the sky. There was no mail-plane due in and the airfield was deserted. Caro, hatless, shaded her eyes with her hand and stared up into the dust-hazed blue. Then she saw the little shape she had been watching for, the stumpy fuselage, the double wings, the tapering tail. . . . Her two loves, David and *Circe*, were coming in together. She swallowed, feeling her throat go dry with excitement.

He banked, turned, came in upwind in a long, controlled glide to land and taxi almost to her feet, where she stood just beyond the Qantas hangar. He kept the nose carefully towards her so as not to spray her with dust from the slip-stream. She rushed forward and patted a wing. Her craft looked as good as new.

Then he was climbing out, in long trousers, shirt and tie, more neatly dressed than she had ever seen him. (He explained afterwards that it was because he thought he might be meeting her mother.) He had pushed up his goggles and undone the chin-strap of his helmet. In two strides he had her in his long arms, holding her close, and everything was suddenly right.

There was no need for words between them.

She took him to meet her mother. They had a hospital afternoon tea on the veranda before Caro announced that they were going up for a short flight while she got the feel of the controls again after the break. Alix liked the doctor, and could see why her daughter found him attractive, with his thick, untidy dark hair, his narrow hips and wide shoulders and those startlingly blue eyes. It was obvious to her that they were lovers. It was in the way they looked at each other, in the lingering touch of a hand as they passed a saucer or a spoon. She was surprised to find in herself a feeling of something like envy. Yet it surely could only end in unhappiness all round. It was a pity; he had a nice smile.

"I hope you appreciate all this man has done," said Caro half-seriously. "First he managed to land in an impossible place without injury to either of us—"

"Only to the aircraft," put in David.

"—and then he found food for us on the beach, and saved me from being eaten by a crocodile—"

"Here, hold on!" he protested. "All I did was warn you against swimming too far out, in case."

"And we found tracks of a big one on the beach just afterwards, didn't we?"

"Ye-es." He had been rather horrified at the newspaper stories, aided somewhat by Caro's imagination, of their "terrifying ordeal on a crocodile-infested beach in the far north."

"I do appreciate it. I worry about her," said Alix, looking into his eyes and letting him understand her double meaning.

Caro set down her cup and said they must go. After the flight David was taking her out to dinner to have two of the biggest barramundi steaks obtainable, the sort of food they'd dreamed about while living on canned sardines.

"So I'll say goodbye, as I'll be leaving with the mail-plane tomorrow for Darwin," he said, shaking Alix's hand.

"And don't wait up, Mum," said Caro. "I'll probably be late."

Caro picked up a warm jacket and her flying helmet and gloves before they drove to the airport. "I want to go up to seven or eight thousand feet," she said, "and be alone with you up there, above the dust."

"I want to be alone with you in bed," he answered, kissing her, one arm round her as he drove.

"We could drive up to the Kajabbi Hotel. Kajabbi is a former mining town, but it still has a pub and a railway station. I couldn't book in anywhere in Cloncurry till late; I'm too well known."

"Does it matter? Do you care what people think?"

She explained about her new appointment as Flying Sister to the A.M.S.; if gossip should get back to the strait-laced John Flynn, her job might be in jeopardy. But when she said that Kajabbi was sixty miles away over a bad road, he objected.

"Let's fly out along the McKinlay road, and find the first town out of Cloncurry," he said. But they would still have to drive, as most small places near town did not have an airstrip.

That was how they ended up at a little place called Leila Vale on the main road. As they drove, with her sitting as close as possible beside him in the front seat, she told him again how angry she had been at finding he had delayed returning *Circe* when she was ready, and how he'd embarrassed her with his telegram, and all the other things she had been saving up to tell him. He pulled off the road and took her in his arms. He had wired her because a letter would hardly have got to Cloncurry before he did. He had kept the plane for two weeks, because there were several serious cases he had to follow up, people who had been waiting for treatment while he had been lost. ". . .And there'll be a cheque coming to you for mileage from the N.T.M.S."

Caro said she understood, but she still frowned.

"You didn't actually need your craft for anything, did you?" he asked reasonably.

"No, but you might have asked. Why didn't you ask?"

"I don't know. I should have. I'm sorry, darling."

He kissed her, and put a hand inside the front of her white dress with its black buttons, and she ceased to care what he had done.

"Oh hell! I'll try and find a side-track," he said breathlessly, driving on. Soon they found a dirt road, and as soon as they were out of sight of the main road they fell together like two waves mingling. He opened one door and laid her along the back seat and in spite of the confined space in Alix's little car they managed somehow to find a consummation all the sweeter for being unplanned.

There was only one small hotel in Leila Vale, for most travellers, having come so far, would go on to Cloncurry to stay. They were shown to a small dark room with a white honeycomb quilt on the bed and a rickety wardrobe. For dinner there was the inevitable roast, and steamed pudding.

"What about our barramundi?" whispered David. "We should have eaten in Cloncurry; they probably never see fish here." (Fresh barramundi from the Gulf came down to Cloncurry by air once a week from Normanton.)

There was a rather old upright piano in the hotel lounge, which was empty of other visitors. David sat down and played her favourite aria, "Your tiny hand is frozen."

"*Che gelida manina. . .*" he sang, and Caro remembered Malcolm's gramophone, and how he'd been rather superior about her liking Italian opera. David launched into "The very thought of you," and Caro thought what a nice voice he had, and that whatever Malcolm had said she still liked Puccini.

David closed the piano and sat her on his knee, murmuring that he couldn't wait to get her into a real bed, if it wasn't too soon after dinner. But when they got between the rather musty-smelling sheets they found that the wire mattress sagged in the middle like a hammock, so that they rolled together helplessly in the hollow. It also gave forth a rusty squeak, so they ended up putting the mattress on the shiny linoleum floor and sleeping there.

The pair left in high spirits next morning, having paid their bill as "Mr. and Mrs. Carson," a name invented by Caro. But the nearer they got to Cloncurry the nearer they came to parting. Nothing had been resolved. David had not made up his mind to leave his wife; he explained that she was rather conventional and would probably never consent to a

369

divorce. When she saw Caro's photo in the Darwin paper—young, fair, and attractive—she had immediately become suspicious. But when he tried to confess what had happened she had covered her ears. "I don't want to hear; I don't want to know about it" was all she would say. And as long as he was at home, she seemed to shut all idea of his infidelity from her mind. He was still fond of her and did not want to hurt her; but now that his plane was repaired he was determined to go back to Katherine.

"She doesn't want an open break; she wants to keep up appearances; but I'm determined not to live at home," he said.

As she saw him off on the late-morning mail-plane, Caro said bravely, "This is goodbye for a long time, then."

"I'm afraid so. I'll write. And somehow we must arrange to meet. Next time I have a call to north Queensland, perhaps you could fly from Normanton, or we might meet on the Territory border, anywhere. I *have* to see you. And I'll try again for an A.I.M. appointment, even if they won't let me fly."

She knew how much that meant to him. More than wife or home.

They had both worried about the consequences of those few days of love on the beach, but she was beginning to feel that there was no need. She did not *feel* pregnant, and she'd had a normal period. So far all seemed well.

CHAPTER NINETEEN

In Normanton in April 1938, the wet season was coming to an end. At
1 A.M. each day, after having gone to bed in sweltering heat under an
airless mosquito net, Caro was awakened in her bed on the hospital
veranda by a dry, comparatively cool south-easterly. She would pull the
sheet over herself and sleep soundly till dawn.

Normanton had a delightful winter climate, she had been told, with
crisp cool mornings and clear sunlight every day. It never rained, and it
was never cold enough for a fire or blankets. Summer clothes, with a warm
jacket for early morning, lasted all the year. Dust and flies disappeared; but
unfortunately the crocodiles that swarmed in the river were still active,
and made the water out of bounds for swimming.

But there was barramundi on the menu; she ate barramundi or trevally
every day without getting tired of it.

It had taken some time to establish her clinics among the Gulf stations
and on Cape York. A supply of serum and antivenin was kept at the
hospital, and Caro carried it with her in a special kit. She always carried
some butterscotch or barley sugar in her pocket, as Alix used to do for
her children's clinics on Cappamerri station. But when it came to
injections for diphtheria and tetanus, the subjects often had to be held
down by their mothers. She would give them a boiled sweet afterwards,
but still smarting from the needle they were not always ready to make
peace.

Two wild little girls, sisters, lived on one station—unable to read or
write except for the station's cattle-brand, which they could scratch in
the dust. They were almost white, with a white stockman father and
half-Aboriginal mother. After the first sister had been inoculated and
retired bawling, the second refused to come forward. She had to be
dragged by her mother and then sat on by Caro while the needle did its
work. Let go, she retired to the doorway and, glaring at Caro, yelled,
"You bloody bugger!"

"Oh dear! I dunno where she get them words," said her mother
apologetically.

There was a big event in Normanton soon after Caro's arrival. The
Governor-General, an English Peer, was making a tour through northern
Australia. Along with Matron and the resident doctor of the hospital,

371

Caro was invited to sit on the official dais where His Lordship was to be welcomed.

The Mayor of Normanton was a large cattleman. Sweating and nervous, he tore off his broad-brimmed hat, grasped the printed Address of Welcome in his huge fists, and began haltingly to read. He was only a quarter of the way through when he gulped, turned to the dignitary and said, "Here you are, your Governorship, read the bloody thing yourself some time. What about a drink?"

Mrs. Brown, wife of the storekeeper at the large Burns, Philp store in the main street, had provided a meal made all of local products. But not content with baked barramundi, she had cooked dugong soup—a great delicacy—and the visitors had two helpings each. Unfortunately this dish was known locally as "Carpentaria Dynamite," and the result was that the Governor-General and his aide made a track to the Gents all night. It was, as he told the locals before he left in the specially chartered Qantas plane next day, "a memorable visit."

There were only two hotels left in Normanton since the days when it was the port for exporting gold from Croydon, and importing stores for the scattered stations, who now ordered their goods by train from Townsville and had them carried from the railhead by motor-truck. Even cattle were beginning to be transported by truck in some parts; but "up north" the roads disappeared each Wet under sticky black or sandy red mud, and bullock-teams and cattle-droves were still in use.

It was during the Wet that the Flying Doctor planes proved their worth, when rivers were up and roads impassable.

A new Flying Doctor, Dr. White, had been installed at Croydon to co-operate with the sub-base at Normanton. As there was no pilot stationed in the town, the doctor drove to as many calls as possible, or radioed Normanton for a pilot. The first time Caro was called by Dr. White, she had a shock. Dr. Jean White—not "John" as she had mis-heard—was a young woman.

Dr. White was plump and good-humoured, with a head of golden curls and a pleasant personality—"You could have knocked me down with a ring-spanner," Caro wrote to her mother. "We get on very well, and have our own little jokes about things—she had never even been in an aeroplane before she took the job—and she trusts me as a pilot and consults with me as a nurse. I am delighted."

Caro was particularly pleased that the A.I.M. had appointed a woman as Flying Doctor, and it gave her great pleasure to fly to a new place and see the hastily hidden looks of stupefaction when two women climbed out of the plane.

She told Jean White how she had hesitated between medicine and flying as a career, but had felt that the medical course would take too long; so she had settled for flying and nursing. "At least you can get a job

372

in a big hospital in spite of your sex," she said. "But there's no chance of my being employed as a regular pilot with any commercial airline, even though I'm fully qualified."

"Things are gradually getting better, you know. Adelaide was the first university that even admitted women med students. But you won't find any women as medical superintendents of big hospitals. Perhaps the Matrons prefer it that way."

"You mean they don't *want* another woman over them? You may be right," said Caro.

She and Dr. White were soon on first-name terms. They had few arguments, though sometimes Caro had to point out that the weather in Normanton was such that it was impossible even to take off, let alone fly farther north.

What social life there was, centred at the hospital, where the Sisters sometimes gave a party, and the Albion Hotel. It was here that Caro heard the northern version of "Click Go the Shears," beginning "Up in the Gulf, where the Norman River flows," its hero a drunken drover's cook:

He raises up his glass, and drinks down his beer,
Then he starts a-yelling in a voice that grates the ear,
"In all this bloody country, wherever you may go,
I'm the best, the best, the best at anything you know.

"The best at cooking corned beef, the best at cooking stew,
In fact there isn't anything that I cannot do.
I can bake a damper standing on my head,
I'm the best, the best, the best, Oh! enough said. . ."

The doctor's role at Croydon was to work part-time at the Croydon District Hospital, hold radio consultations in the surrounding districts, and attend regular clinics. Normanton would be her base at times.

Caro's first flight with Dr. White was to Vanrook Station on the west of Cape York, where they were called to an urgent case of a child suffering from diphtheria. Caro took along her vaccines to immunize any other children at the station who had not had the disease.

The landing-ground was a good one, according to reports. Hundreds of large white-ant mounds had been levelled and beaten into a hard surface over an area four hundred yards long. It was the only cleared space in a landscape of timber, lagoons, and creeks, and swamps now full of water, which in the Dry would be covered in lush feed for cattle.

The homestead was built on stilts above the reach of flash floods from heavy rain. In the Wet, the Gulf stations would be cut off by water for up to three months, and the cattle walked about in water up to their bellies. There were no bridges over the rivers, as they would only be swept away, and the roads were impassable bogs.

As they landed on the cleared strip with its puddles of rain-water, a utility truck came out from the house and stopped on the far side of a running creek. Rolling up their trousers, the station manager and the station cook (whose daughter was the patient) waded across and gallantly carried doctor and pilot across on their shoulders. The cook went back for the doctor's medical kit.

They rushed doctor and nurse to the homestead, where Dr. White performed a tracheotomy just in time, as the membrane was closing over the child's trachea, and inserted a breathing tube. Though it was rather late, she injected antitoxin direct into a vein.

Caro took this dramatic example as a help in convincing the black mothers that they should bring their young children to the clinic for diphtheria shots. She explained that she would have to come back in a month to give a second booster shot. But since there was obviously a carrier on the station, it was imperative that all groups at risk should be immunized.

They stayed all the next day while the doctor checked the patient's condition, and Caro gave the mother lessons in nursing procedure, for the child was very sick. A storm came up in the night and the following day there was a continuous downpour, so they stayed yet another day, calling in from the station's radio to make sure they were not needed elsewhere.

In spite of the Wet, Vanrook was an attractive place. It had a frontage of miles to the Vanrook Creek, which the homestead overlooked from a high bank. The sleeping quarters were upstairs, to get every breeze. Underneath were rooms open to the outdoors, and floored with concrete, the wooden piles treated against white ants. There were no curtains or carpets; all was simple and uncluttered. Large old mango trees shaded the house, and papayas and brilliant flowering creepers grew in the garden. Lying on a path was the skull of a crocodile, with tooth sockets big enough to admit two fingers. The visitors were told that up to two hundred head of stock were taken each year, and some of the horses had scarred necks and shoulders from near escapes. Though so far from the sea, the river was brackish enough for the big salt-water crocs, known locally as "allygators."

Caro and Jean enjoyed fresh roast beef and fresh fruit, mangoes running with juice, and plump papayas.

The little girl was showing marked improvement by the time they had to leave on the fourth day, recalled to Normanton where the doctor wanted to consult with Dr. White over a patient who had been shockingly mauled by a crocodile when trying to swim to his boat in the Norman River while he was drunk. His mates had pulled him out, but his shoulder and part of his chest had been torn away.

"To think," said Caro with a shudder, "that I actually swam in the coastal waters up here, when we crash-landed on the beach! I wouldn't do it now."

When next a call came for the Cape York area, Caro took her vaccines along.

The call was urgent, to a young boy with symptoms that sounded like meningitis. The message had been sent through from Dunbar Station by way of a blackfellow riding a horse and crossing five flooded creeks to the nearest radio. The message did not arrive till early afternoon. By the time Caro had flown the leg to Croydon, the northern horizon was looking threatening, with black clouds massing. They did not take off again till after three. More cloud was working up from three directions as they set a compass course for the Gilbert River.

The farther north they went, the thicker the cloud became. They flew into heavy rain, then out again into momentary sunshine. Dodging round one towering cloud they came to another, and soon there were only a few gaps in the cloud masses. Below spread a great swampy plain with here and there a creek or a lagoon—if they landed there, the plane would have to stay there for ever. Caro was nervous: she'd had enough of wet-season flying and she longed to pass a note to the doctor suggesting they return to Normanton.

But a child was ill, a mother was waiting in an agony of suspense for the sound of the doctor's plane. Caro came down low, knowing there were no obstructions on this course, and watched for the winding channel of the Gilbert. A welcome break in the weather showed a clearing and a group of buildings on a big river. Caro kept the river in sight till she picked up the road, hidden at times in heavy timber, winding tortuously but tending steadily northwest—this was the route she had followed before to Vanrook Station. Flying at only two hundred feet, for miles she skimmed above the tree-tops, fearful of losing this only guide. Then a ground fog began to close in. As it became thicker she saw through a break in the mist the clearing of Vanrook. She circled, passed a note to Dr. White, and pointed urgently downwards. The doctor nodded. It was better to land than be faced with a possible loss of all landmarks. Water lay all over the ground as before, and more rain threatened. She borrowed a big canvas sheet from the station store and pegged it down over her aircraft.

By this time the light was failing, and it was obvious that to go on would only have been courting trouble. The manager of Vanrook gave them careful directions for Dunbar, another hundred miles of flying if only the weather cleared. At four in the morning Caro and Jean surprised each other on the veranda peering anxiously at the sky for stars; and by 6 A.M. it was obvious that it would clear. A breeze had come up from the south. The cook, whose daughter was quite recovered, got up early to make them a special breakfast.

Before they left Caro rounded up the children to have booster shots of diphtheria antitoxin, for it was nearly a month since she had been there. Then, with the sun just breaking through the last of the clouds, they took off for Dunbar.

The little boy at the station was very ill, too ill to be transported to hospital even if they'd had room. Dr. White confirmed meningitis, and managed to bring his temperature down. She had brought analgesics for the headache, but they were not very effective for the sharp stabs of pain which caused the characteristic yelping cry from the patient. A spinal injection of meningococcus vaccine, and complete quiet and rest, were the best she could do. They took off with instructions to send for the doctor again if there was any deterioration.

The father smiled wryly. "It took four days to get the message through last time. We can only pray. But thank you for coming, Doctor. I believe you have saved his life."

Two months later a letter came through to the hospital for Dr. White. The boy had recovered, though he was still weak. "God bless you and the A.M.S.," the letter ended fervently. The doctor showed the letter to Caro, saying, "This sort of thing makes it all worthwhile. I have begged them to install a radio transmitter as soon as possible. Apparently the local telephone link-up stops working in the Wet."

Sometimes Dr. White would come to the base at Normanton by the quaint little rail-motor that rocked slowly over the ninety miles of narrow-gauge track from Croydon. Caro made the trip there and back just to see the countryside, which was thinly covered with scrub among which plains turkeys and tall grey brolgas stalked. The train did not turn round when they got there; the motorman just walked up to the other end, which had the same controls in reverse.

In days when the gold-field near Georgetown was producing, it had been an important daily train carrying large quantities of gold under escort, to be shipped from Normanton wharf. As it entered the Gregory Range the country became rocky and inhospitable-looking, but Georgetown was now the centre of a beef industry.

"We get plenty of beef there," said Dr. White, "but I long for lamb, or even mutton or pork, for a change. But all we get otherwise is goat. There's only goats' milk and goats' butter. . . . It's all right, you get used to it, but it's an acquired taste."

"I know," said Caro. "We lived on roast goat and goats' milk at Birdsville a lot of the time, when I was at school."

Usually Caro flew down to get Dr. White, and they would visit stations on the way back for regular clinics. At one station an Aboriginal child was brought in with a festering ear that had been "fly-blown." A fly had laid its eggs inside the ear. The eggs had hatched into larvae which had burrowed farther in, and then hatched into adult flies.

Dr. White looked rather sick as she probed among the running mass of suppuration, after giving a local anaesthetic. The child made no sound, just looked at them with her big brown eyes. Caro fetched the long-nosed pliers from the plane's tool-box and probed behind the perforated ear-drum. She had seen this condition before, though not so advanced. There was a pocket of dead flies behind the ear-drum, which had hatched and been unable to emerge. The doctor cleaned up the ear, syringed it out, and dusted it with phenyl powder, while Caro washed her pliers in a bowl of antiseptic. The child would be permanently deaf in that ear.

"How could the parents let it get to such a stage, without seeking help?" said Jean White afterwards.

"I've found the natives are very stoical about pain. I've seen a man walking around on the stump of his leg, which was covered with old scar tissue, after he'd lost his foot in some accident. In the old days, if he couldn't keep up on a walkabout, he'd be left to die."

(She hadn't actually seen this case, which had happened west of Alice Springs; her mother had told her about it once. But Caro preferred to tell her stories in the first person.)

CHAPTER TWENTY

The interest of her new job and her new surroundings helped to ease the pain of parting from David. Already it seemed long ago, but so as not to forget anything, Caro went over and over in her mind the five days they'd had together on the beach, and his even briefer visit to Cloncurry. Their innocent swim in the thermal pools at Mataranka seemed light-years away.

A letter came from Darwin, airmail all the way. David had been called to Borroloola on the Gulf for an urgent operation: an old identity, maddened by the heat and humidity, had quarrelled with his mate over a game of cards, and emptied a shotgun into his chest. There was no doctor or hospital, but the local policeman had made the call for help.

> Dearest, I can't be so near you and not see you [wrote David]. I'll hold a clinic for the few inhabitants and any blacks who are around, and then leave for Doomadgee Mission, then Mornington Island to the Aboriginal Mission there. I expect it's on your regular route for child clinics. What if we just "happened" to meet there, say in four days' time? I'll stay overnight at Mornington in case you can't get there till the next day, or are called away on an emergency. (I presume you don't want me to come to Normanton.)
>
> If anything goes wrong I'll send you a wire—don't worry, it will be circumspect. I leave first thing in the morning for the Gulf, so you can't reply to this. I'll just keep my fingers crossed for us both. And you could send a message to the Mission to have the children ready for a clinic—that will tell me you are coming. How I long to see you!
>
> All my love for always. . . .

Fortunately Dr. White was spending a fortnight at Croydon, so after checking with her that the plane was not needed, Caro told her over the radio that she was taking a clinic on Mornington Island, as she had not called there yet, and would be back some time next day.

It was now four days since the letter had been posted. Terrified that an urgent call would come before she could get away, Caro notified the hospital that they could get in touch with her at Mornington, and took off in mid-morning. By good fortune the sky was clear but for a few fluffy white clouds, the horizon ringed with soft blue. As she skirted the brilliant turquoise waters of the Gulf in a westerly direction, she was singing to herself, "Ah, sweet mystery of life! At last I've found you. . ." She felt intensely alive, high on excitement and youth and love and the joy of flying on a clear blue morning such as this. Beneath her the shallow waters of the Gulf were marked by swirls of orange sand marking the undersea currents, looking like wisps of wind-teased cloud in a blue sky. It was only about 120 miles direct across the sea to Mornington, but she preferred to keep the coast in sight for the first fifty miles, so she flew in a wide arc.

Then ahead she saw the first of the islands, with shallower green water around them. Mornington was forty miles long, and she was aiming for the southwest corner.

As she crossed the scalloped coast, each curving bay was lined with a meniscus of yellow sand and backed with a line of greenery. Sparse open forest covered the land. She dropped lower as she came over the Mission buildings and native huts nestled in a beautiful bay, some on the beach itself.

The airstrip had been cleared on a small island just across a narrow strait from the Mission. Her heart leaped as she saw the little N.T.M.S. plane on the ground—the Tiger Moth with which David had replaced his little Avro Baby.

A group of black children waved from the beach as she was rowed across.

"Isn't that Dr. Trenowith's aeroplane?" she asked disingenuously as she was met by Mr. Wilson, the Superintendent. She was told that he had just flown in that morning, and was even now performing an operation on a woman who had fallen down the steps of her high-set house and almost severed her ring finger.

"So the doctor arrived opportunely," he added.

"What a happy coincidence," said Caro with a smile.

"We thought we'd give you both lunch first, if you would like to hold the clinic afterwards."

Caro had a cup of tea that she didn't want; her throat was constricted and her pulse uneven. When she and David met, they were constrained to a warm handshake and a formal "Hello, Sister!" and "How are you, Doctor?" She returned his smile, which brought out the deep laughter lines in his cheeks and the fine lines etched around his blue eyes. She had known prim smiles, "hearty" smiles showing a lot of white teeth, smiles of spurious friendliness in which the eyes were crinkled and the lips smiled, with no human warmth behind them. His was lighted from within by his love of life and his natural friendliness.

Caro was soon at ease, chatting to the missionaries and remarking on the verdant setting and the attractive garden. They explained that during

379

the Dry it was the children's task to keep the vegetable garden watered, as well as the grass around the buildings, which were set among flowering oleanders and poinciana trees. The men caught dugong and fish and turtle and tended the fowl-runs and pig-pens, so that the Mission was self-supporting and the fine-looking, mostly full-blood people well-nourished and healthy.

After a splendid luncheon of turtle soup, baked fish, and fresh salad, followed by sliced papaya with lemon juice—she liked to see how David enjoyed his meal, the gusto with which he ate, like a starved schoolboy—the children were lined up for Caro's clinic in the little hospital building. While the doctor stood by to examine ears and throats, Caro prepared her syringes and vaccines and treated any new cases of trachoma with eye-drops and ointment. David was good with children, talking to them and reassuring them. A shame his wife refused to have a baby!

After the clinic they at last had a chance to talk in private. She asked him about his trip to Borroloola; she had thought he looked tired when she first saw him, with his rough dark hair uncombed and his thin cheeks hollow.

"It was a bit exhausting," he said. "I operated to remove as many pellets as possible, while the Police Constable held the lamp and insects kept falling into the wound. His liver was as full of holes as a colander. He didn't survive the op. It was so hot we had to bury him straightaway, and as the white ants had eaten all the wood around, we buried him in an old tin tub. His mate who shot him was sober by then, and cried at the funeral. The policeman was upset because he'll have to take him all the way to Darwin to be tried."

His hand touched hers as he helped her pack her medical kit. "I can't stand this," he said in a low voice. "Even if we stay overnight, and they're sure to ask us, we couldn't even go for a moonlight walk along the beach together without causing comment. I love you. I want to kiss you. . . . But I have an idea."

He had thought of a plan whereby they both flew off together, ostensibly in convoy back to the mainland for the sake of safety; and then circled the island and met on one of the beaches on the north-west corner, "in the lee of Thabugan Point," said David. "I'll choose a beach which looks possible for landing—the north shore has no mud and mangroves, and hopefully no estuarine crocodiles—and I'll land first. If the surface is all right I'll wave you down. If not, you just keep flying, and report that you saw me make a forced landing, and the Mission will send round their launch. We must just hope no one is fishing round there who'll spot us. What do you say, darling? Are you game?"

"I am if you are. You're the one who'll be risking your craft."

It all worked as he had planned, and even the weather co-operated. Their two little aeroplanes parked in tandem on a long golden beach, they rigged up a shelter under one wing, and spent an idyllic afternoon —swimming in the emerald-green, glass-clear water close to shore, sunbathing and making love, and nibbling on the fresh fruit and tomatoes from the garden that the kindly missionaries had pressed on them both. They had both filled their water-bottles before leaving.

"It's just like the garden of Eden," said Caro, lying back luxuriously and peeling a banana.

"You make a beautiful Eve, without fig-leaf," he said. "Have you ever heard the Mission version of Genesis given in pidgin by a Binghi? It goes like this:

"'Me bin savvy that old man Cod. Him bin look-im-out that feller Atom, bin talk, Dis-one good place allabout, plenty water, plenty everting make-im tucker along you. You bin sit-down dis place longa you missus, call him Eba.'"

She laughed, then sighed.

"It's sad, you know, they *did* have a Garden of Eden, before the white man came. Except for the desert natives, and even they had their oases and rock-pools. But now, at least in the south, every river and lake and waterhole and billabong—all their favourite camping grounds have been taken over by white men and their sheep and cattle."

"Don't worry, these islanders had a hard time in the dry season, with strong south-easterlies so they couldn't fish; or during cyclones in the Wet with no cover but grass or bark. On small islands there were always killings over women and food. The Bentinck natives are still wild men, they've resisted being Christianized or civilized, and they'll try to kill anyone who lands there. Two of them speared a Mornington man, and the missionary sent for the police. The murderers were rounded up and taken to Burketown gaol, and kept there till the Constable could take them down to Cloncurry for trial. They didn't understand; they thought they were going to be killed straightaway.

"Next thing I was called in—the Cloncurry Flying Doctor was away down the Diamantina—to sew them up. The black tracker who took them their food had given them a tin of jam and showed them how to spread it on their bread. When he went back the first man put his hand through the bars, holding two bloody testicles wrapped in the jam-tin label. The other man was busy sawing away at his second ball with the lid of the tin."

"Whyever would they do such a thing!"

"Nobody knows. Perhaps they thought if they punished themselves like that, the police would let them go. No one could speak their lingo."

"What a horrifying story! Like Van Gogh and his ear."

"They were sent off to Aurukun, or Palm Island or somewhere eventually, far from their own country."

"Their own country means everything to them; perhaps that's why they

381

mutilated themselves," said Caro. "Fearing they'd never see their island or their wives again. . . . But even those who haven't broken the white man's law have been pushed out, haven't they, into land we don't happen to want? And even that will be taken if it's found to contain gold or something else of value."

"We have given them something, though—they didn't have anaesthetics or modern medicine in the old days."

"Perhaps they didn't need them."

"Well, the first op performed at the Alice Springs Hostel when it opened was on a blackfellow, for removal of a cyst as big as a football on the back of his neck. A doctor just happened to see him while travelling in the Territory, and persuaded him to come in. He thought the white-feller medicine was pretty good."

"Yes, that's true. But . . . my mother was depressed by Alice Springs when she lived there. The attitude to the black people who'd been dispossessed, who were forced to live outside the Gap away from the springs. I'd like to see it, though; it must be a beautiful area."

"I believe there's to be a full-scale hospital built there soon; the place is getting too big for the Sisters at the hostel. And a new Flying Doctor base, the first one in central Australia. Why don't we try to get work there? You know I'm leaving Margaret. She won't divorce me and it can't be helped. But I'm not going to live with her any more."

Caro kissed him. "There'll be a scandal in Darwin."

"Oh, she'll cover up somehow. I've always been away a lot, with my job. But it means I can't marry you."

"Do you want to?"

"Of course I do!"

"It doesn't matter, you know. It's only a ceremony and a piece of paper. I feel married to you already."

"Then why are we hiding on the far side of this island? Because society won't let us live together openly."

She sighed. "I know. And if we get a job, any sort of public appointment in a small town, it's going to be difficult."

"Perhaps she'll find someone else, and decide she wants to be free."

"Perhaps."

She was drawing idly in the sand with a piece of white shell. He took it from her and kissed her sand-dusted fingers. He said he would give her a ring anyway; it would be a private bond between them. "Are you superstitious about opals?"

"No, I love them. Particularly the ones with green and blue fire."

"Then I'll get you a ring set with Queensland boulder opal. Outback Queensland is the place for opals. Did you know that south of Winton there was a rush last century? An old fellow was found dead, sitting with his back to a tree. And he was sitting on a flat tobacco-tin full of beaut

382

opals. No one knew where he had dug them! Then someone found Opalton."

They lit a very small fire that night for fear it might be seen—it was just the opposite of their situation at Junction Bay, where they were signalling their whereabouts. Their one night here seemed all too short, though they slept little.

They woke to a perfect morning, with an orange sun lifting from a silky sea of lucent pale-blue. (There were not the enormous tides here that carried the sea away out to the horizon on the far north coast, in Darwin and the north-west.) Against the sea a frieze of twisted pandanus palms and feathery, drooping casuarinas was outlined like a painting in Chinese ink. Each footprint in the soft sand was a pool of blue shadow, the ridges between seemed made of rosy gold. The tide had fallen in the night, and the sea was shallow, exposing the coral rock.

Naked as one of the first original black men, David went out on the reef at the point looking for oysters, taking his pocket-knife with him. He came back with four fat black-lipped oysters, "each one a meal in itself," as he said gleefully. He opened them, assuring Caro that once open they were "already dead." They ate them with some of the bananas from the Mission to follow.

"What, no pearls?" asked Caro in mock disgust. She took one of the shining mother-of-pearl-lined shells for a souvenir.

It was time to go. They dressed, exchanged a last desperate kiss, and departed. He spun the prop for her and she took off first—heading for the sea and the firmer damp sand. *Circe* lifted sluggishly from the beach and circled while he swung the propeller to suck in fuel, climbed back and switched on, climbed out and swung it again until the engine came to life, then quickly dodged the turning blade and strapped himself in the cockpit. Caro held her breath till she saw him safely in the air. They both flew north over the sea so as not to be seen from any Mission boats, then, with a last wave and a dip of their wings, turned away in opposite directions —he towards the north-west, she to the south-east.

Though they wrote to each other regularly, they were not to meet for nearly a year.

Alix wrote that she was going down to Adelaide to see her mother, who was, according to her own account, "not at all well." She was still in the same house, with a live-in housekeeper who, she felt sure, "cooked the accounts" and was lining her own pockets. Alix was actually going to fly, in a Qantas plane with three engines and an enclosed cabin, to Brisbane and Sydney; then she would travel in comfort in the MV "Manunda" round the coast to Adelaide. "I am rather tired of life," the first page of the letter ended. Caro felt a shock. Her mother! With all her energy and strength—surely not! She turned over the page ". . . in a bush town, and it will be nice to visit theatres and the Art Gallery, and above all, the shops. You know Grandma and I could never get on, but I expect we have both mellowed with the years. Anyway, she wants me to come. And I don't think I'll be coming back here."

Caro flew down to Cloncurry for a quick visit to her mother before she left. It was one advantage of having her own plane; she could not have used the Flying Doctor plane for such a trip. She noted the grey threads among Alix's soft curls, but they scarcely showed against the light-brown mass. She still had not cut it; she said it was cooler pinned back away from her face.

"I've been thinking of leaving Cloncurry for some time," said Alix. "I've enjoyed it since I've been in charge of the hospital, but now that I'm nearly fifty I'd like a change. The trouble with Cloncurry is that it's too big—it's neither Sydney nor the bush. I'll either stay in the city or go somewhere far out. I saw an advertisement from the Bush Nurses for a Matron at Forsayth."

"Forsayth! That's really at the end of the line. We don't even fly in there, the Gregory Ranges are out of bounds."

"Yes, well, it's just a thought. And I could pop up to Normanton in that funny little rail-motor from Croydon, to see you."

"Oh, I fly into Croydon. The Flying Doctor is based there part of the time."

"Well, there you are!"

"But I was only appointed for a year. I may not be at Normanton next year."

Caro flew back—it was a little over a two hours' flight to Normanton. Unlike her mother, she was not tired of living in a bush town. Now that the Dry had set in, the climate was monotonously perfect. And the hospital on its gravel ridge, its wide verandas shaded by palms, and with louvered walls to let the breezes through, had been a pleasant place even in summer.

The wide main street was almost empty of traffic. A few dogs slept in the shade of the wooden verandas supported by posts which the dogs seemed to think had been installed for their convenience.

The large Burns, Philp store held few customers, and there were only two hotels left, the National and the Albion. There were no Aborigines about the hotels, for they were not allowed under the law to drink alcohol.

Remembering David's story about the Burketown gaol, Caro asked about the Normanton lock-up when she met the local Sergeant having a drink at the Albion, asking him if he had many native prisoners.

"I have three Abos in at the moment," he said.

"What are they in for?" she asked the Sergeant, who was large and red-necked but quite affable.

"Murder. Some tribal business."

"And what proportion of prisoners would be natives?"

"Aw, I'd say about seventy—no, eighty per cent. They're brought in from the smaller settlements round, our mob are fairly law-abiding. Mostly get run in for being drunk or being in possession of liquor."

"And what about the white men who sell it to them? Do you run them in too?"

"Not often," he said with a grin. "Not writing a book, are you, Sister?" asked the Sergeant as she walked away.

"No; just curious."

Caro was not a member of the hospital staff but, like an honorary medical officer, she helped out when they were busy with no payment but for her board, and an unofficial bed on the hospital veranda. With calls to all points of the compass, and fishing trips and picnics on the river, even a hair-raising expedition after wild pig, her life was full and interesting. There was just an aching void at the centre of it that David had left when he flew away.

A beautiful opal set in an antique silver ring arrived in the post. Pleased that it was not of traditional gold and diamonds, Caro wore it defiantly on the engagement finger of her left hand. Interested inquiries about its significance from Matron and Dr. Jean she turned away with a laugh, saying it just happened to fit that finger. She would gaze into its shifting fires of purple and green, peacock-blue and orange as in colder climates she might have gazed into a wood fire—dreaming and seeing pictures of a possible future. She decided to take the piece of opal Alix had sent her from Cloncurry years ago and have it made into a matching silver brooch.

CHAPTER TWENTY-ONE

Frances MacFarlane died in October 1938, in the home where she had lived for more than fifty years. Alix nursed her with professional skill, reluctantly noting the progressive stages of kidney failure until it was obvious the end was near. The doctor wanted her to go to hospital, but Frances refused. She wanted to die in her own bed. Her mind was clear almost to the end.

Alix saw her become disorientated and finally sink into a coma. She was seventy-six; but when Alix, who had been sitting by the bed, got up to close her mother's faded blue eyes for the last time, she thought how youthful and unlined her face looked as it relaxed in death. Alix had thought she was used to death after years of nursing; but this was her mother's, and she could not watch it unmoved.

She walked to the window and looked out at those close and friendly hills she remembered as a child. Their turf was still green at the end of winter, though they would soon bleach to pale gold in the burning summer months. The colour was made more vivid by the yellow light of the declining sun. She remembered how, more than twenty-six years ago, she had built a cairn of stones on top of the nearest hill and dedicated herself to nursing. How idealistic she had been!

And yet, looking back, Alix knew she had brought comfort and help to many. Why then was she so dissatisfied with her life? The trouble was that Cloncurry Hospital had not provided a challenge; though far out west, it was no longer isolated with two passenger trains a week and a mail-plane every other day.

At Cloncurry she'd not had enough responsibility; perhaps she should have applied for one of the little Bush Nurse places, such as Julia Creek, where the Matron used to pull teeth on the hospital veranda, and had only one nurse on her staff.

At twenty-three, thought Alix, she would have taken on anything: even Marree—bare, hot, and dusty, at the start of the Birdsville Track . . . but in those days she'd had Mab beside her; Mab who was buried in that tiny cemetery half-way to Alice Springs. Between them they'd had to be doctor, midwife, dentist, cook, laundry worker, and spiritual adviser.

She was tired of western Queensland, had not liked the Alice; she was close to fifty and felt she was not young enough to take on a desert outpost again. Yet she did not want to live in the city, especially one so far from Caro's field of operations.

Meanwhile she was in no hurry. She would take a holiday, and next year apply for a nursing position in the far north, in what was known as the "Top End". That was Caro's territory, too. At present she was two thousand miles away from her daughter.

After the funeral and all the chores of sorting her mother's personal things and giving away her clothes, Alix dismissed the housekeeper and enjoyed the luxury of being entirely alone. She rose when she felt like it and ate when she was hungry, and hardly ever looked at the clock. But from habit she was usually up early, when the hills were still silhouetted against the clear eastern sky, their stark outlines softened by a delicate fringe of gum-trees as fine as black lace. She would wander round the garden, watching the light grow and listening to the glorious carolling of magpies, their voices clear as dew. As the sun rose, the dew winked from the lawn in jewel colours —ruby, topaz, sapphire, and emerald.

It was years since she'd seen a heavy dew on green grass!

Though she would be comfortably off and did not have to earn a living, Alix did not intend to stay indefinitely in her mother's house. She was no gardener and would soon become bored with nothing to do. Nursing had been her life, and she had no intention of retiring, although from much standing and walking the wards she had developed varicose veins.

What about Darwin? It was isolated enough, a frontier town with a three-to-four-month-long Wet, then months of perfectly dry weather. A supply vessel called once a fortnight, and the weekly train service ended in the middle of nowhere, still seven hundred miles short of the Alice Springs line from Adelaide; and it was completely cut off by road—if you could call it a road—during the Wet. These days it was connected by air with Brisbane, and Darwin Harbour was a base for the big Qantas flying boats bringing airmail from overseas. She remembered how as a child she had been taken to the Outer Harbour to meet some relative arriving by mail-boat from England. The huge ship's side had towered like a cliff above the wharf. Those ships were then the only link with the other side of the world. Now Darwin, with its small white population far outnumbered by Chinese, Malays, Aborigines, and islanders, was to become Australia's front door.

Frances had died just after Caro's twenty-third birthday. When Alix wrote to tell her the sad news, she added that Frances had left her five thousand pounds. "So Grandma has given you a very special birthday present. And I hope," she added, "that you will not spend all the money on an aeroplane; but I expect you will. At least you will be safer in a bigger machine with a second engine."

When probate was granted on her grandmother's will, the solicitors sent a bank draft to Caro's account with the Bank of New South Wales at Normanton. She looked at all those lovely noughts after the five, and realized that now she could buy a brand-new cabin aeroplane and be free of helmet, goggles, and flying-suit forever. Good old Grandma!

Her year's contract with the Aerial Medical Service was nearly over. Though Jean White was staying on for another year, Caro did not apply for an extension. In two months she would be free to leave.

She wrote to David to tell him her news, and that she was planning to buy a new aircraft. It must have an enclosed cabin, a self-starter and brakes, twin engines, and a cruising speed of more than a hundred miles an hour. She preferred a biplane, which she had been used to. By removing half the passenger seats, there would be plenty of room for a stretcher and a mobile transceiver, making a complete ambulance plane. A DH 84 Dragon would cost her between £4,000 and £4,500, and she hoped to get £500 for *Circe*.

David wrote back delightedly:

This should clinch your getting an appointment as Flying Doctor pilot at the new Alice Springs base. You know work has already started on the hospital and they should open early in 1939. The South Australian branch is to be responsible for the new Flying Doctor radio base, and the Commonwealth Government will pay for the doctor's salary and the charter aircraft. As I'm already on their payroll up this end, I shouldn't have any trouble getting a transfer to the Alice. You know Flynn doesn't like doctors to fly themselves, but I'll be flying down in my Moth anyway. (Perhaps you'll let me be pilot sometimes while we're out in the bush!)

Of course, he wrote, she could always get a position on the staff at the Public Hospital if she didn't get the A.M.S. appointment. But he knew how much flying meant to her. He ended:

It would be marvellous if we could both be posted to the same town, and legitimately fly round the country together like we did in Katherine. That was the happiest time of my life, though all too brief. My darling, I can't wait to see you. . .

Caro wrote back:

You know how it is. Flying is my life. But I suppose I could go back to nursing in order to be near you. Though with a beautiful big new kite, how could I bear not to use it? Perhaps I could set up a charter-flight business in opposition to Connellan Air. No, there wouldn't be enough work for both.

I expect the positions will be advertised by the A.I.M. Board in Sydney. We should get priority by offering to bring two more aircraft, an ambulance plane and a back-up plane, with us.

She made some inquiries of the A.I.M. Sisters stationed there about the conditions at Alice Springs. She knew it had grown considerably since her mother's term there, but would like to know more about the town today.

They wrote back that the Alice was still a one-pub town, but the work of the A.I.M. hostel had increased beyond the capacities of the present three Sisters and the limited number of beds. Apart from the locals, there was a stream of transients, disappointed prospectors who had been lured to the Territory by false reports of the Granites and Tanami gold finds, or tales of Lasseter's lost reef, supposed to be fabulously rich. Then there were the fettlers who worked to keep the 'Ghan line in repair, or rebuild it when it was periodically washed away in floods or buried in sand. Others, who fossicked for gold on worked-out fields, wandered in for treatment for every-thing from sandy blight to cirrhosis of the liver. Then there were the mica miners in the Harts Range, and the Aborigines at Hermannsburg Mission. There would be plenty of work for the new hospital, apart from the cases brought in by the Flying Doctor.

So the change was inevitable, the Sisters wrote, though it would be sad in a way to see the end of the work after more than twelve years. They sent their regards to her mother, who was still remembered there.

Caro had ordered a new DH 84 Dragon from De Havilland in England. It was a twin-engined biplane with enclosed cabin for a pilot and six passengers, and even an on-board lavatory. What luxury it would be after the Moth! With greater speed and reliability, yet not too large for landing on small station airstrips.

Caro decided to advertise her Moth in the Brisbane *Courier* and in the larger western newspapers. By luck she found a buyer in a wealthy grazier near Winton; nearly twenty years had passed since Qantas brought aviation to the town, and the locals were becoming quite air-minded.

Caro took a day off and flew down to Winton by way of Cloncurry, where she stopped to refuel. She took the buyer up for a flight, explaining that she could not deliver the machine until she'd finished her stint with the A.M.S. in Normanton. He was delighted with the Moth's performance as she took him through some mild aerobatics, steep banks, side-slips, and dives.

He paid a deposit at once, and asked her to fly the plane down to Brisbane when she was ready and deliver it to him there. He had enrolled for a course at a flying school. This suited Caro very well.

When she had word, late in February, that her aircraft would arrive in Sydney in three weeks, she said goodbye to Jean White and her other Normanton friends, and left the steamy north with relief. She hoped to be going to Alice Springs, in the dry heart of the continent, where the average rainfall was less than ten inches a year, and nearly all of that in the summer months.

Caro had some sentimental regrets at handing *Circe* over to her new owner in Brisbane, but was borne up by excitement at seeing all the aircraft at Archerfield, including the Avro 10 airliner in which she would fly down to Sydney.

In Sydney she watched breathlessly through the big square windows as they flew above the magnificent harbour, with its extended waterways and wooded promontories, the ferries criss-crossing the blue waters, and the giant single-span bridge which now linked the north and south shores. She was still holding her breath as they glided down and landed at Mascot Aerodrome. There had been no amenities on board for passengers except for chewing gum, and paper bags in case of airsickness, but Caro had thoroughly enjoyed the flight.

She spent a week being a tourist, enjoying the city sights. There had still been no word from the A.I.M. Board about an appointee to the Alice Springs base, so she called at their office in Sydney. It seemed a letter had been sent to Normanton just after she left. She had been given the job of pilot. "As you were already an Australian Aerial Medical Service pilot in Normanton who had given satisfactory service, your appointment was the obvious choice." They would charter her new plane at 6d. a mile, with a retainer of £1,650 a year, and provide her with accommodation in Alice Springs.

"Er . . . could you tell me," she said casually, "do you know who the new Flying Doctor is?"

The man consulted a piece of paper with maddening deliberation, while her heart seemed to stop beating with suspense.

"Yes," he said at last, "it seems we have appointed a Dr. David Trenowith, formerly of the Northern Territory Medical Service in Darwin."

The next day she took delivery of her new silver Dragon, with its gold and maroon stripes running from nose to tail. She thought it the most beautiful thing she had ever seen, and she christened it *Fafnir*, after the Wagnerian dragon.

CHAPTER TWENTY-TWO

After she had got the feel of her new craft, flying down the coast and inland over the rugged scarps of the Blue Mountains, Caro decided to get the unwanted seats removed, leaving three for doctor, nurse, and passenger, as well as a patient on a stretcher. Though, as she was a nurse as well, they would hardly need to take one. She could fill the stretcher space with extra fuel and provisions for her long flight to the centre, and, most important, an emergency supply of water. She planned to fly in a wide arc, from Sydney, north-west and west and finally south down the Telegraph Line, so as to avoid the worst deserts like the Simpson.

Across the seemingly endless blacksoil plains she flew, out beyond Bourke and the Darling River, to the red sand-hill country beyond Windorah. But when she came to her old friend the Diamantina, she could not recognize those parched and sandy plains. The whole countryside was covered in water—or if not exactly covered, it was patterned over most of its surface with winding channels full to the brim and flooding over their shallow banks. A late monsoon in the north had sent an almighty flood down into the Channel Country. For the first time she was seeing all its vast spread of braided channels filled and flowing, which she had known only as shallow sandy depressions with lignum scrub or an occasional long waterhole lined with reeds and trees. Only from the air was it possible to comprehend the size of the flood. No need to worry about perishing for lack of water!

The country would soon be covered with a new growth of annual saltbush, daisies, crimson desert pea, and yellow billy-buttons.

Too late for Cappamerri, denuded as it was of its perennial shrubs and nearly buried in sand-drifts. She felt a temptation to make a diversion down-river to see her grandfather, but she resisted it. Her last sight of the place had been depressing. And David would be in Alice Springs by now, impatiently awaiting her arrival.

She made an overnight stop at Bedourie, then followed the flooded Georgina—though its channel in parts was fifty miles wide—up to Urandangie. She was back in familiar country, and soon crossed the Northern Territory border, to follow a stock-route to the Overland Telegraph Line and the track to Alice Springs. It was when she saw this landmark at last, not far from Tea Tree Well, that she relaxed. She had not realized how tense she had been on this long solo flight over so much inhospitable territory. She should have installed a radio in her Dragon before leaving. But flying it was much safer than flying the Moth, with two reliable British engines to keep her airborne, new navigational instruments, and a better speed over the ground. She had twice the horsepower in each of the two engines than in the Moth's one; and the range was greater.

There was no need for anxiety; she had not even used up her spare fuel. It was just that life had become so precious, she had a foolish dread that she would not live to see David again.

Because she had come down the track, Caro had to cross the narrow rampart of the Macdonnell Ranges, which stretched across the land from east to west like a wall of orange-yellow rock. The Alice airport was south of the range, outside the town.

Below were white roofs and the green of gum-trees, a patch of blue water in the sandy, tree-filled bed of the Todd, and there was the railway line from the south, with the road and the Telegraph Line all passing through the narrow Gap like threads through the eye of a needle.

The Dragon bumped heavily up and down in the thermals coming up from the heated ground, the wings quivered like those of a living creature. The air was thin because of the high altitude, for the Alice was two thousand feet above sea-level and in hot weather heavily laden planes had difficulty in taking off. Caro banked and turned below Mount Gillen into the south-east wind for landing.

Someone from the A.M.S. base, where the radio tower and power units were being installed, had seen her coming in from the north and was even now driving out to meet her. She sat quietly and let herself relax, after taking out a mirror and touching up her lipstick. It had become a habit; she felt vaguely undressed without it. Besides, it kept her lips from cracking in the dry air. She still was amazed at the comfort of her new aircraft—no rush of wind, no roar of noise, no helmet and goggles. She had worn her white overalls for practicality and comfort, laundering them at overnight stops. In Sydney the shops had gone to her head, and suddenly realizing she had plenty of money, she had bought a whole new wardrobe. At last there was plenty of room for luggage.

And then after all David was not there.

The person who came to meet her was an old friend of her mother's, Maurie Anderson, who had been in charge of the Cloncurry radio base station for years. He had come to supervise installation of the Alice Springs base in its handsome new building.

It was a project of the newly formed South Australian section of the Flying Doctor Service, still called the Australian Aerial Medical Services. He told Alix he intended to stay to run it. "So there'll be at least two of us from Queensland," he said. "But Dr. Trenowith from Darwin is to be the Flying Doctor, did you know?"

"Yes," said Caro.

"He'll be paid by the Commonwealth to service the whole of the Northern Territory," said Maurie, "or at least the southern part of it, with a four hundred mile radius from the Alice, well over the border into South Aus."

Adelaide, he explained, had always been the closest capital city to the centre, because the early explorers like Sturt and Stuart had started from there, and because the thousand-mile 'Ghan railway joined it with Alice Springs like an umbilical cord. The Alice's Adelaide House, the A.I.M. hostel, had been financed greatly by South Australian contributions.

"I know," said Caro. "I went to a Presbyterian college, and every week we had to give some of our pocket-money to the A.I.M."

"Your mother's connection with the Mission hostels goes back to 1912, I believe—at least twenty-five years."

"Yes, before I was born."

He drove her to see the new base, its big building completed, next door to Adelaide House.

"You can make yourself known to the Sisters when you've unpacked. I'm afraid they've been rather overworked with transferring their patients to the new hospital, and the hostel is no longer the social centre that it was. We're putting you up at the Stuart Arms for a few days while they are furnishing your rooms at the new hospital building. We thought Dr. Trenowith's wife was coming with him, so a suitable house was bought; then we'd thought he might share with his pilot—until we found that the pilot was to be a lady."

He gave her a bright, direct look. Caro, who'd had a wild desire to laugh at these explanations, straightened her face. How much did he know, or guess? After all, he had been a radio man in Cloncurry when she and David were lost together, and when David flew down to return her plane.

"He's not here yet?" she asked, forcing her tone to be casual.

"Not yet. He had some engine trouble, and is waiting for a spare part for his plane to be flown up from Brisbane. He should be here in a few days."

A few days! What were a few days compared with the months of separation that had passed? And yet, after all her excited anticipation, she felt a bitter disappointment.

The resident doctor's wife hailed Maurie from her front step as he was passing. She welcomed Caro to the town, saying she'd heard all about her, and invited her to take a meal with them that night. Caro was pleased to see that Mrs. Reilly—she judged her to be in her early thirties—was wearing casual garb of shirt, shorts, and sandals, but no doubt she would

393

change for dinner. Caro decided to wear one of her pretty new dresses from Sydney.

Already she liked her new home. There was a clear freshness in the air, and as the shadows lengthened, she noticed a faint tinge of blue, too thin to be called a haze, which softened the ocherous colours of Heavitree Gap. It was as though the air itself were tinted with sky-colour. The driest months were beginning, and from horizon to horizon the sky was clear of cloud.

When the sun set there was an instant drop in temperature, as though a giant radiator had been switched off. The stars began to sparkle frostily. She found she needed a long-sleeved jacket over her light summer frock.

The Reillys even had a small fire going, more as a decoration than because it was needed.

"Firewood is so cheap," explained the doctor's wife, who was a small, neat, dark-haired woman with a ready smile, her hair cut unfashionably short. "Our house-boy collects it for us; he enjoys going 'bush' for a day or two. He has a little camp in the back garden and cooks on his own fire."

Caro listened, feeling she must be in Africa. A part-Aboriginal maid in a clean print dress had brought the pre-dinner drinks and waited at table.

"And how old is your 'boy'?" asked Caro.

"He doesn't know. I'd say about twenty-six."

"And what is his name?"

"He's called Pumpkinhead, or Pumpkin for short," said the doctor. His face was brown, but he was indubitably a "White."

Caro was familiar with this way of putting down the Aborigines, as though they were less than men—by calling them "boys," at whatever age, and by using belittling or comic names—Goggle-Eye, Snowball, Sunny Jim, Charcoal—to emphasize their non-status.

"Pumpkin wanted me to take his sister on as a house lubra," said Mrs. Reilly, "and when I asked if anyone would recommend her, and whether she could cook, he said 'No-more, Missus, but him bin in gaol!'"

"Yes, most of them have been in gaol at some time," said her husband.

Dr. Reilly had been until recently Deputy Chief Protector of Aborigines in Alice Springs, a position with rather vague duties.

"Before there was a doctor at Tennant Creek," he said, "I sometimes had to travel by car to Tennant to see a patient too ill to be moved. Nearly seven hundred miles there and back."

They'd had to carry a barrel of water and forty gallons of fuel. At the sandy creek crossings they would let air out of the tyres, and then pump them up again after they'd crossed.

"I used to go with him," said Mrs. Reilly. "It took us fourteen hours to get there; and once, with a very sick boy, we had to make the trip three times in one week."

"Having an ambulance plane stationed here, and a Flying Doctor, will make a wonderful difference," he said. "I know Dr. Trenowith; he's a fine doctor, and a most resourceful man. I'm looking forward to his arrival."

Caro glowed. "So am I!" she said.

"Of course you know him, as you've been working in the far north. I've never been in the Gulf country. What were the flying conditions like there?"

And for the rest of the evening they exchanged stories of their various adventures in the more isolated parts of Australia.

"We'll have a little dinner party to welcome you and Dr. Trenowith when he arrives," said Mrs. Reilly as Caro took her leave. "Nothing big —just a few friends who'd like to meet you. I don't think we've ever had a woman pilot here before, certainly not one who's a trained nurse as well."

A message came to the base the next day from Katherine, saying David would be arriving on Thursday. The doctor's wife organized her welcoming party for that night; Dr. Trenowith was used to long flights and she was sure he would not be too tired.

So on the first night of their reunion, when they'd had time for only a few hurried words before he was borne off by the officials of the town, he and Caro found themselves seated at a table with eight other guests, making conversation and longing to be alone.

David almost ground his teeth. Where he sat, on the same side as Caro, he could hardly hear her voice for the buzz of conversation; he could not see her face to signal his love with his eyes. They might as well have been a thousand miles apart still. Caro, seated on Dr. Reilly's right by the head of the table, wondered if Mrs. Reilly had done it on purpose: placing Dr. Trenowith at the other end, on her own left. A new man in a small town was always of interest to the local women.

After dinner Caro managed to speak with David, who hastily told her where his house was.

"I'm at the Stuart Arms Hotel," she murmured. "Room Ten."

"Your place or mine?"

"Mine, I think."

It was nearly midnight before they were at last alone. There were two single beds in Caro's room. They squeezed into one—"It beats the back seat of a Morris Minor," said David. "Oh, darling! Isn't this wonderful? I've dreamed of you so often."

After, as they lay twined under the blanket (for the night was chilly, the sky frosty with stars) he asked, "Was it as good as the first time?"

She shook her head. "No."

"No?"

Then at his disappointed look she laughed, and said, "Better."

He kissed her neck. "That dinner party! I thought it would never end. And you looked so lovely in that greeny-blue thing."

She had not known whether she was expected to wear a long dress, and the other women had done so; but she'd compromised with a new silk frock with a low-cut back and a finely pleated skirt, in the new fashion colour of teal blue. It went with her opal ring and she wore the matching opal brooch at the neck.

She looked over the side of the bed now and laughed to see the expensive dress crumpled on the floor where she had stepped from it, beside her scattered underwear.

They talked aeroplanes until far into the night, and he approved of *Fafnir* as a name, though he thought it sounded rather masculine. He felt that aeroplanes were feminine—"unpredictable, with lovely lines, and responsive to skilled handling"—and he was longing to try her—him—it—in a short flight if Caro would let him.

"Of course I will. And sometimes, when we go out on a call, it will be better for the nurse to stay with the patient while the doctor flies the machine, don't you think, Doctor?"

"You darling!"

He left well before dawn, meeting no one in the hotel, and found that the town was asleep.

John Flynn arrived by air for the official opening of the new base on April 19. Flynn's "mantle of safety" was spreading in overlapping rings, soon to include Broken Hill in New South Wales as well as the Western Australian bases, while Queensland was to get a second base at Charleville.

Caro moved to comfortable rooms at the new hospital, a bedroom and small sitting-room. No one worried about what time she got in, so she was able to visit David in his house, which was in walking distance. She could hardly believe that everything had turned out so well.

CHAPTER TWENTY-THREE

Their first medical call together was from a station north-west of Alice Springs, almost half-way to the Western Australian border. This had been some of the last land taken up, for the Aborigines were implacably hostile until they had been "subdued," that is, shot into submission.

Old bushmen could describe narrow escapes, when they had slept away from their roll of blankets, and in the morning found the bedding riddled with spears. There was still an occasional murder on both sides; but white men were not supposed to take the law into their own hands these days. Those who did so were actually brought to court by the local police and charged with murder; but they were never found guilty and it would be unthinkable that they could hang.

At Coniston Station a boy had come off a motor bike, landing on a rocky outcrop. His people had radioed for advice, being afraid to move him in case his spine might be injured. David ascertained that it did not sound like concussion, but the boy had vomited blood.

"We'll come at once," he said. "Keep him warm and give him nothing but fluids."

He called Caro, who went ahead of him to the airstrip to warm up the engines and check fuel; then they clawed their way up through the thin air and circled for height to cross the Macdonnells. It was early afternoon. The ground had begun to heat up and the flight was bumpy.

The airstrip turned out to be dusty but with a fair surface. The injured lad was out near Brooks' Soak, his mother with him. The station hands who came to meet the plane would drive the doctor there at once. Caro went along to help.

Mrs. Royston, the mother, was a typical battler, daughter of a pioneer. She was widowed and now acted as housekeeper to old Randal Stafford, who had been at the station since the early days when it had been one of the farthest west. Mrs. Royston had not panicked, but she clasped Caro's hand in a convulsive grip that showed her controlled emotion.

While the station hands lifted the empty stretcher out of the truck, the Flying Doctor was testing for reflexes, and told the mother there seemed to be no spinal injury, or concussion. But the boy was grey-faced and complained of pain in his lower back. David, listening to his sighing breaths, suspected internal bleeding.

397

"I'll give him a shot of morphia and then we'll get him into the utility," he said. "Don't worry, we'll have him safe in a hospital bed by tonight."

While they were loading the boy into the back of the station truck, Caro caught sight of a marble monument enclosed by railings, half-hidden by silvery grass. She walked over and read a short memorial verse, and the inscription:

In memory of Frederick Brooks
Murdered on 7th August 1928
—a true and staunch mate . . .
His old mate,
Randal Stafford

"Only ten years ago!" remarked Caro.

"Yes, this is the spot where Fred Brooks was speared," said the boy's mother. "It's been called Brooks' Soak ever since."

"And what happened to the Aborigines? Were they caught?"

"Oh, Constable Murray went out with a posse and rounded them up. I believe they shot at least twenty, probably a lot more. A big inquiry was held, but it found that the shooting was justified."

As they drove back to the airstrip Mrs. Royston asked if she could come with her son to the hospital.

Caro looked at David, who nodded. He was checking the boy's weak pulse.

Back at the hospital it was found that he was passing brown urine. He had ruptured a kidney and would have died without speedy treatment.

When he was on the mend Mrs. Royston sought out Caro and once more pressed her hand. "Thank God for the Flying Doctor's plane!" she said. "In the old days, he would have died. It's such a relief to us poor mothers who worry about our sons."

They had a few days without any calls, so David and Caro explored the town and climbed Anzac Hill in the early morning; then and at sunset there was deeper colour in the landscape. "It's a land of opal and iron oxide," said Caro, looking at the fiery rocks glowing through the misty blue atmosphere. Hundreds of kites, as always, circled high in the blue, like black cinders rising above a fire. The town's white roofs and green trees spread below.

"Look!" said David, pointing away from the town.

She stood within the circle of his arms, and leaning back against his shoulder followed the direction of his pointing hand. A pair of wedge-tailed eagles was circling into the sky, in wide, sweeping arcs. Their wings were outstretched, unmoving, as they rose effortlessly on the thermal currents as the bare rocks heated up.

"Wonderful flyers!" he said. "A seven-foot wing-span!"

"Yes. And pelicans—I used to watch the pelicans climbing like that at Birdsville when I was eight or nine. I think that's when I decided I wanted to be a flyer, too."

He kissed her. "What a dear little girl you must have been."

The next day they went out to Emily Gap and had a swim between the leaning walls of red rock, where centuries ago an Aboriginal artist had drawn patterns in yellow ochre. When no calls had come by 4 P.M., David asked if she'd like to "come for a spin" with him. He thought she might like to see Barrow Creek, where the old original Telegraph Repeater Station was still standing. It had been built like a fort, but the two men stationed there had been speared to death in 1874.

It was only about a 170-mile hop, he told her, and his little Moth could land beside the Telegraph Line, though there were stony jump-ups all around. The Line had for many years been the main stock-route, with wells at regular intervals, and a strip on either side was bare of vegetation. As they flew above the vast Burt Plain, for sixty miles they seemed to be passing over a field of yellow wheat, with clumps of grey mulga.

"That was spinifex," David told her afterwards when she asked about it. "Spinifex in seed. It grows higher than the bonnet of a motor car."

They passed Tea Tree Well and Connor's Well, following the Telegraph Line, then circled above the tiny township of Barrow Creek and landed beside the old stone buildings of the station. There were a single small pub, a police station, and the store. The sun blazed down on the treeless red soil, and they made for the dense black shade of the station veranda. The Constable came over to see if they were in trouble, but they explained they were just skyborne tourists.

"We're starting to get quite a lot of vehicles through these days," he said. "The centre's not what it used to be. Next thing I'll have to go on point duty to direct the traffic."

After yarning to the policeman for a while, they walked over to look at the memorial stone marking the graves of the Telegraph Station master and the linesman who had been speared. The Constable told them that the place was built in the shape of a fort, with the buildings in a square facing inwards and large iron gates that could be closed. They had not been expecting an attack and were caught outside; one fell dead in the doorway and the other managed to get inside, but died that night after sending a Morse message for help up and down the line.

"Of course, there was a punitive expedition under the Superintendent of black trackers in central Australia; they went out and they shot every black person they came across. For years no blackfeller ever came within miles of Barrow."

"I think I could do with a beer," said Caro as the policeman left them. "I wonder how many really died?"

David shrugged. "In northern Queensland years ago a man was speared and mutilated; they left his severed head in the camp oven at his camp. It was said to be some trouble over a gin. . . . His mate who found him was so moved that he wrote a poem of vengeance:

For every bone in this poor corpse,
A Kalkadoon shall die!

"Do you know how many bones there are in the human body?"

"No. But I'm sure he was being rhetorical."

"More than two hundred. . . I don't know how many Kalkadoons there were, but they were never any problem again. They were 'dispersed,' as the term was in Queensland for wholesale slaughter."

"Yes. I definitely want a beer."

In the dark little bar of Barrow's only pub they drank with three miners in from the copper mines to the east. The miners had heard the plane come in, and learning who the pair were, insisted on buying them a beer.

"A mate of mine was out at the wolfram mines," one of them said. "He fell down a shaft and broke his pelvis, and the doctor from Cloncurry flew over from Queensland and took him back to hospital. The Flying Doctor Service is all right, I reckon."

As they left the bar David explained that wolfram was in demand because of the rumours of war now shaking Europe. It was used to make tungsten for hardening steel, used in armaments.

"There won't be another war!" said Caro. "I just don't believe the world could be mad enough to go through that again."

"I don't know. The League of Nations proved pretty useless in the war in Spain—though that was ostensibly a civil war—and in its attempts to stop Italy invading Abyssinia. The Germans and the Italians have been having a practice run in bombing techniques. If it does come, the aeroplane will be far more important than in the last war."

Right behind the Telegraph Station building the small rocky hills rose, their sides divided by gorges down which the marauding natives had poured when the station was attacked. David and Caro, now that the afternoon was cooler, climbed to the top of one, and as they stood looking out at the view saw a movement on the far side of the level top. A yellow-coated dingo, with a white tip to his tail, was hastily departing down the opposite side from where they had climbed up.

When they took off again the rocks were painted by the richer yellow light of the declining sun. Distant red walls had clefts of deep cobalt shadow, and the trunks of ghost-gums stood out starkly white against them. From the air the ground was yellow, orange, and red, with patches of grey mulga like dark shadows. They landed south of the Gap just after sunset, when the western sky was banded with apricot and pearl, and the blue-misted ridges shone a ghostly red in the afterglow.

They ended their sightseeing the next day, when there'd been no calls by late afternoon, with a picnic out to Simpson's Gap where there was a permanent scenic waterhole among the ranges fifteen miles to the west. They walked far up the white sandy bed of the stream which over the millennia had cut this mighty slice through the Macdonnell Ranges, but which now rarely ran. Because it was a weekday they felt safe from people, and making their way along a little branching gorge, made love in the warm sand in the shade of a pure-white ghost-gum topped with green.

"Strange to think we're in the very heart of Australia," murmured Caro. "A hundred years ago no white man had ever seen it."

"Not quite the centre. Central Mount Stuart is near enough to the middle of the continent. We flew quite close to it near Barrow Creek."

Feeling a need to go behind a rock, Caro walked on farther and squatted behind a smooth overhang of yellow stone. There were no Aboriginal paintings, but a few graffiti. Some idiots had carved their initials, even as they had defaced some of the ghost-gums, for this was a popular picnic spot. Seeing some writing scrawled higher up, Caro stood to read it. The message had been drawn with a piece of orange ochre stone.

She came stumbling back through the sand to join him, her face stiff with shock.

"What is it? What's up?" asked David, taking her hand. She turned her face away. "You look as if you'd seen something nasty up there."

"I have! Something so revolting, I've scratched it off with a stone and sand. In this lovely, peaceful place! How could they?"

"What was it?"

"I don't think I could repeat it. Have you got a pencil?"

He took a small notebook out of his shirt pocket, with a pencil attached. She sat down and wrote:

Near this spot the Mayor of Alice Springs had his first gin. He said afterwards that he'd as soon have fucked a black dog.

"Pretty low!" commented David.

"It's hateful! The utter contempt of it—the denial of humanity—"

"That's just it, I'm afraid. The blacks are not regarded as human beings by some of the locals. I don't think a tourist did it. You've heard it—'Murdering niggers' . . . 'You can't trust a nigger,' and so on."

"Anyway, let's go back to the car. I feel sick."

That night, under the frosty stars, they went to the open-air picture theatre, taking a rug against the chill air and the thin canvas deck-chairs in which the white patrons sat. At the very front of the theatre, which had walls but no roof, the Aborigines sat on straight chairs in the worst seats. A piece of rope was stretched across to mark the boundary between

401

the races. Their seats were cheaper, but no European, not even children, sat in them.

On the wolfram field near Hatches Creek a miner had been taken ill with acute appendicitis. His mates had taken him into the township and called the base at Alice Springs.

It was afternoon by the time they got the message and Caro and David set off to transfer the sick man to the nearest hospital at Tennant Creek. He would need an immediate operation.

Caro sat with the patient, who was in great pain, while David flew the aircraft. At the hospital he consulted with the local doctor, but did not stay to help; it was a straightforward operation. He left, ostensibly to fly back.

Outside, he looked at the declining sun, and then at Caro. "We'd better stay the night, don't you think?"

"Yes, Doctor," said Caro submissively.

Wandering about the town, which had known a mushroom growth in the last few years, they saw outside a store a large wire cage.

"Oh no!" whispered Caro.

A great wedge-tailed eagle was sitting hunched in a corner, its fierce yellow eyes glaring through the netting at the unattainable sky. He did not show any awareness of their presence.

"Oh, the poor thing!" Caro was near to tears. "How could anyone cage such a magnificent bird?"

Its sturdy legs were feathered right down to the grasping talons; its great wings were folded, useless, by its sides.

David stood beside her. "People, on the whole, have no imagination. You and I have a fellow feeling for birds because we know what it is like to fly far above the earth—"

"If 'a robin redbreast in a cage, puts all Heaven in a rage,' the sight of a caged eagle should cause pandemonium up there," she said. "I'm going to let it go!"

"No, wait. You can't." The storekeeper was peering out at them through the door. David pulled her away.

"We'll have to come back after dark," he said.

They managed to book two adjoining rooms in the single small hotel. Someone was celebrating a good crushing with a high yield to the ton, and the party went on in the bar until well after midnight. When all was at last quiet, David and Caro tiptoed out into the cold, clear night. The air, which had been full of dust, smelt clean and fresh.

"We should have gone out to the airstrip and brought the tool-kit back," whispered David. "What if there's a padlock?"

"I didn't see one." Caro felt inclined to giggle. They were like two children on a midnight adventure.

Quietly they made their way along the tremendously wide main street

402

to the store. As they passed one house a dog started barking, and they froze in their tracks, already feeling guilty. They went on quietly in the light of a waning moon. A dark shape in the cage, the glint of an eye, showed the eagle still hunched in the same corner. David examined the lock of the door. There was only a hasp and staple, but no padlock. A second bolt was pushed home higher up the door. Stealthily he opened them both, and set the wire door ajar. It jammed on an obstruction on the ground and would not open fully.

Caro was at the other end talking to the eagle, which ignored her.

"What if he doesn't even notice the door is open?" she whispered as David joined her. "What if he doesn't escape?"

"I could go in and try to chase him out," he said doubtfully.

"No! He would panic, and try to tear you to pieces." She said the noise would wake the storekeeper, whose house adjoined the store.

"We can only hope he'll notice when it starts to get light."

Pleased that it had been so easy, that no one had caught them— "They'd have accused us of trying to steal the bird!" said David—they went back to their rooms to sleep until dawn. They were leaving first thing for the Alice.

In the cold, clear dawn, the town's only taxi picked them up. The way to the airstrip led past the store with the cage in front.

"Er—just go slowly along here," said David. "We've hardly had a chance to see the town."

As the ancient Buick chugged past the store they craned their necks, dreading to see the bird still hunched in its corner. The door still stood ajar, and the cage was empty.

Caro was bursting with delight; they clasped each other's hands in silent congratulation. Soon they'd be on their way back to Alice Springs, and no one would know who'd opened the cage.

As she opened the throttle and roared up into the blue, Caro felt both gratefulness and joy. To leave the earth far below, painted in its soft morning colours, and fly off with the man she loved! She felt she had struck a blow for freedom and against the dead hand of society.

Early next morning while the medical session was on, David received a call from 8TG, Cappamerri Station on the Diamantina. The voice was very faint; this might have been due to atmospheric conditions, although these were usually clearer in the mornings.

"I'm crook, very crook, doctor. Over." He sounded breathless.

"What are your symptoms?"

"Pains in the chest. I can hardly breathe. Over."

"Right. Lie down and rest, or prop yourself up with pillows if it will help you breathe. Try not to panic. Stay absolutely quiet till I get there. I'll come at once. Over."

"Thanks, Doc."

"Better get someone to pack your things, I may be bringing you back to hospital. How is the airstrip?"

"It's—all right. A bit rough. Over and out."

David rang Caro at once. "Can we be ready to take off in half an hour?"

"Where are we going?"

"To Cappamerri Station. It's Big Jim Manning. Your grandfather."

There was a silence while Caro caught her breath. She had not thought of her grandfather since the day when she had flown here, when she'd consciously decided not to call and see him. She hadn't even called him on the radio, as she might have done, using the powerful voice transmission from the base.

"Is it—is it serious?"

"Sounds like heart. I said we'd come right away."

"Did he speak himself?"

"Yes; sounded a bit breathless. Probably someone else doing the pedalling for him."

"Jenny!"

"Eh?"

"No matter. I'll go and check the engines and the fuel."

404

CHAPTER TWENTY-FOUR

When David arrived at the airport he found his pilot poring over a map.

"You know the Simpson Desert lies directly between us and the lower Diamantina," said Caro. "If we go around it by way of Boulia, it will be about a six-hundred-mile flight, and it will take us six and a half hours, with stops for fuel. By cutting straight across the desert we could cut off more than a hundred miles."

"And save an hour and a half."

"Yes. My grandfather may be dying."

"Well, dear, it's your machine and your life. I'm ready to go where you are."

"I'm not afraid when you're with me. Coming up from Sydney I was scared of the desert, and went the long way round, but now I'd like to take the direct route."

The plane was packed with tins of water and emergency fuel supplies. Caro had brought iron rations of dates and chocolate, besides a thermos of coffee and sandwiches.

She had mapped a course along the dry bed of the Todd, and then due east to the Hale River, which petered out in sand somewhere to the south.

This was the last known map point before the edge of the Simpson, which lay between them and the salt Lake Caroline and the dry Hay watercourse 140 miles away—the only reference point before the far edge of the desert near the Queensland border. Bedourie was another 135 miles to the south-east. With a range of four hundred miles, they should make it without having to land to refuel.

"If only the Tropic of Capricorn were visible, like the O.T. Line," said Caro, "we could simply have followed along it right to Queensland."

Caro flew *Fafnir* while David navigated. She claimed that poring over maps while on long flights gave her a headache, though she'd never had a headache on her long solo flights. She knew he longed to do the flying, but she wanted to make this adventurous flight herself—the first woman to fly across the notorious Simpson Desert.

They picked up the Hale without trouble eighty miles out. In less than half an hour they were over the edge of the desert.

They stared down at the long, perfectly parallel sand-dunes, reddish-pink in colour, instead of the dark mulga that had covered the earth

405

before. Between the sand-ridges were long pink stretches of bare sand, here and there mottled with patches of spinifex and grey shrub. Apart from a few bare clay-pans breaking up the regularity of the long sand-ridges, the ground was featureless as far as they could see. It was like flying over a weird, frozen sea of which the waves were pink and red and yellow instead of blue, like something that might be seen on Mars.

Caro looked at David with shining eyes. She swooped down and down to only five hundred feet above the desert, where they could feel the hot breath of the desert coming up to them. Surprisingly, from this height the country looked less desolate; they could see patches of shade beneath the occasional acacias and desert oaks, and clumps of spinifex. But it was too hot and bumpy for comfort; she was just climbing for height when David gave a shout and pointed downwards.

"Tracks!"

"Where?" And then she saw them, the rounded marks in the sand of two camels travelling side by side, at an angle to the dunes. They appeared to have come from the north, and now began to turn back again. With visions of lost explorers, Caro wanted to follow them, but David said they would be wild camels that had entered the desert to browse on the herbage.

She climbed again to the cooler air at three thousand feet. Then they saw ahead and to the south a large salt lake, and beyond it the dry channels of a wide watercourse at right angles to their route.

"The Hay," said David. "Now it's just over a hundred miles to Sandringham Station."

Caro set a compass course due east. At last the true desert ended. As they crossed the Queensland border another salt lake passed below; then the bed of the Mulligan—a winding strip of white sand bordered by eucalyptus. The sand-ridges were more scattered, with stony gibber flats and saltbush and mulga between.

Then Sandringham Station showed up, on a waterhole in a dry watercourse. They turned south-east for Bedourie, only another thirty-five miles. In her relief Caro began to sing. They landed at Bedourie airstrip; with a cruising speed of over a hundred miles per hour, it had taken them three and a half hours.

Caro was exultant. "I just wanted to fly non-stop from Alice to Bedourie."

"Well, now you've done it, what about letting me fly the last hundred miles to the station?"

She hesitated. "All right. But will you let me land? I know the terrain; I've landed on that clay-pan before."

"Okay. We'll change over when we reach the Diamantina."

After a welcome wash and a meal of their remaining sandwiches and coffee, they refuelled and set off on the last leg of the journey with David at the controls, looking happy. He still hated to be a passenger.

As she resumed the pilot's seat over the Diamantina, Caro was surprised to see no water in the channels, only the usual waterholes near Duthie. The flood had already sunk away into the sand. But the gibbers were covered in saltbush and wild flowers. Soon the drovers would be moving down the stock-routes with mobs for Birdsville and Marree. But there would be none from Cappamerri.

As they circled above the station, losing height, they saw a team of Aborigines with straw brooms assiduously sweeping the clay-pan landing-field. The trouble was, they didn't move, but after waving a welcome stood where they were, leaning on their brooms.

"Damn!" said Caro. "I'll just have to give them a fright!"

There was nowhere else to land. Two great hills of salmon-red sand had converged on the homestead from each side, threatening to engulf it. Several of the outbuildings were already buried.

Caro circled, then dived straight at a group of three men. One fell over backwards in his fear, two of them ran wildly, holding their hands over their heads for protection. The others stood transfixed a moment, and then fled. At the last moment she pulled up and away.

David was chuckling. "You sure put the wind up them!"

"It was that or land among them, and risk chopping off an arm or a leg."

"It's very hard to judge something like that. I once tried to frighten some cattle off a runway, and I got hooked in a cow's horn. I nearly crashed, and the cow took off for the horizon."

Caro banked and turned on her landing approach, then came down on the clearest patch she could see. After taxiing a short way the wheels bogged in soft sand, and slewed them to a stop. The blacks hovered nervously in the distance till the propellers stopped turning. Then the older ones crowded round, greeting the "Young Missus" by the title they had used for her mother, when Caro herself was a child. By now a group of children had come up from the camp, straggling over the sand-hill, and all tried at once to hold Caro's hand. She was not wearing either nurse's uniform or flying gear, but a sleeveless green frock, the colour of a pale breaking wave, for coolness.

"Pretty!" said a chubby little girl, holding Caro's skirt in sticky fingers. Caro had brought her usual paper bag of barley sugar for the children.

"This is Dr. Trenowith, the Flying Doctor," she introduced David, who smiled at the children. They looked remarkably healthy, Caro thought, perhaps because, as the station supplies of beef, tea, flour, and sugar were giving out, their parents had gone back to living off the land. With fish and birds' eggs and ducks from the lagoon, lizards and small marsupials from the sand-hills, and their traditional lily-roots and berries, they had a healthier diet. The usual running noses and suppurating ears seemed less apparent.

407

The escort of children stopped at the gate of the garden enclosure. As they walked up the two steps to the veranda, a figure hovered just inside the front door, half in shadow.

It was less than four years since Caro had called on her first journey to Cloncurry, but Jenny, she realized, had put on even more weight and was now quite shapeless, while her face had become more Aboriginal in appearance. There was no trace of the lithe and attractive girl she remembered as a child, when Old Lucy was still running the place. The house now had the same neglected air, with sagging curtains and dusty floors, as on her last visit.

Caro clasped Jenny's hand in both of hers. This was Big Jim's faithful companion.

"Boss very sick?" she asked, as David introduced himself.

"Him very sick. Might-be close-up finish."

Big Jim Manning lay on the double bed in his room off the veranda —the mosquito-net looped up above his head—and propped on some very dingy white pillows. Caro felt sure Jenny would have changed the covers for the doctor's visit, but no doubt they had been washed in discoloured river water from rains that fell hundreds of miles to the north, and the rain-water tanks would be empty.

"Ar there, my girl." He spoke gaspingly. "G'day, Doc. They told me —I was speaking to Monkira Station—there was a new Flying Doctor at Alice—and his pilot was a girl. Guessed it might be you, Caro."

"I should have made a call to check that you were all right." Caro was contrite. "But I haven't been long in the Alice." She leaned over and kissed the weathered cheek, whose deep reddish tan from a long life in the saddle in the centralian sun seemed out of place on a sickbed. His eyes, blue slits set among leathery wrinkles, lingered on her face.

"Good to see you," he said.

"Don't talk now. I want to take your blood pressure and have a listen to your heart," said David.

The skin of Big Jim's torso was creamy white. Above the line of rolled-up shirt-sleeves and below the edge of an open front collar, the brick-red of his arms and neck ended in a sharp line of demarcation. Big Jim had never gone outside without a shirt, or worked in just a sleeveless singlet as many did.

"If you don't need me, I'll just go and see the plane is tied down properly," said Caro, feeling that her grandfather might feel constrained in front of her, seeing her as a girl rather than a nurse.

When she came back Jenny was setting teacups and a covered teapot —incongruously swathed in a smart tea-cosy which "the Old Missus" had knitted long ago—on the table of what used to be the dining-room. Caro tried to recall what elegancies there had been when the grandmother she scarcely remembered was still in charge. With the tea went a wedge of baked damper, no butter. They still had flour, then, but probably no yeast for breadmaking.

There had been no sign of any stock from the air, only a few goats nibbling at the saltbush, which out on the gibber plains had regenerated in part now it was not grazed by thousands of head of cattle.

David, joining her for tea, looked grave. He said Big Jim's pulse was weak, his legs were swollen with oedema, and there was a murmur suggesting a blocked ventricular valve.

"It's progressive heart disease," he said, "leading to heart failure, which is affecting his liver and his kidneys. Hence the retention of fluid."

"What is the prognosis?"

"Not good, especially at his age. I can't do much, except give him diuretics and digitalis, but he has to have complete rest in hospital."

"I don't think he'll go."

"You'll have to persuade him to come with us."

"Well, I'll try."

After a meal of roast goat and damper with tomato sauce, Caro tried to reason with her grandfather.

"I'm not going to any hospital," said the old man obstinately. "Always thought I'd die with me boots on. At least—I'm gunna die—here at Cappamerri—not in some strange town."

"But it's only a small town, Grandpa, and I'll be there, and there are lots of old bushmen from the stations round, cattlemen like yourself."

"No. Once you got me there—I'd never get back. I want to be buried here—on the sand-hill above the waterhole—next to Danny's grave. It was Jenny made me call the doctor, I should—never have bothered you. Coming all this way."

Jenny appeared in the shadows just beyond the lamplight, outside the fly-wire door on to the veranda.

"Come in, Jenny, see if you can make the Boss see sense. He has to go to hospital. There's room for you in the plane, if you'd like to come too."

"No-more, Missus. This me-country. Me no leave here."

"Me neither," said Big Jim.

When David tried to persuade him with no more success, he began to get annoyed at the old man's obstinacy.

"Look, Mr. Manning, we've made a flight of nearly a thousand miles here and back to see you. But I can't help you if you refuse to be helped. You have heart disease, which will lead to complete heart failure unless treated."

"How long—'ve I got?"

"A few more years, with treatment. Without it—less than six months, with increasing disability and discomfort. Jenny, you pack the Boss's things for hospital."

409

He did not argue any more, but shut his eyes in seeming indifference. "I'd like to 've seen eighty," he muttered. "Never mind—I've had a pretty good innings."

In her bedroom, Caro flung herself on the bed and covered her eyes with her upflung arm.

"I feel we've bullied him," she said. "He doesn't want to go."

"Well, he can't stay here with just a black woman to look after him."

"He has his sons."

"You mean her sons? Half-castes?"

"Yes. She's been with him for twenty or thirty years."

After a while Caro got up and went back to the old man. Jenny had helped him to sit on the side of the bed, with his swollen legs and feet resting on the floor. His breathing was less laboured. He could still get to the bathroom unaided.

"You go and get some sleep, Jenny," said Caro. "I'm a trained nurse, remember? I'll sit up with him. Did your daughter go on with her job at the Birdsville Hostel?"

"No-more, Missus. Him bin have whitefeller's baby. Go to Birdsville school now, doin' orright."

When Jenny had gone, Caro helped the old man back into bed. David had given him a light sedative, and Caro propped him up with extra pillows.

He grasped her hand in his big gnarled fist that had held the reins and guided many a horse on long droves and musters. "Thanks for coming, girl."

"Good night, Grandpa."

"Goodbye." He was half asleep.

In her grandfather's room a stretcher had been made up, and Caro, still tired from the long flight, lay down on top of the grey blanket. Big Jim had dozed off. She went over to him once, and found he was sound asleep, so she lay down again.

Some time in the night she woke to find David standing beside her. She started up.

"It's all right, darling. He's sleeping still, and his breathing is easier. Why don't you come to bed?"

"I told Jenny I'd stay with him."

"Please, Caro. I can't sleep for thinking about you."

She said she would come for a little while, and then come back "on duty."

"You know, even if he was in hospital," said David in his room, which was next to hers along the veranda, "there wouldn't be a nurse at his bedside all night. He's only a few doors away."

She had meant to come back within an hour, but she fell asleep in his arms. "Do you realize," she murmured sleepily before doing so, "that I

410

was probably begun in this bed? About Christmas 1914. The same time as the Great War. . ."

She was awakened in the early morning by some loud noise, like an explosion. She had been dreaming about war, and at first thought it part of her dream. But David was already out of bed, pulling on his trousers.

"It sounded like a shot."

She followed him along the veranda to the other bedroom. Big Jim Manning was slumped sideways against the pillows. His eyes and his mouth were open, and a shotgun muzzle rested against his side. Bright-red blood flowed from a gaping wound in his chest. David was feeling for a pulse in his neck, while trying to stanch the blood with a bunched-up sheet. The bedside lamp was still burning.

There came a quick patter of bare feet along the veranda, and Jenny came running in, her eyes and hair wild. She gave a great wail and cast herself on the body, regardless of the blood. "Boss, Boss," she sobbed.

David gently detached her, and closed the eyes and mouth and covered the dreadful wound with a sheet. Big Jim had shot himself through the heart at point-blank range. Jenny stood by like a character in a Greek tragedy, with her blood-stained shift and straight, tangled long hair, emitting high-pitched wails. Caro was crying quietly.

David put his hand on her shoulder. "I'll sign the death certificate, and we'll have to bury him without waiting for the police to get here. When she is calmer, ask Jenny to get her boys to dig a grave."

Caro fetched a bowl of water and asked Jenny for some old towels or cloths. She used absorbent pads and bandages from her first-aid kit to fill the wound. She could get no help from Jenny, who flung her arms about and tore at her hair and face while Caro washed the body.

"Jenny, listen. How Boss want to be buried?"

"Boss tellem me, 'S'pose I die, you bury me longa box, longa big sand-hill.'"

"Right. Where this-feller box?"

"Longa back 'randa." She pointed with her lips towards the back of the house.

Caro asked her to fetch her sons (living in the sand-drifted station-hands' quarters) to put the Old Boss, their father, in his coffin, and then dig a grave for him.

Jenny went away, and soon a loud chorus of wails broke out in the camp.

When David came back, Caro leaned her face against his shoulder. "It's my fault. I should never have left him."

"Nonsense. He'd have done it anyway, as soon as we'd left."

"No. He was afraid we'd force him into going back with us. It's my fault."

"Caro, be realistic. His heart wasn't going to get better. He hadn't

411

much of a life in front of him. This way it was a quick and certain ending."

"I suppose so," she said doubtfully.

At 6 A.M. David had spoken by radio to the police constable at Birdsville, the nearest centre. He said there had been an accident with a gun, that the owner of Cappamerri was dead and that he would sign the death certificate and supervise the burial. For obvious reasons the funeral could not be delayed. He would leave the papers all complete.

Caro was standing by the bed where he had left her, with her arms crossed and her head bowed. "David, he said 'goodbye', last night. Not 'good night', but 'goodbye'. He'd already made up his mind."

Jenny's two sons came in, both big men, one of them much lighter in complexion than the other. Each went up and touched the dead man's shoulder before lifting the heavy body, wrapped in a clean sheet, into the coffin. Caro shook hands with her half-uncles, and went to look for some flowers in the neglected garden.

CHAPTER TWENTY-FIVE

The weather was hot and it was advisable not to delay, so the funeral was held late the same morning. Caro wanted to be present and asked David to conduct the service. They could not stay longer, for an urgent call had just come from the Alice base. The doctor was needed as soon as possible at Woodgreen Station on the Sandover, where the station manager had badly injured his hand in the gears of a boring plant.

Big Jim's two sons arrived at the homestead with a cart, to Caro's surprise, pulled by a pair of black horses.

"But I thought there were no livestock left on the place!" she exclaimed.

"Well, Barney and me, we broke in a few brumbies—made a trap for 'em by the second waterhole. Got a coupler pack-horses as well. Brother Joe, 'e rode orf and got a job on another station."

"And you're staying on? I know the Boss wanted you boys to have the place."

"Yair. Might as well 'ang on long as we can."

"Y'never know, some drover feller might lose a few beasts, an' they might just wander on to Cappamerri," said Barney, looking innocently at the ceiling.

Their mother looked at them proudly.

"They's good boys," she said.

Big Jim was no light weight, and David helped his two strong sons to lift the coffin from the table and get it out to the waiting cart. A stream of natives from the camp followed as they drove to the base of the sand-hill, the women tearing their hair and inflicting "sorry cuts" on their scalps, so that blood ran down and matted their hair. The wailing reached a crescendo as four men lifted out the long box and took it on their shoulders for the arduous climb up and over the loose sand to Danny's grave. But when, after three changes of bearers, they came over the top to the other side, the little gravestone could not be found. It had disappeared under the drifting sand.

They fixed on an approximate site from what the older people remembered, and with shovels had soon excavated a hole in the soft sand in a spot overlooking the home waterhole, now sadly diminished in size as far as Caro remembered. The lowering of the coffin into the grave was the signal for a fresh outburst of wailing. (That night there would be a corroboree to farewell the Old Boss. His name would never be mentioned again.)

David read the Burial Service from an old Church of England prayer-book they had found in a bookcase. Caro stood with her head bent, staring at the wave-patterns made in the coloured sand by the wind; and, beyond the trampled area, the tiny marks, the tracks of hopping-mice, lizards, and small snakes that came out at night and sheltered by day in burrows from the scorching sun. She had picked some everlasting daisies, papery white and gold. In the garden had been nothing but a few hardy sun-flowers. She and Jenny, who stood beside her with swollen eyes, dropped the gaudy sunflowers onto the coffin. Jenny and the old women wailed again as the men filled the grave and stamped down the sand with their feet. Then three heavy paper-bark logs carried all the way from the river were laid crosswise on top to keep out dingoes.

There was no further sound from the dark people. Apart from Jenny, they showed no emotion but chattered among themselves as they ploughed back over the sand-hill, pausing to examine small excavations and pointing to tracks of lizards or kangaroo-mice. Caro paused to stick her bunch of daisies upright on the grave. Everlastings—but nothing lasted forever here, only the endless shifting sand. She intended to have an engraved stone sent up from Adelaide, but it too would soon disappear.

There had been no old friends of Jim Manning at his funeral, for Duthie Station, the nearest neighbour, was nearly a hundred miles away over a track half-buried in sand. It would probably take till tomorrow for the Constable to drive up the mail-route from Birdsville.

Caro and David had to leave at once for Woodgreen.

Because the Sandover River was north of the Alice, they would have to take the long way home. This meant flying back to Bedourie and then north to Boulia before turning west for the border. David was disappointed; he had been looking forward to flying himself back over the desert.

It was nearly midday when the Flying Doctor plane took off. The ground was heating up, and the little craft lurched and bumped in the thermal currents. Four pelicans circled high in the blue.

Caro had the map, but she did not look at it. She sat with her long legs twisted round each other, her arms folded and her shoulders hunched —a defensive posture against the unhappy thoughts and guilt feelings caused by her grandfather's death, and the manner of it.

At three thousand feet the air was smoother. David surveyed the horizon; blue and clear as far as he could see, the sky blended into the darker blue of distance so that they seemed to be ringed with a surrounding ocean. The land directly beneath was bleached with heat, but there was no dust and every detail was clear. He could see for sixty miles in every direction. And the terrain was perfectly flat.

He picked up the channels of the Georgina, still with water in them, and continued north, following its braided channels, to Bedourie, where he landed to refuel. Caro had still not spoken a word. He knew she blamed him for having enticed her away from the sick-room, just as she reproached herself for having gone with him.

"Could I have a look at the map?" he said politely as to a stranger. He followed the course of the Georgina with a long brown finger. "We could keep going north to Boulia, but if we make straight for Glenormiston Station from Marion Downs it cuts off this corner and we get the benefit of the tail wind all the way to the border."

Caro shrugged. "Obviously that's what you intended to do, or you wouldn't have landed here for fuel."

He did not answer. He decided to ignore her mood; he was not going to quarrel. He talked with the Shell gasoline man who had brought the fuel out to the airstrip. They should not need any more before reaching Tobermorey Station over the Territory border, where they could top up with their own emergency supplies.

Listening to the engines running sweetly, looking down at the glinting channels of the remains of the Georgina flood, and around at the wide horizon, David relaxed in his seat and began to sing, "O sole mio. . ." Then he remembered and stopped. Hell, ought he to whistle "The Last Post"? He hadn't known the old man, and he rather admired what he had done. Better to go quickly and cleanly. At least he'd had the consideration not to blow his head off; a shotgun made a terrible mess at close range.

"Would you like some coffee?" Caro was making overtures of peace.

"Thanks, darling. I was thinking, what a lovely clear day."

"Yes. No day for dying."

She came forward and handed him a mug of coffee, resting her hand on his shoulder. A cluster of buildings showed up to the left of the main channel: Marion Downs. They followed the river, before leaving it at Glenormiston and following a stock-route towards Tobermorey along a dry watercourse lined with trees. They were more than half-way when David, checking the instruments, cried: "We're nearly out of fuel! It's not possible!"

"Perhaps the gauge is faulty."

"I don't think so." He immediately climbed for height while he still had power. To the left were rocky hills, but ahead appeared to be a red plain covered with sparse scrub. Then the engines faltered and died. With the tail wind he hoped to get close to Tobermorey Station and find some country eaten bare by cattle. They glided silently, steadily losing height. As they came lower, the ground which had looked smooth and flat from above showed itself scored with small dry creeks and dotted with gidgee and needlebush. At least there were no giant termite mounds. And he had no choice.

"Hold on!" he said quietly as the ground seemed to rush up towards them. "It's going to be rough."

He was nearly down, skilfully aiming for a clear patch among the scattered timber, when a great mound of clay loomed up in front. Though without power, he managed to lift her up and over, and they came down with a bump on the other side, bounced into the air, and landed again, to roll on until brought up short by a shallow runnel in the red sandy soil, filled with wiry lignum bushes that held them without damage.

They sat in silence for a moment, scarcely able to believe that they were down safely. Then Caro, who had been thrown forward by the jolt, came and hugged his neck from behind. "Dr. Trenowith, you are a very good pilot."

"I know," he said, laughing. Then he said soberly, "Caro, do you realize that if your grandfather hadn't died, and we'd left early this morning before the call came from base, we'd now be down in the Simpson Desert?"

"Golly!" said Caro in a small voice.

They found what had caused the trouble. A fuel line had broken, and the petrol had leaked away. They still had their spare fuel on board, but they didn't have any spare pipe. And their radio would not work without power from the engines.

"Let's have a snack, anyway," said David, unperturbed; he had been down in the bush so often before. They gnawed at their slices of damper, and chewed some dates. The chocolate was rapidly melting in the afternoon heat. All round was utter silence; not a bird, not an insect stirred.

There was no way they could repair the break, but if they filled up from their spare tins and took off again for Tobermorey they could make it before the tanks were empty again. The danger was that if an off-balance landing, or an unseen obstruction tipped them sideways, friction with the earth would cause a spark to reach the flowing petrol before it was all used up.

"It would be safer to walk to the station for help," said Caro. "Perhaps a station truck could get through to here."

"Let's toss for it."

"What a gambler you are, David! You call, then."

"Heads."

The penny came down tails. They started to walk.

David carried a water-bag just in case, though if their navigation was right the dry watercourse was Pituri Creek and by following it up they must come to the station. Though winter was well begun, the sun was hot and the red soil gave off heat like an oven. Caro had brought a hat, but David with his thick thatch did not seem to feel the need of one. They stumbled through gullies and prickly shrubs, where possible taking

416

advantage of shade from the thicker timber lining the creek; there was little from the thin gidgee scrub and the occasional "whitewash gum" with its pure-white trunk.

Caro was beginning to feel tired and anxious when David gave a shout. "The border fence!"

There it was ahead, a post-and-wire fence of rabbit-proof netting, a fence that stretched in various stages of repair for seven hundred miles. They went along it till they found a gate, where the earth was trampled to dust by the hoofs of cattle, for although Tobermorey land lay over the state border all its stock were droved into Queensland railheads. To the west the nearest centre was Alice Springs, more than three hundred miles away over rugged country.

Though the sun was declining, Caro was unbearably hot and took frequent drinks from the water-bag. She was also footsore, for her shoes were not sturdy enough for a long walk. She looked enviously at the kites, wheeling effortlessly high in the air.

"Only one mile to go," said David cheerfully, consulting the map.

Once through the gate they began to see some cattle, half-wild beasts that stood with their white faces and sharp, curving horns all pointed towards the intruders, then bounded away through the scattered trees. The homestead could be seen across a perfectly bare stretch, two-storied with the sleeping quarters upstairs and a fly-netted enclosure below. But only the Chinese cook was home. He said the men would be back soon. Meanwhile, "Missie like bathee and cold dlink?"

The sun was sending long blue shadows over the red earth when the three young brothers who worked the station rode in. It was too late to go out tonight, but they were ready to drive David and Caro to their plane at first light and help clear the ground for take-off.

By mid-morning they were on their way down the Sandover, having radioed the base that they'd been delayed by a forced landing. The station people had happily put them up for the night, robbed a petrol pipe from another engine, and sent them off with a good breakfast under their belts and full fuel tanks. After two hundred miles they reached Woodgreen, with a landing almost as rough as the one in the bush.

The injured man was lying down with his arm and hand resting on a blood-soaked pillow. What had been a clean cotton singlet was wrapped around the hand. His face was drawn with pain.

"How did it happen?" asked the doctor as he unpacked his bag. A basin of hot water had been brought for him, and he began to remove the covering from the man's wound.

"We were sinking a new well, ten mile out," said the man's brother. "Bob here got his hand dragged by a steel rope into the big heavy plant and the bones and flesh and everything were mangled in the crown wheel

417

and pinion. It took his whole hand in, and the teeth were worn sharp as razors—"

He began to look sick at the memory.

"Yes," said Bob in a faint voice, "and the silly galoot thought he was winding it out, but he was winding it back in! 'Hey! The other way,' I yelled."

"I was that upset I didn't know what I was doing. We got him back here in the truck and poured pain-killer and disinfectant all over it, and wrapped it up."

"And he didn't even faint?" asked Caro.

Bob grinned. "No way! I'm tough. They call me the Sandover Alligator."

"Well, we'll see," said David. "I'm going to have to clean this up and have a look at it. Do you want a shot of morphia?"

"I don't like needles, Doc," said the tough man, looking anxious.

When David informed him that he would be having an anti-tetanus shot anyway, he groaned. "All right. The morphia first."

Caro held his good hand and had hers nearly mangled as well as he convulsively clasped it in his strong fingers. "Don't look," she said quietly as the bloody mess was revealed.

"I'd rather look at you, any day," said Bob Geddes with the ghost of a leer.

His brother Geoff had not stayed to watch, but when David sought him out while Caro fixed a sling to support the injured hand, he found him sitting in the big airy central room with its walls of open louvers through which the south-easterly blew, warm but refreshing.

"We'll have to take him into Alice for an operation."

Geoff nodded. "Have a beer, Doc," he said. "Kerist, was I glad to see you. They told us from the Alice you were down in the bush somewhere, and I thought of gangrene setting in or blood poisoning or something before you got here."

He brought two cold beers from the kerosene refrigerator.

"I hope they've got plenty of tucker at the new hospital," he said.

"I believe it's good. Why?"

"Well, they call Bob the Sandover Alligator because of the amount he eats. A leg of lamb between two loaves of bread is a sandwich for Bob, they reckon."

When Caro came in he did not stand up, but pushed a chair towards her with his foot. He removed the large-brimmed felt hat that had seemed glued to his head. She noticed that his forehead was paler than the rest of his thin brown face.

"Have a drink, Sister. . . . Here's to the Flying Doctor, the A.I.M. Sisters, and the kero fridge—the three best things ever to come to the outback."

Within two hours Bob Geddes was in bed in the hospital at Alice Springs. Dr. Trenowith and Dr. Reilly conferred over his hand. It was so long since the injury that the hospital doctor feared gangrene might have set in, and it would be safer to amputate. But David felt sure it could be saved.

"I wouldn't like to take the risk," said Dr. Reilly.

"Then I will," said David. And tired as he was, after a short rest he performed an operation with Dr. Reilly assisting, which took two and a half hours. The nearly severed thumb was sewn back, the ragged flesh trimmed away, each suture dusted with antiseptic powder, and the whole carefully bound up with sterile bandages till it resembled a white football.

As the hand healed, the doctor unwound the bandages and sent Bob Geddes to sit out in the sun once a day, letting the wounds dry while he chased away the flies with his other hand.

Chapter Twenty-six

In July the Governor-General, Lord Gowrie, and Lady Gowrie arrived for a visit to Alice Springs, travelling in the 'Ghan all the way from Adelaide. They had a special carriage to themselves. When the train pulled in, the whole town turned out to witness the arrival of the King's representative, though for once it was pouring with rain in the middle of winter.

Houses had all been decorated by the patriotic owners. Even the gaol joined in the festivity, and Caro was amused to see two crossed flags, the Australian and the Union Jack, over the entrance with a large sign saying WELCOME.

Before they went on by road to Tennant Creek, the pair were taken to visit the Flying Doctor base. Lady Gowrie spoke to the listening women over a radius of hundreds of miles, and made their day. The Governor's wife had a gentle manner, but she was not young; and when Caro was introduced to her she noted the dark, tired shadows beneath her eyes.

When war was declared in early September, Caro would not at first believe it. Yet she had heard quite clearly on the radio the clipped tones of the South Australian Governor, saying "This means War!" He was a military man, and he sounded almost pleased.

"How can they—how can they start another war!" she cried. "Not that I remember the last one, but my father died in it—a young man with everything to live for. And now all that suffering is starting over again!"

"It had to come, I suppose," said David. "Hitler couldn't be allowed to get away with any more. And the world governments must have known it was coming. No doubt that's why they sent the poor old Governor-General all the way up here, to stir up a bit of patriotism."

"I only feel patriotic about Australia, and I don't see why we have to be involved."

"And if Hitler conquers all Europe, and then England? Where would we be then?"

"A colony of Germany? Well, let us fight them then, when we're invaded."

"Without the British fleet, and British armaments and aeroplanes, we'd

420

get nowhere. Germany has ten times as many people as we have, and millions of troops."

"I still hate it. David! *You* won't have to go?"

"It depends how tough things get. At present I'm needed more here. A lot of younger doctors, and young airmen, will be joining up, and the Aerial Medical Service is going to find itself short of pilots and doctors. And nurses too, perhaps."

"My mother would have gone to the Front, as it was called, if she hadn't had me. But I won't. I'm not going to do anything to 'help the War effort.' I won't roll a bandage, I won't knit a sock—"

David smiled tolerantly. "We'll see."

The war did not affect life in the centre very much. Naval and Army headquarters were being established at Darwin, and a small Air Force, but as there was neither road nor rail across the continent, Alice Springs saw little of them. Then an Army officer arrived and announced that an all-weather road was to be built from Tennant Creek to Birdum (the southern-most end of the Darwin railway), while the road already in use between the Alice and Tennant would be upgraded to the same standard. The first section would be built in ninety days, before the Wet set in. Medical and communication services would be provided by the Army, and the construction would be done by the civilian road-construction workers.

The locals were sceptical. They felt that the Army did not appreciate the difficulties of the terrain and the climate, with its alternating droughts and floods, sand-hills and mud-slides. An advance party of workmen arrived on the 'Ghan from Adelaide, with truckloads of tools and roadmaking equipment from tractors to steamrollers. It was the beginning of irreversible change for the centre and the far north, and the start of a trickle of motor-borne tourists which was to become a flood in the next twenty to thirty years. Meanwhile a pioneer air service from Adelaide to Darwin was started, crossing the continent in a series of six or eight hops. The *Faith in Australia* made a forced landing on a tributary of the Roper; the passengers had to live on crocodile meat until rescued.

Territorians were more interested in the case against a well-known station boss and his head stockman on a property near the South Australian border. They had been arrested by the officer in charge of the police station at Abminga Siding on a charge of murdering an Aborigine. The officer had eyewitness evidence from several Aborigines, who showed him the body of the dead man. They claimed the man had been dragged for about five hundred yards behind a truck, with a length of wire round his neck.

The two white men were brought to Alice Springs by the Constable, who had been shown the body of "Lucky Legs," and brought his skull back as evidence. (This was usually done in the case of murdered

Aborigines, the flesh removed by boiling to make the Court sitting less unpleasant.)

At the Coroner's inquest he produced the skull which he had personally detached from the body. The five witnesses had to be kept in custody to prevent them from bolting. On the evidence the two white men were committed for trial.

The sergeant in charge at Alice Springs then took the witnesses back over the ground to re-check the evidence, and somehow let them escape. The Constable, who had gone back to Abminga, was asked to go out and recapture them, but they knew they were being looked for; it was a hopeless search.

As he was returning to Alice Springs for the trial he met the two accused men on their way home. The Supreme Court had considered the case before a judge and jury. It had been dismissed for want of evidence.

Caro and David, like everyone else in town, had watched the progress of the case with intense interest. Sides were taken and bets made on the outcome, most being in favour of the accused. Even those who doubted said that old Perce had only been trying to teach a troublesome blackfellow a lesson, and would not have meant to kill him.

There were plenty of witnesses for the defence to give excellent characters for the two well-known and respected cattlemen.

Caro's interest was more personal, for the Constable who had laid the charges was her mother's old friend Jack McGuinnes from Marree and Innamincka. Before he went back down the line to his police station she asked him to come and visit her at the hospital, and took him round to meet David.

"Wasn't there something peculiar about that case, Jack?" she asked. "This business about the skull—the doctor certified that it was a lubra's skull, so it couldn't possibly have been Lucky Legs's. Is that right?"

Jack McGuinnes burst out, "The skull was *not* a lubra's. At least the one I brought in wasn't. The blacks showed me where they'd buried Lucky Legs, and I dug him up and removed the skull from his body."

"I know Dr. Reilly," said David, "and he wouldn't falsify evidence in a Court of Law."

"Well, I'm not in any doubt that there was some funny work went on. When I first got the report of the killing I went out there and made inquiries. The story was obviously a dinkum one. I got hold of several witnesses, three men and two women, after a bit of a search—they were scared stiff and reluctant to come in with me. I had to keep them locked up at Abminga, while we waited for the next train."

"But you weren't here for the trial?"

"No! Yet I was the chief police witness. And the witnesses, who had all gone bush, weren't there either. I was sent out to look for them, and so kept out of town till it was all over."

"And you think the lubra's skull was substituted?"

"Must have been. It wouldn't be difficult to get hold of one."

"So you reckon they were guilty," David stated.

"They were guilty as hell. It was an open-and-shut case. If I'd been present with my witnesses, they'd not have got out of it. That native was dragged behind a truck till he was dead."

The three of them were silent. Caro, feeling depressed, got up and said, "I'll get us some supper," and went out to the kitchen; not realizing that she was showing a familiarity with the doctor's house—and the doctor—that was not lost on the observant policeman. He had heard of Dr. Trenowith's exploits, and liked the look of him. But he'd had an idea the doctor was married.

Afterwards they talked about Alix, and Jack asked hopefully if she might be coming up for a visit. But Caro told him that Alix was bent on nursing in Darwin, and had decided to take a commercial flight all the way from Adelaide to the far northern port.

"The planes land at Alice for fuel, and to give the passengers some lunch," she said. "There's a fly-netted dining enclosure built out at the airport. So I'll see her briefly on her way, I hope."

"Remember me to her, won't you? I've never forgotten her."

The big man was as sturdy as ever, his face as brown and weathered, but his hair was quite grey. It made Caro realize how time had passed since the policeman asked her mother to marry him.

Alix left Adelaide before dawn on the two-thousand-mile flight across the continent. She was a little apprehensive, but no longer really scared of flying. Excitement built in her as she climbed up the slope of the cabin floor, tilted as the big metal plane stood on the tarmac, with its nose pointed up-wind as if sniffing the air, eager for take-off.

There were about nine other passengers, but no such things as air hostesses or in-flight refreshments. They would land at Mount Eba Station for fuel and morning tea, and at Alice Springs for lunch.

The powerful engines, which at take-off seemed to be straining to get the heavy bulk airborne, settled down to a steady vibrating hum. The window vibrated in concert as Alix pressed her brow against it so that she could look straight down at the landscape unwinding below. The sun rose on the right as they flew steadily north; she was on the shaded side.

From Mount Eba onwards the land below appeared like a great sheet of wrinkled orange paper. They were well to the west of Lake Eyre and her old home of Marree; and now they crossed into the Northern Territory and she saw from the air the land she had journeyed by train. The white sandy bed of the Alberga, the intricate dry channels of the Finke flood-plain, unwound below like a map on rollers. There appeared to be not a single cloud over the whole of Australia; and at five thousand feet they could see for a hundred miles all round, to the dark ring of blue that was the ever-receding horizon.

Though the vibration in the glass was beginning to give her a headache, Alix could not stop staring down, watching the cross-like shape of the plane's shadow flitting over the landscape. Nowhere was any sign of water, not even a dam. She thought of Mab's grave at Marree, and how Caro had said her little Moth's shadow had for a moment painted a cross upon it as she took off for Birdsville. She watched the endless barren ribs of red sand passing beneath. How many travellers, explorers, prospectors had perished down there in the heat and glare, while here they were flying over it in cool comfort at five thousand feet.

They were slowly descending; the ground did not look so barren; there was a sprinkling of trees grey-blue against the red soil. Then a wall of orange rock—they crossed it, circled, and came back over white roofs set among green clumps of trees. Alice Springs! They landed south of the range and taxied towards the hangar, sending a cloud of dust flying back from the exhausts.

Caro, in a cool white dress and no hat, was waiting. Alix had worn a blue crêpe de Chine dress and a hat, and even—she admitted she was mad—a suspender belt and a pair of silk stockings. She climbed down the steps and flung her arms around Caro, forgetting to hold her hat, which blew off and went dancing and rolling over the tarmac. An aircraft engineer chased it and brought it back, laughing.

"I've asked them to let me have lunch with you in the passengers' enclosure," said Caro. "There isn't time for you to come into town, I'm afraid. You wouldn't know the place, it must have grown enormously."

"There certainly seem to be a lot more roofs, from the air. Caro, I'm *enjoying* this flight! It's so interesting and the air is so clear! It's like a wonderful geography lesson—we're going right across the centre of the continent."

"Yes, I wish I'd been game to come this way when I flew up to Cloncurry. But I didn't have the range, it's too empty. Even the flyers who came all the way from England alone never attempted to fly straight down to Adelaide, but went round the coast from Darwin. One day I'll do it."

When they'd finished lunch—having entered through two lots of fly-netting to shut out the ubiquitous sticky flies of the centre—and could talk freely, Alix looked straight at her daughter and said, "And Dr. Trenowith? You said he was the Flying Doctor, and you're his pilot again. Is that all you are?"

Caro's face became remote. She looked over Alix's head at the sky. "Why? What else would I be?"

"I believe his wife is still in Darwin."

"So? She happens to like Darwin."

"Caro, don't fence with me. It was always hard to extract the truth from you; but we may not see each other for a long time, and I wish you'd confide in me. Is he in love with you?"

Caro's expression warmed. She looked down at the ground, and then smiled into her mother's blue eyes. "Yes, he is."

"I thought so."

"Oh, Mum, I'm so happy! At least we can be together here. It's not perfect, but—"

"Don't forget this is a small community—oh, I know it's a lot bigger than the ninety or so people when I was here, but it's still small enough for narrow-mindedness and gossip. There could be scandal, a messy divorce—"

"David wants a divorce! He wants to marry me!"

"But his wife won't agree? Apart from anything else, you could lose your position with the A.I.M. It's a Church organization."

"I know." Caro looked stricken. "We are being very discreet."

"Well, I can't say I approve. But I hope for your sake that it all works out. Perhaps he'll join the Air Force."

Caro made a face. "By the way, Jack McGuinnes wanted to be remembered to you. He was up from S.A. on a court case."

"Jack McGuinnes!" Alix looked startled. "I'd almost forgotten him."

"Well, he hasn't forgotten you."

Passengers were climbing back on board. Alix hugged her daughter for a long moment. "Goodbye, darling."

"Mum—you won't become an Army nurse, will you?"

She laughed. "I expect they'd think me too old. No, I'll be working in the civilian hospital, with a great big Red Cross painted on the roof—just in case the war ever comes to Darwin. But it won't."

Caro watched the silver aircraft climbing for height, turning and flying north over the rampart of the Macdonnells, and being bumped about in the thermals. She had a feeling of unease. But of course these big metal craft with their powerful engines were ten times as safe as the flimsy wood-and-fabric kind with one engine she used to fly.

In David's Moth they had made a brief expedition out to Ayers Rock and back, flying in a line due west over Mount Conner, the Rock, and the Olgas; and had even landed on the red sand among the stunted saltbush long enough to take in the stupendous size and presence of the great red monolith which the local tribes called Uluru. It was inside an Aboriginal Reserve and their landing was illegal.

"I'm glad I have seen it," said Caro. "It's extraordinary."

"They say the colour is intensified at dawn and sunset," said David. "Then it seems to be on fire."

They skimmed low over its naked dome in the little Moth, seeing the

425

striations of water-runnels made by occasional heavy thunderstorms, the gleam of a rock-hole at its base. Then they flew on and circled the bare red domes of the Olgas, like the heads of pachyderms buried and thrusting up from below. Mount Conner was different, a residual mountain with a flat top and a "skirt" of talus slope all round. But it was the Rock that compelled the imagination most: with its isolation, the way it rose abruptly from the surrounding plain, its glowing colour, its smooth contours as of a giant pebble thrown down by the gods. In its ancient, mysterious apartness it seemed to symbolize the red centre of Australia.

CHAPTER TWENTY-SEVEN

Looking down through the small window, Alix saw that the painted desert was left behind as they continued north. The sun now came in the port side and made her hot. At Tennant Creek they landed on a strip between low stony hills covered with spinifex and stunted trees. From now on, high above the heat-bumps at seven thousand feet, she looked down on a land hazy with grass fires. At Daly Waters, a fuel stop, the heat hit her in the face like a blow. From Katherine on they flew low over the last leg and could even see the giant red termite mounds standing above the yellow grass. The orange sun began to sink on their left as they circled above Darwin Harbour, drifted with smoke from the twelve-foot grass burning all round. She saw the silvery gleam of the Arafura Sea beyond; she had crossed a continent in one day.

Alix had seen something of the coastal cities, but she had never been out of Australia. Now, in Darwin, she felt as if she were in a foreign country. It was different, exotic. It *smelt* different, warm and spicy, of the mysterious East, which lay just across the silver sea, closer than any Australian city.

Once, there had been ten thousand Chinese in Darwin, and there was still a Chinatown with colourful Chinese characters painted on the shopfronts.

In Darwin the houses were nearly all raised on stumps to get the breeze. Instead of windows they had louvers of corrugated iron or wood that deflected the straight downpours of the Wet without having to be closed. People lived on their front verandas; at night, if they were inside, there were no curtains or closed windows so that from the road the interiors appeared like a lighted stage. And the air was scented with frangipani, coloured with bougainvillaea and flowering shrubs in front of an always present background of brilliant, milky-turquoise sea. Darwin on its peninsula was like a tropical island with its groves of coconut palms and poincianas in brilliant bloom.

In the streets a multi-racial population mixed peaceably—white and black Australians, Javanese and Malays, Chinese gambling-house keepers and Japanese pearlers from Broome; Moluccans, Kupangers, and Torres Strait Islanders, and every mixture between. Alix found it fascinating.

427

The Civil Airport was out near Fannie Bay, to the north of the town; the civilian hospital was at the other end of town, on high land above Doctor's Gully and overlooking the port area. Now, nearly two years after war had been declared, Darwin was at last being put on a full war footing, and a huge anti-submarine net of steel mesh was being installed by the Navy across the entrance to the large sheltered harbour—an opening six miles wide.

The Army was gradually building up to a force of five thousand men, billeted at the barracks on Larrakeyah Peninsula, at Bagot, and Berrimah, where a new Army hospital was being built.

Alix took all this in while installing herself at the Darwin Hospital—an ancient building that was something of a shock to her. It was soon to be replaced, because it was considered to be dangerously situated in case of air attack.

The old hospital was a ramshackle collection of corrugated-iron and concrete buildings, ill-equipped and generally out of date and unsatisfactory. The gate to the Larrakeyah Army Barracks was only a few hundred yards away, an obvious target if the war came close. Morale was low among the nurses, who used to spend all their spare time having parties for the younger doctors and disappearing with them down into the shady walks of Doctor's Gully. But most of the doctors in Darwin now were older men, for the younger ones had joined the Air Force or the Army Medical Corps.

Alix learned that a new modern hospital was to be opened in the new year. It would have 130 beds, an operating theatre and obstetrical wards of the latest design, and an open plan with wide corridors and thousands of fibro louvers in the walls that could be opened to allow maximum circulation of air.

"My dear, we've put up with conditions that they wouldn't believe in the south," said the Matron, a tall, pleasant woman near Alix's age. Alix had taken to her immediately. She had what Alix had only read of— "luxuriant" hair, thick and of a deep, rich red. She wore it in two shining plaits swathed around her head.

"How can you find time, Enid," Alix asked when she knew her better, "to arrange all that hair? I just shove mine into a bun, and I'm tempted to cut it off—it would be cooler and easier to manage."

"I *like* plaiting my hair," said Enid Mackay (like Alix, she had some Scottish ancestors a generation or two back). "I find it soothing to both my hands and my nerves, brushing it out and braiding it. And as for easier to manage, short hair has to be combed all the time, whereas mine stays put all day, even in a strong wind; even when I pull my cap off."

"But if you go swimming—"

"I *never* go swimming. There are all sorts of nasties in the water up here. Crocodiles up at The Point beyond Fannie Bay, and sea-wasps anywhere in the summer—they can be deadly if you're stung."

Alix was determined to swim in that turquoise sea with its twenty-foot tides. She went with some younger off-duty nurses one afternoon for a picnic to Mindil Beach. Carrying beer and sandwiches, they climbed over the sand-hills, and once out of the shade of the bushes, even though it was now July and mid-winter, the yellow sand burnt her feet in her flimsy sandals. The tide was coming in, milky with stirred-up sand, but as it began to fall again the water cleared to zircon shallows.

Then as the sea gradually retired beyond Myilly Point, and the sun set over the water in an orange ball coloured by the smoke of grass fires, and the swift tropical dusk came down, the nurses and their swains disappeared into the shadows at the back of the beach. Alix was left feeling foolish and alone.

Stark against the sea stood the gaunt shape of Vestey's meatworks— an investment of the beef baron, Lord Vestey, which had never got off the ground. Standing empty and unused, it had been taken over by the Army for a supply dump. The farthest point to the south was the tip of the Larrakeyah Peninsula where some of the A.I.F. troops were stationed.

As the troops built up, and the Air Force and Navy headquarters expanded, Darwin became more of a garrison town. Bored troops roamed the streets at night, sometimes throwing bottles and smashing windows for amusement.

The top end of the highway to the south was still not completed. From Adelaide River to Birdum there was only the railway line, and supplies such as beer (regarded by all inhabitants of Darwin as a necessity) had to come by ship.

As Army canteens ran out, there were near-riots. Soldiers roamed Smith Street, breaking windows and shooting out street lights, and chanting their disenchantment song:

The bloody town's a bloody cuss,
No bloody trams, no bloody bus
And no one cares for bloody us
So bloody, bloody, bloody.

The bloody flicks are bloody old
The bloody programmes leave me cold,
You can't get in for bloody gold,
So bloody, bloody, bloody.

And everything's so bloody dear—
Three and six for bloody beer—
And is it cold?—No bloody fear!
So bloody, bloody, bloody.

The men had been too long with nothing to do, in a place which they regarded as a sort of Army Siberia; they would rather have been fighting in Europe or North Africa than kicking their heels in this outpost. The A.I.M., which was Presbyterian, had recently built a club with billiard tables and a library; but because many soldiers were shy or suspicious of "sky pilots" it was not as well patronized as it might have been. John Flynn had been present for the opening ceremony organized by the local minister, who hoped, when beer was short, that servicemen would patronize his tea and coffee bar.

There was little other entertainment in the town, apart from the Chinese gambling dens and opium joints in Chinatown. A visit to these narrow streets with their bright red signs in Chinese characters, their entirely Asian population, was an entertainment in itself.

There was a Services section at Darwin Public Hospital, in addition to the two Army hospitals and the Air Force Hospital. Naval surgeons lent their skills, and some Naval personnel were treated. It was also the only hospital to treat Aboriginal patients, but they were kept in a separate ward.

Alix was nursing a sick baby whose mother had no milk. The child had been on a patent dried baby-food, supplies of which were interrupted, so Alix was trying ordinary dried milk powder mixed with boiled water and sugar. The baby was losing weight, had diarrhoea, and was so apathetic that Alix feared he would die.

Surgeon-Commander Clyde Evans, coming through the ward when Alix was trying to soothe the whimpering child, paused to examine the skinny mite in her arms.

"What he needs is fresh milk," she said. "I can't get his patent food any more, his mother has no milk, and he's not thriving on ordinary powdered milk."

"I can get you some," he said at once. "The Naval mess usually has fresh milk for breakfast; we've got a couple of cows down the line, where there's still some grass left, and there's even been some hay ordered by ship for them. I'll bring you some milk in the morning."

Alix had always liked the distinguished-looking grey-haired Commander; she did not get on with Army types, not the top brass anyway; but the Navy was different. The Commander was solidly built, with a broad head—dependable, Alix thought.

"It's very kind of you, sir," she said, smiling up at him, and he went away wondering why he hadn't noticed before what beautiful blue eyes Sister Manning had. He was lonely, missing his wife and family in Melbourne—but a Naval man should be used to that. It was this place; the heat, the isolation, which was different from the isolation of a ship that moved from port to port. Bloody Darwin! Only the old-timers liked the place, and the Chinese, who could make a home anywhere.

430

True to his word, he brought her two screw-top lemonade bottles of milk the next morning.

"I pinched them from the mess," he said. "A baby's life is more important, even if the late risers have to drink their coffee black."

She thanked him and made up a mixture straightaway, the formula with added water and sugar that was nearest to breast milk. The second bottle she stored in the refrigerator, with a notice, "NOT TO BE TOUCHED. By Order, Matron." She knew Enid would not mind her using her name as authority.

Little Jimmy—was it because his name was Jim that she felt such a personal interest in the baby?—began to put on weight at once, almost growing visibly. Every second day Commander Evans brought a supply of fresh milk, and though she sometimes had to supplement it with milk powder, it was enough to make his little wizened arms fill out and his eyes brighten. Soon he was a healthy, bonny baby. A ship came in with plenty of stocks of Glaxo, and Jimmy was able to go home to his mother.

There were twenty-two nurses at the Darwin Hospital, most of them younger women, though one had been an A.I.M. Sister at Wyndham, and with her Alix struck up a friendship. She was a rugged individualist, plain-faced and blunt-spoken; Sister Ellie Rowan reminded Alix a little of Mab Kingston.

They ventured together into Chinatown, and went out to Fannie Bay in a taxi, passing the gate of the notorious Fannie Bay gaol where Aboriginal murderers and European criminals were incarcerated together. The difference was, according to the taxi-driver, that the white prisoners were allowed out by day to forage for themselves, as long as they came back at night. If they were too late getting back, they would be locked out.

"Locked *out* of gaol?"

"That's right. So they miss their free breakfast, see?"

They had passed through the green Botanical Gardens where the luxuriant coconut palms had to be watered through the Dry, when no rain fell for months. They drove past the Civil Aerodrome at Parap, then along the cliff-top road to the Bay, which ended in East Point, where the Air Force barracks were.

The taxi left them and they climbed over the low yellow sand-hills festooned with purple-flowering convolvulus, keeping their shoes on, for the sand was burning hot. The tide was receding, but there was still enough depth of water for a quick swim.

Two Wirraways droned overhead towards the Air Force station beyond.

"I heard an Air Force man talking to a friend of his in hospital with appendicitis," said Sister Rowan. "He says they've got nothing but a few Wirraways, and five of those are grounded. He said there were plenty of aircraftsmen and airmen and Air Vice-Marshals, but not enough aircraft.

431

They've got eight Hudson bombers, some of them down at Batchelor, and no decent fighters at all."

"Evidently the people running the war don't think Darwin is very important."

"Then why are they building up the Army here, and opening a new Army hospital?"

"I don't know. But the troops are bored. They hate it."

"Yes, an Army Sister was telling me that they are getting a lot of psychiatric cases—it's unofficially known as 'going troppo.' Disturbed soldiers who talk to themselves or walk imaginary dogs, and generally behave oddly."

"Couldn't they be malingerers, trying to get sent home?"

"I expect some of them are. But apparently it is a real problem."

Alix missed Baby Jimmy after he went home with his mother.

"So the little man was well enough to leave?" asked Surgeon-Commander Evans when she told him the supply of fresh milk was no longer needed.

"Yes, he's thriving, thanks to you. He's been putting on about seven ounces a week."

"Well, you might as well keep the new lot I've brought for yourself. I expect you'd like some fresh milk in your coffee for a change."

"I would, thank you."

"And what about a change from hospital fare? I'd like to take you to dinner at the Hotel Darwin when you have a free night. I can't guarantee that they'll have any wine—"

Alix hesitated. "It's very kind of you, sir. But—"

"But you don't want to mix work with socializing, right? Look, Sister, I'm not trying to make a heavy pass at you. It's just that I'm lonely, and it would be nice to have a meal with a woman for a change, instead of my fellow officers. What do you say?"

She smiled suddenly. He really was nice. She liked his calm voice, his air of self-sufficiency without the arrogance that some surgeons developed.

"All right," she said. "Tomorrow night, then?"

Chapter Twenty-eight

After their first dinner together, which they both enjoyed, Clyde Evans and Alix decided to make it a weekly date. On taking her back to the hospital he got out of the Navy Jeep and escorted her to the door of the nurses' quarters. There he kissed her lightly, and said, "Thank you, dear girl, for a most enjoyable evening."

Alix told herself that it was a perfectly innocent relationship, there was no comparison with Caro's situation. Certainly he was a married man, but that need not stop them enjoying each other's company. She found him very attractive, but he had assured her that he was not looking for an extra-marital affair, and she believed him.

Sister Rowan teased her a little about it, for of course she soon knew. "Lucky you!" she added. "He's gorgeous, isn't he."

"He is rather. But there's nothing like that between us. A strictly platonic friendship."

When she met him again on duty his manner in the wards was impeccable, though he smiled at her warmly. She looked at his firm well-cut mouth and thought of that other doctor, at Cloncurry Hospital, with his sensuous mouth and wandering hands and his habit of trying to kiss her behind screens. The Commander would never do that, would never force his attentions upon her. And yet, to be honest, she rather wished he would kiss her again.

She'd had a disturbing letter from Alice Springs, warning her of the scandal Caro and Dr. Trenowith were creating, and had written at once to Caro, a stern letter she now rather regretted.

Meanwhile David and Caro were happy, seeing each other every day and very often at night, unaware in their new-found content of the scandal that was about to break.

By November of 1941 the civilian road crew, with back-up from Army vehicles and supplies, had completed the section of highway from Tennant Creek up to the rail terminus at Birdum. It was now an all-weather metalled road, though unsealed and dusty. They were still working on upgrading the existing track from the Alice to Tennant Creek.

It had deteriorated from extra use as troops and Army equipment and road-grading materials were taken over it, then up the dusty highway to

Larrimah, just past Birdum. The final section to Darwin was by the slow little train called *Leaping Lena*.

Because of the sudden concentration of men in the empty north, the Flying Doctor at Alice Springs was busier than ever, visiting the road camps and bringing back sick or injured men to the hospital. David and Caro were out nearly every day. They now worked smoothly as a team, David sometimes piloting the Dragon on the way back while Caro gave support and comfort to the stretcher case. Sulphonamide drugs were in use and had proved effective against venereal diseases common to the Army, and in helping the rapid healing of wounds and the cure of blood poisoning.

Just as the two of them felt secure in their relationship, Caro first became aware of a coolness in acquaintances such as Mrs. Reilly, the resident doctor's wife, and the Matron of the hospital. At first it was nothing she could put her finger on; she noticed that Matron no longer invited her to afternoon tea in her rooms, and that she had not been asked to dinner at the Reillys' for a long time. When she ran into Mrs. Reilly at the post office one morning, her greeting seemed perfunctory, and she hurried off after a few words, saying she had a hairdresser's appointment. This was surprising, as her hair appeared as if it had only just been washed and set.

Caro was a little puzzled, but thought no more of the incident until David remarked casually as they met at the airport one morning,

"It seems that people are talking, darling."

"Talking?"

"About us. Our names are being linked together, as they say."

"Oh dear! That explains it . . . I mean, I've noticed a certain coolness in the air."

"Yes. I was having a drink with a friend at the Stuart Arms, and he gave me the tip. . . . As a matter of fact, he said 'Half your luck,' or something similar. Apparently it is generally believed in the town that you and I are having an affair."

It was such an understatement that Caro smiled ironically. "Surely not, Doctor!"

"I'm afraid so, Sister."

"Well, I suppose it was bound to get known in a place this size, and where people haven't much to do but gossip. My mother warned me about the possibility. I said we were very discreet."

"I thought we were. The trouble is, when I look at you I can't help it showing in my face—that I love you."

"Me too."

He went to kiss her, but she stepped back. "No, not here, David! I feel we're being watched. And that something beautiful is being pawed over, besmirched by grubby little minds—"

"It was inevitable, I suppose. What now? We can stop seeing each other alone, or we can say to hell with them and live together openly, since the secret is out."

"You know that's not possible. Not if we're staying with the Aerial Medical Service. It's all administered by a Federal Council now, you know. Either one or both of us will be sacked."

"Of course I could join the Air Force. In fact I've been feeling that I should, most of the younger men who can fly have joined already. . . . I couldn't stay here and never take you to bed. If you mean to give me up—"

"David! Darling, you know I couldn't bear it either. But I'd better not come to your house any more. As soon as we get a break, let's fly off in your Moth together, just for an hour. And when we're coming back from a routine immunization flight, there's nothing to stop us landing somewhere on the way back. It will be like the early days when we had to meet on beaches and in the bush. But in town, we'll be strictly on a professional footing."

They flew off together to pick up a patient. At least they still had an excuse for seeing each other. Caro was glad her mother's friend Maurie Anderson was no longer in town to join the chorus of disapproval. He had left to enlist as a Wireless Air Gunner with the R.A.A.F. He might even, she thought, have written to Alix to warn her of what was going on. She didn't want her mother worried.

She and David were being very circumspect, and suffering for it, in the next week. Caro began to feel that perhaps she had imagined the coolness among her women acquaintances. Then a letter came that shattered her complacency.

I warned you about not causing a scandal [wrote Alix], but it seems that is what you have done. Sister Bettens [a former A.I.M. Sister who had married and stayed on in the town] has written to tell me of the situation, and to beg me to use my influence to get you to stop this affair with Dr. Trenowith. She says you are doing harm not only to yourself, but to the image of the A.I.M. Sisters held by outback people. . . . It is only a matter of time, she says, before Sydney hears about it, and either one or both of you will be dismissed. Most likely the doctor, as he is a married man. But either way, you will be disgraced, and will bring disgrace to your profession. I am sorry, Caro, I know how much he means to you, but if you value your career— and my peace of mind—you will end this liaison at once.

Perhaps you could get a posting to a different town, or something. But I beg you to think seriously about it.

Your loving mother.

P.S. Would you like to come to Darwin? I think I could get you on the staff here, but only as a nurse, of course, not as a pilot.

Caro sat staring at this innocent-looking bombshell. So, everyone knew! Her mother knew, and her mother's old friends in the A.I.M., and of course the Matron and the doctor's wife and probably most of the nurses at the hospital. David saw that she was troubled when they met again in the course of their duties. She told him of her mother's letter.

"So! The cat is out of the bag!" he said. "I'm not going to stay to be dismissed; I'll resign. I can always get another job flying, or join the Air Force, but it will be much harder for you to get another pilot's position."

"Because I'm a woman!" said Caro bitterly.

After her mother's letter Caro became increasingly sensitive to the sly looks, the smiles, and the whispers that accompanied her visits to the post office or Pettit's Store.

"It's all very well for you!" she said when David told her to ignore them. "You *like* notoriety; you told me so. But I feel exposed, like a snail without its shell. Even at the hospital, though no one has said anything, I feel the chill in the atmosphere."

"My dear girl, it doesn't matter what people think, as long as you are comfortable with your own conscience."

"I am. I'm not ashamed of my relationship with you. Just I wish it didn't have to cause gossip, and upset my mother. . ."

Caro rarely cried, but her bottom lip began to tremble.

He held her head against his shoulder and stroked her hair, soothing her like a child. "There, there! It's all right, dear. It will all blow over, you'll see."

On one occasion when Alix and Commander Evans shared a bottle of red wine from pre-war stocks at the Darwin Hotel, Alix found it went straight to her head. She was over-tired after a busy day in the ward. "My heart aches, and a drowsy numbness pains/My limbs/as though of Lethe I had drunk," she thought, but not aloud. She had tried her steak and found it good. She began telling him about Cappamerri Station, and how they used to have steak for breakfast, but no eggs.

He raised his glass and smiled into her eyes. "I like to hear you talk," he said.

On the way back to the hospital he parked the Jeep above the sea and turned off the lights. There had been a heavy thunderstorm earlier and the air was humid, but the sky was clear of cloud. The setting moon made a golden track across the sheltered waters of the harbour.

"How many hundreds of thousands of years," said Alix dreamily, "that

436

moon has shone across the water here. Before there were men, or wars. . . ."

"Alix," he said, "I'm giving you fair warning—I'm going to kiss you."

"Oh!" she said, rather breathless, and next moment his firm clean-shaven lips were pressed against hers. Her head sank against his shoulder and for a long moment she was lost in a sensation she had almost forgotten. He lifted his head and looked into her eyes in the moonlight. She said nothing, but he had felt her response.

"I told you, when I first asked you out, that I wouldn't be making a pass at you. But you're so nice, and understanding, and kind, and pretty, it's very hard for me."

"Are you going to tell me you are married, and your wife doesn't understand you?"

"No. My wife is a very understanding woman, and I love her. I promised myself at the beginning of this war that I wasn't going to cheat on her, whatever happened. She trusts me. But . . . Oh hell, do you mind if I kiss you again?"

"N-no."

This time he pulled her right across into his seat, and she clung to him fiercely. But he soon put her firmly back in her seat on the other side of the four-wheel-drive gearbox, and started the engine.

"I'd better take you back, Sister. On duty in the morning?"

"Yes . . . seven A.M." Her voice shook a little.

Back at the hospital he kissed her once more, but said firmly, "I'm sorry about tonight, Alix. . . . No I'm not! I'm glad. But it won't happen again, I promise."

Alix went to bed in something of a daze. Her own response to Clyde Evans had startled and shaken her. She'd lived for so long without a man, become so used to it. . . . But she wished her letter to Caro unwritten. She had forgotten what it was like to be young. What a pompous, po-faced missive it must have seemed to the poor child!

And as for herself, she realized she'd been only half alive. So when Clyde asked her to go on a picnic one Sunday to the Dripstone Caves, she hesitated only a moment. They'd not had another dinner date— apparently he thought it wiser. But a boat trip round the harbour in the daytime—there was no risk in that.

He cast off expertly from the long jetty and reversed the light open boat, which, Alix thought, looked large enough to carry twenty ratings.

"I don't know much about boats," she said over the noise of the engine, "I've lived so much of my life inland."

He brought out a small map and showed her where they were going, north around the various points to Casuarina Beach.

437

"It's about sixteen miles by sea," he said, "and inaccessible by road. You see this tidal creek here, Rapid Creek? The area is all mangroves and crocodiles, and there's no bridge."

They chugged across a turquoise sea towards the smoke-hazed north shore. Alix wore white cotton slacks and an open-necked shirt of pale blue, with a shady hat. At eleven the sun was already hot enough to burn.

She went back to sit beside him in the stern, to ask about the caves they were going to see.

"I don't know much about them," he said. "They sound interesting, though—Dripstone probably means they are limestone caves, with stalactites. I believe there's a little sandy cove where we can beach the boat at high tide."

As high tide was around 2 P.M., they would have to get there in time for an early lunch, and leave again no later than three in order to get back around the rocky headland before the sea went too far out. They rounded the last point and saw ahead the long sweep of Casuarina Beach. A small double headland of limestone jutted out into the sea; at its apex was a perfect little cove with a sandy beach.

"This is it!" said Clyde. "The caves are at the back of the cove, or so I'm told."

They scrunched softly into the sand and he cut the inboard engine. Alix, eager to see the caves, was over the side and scrambling up the beach before he had the kedge anchor fixed in the sand. When he followed he found her staring at two little caverns, about six feet deep and less than that high, in the low cliffs.

"You mean *those* are the famous Dripstone Caves?"

"Er—apparently, yes." He looked apologetic, but suddenly he saw the funny side of it and began to laugh.

"And I brought a torch and spare batteries, and a length of twine so that we could find our way back to the entrance!"

They both sat in the sand and laughed. "Well, at least they're big enough for us to sit in the shade to have our lunch," said Alix cheerfully.

Higher up the cliff were a few little hollows from which water dripped down the face of the rock. "Dripstone, you see," he explained.

"And you said there would be *stalactites*," said Alix in mock reproach.

They made a pleasant meal of cold salmon mousse, which Alix had begged from the hospital kitchen, with salad and a half-bottle of hock.

He climbed up to the first of the damp hollows and collected some of the sweet, clear water for them to drink.

"It would be very handy if you were marooned on the beach around here," he said, "to have drinking water on tap."

"Don't talk about being marooned!"

"Which reminds me," said Clyde, "that we must watch the tide. The given times are not always accurate. In fact I'll take the boat and the

438

anchor out a bit now, in case the water falls and we can't launch her."

They scrambled around the rocks to the next beach, and Alix looked wistfully at the sparkling sea and the clean sand. No chance of having a swim. There were not only Portuguese men-of-war, called bluebottles, but the deadly box jellyfish whose sting could be fatal in minutes. Both came close to shore in the summer months, with the northerly winds.

Clyde had put a stick in the sand at the edge of the water in the first cove. By the time they returned from their walk the tide had started to drop. He had been circumspect; he had not touched her hand until now, when he helped her into the boat. But just through the touch of his warm fingers Alix felt the electric attraction between them.

And then the engine would not start. Clyde swore, and tried the starter over and over, until he had to stop or flatten the battery. He took out spark-plugs and looked at them helplessly. He was no mechanic. But he methodically searched for a loose wire, a loose battery connection, anything. And the sea steadily receded.

"I could push her out into deeper water," he said, "but if the engine doesn't start? She's too heavy to row."

Alix sat petrified. She could not offer any useful suggestions. She could only think, her imagination leaping ahead, of their being forced to stay together in this little cove till someone rescued them—perhaps not before tomorrow. The scandal if they stayed out all night would be as bad as the one brewing in Alice Springs.

The tide fell. The boat tilted on dry land.

"Could we—could we walk back? At least as far as Fannie Bay?" she asked.

"My dear girl," he said rather testily. "There is no way we could get across Rapid Creek even if you could wade it at low tide; it's infested with crocodiles. Then miles of mangrove swamp. . . . If we walk round the coast, it's a lot further, and we'd still have to cross the tidal creeks."

When she suggested lighting a fire as a signal for help, he explained that the Aborigines were lighting fires all the time on this coast, and no one would take any notice. Once it got dark he could signal with the torch, but when the tide was out, no passing boats would be close, and they couldn't come in anyway. There were no other trippers here because of the wartime rationing of fuel.

"This bloody engine!" he said, and gave it a kick. The tide was running out fast, but he tried the starter again, and suddenly the engine burst into life. It must have been something simple, he said, a flooded carburettor or a damp distributor, or perhaps some loose connection that his kick had fixed. But the boat was immovable on the damp sand. He switched off the engine. "I'm sorry, Alix. This is all my fault."

The boat was tilted uncomfortably, so they went back to the caves.

439

"There is one each," he pointed out, "in case we have to spend the night here."

Indeed, it seemed there was nothing else they could do. There was a little bread and butter left from their picnic, and there was plenty of water, so they made a frugal meal.

"The next high tide is at two-thirty A.M.," said Clyde. "We should be able to get the boat off by two. Say two hours to get back, and half an hour to tie up and walk to the hospital. There'll be a moon from ten P.M., and I have the torch so we won't be run down. With luck we might get in before anyone is awake."

"I only hope so!"

"Of course, if the engine refuses to start again. . ."

She didn't want to think about that possibility.

He collected some driftwood and made a small fire. The night was clear and starry, but it was not cold. He spread the thin checked rug which before they had used as a table-cloth.

"You don't really want to wait in a separate cave, do you?" he asked. "At least we can talk."

She was silent, sitting with her face averted, looking at the dark sea.

"Alix? You blame me for this, don't you? I swear it wasn't planned. But since we're here. . ."

He put his arms around her and pressed her head down on his shoulder. The neat bun that she wore was coming loose, and curling strands strayed down her neck. He kissed her ear, and turned her face till he could reach her lips. At first she responded, but when he pushed her back on the rug she turned and buried her face. "You promised. . ." she muttered.

"I know, I know. But it's so wonderful to have a woman in my arms again. I've been thinking about you ever since that night. Alix, I want you so much, you're so sweet, such a dear—"

She sat up, a little apart, and mechanically tidied her hair.

She said in a low voice, "You don't understand. Apart from everything else—and there's your wife, you know that you still love her, and you would regret this afterwards—there's my daughter. Caro is involved with a married man, a doctor in Alice Springs. I wrote to her just the other week, scolding her for causing a scandal, and telling her she must give him up. And now, here am I. . . ! You see? Even if we do cause a scandal here, whatever people think and say, I'll know it's not true. I couldn't face her otherwise; I'd be such a hypocrite."

"But when you wrote, you couldn't have known—"

"That I was going to fall in love with you? No, but that doesn't alter anything. Let's go for a walk around to the next beach now the tide's out, and watch the moonrise. Then I'll have a few hours' sleep, on my own."

"My dear girl, you'll be quite safe with me, now that I know how you feel. You are right, of course. And I would never pester you."

By the time they came back from the beach beyond, they could see the tide had already started on its way in, though it was still four hours to high water. Clyde insisted that Alix should have the blanket under her on the sand in the larger cave. He persuaded her to let him hold her quietly in his arms until she fell asleep. At 2 A.M. he called her. The moon, past full, was well overhead.

The boat was now afloat. Alix held her breath while he tried the engine, but it started almost at once. They set off over the sparkling sea towards Darwin Harbour.

On the way Clyde explained that he'd decided not to go round to the wharf, but to run the boat into Doctor's Gully. From there they could climb quickly up to the hospital grounds.

"She'll be all right on the sand," he said, "and I can take her round to the wharf at three or four tomorrow afternoon."

Soon after 4 A.M. Alix, with her heart beating painfully, crept into the nurses' quarters, using her own key. Back in her room she was overcome by relief, but immediately began to feel hungry. Fortunately she put on pyjamas before going to raid the pantry, for on the way back she met Sister Ellie Rowan on her way to the toilet.

"When did you get in?" she asked. "It must have been pretty late."

"Yes, we ate out, but I woke up feeling hungry."

Alix was surprised at how easily the lies slipped out.

"You look wide awake. Your cheeks are flushed and your eyes are shining. Are you sure you're all right?"

"Perfectly all right. Go to bed, Ellie."

Alix realized how lucky she had been. She could have met Ellie as she was creeping in, fully clothed, with the bottoms of her slacks wet with sea-water.

Chapter Twenty-nine

The British, American, and Australian governments had for some time been aware of the possibility of war with the Japanese, who had been building up their navy and air force and behaving with increasing arrogance. The French Vichy Government had yielded to their demands for bases in Indo-China, and conceded them the use of eight air-bases there. This left Malaya open to attack.

Just before midnight on December 7, 1941, the Japanese began a series of surprise air attacks across the width of the Pacific, from Shanghai to Hawaii, from Hong Kong to Pearl Harbor, and the United States Pacific Fleet was decimated.

A few days later the pride of the British Fleet, the battleships *Prince of Wales* and *Repulse*, were sunk off Malaya. The Australian High Commission in London received a cable on Christmas Day, which read:

WITHOUT IMMEDIATE AIR ASSISTANCE SINGAPORE MUST FALL. NEED FOR DECISION AND ACTION IS A MATTER OF HOURS, NOT DAYS.

And Churchill announced with fine rhetoric, "Singapore will be defended at all costs."

Yet the island was left defenceless, its guns all pointing uselessly out to sea, while the Japanese advanced rapidly down the Malay Peninsula. The British sent a consignment of Hurricane fighters in crates, still not assembled, which arrived when the bombs were already falling.

There had been vague fears of expansion by our northern neighbours for years past. This had been referred to ironically as "the Yellow Peril," but now the peril was real. In mid-December the government in Canberra issued instructions for the evacuation of Darwin, with a list of priorities: women and children first, and each household to take only one suitcase, two blankets, eating and drinking utensils, and a water-bag. Pets were to be destroyed.

Thousands of soldiers spent Christmas and New Year putting barbed-wire entanglements along the beaches. Concrete gun emplacements were manned and armed. As the apparently invincible Japanese moved steadily southward, there was fear not only of aerial attack, but actual invasion.

David told Caro that he was going to join the Air Force immediately.

Her face fell. "David! But—"

"Caro, I must. It looks as if we'll be fighting the Japs in our own country, and I'll have to be in it."

"But there are plenty of young men joining up—"

"Yes, but they need some experienced older men. Besides, I'm a doctor and they'll need medical men in Darwin. Perhaps they'll keep me on the ground, though I hope not. . . . Cheer up, darling!" he said, looking at her woebegone face. "I won't be leaving until they get a replacement, and with so many young doctors joining up, that'll take some time. Come, dear, it was you who said we must stop seeing each other. It will be easier this way."

"It will be easier for *you*, with all the excitement of being in the war, and new powerful aircraft, and travel, and danger—"

"I promise to be careful, and to come back to you."

"Hah! Your middle name is danger. You thrive on it. Promise me, promise me you won't get killed." She clung to him, weeping.

"I promise."

Caro was relieved for Alix's sake, and desolated for her own.

She worried about her mother, who might soon be in the front line. She wrote to Alix to reassure her that David was leaving to join up. Meanwhile, until he was called up, she meant to enjoy every moment with him that she could.

David wrote to ask his wife if she was going south to Adelaide—worried that she might turn up in Alice Springs. But she replied that there was no panic in the town, and she was in no hurry to leave.

She wrote that many women wanted to stay on with their husbands, but unless they were in essential services they would be forced to go eventually. There was tension in the town, but also a sense of unreality. People could not believe that they were in danger from the Japanese, those polite little men seen around the port, or on the pearling luggers. Of course, it was said that they had all been spying on the north coast for years. . . .

Meanwhile Alix had learned from Dr. Evans that there were only five Wirraway fighter planes in Darwin, and they were unserviceable. The other nine were down the line at Batchelor, sixty miles away. As Wirraways had already proved useless against Japanese Zeros, there was in fact not a single fighter to defend the town against an air borne attack. There were anti-aircraft gun emplacements, but no modern Bofors guns. And morale in the Army and Air Force was low.

The new hospital opened in January, when patients and staff moved into comfortable modern quarters at Kahlin. But it still had the drawback of the old hospital, if it came to war; it was just as near to Larrakeyah Barracks, an obvious enemy target. But there was a large Red Cross

443

painted on the white roof. There was also a hospital ship, the former coastal passenger ship *Manunda*, in the harbour to ferry injured patients out of Darwin.

The new twelve-hundred bed Army hospital at Berrimah, nine miles away, was no safer, for it was only a mile from the end of the main runway of the R.A.A.F. aerodrome. It was not yet finished and was only partly occupied when it opened in January.

Alix had been relieving the Theatre Sister in the new Kahlin Hospital, so that she was frequently brought into contact with Surgeon-Commander Evans. He became increasingly worried about the Japanese advance, and predicted that it would not be long before Singapore fell.

The victorious Japanese swept down the Pacific, landing in the Dutch East Indies and taking Ambon Island, from which they could fly to Darwin. "You girls shouldn't be here when the Japanese troops land. You should go south, even if only as far as Katherine," said the Commander.

"We can't go and leave all our patients," objected Alix obstinately. "And surely we can defend Darwin, with a bit of help from our friends."

"We can't rely on the protection of the British Navy any more," he said gloomily. "Their whole Far Eastern empire is falling apart. We can only hope that the Yanks will regard Australia as a great unsinkable aircraft carrier and base for their operations in the Pacific, and therefore worth defending."

During the first week in February, Alix was on night duty. Towards midnight she went out on the hospital veranda for a breath of fresh air. The night was oppressively humid and the sky heavy with storm-clouds. The black clouds were broken into ugly, angular shapes along their edges, and among them she saw the pallid moon, past full, which seemed to her distorted, out of drawing. In spite of the heat Alix shivered. She felt there was something hateful about the night.

She was just turning to go inside when the air-raid siren shattered the quiet.

She rushed to the Surgical Ward she had just left, where some of the patients, being sedated, had not stirred. Others were sitting up in alarm.

"All right; keep calm," said Alix. "If the bombing comes close, I'll get you all to lie under your beds. But we'll wait and see."

Matron came in in her dressing-gown. "Yes, better not do anything yet. It could be just reconnaissance planes," she said. Her hair fell down her back in a long, thick, shining red plait.

They all strained their ears but could hear no sound of aircraft engines or ack-ack guns. After a while they relaxed.

It was more than an hour later when the all-clear sounded, and meanwhile half the population of Darwin—white, Aboriginal, and Chinese—had been sheltering on the beach below the cliffs. Some had brought pillows and blankets. After an hour huddling on the beach, the people decided that a Japanese attack could be only marginally worse than the ferocity of the sand-flies and mosquitoes, so they went home. Not a single aircraft had been heard. The air-raid alert had been a false alarm.

But Darwin was now wide open to air attack, and still without proper defences. Those residents left in the far north felt cynically that the Commonwealth Government, safe in Canberra, had decided to abandon them to the Japanese while they concentrated on strengthening the populous cities to the south.

On February 15, 1942, Singapore fell, and seventeen thousand Australian troops disappeared behind the bamboo walls of prison camps. The Japanese had already moved into the islands north of Australia. Timor would be next, and then Darwin.

Sister Rowan was just on her way to the theatre when Clyde Evans said to her seriously next morning, "I hope you've got plenty of dressings ready in the theatre, Sister. It's only a matter of days before we're raided. I hope the R.A.A.F. knows what it's doing. . . . They've only got those little stumpy-winged Wirraways—home-built jobs. They'll be no match for the Jap Zeros. And they don't have enough range with their Hudson bombers to worry the Japanese bases."

Two days later the anti-aircraft guns nearly shot down some transport planes (bringing troops back from Japanese-occupied islands to the north), mistaking them for enemy aircraft. This incident added to everyone's edginess and did not improve relations between Air Force and Army administrations. The last civilian women had now been evacuated, in theory; but in fact there were still sixty or so in the town, some working in the post office, some part-Aboriginal or Chinese women who had not been counted.

Some of the older men for whom the "Top End" had been home for many years, had practically to be carried, kicking, to the railway station or wharf. Some went south by air liner, but the commercial services to Adelaide were infrequent, while Qantas flying-boats round the coast to Brisbane and Sydney were not considered safe from Japanese attack.

The Administrator's wife and all of her household staff were still at the Residency.

On February 17, a convoy of troopships on its way to Timor turned back after being attacked by Japanese bombers. They steamed into Darwin Harbour on the eighteenth, and those who were expecting the Japanese to arrive any day shook their heads. The enemy knew where the fox had gone to earth. They would inevitably follow and try to finish it off. Among the ships was the American destroyer U.S.S. *Peary*, which would be a prize.

Then on the morning of the nineteenth, a squadron of United States Air Force P40 Kittyhawks, which happened to be in Darwin, returned from an abortive flight to Timor. They confused the issue so that a simultaneous warning from the look-out at Casuarina Beach that a large formation of Japanese planes was approaching was all but ignored at R.A.A.F. headquarters.

"How do you know they're Japanese?" asked the control room. "They could be the P40s."

"Because they've got bloody great red spots under their wings!" came the reply. Within a minute the first bombs fell on the harbour, and the air-raid sirens belatedly began to sound.

The P40 pilots made a desperate, valiant effort to get off the ground again, but most of them were shot down and destroyed before they could get any height. Only one, still in the air, was above the Zeros and managed to bag two. The Japanese had thrown in twenty-seven low-level dive-bombers and twenty-seven high-level bombers, with an escort of Zero fighters that were fast and manoeuvrable. The squadron of P40s was lost, along with the useless Wirraways destroyed on the ground, and the lives of several American airmen.

Darwin and its harbour full of forty-five ships at anchor was a sitting duck.

CHAPTER THIRTY

It was a beautiful warm morning with a gentle breeze off the sea, when the Japanese force of eighty-one war-planes arrived over Darwin. The sun shone, a few steamy white clouds patterned the sky.

The radar warning system was not yet operating. Through a series of bungles and plain incompetence, a radio warning from Bathurst Island twenty minutes before went unheeded. Though a raid had been expected for weeks past, the town was unprepared; people were going about their morning shopping, banks and post office were busy, the Court was sitting, when without warning the bombs began to fall on the harbour.

Inexorably the explosions marched along the jetty to the shore, over the administration buildings, the Administrator's residence, the police barracks. A direct hit on the post office sent up a black cloud of dust and smoke, and ten people, including several women postal clerks, died in the slit-trench where they had just taken shelter. The post-master's body was found sitting grotesquely in a tree, while his wife and daughters had all the clothes blasted from their bodies.

Then it was the turn of the Darwin Hospital, while the Army barracks nearby were not touched. (It was thought afterwards that the enemy pilots had mistaken the hospital buildings for the barracks.)

Sister Rowan was in the theatre preparing for an operation to be performed by Surgeon-Commander Evans. The nurse assisting had gone along the veranda to get the patient from the Surgical Ward. She came running back, shouting that she had seen Japanese planes dropping bombs on the harbour. The sound of the sirens reached them at the same time as the noise of the explosions.

Alix had been transferred that week to Casualty. There she was to have one of the busiest days of her life. First she ran to her quarters to get her steel helmet, then went to help move bedridden patients under the beds and pile mattresses on top for protection, while those who could walk took to the bush or the beach below the cliffs.

Six huge explosions shook the hospital. Concrete and glass were hurled through the air, part of the ceiling fell in, but no patients were hurt. The naval ward and the laundry were demolished, and the theatre was damaged, though it was still usable.

The nurses crouched half under beds. A huge rock came crashing through a window on to an empty bed, bounced off the mattress and rolled away without causing any injury. Alix shut her eyes; her steel helmet felt heavier every moment, but she had little faith in its protection. The noise was terrifying. The roar of planes, the explosion of bombs, and the sound of falling masonry filled the air.

Then suddenly it was over. The sound of aeroplane engines faded into the distance, the explosions sounded farther and farther away. The nurses got up from the floor and began putting the ward to rights, settling patients back in bed, sweeping up broken glass and debris, and dusting bedside lockers.

Within ten minutes of the first bombs falling, casualties began to arrive. The Medical Superintendent told Alix to carry on alone, as the casualty officer was needed elsewhere. She was to give anti-tetanus injections, suture what wounds she could, and send on to the doctors only those cases she was unable to treat herself.

Her courage rose to the occasion. It was many years since she had sutured a wound, and nearly thirty since she had stitched up Jim's abdomen gored by a bull. But her hand was steady and her voice calm as she reassured shocked and burnt patients. The first case, a badly smashed leg, she had to send on to the surgical team. She heard afterwards that it had been amputated.

The first casualties were brought along by Constable McNab, the Reverend Chris Goy of the A.I.M.—he still had shaving soap dried on his chin—and Sergeant Bill McKinnon. Injured seamen were groaning in pain, their bodies blackened by burning oil in the harbour. Eight ships had been sunk and many others beached and burnt. The U.S.S. *Peary* had been blown out of the water, killing eighty of her crew and her captain; but the U.S. seaplane-tender *William B. Preston*, though hit in the stern, put up a smoke-screen and somehow got away to sea.

One Catalina flying-boat managed to escape destruction. Perhaps she was hidden from the Japanese by the pall of smoke from the ammunition ship *Neptuna*, which was burning nearby. The two Qantas captains raced down to the wharf and had themselves ferried out in one of the launches bringing oil-covered and desperately wounded men from the sea. They managed to take off in the flying-boat before the *Neptuna*, glowing red-hot, went up like a giant bomb. Without a crew, they were able to fly the machine to safety at Groote Eylandt. Next day they came back to shattered Darwin to pick up the crew—the same day the Japanese occupied Timor, the last link of the Australia-England air route.

Even the hospital ship *Manunda* had been hit by bombs. Afterwards Alix learned that a nurse she knew had been killed, and another seriously injured.

In Casualty, Constable McNab remained to help Alix by receiving patients, taking their details if they were fit to give them, and presenting them to her in order of urgency. He cleaned the blood off the floor and went for extra bandages and splints. Alix treated some horrifying wounds; one young sailor had his face split open from forehead to chin. She gave him an injection and sent him on to Surgeon-Commander Evans without delay.

She and the theatre nurses had been on their feet for seven hours when they left for a hurried meal in the nurses' quarters. They had not eaten since breakfast. On the way Alix and Ellie Rowan met the Medical Superintendent, who told them that an evacuee train was leaving for the south with all the women remaining in Darwin, as a Japanese landing was imminent.

Alix and Ellie looked at each other. "We can't possibly go, and leave all these patients to look after themselves," they said. With eight other nurses, they volunteered to stay on.

In the nurses' dining room a young Sister rushed up to them.

"Oh, Sister Manning! Have you heard the dreadful news?"

"What, have the Japs landed?"

"No! They've let all the prisoners out of Fannie Bay. And most of them are in for rape!"

"Good," said Ellie, "if the Japanese are coming tomorrow, then give me an Australian tonight."

Half an hour after the all-clear, the warning sirens had sounded again. The Japanese had come back with fifty-four bombers, and this time they concentrated on the Air Force Station, criss-crossing it with precision fire-bombing until every building was a smoking shell and every aircraft completely destroyed. But only six men had died.

The greatest damage was to morale. Airmen and aircraftsmen, clerks and administration staff wandered about dazed and bewildered. Then a message began to spread from group to group: "We've been ordered to go into the bush south of the town, and re-group."

Exactly where, nobody seemed to know—in fact the order, though vague, had specified "a mile out of town and into the bush." A stampede began, and soon the station was deserted. Some of the men turned up at Adelaide River, some at Batchelor, some even managed to get to Daly Waters. After two days there were still three hundred men missing.

Immediately after the second raid an attempt was made to move out all the women and children left in the town. A party of nuns from the Catholic Mission at Garden Point shepherded a flock of part-Aboriginal girls and one boy, who were given transport in an open coal-truck to the south. But Aboriginal women were given no such priority; they were simply told to go bush. Many of them had children at the missions or the official Half-castes' Home, where they could at least visit them, but now they were to be separated by a thousand miles. One old black woman keened to herself as the train departed, with unconscious poetry:

> My kid Ruby leave longa train,
> Missus, she gone longa plane.
> Me can't stay Darwin, me go bush.
> Maybe I die. All-a-same.

Passenger planes leaving were full, and at the airstrip at Adelaide River there was the spectacle of young civilian men elbowing women aside and offering double price for their seats.

The one idea was to put as much distance as possible between themselves and the murderous Japanese. In what became known as the "Adelaide River Stakes," hundreds hurriedly left town in whatever vehicle they could commandeer, including the two town night-carts. It was a panic flight.

CHAPTER THIRTY-ONE

At eleven o'clock the night of the raid, the flow of casualties ceased. During the afternoon an urgent request had been sent to the A.G.H. Army Hospital at Berrimah for some relieving nurses, and four were sent at once. But the back-up team of surgeons which had been promised in an emergency never materialized.

Alix, having taken an hour off for supper and put her feet up on the table in the nurses' dining room, volunteered for duty in the theatre, where Sister Rowan had been on her feet for sixteen hours.

Clyde Evans, his eyes bloodshot but his hands as steady as ever, was still operating. He gave Alix a nod and his eyes smiled at her over his mask. She was startled to feel a surge of love move in her as she watched his sturdy figure. She felt happy standing shoulder to shoulder with him and passing instruments, double-counting swabs with the theatre nurse, and exchanging a few words with the anaesthetist, a younger man who was showing signs of fatigue. The strangeness and tension of the day had somehow speeded up reactions and intensified her feelings.

Watching those sensitive hands with their spatulate fingers moving so deftly, cutting and tying off, probing and stitching, she remembered something she had not thought of for years; her first love, Dr. Hamilton, the god-like surgeon she had worshipped from a distance: a pure and hopeless love, unrequited and unconfessed, yet she had never forgotten him.

Clyde Evans was probing with forceps in a mass of torn flesh, extracting angular pieces of metal.

"Bloody Japs are using daisy-cutters," he muttered. "Anti-personnel bombs, they're called. They whizz along a few inches above the ground after they explode, and can cut a man to pieces."

"'Anti-personnel!'" said Alix. "Wonderful, isn't it, how armies have jargon to reduce their horrors with reasonable-sounding phrases. Like 'over-kill' and 'fire-power' and 'optimum casualties' . . . I hate war."

"I suppose I am trained for it. But I hate it too."

"My husband was killed in the last one."

His tired eyes left his task for a moment to flash her a look of sympathy.

"Well, at least you have your daughter to remember him by."

"Yes . . . I used to worry about her flying, but of course it has become much safer since she first started."

She scarcely knew what she was saying. She could only think, I love, I am in love, and nothing else matters.

It was one-thirty in the morning when they finished. The last patient was slowly waking up in the recovery room, unaware that he had lost one ear and part of his left cheek. The surgeon tore off his mask and theatre cap, and Alix helped him out of his bloodied gown.

"You go and get some sleep, Nurse," she said to the young theatre nurse. "I can clean up here."

For the moment they were alone. He pulled off Alix's cap and took her in his arms, pressing her curly head against his shoulder.

"Dear girl," he murmured. "Thank you for your help."

Alix smiled dreamily against his shoulder. "Do you know," she murmured, "that when I was about eighteen I was in love with a surgeon. He was an honorary at the North Adelaide Hospital where I trained. I loved him dearly. And he was hardly aware that I existed."

"He must have been blind," said Clyde, stroking her hair.

"No—he was much older; I suppose he'd be an old man now. And he was married, you see."

"I see." She felt him grow tense.

"And now I am in love with you. After all these years. It's as though—"

"Oh God, Alix. I'm so tired, I'm not thinking straight. But you know that I still love my wife, whatever I feel for you. You mustn't expect—"

"I expect nothing." She smiled at him serenely.

He kissed her eyes and her mouth, and put her from him.

"Go on, get to bed. You must be dead on your feet."

She had accompanied the patient to the Surgical Ward and checked that his breathing passages were clear, when she heard an altercation in the corridor.

The Medical Superintendent had just returned from a summons to Larrakeyah by the Director of Army Medical Services, which now controlled all hospitals in Darwin. He announced that the Army wanted the Kahlin Hospital evacuated, and all patients removed to Berrimah Army Hospital "for safety."

Surgeon-Commander Evans exploded with anger. He had been under stress for hours, making life-or-death decisions, straining eyes and nerves. Now he insisted that his patients should not be disturbed when some of them were recovering from major surgery.

"I won't allow them to be moved," he said obstinately. "They're under far less risk from being bombed than from complications caused by being moved too soon."

But the Army Medical Director was adamant, and the doctors at the

452

hospital had no choice but to comply. "And let it be recorded that I do so under protest," said Clyde Evans angrily.

"Well, Alix," he said, putting a hand on her arm. "No rest for the wicked, eh? The Army trucks will be here soon, and we've got three hundred patients to get ready for transport."

Matron Mackay began to supervise the move, her head swathed in plaits, not a hair out of place, her uniform spotless.

Sister Rowan, who had just got to sleep, was called and told she had to start work again. "The bloody Army!" she said to Alix. "I wouldn't be an Army nurse for quids."

The walking wounded got themselves to the trucks; the rest, some of them unconscious or still in a state of shock, were carried outside. Fortunately the night was clear.

When they arrived at the A.G.H. in the early hours of the morning, they found that it was full. There were no beds; but the unflappable matron had mattresses spread on the floor in wards and on verandas. The weary civilian nurses stretched out fully dressed on mattresses in the Army mess.

They were not reassured by hearing that one patient had died from a machine-gun bullet while under his bed that day. Looking up, they saw that the roof of the supposedly "safe" military hospital, nine miles from Darwin, was as full of holes as a colander.

Later in the morning nearly two hundred sick and wounded were taken to the harbour and embarked on the damaged *Manunda*, hoping to reach Perth. As they were loaded on the tender, they saw the piles of dead lying on the beaches like stacks of firewood.

There were so many dead, some quite impossible to identify, and the weather was so hot, that something urgent had to be done. It was Clyde Evans who gave the order for them to be placed on a barge and taken out for burial at sea.

Beached and broken ships; smoking hulls; pieces of metal debris from the *Neptuna*, all littered the foreshore. Half the jetty was gone, and the water was choked with shattered craft which were exposed as the tide went out. Many of the wharfies who had been unloading ships at the jetty were dead.

The gaol had not been hit by a bomb but had been strafed and shot up. The eighteen terrified Aboriginal prisoners, some of them on ten-year sentences for murdering the crew of a Japanese pearling lugger, were told to go bush.

"And if you see Japanee-man, orright you kill-em this time. Japanee-man no good."

The bemused natives set off at a run, and probably didn't stop till they got to their own country. Of the European prisoners, at least one had distinguished himself that day in tireless rescue work in the midst of

453

falling bombs and burning oil on the harbour. He later received a pardon and a citation for bravery.

In contrast, by the following morning there were nearly twelve hundred refugees at Adelaide River, the end of the road. They were milling about the railway station where the evacuee train was about to take off for Birdum, one long step on the way to the south and safety. Some of the civilians tried to rush a railway truck and had to be stopped by Army officers firing over their heads or at their feet. The commanding officer then conscripted them into a labour force. Everyone believed that martial law was in force, though in fact the Army had not been given this power. Nor did the Army do anything to stop the looting of empty houses by their own men in the next week.

Bands of Military Police, with no authority but for their arm-bands and pistols, began systematically looting; first the liquor stores, then shops in the main street, and then private homes abandoned by their owners. Men working in key positions in radio transmission or helping at the hospitals went home to find their houses stripped bare.

By now the M.P.s were nearly all drunk, shooting wildly with pistols and threatening owners who protested. Soon everyone joined in the free-for-all: officers and men, Australian and American, Air Force and Army. The nearly new Darwin Hotel was stripped of furnishings, after all the liquor had been taken from the bar and cellars. Even Government House was not exempt. A valuable grand piano belonging to the Administrator's wife simply disappeared.

Senseless destruction went on for days. Many upright pianos were ruined by having beer poured inside the lids. Sheets and curtains were ripped, rifle-bullets were put through ceilings, drawers of papers and clothing were emptied on floors, fibro walls kicked in.

Not only portable goods were taken. Men commandeered trucks to transport refrigerators, sewing-machines, and radios to the wharf to be sent south or sold to ships' crews.

Perhaps it was release from tension, combined with alcohol, and the frustration of not being able to hit back at the Japanese airmen. The ferocity of the two raids had paralyzed the town, but no troops invaded —which was just as well, in the first week of looting, panic, and disappearing down the track.

As the Medical Superintendent at Kahlin Hospital said disgustedly to Surgeon-Commander Evans, "Two hundred Japanese armed with frying-pans could have taken the town yesterday!"

CHAPTER THIRTY-TWO

Caro heard of the bombing at the same time as the rest of Australia: through the morning paper. Though the country had never been attacked since the British landed their occupational forces in 1788, the newspaper headlines were not unduly large.

DARWIN BOMBED, they announced. "Fifteen dead, twenty-four wounded. Enemy planes shot down."

Even as the truth began to filter through, as refugees reached the south with their tale of destruction, the government clung to its lie. Accounts of American losses began to appear in the United States press, which did not tally with the official figures; but Canberra was still bent on playing down what had happened. In fact, 250 people had died—at least. The final figures were never certain, and could have been nearer to a thousand.

Four days later the first refugees since the bombing began to arrive in the Alice, with a very different story. Meanwhile the Flying Doctor Service—as it was to be known officially from this year—had been asked to lend any available ambulance planes to fly out women and children still not evacuated, including children from the island missions to the north and a very pregnant Chinese woman.

"My God, I hope those bastards didn't bomb the hospital," said Caro to David. "I hope Mum is all right. What if the Japanese land in the north? Everyone knows it's not properly defended."

Caro asked the Council in Sydney for permission to fly to Darwin. It was known that the road beyond Adelaide River was unusable, and the few commercial airliners could not cope with the numbers of refugees. She could bring back half a dozen passengers sitting up, and Connellan Airways had offered to make a plane and a pilot available to Dr. Trenowith in an emergency until her return.

It was two days after the raid when permission came through, and she then had to get a clearance from the Army to fly north. The fact that she was both a nurse and a pilot helped. She arranged to refuel at Army depots along the way, and set off at dawn on February 22.

Compared with some of her cross-continent flying, it was easy—no navigation problems as she followed the wide new clearing for the road, even easier to follow than the old Telegraph Line.

Daly Waters had become a back-up Air Force station, and at Katherine

455

there was an Army hospital. She reached Adelaide River, seventy miles south of Darwin, in the early afternoon. She had been directed to land there to pick up refugees because the Darwin airports, both civil and Air Force, had been so torn up with bomb craters and littered with burnt-out aircraft that they were unusable. Caro ignored the direction and flew on as far as Batchelor, eight miles farther north, where the R.A.A.F. Wirraway unit was stationed.

It had just occurred to Caro that she would not be able to see her mother, or even speak to her, for the Darwin Post Office and Telegraph station were gone and so far communications had not been restored. Radio messages from Air Force Command in the south were being intercepted at Batchelor, and then flown on in a little Moth training plane to the R.A.A.F. base in Darwin, as there was no radio communication with Headquarters. In fact communications between the two bases were so poor even before the raid, that the first news the Batchelor unit received of what had happened came over the railway telephone line.

The messages-by-Moth were not much faster than a pony express, the men told her, but they were being flown as fast as possible by the squadron leader, an ace pilot. When Caro heard his name she asked to see him.

Caro had caused a bit of a stir by landing out of the blue in her little Dragon. The Squadron-Leader was intrigued.

She introduced herself: "Caro Manning. Sister Manning, actually. I'm the Flying Doctor pilot stationed in Alice Springs, and I need to get to Darwin."

"Civilians are definitely not allowed to fly in that direction," he said, but he smiled under his luxuriant handlebar moustache, admiring her trim figure in khaki overalls.

"Not even in the Flying Doctor plane? I've been asked to pick up refugees and fly them south."

"Yes, from Adelaide River airstrip, not Darwin."

Caro tried another approach. "You know, she mightn't remember me, but I used to go to the same school in Adelaide as your wife, in fact we were contemporaries. She and I were two of the lucky ones who rode horses to school."

"Caro Manning! Of course, I've heard Maisie speak of you. She's still mad about horses."

"Well, now I'm mad about aeroplanes."

"Yes, I remember hearing about your exploits. You trained at the Aero Club, and bought your own kite."

"I just want to get to Darwin Hospital," she explained. "I want to see if my mother is all right—she's on the nursing staff there. I hope to persuade her to leave Darwin before the Japanese arrive. If you were flying up there with a radio intercept—"

"H'm." He looked at her consideringly. "You look fairly professional in your flying gear, but no one could mistake you for an airman, with that figure. If anyone asks, you'd better be an Air Force nurse flying in as a replacement. The Air Force hospital was badly hit."

He had a reputation as a rather flamboyant character, and unconventional. Caro was not disappointed. An hour later she was seated in the second cockpit of the Moth and skimming over the long yellow grasses and the red ant-hills on her way to the bombed port.

He had explained that he would be landing at Berrimah to deliver his message, and she could inquire at the 119th A.G.H. there, which was near the R.A.A.F. airfield. They would know the position at Darwin Hospital.

Though she was enjoying being in an open aircraft again—she had borrowed helmet and goggles at Batchelor—Caro could not relax for worrying about Alix. Had any nurses been killed?

She could not believe afterwards how well it had all worked out. The little Moth taxied almost to the entrance of the Army hospital; and Alix was actually there, and off duty, resting on her bed.

"Caro! How on earth?"

"Mum! You're all right, then!"

They were both talking at once, laughing and crying and kissing each other. Caro explained how she'd hitched a ride from Batchelor, and had flown from the Alice to pick up refugees: "And I wish I could take you back with me, but there's no room for you in the Moth. I wish you'd go south, though."

Alix explained that she had been offered a place on the last train, but had decided to stay. "Someone has to," she said reasonably. She asked about David, and Caro told her he had joined the Air Force.

Alix looked down and turned a little pink. "As a matter of fact," she said, "I've done just what I was scolding you for, in my letter—fallen in love with a married man. And he will *never* be divorced, and doesn't want to be. Oh, Caro! I feel so alive, so young again. We're both doing important, necessary work here. Why would I want to go south?"

"Good for you," said Caro. "After all, you're not much over fifty."

Alix told of the exhausting day and night of the raid, and how hundreds of casualties had been treated, but things were easier now that so many had been shipped away in the *Manunda*. "Many of them will never make it to Perth, and will have to be buried at sea. But at least it has relieved the pressure on us here."

"But you promised me you wouldn't join an Army hospital."

"I didn't! The Army Medical Director made us all move here, with our patients, in the middle of the night, in case there was another raid on Darwin."

"So you *were* bombed?"

"Yes—red crosses on the roof notwithstanding."

"Is he—this man—a doctor, by any chance?"

"He's a naval surgeon. We worked together in the operating theatre. He's a fine surgeon."

"I'm sure he is. Let's go out in the grounds, shall we? I have to be ready when the Moth comes back to pick me up. Ten minutes, he said." It was then she noticed the bullet-holes in the ceiling.

"And this is the 'safe' hospital, is it?"

"It was only strafed. And they were probably aiming at the anti-aircraft guns on the Air Force base—it's so close."

"That was completely flattened, apparently. We flew over the harbour coming in. It's horrifying, the tide is half out and there are all these skeletons of ships sticking up out of the water."

"Yes. And so many sailors were caught in the burning oil that day. I was in Casualty. There was so much suffering, that after a while you became numb. They were still being brought in until nearly midnight."

They heard the noise of a single-engined aircraft, and the yellow-painted Tiger Moth came trundling towards them, taxiing all the way from the base, dodging craters. Caro hugged her mother. Alix looked bewildered.

"I won't be able to believe this, afterwards," she said. "Here for ten minutes! From nearly a thousand miles away! It's ridiculous."

"Yes, I know. But I just wanted to find out if you were all right. There's no telegraph or mail, and there've been rumours that more than a thousand people were dead. Officially we were told fifteen."

"Hah!" said Alix. "Fifty times that, I would say. And they're still dying of wounds. One nurse has been killed, but not in our hospital."

"Well, you take care."

Caro dodged the turning propeller, climbed into the cockpit, and pulled on her flying-helmet. She waved goodbye as she looked down from the air at her mother in nurse's uniform. Suddenly Caro was blinded by tears. That small white-clad figure looked so vulnerable standing there between the bombed airfield and the strafed hospital.

By the time they got back to Batchelor the sun was setting. Caro was given a service hut with a bed, but got to it late, as the airmen decided to celebrate having such unexpected female company by holding a party.

At Adelaide River next morning, she circled round and pretended she was just coming in from Alice Springs.

Fortunately the pregnant Chinese woman had already found a seat in a passenger plane; Caro would not have been able to attend to her as well as pilot the Dragon if the woman started giving birth. There were four young part-Aboriginal girls and two Catholic nuns and an Italian woman who spoke no English. The nuns tried talking to her in Latin, without much success. The children sat on the stretcher side by side, wide-eyed and silent. They had seen a plane land and take off, but they'd never been inside one. They sucked quietly on the barley sugar that Caro had distributed all round as a precaution against airsickness.

The South Australian Government had been adamant that it did not want a flood of Chinese and part-Aboriginal refugees in its tidy little city, so probably only the Italian woman and the nuns would get as far as Adelaide.

They stopped at Katherine for refreshments and a walk in the fresh air for the Italian woman, whose plump pale face had begun to turn rather green as the ground heated up and the little Dragon began to bump up and down in the thermals. When they landed she explained that the noise of the engines was giving her a headache, or so Caro understood it: *"Ho mal di testa—il rumore dei motori,"* she moaned. It was a wonderfully expressive phrase, Caro thought.

Back at the Alice that afternoon, she handed over her passengers to the authorities. The girls were taken to the home for half-caste girls, and the Italian woman took a job as a cook, while the Catholic Church paid for the nuns to go on by train to stay with a religious order in Adelaide.

As the American presence in the Philippines became less tenable, it seemed that President Roosevelt realized the full importance of Australia as a base for U.S. forces, land, sea, and air. Troops began arriving in Sydney and Brisbane, and much-needed aircraft, from Flying Fortresses to Kittyhawks.

The Australian Air Force was so short of suitable aircraft that the government had been impressing privately owned planes, even DC 84s and little Fox Moths, for transport requirements or conversion for ambulance work. Caro realized that if *Fafnir* were not already in an essential service, she would have been taken by the government—not without some financial compensation, but nothing could compensate her for the loss of her precious plane.

David had not been called during the two and a half days she had been away, except for a consultation with the Tennant Creek Hospital doctor. For that he was able to fly himself in his little Gypsy Moth.

Caro told him about her adventures when they met for dinner that night, defying gossip. Now that he had decided to join up, knowing that they were soon to be separated, they didn't care if they were seen alone together.

"She's so obstinate, she won't hear of leaving, though one nurse has already been killed," said Caro of her mother.

"Now I know where you get it," he said teasingly.

She made a face at him. She had been talking without stop, telling him about the flight, losing no opportunity for drama as she described how she had wangled a flight to Darwin, and the squadron party: "They're so young, none over twenty-two, and they know how short their life-expectancy is. It makes them light-hearted and reckless, not depressed."

"I know. I was young and reckless in the last war, remember?"

"David! Can't you let younger men fight in this one?"

His face darkened. "I'm not all that old, for God's sake! I'll only be forty next birthday."

"And I'll be twenty-seven. My mother was married and a mother by now. When I was little and asked, 'What did you do in the war, Mummy?' she would answer, 'I had you!'"

"And a very commendable achievement, too. She should have got a medal."

"I'm talking too much. Someone once told me that I could talk the hind leg off a donkey. Whatever *that* means."

"I like to hear you prattle."

"PRATTLE!"

"Just a joke. It's been most interesting to hear about Darwin at first hand. Obviously the evacuees are going to have a very different story from the official one. And try not to worry too much about Alix. Now that the Japs have devastated the place, perhaps they'll leave it alone."

CHAPTER THIRTY-THREE

For three weeks bodies continued to be washed up by the sea, burnt and decayed beyond recognition, and were quickly buried without ceremony. The beautiful turquoise waters of the harbour were choked with sunken ships, the sandy beaches littered with burnt-out hulls that had drifted ashore. For a week the smouldering jetty sent up a column of smoke which hung in the humid air.

Though later there were to be some night raids, it became apparent in the first weeks that the enemy preferred daytime take-offs and landings, so that raids tended to occur in the late morning or early afternoon. At first there was a lull, though Japanese planes continued to appear, and the skies were made uneasy with the sound of high-level reconnaissance planes. One day ten Zero fighters circled overhead, but there was no attack. Nor was there any sign of a Japanese landing.

Nerves were beginning to unwind. Nurses no longer hurried patients into slit-trenches or under beds. Then on March 4, eight Zeros came screaming in over the roof at low level for a machine-gun attack on the R.A.A.F. Station. A Hudson bomber was destroyed on the ground, but there were no casualties.

The Kahlin Hospital staff were still quartered in the A.G.H. at Berrimah, though it seemed to be one of the most dangerous places since the enemy were no longer interested in bombing the town or the harbour. The Army in another about-face decided that the A.G.H. staff should go inland and establish a hospital at Adelaide River, admitting at last that their new hospital was badly situated.

Three days later the evacuation began. A convoy of ambulances with fifty patients and twenty-two nurses set off on the sixty-mile journey down the road, to set up a camp hospital in tents, with no proper washing facilities for the nurses and a makeshift operating theatre in a tin shed. This left much more room at Berrimah for the Kahlin nurses and doctors.

A second convoy was to go south in a week or two, for there were still patients, some of them elderly, who had been brought in as refugees from Malaya. One old lady, Mrs. Wilson, had spent all her married life there. Having been used to a retinue of Malay servants, she was rather imperious in her manner of demanding a bedpan. But once she was on her feet she offered to help the nurses, who humoured her though in fact she rather

461

got in the way. She kept mislaying the steel helmet issued to all walking patients.

Then on March 16 the Japanese made a determined attack with fourteen bombers. Again the R.A.A.F. base seemed to be the target. As the air-raid sirens sounded, Alix, hurrying through the front hall, saw old Mrs. Wilson pushing open the fly-wire door. She wandered out on to the veranda, calling, "Has anyone seen my tin hat? I can't remember where I put it. . . ."

Alix followed her and tried to bring her inside, but she stopped by the door like a balky horse.

"Come, Mrs. Wilson, come inside."

Looking towards the R.A.A.F. Station, Alix saw the smoke and debris go up from a direct hit and she knew there would be casualties this time. Then she saw an enemy bomber, hit by a lone anti-aircraft gun. With his plane on fire, the pilot immediately headed back towards the sea, jettisoning his bombs.

Alix could see them; she was sure they would fall short of the hospital. But she gave Mrs. Wilson a solid push that sent her through the door.

She heard the explosion; fearing the approaching shock wave, she went to throw herself into the hall. But before she could do so, something hit her in the back and knocked her flat. At first Alix thought it was just the blast that had hit her, for she felt no pain. But when she tried to move, she found that she could not. Her legs were paralyzed; there was no feeling from her waist down.

She thought, My spine, and knew it was serious.

Then a nurse with short red hair under her cap was beside her, and shouting for orderlies and a stretcher. Alix looked at her vaguely, thinking she was back at Kahlin, and that Matron Mackay had cut off her plaits of long red hair.

"My back . . ." she murmured. She had been flung on her face and rested her cheek on the floor. The nurse reached across her. Alix felt no touch, but saw that her hand, when she drew it back, was covered in blood.

A blanket was pulled under her and then she was slid sideways on to a board, with as little movement as possible, and from there on to a bed in the Surgical Ward. She still lay partly on her face. Sister Ellie Rowan came and touched her hair, with a jocular remark about "that old trout Mrs. Wilson. You saved her life, worse luck, and now she's complaining that you pushed her." But rolling her eyes up and sideways, Alix saw that her friend's face was stricken. Then she heard Matron Mackay's voice.

"Surgeon Evans is coming," she said. "Sister Rowan, you'd better prepare theatre, there may be several cases. An ambulance has just brought two R.A.A.F. ground staff in, but one died in Casualty and the other was dead on arrival. There are sure to be some more casualties."

"Yes, Matron."

Then Enid Mackay was gently touching her hand as it hung limply over the side of the bed. Alix smiled against the low pillow. "You didn't cut your hair off after all," she murmured. Enid patted her hand. Shock and loss of blood, she thought: Alix's mind was wandering. Alix murmured, "I'm thirsty." A nurse was setting up a drip bottle beside the bed.

Enid gave her a small piece of ice to suck.

"Ri-dic-u-lous," enunciated Alix clearly, her mouth feeling less gummed up. "Here am I being a patient, when I should be nursing the wounded."

"There are plenty of nurses," said Enid. "This wouldn't have happened if we'd been back in our own quarters. Damn the Army!" And then, "Here is Surgeon-Commander Evans to look at you."

"Hallo, Alix. What have you been up to?"

He came round and stood by the bed where she could see him, then sat down and began taking her pulse. His strong jaw was painfully set. But the touch of those long fingers was infinitely soothing.

He asked to have the clothes cut away from her back, and drew in his breath sharply as he saw the jagged hole in the white skin. A large piece of shrapnel must have done that, and some of it would still be inside, perhaps resting against the spine. Removing it would be dangerous; yet it couldn't be left there.

"I want the patient prepared for surgery," he said to the nurse, "but let her rest a little and recover from shock. Nil by mouth, and plasma intravenously."

He sat down again and lifted Alix's hand. "Can you close your fingers on mine? Good. Now tell me what you feel."

He stuck a needle into her right leg, then her left; she did not react. "Which foot am I touching?"

"I can't tell. None."

"Mm. Any pain?"

"Not really. I just feel numb. It's my spine, isn't it?"

"I'm afraid so. If it's just pressure from a piece of shrapnel, I may be able to remove it. We'll see."

He held the back of his hand against her cheek in what could have been construed as feeling if she was feverish, but which Alix knew to be a caress. Then he left her and conferred privately with Matron Mackay.

Enid could see by his face that the prognosis was not good.

"There is no sensation in the lower limbs," he said. "The spinal cord is evidently damaged, which probably means she can never walk again. But the wound is so massive, I fear there may be other internal injuries —kidneys, ruptured bladder, the peritoneal cavity. I can't tell till I have a look. As soon as the B.P. stabilizes, I'll operate."

463

"There's already an urgent case in theatre, Doctor. An American serviceman, caught in machine-gun fire. Six others with less serious injuries are on their way in."

"Why don't they send us some fighter aircraft?" he cried angrily. "Do we just have to sit here and take everything the Japs care to throw at us? The Top Brass don't seem to care what happens to us up here."

"Of course not," said Enid Mackay with a grim smile. "This is 'The Top End,' Capricornia, the land fit only for goats. Heaven knows why the Japanese should want it."

"They don't. They just want to stop the Americans using it as a base."

Half an hour later, Alix was wheeled into the theatre. Clyde Evans was disturbed to find that her temperature was up and her pulse had risen. Lying half on her side, she smiled at the anaesthetist, whose wife had stayed on to work the hospital switchboard and had been hit in the leg by shrapnel on the day of the big raid. She had now been evacuated to the south.

Clyde, in gown and gloves, his iron-grey hair hidden by a surgical cap, leaned over and looked into her eyes.

"Alix, I'm going to try and remove the piece of shrapnel that caused the wound. If it's lodged against the spine it won't be in very deep. You'll be out of here soon."

She smiled at him dreamily. They had given her some pre-operation sedative, hyoscine hydrobromide or something, her mouth was dry and her thoughts floated. She felt no fear. She remembered how when she was about eighteen she used to lie awake fantasizing that she had tried to kill herself for love, and that Dr. Hamilton was attending her, too late to save her life, and full of sorrow at her approaching end.

Silly girl that she had been. To have even thought about suicide, when life was so interesting, such a challenge. Who would want to leave it voluntarily?

A little later the surgeon gave a subdued oath. "Christ, look at this!" he muttered. Inside the jagged hole the spine was broken, the left kidney pulped, the piece of metal lodged somewhere in the peritoneal cavity. The smell told him that the bowel was pierced.

He could only do more damage by probing about in there. There was nothing to be done but sew her up again.

When Alix slowly woke in the recovery room, Sister Rowan was by her side.

"Well . . . was it very . . . big?" she asked, her voice slow and halting. "Can I see it—the bit of shrapnel?"

Ellie Rowan shook her head. "It's still in there, Alix. He couldn't remove it."

"Oh." Her breathing was laboured now. Rowan's face was moving in

464

and out of focus in a most peculiar fashion. Alix squinted in an effort at concentration. "That's—bad, eh?"

"It's not good. Don't try to talk now. Commander Evans asked to be told as soon as you woke up. I think he has a soft spot for you."

"Think . . . so?" Alix smiled. She felt her cheek move against the pillow. "Ellie—turn me a bit. So I can see him. It doesn't . . . hurt, honest. I feel . . . strange. Floating."

"You've lost a lot of blood."

But Alix was not fooled. "No. I'm dying, aren't I?"

"Don't talk like that."

"Please—fetch him."

If she still had any doubts, she knew as soon as she saw his face. He tried to smile at her, but his lip trembled, and he bit it fiercely. He took her hand, and lifted it to his cheek.

Sister Rowan discreetly withdrew.

"Tell me . . . It's bad, eh?"

"I couldn't do anything. The wound is too massive. There is extensive damage—" He stopped and covered his eyes with his other hand.

"It's all right. I've had a good life, an interesting life. It's just . . . I wanted to see . . . my grandchildren. Write to her, Clyde. You tell Caro. Tell her. . ."

"Yes, yes. Oh, my dear! Now it's too late, I wish we hadn't been so high-principled. I wish we'd been lovers."

"No. You'll be glad . . . when you go home."

"I suppose so." Her hair was loose, spread in light, soft curls about her shoulders. He twined a curl round one finger. "Such pretty hair!"

She stared up at him. He was gently stroking her forehead. Instead of grey, his hair looked fair, his forehead smooth and high. Dr. Hamilton was at her bedside, taking a regretful farewell, just as she had imagined it. Her pale lips moved in a contented smile. The room seemed to be growing dark, but she could still see his face. Clyde Evans bent his head and kissed her mouth before it became cold.

It was ironic that the very next day the first of three squadrons of No 49 American Fighter Group arrived in Darwin. Two more squadrons of Kittyhawks finally arrived in April, flying from Brisbane by way of Cloncurry, Mount Isa, and Daly Waters. These aircraft had been promised for some time, and when they failed to appear the airmen at Batchelor began to refer to them as "Tomorrowhawks" and "Mythhawks." Once the three squadrons had arrived, a Japanese attack force came in, as usual expecting little opposition, and thirteen of their planes were shot down.

General MacArthur arrived in Australia, flying from the Philippines by way of Darwin, and set up his headquarters in Melbourne. Soon he was to be appointed Commander-in-Chief of all forces in the south-west

Pacific area, and begin an offensive against the Japanese to north and east.

By now the United States Army Air Force had many transport planes at Amberley in Brisbane, and American troops were arriving there daily. The Royal Australian Air Force had four squadrons of Catalinas in Townsville, Queensland, with sufficient range to reach Rabaul, in the Bismarck Archipelago, and return.

Since the March 16 raid all nurses, except the few male nurses in Darwin, were sent down to Adelaide River. The raids continued, but now not without cost to the enemy. Commander Evans, back at Kahlin, looked out and shouted in triumph as he saw two Zeros twisting seawards, the red round suns glowing under their wings as they turned, smoke pouring from them as they plunged into the harbour.

He shook his fist. "That'll show you, you little yellow devils!" he shouted.

He felt a personal hatred for the Japanese since they had got Alix. And he had seen so many terrible burns and wounds. Yet in the past he had treated Japanese pearl divers suffering from the bends, and had admired their courage when they said they intended to go down again.

Darwin had become hateful to him, with its shattered buildings, its beaches strewn with oil and stinking decay. He longed for a shipboard posting, somewhere far away from there, on the clean ocean.

The hardest thing he had to do, next to attending the funeral, was writing to Alix's daughter. He had asked the authorities to let him break the news first, before she was officially informed.

Dear Caro [he wrote]. We have never met, but I feel that I know you. Perhaps your mother told you that in the last few months we had become close. Therefore it is with a particularly heavy heart I write to tell you that on March 16 Alix was caught by a piece of flying shrapnel from a Japanese bomb, and died about an hour later. I tried to operate but found such massive internal injuries that it was impossible to do anything for her.

She felt no pain. This is not the usual reassurance handed out to relatives. She felt no pain because her spine had been severed and she was paralyzed below the waist. She talked to me of you; she even smiled. She died peacefully in my arms. . . .

The A.I.M. padre, the Reverend Goy, conducted the service, and spoke of her years of work in isolated posts in the outback. He quoted a little prayer of John Flynn's: 'God, give me work till my life shall end, and life till the work be done.'

Your mother was a brave and beautiful person, and a gallant comrade through that dreadful twenty-four hours after the first raid. She refused to leave for the south, and worked to the end as she would have wished. Now she is gone, but many will remember her as a friend and a fine and dedicated nurse.

CHAPTER THIRTY-FOUR

Within three months the armada of aircraft carriers and war-planes which had caused such havoc at Pearl Harbor and Darwin was at the bottom of the Pacific Ocean.

At the Coral Sea Battle in May 1942, with combined U.S. and Australian naval vessels, and air squadrons from Townsville and Cairns, the Japanese suffered their first defeat. In the following month at the Battle of Midway they lost four aircraft carriers; 280 planes went down with the ships, and 52 aircraft and their crews were destroyed in combat. It was a loss of ships, aircraft, skilled airmen, and "face" from which they never fully recovered.

Caro rejoiced as she read of this major setback to the hated enemy. The British Government had left Australia to sink or swim while it got on with the war in Europe and the Middle East—aided by Australian troops and airmen—and America had come to the rescue.

Caro's first reaction on receiving the news of her mother's death was one of disbelief, then grief, then anger against the Japanese airmen who had done this. At first she read the letter uncomprehendingly, her mind simply refusing to take in the stark fact. When the full impact hit her, she beat at the letter lying on the table, until she bruised her fists.

"No, no, no!" she sobbed. "Not Mum! It can't be. They've made a mistake. . . ." But slowly she realized that it was true, that she would never see her mother again. She went and lay down on her bed, staring out at the perpetually blue sky, that sky from which the bombs had fallen in a lethal hail.

"Those bastards!" she shouted, bounding up again and pacing round the room. "Oh, I wish I could fly up to New Guinea and have a crack at them!"

They had killed an innocent nurse on the *Manunda*, and now her mother, besides all those girls in the post office at Darwin. Somehow, vowed Caro, she would get into the Air Force in however lowly a position, and help in the defeat of the Japanese Empire.

The official letter from the Army Director of Medical Services was so full of clichés about "the supreme sacrifice" and "our glorious dead" that it was almost meaningless.

Letters also came from John Flynn; from the Flying Doctor administration, as it was now for the first time officially called; from the hospital staffs in both Cloncurry and Darwin.

Matron Enid Mackay sent a moving tribute, but the letter Caro cherished most was the one from Surgeon-Commander Evans.

"This is the man Mum told me about," she said as she showed it to David later. "You can see what a nice bloke he is. But he was married, and there was no future in it, so she said."

"She didn't believe in divorce."

"No; but she didn't judge you and me. She is very fair-minded . . . I mean she *was*." Hot tears scalded her face. "God! I just wish I could join the Air Force and help beat those bastards!"

"You! You're the one who said you wouldn't even roll a bandage."

"That was before they started raiding us. Perhaps we should just let them land in the north, and try to march across the continent. They wouldn't have a clue, in their green little rocky islands, what the heart of Australia is really like. They'd disappear like the Roman legions in the deserts of Persia."

"I don't know. They're tough little men, and adaptable. . . . I suppose you could join the W.A.A.F.s."

"The Women's Auxiliary? No, thanks! It's only for clerks and telegraphists and washer-uppers—jobs that are regarded as 'suitable for women.' I want to be a pilot."

"Dear girl, you haven't a hope. They won't even allow W.A.A.F.s into forward areas."

When David's call-up came through in May 1942 they went for a last picnic in his Tiger Moth, which he was handing over to the Air Force as a trainer. He piloted her north up the highway to the spinifex-covered Burt Plain, then they turned west. Just as some stony ridges began to appear ahead, he circled lower, and there, lying like a perched lake in a rocky hollow, appeared a clear blue pool.

"Anna's Rockpool," he wrote on a slip of paper and passed it to Caro, pointing downward as he did so.

Yes, it looked inviting, but surely he didn't propose to land in this country? He circled again and swooped down past a ruined stone hut. Here the scrub and spinifex fell back and a bare, eaten-out area surrounded it, which had never recovered though the place looked long-abandoned.

He came in low over the crumbling walls and, while Caro held her breath, did a side-slip to lose height and touched down in the red dust. The tail-skid bit into the ground and they pulled up just short of a rocky outcrop.

"Scared you, did I?" he asked complacently as they climbed out. "I checked this place out years ago, when I had a call to Napperby Station, about thirty miles further west. This hut is the remains of Old Napperby."

They walked hand in hand to a second rocky hill and he led the way

469

in a steep climb to the top, by way of an overgrown track. It was hot; she was wearing shorts, and the dry silvery grass pricked her legs.

The south-east Trades had begun to blow for the Dry season, and on top of the hill there was a delightful breeze. And among the rocks, like a natural reservoir, lay a round basin of water, so sheltered that the rocks on the far side were perfectly reflected. It was hard to tell where water ended and air began. Leaning above the water was a group of ghost-gums with pure-white trunks.

Caro stood entranced. It was the most beautiful swimming place she had seen since Mataranka. They left their clothes on the rocks, and swam and sported like two young dolphins, making love in the water. A second time they came together on their spread towels on the strip of red sandy earth. Afterwards David carried her back into the water for a wash: even her hair was red with dust. Then they lay and dried off on the rocks, partly in the gum-trees' shade. High above, kites circled endlessly against the clear blue sky.

"Remember how we let the eagle go?"

"Mm." She felt too lazy and filled with well-being to talk.

Back at the hut, a flock of white cockatoos was perched like a frieze on the ruined stone, perhaps waiting for the intruders to be gone so they could return to the rockhole. They took off in one shrieking, cursing mob.

"Perhaps they're the ghosts of the people who've died round here."

"*Have* people died round here?"

"That's why the old homestead is deserted," said David. "It was back in the early days, 'when the blacks were bad.'

"The two men who took up Napperby were resting inside, with their guns in the wagon out the front. A mob of blacks crept up and threw lighted sticks and set the spinifex roof on fire. You know how fiercely it burns. One man ran outside and was speared; the other tried to shelter under his bed and was incinerated."

"And the blacks?"

"Oh, the locals organized a big 'nigger hunt.' There were not many left around here after that."

"Of course," said Caro softly. "They were defending that beautiful permanent rockhole—as precious to them as life itself. . . . And then the whites went away and abandoned it after all."

She handed him an apple from the picnic basket, and shook out the crumbs of cold Camp Pie and bread. Instantly some big black ants arrived and fell on the bits of meat and demolished them.

"Meat ants," said David. "They're ravenous."

Caro looked at them soberly, keeping her feet well away. Between the eagles and the kites and the ants, there would be little evidence but bones within a short time of any massacre around here.

In June David left for R.A.A.F. headquarters in Brisbane. When the new Flying Doctor arrived, Caro could scarcely keep from staring, as they met for their first flight together and she drove him out to the aerodrome.

Except for a dark tie, Dr. Ray Cantor was dressed in shining whites from the solar topi on his dark curly head to the shoes and socks on his feet: white shirt, white duck trousers with a white belt. Caro was wearing a hat with a thick fly-veil to keep out the swarming flies, so she was able to hide her expression of amused astonishment. He was a young man not long out of medical school, but so enthusiastic, so keen on his work and interested in the people and places of the centre, that she soon grew to like him.

Caro was feeling depressed after David left, but his first letter from Brisbane brought some good news.

You'll never believe it [he wrote], but my wife has fallen for someone high up in the Army. Apparently he helped her to get away during the last panic in Darwin, and she wants a divorce! Of course it could take years, but she's going to start proceedings in Melbourne immediately. Needless to say I won't contest it, but for one thing—I won't have you named as co-respondent. I've written to tell her so, and that I'll give her evidence of adultery. That should be easy enough; I'll get one of the "Brisbane Ladies" down the Valley to earn an easy hundred pounds by saying I spent the night with her. So we'll be able to get married properly after the war.

His next letter came from an undisclosed address in the Northern Territory, because of security regulations. He wrote in disgust that they would not let him do any fighting or even medical work in New Guinea, but had made him Squadron-Leader of an Air Force Ambulance Unit. Some of the planes, he said, were only Dragon Rapides, not much better than *Fafnir*, and one was a Fox Moth, but he had been given a converted American DC2.

I have to get used to having a co-pilot sitting alongside me [he wrote]. It's hard, after so many years as a loner. I wish you could be my co-pilot. We are stationed somewhere near my old field of operations. Maybe I'll get as far as New Guinea. But they won't let me fly a fighter plane. That's for boys of nineteen and twenty.

There are lots of refugees arriving from there and from the Philippines and New Britain, who need ambulance transport down to the A.G.H. at Adelaide River. Just as well the Americans are here. Apparently Prime Minister Curtin begged for just one aircraft carrier, or a few fast planes—thousands of our own airmen are fighting over there for Britain. But they "couldn't be spared." Now the British have offered

471

some squadrons of Spitfires, *next year*. Talk about too little too late! Churchill said, "We will not let Singapore fall." It fell because of British complacency and unpreparedness. You should hear the men who got back from there describe the British Air Force Base: "Acres and acres of playing fields, tennis courts, golf courses, swimming pools, clubs and bars." Oh, it was well organized—for a pleasant peacetime bash.

Caro put in her resignation for the end of the year, and started making inquiries about the Air Transport Command's ferry service for aircraft. She knew that women pilots were employed in Britain by the Air Transport Authority. Her childhood idol, Amy Johnson, had been killed while ferrying an aircraft to England.

CHAPTER THIRTY-FIVE

For months Caro beat her head against a brick wall, trying to get through to Australian Air Force authorities that she was just as competent to ferry aeroplanes as a man, and that she could free a male pilot for combat duties. She was advised to join the Women's National Register, and the Women's Auxiliary Air Force. But women pilots were not wanted. There were now twelve thousand "airwomen" in the W.A.A.F.s—none employed in flying. She went to Brisbane for an interview with the R.A.A.F. officer in command of Air Transport, a man of nearly fifty with many years' experience as a commercial pilot in Australia.

He informed her briefly that women were not allowed into combat areas nor any farther north than Cairns. She could join the W.A.A.F.s, many of whom were stationed in Townsville.

"I don't want to be a W.A.A.F.," she explained. "I'm a qualified pilot and aircraft engineer, and I want to use my skills for the war effort."

"My dear girl," said the officer, "you may be quite a good pilot, but one reason why we don't have women in the Air Force is that as soon as we had trained them to be of use, they would go and get pregnant."

Caro got up and left him. She had heard there was an American Air Force transport unit commanded by a legendary flyer, Captain "Pappy" Gunn, formerly manager of Philippine Airlines. She sought him out at Archerfield Aerodrome in Brisbane, where the unit was based. With a handful of officers and men, and a strange assortment of aircraft from Dakotas to ageing C39s, three Liberators that had just arrived from the States, and a twin-engined Commando, he was organizing the delivery of men to planes without pilots, and spare parts to planes needing repair.

After some hesitation Captain Gunn agreed to take her on, giving her the honorary rank of Flight-Lieutenant, and agreeing that in the present shortage of aircraft even her little Dragon would be of use.

"We're building up an aircraft engine repair base at Townsville," he said, "and they urgently need spare parts transported up there as soon as they arrive from the States."

Caro would have to do a conversion course in flying larger and heavier aircraft. She was issued with a man's khaki U.S.A.A.F. uniform, which fitted quite well after she had turned up the bottoms of the trousers and let out the seams under the arms of the jacket to accommodate her bust. Fortunately her hips were boyishly narrow.

Caro had now learned that David was stationed at Manbulloo, Northern Territory, where an American Mobile Works Squadron was based. They had prepared a series of airfields right down the highway from Darwin to Katherine and Daly Waters, with runways big enough to take heavy bombers.

It was not until August of 1943 that Caro managed to get an assignment delivering a new C47A Dakota to Manbulloo, flying as second pilot in the two-man crew. David was there with his unit.

He looked well, but older, thinner, more serious with the responsibility of leading the Ambulance Squadron. But when he saw her his face folded into its old laughter lines, and he lifted her right off the ground as he hugged her.

"I must say you look terribly smart in your Air Force uniform," she said, inspecting him in his neat dark blue and his peaked officer's cap. He'd always been inclined to fly around in an old crumpled pair of shorts and an open-necked shirt. The fitted uniform enhanced his lean figure.

"We're still transporting refugees to hospital, some are very weak, they've been holed up in the hills of Timor for more than a year," he told her. "And men are still getting killed and wounded in Darwin raids."

He was upset about the numbers of young airmen who had been killed in New Guinea in the last year and a half because their planes were outmoded and outclassed, or their bombers did not have sufficient air cover. Most of them were not more than twenty or twenty-two.

"A chap back from there told me of three Wirraways chasing a heavy Jap bomber, and it simply speeded up and left them behind. Bombers outpacing fighters! It's pathetic."

He took her to dinner at Manbulloo Station, where he said he was always welcome. She could see that it was true. The station people were aware of his many years as a doctor flying his own plane, and more recently as the Flying Doctor at Alice Springs.

They spoke optimistically of the progress in the Pacific War, for the Japanese no longer held superiority in the air, and were being forced back to the north coast of New Guinea. Crack Australian troops, who had fought and sweltered in the desert, had been brought back to fight in the rain and mud of New Guinea jungles.

Caro had to fly back to Townsville in the morning. David put her up for the night in his own hut. The briefness of her visit after so long added a special poignancy, as did the fact that they were back in the Katherine area where, as David said, "it all began."

He took her with a sort of desperation, as if it were for the last time, feeling that one or the other might not survive this war.

After a night of love, David and Caro had fallen into a deep, exhausted sleep towards dawn. She felt filled with love, fulfilled in a new way, as she walked with him to the big Flying Fortress, going back to Townsville for overhaul, in which she would be a passenger. Clinging to his lean, strong hand, she wondered momentarily, What if I conceived last night? She had taken precautions, of course. It was unlikely.

He sent her off with a mock warning: "You realize that you might end up in Brisbane instead of Townsville? These guys are not noted for their navigation. One U.S. pilot turned up in Townsville, stepped out briskly and asked, 'Say, is this Milne Bay?' He was only in the wrong country! He thought he was in Papua."

David did not tell her that now we had our landing fields back, he was flying regularly to New Guinea for wounded men.

When Caro arrived back in Townsville, she was sent north to deliver a spare engine to a Catalina flying-boat just arrived in Australia from New Guinea. With one engine shot out and losing height, the pilot had directed the crew to bail out while still near the coast, then set a course for Cairns, but had been forced to land at Cooktown.

The flight up the coast in clear weather, at only five thousand feet, was beautiful. She flew over the sea for most of the way, looking down at the Great Barrier Reef and its lovely islands, each one surrounded with a shallow coral reef covered in emerald water, and set in a sapphire sea. Cooktown had only a small airport, but the Catalina had landed in the calm sea inside the Barrier Reef.

The policy of the R.A.A.F. was not to allow women to serve north of Cairns, but as Caro was not a W.A.A.F. she got away with it. But she would not be allowed to leave Australia.

She enjoyed her work; she had always liked working with men, and had found the almost exclusively feminine world of hospitals (except for the lordly honorary surgeons) rather stifling. The only problem was in coping with the advances of some very attractive young American airmen. She was tempted more than once, for she was missing David physically as well as in every other way, but she remained faithful. Then, towards the end of November, she realized that she would soon have to resign. Her premonition or instinct had been right. In six months' time she would become a mother.

The first thing she did was write to David to tell him the news. The second was to think about names. Caro had no preferences in boys' names, but she decided, if the baby was a girl, to call her Alexandra.

There was no need for anyone else to know about her condition as yet. She meant to keep on working, and leave for Adelaide in plenty of time to have the baby in her mother's old hospital. Sad to think Alix would never see her grandchild. . . . But Caro realized there could have been worse deaths than that from a random piece of shrapnel.

From stories being brought back by survivors who had escaped from the islands, it seemed that death was preferable to being a prisoner of the Japanese, starved and beaten by brutal and ruthless guards.

Caro was worried because she had not heard from David for two months. Though in her mother's case she had been informed at once, she was not David's next of kin. Instead his wife would be told. He must have got her letter about the baby by now. Then in February 1944, just as she was preparing to leave Brisbane for Adelaide, a long letter came.

He was delighted by her news.

This has made me incredibly happy, and given me a new interest in the future, just when I was feeling very depressed. The bad news, darling, is that I am in hospital in Port Moresby, have been quite ill, and not able to write.

Our ambulance plane was shot down, and in the crash my right leg was badly shattered. The Army got us out, carried us through the jungle on our own stretchers, but I was in a bad way. Gangrene had set in by the time I reached hospital. In short, darling, they had to operate, and I lost my leg. The stump is healing well, but I wish I had you to nurse me. I'll be invalided out of the Air Force, and as soon as I'm discharged I'll make a bee-line for Adelaide to see you and little Alix or Omega or whatever you decide to call him/her.

I wanted them to give me a local anaesthetic so that I could watch the op, but I had to have a general. The nurses and orderlies up here are all men, no pretty nurses to hold my hand.

So, dearest, you'll have a one-legged husband to look after. Not that I mean to let it ground me. I can fly perfectly well with a tin leg. . . .

Caro was swept by a mixture of feelings on reading this letter. Relief that he was alive and comparatively safe, joy that he was returning to her, horror and pity at the mutilation he had suffered. And how he must hate it, while learning to live with it. Such a vital, active man, striding about on his long legs, clambering in and out of his little plane! But at least he had not been killed, he was coming home to her. And the baby would be born in May.

She foresaw the difficulties ahead. For some time he would be in pain, and there could be problems with the artificial leg. He had not said, but she felt sure the amputation was above the knee. That was all right, she was used to nursing, but there would also be a young baby taking much of her time, and David was not the most patient of men. It would be a long time before she was back in the air.

Flying her own little Dragon, Caro left Brisbane at dawn, circling once over the sub-tropical city with its steamy heat and great flowering trees. It was an attractive city, but over-full at present with American troops spending money like water. The bars, the brothels, and the taxi-drivers were making small fortunes by charging ten times their normal rates for alcohol, sex, and transport.

"The Yanks don't know the difference between a pound and a dollar, and what they don't know won't hurt them," said the taxi-driver who had taken her out to Archerfield.

With the sun behind her, Caro flew away from the coast, heading for the Diamantina. Her course was almost due west to Charleville, four hundred miles inland, now a big Air Force refuelling depot and airport for American planes on the ferry route to Darwin. After refuelling she set off for the Cooper crossing at Windorah. The far west of Queensland was baked and dry, in contrast to the lush green of the coastal strip. But there was water in the long billabong at Windorah, shaded by drooping coolabahs. She stopped for lunch and a beer in the little pub. She had been flying for six hours, but she wanted to reach Birdsville that night. It was only a short hop now, 120 miles to Cappamerri, and then a mere 80—though it was longer by road—to Birdsville.

Soon she was crossing long red sand-hills intersected by patches of bare gibber plain. She took no risks, but followed the mail-route by way of Betoota, mindful of the growing life within her. She dropped lower to feel the heat and fill her eyes with the subtle reds and pinks of the sand-hills, the blue-grey foliage of the desert-loving saltbush and erem-ophylla. *Fafnir* was lurching and bumping in the heated spirals of air. She climbed again until she could see the channels of the Diamantina ahead, dry but marked by a growth of lignum bushes, and here and there a long permanent waterhole lined with trees.

Caro turned and followed the river down towards the South Australian border. She felt that she was nearly home, though it was still another eight hundred miles to Adelaide.

She flew over Duthie, and on down the river channel to Cappamerri, or where Cappamerri ought to be.

Where was the station, and the clay-pan airstrip? Could she possibly have passed it without seeing it? She came down to five hundred feet above a long waterhole almost choked with red sand.

And then she saw it, the gable at the end of the house sticking out of a sand-hill. There was no sign of any buildings or fences—nothing was left but the homestead, and it was more than half buried in sand.

She circled, staring down in disbelief. This was all that remained of Cappamerri Station, its thousands of stock and all its inhabitants, white and black. Even the Aborigines' camp was gone.

"Well, look at that!" said Caro, who on the long trip had begun talking, for company, to the six-month-old being she carried. "Somewhere down there lie the bones of your great-granddad, and your great-uncle Danny, and possibly some black cousins-once-removed as well."

The clay-pan airstrip had disappeared. She did not dare try to land, though she would have liked to have a closer look at her old home. Caro flew on towards Birdsville, leaving behind that empty haunted place where the bones of the white usurpers and of the dispossessed tribes lay crumbling together under the shifting sand.